Unraveling Stories

Threads Series Book One

S. J. Garrett

This book is a work of fiction. Names, characters, places, and incidents are the product of the author's imagination or are used fictitiously. Any resemblance to actual events, locales, or persons, living or dead, is coincidental.

Line By Lion Publications
318 Louis Coleman Jr. Dr.
Louisville, KY 40212
www.linebylion.com

Cover Art by Alex R.R.

ISBN: 978-0-9991070-7-2

Other Titles by S.J. Garrett

CHRONICLE Series
Chronicle of Destiny
Chronicle of Summer

ETERNITY Series
Ghost Eyes

DESCENDANTS Series
Shadow on the Sea

3rd DISTRICT Series
The Shaughnessy File
The Carmichael File
The Dease File
The Lucino File
The Taber File

Singles
Until The Dawn Breaks

PROLOGUE

"The light is in the night where the songs will never end; Come with me and tell our tale"

Amid the millions of stars in the universe, and hidden beyond the ends of the Milky Way, was a galaxy ruled by three absolute forces.

Destiny.

Time.

Nature.

Destiny was an absolute force no different from gravity, and the goddess of it commanded all lives on the world of Oriku. She preordained events and people, set every important moment into stone. Her power encompassed all that lived, yet it was only visible by reading the stars. The stars served as the messengers of Destiny. They were the children of the gods. They watched over civilian and warrior, helpless and hero alike.

The stars had not always watched the world directly, however. Destiny had not always taken command. Legend stated that a million years before had found the sky filled with a mirror that reflected the land of the gods. As the people had become selfish and cruel, the gods had filled with grief. When grief had become anger, they had shattered the mirror. All lives had been thus bared to Destiny and her messengers and would forever be under her control.

The shattered mirror had broken into twenty-five pieces. Each had fallen to the land and become known as Pure Relics. They gave their bearer great magic and immortality, but at a very high price. Lesser normal relics spawned from the Pure Relics, and it was only magic that they imparted. No price had to be paid.

Even after a million years, most Pure Relics stayed little more than rumor or mystery. Most hid away, some had been claimed, and a select few others slept peacefully as they waited for their role to fill in history. They had been chosen by Destiny herself to be worn by three different 'heroes' who would be born under the star known as Kaiten.

The Kaiten was the star that shined the brightest in the sky and radiated a light that drew other stars to it. Only six times would it shine. It would shine once on each birth of a hero, and then it would shine again on each hero as they stepped onto their destined path.

It was foretold many millennia before that there would be three wars on Oriku and there would be three Kaiten Stars to lead other destined friends into battle. A battle for freedom. A battle for sanity. And a battle to end all battles: a battle that would be for peace itself.

This story is the story of the first Kaiten Star, and the amazing journey he did not know lay ahead of him . . .

Part One

Take all I know
Turn it into darkened shadows
They'll disappear in the sun
When a new **story** has begun

- Blackmore's Night 'Gone With The Wind'

Chapter One

"Trapped by my birth, I was a bird in cage."

(Ten years ago . . .)

Until his dying day, Liang, tutor and bodyguard to young Lord Tyrian Southerwind, would never forget his first sight of Ben, the boy who would shape Tyrian's future.

It was summer. The sun rose high and so did the heat. The small town of Teasarn sat in the middle of the desert and claimed few trees to give it shade. Buildings stayed small and unadorned. Roofs were built extra-long to provide shade around the edges of walls. It was a town for peasants, though it housed a noble family.

Riding down the middle of the street, Liang held onto Tyrian with one hand and the reins of his horse with the other. At twenty, Liang was twelve years older than Tyrian but he loved the young boy as a father would. The gods only knew that Tyrian's birth father was rarely around. Oh, Donald Southerwind certainly loved his son, but he served as the High General to the Emperor. His duties bound him to the capitol.

Tyrian didn't mind. He was mature beyond his tender years and held a bedrock seriousness that baffled everyone who met him. He could be coaxed into mischievousness by his cousin, Marian, but he could more often be found studying anything he could get his hands on.

"Liang." Tyrian looked up at his mentor. "You went away."

Liang hugged Tyrian tightly. "My apologies, Tyrian."

A smile brightened Tyrian's handsome face. "You didn't call me 'lord' Tyrian!" he noted somewhat triumphantly.

"What would be the point? A certain little terror *ordered* me not to." Liang's voice was equal parts affection and amusement.

Tyrian suddenly went very still. "Liang." He tugged on his mentor's tunic sleeve. "Liang! Look!"

Liang looked and promptly stopped the horse they rode. Before he could blink, Tyrian had clambered down and ran across the dusty street. Liang cursed and followed swiftly. "Don't move him!" he ordered.

Tyrian skidded to a stop next to the prone figure lying on the side of the road but didn't move him as he knelt down. He spotted a dagger sticking out of the boy's shoulder and didn't hesitate to grasp it and pull it out.

"Tyrian!" Liang rebuked.

"If it stays in," Tyrian said reasonably, "then we can't heal it." He put the dagger aside and took off his vest to fold it up and press it to the wound. It was bleeding sluggishly, and that was a good sign. It meant the boy hadn't yet died.

Did *nothing* shake Tyrian? Liang just sighed and looked around. They stood in the middle of a road on the outskirts of the town. There were no people around. No way to know how the boy had come to be there or even why. "We need Marian," he said firmly. "She's a fine Healer."

At thirteen, Marian had just turned old enough to wear a relic and had taken to Medicine Relics instantly. In a few short months, she had become an incredible Magician who specialized in healing magic. Tyrian nodded immediately. "Then we'll take this boy to her."

Liang didn't argue. He simply took off his cloak and wrapped up the wounded boy safely. The boy's skin looked pale and at the same time flushed with fever. He weighed almost nothing, a stark statement about his current health since he was bigger than Tyrian and should have weighed significantly more.

"You ride," Tyrian ordered Liang. "I'll lead the horse."

Again, Liang didn't argue. Tyrian was a natural born leader and issued orders with the maturity and skill of someone thrice his age. If he didn't grow up to follow in his father's footsteps, the Empire would miss out on the greatest general of all time.

Liang got onto the horse and held the boy tight as Tyrian led the horse through the town. As they went, many people stopped what they were doing and turned to watch. "Is something wrong?" a flower seller called.

"A boy was left abandoned near the edge of town," Tyrian told him. "He had been stabbed. We're taking him to Marian."

"Poor child," someone else murmured. Anger sparked in her eyes. "We'll look into where he came from and who attacked him. Teasarn is *peaceful*. It'll stay that way. We don't look kindly on cruelty."

"That's why Lord Donald wanted his family to live here," Liang murmured.

"Pardon?" Tyrian glanced over his shoulder.

"Nothing."

"No it's not." Tyrian frowned. "I thought the Emperor worried that Father would be distracted by me and Mother."

Liang hesitated. Very slowly, he said, "That is part of it. But it is also true that Lord Donald wanted you to grow up in a place that would love you for you and not because you were a general's son."

"I see. I suppose that almost makes up for him never being home."

The words were said without bitterness. As far as Liang could tell, Tyrian held no grudges and no resentment for anyone or anything. He was a rare, rare child. His green eyes burned with an indomitable spirit and iron will that could not be bent or broken. He would lead millions one day. Of that, Liang felt sure.

The door to the house where Tyrian lived suddenly flew open and a pixie-sized female wearing a Healer's jacket and leggings stormed out, her rusty colored pigtails bouncing merrily. "Alright," she said briskly, "who was hurt?"

"We don't know him," Tyrian apologized. "But you'll heal him."

It wasn't a question, but Marian answered anyway. "Of course!" She pointed at the house. "In! It's too hot out here anyway."

Tyrian linked his hands behind his back as he followed Liang into the house. Another servant took the horse to the stable, and Marian shut the front door to keep the heat out. That she took orders from her younger cousin surprised none. She was nearly as protective of Tyrian as Liang.

Annareal Southerwind came rushing down the stairs, and her dark green eyes held concern. "Tyrian! I saw the commotion from the window! What is going on?"

Tyrian sighed and pointed toward the guestroom that Liang had entered. "We found a wounded boy. He had been stabbed. And abandoned." When his mother hugged him tightly, he found a smile for her. "I'm fine, Mother. I'm more worried about the boy."

Annareal was used to her son. "As we ought to be. I'm going to send a message to your father. He will want to come home to hear about this."

Tyrian waited until she had hurried down the hall before going to the guestroom. He peeked inside and saw Marian busy using her relic to heal the boy. Liang stood near, and his face looked carved in stone. When Tyrian walked over to join him, he saw why. The boy's back had been liberally covered with scars from beatings. Without any hesitation, Tyrian said, "He's not going back to where he came from."

"That is for Uncle Donald to decide," Marian reminded him.

Tyrian arched a black brow ever so slightly as if to disagree. He didn't say anything further though, his mind already gathering his arguments if his father disagreed.

It was night by the time they all heard the thunder of hooves outside that meant Donald had returned. Tyrian had been sitting with the boy just in case he woke, but when he heard his father, he brightened and hurried out of the room and the house.

He got to his father just as Annareal did. Donald Southerwind just smiled and caught both of them close. He had missed them madly every minute. "If that was all I was called home for, then I call it a successful trip," he teased. Despite the tone, his blue eyes looked serious. "What's going on? Your message said it was urgent."

"Tyrian and Liang found a wounded boy," Annareal explained as she led her husband into the house. "He had been stabbed and abandoned. When Marian was healing him, she noticed that he had been brutally abused. He rests now, and hasn't woken yet. The wounds that could be healed are gone. He has a cracked rib that should mend soon enough."

Magic could only heal so much, unfortunately, Donald thought. Any anger remained carefully hidden as he went to the guestroom and looked inside. Something sparked inside his eyes as he saw the boy's thin face. "He has to be at least thirteen," he said succinctly. "And he's thinner than Tyrian."

"That isn't saying much," Marian noted. "Tyrian doesn't look eight."

"Fair enough, but it's still evidence that he's been long neglected." He walked over to the bed and looked down at the boy. There was a deep wellspring of magic capacity inside the boy, so he had to be at *least* thirteen. Magic capacity was what allowed people to wear and use relics. The deeper the capacity, the more output potential you had. It only started to manifest after thirteen years of life, though there were occasional exceptions for early bloomers.

The boy began to stir, his brow wrinkled by a fretful frown. Donald instantly reached out to cover his hand. "You're safe," he said calmly. "You rest in the home of High General Southerwind, right-hand to Emperor Albanion. No harm will befall you here."

The boy's lashes lifted slightly. His brown eyes seemed slightly disoriented, yet nonetheless alert as they met Donald's gaze. "You won't send me back?"

Donald pulled up a chair and sat down. "Why don't you tell me where 'back' is? And your name as well, lad."

The boy hesitated. Tyrian promptly walked over and looked down at him. "You don't have to trust us," he said calmly. "But you could at least give some courtesy to the person who took the dagger out of your back."

A rapid blink was his response. Then, hesitantly, the boy asked, "How old are you?"

Donald muffled a laugh. "This is my son. Tyrian is eight years old. I'm afraid that he is far advanced for his age. He issues orders without question." He sighed. "Takes after his old man."

The boy suddenly smiled at Tyrian. "I don't know why, but I feel safe with you. So I'll trust your father as well." He let out a breath. "My name is Ben. No family name."

Donald nodded. That wasn't unusual. Last names were a luxury. Some people had them, some didn't. If a couple married, they often took entirely new last names for their new family. His last name from birth had been Phiriead. "Alright, Ben. Now what happened?"

"I lived in an orphanage in a small town in the woods far from here." Ben's eyes closed. "It was . . . okay. But we were attacked by an army from Foresalia and everything was burned. I was taken prisoner."

Tyrian looked at Donald. "We're under attack from Foresalia?"

His father shook his head. "Not exactly. They periodically try to take towns just as we try to take theirs. We've been enemies since before even I was born."

"So how did you get away?" Tyrian asked Ben.

"Ran. Someone tried to catch me but I lost him. I really don't remember much after he tried to kill me." His eyes opened slightly. "I'm thirteen. Even if I get independence, I can't make it on my own. Are you going to send me to another orphanage?"

It was a justified question. Independence could be petitioned for by anyone of any age under adulthood, but no younger than eleven for combatants and thirteen for civilians, and the one making the petition had to be able to prove they could support and provide for themselves. Ben, lacking any practical or combatant skills, was required to either gain a legal guardian or return to an orphanage until he reached adulthood at eighteen.

Tyrian narrowed his eyes at Donald. The general sat back, thinking quickly, and then said absently, "To my memory, there is no law against adopting homeless children escaping capture. And since there's no law against it, then I can't be doing anything wrong by keeping you, can I?" He got to his feet and gently ruffled Ben's hair. "You've got a home here. You won't go anywhere."

The door shut behind him as he left, and Ben looked at Tyrian in consternation. "You did that," he accused.

"I didn't do anything," Tyrian defended himself. "I *would* have, if needed." He crossed his arms on a scowl. "And I don't like that we've been at casual war for more than thirty years. It's wrong."

Ben studied Tyrian's face intently. In particular, he studied his eyes. He could see it, let alone feel it. The fierce, burning determination to protect others and the powerful iron will that would make him a force to be reckoned with. *Nothing* would break Tyrian. He would fight to his last breath . . . and win.

Ben closed his eyes on a sigh. Finally, at last, he had found the person he needed. "Can I ask for a favor?"

"Of course. We're brothers now." Tyrian smiled as he said it. "I've always wanted a brother."

A smile touched Ben's lips. "Then repeat after me. *Askandi repulsin* Devourer."

Tyrian didn't hesitate; he recognized the language of magic. "*Askandi repulsin* Devourer." He tilted his head as he felt a curious sensation inside his soul, almost a tingling as if something had awakened or taken root. "What did I say?"

"It broke a curse on me, that's all."

Curses were as common as magic, and easily repelled in many instances. They existed as two sides of the same coin. "Oh. Well, are you hungry?"

"A little."

"Okay." Tyrian got to his feet. "Then I'll get something." He paused at the door and looked back, and his dark green eyes burned fiercely. "I won't let anyone hurt you, okay, Ben?" That said, he headed out of the room and let the door swing shut behind him. Ben was family now, and Tyrian protected his family.

It was that simple.

Chapter Two

"My world has broken."

(Present)

"Is it just me," Ben asked idly as he looked out the front window, "or are the flocks of females getting bigger near the house?"

Marian shot a teasing grin at Tyrian who sat with his feet propped on a table. "*Someone* just became legal. And if I wasn't his cousin, I'd be after him too."

As of midnight, Tyrian had turned eighteen and was finally of the legal age for courting or being courted. Of course, that hadn't stopped the young women in the capitol from trying to get his attention since he had moved there two years before. He was tall at six foot, strong in the shoulder, muscular in all the right places, and his black hair and green eyes seemed perfectly paired to his handsome face.

He had been allowed to move to Trinan, the capitol of the Empire, at age sixteen. Ben, Marian, and Liang had moved with him, ostensibly to be his bodyguards as needed, but more because they didn't want him to be lonely. Annareal had been forced to remain in Teasarn to keep from distracting her husband and son alike.

Now, two years later, Tyrian was not only one of the best warriors in the Empire, but he was also on the cusp of stepping into a leadership role. He had already started picking up tasks normally assigned to his father; even Emperor Albanion looked on him with great respect. He was a master staff user, and his magical capacity was so immense that if he ever equipped a relic he would be one of the most powerful users in the world.

"So what is it you're doing today anyway?" Marian asked as she walked over to sit on the edge of the table. She had given up making him put his feet down. She could never order him to do anything.

Tyrian linked his hands behind his head. "Well, apparently the Monk Clans have sent a delegate to the Empire. They want to speak about the uprisings going on. Emperor Albanion is too busy to meet with the delegate, and my father is trying to put down a rebellion in another town. So the task fell to me."

"Monk Clans?" Marian asked curiously. "I've only heard of them in passing. What are they?"

"An impartial faction that belongs to no country, though they have branches in all of them," Liang explained as he walked in. "*Exceptionally* talented combatants who have trained in a specialized form of hand-to-hand combat that even brawlers like myself don't learn. You have to train for years and years to master a monk's skills, and most consider it a very good thing they are neutral in all countries. They would make a dangerous addition to any army, to be sure."

"I suppose then I should be honored I am speaking to them," Tyrian said.

"Don't make light." Liang firmly took Tyrian's feet off the table. "It's a *great* honor to be trusted with this."

"I wasn't making light. I stated facts. I'm not certain I feel honored at all, yet." Tyrian got to his feet with lethal grace. Dark and powerful, his serious nature and intense emotions gave him an unrivaled presence. "And to add another fact, we ought to be going now."

"May I go as well?" Marian asked. "I am considered one of your bodyguards."

"Of course." He glanced at Ben. "What about you?"

Ben smiled. "I have to go get . . . something."

Tyrian eyed his brother warily. "Last time you got me a birthday gift, it left me embarrassed for days."

"No, no. This is a good one. Promise." He glanced out the window again. Wistfully, he said, "Ginnie is certainly lovely."

Tyrian grinned. "Why do you think I dated her?"

"She still laments you never did more than that," Liang murmured softly.

"If she didn't, she wouldn't be outside." Tyrian tied on the green scarf that had become something of his trademark; it had been a birthday gift from Marian, and was his favorite possession since she had handmade it. He picked up his staff from near the door and equipped it on his back using invisible threads of magic.

Orikuans had figured out how to use magic for everything, including carrying items without straps, and they had even created personal pockets that effectively acted like backpacks capable of holding most anything. A lot of people carried weapons there, but Tyrian preferred to have his close at hand. Sure, it only took a moment to take something out of the invisible, weightless pockets, but that single thought could be the difference between life and death in battle.

Much to his vast amusement, when they got outside, Marian swept the crowd and announced, "Unless you can either arm wrestle Liang or out-heal me, you can't have Tyrian."

The crowd cleared.

Quickly.

"Enjoy being single forever," Ben murmured drolly.

Tyrian ignored him as he went down the steps to the road that led to the castle. His manor rested not far from the gates, as was the privilege and requirement of noble birth. In many ways, he envied commoners. They had more freedoms than noblemen.

The guards at the gate were used to Tyrian's presence, and likewise used to seeing Liang and Marian accompanying him. They let all three inside without issue. Tyrian sensed a presence once in the courtyard and turned as he realized someone approached. Seeing that it was the Prime Duke didn't relax him at all. The Duke was the Emperor's closest advisor. "Am I late?" he asked.

"Not at all." The Duke cleared his throat. "The delegate is waiting for you in the first floor drawing room. You can't mistake her. She's an imposing figure with much experience under her belt." He quickly scuttled away.

"That man is deathly terrified of you," Liang told Tyrian.

"That's because I know he's lazy and incompetent. And he knows I know." Tyrian led the way into the castle, his discomfort for the immense pomp and protocol carefully hidden. The castle looked like an exercise in overindulgence of the worst sort. No floor should ever be so polished that he could see his reflection, and no ceiling should ever be held up by dozens of gold pillars. Such a waste.

The first floor drawing room was located between a dining room and a guest bedroom. When he opened the door and walked in, the Duke's warning had him prepared for an older, powerful, and imposing figure dressed in the head-to-toe black that hallmarked monks in formal gear.

To his everlasting shock, what he saw was a young woman who could not be much older than he was. She was also more petite than he had expected, standing a few inches shorter than he did and possessing what looked like a graceful figure. Her thick hair glowed blue-black as it hugged her face, and her black eyes held little flecks of blue that sparkled under the chandeliers. She did wear black clothing, but not the formal gear of the monks. She wore instead casual black leggings and a black tunic. Only the utter stillness of her well-trained body belied her training

The punch of sudden desire slammed into him as if from out of nowhere. His hands burned with the hunger to get into her hair and to shape her body. If he let himself, he could practically know how her lips would mold to his and how her kiss would taste. Her eyes met his and widened with a matching shocked recognition, and he knew he was not alone in his knowledge.

Marian slid a glance at Liang. He didn't look at her, but a little, satisfied, smile curved his lips. Pointedly, he cleared his throat.

Both Tyrian and the monk jolted as if they had been shocked with a Lightning Relic. Tyrian recovered his wits first and offered a formal bow. "Hello. I'm Tyrian Southerwind. I was asked to speak with you on behalf of Emperor Albanion."

A delicate black brow arched. "On behalf of High General Donald Southerwind on behalf of Emperor Albanion, no doubt. I suppose I am lucky it didn't get delegated to the stable boy."

"Don't knock the stable boy," he countered blandly. "He plays a mean game of chesstac." He held out a hand. When she very warily took his hand, he brought her fingers to his lips. "Welcome to Trinan, my lady . . . ?"

"Cassie." Cursing the breathlessness in her voice, she tried to subtly tug her hand free. Despite the gentleness of his grip, it held stronger than any steel. Her heart fluttered and so did something low in her body. Why did he have to be so gorgeous, she wondered frantically. And why did simply *looking* at this man make her feel as if she could climb mountains? She would do anything for him if he would only smile.

"Then welcome to the castle, Lady Cassie." He slowly released her hand but only so he could take her elbow to escort her to the table in the room. "Have a seat before you pace a hole into the carpet."

"It's just Cassie. I'm not of noble birth." It was a warning for him and a reminder for herself. Their stations were too far apart for any relationship, no matter how hot the sparks between them flew. She sat down gracefully on one of the chairs and then flicked a glance at Liang and Marian. They had remained near the door but avidly listened anyway. "Bodyguards?" she asked Tyrian as he sat down across from her.

"Family first and foremost. Marian is my cousin; my parents raised her after her parents were killed in a quake. Liang is my mentor and tutor. He's a second father for me. And," he added mildly, "they also serve as bodyguards, yes."

"I see." She cleared her throat. "Well, let's get down to business. I'm here on behalf of the people of the Empire."

"That . . . is an interesting statement." He crossed his arms. "The Monk Clans are speaking for the people to their own Empire?"

She searched his face and intense green eyes. Nowhere did she see any indication that he knew what she talked about. Slowly, she said, "You don't know what's been going on? Why there is a rebellion?"

"I know what I was told by my father." He leaned forward with his arms braced on the table. "I'd like to hear the other side."

She debated mentally for long moments. "Can I trust you?" she asked softly, mostly to herself.

His hand softly covered hers. "Yes," he said quietly. His eyes met and held hers. "I would never betray you."

Something leapt between them. It flew between their eyes and where their skin touched. It was sharp and wild, as electric as a storm and as powerful as a quake shaking the land that welcomed the rain.

"Gods," Marian muttered under her breath as she shifted her weight. She could *feel* something in the air that made her skin prickle and her relic hum softly. "What is this?"

Cassie took a very long breath to fight the trembling in her body. She had not expected this man to be so devastating to her hormones. "Alright," she said. "I trust you, Lord Tyrian." She turned her hand over so that their palms pressed together. His skin felt hot and wonderful and tempted her in a way she had never been tempted before in her nineteen years. "The people are rebelling against tyranny."

His eyes didn't waver from hers. "The Emperor? Or the Empire in general?"

"There is no difference. For the last year, the Emperor has been choking down on the cities. People are going homeless in effort to pay their taxes. If you so much as accuse the Emperor of having bad breath, you're thrown in jail or worse. The armies that used to be so beloved have become monsters."

Liang started to speak, but Tyrian held up a hand sharply. His eyes probed Cassie's face. He believed her. There was too much intensity in her face for him to do otherwise. "Monsters?"

She drew a deep breath. "We of the Monk Clans were called in to the situation a month ago. A town had started to make noises like they were going to stage a protest against the Empire. To even forestall such a thing, the army rode in and decimated a homeless shelter." Helpless pain filled her voice as she whispered, "A dozen children were killed, amongst many others. The town lives in fear of their every word now."

He gently reached out with his free hand and brushed away a tear clinging to her lashes. "I hate it," he said quietly, "but I am willing to believe you. Is that why you are here now? To plead for the people?"

"To offer an ultimatum. The Monk Clans will side with the people and instigate war unless the Empire ceases its chokehold. And, I assure you, we have the strength to make such a thing difficult for the Empire." She pulled free and got to her feet. "You don't have to believe me," she said quietly. "You can see it for yourself. Visit any town beyond the capitol's walls and you'll see it."

Marian and Liang got out of her way quickly as she crossed to the door. She opened it and then paused and looked back at Tyrian. Aching sadness filled her eyes. "I wish you weren't Tyrian Southerwind. I wish you were a commoner."

The door shut softly behind her. And, not for the first time, Tyrian wished the same thing. His left hand curled into a fist on the table. The fingers of his right hand drummed lightly on the top of the table. His eyes narrowed, and he didn't notice when Liang and Marian came over to sit down beside him.

Marian's glance flicked to his hand. Why he had the mannerisms of someone who wore a relic and yet had no relic was beyond her. She gently covered his hand with hers. "Tyrian," she said softly. "Do you believe her more than you believe even your father?"

His sigh came out long and deep. "Yes," he admitted. "Don't ask me how, Marian. I just do. I just . . . *know* that she would never be capable of lying to me or hurting me. And I could never do the same to her." He lifted his hand and looked at it. "Something inside me . . . recognized her."

"That," Liang said mildly, "was fairly obvious."

The door flew open suddenly and banged against the wall. Panting from exertion, the maid in the doorway barely managed to say, "Lord Tyrian! Come quickly! Lord Ben has been wounded! Hurry, please hurry!"

Tyrian went white and rushed out of the room as fast as possible with Marian and Liang close behind. When he shoved his way through the crowd outside the castle gate, he lost whatever color had been left in his face. "Ben!"

Ben was lying on the ground with blood covering his body, and his shredded clothing bared a horrific amount of wounds. Soldiers knelt beside him and tried to stop the bleeding, but there was just too much damage.

Tyrian scrambled down the steps and knelt beside his brother. "Ben! Who *did* this?" His hand gripped Ben's tightly as Marian dashed forward and knelt down to begin using her relic.

"Didn't . . . see." Ben couldn't see or think straight. Everything hurt all at once. "Drained . . . me. Lifeforce."

A collective gasp rose from those watching, and Marian's hands fell away helplessly as her relic stopped glowing. Tyrian's face went tight and withdrawn as his eyes burned. All relic users had the ability to drain lifeforce from an enemy, but it was considered an incredibly taboo skill; unlike normal wounds, you could not be healed if your lifeforce was drained. Only time could mend such a thing, provided there was enough life left to *be* mended. Some very extreme circumstances made it acceptable to drain lifeforce, such as in self-defense where there were no other recourses, but to use it on a civilian like Ben was outright outlawed. In the Empire, such a thing was punishable by death for being a cruel and unusual torture.

"Where did this happen?" The turmoil inside Tyrian could not be heard in his even voice.

"Teasarn. As I . . . was leaving." His eyes closed. The pain was going away. He wasn't afraid. He had done what he was meant to do. He believed in Tyrian.

His hand went limp in Tyrian's as his eyes closed. A fist slammed into Tyrian's chest with razor tipped knuckles. With precision control, he put down Ben's hand and watched as the soldiers lifted his body to be transported to a holding chamber prior to funeral.

"Lord Tyrian."

Tyrian got to his feet but he didn't turn around. "My liege?"

Emperor Albanion came down a few steps and studied Tyrian's back. He knew that there was no better warrior. He had watched Tyrian grow from a child to an adult, and as an adult, he received certain permissions no child would. "You are free to return to Teasarn to seek your brother's murderer."

Tyrian nodded tightly. "I thank you."

"I trust you will take the appropriate action when you determine who is to blame." Albanion turned to look at the crowd. "Disperse," he ordered. "Leave Lord Tyrian be." To another soldier he said, "Send word to General Southerwind. Let him know what has occurred."

Tyrian said nothing as he went down the steps and headed with purpose toward the stables where his horses were kept. His face betrayed nothing of his emotions, and yet people still got out of his way as fast as was possible. A sort of aura surrounded him as something dangerous and violent, and it reflected in his fierce gaze.

Liang and Marian said nothing as they followed him. They knew he wasn't going to fly off the handle, but they also knew he needed their support more than ever. Marian had to bite down on her lip, hard, to fight the urge to cry. She had loved Ben as if he were her brother, too.

When they had ridden a mile out of the city, Tyrian rode closer to her. He reached over without a word and picked up his smaller cousin to set her in front of him. "Cry for both of us," he said quietly. "Because I can't."

Liang studied his young master in concern as Marian sobbed violently against Tyrian's shoulder. He had known Tyrian was the type who could not break, but he now began to wonder if that meant he could never truly heal either. Not a single tear had ever been shed by Tyrian in his life; instead, it often seemed as Marian cried *for* him. He himself just straightened his back and grew stronger. How long could he continue that safely?

It was not long before Teasarn appeared in their view, and Tyrian felt a little chill ripple down his back. He hadn't been back in two years. All his training and his duties had prevented him from going home at all. He had seen his mother once or twice when she had come to visit him, but that had been it.

The Teasarn of his memories had been a small farm town but deeply loved and cared for by the people. The town before him now looked as if it was on the verge of complete collapse. Streets were broken and in need of repair. The flower seller's shop had closed and looked as if it had been empty for months. No children ran around laughing and playing.

"By the gods," Marian breathed softly. She was once more riding her own horse, now that her tears had been spent. "What is this?"

Tyrian spotted the familiar face of the mayor and stopped his horse. He swiftly dismounted and crossed the street. "Mayor," he said. "What is going on here?"

The mayor blinked at Tyrian for a moment, not recognizing him, and then guardedness came into his eyes. "Lord Tyrian, we were not expecting you."

"I came looking for my brother's murderer," Tyrian explained calmly. "Ben was attacked and drained of his lifeforce in or around town." His sharp eyes saw some of the color leave the mayor's face. "Which alarms you more: that it happened or that I am investigating?"

"That is an outrageous insinuation!" As soon as the outburst left his lips, the mayor looked around sharply. When he saw no soldiers, his shoulders relaxed. "I am sorry, Lord Tyrian," he said quietly but sincerely. "Lord Ben was a good man."

Tyrian said nothing for long moments. His eyes moved up and down the street intently. People who had once always smiled at him now looked at him with distrust. Empire soldiers stood on every other street corner where they watched everyone and everything. It looked like the wartime occupation of a hostile town, not the peaceful protection of an Empire city.

"Tell me what's going on around here." It wasn't a request.

The mayor nodded instantly. He trusted Tyrian, no matter who he worked for. He had always felt that Tyrian had the eyes of a hero, the eyes of someone who would never hesitate to help those who needed it and bring down those at fault. "I am no longer mayor," he began. "I was removed from duty a year ago."

"Then who is in charge?" Liang asked.

"The Emperor."

Tyrian began to drum the fingers of his right hand on his left arm. "So he just rules everything rather than ask the people to elect a leader to report to him." That was new to him. He had heard nothing of it. "What's the current tax rate?"

"Seventy-five percent of all sales, or a minimum of one thousand gold per month, whichever is greater."

Tyrian nearly choked. "Excuse me?" he sputtered, his composure broken with that shocking information. "How can you survive on that?"

"We can't. We've been working together but . . . I'm afraid the last few months have been bad. We didn't have as much to sell to the capitol as usual and so we were short on payment." The former mayor lowered his gaze. "And ever since, there have been soldiers here. Slowly, people are losing homes and businesses."

"I'm not going to sit by," Tyrian said curtly. "I'll talk to my father and make him talk to the Emperor. This isn't just wrong, it's *disgusting.*" His skin prickled in warning, and he saw from the corner of his eye as one of the soldiers lunged toward him. He drew his staff and turned at the same time, and he easily blocked the sword swinging for his head.

"Traitor!" the soldier snarled. "How dare you speak out against our emperor?" He jerked backward and leapt forward again, but Tyrian was already moving. He ducked under the strike and whirled around, and the staff cracked into the back of the soldier's head. The soldier dropped like a brick onto the broken cobblestone.

All hell broke loose. Every soldier in the vicinity came running toward the scene, and all drew weapons. Villagers scrambled to get inside to safety. Tyrian, Liang, and Marian found themselves surrounded in a matter of moments. "Do we have a problem?" Tyrian asked.

One of the soldiers narrowed his eyes. "Just because you're General Southerwind's son doesn't mean you can get away with anything you want to. It is treasonous to speak against the Emperor and the Empire!"

Icily, Tyrian asked, "Is that what Ben did? Is that why you killed him?"

"Ben?" Another soldier scoffed. "We didn't have anything to do with him."

Tyrian did not believe her. That many soldiers covering that much of the town couldn't have *not* seen Ben get attacked. "I see." His hand tightened around his staff. "Well, I'm not going to rescind my comment. The state of this town is deplorable. And I'm not going to accept it."

The soldiers lunged forward with a collective shout, clearly intending to change his mind for him. The first to fall was dropped by Liang's fist in his nose. Another fell when Marian smashed him in the head with her mace. Tyrian's staff was limited in ability at close range, but as soon as he had enough room to start moving, he began taking out the soldiers quickly.

He blocked a sword and slammed the end of his staff into the owner's stomach. As she fell, he sensed movement behind him. He turned sharply but not fast enough. The dagger slashed through his upper arm, biting through shirt and flesh equally. The pain numbed his entire arm and he found himself with only one hand to swing his staff.

Liang didn't realize the trouble until he heard the thud. He turned sharply to see Tyrian sprawled on the street while a soldier stood over him with a raised dagger. "Lord Tyrian!" He started to lunge forward, but he knew in the back of his heart that he wouldn't make it in time.

At the last instant, someone literally materialized in front of Tyrian as if appearing from thin air. The monk wore all concealing clothes, hiding even their face from sight, but they were brutally fast and efficient. They grabbed the soldier's wrist and twisted it so sharply that the breaking of the bone was audible. As the dagger fell harmlessly on the ground, the monk kicked the soldier hard enough that he went flying halfway across the street.

The monk pivoted on the balls of their feet and small star shaped blades flew from their hands. Each found a target. Any soldiers still on their feet hit the ground with meaty thuds. As silence descended, the monk knelt beside Tyrian and helped him sit up. His dark green eyes locked on the face of the monk and then pointedly looked in their dark eyes chipped with blue. The monk paused and then removed the headpiece they wore.

"Cassie." Somehow he had known, even before he had seen her eyes. He lifted his good hand to brush his fingers across her cheek. "Thank you."

"Thank me later," she said grimly. She took his good hand and helped pull him to his feet. Something dark and deadly churned inside her heart as she saw the wound on his arm and the bloodstains on his clothes. She would tear apart anyone who ever hurt this man. Protecting him was as essential as breathing, and somehow she knew it.

"Tyrian, are you alright?" Marian scrambled over and began to examine the wound. She cursed softly. "I need herbs. Magic alone can't handle this one. At least, not my magic."

There came a soft and intricate whistle in the air. Cassie's head lifted sharply, and her eyes flickered around. When Tyrian started to speak, she covered his mouth with a hand. "Be quiet," she told him very softly. "I'm taking you somewhere safe, but you have to be absolutely silent. All of you do."

Liang lifted a brow at Tyrian, wondering if he would take orders from Cassie where he had taken orders from no one else. Yet, somehow, he felt entirely unsurprised when Tyrian gave in and nodded in agreement without fuss. Liang simply fell into step behind them as Cassie helped Tyrian cross the street. There was, indeed, something quite unusual between his young master and the lovely monk.

They passed between two buildings into a small alley. Cassie paused for a moment and then gave a soft whistle that matched the one before. A hidden floor panel lifted instantly to reveal an entrance. Holding the door up was a handsome young man with blond hair and disgruntled blue eyes. "Let's go."

He ducked out of the way and Cassie climbed down first. She was followed by Marian and Liang. Tyrian had to climb down with only one hand, but he managed without complaint. When he got to the bottom, his eyes widened slightly as Cassie grabbed his good arm and dragged him along behind her. "Pardon me."

"Not pardoned." Under her breath, she muttered, "Damned idiot probably wouldn't ask for help if his arm was falling off!"

Politely, he said, "I would hope you're wrong. I certainly don't intend to test it, though." He didn't bother to try to break free. He may have been bigger, but he was fairly sure he wasn't stronger. "If you'd like to tell me where we're going, I'd be happy to walk without being dragged." He eyed Marian and Liang as he heard a snort of laughter from one of them. "And you can both be quiet."

He found himself unceremoniously dragged into what looked like a medical room. "Sit," Cassie ordered as she pushed him at a chair.

He sat, and a smile curved his lips. Marian coughed and hurried to collect the herbs she needed from the baskets sitting around. She wasn't going to say a word about how odd everything had gotten. She just busied herself with cleaning the wound so it could be healed.

"So." The blond stepped into the doorway. Something guarded and hostile lurked in his eyes. "You're Tyrian Southerwind."

"Much to my regret it would seem," Tyrian said quietly. He met the blue eyes studying him intently. "I'm not a threat to you."

"Oh, really?" The blond scoffed. "An Empire minion just *happens* to turn against his own people and conveniently be rescued by us. How do we know it wasn't a set up?" He rested a hand on the hilt of the sword at his side. A Lightning Relic glowed where it was visibly etched into his right hand. "I don't trust you."

"Kyle Raitels!"

He jumped and turned guiltily. "Now, Ophelia," he began.

"Don't you 'now' me, you overprotective ninny!" The slender young woman behind him firmly shoved him out of the way and walked into the room with all the grandeur of a queen. She propped her hands on her hips and studied Tyrian intently. "Well. So you're Tyrian." She looked at Cassie. "You understated."

"Understated what?" Tyrian asked.

Slight pink climbed Cassie's cheeks. "Nothing," she muttered.

Ophelia Goldwind walked over and looked down at Tyrian. "Welcome," she said. "It would seem you're my unintentional guest. I'm Ophelia Goldwind. I'm the leader of the Rebellion Faction."

Tyrian blinked up at her. She looked barely older than his age. "You're young."

"*Thank* you," Kyle muttered distinctly.

"You be quiet!" Ophelia ordered him. She turned back to Tyrian with a smile. "Ignore my fiancé. He's overprotective in immense doses. But he's cute, so I endure." She ignored the pink on Kyle's cheeks and the smirking look that Cassie shot at him. Served him right! "Now, then. I understand that you spoke out against the Empire and got yourself in trouble."

"That about sums it up," Tyrian agreed. He let out a hard breath. "I didn't like what I saw today. I like even less that I believe what I saw was not just a rare occurrence." He looked at Cassie. "I believed you then," he said softly, "and I believe you still."

Ophelia leaned down until they were eye-to-eye. Her eyes looked more yellow than brown and seemed somehow familiar to Tyrian, as if he had known he might see them someday. And yet, they weren't entirely what he expected to see. It was an odd feeling.

For her, looking into his eyes brought a sudden peace and sense of rightness. She had always known that when she met the person with eyes like his that her destiny wouldn't be long in coming. She straightened up and smiled. "Why don't you finish getting healed? Once you're ready, you can come find me in my meeting room and we'll talk."

"Very well."

She turned and looked at Kyle. "He's the same size as you are. Go find a tunic for him to borrow."

He sighed. "Yes, dear." He knew better than to argue with her when she got that look in her eye.

She followed him out, and her long brown ponytail swung merrily as she went. Her choice of clothes as much as the sword at her hip said that she was a skilled swordswoman, but there was a distinct rhythm to her gait that indicated she had been raised by a private school. She had the graceful walk of someone from nobility.

"What have I gotten myself into?" Tyrian asked Cassie with a wry sigh.

She smiled just as wryly. "If I figure it out, I'll let you know." She heard an intricate whistle and sighed. "I'm being asked to gather the others. I suppose I will see you in a while."

He reached out to take her hand as she started to go past. "Thank you," he told her. "For saving my life."

Her breath caught in her chest, and she felt her pulse flutter everywhere at once. Why did his eyes have to be *that* color? Why did his intensity seem to slowly be pulling her in and his fierce will consuming her own? "You're welcome," she managed to say, and then freed her hand and hurried from the room as fast as she could.

"The Great Sage Tanelia is quoted as saying," Liang murmured, "that those who find themselves mired in the weaving of destiny may discover the most tangled threads are those connecting two souls."

"The Great Sage," Tyrian muttered, "isn't kidding."

Chapter Three

"I want to regain the innocence of my youth."

Kyle returned within a few minutes with a tunic for Tyrian. "Thank you," Tyrian told him sincerely. "I know you don't like me."

The blue-eyed swordsman blew out a hard breath. "See, that's the damnedest part. I *do* like you, and I don't know why the hell why. I know for a fact that you're dangerous to Ophelia, so I should really be hating you. But I can't seem to do it."

"Okay," came another male voice. "What's this about us being invaded?"

Kyle sighed and moved out of the doorway. "I said no such thing, Ewan."

As the newest arrival stepped into the doorway, Marian's eyes went wide. Liang lifted a brow. Tyrian could only blink, for once startled past his normal serenity. The young man standing behind Kyle was *huge.* He was six-seven, if he was an inch, and his broad shoulders filled the doorway. His face spoke of rugged lines that, while decidedly attractive, completely ruined any chance he might have had of being truly handsome in the way Kyle was.

He wore the casual clothing of a swordsman with arrogant ease, and a sword rested at his hip. His eyes were a clear shade of yellow-brown that matched his unruly brown hair, and he swept the room with a gaze that felt oddly piercing. "So," he said, and even his voice sounded more rugged than polished, "you're Tyrian Southerwind."

"Wow," Marian breathed. "Grizzly men do exist."

Kyle choked. Hard. Coughing fiercely, he turned away. His friend eyed him intently and then turned to Marian. With a smile that softened his face and a bow that would have done any nobleman proud, he said, "Ewan Grizmar at your service."

"An honor." Tyrian returned the bow. "As you guessed, I'm Tyrian. This is my cousin, Marian, and my mentor, Liang."

Ewan studied Tyrian intently and then smiled half to himself. He could see why Cassie was so taken with Tyrian. Oh, she hadn't said anything, but the way she had bolted out of the base to his defense spoke volumes. "Nice to meet all of you. Or as we say where Kyle and I are from, well met."

"Where are you from?" Liang asked curiously.

Something came and went from Ewan's eyes like a shadow of pain. Kyle touched his arm lightly, and Tyrian very nearly reached out as well.

There was something about Ewan, and Kyle, that drew Tyrian to them as strongly as he was drawn to Liang and Marian. "The former Commune of Soldiers," Ewan finally said.

"Ah." Liang saw Marian and Tyrian frowning at him and explained, "The Commune of Soldiers is its own faction in much the way the Monk Clans are. A few years ago, the main village was erased by a rogue Vampire. The others have tried to pull together, but it's been hard."

"Vampire." Tyrian frowned thoughtfully. "I thought they were peaceful."

"Oh, most are," Ewan assured him. "Millennium Vampires, they're called. They have a valley hidden somewhere. They are very peaceful. But when they go rogue, they become evil. They can't go out during the daylight and they can't consume anything except the blood of the living."

"Yick!" Marian rubbed her arms to fight a chill. "I hope I never meet one."

"Yeah," he said softly. "It's not fun." He brushed off Kyle's hand and straightened his back. "Well, let's go find the boss lady. Once we meet with her, you can explore if you like." Blandly he added, "I'm sure Cassie would show you around."

Tyrian kept his eyes steady on Ewan's. "If she would like to."

They continued down the hall, and Ewan murmured to Kyle, "Gives nothing away, that one, but he's not secretive. I get the feeling he wouldn't be able to lie to a friend convincingly. Hell, I'm not sure he could lie to an enemy."

"Yeah," Kyle agreed quietly. "There's just something about him that gets to me. I think I can see, in part, why Cassie went running out to his defense." He added louder in a complaining voice as they walked into the meeting room, "You're not going to bring home every stray you find, right?"

Ophelia gave a ladylike snort as she looked up from the map she was studying with Cassie. "You're a farm boy at heart, Kyle. You wouldn't mind *that* much."

From the wall to the side, a rumbling male voice asked dryly, "How is it that opposites are so strongly drawn together? A farm boy and a noblewoman. Is it supposed to make sense?"

"Don't help," Kyle muttered as he sat down in a chair at the table. He jerked a thumb toward the speaker. "Tyrian, meet Dylan. Dylan, meet Tyrian Southerwind."

Tyrian studied the tall male sitting near a sewer grate. His eyes were hard emerald color and his hair looked more brown than blond. There was nothing about his appearance that looked overly attractive or trust inspiring, but Tyrian *did* trust him. Inexplicably, without question, and with the same strength with which he trusted the others. It was . . . curious.

"So," Ophelia said, studying Tyrian, "how old are you? What brought you to Teasarn?"

Something flickered in Tyrian's eyes. "Eighteen as of today. My older brother was murdered in this city. He made it back to the capitol by a miracle and died on the steps of the castle. He had been viciously attacked and drained of lifeforce."

"Shit," Dylan said so softly it was nearly inaudible.

"I don't suppose anyone saw anything unusual," Liang asked the room in general.

Ewan frowned. "I know I saw some of the soldiers acting odd. When did the attack occur, Tyrian?"

"This morning I assume. It's only a one-hour ride from here to Trinan. He left early, right before I met with Cassie. He returned not long after she left."

Cassie's sharp eyes noted the pallor under his skin and the buried grief in his eyes as clearly as if he had spoken about them. Pain stabbed through her heart. Her gaze lowered and she saw his knuckles had gone white from his fingers clenching the back of a chair. She moved forward without conscious thought, only sure that she had to comfort him. "Sit down," she told him, gently grasping his arm. "Before you fall down."

Tyrian sat down, and he was unaware of the lifted brows as he did so. When Cassie would have moved back, he took her hand. "No." Holding tight, he turned back to Ophelia and ignored her speculative look.

Kyle drummed the fingers of his right hand on the table lightly. "He had to have been attacked the instant he entered the city. The meeting wasn't *that* long, was it?" When Tyrian shook his head, Kyle leaned back in his chair. "Something smells rotten."

"That's why I came here. And . . ." Tyrian looked up at Cassie. "And I wanted to see what Cassie had been talking about." He turned back to Ophelia. "Because I am fairly sure the soldiers of the Empire know something of what happened to Ben, then I have all the more reason to distrust them. Why don't you tell me more about what is going on?"

"You'd help us?" Ewan asked idly.

"If you were in the right, and if the Empire was in the state you claim it to be, yes. I've already seen what has happened here. I lived here for sixteen years. My mother still lives here. I know it was not always like this."

"Kell?" Ophelia called.

An old man stepped forward from the shadows. On first look, he seemed quite fragile. He stood hunched over a cane, and his long white beard and snowy white hair showed starkly against his dark skin. Wrinkles lined his wrinkles and he moved so slowly that it was a wonder he didn't fall over.

"Do you need help?" Marian asked kindly as she moved to his side.

Tyrian smiled. He didn't know how he knew, but he knew it was entirely an act. "Don't bother, Marian. He's not as bad off as he proclaims."

Kell gave a surprisingly youthful laugh and promptly straightened up. His age didn't change, but the deceptive frailty went away with shocking swiftness. He gave a quick and graceful bow. "An honor to meet you, Lord Tyrian. I am Kell. I work for Lady Ophelia as an informant." He grinned cheekily at a flustered Marian. "Don't be embarrassed. I fool everyone on first meeting."

"No kidding," Kyle groused.

"Is he always grumpy?" Tyrian asked Cassie.

A smile lit her eyes. "Ophelia says he is."

Aggravated, Kyle said, "My fiancée has dragged me into the middle of a rebellion and postponed our marriage—twice! I had only *just* gotten to name my sword when we started this madness, and now I'm defending her life and her virtue at every turn! Of course I'm grumpy!"

"You only had to defend her virtue once," Dylan noted.

"And if *you* hadn't let her leave her sword behind when she met alone with that snake, it wouldn't have been at all!"

Ophelia sighed and smiled at Tyrian. "Kyle is often grumpy where the safety of his family is concerned, but he's also very outgoing and upbeat. He loves to live." Her eyes warmed when she looked at Kyle. "Perhaps it's one of the reasons I love him."

"Name your sword?" Marian asked.

Kyle nodded. "True swordsmen from the Commune of Soldiers are not considered adults until they are given the right to name their sword. Ewan gained his right five years ago but didn't bother to name his sword. I gained my right a year ago." He drew his sword and held it up so that the engraving in the blade near the hilt was visible. It read as only one name—*Ophelia*.

"Most people name their swords for someone they love," Ewan offered. "I've yet to meet anyone I loved enough to name my sword after."

"You seemed serious about Lena," Dylan offered.

A slow red color climbed Ewan's cheeks. He coughed. Hard. "So, Tyrian, what can we do to convince you?"

"Lena?" Tyrian asked delicately.

"She'd be Ewan's wife if he wasn't a coward," Kyle murmured with more than a touch of glee in his voice and eyes. "They had a very intense two-week relationship that made him go running for the hills. Last I heard, she's prepared to hit him over the head with a frying pan if he ever goes near her again."

"So," Ewan said again, this time with a touch of desperation, "what can we do to convince you, Tyrian?"

Kell offered a small spherical shaped glass globe to Tyrian. "This is a Seeing Relic," he said calmly. "I have been using it in various cities to record any events that might be of . . . value to us. You can trust what you see. I am a skilled informant. Hell, I've been a skilled informant since before your father was born."

"Are you wearing a relic?" Ophelia asked.

"No."

Startled looks instantly went to Tyrian from everyone present. "Really?" Kyle frowned. "But you have such a powerful magical capacity. I can sense it so clearly that I thought you had a strong relic."

Tyrian shook his head. "I've never found one that I was comfortable with, but I know that I'm quite strong." He picked up the Seeing Relic. "I should be able to use this without any conflicts."

The evidence of his strong sorcerer potential was clear when the Seeing Relic activated without him fusing it. It hovered over his palm obediently and began projecting images into the air over the table so that everyone could see.

It was disturbing, to say the least. A dozen cities scattered across the vast expanse of the Empire were shown to be in the same condition as Teasarn. Broken buildings, dirty streets, people living in alleys. Soldiers swarmed the crowds. The façade of regular life was simply that.

"So people in other cities are beggared, while people in Trinan live perfectly happy, unassuming lives." Marian's entire body quivered with barely leashed anger. "To think that we were all so happy and carefree while people suffered . . . !"

Liang let out a hard breath. "The evidence is damning indeed. And as much as I want to believe that there must be a reason for this, I can't convince myself that it is a good one." He looked at Tyrian, who was very quiet as he watched the relic. "It's your decision, Lord Tyrian," he said quietly. "You know that I follow you anywhere."

Tyrian put the relic down and the images stopped. With a sigh, he leaned back in his chair and closed his eyes. In that moment, he looked every inch the adult he had been forced into becoming far too fast. "I can't think at all right now. My head is so scattered."

It took every ounce of Cassie's willpower not to lean down and hold him. She bit her lip instead. Why couldn't anyone else seem to see how tired he was?

Ophelia saw Cassie's agitation as clearly as she saw the swirling darkness inside Tyrian's heart. Softly, she said, "Cassie? Take him to a room where he can rest. Introduce him to R.K. too, so he knows who to go to for anything regarding his quarters."

"No problem." Cassie lifted her hand as Tyrian got to his feet. Her eyes missed nothing of the way he carefully concealed his exhaustion and pain. Damn it, did he feel as if he had to hide everything? He didn't need to take everything on himself. "Follow me."

Liang started to get to his feet as they left the room. To his surprise, Ewan firmly put a hand on his shoulder. "He's upset!" Liang protested. "Surely you noticed! He needs someone to talk to or he'll keep it all inside! I've always been his confidant!"

Ewan shook his head with a smile. "Cassie can handle it. In fact, I think she *should* handle it. You saw them together, Liang. If they aren't in love before the week is out, I'll eat my hat."

"Week?" Ophelia smiled. "Ewan, they're already in love. They just don't know it."

All eyes went to the door. "Could be," Liang murmured. "Could very well be."

Tyrian looked around curiously as he and Cassie walked down the hall together. The underground base resembled an underground city built from a series of convoluted catacombs. He had never even known the catacombs existed. If he had, he would have definitely explored them. He loved to wander and see new places. "You guys have really gotten yourselves set up well down here. It must have taken a while to build."

Cassie glanced up at his face. He sounded normal enough, but the darkness was in his eyes again. Instead of answering the unspoken question, she asked, "Is the only thing keeping you on your feet that iron will I can sense?"

"Sometimes, yes," he admitted. He let out a hard breath. "I couldn't even begin to describe how much it hurts that Ben is dead. But I just . . . I just can't seem to cry or grieve. If I tried, then I might never recover. It doesn't make sense, but it's how I feel."

She hesitated and then went with her instincts. She reached out her hand and gently took his. His fingers automatically laced with hers, and the sense of belonging was so strong that both felt it as a literal spark between their flesh.

"How long are you to stay with the rebellion?" he asked.

She gave a little sigh. "It's . . . sketchy. I was assigned this task for as long as it takes to achieve freedom. If we are on the cusp of losing, I'm supposed to retreat back to the Clans to regroup."

"Nice of them to be so specific," he said dryly.

A little smile touched her lips. "Isn't it, though? But I suppose I'm not mad about it. Not as mad as I was. Things have . . . changed."

He glanced down at their fingers. "You're telling me."

She swung around a corner and let go of his hand. "R.K," she called as she approached a long counter where a young man stood, "Lord Tyrian needs a room." She turned to smile at Tyrian. "Lord Tyrian, this is R.K. He's our innkeeper. He keeps track of supplies and maintenance and the like. He also does a fair chunk of the cleaning."

R.K. gave a long-suffering sigh. "I need to find someone to help me. I'm wearing so many hats that I looked in a mirror and thought I was a coat rack." He offered a hand to Tyrian. "It's an honor to meet you, Lord Tyrian."

Tyrian shook his hand with a smile. "Likewise. You seem young for an innkeeper."

"I'm probably only a few years older than you," R.K. admitted. "But my parents were innkeepers, so it runs in the family." At the question in Tyrian's eyes, the innkeeper said softly, "They were murdered by Empire soldiers when they refused to give free room and board to the unit who had massacred the homeless shelter."

"I'm sorry," Tyrian said quietly. He held R.K.'s hand tighter. "I promise, no matter what I decide to do, I'm going to try to change things. Something's wrong. I know it is. So, I promise I'll try to make it better."

R.K. looked at him, a little surprised. "It's odd. Somehow, I believe you. I know you'll do it. You're very . . . inspirational, I guess." He nodded a little to himself as he handed over a key. "If you need someone to talk to, just let me know."

"I will, thank you." Tyrian looked at the key and saw that the number matched the number over one of the doors. He looked around for Cassie, but she seemed to have faded into the scenery. A little sigh caught in his chest. Her monk skills were going to be the bane of his existence. He was sure of it.

He managed to hold onto his composure until he got inside his room and had shut the door. He turned a lamp on low and looked around the small room. It was sparse, but comfortable. The bed looked soft and welcoming and a table had been heaped with books. He would have never guessed he was in a catacomb, under a city being brutalized by the Empire that had helped raise him. Ben would have loved the irony.

Pain stabbed through his heart. He slowly sank down until he sat on the floor. Shoulders shaking, he buried his face in his hands. He couldn't cry. He *wanted* to cry. He wanted to scream and rage, but he couldn't. All he could do was endure the waves of agony washing over his heart and soul.

Soft hands settled on his shoulders, and he looked up sharply to discover Cassie kneeling next to him. "How'd you . . . ?"

"I used the shadows to slip inside. It's a basic skill." She tenderly cupped his face with one hand. "You loved him."

His eyes closed. "He was my brother. Adopted, but after the first year, we both forgot. He was five years older than me. Liang and I found him after he'd escaped a brutal home. I was eight. We brought Ben home and my father and mother decided to adopt him. He was my best friend."

Her heart breaking for him, she leaned in and gently pressed her lips to his forehead. She couldn't bear to see him suffering. "I'm so sorry, Lord Tyrian."

His lips curved a little. "If you don't drop my title, I'll be forced to do something drastic." He opened his eyes and looked at her. She was soft and vibrant in the lamplight, burning with some sort of inner light that he felt rather helplessly lured toward. She was shorter than he was, even kneeling beside him. She should have seemed too small to protect him. But he felt . . . safe. If she was there, he would never be hurt. "Cassie."

Her eyes closed as his hand lifted to frame her face. "I'm supposed to be comforting you," she whispered. "I can't stop myself, Tyrian. I can't. I want to protect you so badly. I feel . . . I feel as if I was born for that sole purpose. When I saw you under attack . . . I went a little nuts."

"You looked amazing." He leaned in and lightly brushed his lips over hers. "I knew it was you. And I knew you'd save me. Even now, I feel safe near you. I should be thinking that you need *me* to protect *you*, but I don't." His lips teased hers again. "Tell me you're legal."

"I'm nineteen." The words were breathless and her hands dropped to his shoulders. She didn't know whether she wanted to push him away or pull him close. Her entire body throbbed with heat. Just the little brushes of his lips were driving her slowly mad. "I'm older than you are."

His lips curved almost wickedly, and she realized in shock that his intense seriousness hid a wildness and reckless danger as deep as the sea. He slowly pulled her closer, and his hands burned her where they curved around her neck and hip. "I like older women," he said softly, his voice huskier and deeper than she had heard it before.

"This is the biggest mistake I've ever made," she whispered in return. "Why can't I push you away?"

"Because I'm not the only one feeling it." His eyes met hers and he found himself falling into the blue flecks that glimmered like gems in the lamplight. "Where the hell have you *been* all this time?" he asked, and there was an aching loneliness in his voice.

It touched a chord inside her. She had never even realized that it had been his voice and his eyes she had been subconsciously seeking. On a desperate sound, she pulled him closer and kissed him wildly.

He tugged her onto his lap and deepened the kiss, his tongue hungrily thrusting past her parted lips. A low sound rumbled in his chest as her taste shot through him. He *knew* her taste. He knew the supple curves pressed so maddeningly against his body. His entire body was burning, his arousal throbbing painfully. He broke free of the kiss and buried his lips against her throat. Her scarf was in the way, and he impatiently removed it so he could taste her skin. "At the risk of being obvious, I want you like hell on fire."

She gulped in cool air but it did nothing for her control. Quivering with need, she dug her fingers into his tunic. "Yes," she managed to say, "that's definitely obvious. And I want you too. Oh this is madness!" She felt his lips moving across her throat and went deathly still as her heart skipped a beat. "Stop."

His head lifted sharply as he heard the fear in her voice. His eyes met hers and he lifted a hand to tenderly examine her throat. His eyes couldn't see anything in the shadows between their bodies but his fingers could. They found the thin scar almost instantly. Something volatile filled his eyes. "Tell me it was an accident." Her gaze dropped. On a rough breath, he caught her close and pressed her face to his shoulder. "I can't handle hearing about it now. But I want to know later."

"There won't be a later," she protested, although weakly.

He remained silent for several moments and then, with a smile, he let her go. "Alright," he said calmly.

Warily, she eyed him. "Alright?"

"I'm letting you have all the room you need to run. When you get tired of fighting the threads tying us together, I'll be waiting." He stole a quick but hungry kiss. "And I won't gloat or hold it against you. I'm willing to wait. I'm a very patient man."

And she was in *deep* trouble. She took a shaky breath and got off his lap. "One day at a time," she said firmly. "We only met this morning. There's . . . something between us. Neither of us know what it is. So we need to take it one day at a time. Before we even think of being lovers . . ."

He smiled. "Cas, we're already lovers. We just haven't consummated the relationship. We both know it."

Shaken, she looked down. "How is this even possible?"

"I don't know," he said simply. "But we'll figure it out. Until then, I'll stop pushing you. I won't promise not to kiss you, though. I'm not *that* strong-willed." A little dryly, he added, "My 'iron will' gives me the ability to withstand any event and keep strong in the face of deep emotional grief and trauma. It doesn't, however, seem to do *anything* to keep me sane about you."

"I better go." Before she climbed onto his lap and begged him to kiss her again.

"Might be a good idea." He caught her hand and brought it to his lips softly. "When's dinner?"

"In," her breath broke as his tongue teased the skin between her fingers, "in an hour or two."

"I'll be there."

She tugged her hand free and suddenly disappeared. Though the door couldn't open the way he was leaning against it, he knew she had left the room. He could feel her presence disappear, and it left him cold and lonely again. He closed his eyes on a sigh. Of all the rotten timing.

There came a light knock on the door. "Lord Tyrian?" Ophelia called. "I thought you might be feeling up to a walk with me."

He got to his feet and opened the door. Oddly, he did feel better. Cassie's unquestioning comfort and support had restored his balance. Nothing hurt other than his desire for her. "I might be amiable," he said by way of agreement.

Ophelia gave him a once over and hid a smile. "We have showers installed if you want to, uhm, freshen up before bed." Her voice was carefully neutral but laughter lurked inside. "The water's almost always cold, though."

He sighed. "Thanks." He fell into step beside her as she began to head down a hall. Much to his surprise, he felt very comfortable with her as if he had known her his entire life. "Where are you from, if you don't mind my asking?"

"I do not mind." She linked her hands behind her back. "I was born in Caschin. I lived there with my parents and my older brother until I was fourteen. My brother is about ten years older than I am. He's an amazing strategist and trains other students. When I was fourteen, our parents died from a plague. Matthias and I ended up traveling."

"Is that how you met Kyle?" he asked.

"Indeed! I'm eighteen, for your information," she offered, "and he's nineteen. Ewan is twenty-one. Anyway, when I was sixteen, we came across the new Commune of the Soldiers. Kyle was there. He . . ." she considered her words, "was a rebel at heart. A handsome prince who desperately needed a princess to rescue. I needed a prince."

"So you fell in love at first sight."

"Uhm, no. We fell in love after I beat him at swordplay and he demanded a rematch every day for a week until I lost my temper and threw him in a river." She smiled when he laughed at her. He needed some laughs. He was far too serious. "We've been together since. When I decided to form this rebellion a year ago, it was hard convincing him. He wanted to wait until I was legal and he could court me. I told him there was no time, so he asked my brother instead for permission, and Matt agreed. Being engaged meant Kyle was my legal guardian for the next few months until I was eighteen."

"And your brother went along with it because he knew how bad things were." He lowered his gaze. "I wish I'd known how bad things were. I still don't even know if I want to help the Rebellion or if I want to go back to the Empire and work on them from there."

"I won't force your decision," she said gently. "I firmly believe it is a decision that you must make on your own. But there is something I have to tell you." She took a little breath. "I always knew that when I met the young man with an indomitable spirit in his eyes that I would soon die. You are that young man. So I will die soon. Very likely, I will be dying for what I believe in, so I don't regret it."

He said nothing for long moments, then, "Does Kyle know?"

"No."

"Ewan or Cassie?"

"No."

"Because they would try to stop it."

"Indeed." She studied him. "You seem amazingly calm for a man who just heard someone tell him that he was the harbinger of her death."

"I'm waiting for the other shoe to drop," he countered wryly. "For you to be so calm tells me you expect something good to happen."

"Something good will happen," she assured him. "I can see it, Tyrian. Freedom for everyone. If I have to die to ensure the world will someday be at peace, then I don't mind it so much."

"And Kyle?"

"I'm not his soul mate." She smiled as she said it. "When I realized it, I was deathly jealous of whoever this mysterious girl that was meant for him was. But then I realized that . . . I don't have a soul mate. Not yet. Something inside me is incomplete right now. So . . . I'm okay. But I need you to promise me something. After I'm gone, let Kyle grieve. When you see the first sign of him pulling back up and on the cusp of being ready to let me go, tell him what I've just told you. It might be years, but will you help him?"

"Without hesitation."

"Good." She leaned up to gently kiss his cheek. There were no regrets in her heart and a curious calm existed inside her soul. Everything was happening just as it was supposed to happen. "Now then, about Cassie."

He sighed. "Neither of us understands a thing about what is happening between us. That being said, however, I'm giving her room to try to come to grips with it. I, of course, will be making absolutely no demands on her."

"Oh of course not," she agreed drolly, tongue in cheek. "You are, after all, a paragon of many virtues including patience and willpower."

His dark green eyes danced as they met hers. "How nice of you to notice."

With a laugh, she swung an arm around his waist. "Let's get dinner. You can help me keep Ewan and Kyle from getting into a food fight with Kell."

Chapter Four

"If it had only been destiny, I could have struggled."

Tyrian didn't sleep that night. He couldn't. With nothing better to do, he stayed in bed and stared at the ceiling while his mind refused to settle or focus. Everything was jumbled up. A part of him wanted to walk away. Another part wanted to stay. The only thing he could be sure of through all of his midnight mental ramblings was that he absolutely couldn't let things continue as status quo.

How the hell had he missed this? Why was his father going along with things? He had to know what was happening. And why was the Emperor suddenly treating his people so cruelly? It seemed out of place. Tyrian had always thought Albanion was a little off in many ways, but he wouldn't have thought he was stupidly and bone deeply bad.

It was dawn before he gave up pretending to sleep. He got dressed in his slacks and borrowed tunic and then left his room. R.K. was at his desk but dead asleep on top of it as if he had simply gone to sleep while working. Tyrian stopped long enough to find a blanket and gently tuck it over his shoulders. The innkeeper clearly needed a keeper.

The entire base remained quiet as he walked down the halls. The base was decent sized, enough so that it even had barracks. A glance inside told him that they had a significant number of soldiers on hand.

A soft voice asked from the shadows, "Looking for an exit?"

He let out the breath he had taken. "Cassie." He rubbed his forehead and kept his voice down as well. "Wear a bell, will you?"

Cassie smiled a little as she stepped out of the shadows. "That would defeat the purpose of my being a monk."

He studied her in bemusement. He had gotten so used to seeing her in black that her loose white tunic and brown leggings seemed completely out of place. He was also impressed; blending in was hard enough without wearing bright colors. "I suppose it would," he concurred. "If I wanted to go outside, how would I do it?"

"I can take you to an exit. You don't want to take Liang and Marian?"

"No. I'm just going to see my mother." He glanced at her. "You can come with me. I'm sure there will be some unease if I'm running around knowing where the base is."

She shook her head. "We trust you, Tyrian. Ophelia trusts you, so we trust you." She hesitated and then went with her heart. "And I trust you," she added softly. "I would trust you even if the others didn't."

He swung around and she walked into his chest. Before she could blink, his arms had gone around her waist. He buried his face in her hair and hugged her tightly. Trembling from the inside out, she slowly lifted her arms to wind them around his neck. He was so strong and solid. Unbreakable and indomitable. But she knew, *knew*, he needed her to keep him that way. Someone had to protect him.

"Thank you," he said softly. "You're the last person I'd ever want to doubt me." He eased back and skimmed his thumb over her cheek. "And I just want you to know that I trust you with my life." He smiled slowly. "Anytime you want to protect me *very* closely, feel free."

She cleared her throat. "Tyrian."

He released her, still smiling. "I never promised to make it easy on you." He caught her hand and swung her fingers up to his lips. "Come meet my mother. As far as she has to know, you're just a girl I met. Has anyone in town seen you around?"

"Well, no. But won't she think you're courting me? You're not, are you?" she asked warily.

"Of course not, Cas."

A frown darkened her face. "Well, why not?" He quirked a brow at her and she felt her cheeks heat. "Never mind! You're not allowed to court me, understand?" He was still smiling at her but she didn't push the issue. "We're just friends," she stressed. "Tell your mom we're just friends."

"I'll tell her we're friends, but not *just* friends. I've never lied to my parents." They had reached a wall, and he studied the nearly invisible ladder. Likewise, the trapdoor in the ceiling could barely be seen as well. "Will anyone see us?"

"I'll check."

He waited patiently while she seemed to disappear into the shadows. When she reappeared, he automatically tucked her hair behind her ear. "Well?"

"It's clear." His fingers were lingering warmly on her cheek. She almost helplessly turned her face into his touch. His hand slid slowly around to the back of her neck and tugged her gently closer. Wanting him, needing him more than air, her lashes lowered as he bent his head and gently brushed her lips with his.

It was the lightest, most tender kiss she could have ever envisioned, and it left some sort of imprint on her soul. She felt it. With that soft little kiss, he had marked her indelibly. She was in love with him. "Oh god," she whispered when his head lifted. "How is this possible?"

"I don't know." He kissed her again just as sweetly. "You don't have to be afraid, Cassie. It's one day at a time. When *you're* ready, then we'll move forward." He smiled. "Should I refrain from kissing you?"

She shook her head fiercely. "No. Oddly, it seems to help clear my mind. Actually, no it doesn't. It completely turns off my mind. But I think that might be why it helps me. I'm thinking too much and not feeling enough."

"Then in that case, I won't have to test my willpower. I don't think it would have held up to restraint for you." He released her and climbed up the ladder. He carefully pushed the door open and peeked out. It was still clear. He climbed out entirely and then waited for Cassie. As soon as she had joined him and the door was once more hidden, he took her hand and escorted her to the end of the alley.

It was barely dawn, but, being a farm town, people were already up and around. Tyrian's sharp eyes spotted several soldiers, but if they recognized him, they didn't say anything. Reading the tension in his shoulders, Cassie murmured, "You don't look like a nobleman right now. The tunic is too casual, and I look distinctly like a farm girl."

"Then this ought to help." He laced their fingers together. "I think I like blending in," he decided slowly. "There's something to be said for not having people look at you with expectations."

She studied his face to memorize every line and feature. "Are there a lot of expectations of you, Tyrian?"

"Where do you want me to start?" he asked, his voice sadly wry. "Ever since I was born, I was expected to train as a warrior. That wasn't so bad; I love the thrill of battle. I was *born* for it. But I've been such a natural leader—bossy is another word—that everyone expected me to follow in my father's footsteps. And they keep expecting me to be the best. So I am. Then they expect more."

"To the point where you wonder if people like you because you're you or because you represent something to them." She brought his hand to her cheek. "I expect you to be you. Stubborn, frustrating, giving, protective, loving, and brilliant. That's all."

A note of strain colored his voice as he said, "Keep saying things like that and you'll find yourself kissed senseless. I'll make up your mind for you." His eyes burned as he glanced down at her. "I have enough trouble keeping my hands to myself."

Knowing full well that his willpower was so strong as to keep him from giving in to even debilitating grief and that it couldn't be shaken by even the crumbling of everything he thought he had known, she realized that knowing she could obliterate his willpower simply by being there was very, very heady.

The house where his mother lived looked no different from his memories, even though he hadn't been back in two years. When he knocked and she opened the door, she looked no different either. "Can we come in?" he asked.

Annareal lifted a brow slightly. "You're asking? At your own home, you're asking?" She stepped back regardless to let them inside. "I'm not sure if it is polite or insulting, frankly." She studied Cassie with a mother's immense curiosity. "I don't believe we've met."

"This is Cassie. She's become my best friend in short time, and I thought you'd like to meet her."

Annareal's eyes dropped to where their fingers were still clasped. A little smile played around her lips. "You thought right. It's nice to meet you, Cassie. I'm Annareal Southerwind." She studied Tyrian's eyes and then her own gaze darkened. "So. It's true, about Ben."

Cassie held tighter to Tyrian's hand when his fingers tensed. "Yes," he said quietly. "It is. That's why I came back here. And, coming here . . . I see so many things wrong. What's going on, Mother? Why are the soldiers here like this?"

Annareal sighed and led the way into the parlor. She waited for them to sit down before taking her own seat. "I don't know," she finally said. "I want to say it just happened out of the blue, but it truly was so gradual that no one noticed until it was as bad as it is now. I didn't really notice because I don't pay taxes; your father pays them directly from his pay."

"Why is he letting this happen?" He rubbed his forehead. "It's just not right! How can beggaring cities and hurting people possibly help the Emperor?"

"You can't pretend to understand what goes on in a ruler's mind," she chided gently. "But you must follow your own heart, Tyrian. If you feel what is happening is wrong, then tell someone. You are respected. They would listen."

He took a long breath. "Thank you."

"You're welcome." She smiled at Cassie. "Feel free to come for dinner any time. Tyrian's . . . friend is always welcome in my home."

Cassie cleared her throat. "Thank you, ma'am." Sensing the sun rising swiftly, she squeezed Tyrian's hand. "We should be going, Tyrian."

"Of course." He got to his feet and leaned down to kiss his mother's cheek. "It was nice to see you. I'll come back for another visit soon." Holding tight to Cassie, he led the way out of the house. As soon as they were outside, he smiled. "She didn't believe that you were just my friend."

"Oh hush," the monk groused. She contemplated her words and then said slowly, "She was wrong about something. You, more than anyone, knows what goes on inside a leader's mind. You have the potential to be the greatest leader ever because you *care* about people, Tyrian. Your compassion is as critical as your intelligence."

"If you keep flattering me, I'm going to get an over-inflated ego." He swung her fingers up to his lips. "That or I might kiss you wherever we happen to be."

"That shouldn't be as tempting as it is," she complained as she led the way toward another alley and another secret passage.

"I warned you." He felt himself relax as soon they entered the catacombs, and he realized something he had not noticed before. Subconsciously, he had been tense the entire time through the village and his meeting with his mother. Here, in the base, he felt comfortable. In that moment, he made his decision.

"Lord Tyrian!" Liang said in exasperation as he came down the hall.

"What's with the 'lord' stuff?" Cassie whispered.

"He likes to pretend he's formal around other people," Tyrian whispered back.

Liang ignored Cassie's muffled snickers as he caught up. Hands on hips, he glared at Tyrian. "You should have woken me. It wasn't safe for you to go wandering around outside."

Before Tyrian could open his mouth, Cassie said with a touch of chill, "Yes, heaven forbid a Tenth Class Monk be capable of protecting him. Why should he even be trusted near her, let alone to be protected by her?"

She disappeared abruptly into the shadows. Liang grimaced. "I didn't mean to offend her."

"I think you unintentionally hit a sore nerve." Tyrian made a mental note to find out what it was. "But she did have a valid point. I'm safer with her than with anyone else. Of that I am absolutely positive." He began to head down the hall with purpose. "If you want to know, we went to visit Mother. I spoke of seeing the village in this state and she told me to follow my heart."

"And?" Liang asked it though he already knew the answer.

Tyrian walked into the meeting room where Ophelia and Kyle stood looking over a huge pile of papers. They glanced up inquiringly and Tyrian said without preamble, "I'm in. I have no reason to believe that anyone at the castle would listen to me. Despite appearances, I'm still just Donald Southerwind's son. But I can't let this go on."

Kyle gave a satisfied smile as Ophelia nodded. "I knew you'd feel that way," she said. "Come join us, Tyrian." When he had stepped up beside her, she gestured to the map. "This is the layout of the Empire. We share a Y shaped border with Melodina and part of Foresalia. But we can't expect help from either. Melodina is having its own internal discord and Foresalia hates us."

"We don't want to be depending on anyone for a rebellion," Tyrian said thoughtfully. "We'll be struggling enough to establish a new leadership without having debts to repay."

"You talk as if we've already won," Liang noted.

"Am I supposed to talk as if we've already lost? If so, then we might as well end here. I'm not going into this thinking I'm going to lose." He picked up one of the papers and discovered a roster. "We have soldiers from assorted places. How well trained?"

"Well enough," Ophelia admitted, "but not nearly on par with the Imperial Army."

"We can train them. I know how the Army operates." He dropped the papers. "I have a tendency to get bossy," he informed her. "Feel free to tell me to shut up if you think I'm getting *too* bossy."

She smiled at him. "You're a better leader than I. Already you're getting us more organized than we were before."

"Ah, so you joined us." Ewan sauntered into the room with Cassie and Kell following him. All three looked unusually tense and there was something dangerously pissed off in Cassie's eyes. "Glad to know you made the choice before you had none."

Ophelia's eyes narrowed. "What do you mean?"

He tossed a poster onto the table. In bold words across the top was 'WANTED DEAD OR ALIVE.' Tyrian's picture blatantly sat underneath it. A reward of up to ten thousand gold or a lifetime free of taxes had been offered as reward. There was no explanation or any legitimate reason as to why Tyrian suddenly had a bounty on his head.

"What the hell?" Kyle snatched up the poster. "Where'd you get this?"

"They're being plastered all over town," Kell offered. "When I asked a soldier why a nobleman's son was being hunted, he said that the Emperor had determined Tyrian was a threat to the Empire itself. Apparently his new consort said Tyrian was destined to overthrow the Empire."

"Consort." Tyrian frowned. "That would be Lady Blaine. I've never met her before. I know *of* her, naturally. She made quite the . . . impression on the court when she arrived. She has the Emperor wrapped around her finger." Something flickered in his eyes. "She arrived little over a year ago."

Ewan's brows shot up. "Conveniently around the time the situation began to change."

"Seems so." Tyrian picked up the poster and calmly tore it in half. "It changes nothing. They'd have been after me as soon as I joined the Rebellion anyway. Maybe that was what she saw. If so, then I feel much more confident about our efforts, don't you?"

"He can make the absurd sound reasonable," Liang apologized to the others. "You'll get used to it."

"Where's Marian?" Tyrian asked.

"Flirting with R.K."

He sighed. "Would someone tell her to go turn her wiles on the merchants and get as many magic scrolls and medicines as she thinks she can get away with explaining? She can use my money."

Kell grinned and scuttled off much faster than a man of his age should have been able to.

"How many troops do we have?" Tyrian asked Ophelia.

"One unit's worth—one thousand soldiers."

Tyrian began to drum the fingers of his right hand on his left arm. Several pairs of sharp eyes noted the action. "We need more troops. But we won't get more people to leave the Empire to join us unless we look serious. We can't go anywhere near the Imperial Army as we stand. They have dozens of units. We need to start small and make big waves at the same time."

"So how do we do that?" Ewan propped his feet on the table.

"We take this city." Tyrian turned to Ophelia. "If we make a bigger show of rebelling and actually let everyone know definitively that's what we're doing, the people will believe us more readily. One unit is enough to hold this town. We rout the soldiers currently here and send those who surrender back to the Empire. If any want to defect and join us, all the better."

"You're that sure they would?" asked Kyle curiously.

"You don't have corruption only at the surface. It seeps into every crack. If the people suffer, then the lowest class soldiers will suffer too. Many probably came from towns just like Teasarn."

There was a long silence. Then, slowly, Ewan said, "It's so odd. When you say things like that, I believe you. If you told me I could storm the castle with a stick and a torch, I'd do it. I'd believe you until you were proven wrong."

Cassie leaned on the table. "This would also have another benefit. If there is an active showing of resistance and success from the Rebellion, then I will be justified in going to the Clans and asking for more help. If we can get even one or two units from the Clans, then we will be very well set."

"And other towns will be more inclined to aid," Liang noted. "What about the civilians in this town? The children in particular."

"R.K. and Kell have befriended all the children." Ophelia pulled out another paper. "We know all of them by name and age. For months now, the kids have known that if they see real fighting break out, they're to come to the catacombs for safety. More than any, the children can be trusted."

"Then I, Cassie, and Kyle will take Marian and work from the inside while our unit comes in from the outside. The Army unit will no doubt be arriving anytime." Tyrian sat down with a sigh. "After all, this was my last known location and they want me dead or alive."

Unable to bear the buried note of pain, Cassie stepped forward and put her hands gently on his shoulders. "Maybe your father doesn't even know yet," she said softly.

Kell and Marian came skidding into the room. "An Army unit approaches," Kell said bluntly. "They're carrying a flag bearing the symbol of the High General. The Empire isn't playing games."

"Tyrian," Ophelia said softly in pain.

He said nothing for long moments and then straightened his back. "Fine," he said calmly. "If anything, this is best. I know how the *High General* works and how he trains his troops." He got to his feet, his face carefully controlled. Only his eyes, and the darkness inside, belied the turmoil inside his heart. "They rely heavily on direct combat. If we attack with subterfuge, we'll have the advantage."

As Kell hurried to the barracks, Marian hissed out a breath. "This isn't right!" she said heatedly. "Why do we have to do this?"

"Because no one else will." Tyrian gave her an even look. "You can leave."

She glared at him for long moments and then walked over and hugged him fiercely. "Not a chance!" she said against her cousin's shoulder. "You're stuck with me. I'm not about to let you get into trouble alone."

A little tension left his shoulders. "Thanks, Marian." He looked at Ophelia. "What about you?"

"I'll stay here with R.K. and Kell and we'll keep the children safe. Ewan, will you and Dylan ride with the unit to command them?"

"Done." Ewan got to his feet and headed out, shouting for Dylan to join him.

Tyrian looked at Liang. "Go find my mother and protect her. If she wants to help us, great. If not, then she can be sent to the castle. If she's really such a potential distraction to my father, then that's all the better for us."

Cassie softly touched his arm. Heaven help the Emperor if Tyrian ever truly let loose of the bitterness he had been saving up for eighteen years. Her eyes lifted to meet Liang's and an unspoken message passed between them. "I'll protect him with my life," she said simply. "I can do no other."

Liang nodded slowly. "I'm beginning to see that. Very well." He turned and left the room.

Ophelia held out a small clear stone to Tyrian. "This is a Voice Relic," she told him. "If you equip it to your earring, you'll be able to use it to talk to us and vice-versa." As he took the relic, her eyes met his. "You call the shots. You know our enemy."

He nodded and removed the small earring he wore to fasten the relic to it. The earring was more than decoration; it was a highly advanced form of magical technology. It could hold small relic fragments—like the Voice Relic—that would allow him access to a multitude of extra amenities. Most, if not all, people wore them.

A soft beep heralded Ewan's voice from the relic as he said, "Enemy in sight. No sign of Donald Southerwind. A lesser lieutenant is riding at the front."

"What's your location?" Tyrian asked.

"Hiding around the edge of town."

"Wait for them to get within range of either arrows or magic, whichever you've got a better shot at landing. After the initial shot, don't wait for them to recover. Go in immediately. Take prisoner those willing to surrender, let those willing to run do so, and remove any who choose to remain and fight."

"I like how you think. Consider it done."

The soft hum faded and Tyrian headed for the nearest exit. "We're going up top to catch anyone who causes trouble inside town. Ophelia, the kids will be sent to you for safety as soon as possible."

"Done." She gave Kyle a soft and tender kiss. "I love you," she told him softly.

Kyle shot her a frustrated look. He had always felt there was something she hadn't told him, and now he was sure. Vowing to pin her down later, physically if necessary, he followed Tyrian and Cassie as they headed up to the streets with Marian close behind.

Pandemonium had broken loose up top. The units clashed outside the city walls with the sound and fury of a full war. The Army was not prepared for the sort of controlled, yet uncontrollable, fury of the Rebellion. For every Imperial soldier that fell, another threw down arms to surrender.

The soldiers in the city were on a rampage. They tried to attack anyone who got in their way, civilian or not. Most of the townspeople were smart enough to run for cover. Children mysteriously vanished from the streets.

Kyle drew his sword. "Which way?"

"Follow me." Tyrian drew his staff and started down the closest street. At the end, he spotted several soldiers trying to break down a door. "Cassie."

He didn't need to say anything else. Throwing stars appeared in her hand and she hurled them with all her might. Her aim was true. Two of the four soldiers dropped instantly. The other two whirled and attacked.

Kyle and Tyrian proved a formidable combination. It was only moments before both soldiers went down. Marian only had to heal a minor cut to Kyle's arm where he had deflected a blow from his head. Now knowing how they worked together, the party made their way through the city, sparing no mercy for those who wanted to fight but willingly taking captive those who surrendered.

They had just cleared the streets when Dylan's voice came over the relic, "We've routed them. The majority are running back for the capitol as fast as possible. We have about one hundred prisoners."

Liang came running down the street and skidded to a stop next to Tyrian. "Lord Tyrian," he said urgently, "I can't find Lady Annareal! I've looked everywhere! She wasn't at home and she hasn't been seen anywhere!"

"*Tyrian!*"

The panicked and very loud shout through his Voice Relic made Tyrian wince. "R.K.? What's wrong?"

"Hurry! The base has been breached! Hurry!"

Kyle went white. "Ophelia."

The nearest entrance to the base was a block away, and the panel had already been pried up. Heart in his throat, Tyrian dropped down inside and ran down the hall. He discovered R.K. and Kell at the end, wounded and covered in blood where they sat slumped against a wall.

Marian made a panicked sound and rushed to their sides. "Hang on, boys! I'll get you healed!"

"Hurry," R.K. managed to say. "Lady Ophelia is in danger!"

Kyle was already running down another hallway. Tyrian and Cassie followed him swiftly. The sound of children crying grew louder as did the sound of fighting. Swords clashing together and soft feminine cursing. Somehow Tyrian knew what he would see.

They entered the room and came to sharp stops as they saw Ophelia locked in combat with Annareal. The older woman was by no means weak as she skillfully parried and blocked Ophelia's attacks. A dozen children huddled near a wall in terror.

"Stop!" Tyrian ordered sharply. "What are you *doing*?!" He was already moving forward as he spoke, and his staff appeared in his hand.

"You can't have both of us," Annareal retorted. "Make your decision, Tyrian!"

There was no decision to be made and it reflected in his eyes. His disgust for his mother was plain and clear. In fury, she whirled and went after the children. Kyle and Tyrian both rushed forward and so did Ophelia. The males didn't reach Annareal, but Ophelia did, and she threw herself in front of the children. Annareal's sword went directly into her chest and all the way out through the back. The soft gasping sound she made permanently imprinted itself in the ears of those present. Even as she fell, the others leapt forward.

Annareal found herself grabbed around the neck, slammed into the wall, and held a foot off the floor by Cassie. "Y-you," she managed to gasp. "What are you?"

"I'm from the Monk Clans," Cassie said in an icy tone. Her grip tightened. "Time for a nap." She jerked Annareal down as she shoved up with her knee. The older woman gasped as the breath was driven out of her lungs and dropped unconscious onto the floor. "Tie her up," Cassie ordered Liang as he stepped into the doorway.

"Oh god." Kyle lifted Ophelia into his arms, his face white with pain and terror. Blood. There was blood everywhere. The wound in her chest looked wide and vicious, and it had gone clear through a horrific spot. Every living creature had a place on their body that equated to an instant death sentence if they were even wounded there. In Humans, it sat an inch to the left of the heart. No Healer, no matter how talented, could heal a wound in a critical zone. "Ophelia! Ophelia!"

Her eyes opened halfway. "The kids?"

"Alive," Tyrian said quietly. "Thanks to you." He was completely unaware of the hand Cassie rested on the back of his neck. Pain boiled in his heart, scalded his soul. "We won the battle. The Army retreated. We have prisoners. Your rebellion is just beginning."

She closed her eyes as she smiled. Her breath caught on a painful hitch and then smoothed. "Yours. It's yours, Tyrian. It was always meant to be yours." She carefully lifted a hand and he grasped it tightly but gently. "You have to free everyone. Please."

"You have my vow."

"I'm glad." She drew a ragged breath. The pain was going away. It really didn't hurt anymore. Everything was warm and quiet. It was okay. She had done everything. No . . . not everything. She needed to do something else. "Tyrian? I need you to say something," she whispered.

"What is it?"

"*Askandi repulsin* Devourer."

He went very still. "Why?"

"Please."

Softly, he said, "*Askandi repulsin* Devourer." He gave her hand a little shake. "Why? Ben made me say that once too. What does it mean? What's going on, Ophelia? Damn it, you can't die and leave us like this!"

She looked at Cassie who hesitated and then nodded a little. Her gaze then went to Kyle. Her eyes softened. "Kyle." She lifted her free hand to touch his cheek gently. "I never regretted loving you." Before he could say anything, her hand dropped and her entire body went slack. Her eyes slowly closed and her breaths stopped.

Ewan began to curse in a soft and vicious voice from the doorway. He had one arm around R.K.'s waist to keep the other man on his feet. He was healed, but blood loss could only be cured by time. Kell was leaning on Marian whose face looked utterly white with devastation. "No," she whispered.

Tyrian put down Ophelia's hand and got to his feet. "Take Annareal to a holding cell," he ordered, his voice quiet and controlled. "Ensure she carries no weapons and no way to get out. She is to be guarded by any two soldiers who won't be enticed by her pleas. Offer the other Army soldiers the option of joining us or returning to the Empire."

"Who is she?" Dylan asked harshly from behind Ewan with a sharp gesture at Annareal.

A bitter little smile curved Tyrian's lips. "Donald Southerwind's wife." He knelt to help Kyle stand. The swordsman had Ophelia's body clutched in his arms. "I won't let her down, Kyle," Tyrian said quietly. "Or you. You can hate me if you wish."

"I can't feel anything right now." Eyes as heavy as his steps, Kyle slowly walked out of the room.

Tyrian almost envied him. He wished he couldn't feel anything right then too.

Chapter Five

"The loneliness of the past, the tomorrow of yesterday."

While Kyle took Ophelia's body to a place to be held until a proper burial could be done, Tyrian went to see the soldiers that had been captured from the Imperial Army. Cassie and Liang accompanied him, both concerned with how he had pulled further into himself. Marian tended to the wounded, but it was clear that she too had been deeply shaken. There was no one who hadn't been affected.

The soldiers were being held in the barracks under close guard by Rebellion soldiers. As Tyrian surveyed the room and the faces, he realized that most of them were barely older than his age and the rest were younger. They may well be new recruits. His father had severely underestimated the Rebellion. "Any trouble?" he asked one of the guards quietly.

"No, Lord Tyrian." The guard shook her head. "They've been amazingly quiet. Maybe they sense the precarious balance."

He walked further into the room. "I'm Tyrian Southerwind," he began, "and I would appear to be the leader of the Rebellion. I'm here to offer you a choice. You can join us, or you can go home. The fight is over. We're not going to kill you in cold blood. If you want to fight us again, however," he added mildly, "then all bets are off."

"Why did you join the Rebellion?" one soldier asked. "You betrayed your Empire and your father."

"Because my Empire betrayed its people. Have any of you talked to your families lately? Do you even know what they are suffering? Teasarn is just an example of the ways that the Emperor is choking his people to death." Tyrian stepped forward and lifted his chin. "I'm not standing by. I refuse to. I'm going to change things. If the Emperor won't listen to reason, then maybe it's time we had a different sort of government."

A little chill went down Liang's back. He had never heard Tyrian so eloquent, had never realized those thoughts were inside him. More still, he saw then something he had never seen before. That glitter in Tyrian's eyes, that indomitable spirit . . . it was the mark of a hero. Liang knew it for sure. In Tyrian's eyes was the glitter of a leader who would do whatever it took to protect his people and his land.

Silence reigned for a long while and then the soldiers began to remove their Imperial jackets. They pulled off the badges from their hats and dropped them on the floor. Then, as one, they all knelt. "You have our loyalty, Lord Tyrian," one said clearly. "We'll follow you to the end."

"Why?" Tyrian asked.

One soldier straightened up as a half-smile twisted his lips. "We're all from small towns too. We had heard rumors but never seen what was really going on. We want to fight for our families and for you."

Tyrian turned to the guards at the door. "See that they are given new clothes and any wounds are treated. We're going to be tight for space for now, but I'll look into obtaining a real place of operation. We can't hide under the streets forever."

"Yes sir."

He headed down another hall, very conscious of the fact that he was still being followed. "Are you going to do this all the time?" he asked on a sigh. "Because I'm fairly sure that it's going to become very vexing."

Cassie and Liang looked at one another for long moments. Liang leaned down to murmur something in Cassie's ear and she nodded. With a smile, he then turned and went the other way down the hall.

Tyrian lifted a brow at Cassie. She shrugged one shoulder. "There's no need to think you need two bodyguards while within our own base. Liang is going to go see how Kyle and Ewan are doing. They and Dylan knew Ophelia the longest."

"If it's safe, why have you stayed with me?" he asked. He turned the corner and found himself looking at his mother, housed in a holding cell. His shoulders tensed.

She softly wrapped her hands around his. "Because you need me. I'm not going to let you break, Tyrian."

He took a deep breath. Oddly, knowing that she was there was enough. Every time he thought he stood at the edge of a precipice, she was there to gently draw him back. Back straight, he walked over to where two guards stood on duty. "Any trouble?" he asked as calmly as he could.

"No, Lord Tyrian. She's been very quiet. Should we leave to give you some privacy?"

"Don't go far though," he agreed.

The two guards moved down the hall to be out of sound but not out of sight. When they had, he stepped in front of the metal grate that served as a cell wall and door. "So," he said evenly. "How does it feel to be a murderess?"

Annareal looked at him in horror. "But I was told . . . !" She sealed her lips shut.

"Told what?" When there was no answer, he added coldly, "I have no reason to treat you with mercy or kindness when you cold-bloodedly snuck into this base and attempted to kill children. You did, in fact, kill a woman I considered to be much like a sister to me though I knew her a short time."

Tears began to roll down her face. She had never seen her son like this. She hadn't wanted to believe he could be like this. "I was told," she whispered, "that if you joined the Rebellion, you would be destroyed. And I see I was right. You're not the Tyrian I knew."

"No, I'm not. Watching my mother commit murder had a strong impact on me."

"It wasn't murder!" She leapt to her feet, fury in her eyes. "I thought I was protecting you!"

"Yeah," he said evenly. "I was in real danger from a bunch of children. If you had been just after Ophelia, then you had no reason to be in that room. You should have taken the fight out, or called her out for a duel. She'd have responded. Instead, you forced a dozen children to witness the death of someone they loved. You went after them on purpose so that she would make herself vulnerable. They'll never forget that moment. *I* will never forget that moment."

There was movement from the shadows, and Kyle stepped forward. His blue eyes looked dark and volatile with grief and fury. A faint tremor shook his entire body. "Let me kill her," he told Tyrian. "Let me have my vengeance."

Tyrian was silent for so long that Annareal lost all color in her face. Finally, Tyrian turned to Kyle. He gently wrapped a hand around Kyle's wrist, staying him before he drew his sword. "No," he said quietly, "because it will do nothing for your pain. If I thought you would feel better, I would open the door right now and look away. But it won't. Killing her right now will make you a murderer as well, Kyle, and I will not see you suffer in that way. It won't bring Ophelia back."

Kyle's eyes closed and he dropped his head on Tyrian's shoulder. Tears slid soundlessly down his cheeks. "I know," he agreed softly.

Tyrian glanced at Cassie who nodded slightly. He then looked at the woman who had given birth to him. "You will be escorted back to Trinan. Feel free to tell them you killed Ophelia. But also feel free to tell them that I will bring the Rebellion to victory. Not just for Ophelia's sake, but for the people." A chill smile curved his lips. "I had already been made second-in-command before the battle began." He gently put an arm around Kyle's shoulders and escorted him away from the area.

Cassie walked over to the grate and studied Annareal. "It sickens me," the monk noted quietly, "that you could hurt your son like this. I don't care what you thought you were doing. It was wrong, and you know it." She pulled up her hood and wrapped her scarf around her face to effectively obscure her appearance. "I will escort you personally, Lady Annareal. And it won't take much of an excuse for me to take the vengeance that we all so dearly wish for. Monks live by a different code than the Commune."

As they walked down the hall, Tyrian said quietly, "I'm sorry, Kyle."

"I don't blame you, Tyrian." Kyle drew a deep breath that came out ragged at the end. "It was always a possibility that one of us might die for this Rebellion. But . . . it just doesn't seem real that this has actually happened. It *hurts*."

"I know." They were the same height, so it was easy for Tyrian to again put an arm around his shoulders in support. "I'm up to three people that I loved dying."

"Three?"

Darkness moved in Tyrian's eyes. "Ben was the first. Then Ophelia. And my mother is dead as well. When she drew a sword against innocent children, she died in my mind."

Kyle remained silent for long moments. "Are we really going to fight for freedom?" he finally asked quietly.

"Yes." Tyrian released him as they reached the meeting room. "And we're going to get it." He walked into the room with his head held high. "Cassie is escorting Annareal back to the capitol. We have one hundred new soldiers in our army, so we're on our way to having a second unit."

As he sat down, Ewan said, "Well, the townspeople stand behind us. We've been checking, but there's not a single person who doesn't support us. However, I'm concerned about their safety. We have to spread out somehow, but if we leave the town unprotected, then people will very likely be killed."

"I was thinking of that myself." The green-eyed warrior frowned thoughtfully. "We need a base. Something big enough to hold everyone we might possibly need to house, but something that is still defendable."

"Well," Dylan offered, "there's an abandoned castle a few days' journey from here. It was once the seat of the Empire, but when it was moved to Trinan, the castle was completely abandoned. If I remember legend right, it withstood a five-day siege from Foresalia over a hundred years ago."

"Isn't it in the middle of a nasty lake?" Liang asked warily.

"Nasty how?" Marian wondered.

"Nasty as in full of very cranky monsters," was Kell's dry explanation. Though still pale from losing blood, the old informant was well on the way to recovery even though the use of his cane was more practical than prop right then.

Tyrian sighed. He had nothing against the monsters of the world; they were more vexing than threatening for any seasoned warrior. They just served to stand as a constant reminder that the world was still being punished for events of more than a million years prior. When the gods handed down punishment, they didn't mess around.

"Well, we've got a solid group of fighters." If anyone noticed that Kyle's knuckles were white where his hands gripped together, no one said anything. "Tyrian, Cassie, I, Marian, and Liang can go check out the castle and try to drive off the monsters. Ewan and Dylan can stay here to keep things in line. If we get the castle, we can move everyone there."

Cassie suddenly stepped out of the shadows. She also startled Ewan who jolted so hard he almost sent his cup of coffee flying. "Wear a bell!" he demanded in aggravation.

"As I told Tyrian, that would defeat the purpose." She looked at Tyrian and then immediately crossed to him. She took his hand gently. His fingers gripped hers tightly though his expression didn't change.

A bit warily, Liang said, "You weren't gone long enough to escort Lady Annareal back to Trinan."

The smile that curved Cassie's lips looked chilling. "I left her halfway. She can walk the rest. If she gets eaten by monsters, it's not our business."

Kyle's eyes shot to Tyrian. His expression hadn't changed, but Kyle had started to understand him very, very well. The amount of emotion the slightly younger man pulled out of everyone seemed almost shocking, yet it was a two-way street because Tyrian clearly cared just as strongly for them in return. With that emotion came understanding. "You stopped me on purpose."

"It's not our fault if she can't hold her own in the wild and that Cassie was needed here with me more than she was needed out there." Tyrian kept his voice neutral. "I showed more mercy than most people would."

And it was cutting him inside. Ewan's eyes met Dylan's in understanding. Carefully, the former said, "Why don't we get some rest before we set out for the castle tomorrow morning? It's been a bitch of a day."

"I'd rather get drunk," muttered Kyle.

"We can do that too," Ewan agreed amiably. He dragged Kyle up out of his chair and shoved him at the door. "Let's see if we can get you to sing like a canary again. Dylan, you coming?"

"I don't sing," the other man said dryly.

"No, but you tell great jokes. Let's go."

"Kyle will be fine," Kell said quietly. "Ewan knows how to handle him. It's a repayment in a way. They've been through one hell together. Kyle helped Ewan pull out. So now he'll help Kyle."

"The Commune of the Soldiers?" Marian guessed softly.

"So I suspect. I don't have all the info." He got to his feet carefully. "Ugh. These old bones are indeed old." He brushed off Liang and Marian when they moved to help him. "I'm old not incapacitated," he groused, waving his cane threateningly.

"Do you want me to go so you can talk?" Cassie asked Tyrian softly.

"No." He brought her hand to his cheek. "I need you to stay close." A bit shakily, he admitted, "I'm about ready to fall apart."

She leaned down to wrap her arms around his shoulders. "I won't let you," she vowed softly. She looked at Marian and Liang who seemed completely at ease with the scene. "You've been amazingly . . . accepting of me."

Slowly, Marian said, "Based on the fact that we've known Tyrian his entire life, we know his mind and ways. So what we see here isn't surprising. It's almost expected, somehow. I feel as if I always knew he'd meet you."

"And," Liang said softly, "I want to apologize, Lady Cassie. I did not mean to infer earlier that you were incapable of protecting Lord Tyrian properly. I have protected him his entire life. So in my mind, the fact that I was not there was all I considered."

Cassie inclined her head in acknowledgment of the apology. "I apologize as well about being touchy. Monks are far too often seen as untrustworthy because we keep so many secrets of our skills and cities. It cut that you did not trust me with Tyrian."

He smiled. "I fully believe you are capable and willing to protect him."

She glanced down to see Tyrian tapping a finger on the top of the table even though his face revealed nothing. "You mean protect him when he can't protect himself?"

Liang's eyes flicked to Tyrian's hand and a smile curved his lips. She did indeed know Tyrian very well after a short time. "Precisely." His smile faded as he let out a quiet breath. "I can't believe all of this is happening, that everything is changing so quickly."

Marian laid her head on top of the table and closed her eyes. "It seems so unfair! Do . . . do you think Ben's death had anything to do with all of this? If he hadn't died, we wouldn't have come here when we did. We might have ended up being enemies with Lady Ophelia and Cassie."

Tyrian didn't respond, but his mind turned over and over again about the 'curse' he had supposedly broken on Ben and Ophelia. He *knew* the words were from the language of magic, and he was fairly sure it had to do with some relic somewhere. It had been after he said it to Ben that he began to pick up mannerisms of someone wearing a relic, and at thirteen, despite his great capacity, he had been entirely too uncomfortable to fuse a relic at all. Now, having said the same phrase to Ophelia, he could feel the skin of his right hand burning.

Someone knocked softly on the door, and he glanced over to see a young soldier standing there. "Pardon the intrusion," she said softly. "But a messenger pigeon just arrived with a note for Lord Tyrian." She walked over and held out the paper.

"Thank you." Tyrian took the note and unrolled it. He recognized his father's handwriting immediately. The note was simple and to the point: *She made it back*. In a murmur, he said, "Never gives away anything. I have no way of knowing what he feels about this, or if he even cares."

The soldier cleared her throat and drew Tyrian's attention. "Lord Tyrian, I just want to let you know, on behalf of everyone, that we believe in you. We know you won't let us down." She gave a little salute and left the room.

Tyrian took a quiet breath and then crumbled the note and threw it over his shoulder. Cassie released him and he got to his feet. "I'm going to try and sleep." Without waiting for anyone to say anything, he turned and walked out of the room with his back more stiff than straight.

Silence fell and then Marian said idly, "He likes brandy."

Cassie shot her a quick look but the other woman was studiously picking at a piece of broken wood on the table. Her eyes flicked to Liang who feigned an absorbed interest in a painting on the wall. Suddenly realizing it was acceptance, she got to her feet. "I better go make sure Ewan doesn't drink everything."

She left the room, and Liang and Marian shared a smile.

Cassie found Kyle, Dylan, and Ewan sitting together at a table in the galley, and all of them were drinking. Dylan was on his way to being drunk and Kyle had already gotten there. Catching the tail end of a decidedly bawdy joke, she felt glad she didn't blush easily. After a study of Ewan, she realized that despite his enthusiastic response to the joke, he was very, very sober.

She walked over to the table, and under the pretext of inspecting the glass, she took a sniff of his drink. It was tea carefully doctored to look like liquor. R.K. played bartender not far away, and she watched as he covertly poured three drinks from two different bottles. "Well?" she asked Ewan softly.

He took his glass back from her, his brown eyes guileless as he saluted her lightly. "Someone needs to make sure he doesn't break his neck when we're done here."

"You're a good man, Ewan Grizmar," she murmured.

"Shh. I have a reputation to uphold."

She smiled and went over to R.K. "Got any brandy hiding back there?"

He ducked under the counter and began rummaging through bottles. "Somewhere, I think. We need a bartender." He came up and held out the bottle. "I didn't know you drank." Something suddenly began to twinkle in his eyes. "Or is this our leader's drink of choice?" When she averted her eyes, he whistled softly. "Nice."

She snatched the bottle out of his hand and turned and stalked out. Everyone was a smartass. Knowing her luck, they would probably start a betting pool. Just because she was attracted to Tyrian didn't mean she would fall in bed with him. Well, okay, it *kind* of did, but it wasn't quite that simple. She was in love with him, and that was a whole new level of trouble. If she had a single working brain cell, she would turn and walk away, go back to the Clans, and have them send someone else.

But when she opened his door slightly and saw him sitting on the side of his bed with his head in his hands, every thought of leaving disappeared. She walked over and sat down beside him. She set the bottle aside and then gently smoothed his hair back from his face. "Tyrian?" she asked softly.

"There was a time when I thought my life was going to be simple." He didn't look up. "There was a time where I thought that my life would be easy. I'd go to Trinan. I'd become a soldier and then I'd become a general. I'd follow in my father's footsteps. Nice and simple and tidy."

"Life isn't simple." She pulled his hands away from his face so that he was forced to look at her. "I wanted simple, too, after my parents died. But it just doesn't work that way."

He looked at her for long moments and then straightened up. He wanted to ask about her family and her history, but he didn't. He could sense pain under the surface. The last thing he ever wanted was to hurt her. Instead, his gaze fell on the bottle. A brow lifted. "You want to get me drunk and take advantage of me?"

She pondered that for long moments. Long enough that his lips began to curve. Seeing it, she finally said, "No, I don't think so. But I'm willing to share a drink with you if you want to pretend for a little while that the world doesn't exist."

"How's Kyle?" He spotted two glasses sitting next to a pitcher of water and retrieved them.

"Telling jokes that would make even your hair curl. But when he pauses for a breath, there's something in his eyes. Hopefully he'll pass out soon. Even more hopefully, he and Dylan won't have hangovers tomorrow morning."

"If they do, Marian knows several cures."

She quirked a brow as she poured the brandy into the two glasses. "Are we intimately acquainted with them?"

He gave her a little salute with his glass. "Ben and I decided to experiment when I was sixteen. To say we never did it again would be an understatement. Of course, Marian laughing at us didn't help."

"I've never been drunk," she informed him gravely.

"Really?"

"Really. Part of the monk code. You don't give away your control to outside influences. Alcohol is the biggest item on the list." She sipped the brandy and wrinkled her nose. "Bleh." She set the glass aside. "On the bright side, I don't like the taste, so I don't miss much."

"Like me and most vegetables."

"You don't like vegetables?"

"Ones grown in the ground at least."

"And this is because . . . ?"

"My illustrious mentor decided to tell me a scary story when I was much younger. It involved someone being buried alive, and when they died, they turned into vegetables. The person who ate the vegetables would get possessed."

"And your mom doesn't know why you suddenly run screaming from carrots and potatoes."

"I wouldn't say I ran screaming." He shot her a grin. "It was more that I hid under my bed and had to be pried out. Liang *tried* to tell me it was just a story, but it didn't help. To this day, I get a chill. If I eat them, they have to be well hidden."

Gravely, she said, "Let us hope the Imperial Army doesn't decide to dress like potatoes before they attack."

"If they do, I'm letting Ewan and Kyle turn them into mashed potatoes. I bet it would be therapeutic."

She tried not to, but the mental image broke her resistance and she began to snicker. She had never realized he had this playful side hidden under the seriousness of his nature. It was highly alluring. She teasingly eyed his nearly empty glass. "You're not the type to get drunk on a single brandy, right?"

"Not hardly." He finished what was left of his drink and tossed the glass to the side. Before she could blink, he caught her in his arms and dragged her across his lap so that she sprawled against him.

Her pulse began to pound. Breathless, she stared up at his face. Only a few candles lit the room. In the flickering light, his face was more beautiful than she had ever seen. His eyes glowed softly with green flecks amid darkness, and she wanted him more than she wanted air. "Tyrian," she managed to whisper.

He lowered his lips without hurry to hers. He softly teased her lips as his hands smoothed slowly up and down her back. She felt so good in his arms. It took all his willpower to not kiss her at every turn. Just looking at her made him burn.

A shiver went through her entire body. She wound her arms around his neck and pressed upward to deepen the kiss. His hands, where they pressed against her back, burned through the layers of her clothes. His right hand was the hottest and made her skin tingle with sheer delight. Every place their bodies touched was pure, torturous, pleasure, but he kept the kiss stubbornly gentle.

Shaking, he finally eased back a breath. His fingers had curled into her clothes and he forced himself to let go. He wanted nothing more than to rip the offending material from her body. She was stark and imposing and beautiful in monk wear, but he wanted her naked in his arms so he could see every inch. "I have never," he said roughly, "wanted anything more than I want you."

"You can have me." The words were out before she could stop them. When she saw his eyes flare with raw desire, she realized just how precariously he held onto his control. "You stopped for my sake."

"You think I stopped for mine?" He buried his mouth against her neck and drew her even closer until she sat on his lap. He hotly trailed hungry kisses down her collar to the edge of her tunic. The tempting swell of her breasts teased and seduced underneath. "Unless you want me to tear this off you right now, you need to stop me."

The sheer fact that he could make the offer to stop when she could feel his throbbing arousal pressed against her was impressive. She felt hot and empty, as hungry for his flesh as he was for hers. But something inside . . . wasn't ready. Her eyes closed. "Tyrian."

He pressed his face to her neck for long moments and then carefully released her. She got off his lap but he didn't move. His hands dropped to his sides. "That damnable monk control issue," he finally said, true humor in the words.

"Do you think that's my problem?" she asked softly. "I want you so badly, Tyrian."

He sucked in a breath. "Kindly don't say that, especially right now."

Her gaze lowered toward his lap. "Oh."

"Oh, she says." He fell over on his back and threw an arm across his eyes. "I'm going to go insane. I know I am." He let out a hard breath. "I think I need a shower."

"The water's always cold," she told him. His green eyes flicked to her, smoldering and volatile. "Oh," she said again. She cleared her throat. The idea of a cold shower sounded rather appealing to her as well. He wasn't the only one on the edge of insane. "I think I'd better leave."

His hand shot out and wrapped around her wrist. "No," he pleaded softly. He sat up. "Please. Stay with me."

The lost note of pain in his voice broke her heart. She had made him forget for a little while, but her inability to be his lover meant that when passion cooled, his mind began working again. If she couldn't give him the most basic comfort of her body, yet, then she could at least offer this. She pressed her hand to his cheek softly. "I will. I promise. I'm not going to make you be alone."

He turned his head to press his lips to her palm. "We should sleep." He studied her clothes. "Can you sleep in that?"

"Comfortably?" she asked dryly.

"That would be a no." He got to his feet and began to unlace his tunic. "Here. You can use this. It's borrowed anyway."

Her mouth went dry as he pulled the tunic off. He was so outrageously perfect that it seemed a crime to even think he wore shirts. Every muscle was sculpted and defined from a lifetime of training. Golden from the sun, too, indicative that he was often outside without a shirt. And where the hell had she been when he was, she wondered crossly at herself. She had been working in various cities since she was fifteen. She had passed both Teasarn and Trinan more than once.

He suddenly pulled her up to her feet. Heart pounding, she wondered what he would think if she started petting and kissing him everywhere. Her body swayed unconsciously toward him but he held her back. His voice strained, he said, "Cassie? You're killing me here."

She got a grip on herself. "Sorry." She took the tunic from him and watched as he swiftly went to the bed and pulled back the covers. He got under them and then pulled the pillow over his face. She had a feeling it was more for his own control than her potential shyness.

She wasted no time in stripping down to her underwear and pulling on the tunic. It covered her more than decently and would be vastly more comfortable for sleeping. Under her breath, she muttered, "I've seen half naked men my entire life. What is wrong with me?" She slid into bed beside him.

"Do you feel more than attraction for me?" he asked as he pulled off the pillow. He fiercely ignored the way the tunic dipped open over her breasts. She was outrageously perfect; all soft curves and fragrant shadows.

"Of course I do."

"Then there's your answer." He turned onto his side and drew her closer with an arm around her waist. "Cuddle in. Save some time. Sure as hell you'd end up here even in your sleep."

She couldn't argue with that. She cuddled in with a soft sigh, and her head found a perfect spot on his shoulder to rest. The utter rightness of being held by him sank into every corner of her heart and soul. Suddenly tired, she could barely keep her eyes open. "I've never slept with anyone before," she murmured. "It's nice."

He went very still. "Never . . . At all? Ever?"

"Never." She tucked her nose more firmly against him. He smelled rich and dark and wild. "Never wanted to before." She gave a nearly jaw-breaking yawn. Her arms curled around him to give as much as receive comfort. "Go to sleep, Tyrian."

He closed his eyes, his heart and mind reeling. He had never even suspected she might be untouched like him. She was nineteen, and she was certainly beautiful and likeable. Were other monks idiots?

Her arms tightened as her body aligned itself to his. Almost completely asleep, she murmured, "Tyrian."

He buried his face in her hair and let everything go, accepting the comfort she readily offered. Oddly, he found it easy to rest as long as she was holding him. Knowing it was important but not really caring, his arms tightened around her as he fell asleep as well. He would *never* let her go.

Chapter Six

"My two sides deceive even my own heart."

(Trinan, Imperial Castle)

The seven generals of the Empire could count on one hand the times they had all been called together to the palace at one time. The six Lower Generals and the one High General knew that when all seven were demanded, it was a sign of grave importance.

When Marcus Quint arrived, he found Alexander Renduex and Vincent Martine in the hall outside the throne room. "Well?" he asked the taller males quietly. "Is it true?"

"I'm waiting to ask General Southerwind." Alex's gaze lowered. "But I suspect it is true."

Vincent let out a long breath. "It's . . . disturbing." His head lifted quickly as he sensed a familiar presence. "Hello, Samantha."

"Well met, Vince." Samantha Yureny sighed. "Or, at least, I wish it was." She ran her hands over her arms to ward off a brisk chill. "There's nothing welcoming about being summoned all at once and with such rumors flying around, I might add."

Gordon D'terio came around the corner in time to hear her last comment. "Agreed," he said. His voice had an odd rasp to it that his fellow generals were well used to hearing. No one asked where it had come from. "It's hard to believe."

"Believe it." The sixth Lower General, a woman named Diamond Cutter, approached from another hallway. "I just confirmed it with a soldier who was released. Tyrian Southerwind is the leader of the Rebellion. Newly, however. He came onboard when he went looking for his brother's murderer."

In a very quiet voice, Marcus asked, "So then why did we issue a bounty for him *before* he joined the Rebellion? Lady Blaine may have driven this prophecy to occur by having a price put on his head."

"And if so," Donald said calmly as he joined them, "then there may as yet be something to be done. For now, if Tyrian is a danger to the Empire then we will deal with him." He paused and then added, "And let your soldiers know that we prefer him alive, not dead. You can't ask questions of a corpse."

"Yes sir." Vincent exchanged a glance with Samantha but neither said a word.

Marcus, ever the one to ask questions, said, "Do you think he's just being fooled?"

"Someone's being fooled in this scenario, that's for damn sure." Donald opened the throne room doors and walked inside. If he felt anything when he saw Annareal standing to the side, his face didn't show it. He crossed the room to stand before the throne and bowed deeply with the Lower Generals right behind him. "You summoned us."

Albanion nodded curtly and his fingers gripped the arms of his throne. Beside him, a hand on his shoulder, was the Lady Blaine. A slender and beautiful young woman, she had long black hair and piercing blue eyes. Something cruel almost always lurked at the edge of her mouth even when she was smiling.

Often, Di had wondered if Blaine's smiles were even capable of warming her icy eyes. Neither she nor Samantha liked Blaine in the slightest. Their male associates had at first, but they had eventually listened and really looked. Now none of them trusted Blaine. They especially didn't trust her power.

"Lady Annareal reports that she removed Ophelia Goldwind as a threat, but that Tyrian Southerwind has taken Ophelia's place." Albanion's fingers flexed and gripped the arms harder. "What in the name of the gods is your son up to, Donald? Is he trying to destroy the Rebellion from the inside or has he truly turned traitor?"

Without hesitation, Donald said, "If Tyrian is in the Rebellion, he is in the Rebellion because he wants to be. He's not the type to use subterfuge and deceit. If he was out to destroy them, he would have challenged them to a duel, one by one, until they surrendered."

"So he has been deceived." Albanion nodded curtly. "Blaine was right."

Di opened her mouth and then closed it. Seeing it, Blaine purred, "Did you have something you wanted to say, General Cutter? You are known to be quite *sharp* and *cold*."

The very subtle digs made Alex and Marcus both tense. Vincent shifted his weight warningly. Gordon's eyes narrowed. Samantha's hands curled into fists. Di just lifted her chin. She had heard every insulting reference to her name possible. "I was merely going to ask if perhaps we drove him there by offering a bounty for him. A self-fulfilling prophecy, if you like."

Albanion paused and Blaine leaned down intimately. "She's just offering a ridiculous opinion. You know it's not true."

He nodded, the frown fading from his face. "Of course." He brushed off Di's words almost carelessly. "Since you seem to believe Tyrian is there of his own will, the bounty stands. We cannot underestimate this boy. We will have to be more aggressive if we want to stop him. If they make a move for other towns, we will try to stop them. However, you, Generals, will focus your attention on the checkpoints."

Marcus blinked. "May I ask why?"

"The mentality of power. If the Rebellion starts to take control of checkpoints, the people will rally around them."

Very, *very* softly, Alex asked, "Do the people have reason to rally around a Rebellion?"

There was a long silence. No one moved or spoke. Then, curtly, Albanion said, "There is always discontent when a ruler does something for the better of his people and they don't understand. You may take your leave, Generals. Keep the checkpoints safe. General Southerwind, I ask for you to remain."

All seven generals bowed and the Lower six left the throne room. As they walked down the hall together, Gordon commented idly, "He didn't answer the question. Not really."

"We serve the people," was Samantha's murmur. "So we need to evaluate what is best for the people." She glanced at Di. "If you'd just marry Alex and put him out of our misery, you could get a new name."

Alex grinned. Di just scowled. "He'd be miserable married to me. And the Emperor would never allow it. We might *distract* each other." She stalked off down the hall, her white hair swinging behind her.

"Not that you're not already distracted by her," Vincent murmured to Alex.

Alex snorted softly. "She's distracted me since we were five. It's been thirty years and I'm not over it. I probably never will be. But thanks for the vote, Sam."

She smiled. "Anytime."

Chapter Seven

"Once upon a time, there was a tower; A place covered with thorny vines."

Tyrian awoke to find he was alone in bed. He lifted his head to look around, but he already knew Cassie wasn't there anymore. He couldn't sense her presence. With a sigh, he dropped his head back onto the pillow. He had slept the entire night through without moving or dreaming. He felt more rested than he had in his life.

Blackmail or bribery, whatever it took, she would share his room and his bed from then on, even if it took them a year to become true lovers. If his sleep had been so restful, he knew hers had to have been as well. The universe just worked like that.

Only a little annoyed to be alone, he got out of bed and went to the pitcher to splash some water on his face. His shirt had been tossed over the end of the bed and he pulled it on. A smile instantly curved his lips. The material had absorbed the scent of Cassie's skin and it deeply soothed him. She would have to borrow more shirts when he had his own.

Finding himself actually hungry for breakfast, he headed down the hall toward the galley. He glanced inside and saw Cassie sitting at a table with two very haggard looking combatants and one who looked as if he had a cast iron stomach. He just smiled. He had figured Ewan wouldn't let himself get drunk if his friends did.

Liang and Marian were with R.K. and concocting what looked like one of Marian's disgusting but effective hangover cures. Kell was nowhere in sight. Liang spotted Tyrian first. "Good morning, Lord Tyrian," he called, careful to keep his voice from being too loud.

Despite it, Kyle and Dylan both put their heads on the table with groans. Tyrian's lips twitched. "Good morning," he said as he walked into the room. He gave Cassie, who was looking at her coffee and not at him, a severe look. "It's rather rude to leave the man you slept with so that he wakes up alone."

She went bright pink. Ewan burst into laughter. Kyle did too and then grabbed his head again. "Owwwww." He punched Ewan in the arm. "Shut up. My head is ringing."

Dylan lifted a hand for a thumbs-up without lifting his head. "Nice job, Cassie."

"*Sleep*," she stressed. "We just *slept*. I was worried he wouldn't get any sleep."

Gravely, Ewan said, "He looks quite rested so you did your job well." He winced as she punched his arm instead. "Ouch. You hit harder than Kyle does."

"One would hope so," the swordsman muttered as he put his head back down on the table.

Tyrian got two cold cloths and walked over to put them across the back of Kyle and Dylan's necks. His eyes danced merrily as he looked at Cassie even though his face remained calm. "Now we're even," he told her.

Cassie fiercely ignored that as she sipped her coffee. She refused to admit that it had taken all her strength to force herself to leave his side. When she had woken up in his arms . . . there were no words for it. She had never rested better. She had never been happier. "Get some coffee."

"Yes'm." He walked over to R.K. and accepted the cup being held out. He carefully eyed the pitcher that Marian still worked on. "Green or blue?"

"I opted for green. No need to make sure they never do this again. I get the feeling it isn't the first time."

"Green or blue?" Dylan asked warily, turning his head enough to eye Marian.

"Good instincts," Kyle groused. He kicked Ewan under the table. "And don't look so god awful chipper or I'll throw you out a window."

"There aren't any windows down here," Tyrian noted as he walked over with Liang and Marian following.

"I'll make one." Kyle sat up and stared at the glass of very ugly green liquid that now sat in front of him. He carefully sniffed at it but there was no immediately discernible smell. He eyed Tyrian as the other man moved to stand right behind him. "What did she put in this?"

"Don't ask."

Dylan eyed Liang, who also stood behind him, then looked at Kyle. His friend shrugged. Fatalistically, both picked up their glasses and took a large swallow. And if it hadn't been for Tyrian and Liang grabbing their shoulders, both would have promptly shot out of their chairs. They started hacking and coughing. "That is *disgusting*!" Dylan managed to say.

Marian put two cups of coffee down in front of them and smiled as they drank them as fast as possible. "Your headaches are gone, aren't they?"

"I almost miss it!" Kyle downed his coffee in nearly a single swoop, and the horrid taste faded from his mouth. It was a miracle he hadn't lost any and all appetite when he'd had the 'cure,' but, to his everlasting shock, the headache was gone and he felt as good as new. He even felt hungry for breakfast. "Okay," he admitted reluctantly, "that's effective."

"Disgusting, but effective." She sat down with a smile. "There are medicines in this world that work miraculous things . . . they just have the worst side effects *ever*."

R.K. came over carrying plates of food. "We need a cook," he said woefully. "I'm not a jack of all trades."

No one said a word even though the toast was burnt. They liked him too much to hurt his feelings.

Everyone had finished eating by the time Kell showed up. The old informant grabbed a seat beside Liang and announced, "The villagers are already preparing for their move. By the time the castle has been claimed, we'll be ready to go."

"Good." Tyrian leaned back in his chair. "Then we should get going soon. Cassie, Kyle, Liang, and Marian can come with me. Ewan and Dylan, I'm counting on you to organize the soldiers just in case the Army decides they want to make another strike."

"Do you think they will?" Ewan asked.

He shook his head. "No. Not yet at least. My father doesn't believe in spilling innocent blood, and if they attacked the town, that's what will happen. However, as soon as we are settled in our new base, you can be sure we'll come under siege."

"Well," Cassie spoke up, "I've sent a letter to the Clans. Hopefully they'll send us some soldiers as well. Every bit of help can be used."

Thoughtfully, Dylan said, "I wonder where the Gunners' Guild stands on this."

"Gunners' Guild?" Tyrian quirked a brow.

"Another faction," he offered. "A very elite, very secretive one—almost a cult, really. They have bases out of all countries. Their primary headquarters is located in Melodina's mountains, I believe. They specialize in technologically advanced weaponry."

"Techno . . ."

Very softly, Cassie said, "Guns."

A chill went down Tyrian's back. Guns were considered to be the ultimate destructive weapon. Unlike most other weapons, even bows and arrows, a gun could kill someone before they ever knew they were hunted. Most cities had standing laws barring the usage of guns without special permission. "So we have an elitist cult of gun users running around Oriku. That's just great. Do we want to attempt to contact them?"

"Lord Tyrian?"

He looked at the doorway to see a soldier standing there. "Yes?"

The soldier saluted crisply. "There is a stranger in Teasarn. He is asking for you. He does not seem to be a threat, but the people are watching very closely."

"Because he is asking for me?"

Softly, the soldier said, "Because he is wearing a gun."

"Well," Tyrian said. "That answers *that* question." He got to his feet. "I'll go up to talk to him. When you're ready to leave," he added to Kyle and Marian, "come find me." When Cassie promptly stood, he added without a hitch, "Find us, that is."

"Good boy." She crossed her arms as she followed him out of the room. She had realized it was a losing battle to fight her desire to protect him, and so hadn't even bothered to try. It was not unlike her battle to stay out of his bed, but far less frightening for some reason. Strange how that worked.

When the soldier left Tyrian and Cassie, they stood on the corner of the market street. People who had been hostile just the day before were once more accepting and open to Tyrian. Seeing it made him remember all over again how badly the Empire choked its people. Anger churned in his stomach. Why wasn't his father doing anything? Didn't he care?

Cassie slipped her hand into his without a word and he took a deep breath as he drew on her unquestioning support. It was becoming more and more critical to him.

"Oy, y'all wouldn't be that Rebellion, would ya?"

Tyrian lifted a brow at the highly accented voice and turned around. He found a young man not much older than himself, dressed in sturdy brown slacks and a black tunic. A brown vest with fringe covered the top, and scarred and well-used boots covered his feet. A wide-rimmed hat pulled low over his green eyes. Around his hips sat a holster. In the holster on each side was a well-crafted lump of metal and stone that Tyrian knew instantly had to be a set of guns. "I might be," he finally offered. "Why?"

The young man shoved his hat back on his head and two locks of dusty brown hair fell in his face. "Well, I might be from Gunner's Guild, friend." The words, clear as they were, continued to carry the drawling rhythms of his native Melodina mountains. "If y'all don't want ta trust me, then it ain't my issue."

Cassie started to bristle but Tyrian held a hand in front of her quietly. His eyes met and bored into the gunner's. It was there again, that inner recognition of a kindred spirit. A friend. Someone he needed to be near and to have near. "I'm Tyrian Southerwind," he said softly. "Leader of the Rebellion." He held out his hand.

The gunner looked at him warily for a few moments and wondered what it was about the other male that seemed to pull so sharply. After a moment, he took Tyrian's hand. "Shots," he offered. "It's the only name I have, let alone answer to."

"Seems to suit you." Tyrian cocked his head. "So what can I do for you? Are you here on Guild orders or on your own?"

"Hmm." Shots considered his words carefully. "I am here under orders to assess the situation and apply my own judgment."

"Ah." Cassie arched a brow. "I see. That way if things go right, the Guild can claim credit, and if they go wrong, they can be absolved."

"Succinctly put, my lady monk." He tipped his hat slightly. "And quite accurate as well. You are . . .?"

"Cassie. I am representative of the Monk Clans for the Rebellion."

His gaze lowered to where she still held Tyrian's hand, the gesture so automatic that neither had noticed at all. His lips quirked. "Always good to stay close to the leader of the Rebellion. And that's what I'm here for. I'm supposed to stay close." He flashed his teeth in a smile. "So y'all will have to get used to my face as it'll be hanging around for quite a while."

"Fair enough," Tyrian said easily. "Can you fight, cook, or clean?"

He blinked. "All of the above."

"Good. You can help us in battle and you can help R.K. He burns toast." That said, Tyrian turned on his heel and walked away.

Bemused, Shots scratched the side of his head. Tyrian clearly expected his orders to be followed, and the damnedest thing was that Shots *wanted* to follow his orders. "What have I gotten into?" he muttered as he followed Tyrian and Cassie.

They found Kyle, Liang, and Marian waiting for them just down the street with several horses. Kyle eyed Shots intently and almost automatically shifted so that he stood more in front of Marian. "Well met," he said carefully.

Shots held his hands up. "Easy, friend Soldier. I'm on your side. The Guild decided that it's better to be friends of your enemy's enemy than not."

Tyrian's eyes sharpened. "The Guild considers the Empire an enemy?"

Shots shut his mouth. Quickly. Kyle studied him for a few moments and then shrugged. "Fair enough. I'll trust you since Tyrian does." He swung up onto the back of his horse easily yet without any of his normal grace.

The gunslinger missed nothing with his sharp eyes. Very quietly, he asked, "Grief?"

"Yes." Tyrian's eyes darkened. "For all of us, but Kyle more." He also got onto his horse. He rode ahead quickly to catch up with Kyle, and though

Shots couldn't hear what was said, Kyle's shoulders lost their tension and he lightly clapped Tyrian on the shoulder.

In moments, all were mounted and riding down the dusty road out of town. It was a three-day ride to the abandoned castle, and in those three days, it became apparent that Shots didn't talk much about himself. Subtle attempts by Kyle, and not so subtle attempts by Marian, only resulted in him changing the subject.

However, in those three days, Shots became aware that he had gotten himself in over his head. He *liked* Tyrian. Hell, he even liked the odd collection of friends the young lord had. He was still wondering what he had gotten himself into when, on the evening of the third day, they came to the end of the road where it dropped off into a thick and disturbingly murky moat.

"That is unpleasant," Liang decided.

"The moat, the castle, or the yellow eyes staring at me?" Marian stepped behind Shots. "Shoot it."

"If it comes out of the water, gladly, little lady."

Tyrian tilted his head back to look at the castle. It was a thick and immense structure of stone and brick that loomed ominously over the muddy gray water. Thorny vines climbed the outer walls and nearly obscured large holes from view. Towers rose in the four corners of the castle walls to give a long distance view in all directions. Another tower rose directly from the center, at the top of which were several large windows with broken stained glass.

"If I remember correctly," Liang said, "these walls house a small city and the castle itself. It's about half the size of Trinan aboveground, and half the size belowground."

"Belowground." Kyle lifted a blond brow. "As in it's a two-story city?"

"Precisely. The catacombs were turned into bustling city roads and domains as well. So the city got twice the size of the land it sat on." He smiled at Tyrian. "What do you think of your kingdom, Lord Tyrian?"

"I think R.K. will need a bigger mop." Tyrian dismounted and walked toward the edge of the moat. "So how do we get over there? The drawbridge is raised and that moat is full of some distinctly unhappy monsters."

"I could shoot the chains," Shots offered. "Drop that bridge right quick, Lord Tyrian."

"We'll call that a last resort." Tyrian walked along the edge of the moat and tapped the ground lightly with his staff. Eyes surfaced in the water and watched him intently as he walked. As he moved away, the eyes moved through the water and followed. Slowly, one after another, the monsters surfaced to follow him.

"Are you *sure* he doesn't have a relic?" Kyle asked softly.

Marian shook her head. "Positive." But she was frowning as she said it.

"Pardon?" Shots asked.

"Oh, sorry. Forgot you don't use relics." Marian rubbed a hand over her relic mark. "What Tyrian is doing is called 'monster singing.' It's a technique a relic user can use to lure monsters into docility. The theory is that monsters are born because of the sin of mankind, and relics come from the shattered mirror. So you're reminding the monsters of whence they came. The stronger the magic, the longer the monster can be docile."

"And he doesn't have a relic." Shots filed that away mentally. "He's got some strong magic capacity though."

"Yes. He does."

Tyrian started to disappear around the side of the castle, and Cassie moved forward quickly. In a blur of black, she suddenly appeared at his side. "Do you know what you're doing?" she asked him softly.

"Yes." Eyes darker than usual, he added, "I just don't know how I can do it."

By the time they circled the castle and returned to the others, every monster in the moat was following the sound of his staff. When he stopped walking, they stopped moving. After a few moments, many of the eyes sank back under water. Slowly, one by one, the rest of the monsters went under water as well.

"Don't tell me he permanently made them docile." Shots swallowed hard. "Seriously, t'ain't possible, is it?"

"One way to find out." Tyrian knelt beside the water but was pulled back to his feet by Liang.

Instead, Liang knelt and put his hand in the water. A tense couple of seconds went by, and nothing happened. He let out the breath he had taken and pulled his hand out. "Nothing even tried to attack me." He narrowed his eyes on Tyrian. "Never put yourself at risk again."

Since it was better to be silent than make a promise he would never keep, Tyrian said nothing. Cassie's elbow, however, landed sharply in his side. "Ow." He shot her a dirty look. "Fine. I'll *try* not to put myself in danger."

"Thank you." She looked at Shots. "Shoot the drawbridge down, please."

"Yes'm." Shots drew his guns and took aim. The loud crack of the bullets firing made several of the monsters blow bubbles in annoyance, but nothing surfaced.

The chains holding up the bridge snapped and the immense stone and wood slab began to lower quickly with a screech of metal on metal. It landed on the bank hard enough to make the land shake and send billows of dirt in the air. When silence descended again, the passage was clear into the castle grounds.

With Tyrian in the lead, the team slowly made their way across the bridge with the horses following obediently. The bridge was strong and sturdy despite disuse and held firm without a shake or shudder.

The city lay in disarray inside the castle walls. Buildings that were made of stone still stood mostly solid. Buildings of wood had broken and crumbled under the elements. Every pathway was overgrown with weeds and vines. A broken fountain in the center of town still ran with water, but it sprayed into the air rather than flow down the sides.

The castle itself sat situated in the very center of the town. On most street corners stood broken hatches leading to the Belowgrounds. Tyrian frowned thoughtfully. "Let's split up. Shots, you, Kyle, and Marian check out the Belowgrounds. Liang and Cassie will come with me to check the castle itself."

"You're the boss, boss."

Tyrian led his two guardians toward the broken double doors leading into the castle. His shoulders braced for what he would see inside, but it was, somehow miraculously, in nearly perfect shape. Only a little rubble stood in places, and other than a severe need for a washing, it seemed ready to be moved into.

A total of four stories made up the castle. The first floor housed a throne room and a kitchen among many other small rooms that could be used for just about anything. The second floor had even more small rooms as well as a meeting room, grand ballroom, and formal dining room that was as big as the throne room. The third and fourth floors held more bedrooms.

"No royal chambers?" Liang asked dryly.

"Hmm." Tyrian looked at the tower. It sat right in the middle of the courtyard with the only entry accessed from the first floor. It went up two stories over the top of the main castle. "Let's check that out."

At the bottom of the tower was the start of a long circular staircase that had severely broken down. The stairs led all the way to the very top where, finally, a room could be found.

When Tyrian opened the door and walked inside, he instantly felt at home. The large circular room was five times the size of his room back home, and it had a smaller bathing room off to one side. The broken stained glass windows let in floods of light, and on the opposite side sat a set of doors opening onto a balcony.

"A little paint, a new floor," Cassie murmured. "Some new furniture, and it'll be perfect for you, Tyrian."

For us, he thought, but the words didn't pass his lips. "Mmm." He walked over to the balcony doors and opened them. He stepped outside and realized the balcony went all the way around the tower. He could see anywhere in the castle walls that he wanted. He could see the people he fought to protect.

He hadn't even realized his hands had tensed on the rail until Cassie's hand covered his softly. He tugged her into his arms without a word and buried his face in her hair. She paused for only a moment before wrapping her arms around him to comfort him in the only way she could.

Observing them, Liang's gaze was drawn up to the sky where the stars had begun to emerge. Two seemed to be shining brighter than usual. One of the stars shined especially bright as it fell on Tyrian's shoulders. The other shined on Cassie. Where the stars were located in the sky, it almost seemed as if the star shining on Cassie also strove to shine on Tyrian's star to shelter and protect.

It was a curious, and yet somehow familiar, omen.

Chapter Eight

"I'm going to become strong and bring a new future to everyone."

By the time the villagers from Teasarn arrived with Ewan and the others, the castle had started to look more inhabitable. With the sudden influx of hundreds of new people, civilians and soldiers alike, the castle soon bustled with activity. Every able-bodied person began to clear away rubble and weeds, while those who couldn't carry began to clean. When the clearing was done, rebuilding began.

On the morning of the seventh day in the castle, Tyrian found himself kicked out of the tower that he had been using for his room. Befuddled, he nonetheless went to find other things to do rather than try to go over maps. He ended up helping some of the soldiers set up training grounds behind the palace.

When Cassie went to find him that evening, he was covered in dirt and his dark hair clung to his head with sweat. He was also the most incredibly beautiful thing she had ever seen. Even this way, dirty and sweaty, she wanted him until she was mad. "I'm in such trouble," she groused under her breath as she walked over to him.

"Hey, Cas." His smile came slow and dangerously. He had seen her watching him. "Sure you're not going to change your mind?"

He had offered to let her share his room every night. Every night she had said no. And every night, he had smiled and let it be. She put her hands in her pockets. Fast. "No," she said, but her voice quivered slightly on the word. "I'm just here to escort you to your room."

"What, I can't go by myself?" he asked dryly. He scrubbed a towel over his face as he fell into step beside her. "What the hell has been going on up there? Every time I glanced at the balcony, I could see people moving around. I also heard banging. What gives?"

She smiled. "Oh, you'll see." She watched him from the corner of her eye as they walked through the castle. The strain under the surface of his tranquility seemed to be blatant to her, but no one else had noticed at all. She couldn't even be sure that Liang had noticed, and he wasn't much less sharp than she was for Tyrian.

Tyrian was unaware of her scrutiny, so she admired him at her leisure as they made their way to the central tower. He had a smile for everyone, something to say. He always knew the right words for any given person. Charisma? That was one word for it, but it seemed more elemental than that. She couldn't put her finger on it, yet she knew it was a special quality only inside this one man.

Two guards stood attentively at the doors at the base of the tower. They saluted with smiles when they saw Cassie and Tyrian and then moved aside so they could access the stairs. Tyrian quirked a brow, though he didn't say anything. The guards had been there ever since he had taken the tower for his own. They rotated out daily, but he knew all of them by name.

The stairs had been meticulously repaired, and there was now a handrail. The stairs had been rebuilt from stone, much less likely to break than wood, and someone had painted a green and black 'carpet' down the middle. Tyrian liked it. It added color without being excessive.

The door to his room at the top of the stairs was now properly mended and hung on the hinges as it should. It was bright and clean and looked very welcoming. Fairly sure as to what he would see, he opened the door with a wry smile.

Sure enough, his room was in pristine condition. The floor had been completely stripped and rebuilt and no longer creaked warningly when walked on. The room had been creatively sectioned into two halves with a three-quarters tall wall splitting it down the middle. On one side, behind the wall, was the actual bedroom. The front area was now a sitting room. A fireplace had been installed and already crackled welcomingly to cast light and heat through the room. A table with two chairs sat near it while a plush rug lay directly in front of the protective grate.

"Well," Tyrian said. "Now I see why there was a lot of banging. Where'd all this come from?"

"We've had some busy builders over the last few days," Cassie offered innocently. She leaned in the doorway and watched with a smile as he curiously examined every inch of the room. He was being his normal mature and serious self, but she could tell he was pleased. A sudden relaxation in his eyes and shoulders implied a heavy weight had been lifted. She had wanted nothing more than that and had in fact personally picked every item in his tower for that very thing.

He didn't need to ask to know she had done everything. He couldn't have asked for anything more, and she knew him better than anyone. He curiously peeked around the wall and discovered a large closet and bed. A smile teased his lips as he wondered if she had realized she had picked both with enough space for two.

The bathing room was also spotless, and it held a large tub that he eyed wistfully. If there was any one luxury he had always appreciated for his station, it was to have hot and cold running water. As Cassie came up beside him, he asked, "Is the whole city outfitted?"

"They're working on it." She smiled. "We figured you'd want it."

"You figured correctly. It's one of those things that shouldn't be enjoyed by just the nobility." He blew out a breath. "Or former nobility. I'm pretty positive that I've been disowned by now, traitor to the Empire that I am."

"You'll still be Lord Tyrian to everyone," she said gently. "But not because of your birth, Tyrian. Because you have earned their respect." She rested her cheek on his back and wrapped her arms around his waist. "More expectations are being placed on you, but at least they are placed by people who love you. We want you only to be yourself."

He turned to skim his hands through her hair. When she held him, he felt indomitable. "It's a curious thing. I never questioned how much I loved Liang and Marian, or how much they loved me. We're family. Then I met you. And Kyle. And Ewan. And R.K. . . . Dylan and Kell. Shots."

She softly smoothed his hair out of his dark eyes, her fingers lingering warmly on his cheek. "It's mutual, you know. We're not questioning it. We're just accepting it."

He caught her hand and his eyes darkened with an intense hunger that took her breath. "There's something different between you and I," he said softly. "It's not the same. I need all of you, but I need you more. Don't ask me to qualify how. There are too many ways." He bent his head and skimmed his lips down the line of her jaw. "And it's not the same for you," he added huskily.

Her lashes lowered on a helpless surge of desire. She wanted so terribly to be his lover. To keep him safe in her arms. She couldn't even tell if the two prongs of hunger were separate or part of each other. She couldn't tell where her need to protect him ended and her need to have him for her own began.

His right hand curled around her waist, and the skin felt hotter than usual, even through her clothes. Her breath wedged in her chest. It was as if his heat seared her, branded her. She could *feel* the delicious tingle of magic, but he didn't wear a relic. It was impossible that he do the things he did. "Tyrian."

The way her voice hitched on his name sent a shudder through his body. He trailed his lips lower until he found the edge of her scarf. If she wasn't wearing it, she wore high-necked tunics. He had yet to see the scar that marked her. He *needed* to know everything about her. "Trust me," he urged softly. "Trust me."

"It's ugly."

"Let me be the judge of that." He lifted his head and stared down into her eyes, his force of will so strong and powerful that his eyes seemed to glow like gems. "You don't have to tell me about it yet. But let me see."

She closed her eyes in acceptance, unable to fight him over something minor. All her will was on fighting her own fear. What was wrong with her? Why couldn't she just give in? What was that thing inside that balked so fearfully at the idea of surrendering to her own heart and body? Her own soul.

He caught the ends of the scarf and untied them so that he could unwind the cloth. In the light coming in the windows, she was perfectly illuminated. Her pale skin looked ridiculously soft for someone so powerful, and that seemed to be what made the tiny scar that much more vivid. It was little more than a white line, but it crossed from one side of her neck to the other. Shaken, he touched it lightly. This was no accident, no lingering wound from a fight that magic couldn't heal. Someone had once tried to murder her.

She caught his hand and brought it to her cheek as she saw his body tremble. "I survived." She framed his face and tugged him down so that she could kiss him tenderly. She felt naked and exposed, both external and internal scars showing, and yet she felt safe, and driven to comfort rather than be comforted. Somehow, she knew that he held a deep hatred of scars not earned in battle.

He remained stiff for a few moments and then the tension fled his shoulders and he cupped the back of her neck so he could softly deepen the embrace. For that moment, time seemed to stop. He could have stayed there kissing her forever.

Reality intruded with the sound of a soft bell chiming. She slowly eased back a breath and whispered, "Inter-castle communication via Voice Relics. The contact point is near the door. Someone wants your attention."

He nipped at her lower lip. "I want *your* attention."

She managed a shaky laugh. "Trust me. You have it. You're a dangerous man, Tyrian Southerwind."

"A patient one," he reminded her. He slowly released her, and his hands deliberately caressed her body as he did. "Infinitely patient."

She pressed her fingers to her swollen lips, which were curving against her will. "I can only imagine what I'd be going through if you were the impatient type."

Humor edged into the hunger in his eyes. "You'd have been naked in my bed that first night. That I promise." Because there was another bed sitting temptingly close, and she looked outrageously soft and sultry, he wisely went around her to where the contact point was located. It looked like a box embedded in the wall and had a button that said 'talk.' He pushed it. "Hello?"

"Ah ha!" The voice that emerged belonged to Kyle. "This thing does work. We weren't sure. We've had some crossed signals around here. Kell tried to get Shots' room but got Marian's. When she tried to answer back, she got R.K.'s inn. At least one of them is working right."

"Seems so. Is this just a test or did you need me, Kyle?"

"Both. C'mon down to the meeting room. Have Cassie show you where it is." Blandly, he said, "I assume the delay in answering was because she is still there."

Tyrian didn't respond to the light teasing. He felt far too grateful that Kyle was making an effort to keep his spirits high. He looked over his shoulder and smiled at Cassie. She had put her scarf back on, and had smoothed her hair, but she still looked as if she had been soundly kissed. He said nothing about it. "Well?"

She cleared her throat. "Follow me." Studiously ignoring his smile because she was going to kiss him again if she didn't, she led the way out of the tower and back down into the castle once more. They crossed down two halls, went up another flight of stairs, and then went down two more halls before reaching a set of double doors. "It used to be the throne room," she explained.

The guards outside opened the doors and Tyrian walked in curiously. He could definitely tell it had once been a throne room, but it had been turned into a strategic meeting room. Maps and charts hung on the walls along with a roster of soldiers and combatants. A long meeting table resided in the center of the room with chairs spaced around it.

Ewan sat in one of the chairs with his feet propped on the table. Kyle leaned on the table beside him. In another chair was Kell. Also present were Liang and Dylan, both of whom were having a lively conversation with a slender young woman possessing pale blonde hair.

She was new, Tyrian noticed immediately, since she was unfamiliar, but she wasn't entirely a stranger. He could feel that instant tug inside his heart and soul, that familiar feeling that told him this was another person he needed to have near. Someone who would love him for being himself.

"Ah, there you are," Dylan said. "Lord Tyrian, Lady Cassie, this is Hawke. She's coming to us from a distant village. Her brother is in our army. She wishes to join as well."

Tyrian smiled. "Nice to meet you, Hawke."

She smiled back and gave a jaunty bow. She looked to be barely courting age, but there was a confidence in the way she moved and held herself. The belt around her hips held not a dagger or sword but a set of slingshots and a bag of ammo. An unusual, yet quite useful, weapon. "Greetings, Lord Tyrian and Lady Cassie."

"Just Cassie," the monk said hastily. "I'm not nobility."

"Guilt by association," Ewan said idly. "Everyone's calling you it, Cassie. Just bite the bullet, as Shots says, and accept it graciously."

Cassie said nothing and crossed her arms. Tyrian just smiled and leaned against the table. "We'll be glad for the extra specialization," he said to Hawke. "You'll be a big help to us."

Hawke studied him for long moments, vastly fascinated. It was like finding a long lost friend or something. She absolutely *had* to protect him and keep him smiling. He needed her. She felt sure of it. The depth of emotion he tugged was amazing. "You make me really feel like I'm needed."

"Lot of that going around," Liang murmured.

"Well," she said briskly, "I guess I ought to go scare up a room. Unless you need me right now?"

"If I need you, you'll know." Tyrian lightly touched her shoulder as she went past and was rewarded with a smile. He suspected he knew who her brother was; they looked as alike as two peas in a pod. "One of the few vegetables I like," he muttered to himself.

Liang coughed before he laughed. Cassie bit her lip. Ewan quirked a brow at Kyle and Dylan, who shook their heads. "Mmkay, well moving on," Kyle said, "it's time we start talking about the next city we want to liberate. We're going to need to increase the army dramatically if we want to hold it and still be able to move on to other cities."

"I've sent a message to the Clans. There's no knowing what they'll send or how long it will take for word to get to them and back," Cassie noted. "Shots has also contacted the Guild to see if they'll spare anyone. He said not to count on it, though."

"I think," Tyrian said slowly, "that it might not be as hard as we think. Look what happened with the last engagement with the Army that we had. A fair chunk of them chose to surrender and cross to our side. I fully believe it will continue to happen."

"What about the Lower Generals?" Ewan asked. "Word has it that they've spread out to the checkpoints. We won't want to go after them just yet."

"What makes the checkpoints so important?" Cassie asked curiously. "I'm not sure I've ever known that."

"They're the four entry points into the country," Kell explained.

"General laws of engagement state that holding a country's checkpoints means you hold the country. You have full control over the import and export of all goods and supplies. It would be very easy to completely choke a country if you had the checkpoints."

"I see. So by guarding the checkpoints with the generals, Albanion is stating that he's not taking any chances." She pursed her lips. "This prophecy of Blaine's must have really spooked him. He must really believe Tyrian is capable of overthrowing the Empire."

"Well, he's making it easier," Tyrian said softly. "Because you can also control a country by taking the cities on the inside. He'd be putting up a more effective block on me if we weren't from the inside. More still, the people are going to rally around us. He's fighting against his own country. There won't be enough naysayers who like his policies to stop us."

"I don't think anyone truly wants someone else to suffer," Kyle noted. "So even if high class nobility hasn't noticed anything personally, they will have likely noticed everyone else suffering. And unless they're bad to the bone, they won't like it."

"We need a professional strategist," Kell added. "I've got some feelers out to see if there's any out there that aren't happy with the current status quo."

Kyle's fingers briefly tightened on the edge of the table. "Ophelia's older brother. Matthias Goldwind. I'm not sure of his current location. I'm trying to find him to tell him . . . to tell him what has happened. I want him to hear from me, not someone else. If we can find him, he may be able to help us. I don't know if he'll want to, but he's the best strategist on Oriku."

"I'll start looking for him," Kell said promptly.

"So, what next, Tyrian?" Ewan asked.

Tyrian raked a hand through his hair. "As was said, we don't want to go after checkpoints yet. We need to start with the small cities and move bigger. Small ripples to become big waves. There's another city not much different in size from Teasarn that's a few days away from us in the other direction. Lupine, I believe is the name. Let's have our most experienced soldier take a few of the others incognito and scout out the town to see the current state."

"I'll go tell her," Dylan said. He got to his feet silently and headed out of the meeting room. He was beginning to be fascinated by the events, even through the grief that still held his heart. They would do it. He knew it. He knew that Tyrian would never let Ophelia down. He would never let any of them down. They wouldn't let him down either.

"It'll be a few days until we have any information either way," Liang said as he got to his feet. He firmly removed Ewan's feet from the table and then looked at Tyrian. "It's getting late. The kitchen is being renovated to provide enough food for the army, but R.K. said we could use the inn's kitchen in the meantime."

Tyrian almost said that he wasn't hungry, but every pair of eyes in the room seemed to glare at him at the same time. He bit back the words and sighed. "I suppose you are right. I'll head over there. I need some air." He didn't wait for assent before walking out of the meeting room. Cassie followed closely behind.

"He's tired already," Kell murmured. "He didn't even bother to turn stubborn, and the gods know that he certainly can. If he digs in his heels, we won't be able to change his course at all."

Ewan got to his feet. "Cassie will. It's why he has her. C'mon. I'm hungry too. Marian brags about your special porridge," he told Liang. "Can I bum a bowl off you?"

Liang smiled. "With your size, you'd need to bum two."

The inn was quite busy since not everyone had their homes built, and the soldiers had nowhere else to go for food just yet. R.K. was doing his best to keep up, and he had lucked out in hiring some kids to help with cleaning and an elderly woman to help with the cooking. Both were more than willing to let Liang take over the kitchen.

It wasn't long before the entire dining room smelled decadent. Cassie sniffed the air appreciatively and then sighed. "Home cooked food. I haven't had that before."

"In a long time?" Ewan asked curiously. He poured Tyrian a brandy and then poured himself and Kyle both ales. Kyle, thankfully, wasn't in any further need of getting drunk, but the ale helped him sleep. Ewan knew when he saw Kyle stop drinking in the evening that it would be a sign that the pain had finally loosened. Gods knew Ewan had gotten drunk every night for a long while after the attack on the Commune.

"Ever." As even Tyrian looked at her in surprise, Cassie swirled her glass of juice. R.K. had teasingly made it look like a cocktail though there wasn't a lick of alcohol in it. "I was raised by our Clan Master after my parents died. He was a good father, but we didn't exactly have a typical family life."

"How old were you?" Kyle asked softly.

"Five."

Tyrian instantly covered her hand under the table, his fingers lacing with hers securely. When she had mentioned losing her parents, she hadn't before mentioned just how young she had been. He could even see her in his mind, just a little girl with dark eyes chipped with blue. "Give Liang a chance and he'll make up for lost time."

She smiled. "I thought he was just your tutor and mentor."

"And he frequently took over the kitchen." Marian plopped down at the table between Tyrian and Kyle. "We've told him for *years* that he needs a restaurant. But, no, he's determined to keep Tyrian safe until he gets married, just as he promised Uncle Donald."

Ewan saluted Cassie with his glass. "Marry Tyrian so Liang can open his restaurant and feed us."

She kicked him under the table hard enough that he yelped. Gathering her dignity, and ignoring the slow grin on Tyrian's face, she sipped her juice. She wasn't going to deign to give any of them a response. Marriage? She was having enough trouble fighting her own fear so she could be his lover! Was it really her control issues like Tyrian said?

Liang shortly served them bowls of porridge that smelled so good that people at other tables became instantly interested. As orders came in, R.K. said to Liang teasingly, "Can I pay you to make that for dinner rush every now and then?"

At not so subtle pushing from Tyrian and Marian, Liang gave in. He went back into the kitchen to make a bigger batch for everyone else. Marian just shook her head. "We need to find him a wife," she said decisively. "Someone who needs to be protected, but someone who won't let him get away with murder. Maybe a woman who was married once already." She pursed her lips as she thought about it. "A widow. One with a kid. A daughter." She nodded decisively. "That's what Liang needs."

Marian knew people and could be nearly prophetic at times. Tyrian took her words as being fact. He also hoped that just such a person not only existed, but also came across their path soon. She would be a great distraction to keep Liang from following him everywhere. It was as if he didn't remember Tyrian could take care of himself.

Dark had fallen by the time they finished dinner and split up for the evening. Cassie fell into step beside Tyrian as they walked back into the castle. She had a room on the first floor that was one of the ones closest to the tower. It was a privilege that was reserved for her, Marian, and Liang. If she looked out her window, she could see directly up to Tyrian's balcony doors. They often stood open, and she knew it was an invitation. Who else around there could scale a building that tall from the outside?

Twenty feet from the tower doors, they stopped walking. Tyrian gently cupped her cheek and then skimmed his thumb over her lips. "Stay with me," he said softly. "Nothing will happen unless you want it to. But I need to have you in my arms. I need you to hold me." He lowered his forehead to hers. "I can't sleep without you, Cas. Trust me."

"I trust you," she managed to whisper around her tight throat. "But I don't trust myself." She framed his face almost helplessly. In that moment, she hated herself for not being able to give him what he needed. She existed solely to protect him, to be his salvation, and she couldn't do it.

He took a deep breath and struggled to find the willpower to let her go. The sight of him fighting so visibly made her entire body quiver with a combination of fear and desire. She could push his limits. This man, who seemed to have no limits, was pushed to the edge of his endless iron will by his feelings for her. "Soon," she promised huskily. "Please, Tyrian. I'm trying. Keep doing what you are. Let me try and muddle through, else you hate yourself for taking the decision from me."

His green eyes looked nearly black in the light of the stars and it seemed as if some had gotten caught in the depths. He framed her face with his hands, tugged her onto her toes, and kissed her as if the world was ending around them. When her body went limp against him, he released her and took a step back. "Good night," he managed to say, his voice little more than a rasp.

It took *her* willpower not to run. Whether it would be to him or away, she didn't know. Instead, she took a deep breath and walked to her room. She kept her chin up even though she felt her cheeks heating. There were many fascinated and yet sympathetic guards wandering around and watching.

Tyrian did not feel embarrassed nor did he care if there was a betting pool going on—which there was. He felt as if he fought for his salvation. Cassie had been trained from her childhood to not lose control, to complete every job with cool control and calculation. It was simply the way monks had to live; theirs was a dangerous lifestyle. Having never lost control in any way, the loss of herself to the explosive force of desire between them was as terrifying as any enemy she would have faced down. More, perhaps.

He was still thinking about it as he took a cold shower, and it was still tumbling through his head as he dressed for bed and then went to stand on the balcony. Cassie knew that what she fought was both inevitable and irrational, and she was trying to get past it. Knowing was half the battle, but that didn't make the rest easier. But just what the hell was it that was so profound between them? It was *nothing* Tyrian had ever imagined. He was as out of his depth as she was. Why did he need her so much more terribly than the others, and in this way? He was in love with her, and he couldn't even pinpoint when it had happened. He needed her smile, her laughter, her love. Needed her to protect him, to keep him safe emotionally and physically. Needed to touch her, taste her. Needed to feel those strong hands on his body. "More than air," he murmured, "I need her."

"Such is the way of your destiny."

The soft feminine voice was entirely unexpected and wholly unfamiliar. And yet, he didn't feel alarm. He turned from the balcony and walked into his room as a soft lavender glow began to appear. The glow seemed to softly spark with bits of lightning and rolled like storm clouds. When the glow faded, it left behind a shockingly beautiful woman with long black hair that had wings of reddish-orange scattered within.

Her hands linked together inside her long white sleeves, and she wore what looked like an ancient Magician's robe. Lightning bolts hid within the material, and her face was as ageless as it was lovely. Her eyes glowed the haunting color of the twilight time when day met night.

He did not know who she was at first, and then his gaze lowered and he saw the relic mark etched into the skin over her heart. It was so vivid and detailed that it could only be the mark of a Pure Relic. Its shape resembled that of an elaborate hourglass, and so had to be the Pure Relic of Time. Only one person had ever possessed that relic. "Lady Tanelia," he said softly. He bowed gracefully. "You honor me."

She smiled. "I knew I would not surprise you."

He tilted his head slightly. "It's odd. It's as if I knew I'd meet you eventually." He studied her eyes and saw a wisdom as ancient as time, as if she was truly as old as people suspected. Some thought she might very well have lived when the mirror had been whole. He was beginning to believe it himself.

"I have been watching you a long time, Tyrian," she said gently. "Your birth was preordained many millennia ago." She walked over to the balcony and gestured toward the stars in the sky, one of which seemed to be glowing the brightest. "That star. That star is yours alone, Tyrian. It shone on your birth, and shines now as you find your destiny."

"And what is my destiny?" He walked over to join her, nothing in his voice or eyes giving away how he felt. Yet there was an intensity inside him strong enough to be felt. He needed to know what she was telling him. Perhaps it would all make sense.

"You are destined to be a hero." She took his right hand with hers. "You are the first Kaiten Star, Tyrian Southerwind. Blessed by the stars themselves, you will bring freedom for those who are oppressed. Yet it is not a burden to be borne alone. See there in the sky, those many other stars that draw in? They are the Destined Stars, the stars that shone on the birth of those who will be your companions. Of all walks will they come, with only their love for you in common. They will love you enough to die for you, just as you will love them enough to fight for them."

He took a long breath and looked at the sky. There was one star in particular that shone close to his, so close that it seemed to be sheltering the brighter star. "And that is Cassie, isn't it?"

Her smile came quickly. "You are as bright as your destiny. Yes, that star is Cassie. She is the Kentei Star, your fiercest defender and destined lover. She, more than any other Destined Star, will want you to be safe. She will hold you together even when you are on the brink of devastation." Her hand tightened around his. "The price of such a great iron will. You can endure, can go to the breaking point, and can go beyond. But . . . because you cannot break, you cannot truly heal. Should you break, there will be nothing left. The Kentei Star exists solely to keep the Kaiten Star together."

He remained silent for long moments and then his breath slowly unraveled. "Thank you," he said softly, sincerely. "I think things are finally beginning to make sense." He tilted his head. "How many Destined Stars do I have?"

"There are one hundred and eight to share the skies with you. When you have found them all, you will be strong enough to turn this rebellion into a republic, to remove the chains of oppression."

"The first Kaiten Star," he murmured. Her phrasing seemed to imply there would be others. He didn't ask. There was only so much to be taken in at a time. "What of Ben?" he asked suddenly. "All of this began with Ben."

"In more ways than you know." Sadness filled her eyes. "Ben . . . I would have stayed the hands of time had I been able, but I could not change what had to occur. Return to his gravesite, Tyrian. There you will find the answer behind his finding you, his death, and the madness behind the Emperor."

He nodded briefly. "I will do so. I will find my companions, and I will free my country. How will I know when I am ready?"

"You will know," she said simply. "And on the eve of the final battle, I will come to you again. If you need me before then, simply call to me." She rose on her toes and tenderly kissed his cheek. "I waited a long time to meet you, Tyrian. Every minute was worth it."

He smiled as she disappeared in the same lavender light that had heralded her. She was not as imposing as he had always assumed she might be. There was something eternally sad in her eyes, something that made him hope she was also freed someday. Freed from what, he did not know. But she, too, was trapped.

Thoughts tumbling in his head, he went to bed. He had no idea if he would sleep or not, but there was a certainty gelled inside his heart. By guile, bribery, or blackmail, his Kentei would share his bed from then on. She could have her time, but he would have her close.

You couldn't fight destiny.

Chapter Nine

"This moment building up with pressure climbing ever higher."

Early in the morning, Tyrian got dressed and left his tower. He hadn't slept very well after being tormented by dreams and memories and thoughts of what was to come. He had been awake before dawn and formulating a plan of attack, and he was ready to take action. He would sneak back to Trinan, find Ben's grave, and seek his answers.

First, he needed to tell the others just what was going on. It wasn't something to be kept a secret, and it could turn out to be advantageous. He didn't want to be a hero, but he was well aware that he had been headed that direction before he had known it was his destiny. The simple fact remained that there was no one else who could do what he was doing, and it needed to be done.

He went directly to Cassie's room but didn't bother to knock. He just walked inside. She deserved to know the truth of things before the others were told. And if he could catch her sleepy and vulnerable, possibly susceptible to suggestion, it was all the better. He was a general at his heart; he knew how to fight any war he wanted to win.

The room was of larger size considering its location, and it had also been divided between a sitting area and a sleeping area. The division had been made by tall screens that had symbols from the Monk Clans etched into them. Just beyond them, he could barely make out the shape of a bed.

A little smile on his lips, he went around the screens. The bed was much more simplistic than his own, and much smaller. Cassie slept on her stomach. She had one arm thrown over the side of the bed, and the blankets tangled around her hips. She wore an oversized tunic for sleeping and it dipped down over one slender shoulder.

The fist of need hit low and coiled hard inside his body. He stopped breathing entirely as he moved silently closer. Those ridiculously kissable lips seemed to be begging for his. Her body was perfectly formed for his hands. His entire body throbbed with the desire to claim her, even his jaw aching as he struggled for control.

He bent down, intent on kissing her awake, when her eyes suddenly opened. Before he could blink, she lunged upward and sent them both tumbling onto the floor. As the dust settled, she was sitting across his hips with a dagger at his throat. Feeling a bit stupid for forgetting she was a monk, he didn't move. "Cassie?"

She blinked at his voice and then the sleep cleared her brain and eyes alike as she realized who she had attacked. "Oh gods. Tyrian." She hastily tossed the dagger aside and glared at him furiously. "You idiot! Never sneak up on me like that! What were you *doing*?"

He smiled. The display of anger only made her more beautiful to him, and it was a welcome thing to see that she *could* lose her temper. It was a sign of her control issues diminishing. Too, the way she was perched over him allowed him a generous view of her tempting body. The tunic dipped delightfully low over her breasts. "I was intending on kissing you. But I don't argue the outcome."

She opened her mouth and then closed it. Abruptly she realized the position they were in. Her breath wedged in her chest as she stared down at him. The firelight flickered over his face to sculpt lines and planes. His dark eyes shimmered with green highlights and the longing inside clenched her heart and soul. Her hand slowly framed his face against her will.

"You have me at your mercy," he teased huskily. His hands settled hotly on her legs, and his right hand burned with that delicious tingle of magic. "What will you do with me, my lady monk?"

A bit helplessly, she bent her head and kissed him. She couldn't bear it. She had to taste his smile, to claim it for her own. She needed him so badly. His right hand slid up her body, trailing fire in its wake, then buried in her hair to pull her closer. As the kiss deepened, his tongue teasingly tangling with hers, something broke inside.

Her body quivered and then fiercely arched to press against his. Something like a tortured groan came from his chest and he instantly rolled to pin her to the carpet. His hands went everywhere as his mouth devoured hers. The tunic tore as he jerked the laces apart to find the flesh beneath. Somehow, he broke free of the kiss so that he could see what he had uncovered.

She was pale skin and supple curves and nearly flawless. *Nearly*. Small scars from unhealable wounds scattered across her skin and marked her indelibly as a warrior who had fought for her life more than once. The sight of it made something inside his soul quiver violently with complex emotions. Pride. Sympathetic pain. Love. Safety. Seeing the reminder of her monk lifestyle reminded him how safe he was in her arms. Nothing and no one could ever hurt him so long as she was there. "Hold me, Cassie," he whispered thickly. "Don't let me go."

She threw her arms around his neck fiercely and held on with all her strength. "I won't let anything happen to you!" she vowed intensely. "I won't let you go, Tyrian. Ever!" She turned her face up for his kiss, needing his taste imprinted inside. Whatever had broken had broken with a vengeance. Nothing was more important than the man in her arms. She loved him more than any fear could override.

He tore his mouth free and said thickly, "We better stop, Cassie. There's no time for what we both need."

She nipped at his chin. "Will there be time later?"

"I'll make time. Steal it." He kissed her between every word, unable to resist the lure of her swollen lips. "Cassie. My Kentei."

Her eyes, more blue in the firelight than black, blinked at him in sudden confusion. "Your what?" She searched his eyes, saw the core of determination inside, and tightened her hold on his neck comfortingly. "I think we need to talk, Tyrian."

He suddenly smiled. "I came in here intending to talk, actually."

She snorted at that. "Sure you did."

"I did. It was on the list." He rolled off her and up to his feet in a single lithe movement. He offered a hand to assist her, but she flipped nimbly to her feet. He had to be impressed; he didn't know anyone else who could do that. Her tunic was hanging open, tempting him, and he firmly pulled the edges closed. "I'll wait around the screens," he managed to say. "For the sake of my sanity, please cover yourself."

She took over holding the tunic closed and waited for him to move out of sight. Quickly she stripped off the tunic and pulled on her regular monk wear. It was not only her most comfortable thing to wear, but it also hid the most of her body.

When she went back around the screen, he was opening the curtains to let in the rising sunlight. He had also lit lamps. She spotted where her dagger had landed and scooped it up with a sigh. "You really should have known better."

He grinned sheepishly as he sat down at the table. "I suppose I should have." He held out a hand to her. When she crossed to his side, he tugged her down onto his lap. She gave him a flustered look, but he merely looped his arms around her waist. "I like you right where you are." There was just enough of a height difference that they were eye level when she sat on his lap. "Will you sleep with a dagger under the pillow when you're in our bed?"

She touched her forehead to his with a smile. "Yes, because there will be something far more precious than my life in it with me." She sighed softly as her fingers traced his lips. They were still flushed from their kisses. "I give up, Tyrian. I don't know what you did to me, but I'm not so afraid. Or perhaps, I'm more afraid for you than for me." She smoothed her fingers through his rumpled black hair. "I need you to be happy. And I feel like I'm the only one who can ensure you are."

"You are." He took a long breath. "We're destined, Cassie. Lady Tanelia came to me last night. She told me that my birth had been preordained, that I was born under a star known as Kaiten. It's my destiny to save our land. To be a hero." He rubbed his thumb over her cheek. "As repayment for what I am being asked to do, there are one hundred and eight other Destined Stars to share the sky with me. All to be my friends, to love me and support me. You're one of them, but . . . you're more."

"You called me your Kentei Star."

"The name given to the star that shines closest to the Kaiten, the star that shelters and protects. My lover. Lady Tanelia said you were the one being who could hold me together and keep me from breaking." He let out the breath he had been holding. "Seems that my 'iron will' as we've all called it, is a double-edged sword."

"That, I knew." She framed his face with her hands and softly feathered kisses over his face. "I will always hold you together, Tyrian."

"It doesn't bother you?" He searched her eyes intently.

"Why should it? It's what I want." She brushed soft kisses across his eyes. Those beautiful eyes with their indomitable spirit and fierce glitter. The eyes of a leader, a hero. The stars had chosen their emissary perfectly. While she would not have wished the burden on his shoulders, at the least she was there to lift it again. He made her believe that anything was possible.

He caught her chin and tugged it down so that he could kiss her tenderly. "Thank you," he said softly. He curled a lock of her hair around his finger, loving the silken resilience. He wanted to see it tumbled across his pillow. "Move into my room with me," he asked. "Please. I will beg if needed, Cassie. I *need* you."

"Alright. Alright." She grinned. "But we don't want to consummate the relationship yet."

He slowly arched a brow. She looked far too mischievous suddenly. "We don't?"

"Not for at least a week. That way Kyle wins the betting pool."

"You honestly think that I'm going to be able to have you in my bed for a week, knowing you're mine for the taking, and not make love to you the way we both so terribly need? And you honestly think people will believe that I don't?"

"They'll believe it," she countered dryly, "because we're both going to look frustrated and miserable. I mean, more than we do. And I think you can find the control if it is for Kyle. He wants the money to buy a gravestone for Ophelia."

He took a long breath. It would be an interesting test of his willpower, but for something like this, he was willing to try. He predicted one hell of a lot of cold showers, though. "Thank god for running water."

She hid a smile. She didn't need to ask to know. "Was there anything else Lady Tanelia told you?"

"Yes, but that can be told to everyone. There's something I have to do." His eyes darkened. "I have to return to Ben's grave. She told me the answers are there."

She grimaced. The logistics of sneaking into Trinan when everyone there knew Tyrian's face were horrible. Everything that made her his Kentei Star rebelled at the very idea of letting him walk into the lions' den. But if Tanelia said he needed to go . . . "I'm going to hate this. And so is everyone else."

He let her go so she could stand and then let her tug him to his feet. "Let's see if we can't get those communications panels to work properly and get everyone to the meeting room. Think R.K. is awake and can bring us breakfast?"

"No doubt." She cleared her throat. "And I suppose I need to ask one of the castle maids to move my things to your room. What do we tell people if we're not lovers yet?"

"We're taking things one step at a time. And we are." He caught her hand and brought it to his lips before pressing it to his heart. "Even if your fears hadn't broken, we would be doing this. You need to trust me."

She shook her head. "I do."

"Not as much as you should," he countered gently. "This morning proved it. If you truly trusted me with your body as much as your heart, you'd have known my presence and not been alarmed."

She opened her mouth only to close it thoughtfully. "You know," she said slowly, "you may very well be right."

"I know I am." He stole a quick kiss and headed toward the door.

Bemused, she shook her head. "You have a hidden arrogant streak. I can tell you're a spoiled rich boy."

"I just like having my way." Already feeling better because he knew that she was going to be in his arms every night, as she should be, he was smiling as he headed through the castle and to the meeting room. A brief study of the voice-box told him how to use it and he began buzzing the boxes in the rooms belonging to his current Destined Stars. Including himself, there were eleven Stars counted for. It seemed daunting and impossible that there would be more.

Kyle was the first to stumble into the meeting room not long later. He was shortly followed by the others, most of them barely awake. Shots was alert, as was Marian, but Liang and Ewan were drinking cups of coffee as if their lives depended on it. Dylan and Kell yawned around every other word. Cassie arrived with R.K. and they carried trays with breakfast for everyone. Hawke was just alert enough to help pass them around the table.

"What gives?" Shots asked as he propped his feet on the table. He saw Liang eyeing him and hastily took his feet down again. "Y'all made it sound so serious, Lord Tyrian."

Tyrian sat down at the head of the table. He didn't have a choice since they had pointedly left the seat open for him. The only consolation he had was that Cassie sat to his right and Liang to his left. "Last night, I was visited by Lady Tanelia, the Great Seer."

There was silence and then Hawke told Cassie, "See, you need to sleep with him so strange women don't drop in unannounced."

"I'll be sleeping with him tonight," Cassie countered dryly, "but we'll only be sleeping."

"It's one step at a time." Ewan patted her shoulder companionably. His brown eyes twinkled merrily. "True love is scary stuff."

"Y'know firsthand?" Shots asked.

"Lena," Kyle, Kell, and Dylan said as one.

"Shut up!" Ewan muttered.

Tyrian had a feeling he would like Lena if he ever got to meet her. Any woman who could make Ewan run scared was well worth knowing. "Lady Tanelia told me that I am the Kaiten Star," he explained. "And I think what she told me might very well be what Blaine foresaw in her prophecy. Seems it was foretold a long time ago that I would be born and become a hero for my people. I was born under the star known as Kaiten. The stars themselves have chosen me."

"No one else at all was born the night that star shined?" Kyle asked with a touch of skepticism.

"Based on what she told me, no." He kept silent on the idea that there might be other Kaitens. If there were, it was possible the star had shown again in the intervening years on another child's birth.

"So you mean you didn't even have a choice?" Marian bristled. "You're being forced to just . . . just take on the burdens of the entire country? It was different when it was for Ophelia. You made that choice! But now it sounds like you're saying . . ."

"That Ophelia was meant to die." Kyle could barely get the words out. His eyes felt dry and burning. He couldn't cry anymore. There were no tears left. "She had to die so you could save everyone."

Tyrian searched his eyes and could see that Kyle was nowhere near ready to hear that Ophelia had known all along—which also made sense now. "I was already taking over before she died," was all he said. "We can't know what's destined and what's not. Even if we say it's my destiny to save everyone, that doesn't mean that we can just kick back and let it happen. We have to make it happen."

"So then what makes it so destined?" Hawke demanded.

"If Lord Tyrian walks away," Kell said softly, "then any number of events could happen to force him back. Terrible events. Things he will never be able to turn a blind eye to. Some have as yet happened."

"Ben," Marian whispered.

"Lady Tanelia said my destiny began with Ben." Tyrian took a deep breath. "She also said that if I go to his grave, I will find my answers as to why he died, and why his role was so important in my life."

"Time out!" R.K. sat up quickly. "You're intending to sneak back into Trinan where everyone there likely wants you dead? Over my dead body!" He stopped suddenly and got an odd look on his face as the others stared at him. "I have no idea where that came from."

"Everyone at this table," Tyrian said softly, "is what is known as a Destined Star. You were born under stars that draw close to mine. I need you to keep me strong. You give me the support I must have if I want to endure through my destiny. The stars have burdened me, yes, but they gifted me at the same time."

"Well, hot damn." Ewan crossed his arms. "That makes sense of *everything*. Why all of us, even R.K. and Kell, who don't fight, want to make sure you keep your ass safe and alive. Why we all feel so much more powerful because you believe in us. Count on me, Tyrian! My sword is at your command. If you need me to scale the walls of the castle, just toss me some rope and I'll go."

"Let's hope it doesn't come that," the Kaiten said dryly.

"What of Cassie?" Dylan asked. "She's not like the rest of us. Not truly."

"No, she isn't." Tyrian looked at Cassie, his eyes dark with his emotions, all of which seemed too complex for anyone else to understand. "She is my Kentei Star. She is the star closest to mine, the one that shines to shelter me. My greatest defender. The one person who can keep me from breaking."

"He has a breaking point?" Hawke whispered to Shots.

He pulled his hat low over his eyes, his stomach clenching with dread at the idea of what might happen to Tyrian if he broke. "No, little lady. And that's the whole problem. If someone like Tyrian breaks, it's like dropping glass from the tower. There's no repairing it."

Her hands gripped together briefly. She took a long breath and then nodded briskly. "Okay! Okay, then you can count on us, Tyrian! We'll support you no matter what. You want to go to Trinan, then we'll take you there."

"We can't take a full party," Liang protested instantly. "We need to be much stealthier. Cassie, I, and Ewan will accompany Tyrian back to Trinan. Ewan's face isn't known there. He can move around the town safely from the streets while Cassie looks from the shadows. When they can find us a safe opening, then Tyrian and I will join them."

"I don't like this," Dylan muttered.

"Join the club," Kyle and Shots both muttered back.

Tyrian got to his feet. "It has to be done. I trust Lady Tanelia. And . . . I have to know. Ben was my brother. If he died for my destiny, then I need to know why. And I need to know who his murderer is. It's all connected somehow."

Everyone at the table recognized instantly that he had dug in his heels. Only Cassie would possibly be able to change his mind, but she was the last person who wanted to try. Nothing more to be said or done, everyone split up. Liang and Ewan went to their rooms to pack a bag for the nearly weeklong trip, and Cassie found herself going with Tyrian to his—their—room. The maids had moved very fast, as if they had just been waiting for the chance.

Tyrian hid a smile as she walked with him up the stairs of the tower. "The guards didn't look surprised. They looked very pleased."

"I think it is a general feeling among everyone," she agreed ruefully. "Now the bets will really fly as they try to pin down just when their Kaiten and his Kentei actually become lovers. I ought to be embarrassed that my love life is on such display, but I'm beginning to be amused by it. Perhaps because it doesn't scare me as much anymore."

"And it's the price to be paid for being with me." He tucked her hair behind her ear. "I'm living in a fishbowl. Now you're in it with me. I'm sorry, Cassie."

She looked up at him, the blue flecks in her eyes glimmering like the stars that blessed their birth. "I'm not."

It was still a little bit unnerving to open the closet and see her clothes hanging neatly beside his. It seemed so intimate, almost more intimate than when they had shared a bed before. "This will take some getting used to," she conceded.

Once they had both packed their backpacks with anything they needed, they headed down to the courtyard to meet up with Ewan and Liang. They retrieved horses from the stables and then headed out of the city entirely. The gates shut behind them, and guards along the walls waved encouragingly.

It was almost five days before they reached the edges of Trinan. It was three days from the castle to Teasarn, and an hour from there to Trinan, but there was every chance that Teasarn had soldiers in it just in case someone came back. Therefore, the longer route had to be taken. No one complained. Ewan had a lot of hilarious, if hair-raising, tales to be told.

When they reached the city, Liang and Tyrian found a place to hide. Ewan entered the city as plain as day, and Cassie slipped into the shadows that were such an integral part of her life. People spoke candidly with Ewan and told him all about the rumors and the speculation that flew. No one seemed to want to give their opinion of their own living, but Ewan sensed a certain tension under the surface.

As he was about to leave the tavern, he heard a soft musical voice say, "Care for an ale?"

Startled, he looked to the side to see a woman sitting at a table out of the way. She was surprisingly tall and shockingly gorgeous. Her long white hair was scooped up in a ponytail, and her eyes shimmered a fascinating shade of purple. An ageless wisdom lurked inside as if she seemed to know everything. "I might," he said slowly, sensing a kindred spirit. He slowly sat down across from her and studied her intently. She wore the familiar plate armor of a heavy-duty warrior. On her right hand was a Lightning Relic. On her left was an unfamiliar relic that looked like a musical note. "What do you recommend?"

"Hmm." She slid a glass across to him. "A dose of reality? Pity no one else around here has had any."

He sipped the ale and watched her over the top. "I've been drinking the stuff for months. You get used to the taste."

"After a while, anything else tastes terrible. Reality isn't always great, but better to be honest than blinded." She ran her finger around the edge of a water glass, and a softly beautiful humming sound echoed in the air. It lingered like wine on the tongue. "What do you think of the guards in Trinan?"

"They do their jobs well," he conceded.

"Very well, indeed. But sometimes they can be a little lazy. Some even take naps when they shouldn't. I'm surprised no one has snuck into the city, what with that new marble gravestone. It's no doubt worth a fortune."

His eyes sharpened. "I assume it's guarded too."

"Amazingly, it's not." She got to her feet gracefully and dropped a few coins on the table. "The drink is on me. It's always nice to talk to someone else who can read the stars."

She walked away soundlessly, even her armor silent. Her body moved with the precision and control of a long-trained warrior. Much to his surprise, there was a claymore equipped on her back. He had not met many combatants who could wield one, but then, she was *definitely* taller than average. The long and heavy blade would not impede her.

After a moment of thought, he left the tavern as well. It didn't take long before he sensed Cassie join him, and together they left the city. They returned to where Tyrian and Liang hid and hunkered down to wait for nightfall.

"Well?" Liang asked.

"I met a very interesting person at the tavern," Ewan said. He recounted the conversation and then added, "She's one of us. I'm not sure how I know, but I do know it. And she certainly knew who I was. I got the impression she even knows where we are right now." He cocked his head thoughtfully. "She wore an unusual relic."

"What did it look like?" Cassie asked.

"A music note."

"Oh, it's a Music Relic." She looped her arms around her legs. "You know how Voice Relics are considered the bastard child of the Pure Relic of Listening since they're one of a kind but not actually Pure? Well, Music Relics are like the Voice Relic."

"What do Music Relics do?" Tyrian asked curiously.

"Musicians use them to enhance their performance. Some think that someone of enough magical capacity could even use one as a weapon. I can't say how, but it would no doubt have to be quite extraordinary."

Ewan thought of the way the woman had moved and spoke and how everything she had done had been like music itself. He had a feeling it had nothing to do with her relic. "I think she might qualify."

Under the cover of darkness, with Tyrian and Liang hidden in cloaks, they made their way to the city limits once more. A lingering soft pulse of music in the air alerted them to which direction to take, and it wasn't long before they found where several guards contentedly slept away at their post. The gate stood open just enough for even Ewan to slip inside undisturbed.

It could have been a trap, but inexplicably, Tyrian knew it wasn't. That music he could sense was soothing to him, in a way not dissimilar from the way he felt when his Stars were near. It seemed to tingle along his soul.

The graveyard was as silent as, well, death. It was a peaceful place, serene and calming. Both nobility and commoner could be buried there. The class difference didn't matter in your death, Tyrian thought. Only in your life. It was a saddening thought.

Near the edge closest to the city walls, they found a marble gravestone. Tyrian's whole body trembled as he lightly traced the words carved into the cool stone. *Ben Southerwind: son of Donald & Annareal, brother of Tyrian.* "We shared no blood," he said softly. "But we never remembered. No one ever assumed otherwise. People were always surprised to learn he was adopted."

A soft wind rustled the trees melodically. Cassie lifted her head quickly. "Tyrian, be quick," she said softly. "We're being warned that time is short."

He knelt down to study the grave. There was nothing out of place. He had no idea how he was supposed to find answers there. He smoothed his hand lightly over the flowers blooming on the grave, and green light suddenly started to emerge from the grave.

"Get back!" Liang dragged Tyrian back quickly even as Cassie and Ewan swiftly moved aside.

The green glow pushed its way up through the soil and became the familiar shape of a relic. The sphere of glass held the symbol of a multi-edged moon scythe deep within it. The entire thing pulsed with a strong power that everyone present felt inside. Tyrian, more than the others, felt it the sharpest. It was a familiar feeling. He knew this relic.

Without conscious will, he slowly walked closer to the relic. He lifted his hands toward it and felt his soul eagerly soaking up the power being expended. He grasped onto the relic, intending merely to take it from the air, but the decision was taken from him the instant it touched his right hand.

The relic fused forcefully to his hand with a sharp cracking sound. It seemed to shove its way inside his very soul, filling every drop of his magical capacity. It tore at his soul and seemed to claw it apart in an effort to find its place. The pain was all-consuming, staggering, and then the rush of raw power slammed into his head. With it came memories that were not his. They were Ben's.

"Tyrian!" Cassie leapt forward and caught him in her arms. She was strong, but he was heavier than she expected, and she fell to her knees with him cradled close. He looked pale as salt, sweat slowly sliding down his face. She could feel how every muscle in his body had knotted violently in response to the relic's forceful mergence. Terror made her mouth dry as she stared at the back of his right hand where the mark had appeared.

"What the hell?" Ewan's voice was shaky. "I've never seen a relic do that! I've seen people fuse relics! They don't hurt!"

"Regular relics don't." Liang could barely get the words out. "But . . . but legend states . . . states that Pure Relics do."

Ewan went still. "That's . . . that's a Pure Relic?" He looked at the scythe on Tyrian's hand and could see how it was much darker, much more brilliant than a normal relic mark. "Wait, don't Pure Relics give immortality?"

Cassie looked up at the stars, her eyes going instantly to the ones belonging to her and Tyrian. His was dimmer than usual as if it responded to what he endured. Her arms tightened around him, and her star shone ever brighter. She thought of her adopted father, her promised legacy, and then looked at the Pure Relic her lover bore. Destiny did, indeed, plan for everything.

Tyrian was only distantly aware of their voices. It was only the sound of Cassie's heartbeat that kept him sane. It was the only anchor he had as he came under full assault from the memories left inside the relic. He could barely sort them all.

But then, Ben's image appeared in his mind. *Tyrian*, he said softly, *if you are seeing this, then I am gone, and the Devourer is in your hands where it belongs. I gave my life to protect this relic for you. When I met you, I knew you were the one meant to be its owner. I carried it inside, safely protected where it could not be sensed. From that day I asked you to 'break a curse on me,' I had the relic attuned to you. That is why you could never wear another relic. Already, you were wearing one. A Pure Relic user cannot equip any other relic. A Pure Relic fills every aspect of your magical capacity.*

Is that why, Tyrian asked his brother's image. *Is that why my capacity was so great?*

No. That potential was there to take in the Devourer. But it is why everyone was able to sense it so clearly, and why you acted like you had a relic when you didn't. The Devourer . . . its burden is great. But you have the will to endure. You must endure!

Who did this to you? Tyrian nearly shouted the words, driven beyond his control, his will shaken. *Why did you have to die? Who killed you? Why?!*

Rather than words, memories separated themselves and became images. Tyrian watched very clearly as Ben's birth parents gave him the relic for safety before they were murdered. Ben, and Tyrian, saw the murder. Ben was barely more than five at the time. Life at the orphanage was not better over the next eight years, and then, Foresalia had attacked.

Tyrian felt his heart break as he watched his brother flee for his life from the army only to encounter a more sinister figure. It chased him across the hot desert of the Empire until it finally wounded him and left him for dead inside Teasarn. Tyrian could even see himself in the memory as he rode closer with Liang. It had only been he and Liang that had saved Ben that time.

Then, only a short time ago. The memories came in faster for being more recent. Ben arriving at Teasarn to get Tyrian's birthday gift and coming under attack from that shadowy figure. This time it revealed itself to be a haggard and decrepit old woman that looked, somehow, frighteningly, familiar. She screamed at Ben again and again to give up the relic, but he just laughed at her. Said she would never find it. Her rage welled and she grabbed onto his throat to begin draining his lifeforce.

Shock ripped through Tyrian's soul and mind as he saw the old woman use the lifeforce to change her appearance. Shining hair, striking beauty. Eyes as cold and dead as ice.

Lady Blaine, Albanion's consort.

The shock of what he had seen was enough to shake off the effects of the merging, and he opened his eyes as fast as he could. They felt as if they were weighted in lead. His entire body hurt from head to heels and he couldn't find any control over his muscles. He might not have minded it so much if he hadn't opened his eyes to find them surrounded by more than a dozen armed Empire soldiers.

Ewan had his sword drawn, and Liang's hands had lifted in a fighting stance, but there were too many bows and arrows aimed at Tyrian for them to risk moving. Cassie's entire body was tensed.

"We should have known you'd come back," one soldier said in satisfaction. "You lit up the sky like a lantern, Lord Tyrian. That wasn't very subtle of you. Now get on your feet."

"He can't," Cassie said curtly. "Relic weakness."

"Bullshit. Get on your feet, traitor."

"Help me," Tyrian managed say softly to Cassie.

She hesitated and then put all her strength into helping him gain his feet. He managed to stand, but all his weight rested against her. He couldn't even hold up his head. Terror churned inside her stomach. He was so weak! So vulnerable. "Someone has to help me," she said. "You can see he's sick!"

One soldier sighed and put up his bow. "Fine." He walked closer and grabbed Tyrian's right hand with the intent of helping to take his weight. Instead, Tyrian's relic sent out a shockwave that tore through the soldier's entire body. The energy of the relic seemed to completely devour the soldier's lifeforce. He was dead before his body hit the ground.

"Shoot him!" the lead soldier shouted.

Without hesitation, Cassie threw her arms around Tyrian and knocked them both down. One arrow slammed into her arm. Another into her leg. A third struck her in the back. Tyrian, strength returning with the energy his relic had consumed, managed to sit up with her in his arms. "Cassie!"

Ewan and Liang went after the closest soldiers, all of whom were still shell-shocked. Others leapt for Cassie and Tyrian. They never made it. The woman from the tavern appeared from out of nowhere and sent the soldiers flying with a swing of her sword. She lifted her right hand and massive bolts of lightning dropped from the sky. Any enemy still standing was knocked back several feet.

"You!" Ewan said.

"The name is Laia." She turned quickly, assessing the enemy as soldiers carefully got to their feet. "Laia Mitakel." She whistled intricately into the air, and an answering whistle returned shortly. "The way is clear. We just need to make a break for it. Grab the wounded."

Tyrian slowly looked up from Cassie's prone body. Blood stained them both, and some had spattered across his face. Agony moved in the depths of his dark eyes. He focused on the soldiers closing in, and something nearly unholy crossed his face. "Go to Hell," he said very softly, so softly that only Laia truly heard him.

The Devourer glowed and activated as a glowing runic circle opened around his body. The circle of magic existed wholly unique from user to user, and Tyrian's resembled black and green fog. Rolling waves of black energy swept across the land and consumed the soldiers. When the energy faded, there was nothing left at all.

"Shit," Ewan breathed. He had never seen a power like that before.

"Stop gawking," Laia snapped. She knelt and removed the arrows from Cassie's body with swift competency. She grabbed Tyrian's cloak and tore strips from it to bind the wounds as best she could. "We need to haul ass!" She cupped Tyrian's cheek and forced him to look at her. "Tyrian," she said softly, "Cassie will live." Her Music Relic glowed softly. "Sleep."

He slumped over instantly, too weak to resist the spell. Liang wasted no time in lifting Cassie into his arms. Ewan carried Tyrian. They swiftly followed Laia through the stirring city, ignoring the voices rising in fear and confusion. Laia didn't lead them to the same gate they had entered through. She went to another. Waiting there was a man roughly the same height and size as Ewan. "Horses?" she asked.

"Ready," the man countered. "Let's go."

Liang looked at the male with the golden eyes and realized that he had to be the same as Laia. "You're both . . . Destined Stars?"

"Name's Rourke Mitakel. You might be surprised to learn that there are quite a few of us who knew before you did just what is going on." He held Tyrian long enough for Ewan to get on a horse and then gently handed their precious Kaiten over. "Laia is a Healer as well as a warrior. She can tend to Cassie on the way to base."

Liang glanced back at the city as they raced away through the night. "Just what the hell happened?"

"You already said it." Laia's purple eyes looked nearly black in the moonlight. "Hell happened."

Chapter Ten

"There is nothing left in my heart."

When word reached Albanion and Blaine about the incident in the graveyard, the Emperor was more than a little nonplussed. Blaine was infuriated. Somehow she managed to hold onto her smile as a soldier recounted the events. She wanted to rip out his heart even though he was not at fault. "You're sure it was a Pure Relic?" she demanded.

The soldier kept his head bowed, sweat sliding down his back. He hated talking to Blaine. He always felt as if his life was in danger. "Yes, my lady. The Relic Masters in town are certain they recognized the strength of the power. The one body we recovered was branded with the mark of a scythe."

The Devourer! Blaine bit back a snarl of rage. That cursed Ben had been holding it all along! He had taken the secret to his grave, literally, and now it was in the hands of the one person it should never have gone near. The bloody Kaiten Star. Icily, she said, "The Devourer Relic is indeed a Pure Relic. It is a dangerous one. If we're lucky, it will do as its name implies and devour Tyrian Southerwind."

Albanion looked at her speculatively. "Would it?"

She shrugged. "It could." She wasn't holding her breath for it. The very iron will that made Tyrian the destined Kaiten was the very thing that might save his life. "If it doesn't, he has just become far more formidable than he ever was before. He is an army himself."

Albanion waved a hand and the soldier hastily fled from the room. The Emperor settled back on his throne and stared thoughtfully across the room. "I like not that that boy has gained such power. Perhaps a ceasefire needs to be arranged."

Blaine's nails bit into her palm as she struggled to hold her smile. Albanion was a slimy coward. He had no idea what she had endured, what she was willing to do to get her hands on a Pure Relic. She would rip it from Tyrian Southerwind's dead body with her own hands if she had to. In a sibilant purr, she ran a hand down his arm. "We will handle him."

He fell under her spell without a whimper and nodded. "Indeed. We hold the checkpoints. The cities are under guard. This puny rebellion will fall, Pure Relic or not."

And when it did, when the relic was hers at last, she would have everything she had ever wanted.

Chapter Eleven

"Even if it's painful, I'm supported as I cross over a sea of stars."

When Tyrian woke next, he woke all at once. He sat up sharply, his heart pounding hard in his chest. It was nighttime still, but he was no longer in Trinan. He seemed to be lying in a campsite in the middle of the sandy plains. The night felt calm and peaceful.

He slowly looked down at his hands and saw the mark branded into his right hand. He hadn't dreamed everything. His head jerked up at the thought and he looked around sharply. Where was Cassie? She had been nearly killed trying to protect him.

"She's fine," a familiar woman's voice said.

He swiftly turned his head and spotted the white haired woman who had saved them. She was no longer wearing her heavy plate armor. Instead, she wore regular leggings and a tunic. As she sat down beside him, he was suddenly amused to realize she was his height. "You're very tall."

She smiled. "That's what everyone says. My name is Laia Mitakel. I'm one of your Destined Stars. I share my destiny with my husband, Rourke. Our star is a shared one."

He took a long breath. "You would seem to know more than I do about everything."

"To some extent. I've always been a studier of the stars, and Rourke is a walking encyclopedia for legends. It's his life study." She leaned back on her hands while the night wind teased her white hair. "I can answer some questions, to be sure. But others can only come with time."

"Where's Cassie? She was hurt."

"She's out scouting the area, only minor scars as badges of her love for you." She hooked a finger in the edge of her tunic and tugged it down slightly to reveal the familiar relic mark of Medicine right over her heart. A darker outline around the mark implied it had been overclocked to its max ability. "I am as good with healing as with my sword, but without herbs, even my magic isn't infallible. Only the Pure Relic of Healing would have done any good without herbs."

He studied her. He just somehow felt unsurprised that she was powerful enough to wield three relics, particularly three that had been heavily overclocked; both the Music and Lightning Relics she wore had the same outline as her Medicine Relic. Something felt so instantly peaceful about her presence that all tension left his shoulders. He felt nearly as safe near her as Cassie. "Thank you," he said softly.

"Don't mention it." She fell over onto her back and linked her hands under her head. "There are no doubt many like me and Rourke. If you know legends, and you know how to read the stars, then it's like looking at a map. I saw you in town a few years ago and instantly recognized you for what you were. I really wanted to tell you, but I knew I couldn't. I hated it."

"How old are you?" he asked curiously.

She shot him a grin. "Twenty-nine."

She seemed nearly ageless. His eyes said she should be younger, but *her* eyes said she should be older. He slowly rubbed his left hand over his right and felt the dull throbbing inside his soul that was healing. There was something . . . insidious inside this new power. It was under rigid control, but it was dangerous. He knew it. "I killed those soldiers."

"Which doesn't bother you as much as the fact that you don't regret it." She sat up. "You shouldn't regret it, Tyrian. Pure Relics are affixed to the soul. When Cassie was wounded, your soul reacted. It had the power to do something, so it did. You acted within both the laws of engagement as well as the Empire's own rules about taking lifeforce from someone."

"Hell." He held up his hand. "It's an ominous feeling to know the first level spell of this relic is called Hell and can do what it did. What will it do when I reach the fourth and final level?" He dropped his hand into his lap. "Tell me honestly, Laia. You have to know. This Pure Relic . . . the Devourer. It is a part of my destiny. I had to take it."

"Such is the path of a Kaiten Star. Your reward for everything you will do and endure and survive is to have the gift of immortality. But it is a double-edged sword, Tyrian. Pure Relic bearers are sterile. Even if you ever removed the Devourer, and I can't be sure you even could, you would remain sterile. You will not have children."

"And people I love will die when I do not."

She smiled. "They would find you again. Where a Kaiten Star is, their Destined Stars will gather. Once you've shared the skies with someone, you will never be free of them." When he only looked at her, she got gracefully to her feet. "The Kentei Star is . . . special, Tyrian. And I don't think Cassie has played her cards." She linked her hands behind her back as she walked away. "I once trained with the Monk Clans. There's something she has not told you."

He let out a soft breath. Oddly, he felt a little better that she had understood the question he had been afraid to ask. An eternity without Cassie was not one he wanted. He was barely over eighteen. It was hard enough to imagine himself in twenty years let alone two hundred. He didn't doubt that would change; as he acclimated to his relic, he was sure he would feel physical changes too.

"Hey, you're awake," Ewan said in relief as he walked over. "Laia said you were." He crouched down beside Tyrian and ruffled his hair. "How do you feel?"

"Better than expected." Tyrian pushed aside the blankets and got to his feet. His staff leaned against a tree and he grabbed it to equip it once more. It seemed only his soul still hurt. "Where are we?"

"About a day away from base. You've been out of it for a few days. Cassie's been just fine since a day out."

Tyrian frowned a bit. "How did I sleep for days without need for food or water?"

"Laia says that that is a natural effect of relic exhaustion. When you hit that point, where your body can't handle the stress anymore, the relic basically shuts down everything except your breathing. As you recover, your body comes back under your control. Sometimes you'll wake in spurts, and that's when you need to eat and drink, and then you'll sleep again." Ewan sat down on the ground with a sigh. "Other times, like this, you'll just stay under until you recover wholly. It's safe, and natural. She said some doctors will deliberately induce a relic sleep for some critical patients."

"That makes me feel a little less unnerved, thank you. How did you get me here?"

"You've been riding with Cassie. Rourke and I have taken turns putting you on her horse."

"Rourke. Laia's husband."

"Yep. Can't miss him. He's my height and build. We're both descended of Northmen, so not a surprise there."

The Northmen, like the legendary Summarians, were a race long extinct, though not for the same reason. No one really knew anything about the Summarian race or what had really happened to them. On the other hand, the Northmen had migrated from high snowy mountains in Melodina a few thousand years before and settled across the world where they had mated with Humans and their bloodlines had diminished. Only a few descendants, such as Ewan and Rourke (and maybe Laia) truly showed their heritage. They had been a large race.

With a little breath, Tyrian said, "I'll meet him shortly. Where's Cassie? I need to see her."

"She's scouting the area. Bet you gold that you leave the camp area and she'll come to you." He hid a smile as Tyrian walked off determinedly. The confrontation was inevitable; the only reason Cassie had left his side at all was because they had sensed monsters approaching. Or rather, Laia had. She seemed to have some sort of radar for them.

Tyrian swung around a stack of tall rocks with the intent of climbing them for a better view when a figure materialized out of the darkness and caught him with an arm around the neck. He simply let out a long breath, relieved she was well enough to be up to her usual tricks. "Don't expect me to be afraid of you. I never could."

Cassie curled her other arm around him so that she was holding him and buried her face in his hair. "I wasn't intent on scaring you. I've been scared enough lately *by* you." She released him when he pulled free, though it was reluctantly. Her perch on a rock put them at eye level, and she framed his face with her hands. "How do you feel?" she asked softly. "You look relatively normal." Relatively, for even in the moonlight, his eyes seemed more haunted than usual.

He lifted his right hand and cupped her cheek. She very nearly shivered at the heat of his skin burning through her as the tingle of magic teased her nerves. "No wonder," she said softly. "No wonder it always seemed as if you had a relic. You were primed for a Pure Relic."

"More than you know," he murmured, thinking of Ben. Thinking of his brother naturally led him to thinking of Ophelia. She had made him say the same thing Ben had, but how had she known? There was still something more going on. Maybe Rourke would know, if he knew as many legends as Laia implied. Thinking of legends led him to thinking of destiny, and circled his mind back to the events in the graveyard.

Cassie started to ask a question, but the words tangled in her throat as his eyes suddenly landed on her and seemed to look all the way into her soul. A little shiver of trepidation went down her back as she realized he was very, very close to losing his temper. Slow burners tended to be the most dangerous. "Tyrian?"

"What the hell were you doing?" He gave her a quick shake. "You nearly died for me!"

"Yes. I did." She held his eyes evenly. "I am your Kentei Star, Tyrian. I exist to protect you." Her eyes widened as he dragged her down off the rock. On even ground, she was shorter than he was, and it put her at more of a disadvantage. She would have to get creative with him if his temper got the better of him. "Tyrian, be reasonable," she tried to say soothingly. Her heart pounded hard. Strangely, the threat of danger inside him was wildly seductive. Perhaps because she knew it was not a danger to *her*. "I'll do it again if I have to. You can't stop me."

"The hell you will!" he snapped. "Do you think I even *want* to keep going without you by my side? If you die, then what have I got left, Cassie? Protect me if you have to, but your life is not a commodity!"

She opened her mouth to give him a piece of her mind, but the words never made it. He dragged her onto her toes and took her mouth with his. There was no gentleness in him this time. He devoured her, forcing her to accept his feelings or flee. Accepting what he wanted, needed, was terrifying. More terrifying was the idea of running.

She warred with herself until his right hand tightened around her arm. The blast of hot magic streaked through her body and reminded her of his even heavier burden. Resistance crumbled and she pressed upward into his kiss. His taste was wilder, sharper. The promise of wild romance and happily ever after. "Let me go," she whispered when he buried his mouth hotly against her neck.

"Never!" It was almost a growl.

"I'm not running. I want to hold you." Her arms were instantly free and she wrapped them around his neck. She feverishly trailed kisses over his face, softly breathing her love with every word. It wasn't just the hunger of their bodies. She could sense the lingering icy grasp of fear inside him. "There's barely a mark on me." She caught his face in her hands. "Do you want to inspect me personally?"

His green eyes seemed to glow in the light of the stars. "Is that an offer?"

"When we're home." She kissed him again, unable to get enough of his taste. For someone only recently eighteen, he certainly knew how to kiss like an expert. "Practicing?" she whispered huskily.

"I don't kiss and tell. You can't be courted until eighteen, but you can date at thirteen." He kissed her thoroughly to savor the way her body went weak and she arched into him. "I was rehearsing for you. If I can't keep you at my side through force, maybe I can seduce you."

She wasn't sure that would work either, though she was more than willing to let him try. What bound her to his side was so much more powerful than anything she could imagine. Her heart, her soul, and her destiny. Her very birth bound her to him. How she had been chosen for such an honor, she didn't know, but she would protect him with everything she was. Always protect his smile. Her Kaiten. "Maybe we should go back to the camp." She trailed her fingers over his face. "Else Ewan think he's won the bet."

"Can't have that." He slowly released her with visible reluctance. "I'll wait until we're home, Cassie, but not a minute more." He skimmed his fingers down her cheek. "I don't care about the betting pool anymore. I'll give Kyle the money myself. I just want you. I need you."

The nerves had fled entirely. There was nothing except a matching need inside. Nothing except the overwhelming tangle of emotions that had taken over her life. "I'm yours," she said simply.

Hands linked, they walked back to the campsite. The other four were already there. Liang was cooking something over the fire, and Ewan and Rourke traded war stories. Laia sat close by, sharpening the lethal claymore she used. She glanced up when she heard their approach and then looked down again quickly to hide a grin. "Told you she was fine."

"Some things you need to see for yourself. You'd understand."

"I would," she murmured. "I would indeed." She smiled when Rourke almost automatically curled a hand around the back of her neck. "Tyrian, meet Rourke Mitakel."

"Well met," Rourke said with a smile.

Tyrian's brows lifted. "You're from the Commune of Soldiers?"

"One of the Melodina branches, yes."

Tyrian studied him and saw no sword. In fact, he possessed no visible weapon, implying that, like Liang, his fists *were* his weapon. It seemed to suit his personality, and it made him an obvious balance for Laia. "As you say, then, well met. You're a Scholar, Laia tells me."

"Mm."

"Do you know the language of magic?"

Rourke's handsome face remained calm, his golden eyes watching Tyrian. "I do, in fact, know the language. I know most languages."

Tyrian took a long breath. "*Askandi repulsin* Devourer." As he said it, he felt a warm pulse inside from his relic responding. For a moment, just a moment, he was sure he felt both Ben and Ophelia's presence. "What does it mean? Why was I twice asked to say it, and to two people who have since died? Is it my fault?"

"No," Rourke said instantly. "*Askandi*, in literal translation, is 'essence of life taken.' *Repulsin* is a verb variant of *'repulsinen'* which means 'to reject.' So what you have said is a command to the Devourer, proven by your use of its name. You're telling it to reject the essence of life of whomever you're addressing."

"Why is that so important?" Liang asked quietly.

"The Devourer earned its name. You all noticed it already. It devours life energy. That's where it gets its power. Anyone exposed to it or its wielder for too long will automatically have their lifeforce absorbed by it upon their death, and often, their souls will be consumed as well."

Tyrian's hands clenched in his lap. Shadows swirled in his dark eyes.

"Ben and Ophelia both knew they would die. And they both knew that they had been exposed to the relic or me for long enough that they would be absorbed. They didn't want that burden on me. Then why do I still feel them connected to the relic?"

Rourke hesitated. He and Laia shared a long look, as if communicating without words, and then he finally said slowly, "You rejected them, but their souls might as yet linger before rebirth. It is possible that until you're strong enough to fully command the relic, neither of them will be fully freed. You would need to talk to a Relic Master to be sure. I can only give you speculation."

"It's enough, for now, to know I didn't kill them." He looked up at the sky and found his star. He recognized the Kentei Star and was fairly sure he recognized the stars belonging to the companions he had already found. Ewan's and Kyle's were in fairly close proximity to each other, of course. "Which is yours?"

"There." Laia pointed to a star that seemed to shine with a touch of purple hue. "Both Rourke and I were born under that star, on the same night, three years apart. There are others who share stars, in fact. It can happen between lovers or family. Just sort of depends where your destiny falls, I suppose."

"So what else can the stars tell me?" he asked curiously. "I'd like to learn if you can teach me. Perhaps I won't be at so much a disadvantage. This whole thing of not knowing my own life anymore has grown very tiring."

"Hmm." She studied the skies. "Okay, see that one?" She pointed to a star with a soft light. "See how it moves closer? That will be one of your next Destined Stars. It has three points, so it will be female. And . . . hmm. It's on an eighty degree axis, so the person will be roughly around your age."

"That's amazing!" Ewan said. He looked up at the sky and was sure he spotted two other stars creeping in. "There are two more, right? Another with three points, so it's a girl, and since the other has six points, it's probably a boy, right?"

"Right!" Laia grinned at him and then pointed to the star that was his. "That's yours. See how it doesn't move? It's known as a fixed star. No one else will be born under it except you, ever. Your friend Kyle Raitels has a fixed star as well."

"So can you see my future or something?" he asked curiously.

She hesitated for a moment and then said slowly, "The things I read in the stars are not always able to be put into words. And there are things I see that I can't tell anyone about." She looked at Tyrian. "Some stories have to be told in their own time."

He nodded a little, knowing she referred to the possible existence of more Kaiten Stars. It was too much to think about their own war let alone any further wars. Especially wars that Ewan, and Kyle, might be destined to fight in by nature of their fixed stars. Tyrian hated the very idea. Why did there have to be war? Why couldn't there be peace for everyone?

It was late the next day when they finally returned to base. A great sense of relief arrived to just be within the walls again, and Tyrian looked at his tower with longing. It was a refuge, and he very badly needed a refuge right then. Unfortunately, it would have to wait. Everyone was cheering, and both civilian and soldier clamored to see he was alive and well.

"He's fine!" Ewan called as he and Rourke shoved their way through the crowd. "Now let the poor guy catch a breath. It was hell out there." He winced wryly. "Sorry, Tyrian. Poor choice of words."

Tyrian found himself smiling. "No offense taken."

The crowd was still pushing in, and Cassie scowled. "Damn it, we'll never make it to the castle at this rate."

"Everybody *back off*."

Laia didn't raise her voice. She didn't have to. It carried through the crowd like the crack of a whip so that everyone went silent. People pulled back a bit sheepishly and allowed for the party to move through easily.

"Where have you been my whole life?" Ewan asked.

Rourke bonked him on the head. "She's taken. Get your own woman."

"He has one," Cassie offered.

"I do not." It was half a mutter, half a growl, as Ewan beat a hasty path toward the castle. His desperation to escape the conversation was very, very obvious.

"So about his destiny . . .?" Tyrian said to Laia with a lifted brow.

She shot him a grin. "Varied, complicated, and potentially highly amusing for anyone in the vicinity. You'll see it. I probably won't. Do send me letters to keep me up to date."

When they arrived at the meeting room, Ewan had already gotten there. Kyle and Kell were also present, and so was Marian. She spotted her cousin and promptly ran over to leap on him for a hug. "Oh god!" she whispered into his shoulder. "Oh god! You scared me! Word has spread fast about what happened." She grabbed his right hand and stared at the relic, stricken. "It's Pure."

"It is," he said simply. "Ben held it for me. He gave his life so that I would have it. I can't reject it, Marian. I owe it to him." He hugged her for a moment and then looked at Kyle and Kell who were eyeing Laia and Rourke in fascination. "More Destined Stars. Laia and Rourke Mitakel. She's a paladin, he's a brawler."

Kell sighed at Laia wistfully. "You make me wish I was forty years younger." He winked saucily and was rewarded by an answering wink. He had always liked sassy females with as much brain as they had beauty.

Kyle offered a hand to Rourke with a smile. "Well met."

"Well met, friend."

Introductions over, Laia and Rourke took their leave to secure rooms. Marian saw Tyrian's thoughtful frown and smiled. "Don't worry," she told him. "Since you know you'll have one hundred and eight Destined Stars, we've made sure that there are as many rooms as will be needed. If any are like R.K. and own a shop or something, we'll have somewhere for them to be as well. Those who need rooms will have them."

"Good," Tyrian said with a sigh. "That's one less thing to think about."

"So let's hear what really happened in Trinan," Kyle said softly.

It didn't take long to recap the events, and Tyrian filled in everything he had learned from Ben's memories. His voice remained steady, but his hands clenched together under the table. Cassie's hand curled around his wrist was his anchor. The others knew it, just as they knew by the shadows in his eyes that a lesser man would have already broken.

"Then we were right in thinking Blaine is the one who started the problems." Kyle drummed the fingers of his relic hand on the table. "What does she get out of making Albanion choke his people? If she hadn't done that, then we wouldn't be here."

"There's no knowing," Liang said. "It could be simple greed. Maybe she wanted the Pure Relic for power, but not knowing where Ben was, decided to get power in another way. Ben came into sight and . . . here we are."

Marian rested her arms on the table and put her head down. "I can't understand why the generals are going along with things. Uncle Donald, first and foremost, but the Lower Generals as well. They've done so much for the people."

Kyle paused and then asked slowly, "Correct me if I'm wrong, but have any of *their* troops been the ones causing problems in towns?"

Tyrian frowned thoughtfully. "No . . . the armies of the six Lower Generals are specialist troops. They handle the defense of borders and checkpoints. They only go into towns where there is a dire need."

"Like when the Commune of Soldiers was attacked," Liang said. "It was General Cutter's division that went in to clean up the devastation, wasn't it, Ewan?"

"I believe so. I try not to remember that time period much, but I think she was the one who helped take control of things. There were no survivors to be found, but the city could be saved," he added much softer. Kyle touched his shoulder, and he covered his hand. They were more like brothers than friends.

"To my knowledge," Kell said, "it has been the Imperial Army of the Empire that has been causing the trouble. The units directly under the command of the Prime Duke. They're dispatched for regular peacekeeping and patrol." He paused for a moment. "I see what you might be thinking, Kyle. Perhaps the corruption is only at the top. If we can talk to the generals, we might make them see reason."

"We eventually have to go to a checkpoint," Cassie decided. "If we can get our hands on a Lower General and make him or her sit down with us, then perhaps we can stave off further bloodshed."

"It's a start, though I still feel a bit like I'm stumbling around." Tyrian looked at Kell. "Strategist?"

"Still looking. Professor Matthias used to run a school for strategists, but the school closed last year when he had to expel one of his students. He only had one left, so he might be taking him or her on a hands-on journey of experience."

"How did Lupine go?"

Kyle leaned back in his chair. "Relatively well. It's in the same condition as Teasarn, and our soldiers noted barely a single unit's worth of Empire army there. We should be able to take it fairly easily."

"I'll go along to the battle. I have to," he added when the others started to protest. "I'm the Kaiten Star. I have to find my Destined Stars. They can't all come to me. And . . . we can use my being the Kaiten Star and a possessor of a Pure Relic to our advantage. I'm not just a traitor now, leading some little rebellion."

"I'll start dropping rumors," Kell said instantly.

The meeting room doors suddenly flew open, and a young boy hurried into the room. He was barely thirteen in age and very slender over all. Blond hair capped a face that might eventually be handsome. He wore sturdy traveling clothes and had multiple backpacks strapped to his back with scrolls and maps sticking out of every opening. "Lord Tyrian!" he said urgently. "I need to find Lord Tyrian!"

Tyrian found himself smiling as he recognized the tug inside. He stood and moved around the table to be less imposing. "I'm Tyrian Southerwind. Do you need help?"

"My name is Thomas!" The boy stuck out a hand, saw it was filthy, and hastily retracted it. "I'm a mapmaker!"

"Thomas?" Ewan's brows shot up. "Wait, you're the guy who has made the majority of the maps of the world? But you're a kid!"

"Well, yeah. I'm technically Thomas Junior. My dad is the original mapmaker." He looked at Tyrian intently. "He's old and sick, and the world is changing. I have to be here to make note of it so I can make new maps for everyone! You can count on me to make sure you don't get lost, Lord Tyrian!"

Tyrian smiled. "I have every confidence in you, Thomas. You won't let us down. Maybe you can look at the maps we have here and make sure they're as recent as can be. Oh." He took off the tiny relic attached to his earring. "This has my maps in it. Can you update it too?"

"Yeah!" Thomas nearly bounced on his toes with happiness. He had known, just known, the instant he heard about Tyrian Southerwind that he had to be there. Meeting Tyrian, he felt it more. Lord Tyrian needed him. Thomas wasn't a warrior, but he absolutely wanted to protect Lord Tyrian and make sure he was happy. And if keeping him from getting lost would do it, he would rewrite the maps of the world.

To the surprise of all present, a glowing white star appeared on Thomas' shoulder. It was answered by an echoing glow from Tyrian's relic. Startled, Tyrian looked at his hand. He looked at the others, and he realized that all of them bore the white stars on their shoulder. Some were hidden by clothing, but the glow still came through. "Marked by destiny," he said softly. "We'll always know each other once we've shared the skies." Laia was officially one of his most unnerving Destined Stars. How did she *know* this stuff?

"Well, it's late." Ewan got to his feet and scooped up Thomas under an arm. "Let's find you a room, kid. We're going to be keeping you busy!"

"Let's get some dinner," Marian said. "You must be starving after being on the road for almost two weeks!"

"I'd rather eat in my room," Tyrian said with a shake of his head. "I need the quiet." He looked at Cassie, and something heated moved in his eyes. "Can you bring something with you on your way up?"

"Of course." She was barely breathing as he walked out of the room. The *way* he looked at her was enough to take her breath away. That intensity inside him was a very potent thing when turned on a woman directly.

"I get the feeling he'd rather have *you* for dinner," Marian said with a soft giggle. "Are you finally going to put everything the way it's supposed to be?" When Cassie glanced at her, Marian smiled. "Well, of course I accept you! Tyrian needs you. And you make him happy. And you could easily beat Liang at arm wrestling."

Cassie opened her mouth and then closed it. She had the strangest feeling that she really didn't want to know.

CHAPTER TWELVE

"It's painful to love someone this much, I know."

Tyrian's reference to a fishbowl was very correct, Cassie discovered as she made her way back from the inn with dinner. People either knew or at least suspected what would be the outcome by morning. If anything, everyone assuredly knew she was now sharing Tyrian's room. Much to her relief, people seemed to be quite glad for it. Kell had done his job well. Everyone was talking of the Kaiten Star and his Kentei protector.

As she crossed the courtyard toward the tower, she looked up at the balcony. Her heart clenched in her chest with a swell of emotion. Tyrian was leaning on the rail as he looked out over his city. He looked unbearably alone in that moment. So much was being asked of him!

The guards at the base of the tower opened the doors for her since her hands were full, and they were either good actors or just too tactful to grin openly. She certainly could tell they looked a bit on the gleeful side.

When she got to the room at the top, she nudged the door open with her foot. As she walked inside, she said, "I've never seen so many sly winks and giggles in my life." She put the tray down on the table. "Even the kids were doing it."

Tyrian had to smile as he straightened from the railing. She always seemed to know just what to say to him. He walked into the room and went to get the fire stoked. It was still cool enough at night that the room got chilly without it. The sun had set and the moon was rising. He lit a few lamps for light and then sat down at the table gratefully. "Liang was cooking."

"R.K. made him. Said he liked us too much to risk poisoning us on a night like this." She sat down across from him and then stood again as she realized she still wore her monk wear. "I really should change."

He caught her hand. "Don't. I've wanted to peel that gear off you from that first day when you saved my life and I realized there was no one who I was safer with."

Her eyes softened. "Well, how can I turn that down? Forgive me if I laugh at you as you attempt to decipher how it goes together."

He saluted her with his glass of brandy. "I'm a quick learner. Besides, the longer it takes, the more we'll enjoy it."

She just shook her head. "You are a rake and a terror, and I can't imagine why the girls in Trinan weren't mobbing your door."

"They were." He grinned when she lifted her brows. "Right on my birthday, there was a crowd outside the door. Marian scared them off. She said that no one could have me unless they could out-heal her or beat Liang at arm wrestling."

Well, that explained *that*. She thoughtfully stirred her porridge. "I'm not much of a Healer, but I think I could beat Liang. I'm smaller than he is, but I'm stronger. And sneakier. So does that qualify me as eligible? Can I cut to the front of the line?"

"There's no line." He covered her hand and waited until her eyes lifted. "I've been waiting for you," he told her softly. "There were no others I wanted until you. If there's one thing I don't regret about anything that has happened, it's you. You brought me to life."

She curled her fingers into his. "You're immortal now," she said softly. She took a deep breath and let it out again. "There might be a way for us, Tyrian. I'll have to go through my own hell to do it. But I will. I'll do anything to be with you. I can't stand even the idea of you being alone through eternity, and I don't think the stars would give us a destiny that would be so short. There is a way, and I just have to find the courage to do it."

"I'll wait." He slowly smiled. "I'm very patient."

Her eyes lit with sudden humor. "You are the very paragon of patience. And my sanity thanks you for it. I needed to be here on my own. I needed to be able to say that this was a choice as much as it was destiny."

"You choose me?"

She drew his hand to her cheek. "I love you." Her eyes widened as his hands suddenly curled around her wrists and then she laughed breathlessly as he dragged her out of her chair and onto his lap. He was much faster than she had imagined, almost as fast as she was. It was a thrilling realization. "You had to know."

He framed her face and held her eyes intensely, his gaze dark with rioting emotions. "I love you," he whispered. When her entire body trembled, he brushed his lips tenderly across hers. "You had to know."

Knowing and hearing, she realized then, were entirely different things. She curled her arms around his neck and smiled as he stood with her in his arms. She had never been carried before. It was rather enjoyable. "I won't run." She feathered her lips over his throat and savored the taste of his pulse. It beat as hard as hers did, but his hands remained gentle. "Promise."

He went around the wall separating their bedroom from their sitting room and slowly let go of her legs so that she could stand. As her body slid along his, her eyes darkened to a stormy color with the blue overtaking the black. For a moment, she simply held onto him. His arms tightened around her, and their bodies seemed to be perfectly made to fit together.

He slowly released her and set her back a step to study the clothing she wore. It covered her from neck to toes, tied in some places, buckled in others, and wrapped or folded in the rest. There wasn't a lace or button anywhere in sight. "Hmm."

As his hands slowly shaped her body, hot through even her clothes, she stopped breathing. Her eyes closed helplessly in delight as ripples of pleasure followed in the wake of his touch. The heat of his relic hand, that wonderful sting of magic, lingered even when his touch slowly, maddeningly, moved on.

He bent his head and took her mouth unhurriedly. The sigh she gave was sweet. Hunger rode hard, but he ruthlessly held onto his control. He needed to know everything about her. Every secret. Memorize every perfect curve. Map the marks of her life, banish the memories. Need. He had never truly understood what it meant to need anything until he had met his Kentei.

When he lifted his head slightly, she realized that the first layer of her gear had been removed. The overlaying garment was knotted and wrapped around her upper body to diminish her curves. Somehow he had gotten it loose without her knowledge. "It took me years to learn to wrap that," she said huskily, "and you undid it in minutes."

He smiled and tossed the material aside. "I have more incentive." He studied the next layer, which was some sort of sleeveless, snug, tunic tucked into the bottom half of her clothes. "Like opening a birthday present," he said softly. "While tearing off the wrappings to get to the prize appeals, there's something to be said for enjoying the scenery."

She eyed his tunic with some frustration. That she was slowly losing her clothes, and he wasn't, seemed entirely unfair. "I'm going to skip to the tearing part if you don't get rid of that top." When he laughed, her heart clenched wildly. He almost never laughed. That very seriousness that was so much a part of him seemed to reject laughter. His laugh sounded beautiful. Young and carefree. She would do anything to hear it again.

He stripped off his tunic and tossed it aside, leaving him gloriously bare on top. She slowly spread her hands across his chest. "I've wanted this from that first night," she confessed. "You're beautiful, Tyrian." She trailed her fingers across a small scar and then traced the line of a powerful muscle. "Tanned. When did you run around without a shirt?"

"I don't like clothes," he confessed. "Especially if it's hot. Half the time during summer, when I'm alone in my room, I don't wear anything."

"I'm going to become very fond of summer." As he laughed again, she rose up to kiss him fiercely, wanting to taste that beautiful sound. She caught his hands and lowered them to where the buckles on her outer legwear hid.

It only took two tries to figure out the trick to them. The heavy material dropped to the floor and revealed snug black leggings that molded faithfully to her long legs. The snug tunic went over the top to her hips. She looked like some sort of graceful and powerful sleek black cat. "How much more is there?" he managed to ask.

Her lips curved. "Not much." She lifted her arms helpfully as he stripped the tunic up over her head with a swift gesture. She could sense let alone see that his control slowly corroded with every passing minute.

He knelt to strip away the leggings as well and then straightened. His breath lodged in his lungs and remained there. Every muscle in his body seemed to tighten at once as he stared at her. The scraps of black silk that tried to act as underwear and bra clung to a body more perfect than he remembered.

But only in proportion was she truly perfect. Bare to his eyes, he could see the tiny flecks of white that dotted her skin. The biggest and most obvious was the one across her neck. Other much smaller ones scattered across her pale skin. Where the arrows had struck were the most recent; the scars looked a pale pink as they finished healing. He lightly touched where the one had hit her arm and then bent his head to press his lips there.

Her legs went weak with delight as he began to find and caress every scar with his lips. As he pressed a hot kiss to one on her stomach, she grabbed his shoulders for balance. "Tyrian." It was all she could say.

He stood and lifted her into his arms. Rather than tumbling her onto the bed as she expected, he put her down slowly, almost reverently, his dark eyes glowing in the lamplight. "Mine," he breathed. "Finally, mine."

His relic hand curled around her waist, and she took a sharp breath as the whiplash of pleasure streaked through every nerve before coiling deep in her body. Skin to skin, there was nothing to muffle the power in his blood. He slowly glided his hand down her leg, leaving a wave of tingling delight, and her entire body quivered. "Cheater!"

"I may grow to like this relic." He buried his lips between the curves of her breasts. Her skin was slightly damp with sweat and tasted salty and sweet all at once. Her hands buried in his hair to drag him up again but he resisted the effort. "I'm not done yet," he said roughly as he stripped her bra away. "Let me know you."

A moan was all she could manage as his mouth closed over one tight nipple. His relic hand cupped her other breast and she arched against him wildly. The laziness had been melted in fire. The gentleness in him was burning away. She was burning too, her entire body aching with need.

He trailed his fingers down her body slowly, somehow finding nerves she had never known she had. The magic in his skin acted like a beacon. She opened her mouth to beg him to stop tormenting her when his hand slid between her legs. The words became a soft cry as the throbbing increased rather than lessened.

He softly caressed her, teased hidden nerves, his mouth seeking other points until she quivered almost violently in his arms. With a sudden surge of strength and a lithe twist of her body, she tumbled him over and reversed their position. She pinned his hands beside his head. "My turn," she warned huskily.

She looked rumpled and flushed with her hair tumbling around her face and shoulders. The blue chips in her eyes had melted into a sapphire pool. His aching arousal hardened to the point of pain as he stared at her hungrily. She was wild, untamed, and beyond control. There was nothing sexier than his beautiful monk out of control.

She returned every kiss, every embrace. Her lips and fingers memorized his body, sought each little scar and erased it with a kiss. She nimbly unfastened his pants and tugged them down his body. As she did, he managed to tease, "You seem to know what you're doing with other combatant styles of clothing."

"I've worn them." She nipped at his flat stomach and savored the way his muscles bunched and rippled under his skin. "I have a lot of stories to tell you. Want to hear them?"

Her fingers trailed lightly over his erection and he groaned. "Later. Damn it, Cassie!" Her fingers curled around him, learned him, and he shuddered. "Stop." Her body slid against his temptingly as she nipped at his chin, and he grabbed her fiercely. "Stop!"

He twisted and rolled her under him, and she wanted to laugh. It seemed impossible to be so happy when her body was so frustrated and needy. But she was happy. To be free to love, to be loved . . . She wrapped her arms around his neck fiercely. "I won't let you go!"

He couldn't answer with words. He simply moved between her legs, caught her close, and slowly began to press inside her beckoning heat. He struggled to be slow, to give her time if she needed it, but she was hot and wet and perfectly formed for him. Her legs tightened around his hips and he surged forward completely. Her breath hitched and he froze. "Cassie?"

She couldn't find the words for how she felt. Elation, euphoria.

Wonder. Joy. Too many words, too many emotions. There was no way to tell him how *right* she felt. It was as if her world had been set right for the first time. All she could do was catch his face in her hands and pour herself into kissing him, needing him to know.

He did. He caught her closer and pulled her arms around him again, needing her to hold him. He took her again and again, the hunger rapidly going out of control. He couldn't have stopped. Her soft cries muffled against his shoulder, but imprinted themselves inside his soul. Her entire body tensed and her nails bit into his shoulders with sudden alarm. "Let go." He breathed the words against her lips. "I'll catch you."

The cataclysm started deep and spread outward without warning. The sudden ecstasy was shocking only for an instant. She trusted him. She tightened her grip on him with arms and legs and let it take her in wild waves of pleasure. And when it took him as well, it was she who caught him as he took the final leap.

He had enough presence of mind to catch his weight on his arms, but that was the best he could manage. "Legs," he managed to say.

She belatedly realized her legs were wrapped around his waist and slowly let them slide down his hips. As she did, he let his weight rest more fully against her as he relaxed entirely. He made a wonderful blanket. Who knew a sweaty male body could smell and feel so delicious? She buried her fingers in his hair on a contented sigh. "I'm flexible."

"I'm grateful." It was muttered against her breast, his voice drowsy and amused all at the same time. "Mind if I stay here a few minutes?"

"Take your time." She closed her eyes to savor the way her body felt. There were a few aches making their presence known, but she had to assume it was like any new muscles being used. Practice would make them get used to it. At least practicing with these muscles was bound to be a great deal of fun.

He lifted his head, a bemused smile on his face. "Did you just giggle?"

She had. "Maybe I'm happy." She framed his face and searched his eyes. There was a peace inside him that she hadn't seen before. He looked relaxed and young and unburdened by life. "What about you?"

He kissed her softly and tenderly. "Very happy," he said against her lips. Reluctantly, he disentangled their bodies and rolled to the side onto his back. She promptly curled up against him with her head in its place on his shoulder, and one of her arms wrapped around his chest. He felt himself relax entirely on a contented sigh. "Wonder who won."

She smiled up at him. "I think we did. Is it midnight?"

"Possibly. I can't see the clock from here."

"I'll check." She kissed his chin and slipped from the bed. She hesitated only briefly as she stood and then walked with her usual grace around the wall. When she returned, she carried their forgotten dessert and his brandy. "It is officially after midnight. Whoever had money on what is now today is the winner."

"All's fair." He piled the pillows so that they could both sit up in bed. "Dessert in bed, hmm? Now that's my idea of service."

She just smiled as she got back into bed. "Well, I was hungry. I assumed you might be as well." She laughed and batted at his right hand as it skimmed over her arm. "Don't you dare, you fiend!"

When dessert had been finished and the plates put aside, they snuggled together under the covers. She rubbed her cheek against his shoulder and he gently covered her hand on his chest. "Kyle will be alright," he admitted softly. "Ophelia told me . . . she told me she knew she would die when she met me." He closed his eyes. "But she said that something wonderful would happen someday if she did. And she said that Kyle wasn't her soul mate. She didn't have one yet."

"Will you tell Kyle?"

"When he can say her name without a haunted look in his eyes, yes." He turned and braced himself over her, and his free hand slowly smoothed down her body. Her breath caught as he lightly touched her lips with his. "Just how flexible are you?"

Her lips curved. "I'm sure we'll find out."

They were awakened the next morning to the sound of knocking on the door. Cassie drowsily lifted her head from Tyrian's shoulder. He made a grumpy noise and she tightened her arms around him. "Someone's at the door," she said softly. He muttered something under his breath, and she found herself smiling. "I hadn't realized you're not a morning person."

The door opened and a maid called, "It's just Merilyne, Lord Tyrian. I've brought breakfast for you and Lady Cassie, and I'm taking your clothes to be washed." There was a pause, then, with a giggle in her voice, she added, "And mended."

Cassie pinched Tyrian lightly as she sat up. "You owe me a bra," she whispered. "And underwear." Louder, she called, "Thank you, Merilyne. And for those who are sure to ask you, yes, it was after midnight."

Giggling the entire way, the maid hurried from the room, and the door shut with a thunk behind her. Tyrian opened his eyes to see Cassie smiling at him, and his world aligned properly. He had slept, truly slept, for the first time in a long time. He couldn't break apart so long as she held him. "Sleep well?" he asked her. He brushed her tangled hair out of her eyes.

She lowered her forehead to his with a smile. "When someone let me sleep."

"I've got a fondness for flexible monks with really sexy smiles. You can't blame me if I can't keep my hands off you. Your stamina is better than mine though." He tugged her in for a kiss. "But I'm trainable."

There was a playful streak in her lover hidden under his normal intense seriousness. She looked forward to teasing it out more. "Practice makes perfect, as they say." With much reluctance, she released him and got out of bed.

He got out of bed as well and watched as she pulled on her normal gear. Even knowing how to take it off her again, it was fascinating to watch her put it on. He understood the practicality, but he liked her body too much to want it covered.

He smiled as she stepped closer to tie his green scarf around his neck for him. "Thank you." She then used the scarf to tug him down for a kiss, and he was happy to oblige. "Thank you for that too." He curled a lock of her hair around his finger and then slowly released her. "We'd better eat before I give in to the urge to practice getting that stuff off you again."

She slowly stepped back. The idea sounded very tempting to her as well. If this was what an eternity with him would be like, it would be a very, very enjoyable eternity. But eternity was not hers to be had yet. She knew what she would have to do to claim it, and the idea still terrified her.

His fingers skimmed down her cheek. When she looked at him, he kissed her warmly. "Don't think about it," he said softly. "There's time. And that's not just the newly made immortal talking. Five years, ten years, twenty years. However long it takes you, Cassie. I'll be waiting."

After they finished breakfast, they headed down to the meeting room. Kyle and Kell had beaten them there, and they were talking together over coffee. The two males looked up, studied Tyrian and Cassie, and then looked down with grins.

"Is it that obvious?" Cassie asked dryly.

Tyrian curled his arm around her waist. "I've been told it is very obvious to a knowing eye. We'll be able to spot it from now on too." He nuzzled her hair. "I think it will be a real test of my control if I ever see Marian looking like we do. She has a soft spot for villains, and I'm terrified her Healer's heart will get broken."

"And you'll break heads if that happens?" Kyle asked dryly.

"Very likely. For now, my sanity is maintained since she has yet to find someone to court or date." He sat down at the table and then glanced at the door with a smile as Liang and Ewan walked in. "Good morning."

Ewan walked over to Kyle and handed him a bag that made a thump when it hit the table. "It was after midnight. You win the pool." He grabbed a cup of coffee and sat down with a contented sigh. "Morning, Tyrian. You looked nicely rested for once. Cassie, well done."

She felt her cheeks warm slightly but just shook her head. He was incorrigible. "Thanks. So what's on the agenda for today? Are we going to go to Lupine?"

"We might as well make our way there." Tyrian drummed his right hand on the table. "I, Ewan, and you will lead our unit into the battle. If we're lucky, we'll have many more Army members come to join our side. A couple hundred more and we'll have two units worth, even if we leave some behind to hold the town."

"Lupine has its own militia unit," Kell spoke up. "Word reached me last night from one of my contacts. Rarely do the smaller cities have them, but Lupine does. They were retired when Albanion sent in the Imperial Army, but they stand ready to join the Rebellion if we can route the Army."

"Then they could hold the town themselves and we'd still have two units for battle." Tyrian raked a hand through his hair. "We're going to need a high class Weaponsmith and Armorer soon. We'll need our soldiers to be as upgraded as possible."

A guard knocked lightly on the door and then opened it. Tyrian turned around curiously only to get to his feet as a newcomer walked in. She was unassuming in appearance, a bit on the plain side, and though quite slender she also seemed quite strong. She couldn't have been much older than he was. "Hello," she said softly. "Are you Lord Tyrian Southerwind?"

"I am." He smiled as he felt the familiar tug inside. It seemed much simpler to find his companions than he had thought it would be. He didn't doubt it would slowly get harder, but the task was beginning to feel less daunting. "What can I do for you?"

She suddenly smiled at him. "It's what I can do for you. My name is Mouse, Lord Tyrian. I am a Weaponsmith."

Ewan looked at the ceiling. "Okay, next we want the Army to surrender."

"It only works when Lord Tyrian does it," Kell told him dryly.

"If you'd like to see some of my work, I can show you some examples," Mouse offered to Tyrian. "Oh." She frowned thoughtfully. "Wait, is Laia here?" At the nod, she smiled again. "Then you have seen my work. I created her claymore."

Tyrian thought of the brilliant and masterly made weapon that Laia wielded. Oddly, he wasn't surprised that it was one of Mouse's creations.

"Done," he said instantly. "Do you work solely in metal, or do you work with wooden weapons as well?"

"I can make anything you ask of me," she said simply.

Tyrian offered his relic hand, and as she clasped it, his relic glowed and the answering star appeared on her shoulder. "Thank you," he said simply. "We have several empty shops both on ground level and in the Belowgrounds. Whatever suits you best, please choose. Any help you need to get supplies or to get set up, just let someone know."

She squeezed his hand tightly for a moment. "You can count on me, Lord Tyrian. As soon as I am set up, I will start upgrading weapons for those who need it."

While she hurried out to find a place to set up, Tyrian turned to look at the others present. In particular, he looked at Ewan and Cassie. "Would either of you like to bet that Laia knew precisely who she was referring to when she was telling us about the stars?"

"No," they both said promptly.

With Kyle to hold down the base, Tyrian, Cassie, and Ewan headed to the barracks to pull together their unit. Tyrian did his best to balance out the capabilities of his soldiers, but he knew that eventually they would need more mages and more healers. If he could get even one unit each of magic, combat, ranged, and healing, then the Rebellion would be far more ready to take on the Imperial Army.

They had barely ridden out of the gates when he spotted a figure running across the field toward them. He couldn't quite make her out clearly, but he suspected it was a female if only because of the clothes she wore. She was also being chased by a swarm of monsters. "Ewan! Grab her, and we'll grab the beasts!"

Ewan kicked his horse and shot across the ground toward the girl. "This way!" he shouted. She diverted and ran toward him, and he leaned over the side of his horse to scoop her up under an arm as he went past.

The monsters couldn't change direction in time and ran directly into the middle of the unit. It took only a few moments for all of the beasts to be destroyed. As Tyrian reequipped his staff on his back, he turned his horse toward where Ewan approached. The girl on the horse in front of him was in her early teens, and very lovely. If her vibrantly colored clothing and wildly curly hair were any clue, she was a bard of some kind. "Are you okay?" he asked gently.

Ewan lifted her down onto the ground, and she brushed out her skirts with shaky hands. "I am now!" she managed to say with a laugh as shaky as her hands. "Where am I?"

Tyrian opened his mouth and then closed it. In consternation, he looked at Cassie and said, "I need to name this place, don't I?" He frowned thoughtfully. He had never liked the name 'Rebellion Army' because it didn't fully encompass the entire situation. Rebellions could occur even when they weren't warranted. "The home base of the Liberation Army," he finally said.

Ewan gave him a thumbs-up and the soldiers began to murmur excitedly. The bard smiled with relief. "Then I think I'm in the right place. My name is Myrroria, but everyone calls me Myr. I'm a bard from Rubentia. I am here to seek your aid, Lord Tyrian. Rubentia is being strangled to death. You have to help us! Our fields are dying and our people are starving. The Army won't do anything to help!"

"That's a long way to come from," Cassie said softly. "How old are you, Myr?"

"Fifteen. But I'm strong." She lifted her chin. "I know my appearance doesn't seem to prove it, or my entrance, but I'm strong. I can fight. I can fight in small range or large combat. My daggers are always accurate." She reached up to take Tyrian's hands. All she knew for sure was that he needed her as much as her city needed him. "If you need me to fight, I will. If you need me to dance or sing for the troops for morale, I can do that too. Let me join the Liberation Army. I want to help you help our country!"

Though her long golden sleeves covered her shoulder, the glow underneath was as obvious as the flicker of Tyrian's relic. "I'm glad to have you on board, Myr," he said softly. "When I form a ranged unit, you can be sure I will turn to you for advice. You're the first battlefield ranged combatant that I have found. Until then, your songs and dance will keep everyone's spirits up. Including mine."

She brightened. "Thank you, Lord Tyrian! You won't regret it!" She peeked at the moat warily. Though the water was a lovely blue, she could see monsters swimming under the surface. "Uhm."

Ewan grinned. "They're tame. They won't be looking for musical snacks." He whistled loudly, and when someone peered over the top of the gate, he called, "Open the gate for Myr! She's one of us!"

The guard saluted and promptly had the gate lowered. Myr wasted no time in hurrying into the castle. She had a lot to do to get herself settled in. She needed to come up with new songs and stories for the soldiers!

"One wonders what we'll find next," Cassie murmured.

"It takes all kinds," Tyrian said with a smile. "No two stars in the sky are alike, so no two people, even if they share a star, will be alike. I wouldn't want it any way else, truly. If someone is my Destined Star, then it must be because I need them."

Uncaring that the soldiers were watching, she leaned across their horses and softly kissed him. She was sure it wasn't just her that felt proud to be chosen to share his sky. And as the soldiers cheered, she found herself laughing. "Fishbowl."

His green eyes sparkled. "At least no one is bored."

Chapter Thirteen

"It's one step, one small step, in one small world of us."

From a distance, Lupine looked very much like Teasarn indeed. It was of similar size and scope, and it had buildings of much the same layout and design. The biggest difference lay in that Teasarn had embraced its desert land, and Lupine had cultivated theirs to be covered in lush grass and trees.

Tyrian couldn't miss the rundown state of the buildings and streets even from outside the city. Soldiers stood on every corner. It made him sick to his stomach to see it. How could anyone live like this? The Emperor had been corrupted by Blaine, but that did not absolve him of guilt. Only a heart that was on the edge of corruption could be taken over.

Hopes suddenly raised inside the city as the approaching unit was recognized. There was no mistaking the green and black colors worn by the soldiers, and the young man riding at the front wore the distinctive mark of a Pure Relic.

The Army gathered swiftly to form into a unit and left the city edges to engage the rebellion. The lieutenant riding at the front touched the Voice Relic on his earring and said curtly, "Tyrian Southerwind, surrender and there will be no bloodshed."

The cool voice that responded said only, "The only blood spilled will be yours. Do you serve an empire that will starve its people and choke its life? The Liberation Army stands ready to breathe air back into this land."

A little chill ran down the lieutenant's back. The rumors of a legendary hero chosen by the stars, the mythical Kaiten Star, had reached even his ears. He had dismissed it out of hand as foolish hope-mongering by civilians. He could no longer dismiss it. It was there in Tyrian's voice, the will to save those who could not save themselves.

With a curt gesture, he beckoned for his unit to move forward. Soldiers rushed across the land on foot and on horse, ready to engage the enemy. The Liberation Army, all mounted, rushed forward as well. The lieutenant kept his eyes sharp on the field as he looked for the green scarf that marked Tyrian. When he spotted it, he drew his sword and rushed forward to engage him.

"Incoming!" Ewan said. He knocked an enemy soldier off his horse, and when the man held up his hands in surrender, stayed his sword from striking him down. "Tyrian, the leader is approaching you quickly!"

"So I see." The battle raged around them, the land a sea of shouts and clashes of weapons. It seemed a familiar location for Tyrian though it was his first real experience in actual war skirmishes. He felt very much at home on the battlefield. He had been born for it. "Cassie will cover my back."

With his Kentei following closely, he turned his horse and rode forward quickly to meet the lieutenant directly. He was more than proficient as a horseman and did not need to hold the reins to direct his mount. That left his hands free to use his staff, and as they drew even, he struck sharply. The blow glanced off the lieutenant's shoulder and knocked him off balance though it did not knock him down.

The lieutenant, needing one hand to steer, only had one hand with which to wield a sword. At a disadvantage, he dismounted. "A duel, Lord Tyrian! Meet me on even ground!"

Since some wars were ended by duels between opposing leaders, Tyrian had no hesitation in dismounting as well. The less blood spilled, the better. He moved forward quickly to be on even ground and into his Voice Relic said, "Cease fire! Both sides, cease fire! A duel is commencing!"

All soldiers lowered weapons and backed down. A handful of soldiers had been lost on the Imperial Army's side. Only injuries dotted the Liberation Army. Nearly two hundred Imperial soldiers had already surrendered and switched sides.

The lieutenant lunged for Tyrian on a shout with his sword raised over his head. Tyrian held his ground until the last minute. He ducked under his enemy's attack and came up swinging his staff backward. The wooden pole cracked into the back of the lieutenant's head. As the soldier staggered, Tyrian turned sharply and went on the attack.

The staff was little more than a blur as he whirled it over his head to gain momentum. The lieutenant managed to duck the first blow, but discovered too late that it had been feinted. Tyrian ducked back around, swinging as he went, and the staff slammed into the lieutenant's back and sent him tumbling across the field.

A murmur began to move through the soldiers on both sides of awe and respect. Tyrian's mastery of his weapon was very obvious. Other staff users on the field couldn't do half the things he did, and many were older than his eighteen years.

As the lieutenant continued to lie on the field, Tyrian spun his staff one handed and then sheathed it on his back once more. He walked closer to the fallen enemy leader with the intent of calling victory when the lieutenant suddenly lunged to his feet. He leapt forward with a dagger in his hand, and Tyrian's body tensed as he prepared to dodge.

He didn't have to. Three distinct projectiles struck the lieutenant in three different places, each with the intent to kill. His forward momentum threw him into the dirt where he did not move again. Blood pooled under his body.

Tyrian recognized the throwing star in his neck as coming from Cassie. The two arrows protruding from his back and his head were not familiar. He looked swiftly to the side toward the city and saw two figures crouched on rooftops. Both wore the familiar clothing of archers; snug leggings and tunics to cut down wind resistance and vests to provide support for the quivers they wore. The one who had a pink ribbon in her hair saluted with her bow.

He turned to look at the field. Evenly, he said, "The Liberation Army is the victor by rules of the battlefield. Those who wish to surrender and join us may do so. Those who do not are given the option to flee back to the capitol. If you persist in resistance, by laws of engagement, your lives are forfeit."

Several hundred soldiers put down arms and surrendered. The rest fled the scene as fast as was possible, and in such a hurry that they left their dead behind. It sickened Tyrian. When Ewan rode close, he said, "Have the bodies identified so families may be notified. The bodies can be buried on the field where they fell and retrieved later if so needed."

"Yes, sir. What about the new soldiers?"

"Our soldiers can keep them in line until we take them back to base. Cassie and I will go into the city itself and find the mayor." He glanced at the rooftops where the two archers now stood together. "I suspect we may shortly have more experts in setting up a ranged unit for us."

Cassie rode up leading Tyrian's horse and then dismounted as well. She would never regret any action she took to protect his life. The lieutenant had broken the laws of engagement by using subterfuge in a fair duel. "Sanity among the insanity of war," she said to Tyrian.

"I want a world where we don't need it. Is that naïve of me?"

She gently cupped his cheek. "No. It'll happen someday. And just think, you'll be here to see it." She eased up to lightly touch his lips with hers and then straightened his scarf for him. "Let's go meet our new allies. They're quite good with those bows."

The archers were waiting for them at the edge of town. One was male, the other female. They looked as identical as male and female could be, with similar lively faces and brown eyes. The female had her brown hair tied on top of her head with a pink ribbon. The male kept his hair hanging loose to his waist. Tyrian estimated them in their mid to late-twenties, and the recognition inside his soul and relic was not unexpected. "Thank you," he said. "I'm in your debt."

"Not at all!" the woman protested. "We're in *your* debt, Lord Tyrian!" She bowed gracefully. "My name is Emma. This is my brother, Olan. We would be honored if you would let us join you in your fight."

Olan nodded swiftly in agreement. "You can't beat having a ranged unit in battle, and we're two of the best. Please, let us join you."

"Gladly." Tyrian held out his hands and smiled when they each took one. His relic glowed softly and echoing stars glowed from their left shoulders. "There's a young bard at the base. Her name is Myrroria. She is a dagger user. The three of you can work together to give me the ranged unit I need."

"You can count on us!" Emma saluted swiftly. "We'll gather our things and head for the castle! Oh, and if you want to talk to the mayor, you need to talk to Winifred."

"Winifred," Tyrian repeated.

"Right. She's the keeper of the storehouse in town, you know, where the supplies and valuables are kept."

Tyrian began to smile. "I assume that the mayor is among the valuables she has been keeping lately?"

"He wasn't happy," Olan conceded.

As they hurried off, Cassie frowned thoughtfully. "Lupine . . . let's see. The mayor is a man named Leonard. He has a son named Sean. He should be . . . thirteen about now. Leonard has been mayor since just after Sean was born; his wife was killed by bandits during a time when there was no one in charge. I believe it was General D'terio's army who came in to assist."

Tyrian smiled at her. "You're going to give Kell a run for his money."

She smiled back. "Where do you think I get my information?"

The soldiers from Lupine were coming out of the woodworks. None wore uniforms but were clearly soldiers all the same. They moved swiftly to set up borders and secure their city. Others as yet raided the Imperial Army's leftover barracks for anything the villagers could use.

It wasn't hard to find the storehouse. It was the place where the shouting came from. Tyrian closed one eye in a wince as he approached the sound of arguing. Sitting outside the doors was a young teenage boy with bright golden hair and a handsome face. The boy spotted Tyrian and sighed. "Hi."

"Hi." Tyrian knelt down to his height. "I'm Tyrian Southerwind. Are you Sean?"

"Yeah." Sean eyed him owlishly. There was something about Tyrian that tugged at him. He wanted to make sure he was always happy and smiling. It was a weird feeling. "You here to see my old man?" He winced as glass shattered. "Oopf. Aunt Winny isn't happy."

"Aunt?"

"Eh, sort of. She was my mother's cousin." He got to his feet and brushed off his slacks. A sheath with a sword hung around his hips and he moved with the cocky arrogance of a boy trying too hard to act like a grown-up. "Follow me." He pushed the door open and then ducked hastily as another vase went whizzing by. "Hey! Pop! Aunt Winny!"

The man in the room was obviously Sean's father since they shared matching golden hair and blue eyes. He, too, wore a sword, and his son's name showed as visibly engraved near the hilt. The woman facing him down was short and scrappy, and her kerchief kept her black hair out of her face. She promptly scowled at Sean. "How many times have I told you not to call me Winny? I'm going to tan your hide!"

Sean jerked a thumb toward Tyrian. "Nice first impression, Aunt Winifred. Meet Tyrian Southerwind. Tyrian, meet Winifred and Leonard."

Leonard rapped his son in the back of the head. "*Lord* Tyrian. Try not to act like the hooligan you are." He sighed and smiled wryly at Tyrian. "Lord Tyrian, I apologize for the display. Win and I are friends, I assure you."

"If you can't yell at friends and family," Tyrian said reasonably, "then who can you yell at?"

Leonard grinned. "I'm going to like you a great deal." He bowed gracefully. "Well met, Lord Tyrian. I am Leonard. The once and again mayor, so it would seem. Thank you for freeing my people. When the Emperor removed me from my post, I feared for the worst."

Winifred grabbed a broom and began to sweep up the debris. "He was always mayor since we always answered to him first. The Emperor knew it, but let it slide until the rebellion formed. He knew Leo would join you in a heartbeat, and we knew that meant he was in danger. So we made him hide."

"Threw me into the storehouse!" he muttered.

Sean grinned. "And literally! He bounced on his ass," he told Tyrian with a touch of glee.

His father sighed and caught him in a headlock. "Ignore him. Every attempt to install manners has failed utterly. He's a smart kid, and already gifted with a sword, but he never knows when to shut up."

"Takes after his father," Winifred said under her breath. Leonard glared at her, and she shot a sunny smile to Tyrian. "Nice to meet you, Lord Tyrian. Tell me, do you have a Storekeeper at your castle?"

Tyrian and Cassie shared a smile. "Not yet," Tyrian said.

"You do now." She nodded decisively. "You can count on me to keep the supplies safe and organized. I'll get myself packed up here and head out for the castle."

"Thank you," Tyrian said softly. He lightly touched her shoulder and the star briefly appeared in acknowledgement. "I know I can count on you."

She found herself smiling. Tyrian Southerwind was a very powerful young man for reasons that had nothing to do with the relic he wore. When he said he believed in you, you couldn't help but believe in yourself. If keeping a storehouse for his castle would keep him smiling, then that's what she would damned well do.

Leonard studied the star on Winifred's arm and then looked at Tyrian. He studied the relic he wore before murmuring, "I don't suppose we could sit down for a few minutes, Lord Tyrian."

"Naturally." Tyrian fell into step beside him as they left the storehouse with Cassie and Sean following closely. The boy was brimming with questions for a monk, but Cassie was an expert at deflecting questions about her clan without offending anyone. Tyrian hid a smile as Sean clearly tried to figure out how the conversation kept detouring to the weather.

When they reached the city hall, Leonard held the door for everyone and then led the way to the meeting room. "Lord Tyrian," he said as he sat on the edge of the table, "is it true that Ophelia Goldwind is dead?"

Tyrian's eyes darkened. "Yes." As Leonard closed his eyes in pain, Tyrian studied him closely. It wasn't the first time that he had felt an understanding of his Destined Stars that should have come from years of friendship rather than mere minutes. And he knew that Leonard and Sean were, indeed, his as well. "You knew Ophelia. You're already a member of the Rebellion."

"I see," Cassie said softly. "That's why the Emperor perceived you as a threat. He knew you knew Lady Ophelia."

Leonard buried his face in his hands, looking older than he had only moments before. Grief aged his eyes and face alike. "Ophelia was one of my dearest friends. Ewan and I have been friends for ages. I'm about fourteen years older than he is, but we stopped counting when he was a teenager."

"You met Ophelia when she came to the village and met Kyle?" Tyrian asked.

"Mm, after. When she started the Rebellion, they naturally asked Ewan to join. I was home visiting at the time." He sighed. "Ewan and I protested very loudly and very vehemently against it. She was too young. She was too weak. She didn't know anything about war."

Tyrian winced. "Uh-oh."

"She kicked our asses, made Kyle tend to our bruises, and then demanded we put our hot heads to better use." He slowly straightened. "I have never respected anyone more than I respected her until today when I met you. Lord Tyrian, I wish to fight at your side as well. I am a proficient unit leader, and I have some talent as a strategist."

"For Ophelia?" Tyrian asked softly.

"For her. And for you." He blew out a breath. "If the way I felt when I saw you was any clue, I suspect I am tangled within your destiny."

Tyrian held up his relic and Devourer glowed softly. Answering stars glowed from both Leonard and Sean's shoulders. "You're both mine," he said simply. "Destined Stars who share the skies with me. If you will fight with me, not *for* me, then I can be strong enough to help our land."

Leonard smiled at Cassie who smiled back. Despite Tyrian's insistence to the contrary, every Destined Star fought *for* him as much as they did with him. Even those who did not actually fight, like Winifred, were fighting for him. "I never imagined I would have a destiny to fulfill," Leonard said musingly. "It's a curious one, particularly when I have this feeling that I knew inside I'd meet you someday, or that I already had. Or met someone like you, perhaps."

"There's a lot of that going around," Tyrian admitted. "For all of us. It's a learning curve for all involved." He started to say more when his entire head went light. The weakness was swift and powerful and took all strength from his body.

He staggered and Cassie leapt forward to catch him. She had enough strength to gently lower him to the floor, though she couldn't carry him. "You pushed yourself too hard," she said softly as she smoothed his hair from his face. "You've only just unlocked your relic's first level, Tyrian. A week is not enough for your body to recover from so much power and trauma."

Leonard knelt beside them. It tore at his heart to see Tyrian so weak and tired. "He needs to go home and rest. I'm not sure I have the strength to move him, though. I'm only a little taller than he is."

"Ewan can move him. He was with the unit." She looked at Sean. "Fetch Ewan. Quickly, Sean."

He nodded, his blue eyes wide with worry. "Okay!" He turned and rushed out of the city hall and the door banged shut behind him. Tyrian had to be okay. It was too scary to think of anything else.

Tyrian was barely cognizant of the goings-on. His mind had completely scattered from exhaustion. It almost felt as if *he* was being devoured. He dimly noted when Ewan arrived to help move him, and he was aware of being put into a wagon for the trip. As soon as blankets tucked around him, he slipped into the waiting darkness of sleep.

When he woke much later, he found himself in his room at the castle. He had been tucked securely into bed and the sun was either setting or rising. It was hard to tell which at the immediate moment. Cassie was nowhere in sight, but he could feel her presence inside and that meant she had to be near.

"Hey."

He looked toward the entry at the sound of her voice and saw her leaning against the edge of the wall. She wore casual clothes, and a slim black choker covered her scar. She looked soft and welcoming, like a respite from the world. "Hey," he said. He held out a hand, and when she crossed to take it, he tugged her down onto the bed with him. "How'd they get me up here?"

"Ewan. He's stronger than even he realized." She wrapped her arms around him and rested her head on his shoulder. "We're now looking into finding the inventor known as Tedium. He invented those newfangled lifter things."

"An elevator?"

"That's the one. We're going to sacrifice the stairs to put it in. Theory being that you and I don't need stairs to keep in shape, and as you have three more relic levels to go through, we're going to need to make it as easy as possible to get you up here." She rubbed her cheek over his shoulder softly. "How do you feel?"

"Still a little tired, but otherwise I feel better. What time is it?"

"Early morning the day after we liberated Lupine. The army unit of Lupine is officially wearing your colors and calling themselves a part of the Liberation Army. We're working on designing a flag. Luckily, Myr has some aesthetics. She and Mouse are trying to brainstorm." She sat up and smoothed his hair out of his face. "Hungry?"

His stomach rumbled loudly and he smiled sheepishly as she grinned at him. "I think that's a yes," he said. He watched curiously as she got to her feet and disappeared, then his eyes widened as she quickly returned with a tray heaped with breakfast. "You're going to spoil me rotten at this pace."

"Good. Someone has to." She sat down beside him and picked up a piece of toast. "We've got Hawke out on reconnaissance with Laia to investigate the next few towns that are closest to us. We're also trying to find a Magician who has the ability to transport troops into battle. It would save us so much more time if we can have that."

Transporting mages were well versed in sending entire units to precise locations based on their knowledge of maps and the way magic moved in the land. When battle was done, the troops could be transported back the same way. It made life much simpler when trying to battle a far distant enemy. It had been long before learned that thirty thousand troops marching somewhere did more harm than good.

"What about Matthias Goldwind?" he asked.

"That's the only really good news we've got. Leonard knows where he is. There's a really, *really* tiny village of less than a hundred people living in the mountains. That's where Matthias has gone to with his last student. He says we should be able to get there in about two weeks via horseback."

Daunting, but necessary. "What about Rubentia?"

She grimaced. "We need Professor Matthias if we want to take it on. It's being guarded by three units worth of soldiers, and they have a lot of magic users in one of them. That's going to take a level of strategy well above any of our skill. But if we can take it, then we'll increase our own army by another two units thanks to Rubentia's personal army."

"So we're looking at Rubentia as being the first real test of the Liberation Army." He pushed the tray to the side. Strength was pouring back in rapidly thanks to the rest and the good food. "I think we need to get started toward Matthias as soon as we can. No later than today."

"Full party?"

"For a two week journey? Absolutely. It'll be you, I, Liang, Marian, Kyle, and Emma. Kyle and I both have relics with attacking magic, and Marian is a Healer. Emma can handle ranged combat, and most of the rest of us can get in close."

"I'll gather everyone if you'll pack what we need." She moved the tray to the table beside the bed and started to stand. His hand curled around her wrist to keep her where she was, and she looked at him in surprise. "What?"

In answer, his other hand slid into her hair and drew her close for a tender kiss. She melted against him with a little purr of delight that went to his head better than any rush of power ever could. "Too long without your taste," he murmured against her lips.

"Less than twenty-four hours," she whispered back, her fingers tracing his features.

He slowly smiled. "Too long." He tugged her up higher so that he could taste the fragrant skin of her breasts bared by the opening in her tunic. "In fact, I don't think we need to leave until this evening. Maybe tomorrow morning."

With a sigh of surrender, she curled her arms around him happily. He was definitely feeling better.

Chapter Fourteen

"We can only go forward even if the path winds backwards."

Early the next morning, the party gathered at the gates to set out toward the village known only as Acre. It was little bigger than its name implied, so small that the Empire didn't even really consider it a town at all.

Kyle glanced to where Tyrian was studying the newest map that Thomas had provided. "Matthias probably moved there when he noticed the trouble with the cities was escalating," he offered. "He knew Ophelia was running a rebellion, and as soon as her name was leaked, that he would be useable against her."

Emma glanced over at him. "You think he'll hate you, don't you?"

His hands clenched together. "I failed her. How could he do otherwise? Right now, I hate myself as well. I should have put my foot down and told her no. Then I see the good happening, and I hate myself for being selfish."

There was nothing any of them could say. This was something he needed to struggle through on his own. All they could do was be there to support him. He took the watch every night on the trip, only sleeping very lightly when Tyrian forced him to take a break. Even without the iron will that marked his Kaiten, Kyle had a long breaking limit. They all prayed he reached it soon so that healing could begin.

The two weeks went by swiftly. They couldn't go near well-traveled roads and had to avoid any other cities they might have otherwise passed through. There were two along the way to the mountains, and there was a checkpoint not much further away since where the mountains ended was where the Y Border began.

Things got a little easier once they finally entered the mountains. There was more coverage than the scant trees and very few forests that dotted the Empire. The whole country was mostly a desert. On Oriku, the majority of forests belonged to Foresalia and the City-States of Arinsberg.

Acre was tucked safely on a plateau that had a beautiful view of the land below the mountains. The people grew everything they needed and traded between each other for what they didn't have. It was a fully self-sufficient little town, and it looked like what the other cities had before the change.

When they entered the town, the people milling around took immediate notice. Word spread very fast on Oriku, and the people there instantly recognized Tyrian by the sight of his green scarf and distinctive relic.

Tyrian took a quick breath as he stopped beside someone tending to a garden. "Pardon me, sir," he said calmly, "but can you direct me to Matthias Goldwind?"

The old man studied him intently for a moment and then smiled. "Certainly, my lord. If you follow the path, it winds around a cliff to where Professor Matthias resides." He paused, considered his words, and then asked hopefully, "When we have our new government, can Acre finally be considered a real town? We'd like to be free to engage in formal trade with others, but we're not allowed to."

Kyle and Emma shared a grin with Liang and Marian. Tyrian felt the tension in his shoulders melt away as he realized that Acre, though neutral of the conflict, was in fact pulling for the side of the Liberation Army. "I can't make promises," he said with a genuine smile, "but you'll have a much better chance of it."

Leaving the old man very happily tending to his fruit plants, the party moved down the path toward the edge of the cliffs. It was too small to really be considered a road, but it served as the town's main 'highway' for both horse and foot traffic.

When they rounded the edge of the cliffs, they found themselves approaching a plain house of unremarkable appearance. The owner had done nothing to make the place stand out, though it was kept in good condition. Flowers planted cheerfully along the fence added color.

Kyle felt his stomach churn. Almost as soon as he realized it, Tyrian gently rested a hand on his shoulder. With a little breath, Kyle covered his hand in gratitude. "I want him to know," he said softly, "but I want to be the one to tell him. I can't figure out which is worse."

The front door suddenly opened and a young girl with vibrant red hair peered around the edge. Her large eyes were a haunting shade of blue, and they seemed almost reflective behind the lenses of the glasses she wore perched on her nose. Tyrian guessed her to be barely a teenager, and thought the world in for a surprise when she grew up. She already had a striking loveliness to her that felt almost ethereal.

She was also very smart. "Hello, Lord Tyrian," she said formally. "Please, come in. We've been waiting for you. Professor Matthias is making some tea." She gave a little curtsy. "My name is Cherry. I am Professor Matthias' protégé."

"I've got the horses," Emma said. She gave Kyle a nudge. "Go," she urged softly. "You know Lord Tyrian will stand beside you."

While she kept the horses from wandering off, the others went inside the house behind Cherry. The front area was a sitting room, and off to the side sat a table and a desk covered with books and papers. It was much warmer inside than Tyrian had expected, and he felt his shoulders relax slightly.

"Professor Matthias!" Cherry scolded as she hurried to the man standing at the stove. "I said I would make the tea!" she said fretfully.

The man at the stove smiled at her with obvious affection. Looking at him was painful for more than just Kyle. It was painful for Tyrian and Cassie as well. Matthias Goldwind looked very much like his little sister, with the same nearly yellow eyes and thick auburn hair. "I am perfectly capable of making tea," he told her. "And you can't reach the stove safely in either case." He rested a hand lightly on the top of her head as he looked to his guests. "Greetings, Lord Tyrian. I am Matthias Goldwind. Hello, Kyle."

Kyle took a deep breath that shook at the end. "Matt . . ."

Matthias shook his head. "No, Kyle. I already know. I knew it was a possibility. She did too. She made the choice to put her life at risk for the people she loved. We can only honor her memory and move on. I do not blame you, nor do I feel you failed her." He looked at Tyrian. "And I do not blame you either, Lord Tyrian. I don't believe in the sins of the fathers . . . or mothers."

Tyrian let out a little breath. "Thank you, Professor Matthias."

"Just Matthias, Lord Tyrian." He handed the pot of tea to Cherry. "Gentle with that. Do not spill it on yourself." He took the cane leaning against the wall and used it to walk slowly over to where the others waited. Without any conceit or pride, he let Kyle and Liang assist him in sitting on the couch. "Thank you."

"Are you injured?" Marian asked anxiously. "I am a skilled Healer. I can aid you."

"Thank you, but no magic can heal what is wrong with me." He smiled at her. "It is simply something I must live with. It's vexing, certainly, to move like an old man when I'm not yet three decades old, but I'm not a warrior to begin with. I am a strategist." He gestured to the chair across from him. "Which is no doubt one of the reasons you are here."

Tyrian sat down in the chair and leaned forward to brace his arms on his knees. The others sat down as well once he was seated, except for Cassie. She moved from window to window with a restless energy, her eyes probing the landscape for signs of a threat. She couldn't shake the tingling sensation in the base of her skull. It was a familiar feeling that always warned when danger lurked nearby.

"I need a strategist," Tyrian told Matthias. His green eyes looked dark and intense, his voice the voice of a leader. "The Liberation Army needs your brilliance to free our country from tyranny. We're at the place where simply guessing and hoping won't do it any longer. Too much is riding on this. If we somehow fail, then all those who sided with us will suffer the worst."

"You would ask me to join on my sister's behalf?"

Tyrian met his eyes directly. "I would ask you to join on the behalf of your destiny. You are another who shares the skies with me." He held up his relic hand and stars appeared on both Matthias and Cherry. "I need you both. I can't do this without you."

Cherry grasped Matthias' sleeve, her eyes anxious. "Professor Matthias, we have to help. Can we?"

"Easy, Cherry." He covered her hand with his without looking away from Tyrian. "What did Ophelia tell you about me, Lord Tyrian?"

"Little," he admitted. "What I know of you, I know now by meeting you. I may well know things that even she did not. I know you share a similar destiny to be played out in different fashions, though both connected to me." Darkness moved across his eyes for a moment. "A future with peace for all."

Matthias let out a soft breath as he realized what Tyrian knew and understood. Ophelia had, indeed, been frank with him. Matthias had always known his sister would die young; he had long had time to grieve for the day when she would leave him. And he knew, too, that his own future, his destiny, was tangled up within the Kaiten Star. He could not let Tyrian face this alone. "It won't happen in my time," he said softly, "but it will happen." His chin lifted. "And I will be the one to guide you to victory, Lord Tyrian."

Cherry brightened. "We can help Lord Tyrian?" When Matthias smiled, she turned a quick and shy smile to Tyrian. "I'm still learning, but I know I can help as well! I'm a quick study and I don't make the same mistake twice!"

"She doesn't." Matthias affectionately tugged on her hair. "She also learns from her mistakes, unlike a former student of mine." When her eyes filled with tears, he gently rubbed them away. "He will learn some day," he said softly. "There is a . . . hole in his heart, Cherry. It will fill. There was nothing more I could do for him."

She wiped at her eyes and nodded swiftly. "I know." She took a quick breath for composure and then got to her feet. "I'll go pack our bags. Don't stress yourself!" she ordered him.

She disappeared down a hall, and Liang grinned at Matthias. "She's a bit bossy, isn't she?"

Matthias sighed fondly. "My little tyrant. I took her on as a student two years ago when her parents died. It was right after I had left Ophelia in Kyle's care within the Commune of Soldiers."

"You needed someone to take care of," Marian murmured.

He laughed. "Very probably! I had another student named Seymour at the time, but I couldn't turn Cherry away." He sighed deeply. "And I had to expel Seymour last year. It was the last time I saw Ophelia, too. She had words with Seymour, but I don't know what." He looked at Kyle. "Do you?"

"No. I saw her talking to him, but she never told me what she said. Just said something about wishing someone would slap some sense into him someday. If she'd been more temperamental, she might have done it herself." Kyle forced his tone to remain light, but his hands curled together.

Cherry returned lugging three bags, and Liang and Kyle moved quickly to take them from her. "Those are bigger than you are," Liang scolded her. "Grow another foot taller and you can take them."

"Deal." She moved over to Matthias' side to help steady him as he got to his feet. "Should I go ask Beatrice for your horse?" she asked. When he smiled, she hurried out of the house quickly.

They all went outside, Tyrian keeping a hand on Matthias' arm to help steady him, and discovered that Emma had disappeared with the horses. Since there was a stable in town, it was logical to assume she had headed that direction. Tyrian studied the way Matthias moved and was absolutely positive that an elevator had to be installed quickly. He would also insist on a room for Matthias on the same floor as the meeting room.

Cassie's agitation only gained in force. Her restless energy had transmitted itself to others to the point that Kyle walked with a hand on the hilt of his sword, and Liang moved closer to Tyrian and Matthias. Marian had her wand in hand without conscious thought.

Abruptly, Cassie's head jerked upward. "Down!" she shouted. She leapt for Tyrian and sent them tumbling across the ground.

Kyle took Matthias down in another direction as Liang dragged Marian backwards swiftly. Arrows engulfed in flames struck the land where they had been moments before, and the fire consumed the dry foliage close by. The inferno was out of control before anyone really noticed it had begun.

Tyrian scrambled up to his feet and looked to the cliffs higher up. He instantly saw soldiers wearing the colors of the Imperial Army. The archers were readying more arrows. "Take Matthias away!" he ordered Kyle and Marian. "Swiftly! Liang, find Cherry and Emma!"

His Voice Relic beeped softly, and Emma's voice said, "I have the red-haired girl and the Stablemaster. We're running down the mountain with the horses for cover. Don't worry about us!"

A young woman came running up to Tyrian with a hat held over her grassy green hair. Her hair color as much as her pointed ears implied an Elfish bloodline. "Lord Tyrian!" she said. "Come with me! We have a secret escape route to take! Hurry! The villagers are already fleeing!" She looked at Cassie. "Can you cover us?"

Cassie pulled out an odd little marble from her pocket and hurled it to the ground. It exploded into plumes of smoke that merged with the smoke of the fire and made it impossible to see. Tyrian did not want to go. He wanted to hold his ground and fight, but he couldn't. Cassie was shoving him, and Liang and the young woman had his arms and were dragging him. Against his will, he went with them.

The secret escape route was through a tunnel hidden under the bakery. The sound of echoing footsteps told them that they were not far behind the rest of the town. It made Tyrian sick to his stomach, and fury began to burn inside his heart. Just to get him and Matthias, the Army had been willing to attack innocent villagers. If not for the escape route, many might have died. Their homes and lives, at the least, had been destroyed already.

They climbed up a ladder at the end of the tunnel and found themselves partway back down the mountain. The villagers were dirty and soot-covered, but they looked relatively unharmed. The few injuries that had been sustained were quickly healed by Marian and the couple of people who had Medicine Relics.

The sound of hooves had Tyrian turning to see Emma approaching with a herd of horses. Cherry was riding on one of them, clinging onto its mane for dear life, and an older woman rode another. When they were close, Tyrian reached up to pull Cherry down and hugged her tightly. "Are you okay?" he asked.

She held onto his neck tightly, her blue eyes wide with a lingering echo of fear. It was her first real taste of what war was like, and it was daunting. "I'm okay. Are you?"

"Perfectly fine." He turned as Matthias approached as quickly as he could and handed Cherry over. "She's fine."

Matthias hugged her fiercely for a moment and then put her down. He would have asked for her initiation into war to be much gentler, but he knew she was strong. She had been given a very great destiny; hers was a star fixed in the sky, unlike his, which would wane. She would endure.

The other woman dismounted with casual expertise. She was

probably in her late forties and looked fit and agile. Her walnut colored skin glowed in the light from the fires further overhead and her black hair had been braided severely to keep it out of her eyes. "Good riding," she told Emma. "And good thinking!"

Emma gratefully let Liang help her down from her horse. "We'll call it dumb luck and leave it there."

Tyrian studied the Stablemaster and the woman who had helped him in equal turns. They were both Destined Stars if his feeling was correct. It had yet to be wrong, so he certainly trusted it when he felt the fierce yank inside. "Thank you," he said to the green-haired woman. "What's your name?"

She pulled off her hat to shake out the soot. She seemed a very lovely Elf, but most of the race was exceptionally attractive. She wore leggings and a snug bodice that revealed her trim belly, and a belt hung around her hips sassily. She had no relic and no weapon. "I'm Taurus," she said with a smile. "I'm the lead singer for the band Café Latte."

His brows lifted skyward. Café Latte was one of the most well-known bands on Oriku. They had traveled through all lands, and their songs had been recorded onto relics for people to listen to at home. Few didn't know their name. "What are you doing out here? Where are the others?"

"We're on vacation and decided to see our hometowns." She sighed gustily. "Aries is going to have my head. I swore I wouldn't get into trouble, and now I'm about to get into a *lot*." She lightly touched her heart. "Lord Tyrian, I wish to fight by your side. Let my music be what empowers you in battle. I will sing the songs that keep everyone's spirits up!"

His relic glowed softly and the star glowed from her shoulder in response. He smiled. "I would be honored, Taurus, thank you." And as he was beginning to understand the ways of destiny, he had no doubt that the other three members of the band would show up eventually and join as well.

"I'm Beatrice," the Stablemaster said, drawing his attention. "And you can count on me too, Lord Tyrian! I'll keep track of all your horses and make sure they get the dedicated attention they deserve! Do you have a stable?"

"A small one," he conceded. "Most of the horses run freely in the land around the castle. They always come when we call them, but there's been no one I could spare to give all their attention to them. I would be very grateful if you could take that duty on, Beatrice. I know you're the best for the job."

She smiled in bemusement. "When you say that, I feel like I could take care of the Valley of the Unicorns single-handedly. Leave it to me!"

One of the villagers walked over to Tyrian and said, "Lord Tyrian, we would ask to join you as well. We don't dare return home. Well, what little remains of it. When you have won this war, we can come home and rebuild. There aren't many of us. We can find room, and we can be useful."

"It's a two-story city," Tyrian said wryly, "and it's not yet half full. There's plenty of room. And if I'm wrong, we can just expand the walls. Anyone good with a hammer?" Several hands lifted. "There we go. Problems solved. Let's get moving quickly. There's no knowing how long it will take for them to sort through the debris and confirm that I'm not there."

The trip back to the base took less time than the trip out, even with so many more people. They barely paused to rest at night, trying to cover as much ground as possible. Children who were too young to walk rode with the adults who couldn't walk either. Matthias was one of them, and he carried two or three of the littlest ones.

It was the middle of the day when they finally reached the base. While the villagers were welcomed happily and people already there began to help them find homes, Beatrice took over the care of the horses and took them to the stables. Taurus went to find a room inside the castle, as she had been ordered to do, and Emma went to reassure her brother that she was alive and well.

Matthias looked at Tyrian and said, "I can get settled in later if you wish to begin the strategy for Rubentia."

Tyrian nodded. "The sooner the better." He looked at Kyle. "Grab Ewan, Leonard, and Kell, please." As Kyle hurried off, he eyed Liang and Marian. "Go rest."

"You're funny," Marian said. She crossed her arms. "Not until you do."

Her cousin sighed and began to lead the way into the castle. He knew better than to argue with Marian when she got that look in her eye. He knew he could out-stubborn her, but it wasn't worth the effort right then. He *was* tired, yet there was still too much to be done. Cassie's hand slipped into his and he held on gratefully.

He helped Matthias navigate the stairs and again determined to find the inventor who made elevators. When they reached the meeting room doors, he said to one of the guards, "Please find quarters on this floor for Professor Matthias and Cherry. Make sure they're near to each other."

"Yes, sir!" The guard saluted and hurried down the hall.

He walked into the room and then hastily shot across the floor to grab the chair that Thomas was standing on as it wobbled dangerously.

"Tom!" he scolded. "What are you doing?"

Thomas' cheeks turned pink. "I was just trying to hang the new map on the wall, Lord Tyrian!" He got down off the chair and handed over the map so that Liang could hang it for him. "I want to be taller," he complained. He studied Tyrian intently and then frowned. He didn't like how tired the Kaiten looked. "I'll get you a snack!" he promised as he hurried out of the room.

"That bad?" Tyrian asked the others.

"That bad," Liang and Cassie said at the same time.

"So, Rubentia." Matthias sat down in a chair with a sigh. "Tell me what you know."

"Allow me," Ewan said as he walked into the room. "Hey, Matthias. Long time." He plopped down into a chair and propped up his feet. "The situation has changed as of last week. The Emperor knows that Tyrian got out of Acre and that he has the best strategist in the world."

Tyrian rubbed the back of his neck. "I'm not going to like this, am I?"

"General Gordon D'terio," Leonard said as he sat down. "The troops at Rubentia have been retreated and replaced by his elite units. We have two units and he has four. We're outnumbered two to one, *but* he doesn't have a magic unit. Myr and Olan have organized our soldiers. We have one ranged unit, and the other is close-range combat. Only about one-eighth of our soldiers are mages. Mostly they serve as supplemental support."

"General D'terio is not one to use subterfuge," Matthias mused. "The only general who is versed in the ways of undercover combat would be General Quint. We lack the ability to as yet transport soldiers to the field so we can't move in from behind."

"We also think the generals might be willing to listen to reason," Kyle spoke up. "Their armies, until now, have not been directly involved in the situation. They are not at fault for the oppression of the people. They serve the people, so . . ."

Matthias tapped a finger lightly on the table as he thought about things. "What sort of combatants do we have as unit leaders, Lord Tyrian? Which are the most capable?"

"The best three swords users I have are Laia Mitakel, Ewan, and Kyle. The best hand to hand are Liang, Rourke Mitakel, and Cassie, though she's needed at my side more than anywhere else. Marian is our best Healer. Our best ranged are Myr, Emma, and Olan. Shots and Hawke are also ranged users, but they are best suited for small combat, not large; Shots is a gunner and Hawke uses a slingshot. And while we have relic users all over the place, we have no actual Magicians. The most powerful magic we have in a combat sense comes from me, Laia, and Kyle."

"We're going to end this without a drop of blood being shed," Matthias decided. He looked at Ewan. "Fetch Myr and Shots."

* * * * *

Rubentia sat a day's journey away from the base being used by the Liberation Army. It was a large sized town of ten thousand civilians and three military units for a total of thirteen thousand total residents. The four units belonging to Gordon spread out around the borders of the town so that no direction could be approached unseen.

Travelers were still admitted, though they had to go through Gordon's personal unit to enter. The town went on with what little business it could still go on with. When he had arrived to take over for the Imperial units, he had been sickened to see the state of the town. People flinched from his soldiers, and that was unacceptable.

He caught sight of movement and focused his gaze on the road. Coming down it was a horse and two people. A girl rode the horse, and a young man led it. The girl was bedraggled and dirty, and she looked as if she had been through hell and back. Gordon moved forward with a frown. "Halt," he said, though gently. "What business brings you to Rubentia?"

"There's a Healer here," the young man said, his words flavored with the clipped accent of Melodina's mountains. "Halkern is his name. My sister was set upon by monsters when we were trying to get home. This is the closest city. Let us in, sir. I beg you. We're not going to cause trouble."

Gordon studied them, sensing something under the surface like a feeling of meeting a kindred spirit, but not seeing anything to make either of them stand out. The young man didn't even wear a weapon. The girl had a dagger sheath around her hips, but the daggers were missing. He had to assume they had been left behind in the monsters she had tangled with. "Come in," he said kindly. "And hurry to the doctor. Do you need an escort to find him?"

"I can find it. Thank you so much!" The young man wasted no time in hurrying into the city with his sister.

A few minutes later, one of the soldiers said, "To the west! The Liberation Army is approaching! We can see one mounted unit and one unit on foot. The foot unit looks like a ranged unit."

"Ah, so he has one now," Gordon murmured. "Who rides as unit leader?"

After a moment, the soldier said, "Ranged unit is commanded by two archers and a girl. The mounted unit is commanded by Lord Tyrian Southerwind. Riding with him is the delegate from the Monk Clans and Matthias Goldwind."

Gordon lightly touched the Voice Relic he wore. "Greetings, Lord Tyrian," he said calmly. "It's been a long time. Are you well?"

"Well enough," Tyrian said in response. "And you, General D'terio?"

"I can't complain. Professor Matthias, it is an honor to greet you as well. I have heard much of your brilliance."

"My thanks, General." Matthias' voice was very calm and unruffled. That Gordon would take the time to greet them sincerely was yet another sign of the bedrock decency inside the other man. "We ask for your surrender before blood is shed."

Gordon arched a brow. "When you are outnumbered two to one?"

"We're not at as big a disadvantage as you believe."

Before Gordon could ask what he referred to, he heard the distinct sound of something locking into place. He turned his head sharply and discovered that the young man of before was crouched less than a hundred feet away, and he had a weapon in his hands aimed directly at Gordon's heart. Gordon knew instinctively that he looked upon the gunner from the Guild who had joined the Liberation Army.

It was an underhanded move to plant a sniper to take out an enemy leader, but completely within the laws of engagement. Gordon could have called their bluff and challenged whether or not they truly intended to kill him without a fight. It could have been just a ploy to force a surrender. But if he was wrong, and he was killed, there would be no one to determine the fate of his men.

He slowly lifted his hands over his head. "I yield, Lord Tyrian. Professor Matthias, you are, as rumored, quite brilliant. Put down your weapons," he ordered his men. "Those who wish to retreat may do so. I will remain as Lord Tyrian's prisoner. I wish to speak with him."

"We stand by you, General D'terio!" one of the lieutenants said fiercely. "We will follow your commands! If you stay, then we will stay. What you choose to do is what we choose to do. Lord Tyrian may hold us as well. We won't give any trouble."

Tyrian let out the breath he had been holding. Word was going to spread rapidly that he had defeated a Lower General without a fight. Albanion and Blaine would know that that meant the tide was suddenly turning in favor of the Liberation Army and they would endeavor to tighten their grip on the checkpoints and the other cities. There would be no more one-on-one unit battles and precious few more chances for such subterfuge.

It would be nothing but uphill from there on out. There was no going back.

Part Two

"Faith is the daring of the **soul** to go farther than it can see."

-William Newton Clark

Chapter Fifteen

"Touch and go, stop and go, it's always the same."

Liang and Laia had been among those in the mounted unit, and as soon as Gordon surrendered, they made their way to Tyrian's side to join him, Cassie, and Matthias. "Nice," Laia said to Matthias. "We'll just go along with you guys to talk to General D'terio." There was something in her purple eyes that made it less of a suggestion than a strong encouragement.

Tyrian knew better than to argue. As Shots and Myr came running up, he smiled at both of them. "You did a wonderful job, both of you. It was very brave to ride so boldly into the middle of an enemy unit."

Myr swiped at the dirt on her face and smiled. "I'm not above taking advantage of the fact that everyone thinks I'm so sweet and innocent." She took Laia's offered hand and let the older woman tug her up onto the horse with her. "I'm still a little stunned at how well it worked."

Liang helped Shots up to ride with him, and they followed Tyrian, Cassie, and Matthias as the three set out across the field toward where Gordon waited. The Liberation Army was already rounding up the defeated soldiers, all of whom had made it clear by putting down their weapons that they had no intention of causing trouble.

Gordon was being guarded by two Liberation Army soldiers, but he was not restrained and his crossbow had not been taken away. He looked toward where Tyrian approached and studied him intently. He had known Tyrian for nearly as long as the younger man had been alive. He was one of the older generals at thirty-eight, with only Donald Southerwind being older at forty. The youngest was Marcus at thirty.

Tyrian Southerwind had more battle instincts than all of their years combined. The man that Gordon looked upon now was nothing like the boy he had known only months before. There had always been something about Tyrian that pulled at Gordon and the other generals, but it had never been as powerful as it was in that moment when he looked into Tyrian's dark eyes and saw the iron will of a hero.

"May I?" he asked when Tyrian got closer. Tyrian held up his relic hand and Gordon studied it intently. It was, indeed, a Pure Relic. "So I see the rumors are true. The whispers of the legendary Kaiten Star. Perhaps Lady Blaine's prophecy was self-fulfilling after all."

"The legend of the Kaiten Stars has been around for as long as Lady Tanelia has been alive," Laia countered quietly. "She first spoke of the legend a million years ago. It has been forgotten into time, known only to those who read legends. When the Kaiten Star shone in the sky eighteen years ago, those of us who read stars knew what it meant. Blaine put her own twist on it."

"That is not hard to believe, Lady Laiaeariel."

Liang looked at Laia in surprise. "You're titled?"

She grimaced. "Don't remind me!" She scowled at Gordon. "And don't call me that. My parents just *had* to give me an Elf name."

Tyrian hid a smile. "You know each other, then?"

Gordon sighed. "I made the rather naïve mistake about ten years ago in thinking that a newly made general could easily challenge a young paladin to a duel and win without effort. I do believe that I can *still* feel the bruises even a decade later."

"Can I be you when I grow up?" Myr asked Laia.

Matthias hid a smile. "General D'terio, please join us in the city for a conversation. There is much we would like to talk to you about. I'm sure you have questions of your own."

"I do indeed. The widow who owns the town garden has offered me room if needed. I do not think she will mind if we borrow her dining room for our discussion. Best to not cause a stir. Well, more than we have already."

The mood in Rubentia was already lifting dramatically. People were beginning to laugh and talk. They still watched Gordon's soldiers warily, but they greeted the Liberation Army warmly, the way they had once greeted the Imperial Army. Gordon and Tyrian both saw shops that had been closed beginning to prepare to open once more. The inn was opening its doors to people who had lost their homes, and others were as yet taking their homes back.

The garden resided in the center of the city. It covered a fair amount of size since it provided all the fruits and vegetables for the townsfolk. At the center of the garden was a lovely little house. A tiny little girl with silvery brown pigtails stood at the fence surrounding the property, and she brightened when she saw Gordon. "Hi Gen'ral!"

Gordon grinned as he dismounted his horse. "Hello, Tavi." He knelt down to her height. "Is your mother busy? Will she mind if we have a meeting in her home? Do you mind?"

Tavi studied the others with Gordon intently. They all looked like nice people, and the man with the green scarf instantly caught her attention. She looked at him closer, liking his handsome face and serious eyes. She really wanted to hug him and say it would be okay, and she wasn't even sure what was wrong with him. She just knew that something was.

At the intense way she looked at Tyrian, everyone except the Kaiten and Matthias looked at Laia in shock. They all recognized that look and had felt the emotions in Tavi's black eyes. "A kid?" Shots demanded. "A kid? Why a kid, Laia?"

"Because she is needed," was all Laia said simply.

Tyrian dismounted his horse and knelt down to be more on level with the little girl. "Hello, Tavi," he said softly. "I'm Tyrian." His hands itched to pick her up for a cuddle. He had always wanted a little sister or little brother. His littlest Destined Star. He had to protect her future. "Do you mind if we come inside?"

She looked at him solemnly and then went on her toes to hug him around the neck. She cuddled close and rested her head on his shoulder as he stood. "Mommy won't mind. And it's my house too." She focused on Liang and was instantly intrigued. "Who're you?"

He smiled. She reminded him a little of what Tyrian had been like as a child. "My name is Liang. I am one of Lord Tyrian's guardians."

She was happy with that. He looked really nice, and she liked his voice. She thought he was probably more like Tyrian's papa. He looked like he should be one. She envied Tyrian. She wanted a daddy too, so her mommy wasn't so tired all the time. "Okay."

Gordon opened the gate, and Myr and Shots stayed behind to take care of the horses while everyone else dismounted to go inside. Beyond the gate was a path that wound through the garden as it made its way to the house. The closer they got, the easier it was to see the woman standing on the porch waiting for them.

Liang took one look at her and felt a sudden gut punch of shocking desire and emotion. Her haunted blue eyes seemed to look directly through him, stirring up a fierce longing to make right everything in her world. She was unbearably lovely with her silvery brown hair coiled tightly on top of her head. She wore sturdy gardening clothes, but they only emphasized her delicate beauty.

A widow, he remembered Gordon saying. His heart wept for her. She couldn't have been very old, mid-twenties at most, and already she had suffered something so painful. She was single-handedly providing for her city, and she was raising her daughter at the same time. He wanted very badly to take her away from it all so that she never had to struggle alone again.

Tyrian very slowly lifted a brow as he looked at Liang's face and then looked at the widow on the porch. He then looked at Cassie. She was slowly beginning to smile. Marian might just come close to tying Laia for her unnerving way of knowing things she shouldn't.

"Serentia," Gordon said, "I hope you do not mind the intrusion. We would be very grateful if we could borrow your dining room for a quick meeting."

Serentia Tuone smiled instantly. "General, I already told you that you were welcome in my home. You saved Tavi's life. The least I can do is show some hospitality."

"What did you do?" Tyrian asked Tavi.

She looked at him innocently. "I just climbed a tree."

"And got stuck," Gordon muttered. "Nearly gave my soldiers heart failure when they saw her." He sighed. "Serentia Tuone, allow me to introduce Lord Tyrian Southerwind. Lord Tyrian, this is Serentia."

Tyrian looked at her and felt the familiar and unsurprising fierce tug inside. If Tavi was a Destined Star, why shouldn't Serentia be one as well? He wouldn't have been surprised if they shared the same star in the sky. "It's an honor," he said softly.

Serentia looked at him with a bemused expression on her face. She had never felt such a surprising attachment to anyone on first meeting. In fact, she had never felt anything quite like it before at all. It was almost like her love for her daughter. She wanted to protect and shelter, to make sure he was happy and safe. He needed her. She felt sure of it. "Likewise, Lord Tyrian. Do come in, everyone."

"The monk is Cassie," Tyrian said as he stepped inside and put Tavi down. "The paladin is Laia Mitakel. The man with the cane is Matthias Goldwind. The other man is Liang."

Serentia smiled at both Cassie and Laia and then turned to smile at Liang. As she did, she felt her heart skip several beats at a time. Breath held, she averted her gaze as she felt the unexpected stir of desire. It was somehow more shocking than the feeling of her heart stirring as well. She had not felt either in years. "It's nice to meet you. Is anyone thirsty? I can make some tea."

"Liang can help you." Tyrian looked at his mentor pointedly. "Can't he?"

Liang cleared his throat. "Certainly. Please lead the way, my lady." Serentia eyed him with more than a touch of shyness before hurrying down the hall. Liang shot a quick look at Tyrian and then followed her.

Tavi threw open a door near them and announced, "Dining room!" She beamed up at Tyrian as he ruffled her hair. "I'll get snacks too!"

The table was big enough to seat four people, so Matthias, Tyrian,

Gordon, and Cassie sat down. Laia leaned against the wall where she could see out the window. Gordon folded his hands on the table and looked at Tyrian intently. "Alright, Lord Tyrian. I would like to hear your side of things."

"Perhaps it's best if we show you." Tyrian pulled out the Seeing Relic he had been carrying in his backpack. It floated up over his hand and began to obediently project the same images that had been shown to him the first day. More had been added recently since Cassie had been carrying it while they were in Acre and Lupine.

Gordon pressed his hands to his eyes as he lowered his head. He felt ashamed of himself as a general. They had been so busy worrying about Foresalia that they hadn't even realized what was happening to their people. The threat was not from over the border. It was not from the Kaiten Star. It was from within the Empire itself. It sickened him.

"General D'terio," Tyrian said softly, "join us. You have said many times that you serve the people. You have a chance to do it now. Lend your skill to us. I can't do this without you." As soon as the words left his mouth, he sat back in surprise. It was a surprise that also reflected on Matthias and Cassie's faces. "You're a Destined Star."

"I see. That explains a great deal, actually." Gordon straightened his back. "You have my aid, Lord Tyrian. I will help lead your troops to victory. If we can speak with my fellow generals, then I am certain they will join as well." He saw the darkness move in Tyrian's eyes and said gently, "General Southerwind has been kept close to the capitol. You may not have to endure facing him for a while yet. And I am certain he will listen to you when you do. When we met with the Emperor after Lady Ophelia was murdered, General Southerwind told us to insist to our soldiers that you were to be taken alive."

Tyrian let out the breath he had been holding. It was a small, but welcome, bit of relief. "Thank you."

Serentia and Liang walked into the dining room with two trays loaded with tea and cups. Tavi followed with a much smaller tray that had snacks on it. "L'ang made them!" she announced. She wrinkled her nose. "I can't say your name right," she told Liang. "It's a funny name."

"Speaking of Elf names," Laia grumbled. The use of multiple vowels right next to each other made them difficult for non-Elf races to speak. She had always been grateful her name could be shortened to a much easier variant.

Liang knelt down to Tavi's height. "Lie-an-gh," he pronounced. "The 'gh' is soft."

"L'ang!"

Tyrian smiled. "Don't worry, Tavi. That's what I called him for a long time, too." He gratefully took the cup of tea that Serentia held out. "Thank you."

Gordon stood and offered his chair to Serentia. "Sit down," he told her. "Please. I must speak with my soldiers as to my decision." He looked at Tyrian. "If they wish to return to the Empire . . ."

"They are free to go," Tyrian said. "Laws of engagement. They are not held to the decision you make. If they wish to follow you, and therefore me, then I am grateful for their addition."

Gordon bowed gracefully and left the room. The front door shut behind him, and Matthias looked at Serentia. "You know," he said, "we have need of someone with your talents at our base."

Her brows lifted. "Me? Professor Matthias, I am nothing but a gardener."

"And we have none. We have a large overgrown patch of weeds and dirt," Tyrian admitted dryly. "The garden that once belonged to the castle is a rat's nest of desolation. No one has any clue what to do with it. And with so many to feed . . . growing our own crops is critical." He held out his relic hand to her. "Please, Serentia. I need your help for this."

Tavi tugged on her mother's sleeve and said fretfully, "We have to help, Mommy. Lord Tyrian needs us!" She looked at Tyrian hopefully. "I keep my room clean! An' I can take care of the castle dogs! Do you have dogs?"

"A few are running around," he said. "We have a castle guard dog with no royalty to guard, so he could use someone to take care of him."

"I'll do it!" She bounced on her toes as she looked at Serentia. "Mommy, see? We're needed! We have'ta help Lord Tyrian and L'ang! He said he makes yummy snacks, and so we have to grow the 'gred'ents so he can keep Lord Tyrian healthy! Right?" She looked at Cassie and Laia for help.

Cassie couldn't respond because she had a hand over her mouth to hide a smile. Laia wasn't so polite. She was outright grinning. "Right, kid." She winked at Tavi. "We have to keep our Lord Tyrian safe, don't we?"

Serentia sighed and then suddenly laughed. "I can't fight all of you, and I can feel that you mean it, Lord Tyrian. I know you need me. And I have to help. It's a curious feeling, but I can accept it. I would be honored to come take charge of your garden. You can leave it to me." She grasped his hand tightly.

His relic glowed softly, and the matching stars appeared on Serentia and Tavi's shoulders. Tavi stared at the glowing mark in awe. "What does that mean?" she asked Matthias.

He smiled. "It means that we are destined to share the sky with Lord

Tyrian. It was a gift given to the special people that he truly needs in order to save everyone." He looked at Tyrian. "There might as yet be others in town. Would you like to look before we return to base? Serentia and Tavi will need time to pack."

"I'll help," Laia offered. "And so will Liang. Won't he?"

Liang smiled at Serentia. "If she needs the help." It took a lot of control not to tuck her loose hair behind her ear. Having her at the castle would be an exercise in torture if he couldn't manage to get a hold of his emotions and hormones. He didn't even know how long she had been a widow! Tavi was only four years old.

She pressed her hands to her stomach under the table. The fluttery sensation of need was almost foreign after three years. She had forgotten what it felt like to want a man, and she had never wanted Civ like this. At the least, it told her that perhaps she was finally healing. She had thought she never would. "There is a lot here," she admitted. "Any help is appreciated."

"We'll send some soldiers with a wagon to help as well," Tyrian said as he got to his feet. He helped Matthias stand as well and held him steady so he could grab his cane. "If you need anything, tell me immediately."

"I will. Thank you, Lord Tyrian."

Once back outside, Matthias let Tyrian assist him back up onto his horse. "We can stay at the inn for the night and set out tomorrow morning," Matthias told Tyrian. "I will secure a room for you and Lady Cassie."

"Y'all looking for more Destined Stars?" Shots asked. When Tyrian nodded, he said, "Well, I'm not the fastest bullet in the chamber, but I'm startin' to see some patterns. People like us just sort of stand out in the crowd, y'know? So you might try talkin' to that Healer in town that we used as a cover. Halkern."

"I think I saw one of Taurus' band mates at the Item Shop," Myr spoke up. "The guy with the really red hair. Bet he'd be glad to know where she is. We'll help Serentia and Tavi get their things together."

Tyrian felt bemused as he watched everyone except Cassie scatter to get things done. "So many different people," he murmured. "But we share the skies."

She cupped his cheek tenderly. "We wouldn't work so well together if we were all the same." She went on her toes to kiss him softly, and her lips curved as they heard a couple of soldiers catcalling. "You employ smartasses, *Lord* Tyrian."

"I have one for a lover as well. I must like them." He kept an arm around her waist as they began to walk through the city. He didn't mind that everyone knew who he was. He didn't want to be some unapproachable figure. He was fighting for the people, and the people needed to be able to talk to him. Still, he missed the peace of his tower room.

The Item Shop wasn't hard to find. When they asked someone for directions, they were informed, "Just listen for an explosion, and then find the smoke."

Any questions as to what that meant were answered when they did indeed hear a loud bang and see smoke drifting up into the air. Not a single person on the street batted a lash, though the Liberation Army soldiers looked nonplussed.

Tyrian made his way to where the smoke was coming from and found the door hanging open on one hinge. He covered his mouth with his scarf even as Cassie pulled up her hood and faceguard. "Hello?" he called into the building. "Is everyone alright in here?"

A bedraggled young man with very dark red hair stepped out of the smoke, his face and clothes liberally covered with soot. He coughed. "We're alright. A little smoky, but it just adds flavor. Don't mind the mess."

"Aries!" a young girl's voice called. "Turn on the fans!"

"They better not blow up!" he muttered as he moved toward the two large devices sitting on the floor. The blades affixed to them began to spin swiftly and kicked up a breeze that began to blow the smoke out. "Hey, something that works around here!"

Tyrian found himself smiling. "You're Aries? You're in Café Latte, correct? With Taurus?"

Aries looked at him swiftly. "You know where she is? I'm going to tan her hide!" he said fiercely. "'Oh, don't worry about me! I can handle a little trip by myself!' Feh! I'm boxing her pointed ears. Scared me senseless when I heard about Acre!"

"She's at my castle," Tyrian said helpfully. "I'm Tyrian Southerwind, leader of the Liberation Army. She asked to join me, to provide strength to my troops and to me. I would ask that you help as well, Aries. You're needed. I've heard the music you play. It will lift everyone's spirits."

Aries looked at him oddly and then suddenly smiled. "I'm one of them, too? Those Destined Stars that people talk about. I have to be. I can just feel it that you need me, and if you're Lord Tyrian, then . . ." He nodded swiftly. "You can count on me, Lord Tyrian. Café Latte will keep your castle full of the music of freedom!"

Tyrian offered his relic hand and Aries grasped it. When he did, the glowing star appeared. It was a star echoed on the shoulder of the young girl who walked out of the lingering smoke. She stared at her arm before looking at Tyrian. "Well, I guess me too!" she said decisively. "I'm Yumi! Don't let my age fool you; I can fight too. My Mechanobot is a great weapon! I'm the pupil of the Great Inventor Tedium! Let me fight with you, Lord Tyrian. I know I can be of help!"

Tyrian smiled as he studied her. She was probably around ten years old, but she looked strong for her age. She wore shorts with a cropped leather vest buttoned over the top. Tipless gloves covered her hands, and she wore a hat with a pair of goggles on them. Boots covered her feet. Even if she hadn't said she was an inventor in training, he would have known instantly based on her choice of clothing style. "I'm counting on you, too, Yumi."

"You can also count on me," an older male voice said. "Come on into the back room, Lord Tyrian. If you can find the door, that is." The voice chuckled merrily.

"Oh, man." Yumi rolled her eyes. "Now he wants to try and make you look silly! C'mon, Tedium! Just tell him where the entrance is! It's Lord Tyrian! He's not just some poor guy like Aries that you can bamboozle!"

With the smoke cleared, the early evening light was able to get in the windows. Tyrian studied the room curiously and then focused on the walls. They looked relatively normal, but since he was dealing with a world famous inventor, he wasn't counting on anything being what it was supposed to be.

Cassie glanced around as well and her sharp eyes spotted a slightly blackened outline in the rough shape of a door. She pointed, and Tyrian followed her direction. Even the slightest of openings, such as around a door, would have attracted extra soot. He walked over to the wall and tapped it lightly with his hand. It was definitely hollow.

He glanced up and saw a lever over his head. He looked at Yumi and she grinned with a thumbs-up. With a jump, Tyrian got hold of the lever and pulled down. As he dropped back to his feet, the hidden door slid upward to reveal a lab beyond. "That wasn't very hard," he scolded the man standing at a table.

Tedium pulled off his goggles and stuck them on top of his head. He wore a pair of pants and a leather vest not dissimilar from Yumi's gear though he also had a belt equipped with all manner of things that Tyrian was fairly sure he couldn't recognize let alone name. The white star still lingered on his shoulder in response to Tyrian's relic. "So it wasn't," the inventor conceded. "Greetings, Lord Tyrian. I am Tedium."

"Thank god," Tyrian said instantly. "We've been trying to find you! We need an elevator at the castle, possibly two, and I hear you're the man to ask. Can I count on your help?"

"Naturally." Tedium bowed swiftly. "After all, I can't exactly create inventions to better lives when no one has any life to better, correct?" He smiled. He would have gone to assist Tyrian Southerwind even if an elevator wasn't in such need. He had waited many years to meet his Kaiten Star, ever since the day he had realized just what the stars in the sky truly meant. "If you have room for a lab, I'll be a happy inventor."

"No explosions, please," Cassie said dryly.

"I shall do my best. Leave it to me, Tedium, to make your life easier!" He sighed. "Yumi! Get in here and help me start packing! And bring that good-for-nothing musician we've been feeding."

Tyrian hid a smile as he and Cassie left the shop. Explosions were inevitable, but potentially entertaining and useful if Tedium could indeed find ways to make things easier for the army and the civilians. Outside, he said, "Let's find the Healer."

"No need."

At the voice, Tyrian looked down the sidewalk to see a Magician approaching. A mace was hooked into a loop on his belt, and he wore both a Medicine Relic and a Resurrection Relic, one to each hand. He wasn't much older than Kyle or Ewan, and he moved confidently. "I am Halkern," he said with a bow. "Someone said you were looking for me, Lord Tyrian?"

"I am," Tyrian agreed. He felt unsurprised to discover Shots had been right. He, too, was beginning to see the pattern. "I have a distressing lack of Healers. I have only one right now, and as my army grows, so does my need for someone who can tend to wounds on or off a battlefield. Will you join me?"

Halkern studied him, thinking about all the things he had heard about Tyrian Southerwind. He was much younger than would be expected of someone with such a heavy burden, but his presence was inspiring. You could believe that anything was possible so long as he believed it. With a nod, Halkern offered a hand. "I will gladly join you. You can't win a war without a little healing magic, no matter how good you are. I'll be there to help tend to all your wounds, Lord Tyrian."

Tyrian took his hand and the familiar star appeared. "I'll call on you the instant I need you," he promised. He let out a little breath as Halkern turned and hurried toward his home to get ready. With a rueful smile to Cassie, he said, "It's somehow easier and somehow scarier than I imagined it would be when Lady Tanelia first told me what I was to do." He tucked his hands into his pockets as they walked down the twilight streets toward the inn. "I've forgotten what a normal life is like, Cassie." He closed his eyes on a smile. "Though I suppose normality is relative. Your normal is different from mine."

She wrapped her arms around his and leaned her head against his shoulder. "Normal for me isn't fighting wars. My normal life is to occasionally pass through cities to make sure nothing has changed status quo and to take out bandits."

"Bandits, huh?"

"Mm. Our main source of revenue. We also serve as assassins when needed, when justice can't touch those who have horrendously broken a law." She glanced up at him. "It doesn't alarm you?"

"Why should it?" He drew her fingers to his lips. "There's a place for everyone and everything. It scares me a little to think of you having been in so much danger, but I fully believe that it is what makes you my perfect Kentei. Tell me about the dumbest bandits you've ever met."

She smiled as she thought about it. "There's this pack in the far eastern area of the mountains, right near where the checkpoint for the east coast is. They would steal from people, but then take most of it back if they didn't need it. Their leader is a girl about my age. When she heard I was on the hunt, she asked me to tea." She laughed. "We had a great conversation, and she agreed that her brothers were idiots. I liked her so much that I let them go with a warning."

He grinned at the mental image of a bandit sitting down to tea with the monk sent to either destroy or defeat them. "Did they clean up their act?"

"Last I heard, they were only targeting the Imperial Army, so I suspect they took my warning seriously." She rubbed her cheek against him softly. "What's your normal life, Tyrian?"

"Hmm. Studying to follow in my father's footsteps. Combat training. Doing errands for the Emperor or for the Prime Duke. Ignoring the girls who keep coming past my house since I'm not interested in any of them."

The last was added teasingly. She smiled. "What would you have done if it had been a bandit-hunting monk coming past your house?"

"Attached myself to her heels until she agreed to have dinner with me." He trailed the fingers of his relic hand down her arm. "And then I would have worked wholeheartedly on seducing her."

"We can try dinner tonight." She pressed a kiss to his chin. "Then you can seduce me after. We'll try your normal world. And if we find some bandits later, we can try mine." She blew out a quick breath as they stopped in front of the inn doors. "I'm not exactly *dressed* for going to dinner, though."

Myr popped out of the doors and startled them both. "I can help!"

she said cheerfully. She grabbed Cassie's wrist. "Come with me, Lady Cassie! I know just where to go to get you something really pretty to wear!" Over her shoulder, she called, "I'll have something sent to you as well, Lord Tyrian!"

Tyrian blinked and then shook his head as he went into the inn. He stopped at the front desk to speak to the innkeeper, and she handed him a key and cheerfully pointed out the direction. His room was on the second floor, and it was one of the ones that had running water. Laia and Liang were in the rooms beside his, and that didn't surprise him either.

Dinner was already being served, so he hurried upstairs to get cleaned up. It felt good to scrub away the remnants of the day's journey. They had set out before dawn to make it by the late afternoon, and he was certainly feeling the effects of a long day.

He had finished bathing by the time someone knocked on the door. It was Shots, and he winked as he handed over a box. "I saw your Kentei," he said cheerfully. "Yer one lucky guy, Lord Tyrian. She's one fine looking lady." Whistling, he headed down the hall to his own room.

Tyrian opened the box to find a pair of formal slacks and jacket. Matched with them was a finely made shirt. He had grown up with fine clothes, but just a few short months had made him forget entirely what they were like. He had gotten used to casual tunics and pants, or his regular wear for battle.

He changed clothes quickly since he knew that Cassie already waited for him and then left his room and headed for the stairs. He was halfway down them before he spotted his lover, and he stopped dead in his tracks when he saw her. He very nearly stopped breathing.

Gone was his dangerous and powerful monk. In her place was a lady of high class, looking too impossibly delicate and beautiful to be as deadly as he knew she was. She wore a slim black dress that clung to a good deal of her body before flaring around her knees. A black velvet choker circled her neck, and someone had tousled her thick hair. It shone more blue than black in the candlelight of the dining room.

As she felt the gaze, Cassie glanced up nervously, trying not to fidget. She had never worn a dress in her life! When she saw Tyrian, her breath stopped. He looked like the lord he was, as noble as his birth implied. Yet it wasn't just his birth that made him noble, and she knew it. He carried himself like a king. The hunger in his eyes made her forget her nerves, made her feel beautiful and desirable. "Your normal world has some merits," she said softly when he stopped in front of her.

He took her hand and slowly brought it to his lips with a deep bow.

Flustered, she tugged at her hand, but he held firm. His eyes glowed like green gems as they watched her, and the slow smile curving his lips made her want to kiss him in front of the entire room. "You're making a scene," she whispered.

"Yes, I am." He tucked her hand into the curve of his elbow as he walked into the dining room. "Don't expect me to turn loose of you just yet, Cas. I'm worried you'll disappear as if I've dreamed you up. Can you dance?"

"A bit." Her breath caught as he pulled her toward the space where other couples danced together. "Not that well," she added hastily. The words disappeared as he pulled her into his arms. There was something in his eyes, something that had finally relaxed and let go of the stress he lived under daily. This was a chance to forget. She loved him too much to not let him have this night.

Everyone who watched Kaiten and Kentei dance together had to smile. At a table to the side, Matthias shared a satisfied smile with Liang and Laia. To the Destined Stars, the war was secondary. What mattered solely was the happiness of their Kaiten. As long as Tyrian was happy, nothing else was important.

War could wait a little while longer yet.

Chapter Sixteen

"Now rose-colored glasses turn everything to blood red."

Word of Gordon's defeat and the subsequent loss of all four of his units reached Trinan very quickly. When word arrived, Albanion and Blaine were meeting with the Prime Duke. Donald himself brought the news to his emperor, and it was not unexpected news to him. Everyone underestimated Tyrian.

He walked into the meeting room and bowed respectfully as those within looked at him. "My apologies for the intrusion."

"What is it, General?" Albanion asked.

"Word has arrived. General D'terio was defeated in combat by the Liberation Army. To spare the lives of his soldiers, he has chosen to fight now on their side. With the capture of Rubentia at the same time, the Liberation Army now stands at eight units in strength. They have one unit in each Rubentia and Lupine to hold them."

"And they have Matthias Goldwind." Albanion drummed his fingers on the table. "And now they have General D'terio. Damnation, Donald, what is wrong with your boy? Why is he causing all this trouble over something so trifling as taxes?"

"Tyrian follows his heart," Donald said. "If he believes what he is doing is right, then he will continue to do it. And . . . the legend of the Kaiten Star is not as new as we believed. I have found some information indicating that the prophecy of a Kaiten Star was first handed down a million years ago. Lady Tanelia herself predicted his birth as a hero meant to save his land."

Hatred flickered across Blaine's eyes as she stared at Donald. How *dare* he speak that name in her presence? "Tanelia is a senile, reclusive, and pitiful excuse for a sage," she bit out between her teeth. "All those years wearing a Pure Relic have corroded her mind. She knows nothing. Nothing! Never speak her name again!"

"Destiny," Albanion muttered to himself. It couldn't be fought. A prophecy handed down a million years ago was a pretty heavy one. The earlier a prophecy was told, the more important it often came to be. Blaine had seen Tyrian would overthrow the Empire. For many people, perhaps that was indeed being saved. "Are the people siding with him?" he asked.

Blaine curled her hand around his arm and her nails bit lightly into his skin. "It doesn't matter," she purred, though her eyes remained cold.

"You know what is best for your people."

He nodded. "Naturally. General Southerwind, send for General Yureny. Perhaps it is time to strike directly at the Liberation Army itself. We know where their base stands. They have eight units. General Yureny commands nine,, including two made of magic users. We will take them before they take any more cities."

Donald bowed and left the room. As he stepped into the hall, Annareal stepped out of the darkness. Her eyes looked wide and distressed. "Donald," she said softly, "you must tell me what is going on! You haven't spoken a word to me in months!"

He barely spared her a look. "What you did is unforgiveable, Annareal. I know what happened in those catacombs. If you had truly been trying to protect our son, you would have called Ophelia Goldwind out honorably. That he spared your life is a sign that he is a better person than his father. I can't even be sure I would have done so in his shoes. Who really destroyed his life, Annareal? Ophelia Goldwind . . . or you?"

She slowly sank to the floor on her knees, tears gliding down her face as her husband walked away. For the first time, she looked at what she had done from an objective standpoint. Nausea rolled and her stomach rebelled as she went sick all the way to her soul. She covered her mouth with her hand as she rushed from the palace. She made it to the gardens before the violent retching consumed her. What had she done to her family?

Blaine watched her from the window, disgusted. Such a pitiful and weak woman Annareal was! It was hard to believe she had given birth to the Kaiten Star. But then, Blaine had already seen that Tyrian was much like Donald. She didn't trust the High General's loyalties one tiny bit. She knew his family came first. He would no doubt forgive Annareal now that she had repented.

She curled her hands into fists so hard that her nails cut her palms. Things were getting out of hand. She held no illusions of General Yureny being able to take down the Liberation Army; the Commune Soldier had too much bedrock integrity, just like those other accursed generals.

The feel of blood sliding down her hands made her lift them to see the wounds. She needed something to fight against Tyrian that would not be swayed by reason. Something that would have the power to confront a Pure Relic and not be easily defeated. Something that would kill indiscriminately and be the perfect monster of any army's nightmares.

Something . . . undead.

Chapter Seventeen

"My family of you, always small, always cherished."

Everyone set out for the Liberation Army base in the morning. Many had gone on ahead the night before, but there were still a lot to take back during the day. Tedium rode in a wagon with Yumi and Tavi, and he worked feverishly on his newest plans for an invention. He wanted to invent something that would do the work of a Magician and be able to transport units to battle and then back again. Aware that the soldiers were skeptical, he said, "I'll test it on sheep first, I promise!"

Tyrian mentally envisioned a unit of sheep unceremoniously appearing outside a city and hastily coughed into his scarf to keep from laughing outright. That would certainly lift the troops' morale.

It was yet again evening by the time they were home. More than one soldier was happy with Tedium inventing a machine to transport them. The marching was wearing on everyone. They needed to be strong to keep fighting for Lord Tyrian.

The sudden increase in the size of the army was more than the immediate barracks could handle. Tyrian climbed up to the top of one of the corner towers with Gordon and they looked out over the area around the city limits. There was plenty of room for expansion. "I say," Gordon said, "that we tear this wall down and push it out a half mile in all directions. We can leave the moat as is and just build bridges over it." He peered down into the water. "I wouldn't want to make them unhappy."

Pushing out a half mile in a circle would provide more than enough room for up to fifty thousand units. It was a daunting number, but very plausible to reach. It would also remove the need for the current barracks and the space could be changed into more room for civilians. There were more than Tyrian had expected. He actually had a full-sized city under operation with people arriving daily from other cities. "Let's start building the new wall before the old one comes down," he decided. "We wouldn't want to be caught with our pants down. Or rather, our wall down."

Gordon laughed and clapped him on the shoulder. "You had it right the first time, Lord Tyrian." He leaned on the window ledge and looked down at the city. It was bustling even as the sun set. He had almost forgotten what a happy city looked like. "How did we never notice?" he murmured. "The pseudo-fight with Foresalia is no excuse."

"Absolute power corrupts absolutely," Tyrian said. "I'm not saying that a single ruler can't rule well. Albanion was a good emperor before Blaine came along, and my understanding of the history of the Empire indicates that we've had both bad and good. But the bad has, before, never been like this. Inept, not cruelty. It's a sign of a need for change."

Gordon studied him. "What would you make, Lord Tyrian?"

"A republic." Tyrian had been thinking about it a lot. "A republic of the people. Elected leaders who answer to the people in the end. It won't be as hard as you think. We were already on the road, what with mayors of cities taking care of their towns and reporting to the Emperor. This time, however, the leader of the country won't be able to arbitrarily take over. There are a lot of details to be worked out, but that can be decided when the new leader is elected."

"It won't be you?" Gordon asked softly. "You know that that is surely what the people are looking for. You lead so naturally, Lord Tyrian. And you truly serve the people."

"And I have eternity," he said simply. "If I did not wear this relic, perhaps I would be standing here saying I would lead. But I am beginning to feel the effects of the Devourer being Pure. A very long future lies ahead of me, Gordon. Even the idea of being tied down is somehow distasteful."

It did not surprise Gordon. From what he knew of the few Pure Relic users known in the world, none of them could stand to be in one place for very long. They all had secret retreats where they went to be away from normal life. It was a heavy burden to watch time pass around you without being a part of it. And when it was Tyrian, it was a great loss to the Empire. He would have been a leader the likes of which no country would ever know.

They made their way back down to ground level and Gordon went into the castle proper to find his room. Tyrian headed for his tower. He had seen Cassie's silhouette through the curtains and knew she waited for him.

"Lord Tyrian!"

He turned with a lifted brow as a guard approached with two young women following him. One was dressed in the familiar split skirt and bodice of a female dagger user. The other dressed like a civilian, and her clothing had the formal flavor of someone who had been born in a much larger city. The sight of them both tugged at that familiar place inside him. "What can I do for you?" he asked.

The dagger user saluted sassily. "You can let us help you, Lord Tyrian. I'm Cleveland, but everyone calls me Vee for short." Her voice rolled and softly shimmered with the accent of the Melodina valley. "I throw a mean dagger, and I can help you in battle both small and large. As soon as I heard about you, I just knew that I could help. And Eve couldn't get here alone."

The other woman smiled. "Well, I swing a mean frying pan, but it doesn't do much against monsters." Her blue eyes twinkled as she bowed. "My name is Evelyn Winters. I'm a chef."

Tyrian stared at her, certain he was hearing things. "You're a chef. You can cook on a large scale? As in a *very* large scale?"

"Just give me a very large kitchen!" she said cheerfully. She laughed as the guard escorting them let out a distinct whoop of joy. "I take it we haven't got anyone to cook for the soldiers? Leave it to me! If you give me the space for a big restaurant, then I'll make enough to feed as many people as needed! You can count on me, Lord Tyrian."

He looked between them and realized that they were among the few who already knew of their destiny. They had come looking for him solely because they had known he needed them at that very moment in time. "Where a Kaiten Star is," he murmured, "their Destined Stars will gather."

Evelyn and Vee shared a smile. There wasn't a single Destined Star who regretted being chosen. Destiny picked her emissaries carefully, and it was an honor to be made as one. If you were given a destiny, it was understood that you had been blessed. Hard or painful it may be, in the end, you were the person you had always been meant to become.

Tyrian shook it off and looked at the guard. "Show Eve to the inn. She can use R.K.'s kitchen for now, and have some people prepare to start whipping the castle kitchen into shape. It's ridiculously big. The formal dining room can be turned into a restaurant."

The guard saluted and led Eve away. Vee was content to follow another guard to pick out a room she could use. Tyrian watched them go and then went to his tower. He had to climb the stairs cautiously since Tedium was already working on tearing them out to put in an elevator. As he walked into his room, he complained, "At this rate, we'll be scaling the tower with a rope from the balcony. Couldn't he wait until we were gone for a few days?"

Cassie looked up from where she sat in front of the fire and smiled. "He assured me he was just laying the groundwork. He'll do the one in the castle first, and then when we're gone for a while, he'll tackle ours." She got to her feet and went to go into his arms. She rested her head on his shoulder where it belonged. "I saw you from the balcony," she said softly. "Talking to Gordon."

"Deciding what to do about the soldiers. Talking about the new government we're trying to build." He grimaced. "People want me to lead the new government. Somehow, I can't stomach the idea of it. It's already growing harder and harder to be boxed in, even with this tower. Time has stopped. There's so much for me to see and do."

He buried his face in her hair, and she softly smoothed her hands up and down his back comfortingly. She, too, was aware of the difficulties that Pure Relic bearers wore. "There is time for everything, as Laia might say," she said gently. "When we come through this, there will be an entire world for us to explore."

He let out a long breath and relaxed. His arms slid around her waist as he let her comfort him. She was his sanity in this insane world. If she hadn't been there, he would have broken long before. Without further words, he lifted her into his arms and carried her to their bed. He could lose himself inside her arms, and for that short time, his world could be perfect. Her love was his salvation.

They were awakened the next morning to the sound of a knock. The door opened and Merilyne walked in saying cheerfully, "Good morning! Professor Matthias requests your presence in the meeting room! I've brought coffee from Eve's kitchen. Breakfast will be waiting for you at the meeting room." She scooped up their dirty clothes and headed back out with a whistle.

"They had to give us the most cheerful maid in the city," Tyrian said into the pillow. He didn't bother to move.

Cassie leaned over his shoulder and smiled. "You wouldn't wake up for anyone else. If we had a grouch, you could ignore them." She rested her chin on his shoulder. "I would never have guessed you weren't a morning person."

He opened his eyes and glanced up at her. The morning light coming in over the wall illuminated the blue in her hair and eyes alike. She was soft and welcoming, warm and fragrant. "I'm growing fond of them," he said huskily.

She made a quick dodge and scooted out of bed quickly as he reached for her. "No, you don't!" she said breathlessly, trying not to laugh. "You'll make us late, and we'd never live it down." She grabbed fresh clothes and held them like a shield. "Tyrian Southerwind, you get out of that bed and stop grinning at me."

He rolled out of bed and then darted forward and snatched her up into his arms for a wild kiss. She went limp in his grip, her arms wrapping around his neck as she eagerly responded. She never held anything back, giving herself to him body and soul. "It's a wonder I ever keep my hands off you at all," he said roughly as he lifted her higher and tasted the curve of her breast.

The voice-box by the door beeped and Ewan's voice said dryly, "If you're not downstairs in five minutes, I'm going to come get you. And you'd better have clothes on, or I will drag your naked ass downstairs."

Tyrian sighed and put Cassie down. "Spoilsport."

Since they knew Ewan meant what he said, they quickly got dressed, grabbed their coffee, and hurried downstairs. Breakfast was just arriving when they got to the meeting room. It smelled even better than it looked, and Evelyn handed out plates contentedly. "Just wait until I get that big kitchen I was promised," she said as she gave Kyle his breakfast. "Serentia has already promised to put in an herb plot in her garden for me."

Present in the room were Kyle, Ewan, Matthias, Cherry, Leonard, and Gordon. Much to Tyrian's surprise, Liang wasn't there. "Where's Liang?" he asked curiously as he took his plate and sat down.

"Speaking of Serentia," Kyle noted idly.

Solemnly, Gordon said, "She's trying to remove the rocks in the garden because they're taking up space she needs. They're too heavy for her, so she was looking for help. Liang volunteered himself before I even opened my mouth to offer some soldiers."

Evelyn wheeled her cart out, and Matthias sighed contentedly over his coffee. "I'm very glad Eve found us when she did. We're going to need the fuel."

"What's next, then?" Tyrian poked at the orange bits in his food, realized they were carrots, and pushed them aside hastily. He would have to find a way to ask Evelyn to not include them without making her laugh at him. He knew it was a silly phobia.

"Caschin," Cherry said. She hopped to her feet and pointed at a town on the map. "It's about the same size as Rubentia. We're slowly making our way toward bigger cities. After Caschin, we're looking at Dry Basin. It's twice the size of Rubentia, and it's guarded by ten units. It'll keep getting bigger as we go, because the Empire will pull into itself."

"And we will need to start looking at the checkpoints as well." Matthias leaned back in his chair. "Gordon wants to try to contact his fellow Lower Generals on the side, so we are going to postpone the checkpoints as long as possible. The two biggest cities in the Empire, Pardue and Larksville, will be our very last targets before we face Trinan. At over a hundred thousand people each, they're far beyond our current scope."

"A stone rolling downhill," Leonard offered. "It gains momentum the closer it gets to the bottom."

"So, Caschin." Tyrian studied the map. Caschin was many days away. "Isn't that your hometown, Matthias?"

"It is, indeed. It is to our advantage, as I know the layout intimately, as well as the secrets it hides. It is guarded by three units from the Imperial Army, one made of magic users. Cherry checked earlier this morning, and we have enough soldiers to make one magic unit. We have no specialists to lead the unit other than you, Lord Tyrian. You're the closest thing to a Magician we have, and your relic is attack based. It doesn't cast typical magic spells." Not to mention that Tyrian refused to actually cast his relic's spell. He only used raw power.

"I have to admit, it'd be handy to see Hell unleashed on the enemy, but we want to take as many alive as we can," Ewan said.

"Ah, but we're the only ones who know what Lord Tyrian's relic can do," Matthias noted. "No one knows what it involves. There is only speculation as people whisper the name of the Pure Devourer Relic. Only Relic Masters would have a good shot at knowing what it can do, and I suspect there are none who would be willing to go up to the Imperial Army and tell them."

"Can we put up a 'Help Wanted' sign for mages?" Kyle muttered.

Cassie frowned thoughtfully. "I'm still waiting for word from the Monk Clan. My messages had to have reached them by now. With the rate we're growing, Master Kotan should be convinced to send us at least two units. And . . . with my destiny tied to Tyrian's, he will want to give assistance for that alone."

"He's your adopted father, right?" Ewan asked. When she nodded, he whistled softly. "Yeah, I sure would want to help my daughter out if she was tangled up in a mess like this."

"Ewan with a daughter." Leonard snorted softly. "Scary thought. Let's hope she doesn't have her father's temperament."

Ewan grinned. "I can't be offended by the truth, Leo. But for your sake, I hope she does. Would serve you right, old man." He suddenly scowled. "Why are we talking about my daughter when I don't even have a wife?" When Kyle opened his mouth, Ewan shot him a glare. "Don't even say her name or I'm throwing you in the moat to be a chew toy for the monsters!"

Matthias ignored them as he looked at Tyrian, though he had to agree with Leonard. "I think we can take Caschin with three units, and we'll have you ride at the head of our magic one. Laia and Cassie can ride with you. Cassie does not have magic, but she is your Kentei."

Where the Kaiten went, the Kentei went as well. Tyrian nodded. "Laia is lethal with her Lightning Relic, more than even Kyle, and she says she can use her Music Relic in battle as well. I'm curious to see it, in fact."

"And she also has a Medicine Relic," Cherry added, "so she can serve as a Healer. I've never met anyone with such a versatility!"

"We can make the other two units be our ranged unit and close-combat," Matthias said. "Who would you like as unit leaders, Lord Tyrian? I will ride with the ranged unit since they will be mounted."

"Emma and Vee will work to ride with you. That covers both arrow and dagger expertise. For close combat, we'll take Ewan, Rourke, and Sean." He looked at Leonard. "I know Sean is young, but I believe he will do just fine out there. Ewan can show him the ropes."

Leonard nodded instantly. "He's got a big mouth, but he's not stupid. He'll listen to what Ewan tells him. Thirteen is the minimum age for engaging in field combat, and he's just over that. It's as good a time as any to learn."

"Is he training in the tradition of the Commune?" Ewan asked.

"He is."

"Then I'll definitely keep an eye on him for you."

"What about getting there?" Gordon asked.

The doors flew open and Tedium burst inside. He was covered in soot, and sparks crackled over his hair where it stood on end. Behind his goggles, his eyes had gone bright with excitement. "It works!" he exclaimed gleefully.

Yumi peeked around his arm and said, "We lost a couple sheep, Lord Tyrian. They ran away before we could retrieve them."

Matthias opened his mouth and then closed it, for the first time at a loss for words. Tyrian cleared his throat. "Are we talking about a machine that can transport troops to battle and back again?"

"We are indeed!" Tedium was almost dancing in place. "I rounded up people with relics and had them give me their input. We've equipped the machine with the relics normally used by mages for 'porting, and *it works*! We sent a herd of sheep to Rubentia and brought it back safely!"

"The mayor said that we need to warn him next time," Yumi added solemnly. "They thought they were under attack."

"From sheep?!" Ewan's head hit the table with a thump.

Tyrian's stomach quivered as he tried desperately to keep a straight face. He really didn't want to laugh in Tedium's face. He had done a great thing. "Is it safe for sentient use?"

"It is now." At the brows that lifted, Tedium said hastily, "They weren't hurt! They just, er, landed without their clothes. Their clothes joined them a few minutes later. When we brought them back, their clothes were inside out. The third test went fine."

"I'd run from a naked army," Leonard said to Ewan who beat his head on the desk again. "Did their weapons make it at least?"

"Curiously, yes. But, as I said, the bugs are out. The last attempt got our soldiers to a city and back without anything more than a bad case of hat hair." Tedium swung around and almost knocked Yumi over. "The Mechanoportal is in the area near the barracks. I'll be there to operate it. I am a genius!" he proclaimed.

Yumi hurried after him and the doors swung shut. Ewan was still beating his head on the table, and Matthias was still at a loss for words. Kyle pinched the bridge of his nose and said, "If he could combine the two issues, then we could send pre-sheered sheep to the cities and make a fortune in the butcher business."

That did it. Everyone started laughing. When Matthias managed to get a grip on himself, he said to Tyrian, "If you're ready to risk the threat of hat hair, then I say we gather the troops and put our lives and personal style into Tedium's hands to get to Caschin. Before we transport, however, I wish to talk to Laia. She will be critical to my plan."

While Kyle held down the fort with Leonard and Gordon, the others made their way out back to where the Mechanoportal sat. Emma, Vee, Sean, Rourke, and Laia had already gotten there, drawn by the knowledge that their Kaiten needed them. They regarded the large device with some caution, and Tyrian didn't blame them. It looked like a mass of gears and wires and metal with steam rolling out the top and relics glowing over the sides.

"Rally your unit," Tyrian told Emma and Vee. "Matthias will be riding with you."

"Yes, sir!" They hurried off quickly.

Ewan, Rourke, and Sean moved to go take command over their unit as well, and Laia quirked a brow at Tyrian. "So I'm being called upon for my magic this time, eh?" It wasn't really a question since she did not wear her plate armor. She wore her claymore, but the plate had been exchanged for something lighter.

"Indeed." Matthias moved to the side and gestured for her to join him. He spoke softly enough that Tyrian didn't hear a word he said, but Laia looked intrigued. When she grinned and nodded, Matthias turned back toward Tyrian. "We are ready when you are, Lord Tyrian." He gladly accepted help from a soldier to get onto the horse Beatrice was holding for him.

"Leave it to me," Laia told Tyrian. "Just follow Professor Matthias' prompts. I'll take care of the rest."

Interested, Tyrian tucked away his curiosity and joined the rest of the mages as they gathered. The Mechanoportal belched out more steam and made a very loud creaking noise as the relics flashed brightly and blinded everyone. When Tyrian's sight cleared, he found himself standing in the dusty landscape outside Caschin . . . and his scarf was on top of his head. He felt lucky to have escaped with just that. Laia had not fared so well; her white hair had suddenly turned into a riot of curls. She looked like a bard herself.

Cassie made it through unscathed, miraculously, and for that she was grateful. She pulled a black bandana out of her pocket and offered it to Laia to tie back her hair. "Here," she said. "I think you could use this."

Laia tied her hair up into a ponytail and then blew a lock of hair out of her eyes. Even with it tied up, it was long enough to reach her waist in the back. Only the bandana kept her hair from getting thoroughly in her way. "Curls!" she said in aggravation. "Why do you think I let my hair get this long?"

That was the bad news. The good news was that all three units had made it safely to the field. The opposing forces of the Imperial Army looked more than a little surprised to see them arrive. They had been so sure that the Liberation Army lacked transport capabilities. The lieutenant in charge touched his Voice Relic and said, "Surrender!"

"Drop off!" came the retort from the white-haired paladin. "You think we came out here just to hand over the keys? Ha!"

Several soldiers on both sides had to muffle laughter. Even Matthias smiled. Laia's distaste for stupidity in military forces was quite known to everyone in the Liberation Army. Matthias calmly touched his Voice Relic and said, "Lady Laiaeariel is correct. We are not here to surrender. Prepare for engagement." To Tyrian only, he said, "You are now calling the shots, Lord Tyrian. You give the commands for attack. When I see the opening I seek, I will speak up. Laia has her orders."

There was already some unease on the Imperial side. Quite a few mages and fighters alike had recognized Laia's name; she had been very well known in Trinan. The Imperial Army had tried to recruit her for years.

Tyrian tucked down his nerves and took a breath. "Close-range, move in. Ranged, start your attack. Fire over the top of close-range to make it difficult for the enemy to move in. Emma, watch the mages. If they move in, switch targets."

The Imperial Army did not have ranged attack if you discounted the mages. They were forced to come in close to attack, and the arrows raining through the air made it risky. It was a risk they had no choice but to take.

The magic unit tried to move into position to attack Tyrian, but the Liberation Army's ranged unit promptly started showering them with arrows.

The fight between close-range units was bloody and fierce. Even outnumbered, the Liberation Army was far better trained, thanks to the additions of Gordon's troops. As several soldiers went down anyway, Matthias said calmly, "Healing magic, mark three."

Laia lifted the hand with her Music Relic and then pressed it to the mark of her Medicine Relic. A glowing purple circle of magic opened under her feet, and the combined symbols of Music and Medicine appeared over her head. A soft harmony of music swelled in the air and rippled across the entire field, bringing with it her healing powers. Even those whose wounds could have been mortal were promptly healed.

A ripple of agitation ran through the Imperial Army. The lieutenant's hands went damp with sweaty fear. "Take out the mages!" he ordered one of his close-range units. "Aim for the unit leaders! Take down either Lord Tyrian or Lady Laiaeariel!"

The unit went after the mages, which meant the other close-range unit was immediately overwhelmed by the Liberation Army. The several hundred still standing on the Imperial Side threw down their arms in surrender. "Lord Tyrian," Matthias said so that everyone heard him. "Why don't you show them what a Pure Relic can do? Link to Lady Laiaeariel's Music Relic."

Tyrian studied Laia and then looked at the hand she offered him. It was not her Music Relic. With a little smile, he touched his hand to hers. A combined runic circle that glowed with the purple musical notes of her power and the green and black fog of his opened around them both. The mark of the Devourer appeared in the air large enough to be seen by the enemy. What they did not see was the smaller mark of Lightning underneath it.

As massive bolts of lightning began to roll across the field and threaten to consume everyone out there, the lieutenant said hastily, "Yield! We yield! Throw down your arms!" he ordered his troops sharply. "We cannot stand to a Pure Relic!"

The Liberation Army moved in swiftly to take the enemy units under their control. Matthias joined Tyrian and Cassie to cross the field to where the enemy lieutenant waited. "A Pure Relic," Matthias murmured, "no, not likely. But other than a serious singeing, I do not believe they would have been decimated by a Lightning Relic's Electrical Storm spell, even from a Magician as talented as Laia."

"It just makes a big noise," Cassie agreed. "Very clever, Matthias."

"That's why I am here." He studied the lieutenant as he was escorted closer by Liberation soldiers. He appeared much younger than Matthias had been expecting. "Who stationed you here?" he asked.

The lieutenant sighed. "General Cutter requested I lead my units here. I don't believe she expected you to have a magic unit yet."

Speculatively, Matthias said, "I need to speak with General D'terio about General Cutter." His instincts told him that Diamond Cutter had deliberately chosen a green lieutenant so that the battle ended with the Liberation Army as the winner, and only Gordon could confirm if that was her style.

Tyrian looked at the lieutenant and said calmly, "Laws of engagement, lieutenant. You and your troops are free to retreat to Trinan, or you may join my side. We will not force your decision either way, but you must have noticed what Caschin looks like."

"I am loyal to the Empire!" the lieutenant said hotly. "I am not a traitor!"

"And neither am I." Tyrian sat up a little straighter and the sunlight glimmered across the glitter in his dark eyes. "I am loyal to my country, to my people. I fight for them. I will not serve a ruler who would turn a blind eye to the suffering of his land. Only a coward would take the safe route, take the route that allowed him to pretend everything would be all right if he ignored it. If the Emperor wishes to be a coward, then we will find a leader brave enough to make change when change is needed."

Silence fell for a long time and then, softly, the lieutenant said, "It hurts to see through the eyes of another what we have done. It is easy to say that we thought we were doing good for the people. But it is not easy to see that we were wrong." He lifted his head and said to his troops, "Laws of engagement. Those who want to return may do so. I stay."

Most of the troops chose to return, but more than a unit's worth remained behind. They removed their badges and hats, and they accepted the mantle of the Liberation Army. Tyrian did not begrudge those who chose to continue to believe blindly. Once blinded, finding your sight again was nearly impossible.

Laia grimaced suddenly and held up her Music Relic. "Pray for us," she said. "I'm sending the signal for Tedium to call us back. I'm throwing him out of the tower if I end up bald or something."

A few moments after she sent the signal, the troops began to disappear from the field. It wasn't long before only Tyrian, Cassie, Ewan, and Sean remained. They would be the party that went into Caschin to touch base with the mayor and search for those whose destinies aligned with their own. They wouldn't be able to transport back without the troops, but at least it would only be a one-way trip.

Sean remained remarkably quiet as they walked into the town, and Tyrian lightly clapped his shoulder. "You did a good job," he said softly. "It's scary out there, isn't it?"

Sean nodded. It made him feel more than a little better to know that Tyrian had been worried on the battlefield before. He had never experienced anything like that: people running, and shouting, and trying to kill each other. It was different when it was small combat.

Ewan caught Tyrian's eye and nodded slightly, indicating that Sean had taken out more than one enemy and that also added to his agitation. Even when the other person was trying to kill you, that first victory in battle was always the worst. "You served your Kaiten well," Ewan told Sean. "I'm proud of you, and Leonard will be too."

Sean opened his mouth and then closed it as the sound of a loud argument reached their ears. "Whoa." He peered into the windows of the Item Shop they stood beside and said, "Man, the two owners are going at it! Yikes!" He ducked as something hit the window. "Her aim is worse than Aunt Winifred's."

Ewan carefully opened the door and held his hat inside on the end of his sword. When nothing happened, he looked inside. The fighting was once more verbal, so he moved aside to let Tyrian enter.

The shop was split into two segments, which wasn't uncommon for some bigger shops. The woman stood behind a counter that had the universally recognized sign with a backpack on it that meant she sold traveling supplies. The man stood behind a counter with a sign that had a bottle on it, meaning he sold potions and herbs. Both owners were likely in their later years, but they acted as lively as someone half their age.

The woman spotted Tyrian first. "Oh!" She straightened hastily. "Lord Tyrian! What an honor to have you in our shop! My name is Sharmie. I'm a traveling supplies seller. The idiot across the room is Yagi. He sells potions."

"Ignore her," Yagi retorted. "She's just pissed because her boyfriend dumped her."

Sharmie's cheeks flushed. "I am not!"

Tyrian quickly held up his hands. "Hold it!" he ordered. They both fell silent and looked at him, and he shook his head in bemusement. "Is there any way to keep the peace in here? Why do you share a shop if you're going to fight like this?"

"No other space in town," Yagi grumbled.

Tyrian smiled. He could have asked them to join on the basis of their destiny, but he much preferred to be able to offer them something they needed or wanted. It was becoming a game he played with his Stars where they knew the real reason they joined, but they pretended they didn't. "There's room at the Liberation Army base. Actually, we don't have any Item Sellers at all, and we could assuredly use both of you."

Sharmie and Yagi shared a smile. They both turned to Tyrian and said, "We'd be honored!" Hopefully, Sharmie asked, "Would we get our own shops? No more sharing with each other?"

"To keep peace at the castle? Certainly! I'll have some soldiers come help you pack up and make the move out." He blinked in surprise as Sharmie handed him a wrist bracer. "What's this?"

"Latest style of accessory," she told him. "It has properties to increase your speed and strength. Some Armorers are working on taking it to the next level and actually turning these into armor for those who don't want full gear. I have this one because I was thinking of stocking them, but I'm not sure I want to branch into accessories."

Tyrian fastened the bracer around his left wrist and liked how it felt. He could also feel the tingling sensation that meant it was taking effect. "Maybe now I can outrun Cassie."

His lover just smiled. He hadn't even seen what she could fully do, and she intended on keeping it that way. As long as he stayed out of trouble, he didn't have to know just how strong and fast she really was. She had earned her rank for good reason.

Leaving the owners yet again fighting, the team moved down the street. There were signs to point them toward the mayor's place, so they followed them. The mood in Caschin had lifted dramatically, and people already worked to put their lives back in order. People brightened and called out happily to Tyrian, and some even cheered when they spotted him.

"It's the scarf," Ewan said gravely. "There's nothing else about you that stands out. You look completely normal otherwise."

The tension left Tyrian's shoulders and he smiled. Though he had no true 'favorites' among his Stars, he was closer to Ewan and Kyle than any others beside Cassie; not even Marian and Liang knew him as well. The two swordsmen had become his best friends, and even felt more like his brothers. "Thanks, Ewan." He shook his head. "It's been too easy. I'm waiting for the other shoe to drop."

A young man suddenly came out of nowhere. A cap of pale blue hair sat atop his pointed ears. He grabbed Tyrian's hands. "You're Lord Tyrian?" he asked eagerly. At the nod, he let out a quick breath of relief. "Great! Then my sister and the overprotective redhead we call a guitarist are at your castle in your army! My name is Virgo. I'm from Café Latte! I'm joining too, and you can't tell me no!"

He zipped off so fast that he kicked up a dust cloud. Sean and Ewan looked at each other in surprise. Cassie shook her head. Tyrian just smiled. "I think it just depends on your personality. And his doesn't surprise me. Taurus is very upbeat, Aries is very serious, so Virgo would be energetic. Who is the fourth member?"

"Capricorn, I think is his name." Cassie tapped a finger on her chin. "Based on your theory, we can assume he'll be the mature one of the lot. It would be ironic if he wasn't a Destined Star."

"Ironic, certainly, but that wouldn't stop him from joining anyway. We have his friends." Tyrian turned right at the street corner and spotted the mayor's house sitting between two others. It even had a sign outside. It said, '*Yes, I'm still in charge. Shut up and come inside.*'

There was an old man sitting on a bench outside the house, and pigeons covered the bench beside him. He was old indeed, with wrinkles inside his wrinkles and time sitting heavily on his shoulders but happily borne. Seeing him made a funny sensation flutter in Tyrian's stomach as he remembered, again, that he would never age. He might mature a little further, but not age. He would forever be young.

Cassie slipped her hand into his and laced their fingers together as she sensed his unease. Sean and Ewan had sensed it as well, and both were pretty sure they knew why. The former said softly, "Y'know, a lot of people would kill for a Pure Relic's eternity, so you have to count yourself lucky, Tyrian."

"*Lord* Tyrian," Ewan said with a thump of his hand on Sean's head.

"You don't call him that!" the boy complained.

"I'm older."

The old man sitting on the bench looked up and his faded gray-green eyes warmed. "Ha!" he cackled. "So there you are! Took you long enough. I thought I'd be buried before I ever met you." He shooed away several pigeons so that there was a place for Tyrian to sit down. "My name is Tod. If you want rumor and story, caught or spread, I'm your man! My cronies are spread out in other cities, so you'll meet them too." He nodded briskly. "Is that old fart Kell still scuttling around calling himself an informant?"

Tyrian hid a smile. "He certainly is, and he does a fine job at it. You know him."

"Known him for fifty years, I have." Tod thumped his cane on the ground. "Bastard stole my girlfriend when we were kids and then didn't have the decency to marry her. Said he got cold feet." He sighed gustily. "Ah, Grace. I still remember her smile." He eyed Tyrian. "You going to marry that lovely monk over there?"

"Eventually," Tyrian said amiably. "I'm not the one with cold feet."

Cassie felt her cheeks warm and ignored the two swordsmen who elbowed her lightly. She was still fighting for the courage to claim the eternity she could have for her own, let alone contemplating marriage along with it! It was so . . . permanent, and no matter how fiercely she wanted to be by her Kaiten's side, that didn't take away the nerves.

"Well," Tod said briskly, "since you're here, it must be my time. I'll make my way to the base. I'll touch base with old Kell. If you need to get a message anywhere, you can come to me. My pigeons never go off track."

"I'll leave it to you." Tyrian got to his feet and went to rejoin the others. He tucked Cassie under his arm and said into her ear, "One day at a time. One year, if necessary. As far as I'm concerned, it's just a formality. You're stuck with me for eternity, Cassie." He brushed his lips over her cheek. "Our stars will share the sky forever."

Ewan smiled as he watched them. There was something incredibly beautiful about the Kaiten and Kentei. Something in the way they smiled, and talked, and looked at one another. He couldn't imagine anyone looking at them and thinking they didn't belong together.

The door to the mayor's house stood open in the universally accepted gesture to enter, so they walked inside. "Hello?" Tyrian called.

A young woman dressed like a maid hurried forward. "Yes?" She broke off in shock as she spotted Cassie, and the monk stared at her equally. "Cassie?!"

"Yhalenia?!" Cassie grabbed her arm and swung her around. "What the hell are you doing?" she demanded softly. "You're an assassin! What are you doing here in the mayor's house? Don't tell me he's your target!"

"I was after a bandit in town," Yhalenia hastily assured her. "I took care of things the other day. I've been waiting for a chance to quit and make my way back to the Clan." She eyed Tyrian with interest. "However, plans may have changed."

Cassie instantly stepped in front of Tyrian. "Mine," she said softly, her voice so chilling that even Tyrian felt a little ripple of danger. He often forgot her lethality because she acted so gentle with him. "I'll make sure you have to change your methods if you even think of trying your wiles on him."

Yhalenia held up her hands quickly. "Easy, Master Cassie! I get the message!" She smiled. "But I have to be here anyway. That feeling." She touched her heart. "That feeling I felt when I looked at him. It means I'm destined too, doesn't it?"

Tyrian held out his relic hand. "I think we can find use for an assassin who would sooner charm an enemy than attack from the shadows. Subterfuge comes in all types, and we could use more of this one."

Yhalenia took his hand and the star briefly appeared on her shoulder. "Well, keep my cover. Far as Mayor Parkin is concerned, you needed a well-trained maid. Never know when I might have to come back here."

She hurried off, and Sean asked in awe, "She's a monk?"

"An assassin in fact, and a very good one," Cassie assured him. She shook her head. "I should have guessed! Ah, well. It'll be nice to have someone to train with. Just because she chooses to seduce her target rather than fight them doesn't mean she isn't fully trained. I've missed having someone to work out with." She scowled. "And we're going to test Tod's claims. What the hell is wrong with my father?"

Tyrian found himself laughing. She had more facets than a diamond, and he loved all of them. An eternity with her would be sweet indeed.

Chapter Eighteen

"Cry to me, sing to me of salvation."

Mayor Parkin was a humble man who felt more than a little awed and impressed to find himself with the legendary Tyrian Southerwind in his house. He promised to have the three units belonging to Caschin start wearing the colors of the Liberation Army and to send two of them back with Tyrian to increase the army. Even better, one of the units to go back with Tyrian was as yet another ranged unit. That gave him a total of three ranged and one magic, and the other six of his army were close-range combat.

They would have to do something about their lack of specialized Magicians who used attack magic, Tyrian thought to himself as they walked through town. He had no doubt that he would have some who were Destined Stars; he just hadn't yet found them. He could only hope they wouldn't take much longer to cross his path. Matthias was brilliant, but he could only pull so many tricks before someone would be on to them. Brute force would be needed soon enough.

Tyrian glanced up curiously as they passed by a darkened alley, and a sensation of power shivered down his back and resonated into his relic. He stopped walking and looked into the alley intently, his green eyes probing the gloom. "Who's there?" he asked softly.

A figure moved in the shadows and both Ewan and Sean drew their swords, their bodies tensed as they prepared to defend their leader. Cassie stepped slightly in front of Tyrian, and throwing stars appeared between her fingers.

The man who stepped out of the shadows did not reassure any of them. He was almost as big as Ewan, and he wore heavy-duty plate armor from head to heels. His helmet came down over his face entirely so that only his piercing blue eyes remained visible. A lock of golden hair could be seen under the visor of the helmet, but his age and his origins were impossible to determine. He could have been anyone, and he wore power in the same way others wore perfume.

Inexplicably, Tyrian trusted him. Instantly, without question, and immortally. He touched Cassie's arm to make her step aside and then lightly touched Ewan and Sean's wrists. "Swords down." He stepped forward and held up his relic hand. "I am Tyrian Southerwind."

There was a smile in the man's deep voice as he said, "I know." His voice seemed to rumble softly in the air, but pleasantly. It was a voice with an oddly strong cadence not dissimilar from Laia's. "I am called Agrime. It is the only name I know. My star is fixed, Lord Tyrian. It is my honor to serve the Kaiten."

Tyrian nodded slightly. There was a sadness inside Agrime that made him want to reach out. What had this warrior seen in his life to make him shut away so much? "But . . .?"

"But you are not yet ready for my power. You will know when you need me. When you see the Golden Scourge, you will know to return to me. I hunt the Scourge. I seek the lost remnants of the Summarian race."

Questions welled but Tyrian withheld them. "I will return," he promised. He turned and walked away, and his three Stars followed him. When they were out of earshot, he said softly, "I don't know much about the Summarians."

"No one does," Cassie admitted simply. "They simply vanished a thousand years ago. Some of their lost temples and cities have been since unearthed, but they yield precious little information. All we can know for sure is that they were a *very* powerful race, so powerful that they could not bear children with Humans."

Humans were the most versatile race on Oriku. They could crossbreed with all other species: Elves, Merfolk, Faeries, Mongra, Fliers, Dragons, and Grimalkin. That they could *not* crossbreed with the Summarians indicated the lost race had, indeed, been very special. "Could they crossbreed with others?"

"It would seem so, but the person in question had to be *very* strong. There are some people who are suspected to be descended of Summarian," Ewan offered, "but if they're Human, you know there's something else thrown into the mix somewhere. It's said that it would take at least five generations before the blood of the Summarian thinned enough to allow Human blood to enter. Of course, after a thousand years, you can bet we're well past the five generations mark. I doubt there are any purebloods left."

"A seeker of the lost remnants," Sean said softly. "I wonder what remnants he seeks."

Tyrian didn't know either, but he couldn't shake the feeling that his path and Agrime's were meant to cross more than once in the future. More than any other Star besides Cassie, Tyrian had the unmistakable feeling that he had been meant to meet the dark seeker. It was curious. What was the Golden Scourge?

By the time they reached the base once more, the new wall had nearly been completed. The towers were to be stationed like the numbers on a clock, with points at one, three, five, seven, nine, and eleven o'clock. Most of them had been built, though none of them had roofs yet. A new moat was being dug around the outside of the wall and it connected to the old moat via a short channel. The monsters were also happy to have more room, and they helpfully fished out any workers who fell in.

Since the push outward had taken the base up close to one of the primary rivers that ran through the Empire, watch towers were being stationed just in case the enemy decided to sail right up to their door. There was some talk of digging a diversion for the river that would allow them to have a dock *inside* the castle. Ship access might be critical since two of the checkpoints resided along the ocean. The river, heading south, eventually reached the sea.

Sharmie and Yagi got themselves their shops and got to work providing the items needed by soldiers and Stars alike. Evelyn's kitchen had been overhauled and the dining room was now a lively restaurant. The lightened burden on R.K.'s shoulders was noticed by all; he downgraded to just a bar at the inn, and no longer got the orders mixed up. He still fell asleep behind the counter, though, and Tyrian was still sure he needed a keeper himself.

Discussions launched over the best route to take toward claiming Dry Basin. It was large, it was further away, and it was guarded by a lot more units. They had ten units around the city, and Tyrian also had ten units, but the lack of specialization in magic left them highly disadvantaged.

It was early in the morning a few days after Caschin's freedom. Tyrian was in the meeting room with Matthias, Cherry, and Gordon. Ewan and Kyle had come and gone multiple times; they were helping train the soldiers who used swords. Cassie occasionally came by to make sure Tyrian was not overworking. She was otherwise training with Yhalenia. After watching one match, Tyrian had been suitably impressed by monks in general, and his Kentei in particular.

Noticing Matthias rubbing his leg, Tyrian frowned. "Is it bothering you more today?"

"Every day seems to make it worse," Matthias admitted. "Do not let it worry you, Lord Tyrian. My brain is as fit as it ever was. However, I may not be able to ride with the Army for much longer." He looked at Cherry. "You will have to be my voice, Cherry."

It was a bit daunting, but she nodded instantly. "I will do my best."

The doors suddenly banged open, and Yumi and Taurus tried to rush in. They got stuck in the doorway and then broke free and scrambled inside. "We're under attack!" they both blurted.

Tyrian shot to his feet. "What?"

"We were in the tower," Taurus said breathlessly. "Yumi was showing me the really fun gadget she built that could fly like a bird. We were watching it fly in circles when we spotted a shadow in the horizon. It really quickly became an army. They have General Yureny's flag!"

"So Samantha Yureny has been dispatched directly." Matthias sat back in his chair. "She didn't just transport in outside the gate."

"It's not her style," Gordon said. "She prefers her enemy to know she approaches. She once said that winning a battle by default was not a win at all."

"Is she from the Commune of Soldiers?" Tyrian asked curiously. "That sounds like something I've heard Kyle and Ewan say before."

"Quite so." Gordon got to his feet. "How many units did it look like, ladies?"

Yumi bounced on her toes, yet her face was worried. "I heard one of the soldiers saying there were nine, including two magic." She grabbed Tyrian's arm when he patted her head. "I can help! Let me help!"

"You're too young, Yumi," he reminded her gently. "You're not allowed on the field." At ten, she could enter small combat only.

"No, but I can do other things! I have an invention that can help, I mean it!"

Matthias opened his mouth but Tyrian held up a hand. He knelt down to Yumi's height and looked at her seriously. "What invention do you have? I know you're just as good as Tedium, if not better. I haven't heard *you* blowing anything up."

She took a deep breath. "It's a machine that makes mirages. I can make copy images of things. You know how people said they thought the inn was haunted? That was my fault! I was testing it out, and the copies weren't solid enough. But I've tweaked it. Unless you're *really* close to them, you don't know they're not real! I know it could help!"

There was a shrewd look in Matthias' eyes as he rubbed his chin. "How many people can you copy at one time, Yumi? Do you suppose the machine might be able to make a copy of an entire unit? Maybe multiple?"

She tilted her head and her hat fell over her eyes. She shoved it back into place quickly. "I think I can do it!" she said firmly. "I haven't tried it yet. But I tested it on the flock of sheep we used for the Mechanoportal."

"Those sheep are going to have issues," Cherry grumbled.

"Yumi," Matthias said softly, "you may just have handed us another win."

Samantha Yureny was quite impressed when she saw the state of the Liberation Army's base. She had to give Tyrian credit for choosing the old castle as his territory; it was situated perfectly with how close it was to the river, and his way of expanding the walls was evidence of a shrewd mind at work. He was a chip off his father's block.

She had almost left her magic units behind, but she wanted to see what he and his strategist could really do. Outwitting Gordon was clever to be sure, and Samantha was dying to match wits with the Kaiten Star. She had always adored Tyrian, and she thought Destiny could have chosen no better emissary.

The Liberation Army suddenly appeared on the field, the units coming from within the walls in a well-ordered formation. She recognized many of the unit leaders from the close-range units, including Laia Mitakel, Ewan Grizmar, and Kyle Raitels. In one of the ranged units, she recognized Gordon. The magic unit had the young protégé of Matthias', Master Cassie of the Monk Clans, and Tyrian Southerwind. She lightly touched her Voice Relic. "Well met, Lord Tyrian."

"Greetings, General Yureny." His voice sounded calm. "Out for a morning walk? You're quite a ways from home. To what do we owe the pleasure of the visit?"

Clever, clever boy. "I thought I might see if you were willing to surrender and end all this fighting. Emperor Albanion seems to believe I have what it takes to bring you down from your high horse, and as I outnumber you, it does look as if I have the winning hand. Do you play chesstac, Lord Tyrian? I believe this is called a check."

To be in check in chesstac was to have either your king or queen close to being forced into a corner of the board. If that occurred, you lost. Tyrian had played chesstac for many years and enjoyed it. "Really?" he countered. "I don't see myself anywhere near a corner."

Samantha turned her gaze toward the cap of red hair riding beside him. Her voice gentled. "It is an honor to meet you, Cherry. I hear you are Professor Matthias' most prized student. He must trust you a great deal to send you out to face me. Or is his health failing him once more?"

Tyrian lightly rested a hand on Cherry's back and she found her courage. She lifted her chin. "His health wanes lately, but I believe I am capable of leading Lord Tyrian wisely. Do not let my age fool you, General. I am a worthy opponent."

"Tough kid," Samantha's main lieutenant murmured.

"Indeed! Well, let the engagement commence then." She turned to her troops. "Magic units, move in toward Lord Tyrian. We have the advantage. Close-range, go after close-range. Be wary of those ranged units on their side. Get in close and their arrows and daggers will not be so effective. And watch out for General D'terio! He has the longest sniper range of anyone you'll meet."

The close-range units rushed toward each other across the field and the fight started swiftly and violently. Cherry watched intently to study how Samantha's troops were trained, and she discovered that they did not strike anyone who was already down. Because the Liberation Army operated under the same principle, those who went down, but went down alive, stayed in that condition. Only a handful of soldiers on either side didn't get back up again.

"Ranged units," Tyrian ordered his troops, "aim for General Yureny. Shoot to wound, not kill. We want her alive. General D'terio, I leave it in your hands."

One of the close-range units on Tyrian's side was taken down entirely by a well-placed blast of magic from Samantha's units. Laia, rather than lose her soldiers, immediately held up her hand in a gesture of yield. It removed her unit from capable battle, only able to wait out the outcome. She did not wait passively and instead began to work on healing her soldiers.

As units closed in toward Tyrian, Cherry said calmly into her Voice Relic, "General Yureny, we ask for surrender."

Samantha arched a brow. "Oh, do tell. Why should I surrender when I am winning?"

"Because you're not winning at all." She held up a hand. "Second wave, report in."

To Samantha's immense shock, three units appeared on the field and flanked her in entirely. One was of magic users, another ranged, and the third close-range. She recognized none of the unit leaders. Every arrow in the ranged unit aimed directly at her, and when she saw a glint of sunlight, she turned her head sharply to see Gordon kneeling in the field with his crossbow calmly aimed at her heart. She knew full well that they would rather take her alive, but calling their bluff would only delay the inevitable. She drew her sword and threw it onto the field. "Yield."

Gordon and Ewan immediately crossed the field to take her captive. Ewan picked up her fallen sword and held it out to her as she dismounted her horse. "Here, hold onto this. After all the trouble you went to name it, you might as well not get it dirty."

She smiled and re-sheathed the weapon at her side. Engraved in the familiar place was a name that seemed oddly familiar to several people, though they could not place why. "Well met, Ewan Grizmar. I've heard much of you." Her eyes darkened with empathic pain. "I would have returned to the Commune to give my aid if I hadn't been dispatched to the City-States at the time. General Cutter went on my behalf." She glanced up as she heard footsteps and found Tyrian approaching with Cherry and Cassie. She smiled as she looked at the monk warrior. She should have known that no normal woman would ever work for Tyrian. She would have to be a stubborn sort to handle him. "Lord Tyrian, well played." She looked at Cherry. "But you have to tell me where those units came from! I thought you were maxed on eight."

Cherry suddenly grinned. Into her Voice Relic, she said, "Yumi, kill it."

"Okay!" came the cheerful response.

The three 'units' suddenly disappeared into the morning sun and left behind the unit leaders . . . and a lot of sheep. Samantha blinked, blinked again, and then suddenly began laughing. "I surrendered to a flock of sheep! Well played, Cherry! Well played, indeed!"

"Please come with us into the base," Tyrian offered. "We have much to talk about. Your troops may go free if they so wish."

Samantha didn't get the chance to give the order. Her main lieutenant muttered very distinctly, "Don't even think about it. We're staying. We'll sit out here and play cards until you tell us we're officially in the Army."

Tyrian hid a smile as he led the way back in toward the castle with Cherry, Cassie, Gordon, Ewan, and Samantha following him. In a soft voice, Gordon asked Samantha, "Why don't you just marry Lieutenant Colin, Sam? The man is miserable."

She rolled her eyes. "He already hates taking orders from me. He'd hate it more if he was married to me."

"Should we make sure your room is big enough for two anyway?" Ewan asked blandly. He grinned when she shot him a dirty look. "C'mon, you can't tell me I'm not right. You named your sword after him! And we both know your bullshit about why you won't get married has nothing to do with his ego. It's that crap about the generals of the Empire being 'distracted' by their loved ones. You saw what Tyrian's dad went through."

"Ewan." Tyrian shook his head. "Your love life is your own, General Yureny." He suddenly smiled. "But the government we hope to instigate will remove that barrier, if it is indeed one." He let the guards open the meeting room doors and then walked inside. "General Yureny, meet Matthias Goldwind. Matthias, this is Samantha Yureny."

"Your protégé served you well, Professor Matthias," Samantha told the strategist. "She didn't lose her composure and handled herself with the skill of someone twice her age."

Cherry flushed happily as she hurried to sit down. The others took seats as well, and Tyrian lightly drummed the fingers of his relic hand on the table. "I am sure you have questions for me, General. I will answer them to the best of my ability."

"For starters, how did you pull that off out there?"

Tyrian smiled. "One of my Destined Stars is a ten-year-old genius. She invented a device that did exactly what you saw it do. I expect Yumi to surpass Tedium's skill within a few years, and so does he."

"And that leads me to another question." She studied the relic burned into his skin. It was an oddly frightening design, and yet also very familiar. She felt as if she had always known she would see it. More than ever, she felt the fierce tug bringing her to his cause. She needed to protect and defend, to carry his banner into battle so the burden was not his alone. "How do you know your Destined Stars?"

He smiled and held out his hand. "I just do." When her hand lightly touched his, the star appeared on her shoulder. "We share the skies," he told her very seriously. "Your star follows mine. I can't do this alone. You've surely seen the cities, seen what has happened to our people. Lady Blaine was the catalyst to cause this change, but I believe it would have eventually happened anyway. It just happens to have fallen on our shoulders. Lend me your strength, General Yureny."

"Sam or Samantha," she corrected absently as she let go and sat back. She frowned thoughtfully. "It explains so much, it truly does, that I am also a Destined Star. From the day I met you, there was just something about you that tugged at me. And it's not just me." She looked at Gordon. "It would be all of us. All of us always panicked if you were in trouble or hurt."

"Did he get in trouble a lot?" Cassie asked.

Tyrian smiled. "Unintentionally. Liang swears I gave him and my father all their gray hair. I just wanted to learn things. It wasn't my fault that I didn't realize my curiosity might be hazardous to my health."

"And our sanity!" Samantha blew out a breath. "I am a general of the people. I serve the people. They want freedom from tyranny. I can do nothing less than give it. I wish to follow your path as well, Lord Tyrian. You may count on me to help lead your units into battle."

Cherry looked at Matthias excitedly. "Doesn't that mean that we've just doubled our army?"

"If her troops will follow her, yes," he said. "They will be given the option of leaving, but I am quite certain they will follow General Yureny just as General D'terio's units followed him." He sat back in his chair. "I must wonder what the Emperor will do next. He has the other four Lower Generals on the checkpoints. High General Southerwind has been restricted to the castle." He looked at Samantha. "Does he believe that General Southerwind will seek to aid Tyrian as well, and bring all twenty of his units with him?"

"It is possible," Samantha said instantly. "But Emperor Albanion is not who we should be most concerned with."

"Lady Blaine." Tyrian tapped his fingers on the table. "Tell me what you know about her, Sam. She killed my brother for this bit of glass I bear."

Finding out Blaine was behind Ben Southerwind's murder came as no shock for Samantha. She had never liked Blaine from the beginning. No amount of beauty on the outside could hide the ugliness inside. "She is frighteningly powerful. I've seen her use magic and spells the likes of which no other person can, and without a relic I will add! I believe she truly has visions, but I also believe she manipulates them to her needs. Why did she kill Ben?"

"The Pure Relic."

"Then she wants eternity." Laia was leaning in the doorway with her arms crossed. "You spoke of her looking like a haggard old woman when she attacked Ben. That may be her true form. She can only maintain her youthful appearance by subsisting on the lifeforce of others. A Pure Relic would give her back the youth she wants."

"Would it reverse her age?" Tyrian asked in surprise.

"A Pure Relic preserves a person at the peak of their personal maturity. It's conceivable that it would reverse age her."

"I think an investigation into Lady Blaine's history is needed." Matthias looked at Ewan. "Have Kell start looking, and have him look at the other countries as well. She can't have just come from out of nowhere." As Ewan left the room, Matthias eyed Laia. "You have uncanny timing, Laia. What brought you here at this moment?"

"Oh, there's a Kraken in the river that wants to talk to Tyrian."

Silence fell. Then, "How can she say that with a straight face?" Gordon muttered. "A *Kraken* wants to *talk* to Lord Tyrian?"

"You heard me." Laia linked her hands behind her head as she turned away. "It was quite polite too. Even tossed one of the soldiers back on shore when he fell off the dock."

Tyrian got to his feet. "Well, I guess I had better see what it wants. Cassie?"

"Oh, I'm coming, if only for entertainment." She fell into step beside him as they left the meeting room and began to make their way toward the dock in the process of being built. The channel from the river was only half dug, but it was still the shortest route to the river.

When her fingers slipped into his, he let out a long breath. "I have a bad feeling, Cas. I can feel it. There's something bad stirring. I've never felt this before." He pressed his free hand to his heart. "Dread. There's no other word for it."

Closely bound to Destiny as he was, it wasn't too surprising for him to begin to feel fluctuations in the flow of things. She didn't have to like it, though. There was enough weight on his shoulders without him needing to begin to sense things like this. "I'm here for you," she said softly.

He turned and caught her in his arms and buried his face in her hair for a moment. "Thank you," he said softly. He eased back and kissed her tenderly but by no means lightly. He had no care for the fact that they stood in the courtyard surrounded by their friends and soldiers. In fact, if there hadn't been a Kraken knocking on the door, he would have quite happily carried Cassie back to their tower. They had an elevator now.

Watching from the meeting room window, Gordon murmured, "They glow."

"Beautiful, isn't it?" Matthias picked up his cup of tea and ignored the throbbing pain in his leg. It gained force with every day that passed. He fought it. He would see the end of this war come Hell or high water. "I imagine once Lady Cassie has her own eternity, we will see something truly spectacular." At the curious look from Gordon, he smiled. "You will see what I mean soon enough, General."

"Get a room," Kyle said dryly as he went past Tyrian and Cassie.

Tyrian reluctantly released Cassie, but it took all his willpower. She was flushed and very kissed, and so outrageously sexy that it drove him mad. His hands lingered enough as he stepped back that her eyes darkened to midnight blue. "Kraken," he said, his voice strained.

She took a long breath and pressed her fingers to her lips. The power of his kiss eclipsed any power any relic could ever produce, and as he grew stronger, his intense need for her seemed to grow as well. What would it be like when she claimed eternity as well? She wasn't sure if they would survive, though she was willing to try.

His breath hissed out. "Stop smiling at me like that."

Her lashes lowered as she walked past him. "Like what, Tyrian?" Her voice was a little huskier and deliberately enticing. She had never before tried to seduce him, and it was much easier than she had imagined. She didn't feel shy or awkward at all. It was hard to be shy with a man who knew you so intimately.

He stuffed his hands into his pockets as he moved to catch up. "You're going to get in trouble when I get you alone, my lovely monk."

Her lips curved further. "I'll hold you to that."

When they reached the place where the river ended at the half-built channel, it wasn't hard to mistake the Kraken at all. It very patiently floated in the water, watching for their approach. Krakens were among the most intelligent of beasts in the world, though they typically caused more trouble than not. Few spoke any sentient languages and were only understood by someone wearing a Listening Relic.

This Kraken, however, said very politely, "Greetings." Its voice, sounding male, didn't necessarily mean that he was actually a male Kraken, but it was a strong possibility.

"Greetings." Tyrian crouched at the edge of the half-built dock, fascinated as he felt the tug inside. It truly took all kinds. "I'm Tyrian. You were looking for me?"

"Yes, I wish to help your fight." The Kraken waved one of his eight arms in the air. He was mostly shaped like an octopus, but his head was of a different shape, covered in feathers, and he had a beak. "The Imperial Army hunts my kind for sport. For sport! They wouldn't do that to Dragons, now would they?"

"Dragons would eat them," Cassie said dryly.

The Kraken sulked. "So we're more civilized. Lord Tyrian, please allow me to fight at your side. When the battles take to the sea, I will guide your ships. And I will defend this port with my very life."

Tyrian's relic glowed softly and a star glowed across the top of the Kraken's head. "Do you have a name?" he asked.

"Infine, I am called." He fluttered his arms. "I would bow like you two-legged races, but I have no waist."

Tyrian smiled. "The thought is appreciated. Thank you, Infine. I know I can count on you to protect us from the sea. I'm sure no one knows it better."

"Naturally not!" Infine sank down underwater and disappeared under the dock to lurk like a shadow. Barely any bubbles surfaced. If you didn't know he was there, you would have never seen him. Any Imperial unit dumb enough to sail up to the castle would be in for quite a surprise.

Cassie tilted her head. "In the end, it really is easy. How many does that make, Tyrian?"

"Including you and me, forty-one. I don't expect it to be easy forever. It's not easy to accept, and I know that some of you are still a bit flabbergasted by the way you feel." Wind ruffled his black hair as his eyes stared at a future only his eyes could see. "But I need you. All of you. I think that if any one of you was not here, a piece of me would be missing too."

She wrapped her arms around his waist and rested her head on his chest. She had a strong feeling that that was what Tanelia had meant when she had said he needed to unlock his relic as well as find his Destined Stars. A relic was only as powerful as the heart of its owner. His heart grew stronger with every Star, and therefore so did his relic. It would not be long until the second level unlocked, and she feared it. What sort of toll would it take on him then?

He suddenly lifted her off her feet and she held on tightly. "It's the middle of the day!" she protested breathlessly as he purposefully carried her toward their tower while people grinned at them. "We have strategy to discuss with Matthias!"

"It can wait."

Sensing his stubbornness showing its presence, she sighed and gave up with a laugh. Some fights weren't worth fighting.

Chapter Nineteen

"In the dark night, evil creeps across the face of the moon."

It was the middle of the night. Cities slept across Trinan. The moon hung high in the sky. Blaine stood in her tower and stared out at the moonlight scenery. A chill wind blew through the open windows but she did not shiver. She turned from her window and looked toward the one that stood on the other side. Sitting on the edge was a bat. "So you came."

A sinister red glow flickered and the bat became a man. He was tall and beautiful, and his long dark hair was tied at his neck. His body, though perhaps not expressly powerful, was still trim and fit. A woman would look happily at him more than once . . . unless she saw his eyes.

Even Blaine did not like his eyes. They were narrowed, cruel, and dead. The smoky gray color should have been appealing, but there was nothing inside it. His eyes were as dead as his heart. The only heart that beat in the room belonged to Blaine.

The man bowed elegantly as his dark cloak flared around his body. He took Blaine's proffered hand and brought it to his lips. A bit of light glinted off his teeth as he smiled. "I always try to answer when a beautiful woman summons me. Are we having a drink together?"

"Save your wiles, Lord Beelzebub." She tugged her hand free. "My blood is of no use to you." She sat down on the side of her bed and crossed her legs. The silk of her robe slid over her skin enticingly.

He eyed her legs with a touch of wistfulness. He had always liked long legs on a woman. They ran so fast that the chase became that much sweeter. He knelt briefly and then stood. "Why have you summoned me, Lady Blaine? I would not think that any deliberately ask for my presence. How did you find me?"

"You have been in hiding," she said coolly, "but you leave a trail when you seek prey. I am offering you a deal. The Imperial Army will turn a blind eye to anything you choose to do if you will remove the thorn in our side. I want Tyrian Southerwind's head." Hate gleamed across her eyes. "And his relic. The rest of him is yours to deal with. I know you don't like men, but the blood of a Kaiten Star must surely interest you."

The blood of a Pure Relic user. He was, indeed, intrigued. "Is that my repayment? Ha. Lady Blaine, surely you can offer more. Why should I care if the Imperial Army pursues me or not? They have not caught me in five years, have they?"

"Let me put it this way: I care not for the Empire. It may rise, it may fall, it may become your own personal buffet of terror and blood." Her eyes narrowed. "I want only the Pure Relic. When I have that, you may do whatever you wish with this pitiful land. I have something more important to tend to."

The thought appealed. He was tired of hiding. His castle buried in the mountains would look so much lovelier in the middle of the country. His own personal valley. He would turn it to endless night. "You do have my attention, my lady. Is there anything else I should know?"

"Ewan Grizmar is a Destined Star."

His dead eyes lit with hate and anticipation alike. "My loose thread," he purred sibilantly. "How delightful. 'The last survivor of the Commune.'" He chuckled deeply, though the sound held no amusement. "The one person I was looking to destroy was the very one who survived. Lady Blaine, my services are yours. How should I draw out our enemy?"

Her teeth bared in her smile. "Do what you do best, my lord."

When his teeth flashed in his smile, the moonlight glinted off fangs. "I was hoping you would say that." He drew his cloak around himself as he turned and a flash of light transformed him once more to a bat. He flew out the open window, and the chill wind went with him.

Blaine shut the windows and went to bed. She had no doubt that she would sleep quite peacefully now. Things were looking up.

Chapter Twenty

"And when I cry, the tears are red with the way you have made me bleed."

The feeling that woke Tyrian a few days later was indefinable. All he knew was that he was suddenly awake. The room felt quiet and peaceful. The dim light from the fireplace flickered over the top of the wall. The balcony doors stood partially open and let in the sounds of the night. He could hear the wind and he could hear the chirping of crickets. It was a chilly night if they were to be believed.

Cassie slept in his arms, and one of hers wrapped around him protectively. Her breathing was soft and even, her face unlined with worry. Whatever had woken him did not come from her.

He lightly skimmed his fingers down her cheek, marveling that she was truly his. He couldn't even really remember what his life had been before she had come into it. From that first moment when they had met inside the castle, he had known this moment was inevitable, though he would never have imagined everything would be so complicated.

She stirred as he slid from bed, and he softly brushed a kiss over her lips. She snuggled into his pillow, and his heart clenched fiercely with emotion. If there was any bright spot in his world, it was his Kentei lover.

Still unsure of what was wrong, he got dressed and left the tower. The elevator was silent as it moved, and it was swift. The guards outside the tower looked a little surprised to see him when it was barely midnight, but neither said anything. They had learned that their leader was an unusual and gifted man. Everything he did had a purpose, even if he didn't know it.

Hands tucked in his pockets, Tyrian left the castle and ambled into the city. It was mostly quiet with only the occasional light on. There were lights on at the inn, yet that wasn't so unusual. People traveled to and from the base frequently as they came from cities that had been liberated. The base *was* a city now, and he was still trying to figure out what to call it.

He went into the inn and sighed as he saw R.K. asleep at the counter. He fetched a blanket and tucked it around his shoulders. With a shake of his head, he went into the bar area. Somehow, he was entirely unsurprised to find Ewan there. The older male sat at a table with a glass of ale and watched the moon quietly. "You should be asleep," Tyrian scolded.

Ewan smiled crookedly. "Look who's talking." He gestured to the other chair. "Join me."

Tyrian grabbed a glass from the bar and walked over to sit down. He poured himself some of the ale and then sat back to study Ewan. He had never known him to drink alone, let alone this late at night. At the least, he understood better the feeling that had woken him. There was pain in Ewan's eyes as he looked out the window.

Tyrian said nothing, and the silence remained companionable. After a while, Ewan asked, "Has anyone told you yet about what happened at the original Commune of Soldiers?"

"No. I know the bare facts about it. And I know you are the sole survivor other than Kyle, but he was nearly dead, so he doesn't count."

Ewan looked at him, though he wasn't truly surprised. "Did Kyle tell you?"

"It was just a hunch. The way you look when the subject comes up. And Kell mentioned that you pulling Kyle out of hell was much like what he had once done for you. It just made sense." Tyrian let out a long breath. "What did happen?"

"The main Commune was located in the mountains. We were the biggest and the best. Probably about ten thousand people lived there. I was one of them. Kyle was another." He swirled his ale broodingly. "Kyle is a more diverse swordsman than I am because of his magic, but I'm more skilled overall. I'm also older. I was considered a full warrior by the time I was sixteen, which was quite unheard of. Kyle was eighteen when he was given the right, which is above average but not truly unusual. The average age is twenty."

"You could be an adult by law, but not a true adult in the Commune's eyes."

"Yeah." Ewan took a deep breath. "I was an adult, so I promptly went out into the world. I was sixteen and stupid. Cities accepted me as an adult despite my age, so I did stupid adult things." He briefly saluted Tyrian with his glass. "Discovered the joys of women, so I can't say it was all bad."

"And?"

"People talked about me. About my skill, about how young I was. Mostly with respect and awe. You'd think that was a great thing, but apparently it wasn't." His eyes darkened and his hands tightened on the glass. "I met a Millennium Vampire named Riki. She was amazing. She looked like a normal person, but she sunburned quickly. She ate only natural foods, and her main nourishment came from blood. I offered mine because we were friends. We were hanging out together, and it was more convenient. And as long as her blood didn't get into *me*, I was in no danger of being converted." He shook his head. "Weirdest thing I've ever experienced. I didn't even notice she was biting me and I was watching her."

His breath unraveled hard. "She recoiled fairly hard as soon as she tasted my blood. Not in fear for herself. Fear for me. She grabbed my hands and, and I remember this clearly, she looked me in the eye and said 'the Night sky watches you with the eyes of Eternity.'"

"The sky watches you?"

"Confused me too. Then she told me a legend. The legend of the Midnight Moon Sword. A sword so powerful that it has a sentient will. It has the power to strike down rogue Vampires and so is treated with great respect by the Millennium Valley. No hands had ever wielded it. But she sensed the sword's presence near me. She said it had chosen me to be its first wielder. And that because it had, I was in danger."

He closed his eyes. "There was a rogue known as Beelzebub. His name said it all. He had chosen to give himself to evil. Some think there was no giving; he was always evil. He just finally embraced it. He had preyed on cities across the world. If someone disappeared in the night, they were often found dead the next morning. Drained of blood and their hearts carved out. Selene, the Mistress of the Millennium Vampires, had told him he would find his justice at the end of the Midnight Moon Sword."

Tyrian's lungs froze as he began to understand. "Which wasn't a problem, until he started hearing about this great swordsman who was doing many things that a boy his age shouldn't be able to do. Someone of legendary skill."

"I just had this . . . feeling. God, Tyrian. I can't describe it. I was sick and I was terrified. I just knew something terrible was happening. I rushed back across the country to the Commune. Riki went with me. When we got to the Commune, it was midnight." His eyes opened, dark and blind. "And the night was red.

"Blood ran down the streets, dripped from eaves. Bodies lay like discarded dolls with holes in their chest. I could hear those who still lived. They were screaming. I still hear them screaming. I found Kyle. He was alive. It was a miracle amid a massacre. As I was dragging him out, I saw *it*."

Tyrian covered Ewan's wrist and held on. His stomach rolled but he did not protest. Too long had it been bottled inside his friend. "Beelzebub."

"It looked like a man. It walked like a man. It even talked a man. But it was a monster. He saw me too. And he laughed. He stood there over a pile of bloody hearts and laughed at me. 'You're late,' he told me. 'I started the party but the guest of honor was missing.'" The glass cracked as Ewan's hands tightened. "He had killed the entire village just to find me. I lost it. I went after him, even with Riki shouting at me not to. I did good at first. I even wounded him. But he was rogue. I had a normal sword. To be honest,

I don't remember what happened when he came after me.

"I suddenly opened my eyes and he was standing over me. My chest hurt. It was horrendous. When I looked down, he had actually cut me open while I was alive. He wanted me to see him take my heart." The glass shattered between his fingers and the fragments drifted to the table. "I threw my sword in his face. Gouged out an eye. While he was screaming, I hauled my ass away. I grabbed Kyle and dragged him out of there. Riki helped me escape. I passed out with the screams in my ears. Woke up a week later in another Commune. Most of my wound had been healed, but the scar lingered. Kyle was recovering fine with no marks remaining. He didn't even remember the events; Beelzebub had gotten to him in the first wave of attack. Probably went right after him because he was my friend."

Tyrian got to his feet and walked to Ewan's side. He wrapped his arms around the larger male's shoulders and held on tightly, hurting for him. His throat was tight with pain. He couldn't even imagine how Ewan was sane. This war was so much less than what Ewan had endured, and Destiny thought *Tyrian* needed help? "What happened to Riki?"

"She hides within the Valley now. She does not dare emerge unless Beelzebub is gone for good. He would destroy her, and she would stand no chance. I haven't spoken to her in five years, though I think I've sensed her presence now and then." He let out a long breath and leaned against Tyrian. "Kyle helped me get drunk and get through it. I've always been aware that Beelzebub is out there, but at the least, he has not come for me. He hides away, so I hear." His eyes opened and the promise of violent revenge churned. "If I ever see his face, I'm finding that Midnight Moon Sword, and I am cutting out *his* heart."

Tyrian hugged him tighter. "Here I stand worried about things much less than your pain, and you're still laughing and smiling."

Ewan straightened up and turned to scowl at him. "I didn't tell you to make you think that your suffering is less than mine." He tugged Tyrian down into a chair. "Tyrian, look at what you're going through. Look at it from our eyes. See what you've gone through. What you're *still* going through, and what you have yet *to* go through. It eclipses anything that happened in that Commune. Will I forget? No. But I didn't have to go through months of endless war, the needs and hopes of every life in the country on my shoulders. I didn't need to always be strong and pretend that I didn't want the world to go away. I didn't have to look at the destruction of thousands of lives and know that I was the one who had to fix it because no one else could."

Tyrian shook his head and Ewan rapped him smartly. "Shut up," he ordered. He dusted the shards off his hands and grabbed another glass to pour fresh ale out. "It's two completely separate experiences, and you can't compare them in your head. Look at it this way. What hurts more? Falling down or falling down stairs? Both hurt, but the stairs take longer and do more damage in the end. I fell down. You're still going head over heels down those stairs, and they just keep getting longer." He took a drink of his ale and then smiled. "And anyway, I get to grow old and cranky and tell war stories to my grandkids. I'm luckier than you."

Tyrian had to smile. "Will you grow a beard?"

Ewan rubbed his chin. It was rough, but he kept the threat of a beard away. "I tried that last year. Ophelia laughed her ass off at me every time she saw me." His smile turned sheepish. "Marian called me a grizzly man. Let's just say the beard didn't help!" He tossed back the ale and then got to his feet. "Let's walk some of this off. I think I can finally sleep."

As they fell into step together, Tyrian murmured, "Night isn't restful for you. You know too well what evil lurks in it."

"I always fear the day when evil can walk in the daylight."

A guard suddenly leaned over the castle wall and said urgently, "Lord Tyrian! Come up here quickly!"

Tyrian climbed up to the top of the wall and looked in the direction that the guard pointed. He spotted instantly what the guard had. There was a small group of people running flat out for the base. Tyrian's eyes, much sharper than average because of his relic, were able to clearly see that all of them had been wounded.

He leapt down off the wall. "Wake Halkern, Marian, and Laia!" he ordered another guard. "Lower the gate!" he shouted to the ones in charge of the mechanism. He turned as more guards approached. "Roust R.K. and have him clear space at the inn!"

The gate lowered swiftly and Tyrian ran out of it as fast as he could. Ewan was right on his heels. When they saw the state of the lot, Ewan began to curse violently under his breath. There were two adults, one teenager, and two children. All of them looked bloody and wounded. The teenager, a girl, was nursing what looked like a broken arm. The little boy clutched in the woman's arms was barely breathing. "Please!" the woman begged. "You have to help us!"

The teenager fell and Tyrian lifted her into his arms. "You're safe," he said softly. "Come inside, quickly!"

By the time they reached the inn, the city had stirred and people were waking as they heard the commotion. Marian got to the inn first and paled when she saw the tableau. She spotted Laia and said urgently, "Go to

Yagi's shop! Wake him and get the herbs we need!" While Laia diverted and went another direction, Marion picked up the little girl.

Halkern arrived moments later and took the boy from the woman. Kyle and Liang had arrived as well, and Kyle took the teenager from Tyrian. Ewan and Liang helped the man down the hall toward the rooms that Marian and Halkern had gone to. The man was in no condition to walk on his own; his leg looked a bloody mess and gouges bit into his chest.

The woman was relatively unharmed and had only minor injuries to mark her body. She stood in the lobby, shaking like a leaf, her brown eyes wide with the shock settling in. Tyrian felt a sudden powerful fury sucker punch his soul and realized that he looked upon another Destined Star. A warning pulse of deadly magic flickered over his relic but his hands stayed gentle as he forced her to sit down in a chair. He knelt beside her to be less of an imposing figure. "What's your name?" he asked softly.

"Persephone." Tears slid through the blood staining her face. "I'm a pub owner. Best drinks in the Empire. Our city is out of the way, but people would come just to try my concoctions."

Laia knelt on her other side and began to softly and efficiently wipe the blood from her face so she could see the wounds. Her musical voice sounded soft and soothing as she said, "I've been to your pub, Persephone. Your youngest wasn't yet born. You balanced a drink on your belly and dared anyone to flip a coin into it without knocking it over. The only one who could was a kid."

Persephone's shoulders relaxed slightly as she responded to the power of Laia's voice. "I told him to come back when he was old enough to get his free drinks." Her lips trembled. "There's nothing to go back to. It's gone. Like a river of blood washing it away . . ."

Matthias stepped into the doorway with Ewan, but neither said a word. Tyrian covered Persephone's hand gently. "The Imperial Army?"

Her laugh was more of a sob. "Oh, if only it had been so! They were occupying the town, but they just up and left at sunset a few days ago. We thought that maybe we were no longer important enough to need a guard. We numbered only a few hundred." Her eyes clouded. "The moon had risen when *it* arrived." A chill wind ran through the room. "It looked like a man, but it was a monster."

Tyrian's heart froze and he could feel the sudden stillness inside Ewan. Neither said a word. Persephone didn't notice, nor did she notice as more people arrived, including Cassie, Cherry, and Samantha. "He didn't say or do anything. Just looked around and walked out." She shuddered. "The screams started then. We didn't know what was happening. We just barred the doors and prayed. But he just . . . broke the door open. He stood there covered in blood, blood dripping down his chin, his eyes dead and a smile on his lips. He asked me for a drink. Blood ran in the door behind him."

"*Fuck!*" Ewan snarled as he slammed out of the inn.

"He toyed with us. He broke Daria's arm. Just . . . tore at us. We got away. I don't know how. We've been running since. We knew . . . we knew we could come here, to Tyrian Southerwind." She doubled on a low sob. "Why did it come for us?"

There was a sick feeling in Tyrian's stomach. He did not believe in coincidence. The Army had left exactly at sunset before the attack. "Persephone," he said softly, drawing her gaze. He took her hands tightly with his. "I'll get rid of this monster but I'll need your help. You'll need to give me your strength. I know you're strong enough for this."

She drew a ragged breath and drew on the strength inside him. It seemed to pour off him in waves, making it possible to believe in the impossible. She could feel it. He did need her. "I guess I can open another pub here."

"Take over the bar here," Laia suggested warmly. "R.K. will thank you." Her left hand smoothed across the shorter woman's face. "Sleep," she said softly, her voice melodic and hypnotizing. "And do not dream."

Persephone slumped over and Laia lifted her easily. She disappeared down the hall, and Marian and Halkern appeared in the doorway instead. Both looked drained and haggard, the pallor to their skin evidence that they had been pushed to the limit of their magical capacity. "They'll live," Marion said, her voice slightly slurred, "but we could not do everything. We didn't even know *how* to treat some of those wounds."

Liang stepped up behind her and wrapped an arm around her waist to keep her on her feet. "You both need rest," he said. "Let Laia tend to the rest."

Kyle had returned as well and moved to help Halkern. Together, he and Liang aided the two Healers to a room where they could rest and recover. While they did, Tyrian slowly stood. The others looked at him and could see the darkness churning in his eyes stronger than ever. Cassie wrapped her arms around him and was alarmed to realize how cold he felt. When she had woken without him, she had known there was something wrong. "You're freezing!" she said.

Tyrian didn't immediately respond. Ewan stepped back into the doorway and said fiercely, "If I hear one bloody word from your mouth about this being your fault, I'm rearranging your nose!" His breath hissed out. "If it is anyone's fault, it's Blaine's! We know it is! She wants you dead, and she knows that she will never have it from the Lower Generals!"

"What are we talking about?" Samantha asked quietly.

"The rogue Vampire," Ewan bit out between his teeth. "Lord Beelzebub himself." Knowing his hated enemy was close enough to go after was not something he felt excited over. Another innocent village had been slaughtered, and no words would ever tell Tyrian that he was not at fault. Seeing his beloved Kaiten standing on the edge of shattering, destroying Beelzebub became very, *very* personal for Ewan.

That Tyrian was on the edge was evident to everyone. They all held their breath. Cassie found herself unusually calm. She framed Tyrian's face and forced him to look at her. "Tyrian," she said softly. "We are not guilty for the sins of others. Yes, the village would have been spared had Blaine not enlisted a rogue to draw you out. But that does not make it your fault. If you were not here, there would be nothing to stop her at all."

A shudder ripped through his body and he caught her in his arms fiercely. He buried his face in her hair and held on as if his life depended on it. The others slowly let out the breaths they had been holding, and Cherry held onto Matthias' hand tightly. He gently squeezed her fingers and then said softly, "We need to go to the meeting room and discuss this." When Kyle and Liang returned, he said, "Kyle, Liang, please come with us."

No one said a word as they walked through the city to the castle. Liang and Cassie flanked Tyrian so close that their arms brushed. Kyle and Ewan walked very close behind. The four of them closed Tyrian inside their protection. Samantha and Cherry helped Matthias move quicker than he normally could, the general aiding by taking a good deal of his weight off his bad leg.

Gordon and Leonard waited for them in the meeting room. Leonard took one look at Ewan and stopped breathing. "No."

"It would seem so." Ewan sat down heavily and buried his face in his hands. He was only dimly aware of Kyle's hand on his shoulder in support. "I always knew this day was inevitable, but I didn't expect it to happen like this."

"What are we discussing?" Gordon asked quietly.

Tyrian took a deep breath and sat up straight. "It would seem," he said calmly, "that Blaine has determined that the Lower Generals are men and women of integrity and morals. She may have even guessed that all of you may or may not be Destined Stars. And because she knows those things, she knows that if she wants my relic, she needs someone or something that won't be swayed by reason."

"After sundown a few days ago, a village was massacred by the rogue

Vampire Beelzebub." Ewan's voice was not neutral though it managed to remain calm. "The Imperial Army occupying the town mysteriously abandoned it right at sunset. You can't tell me it was coincidence."

Gordon and Samantha paled. It was horrifying to think that any soldier in the Imperial Army, let alone whole units, would simply leave innocent civilians as play toys for something as evil as Beelzebub. It was more horrifying than the images they had seen of the Army doing destruction themselves.

Matthias took a long breath. "This is unexpected, and beyond my scope of knowledge. What is a rogue Vampire?"

"A Vampire that has given in to evil and rejected their gifts in exchange for greater power. In turn, they become undead and cannot stand the sunlight." Ewan's hands curled into fists.

"Then what do we know of Beelzebub specifically?"

"He's afraid of Ewan." Kyle sat down beside his friend. "Does anyone know the legend of the Midnight Moon Sword?"

"I do." Rourke stood in the doorway and his golden eyes were dark. At the startled looks, he said, "Laia said you might need me, Professor Matthias. My knowledge is yours."

"Then please tell what you know."

Rourke walked in and sat down at the table. As he passed Tyrian and Ewan, he lightly touched their shoulders in silent support for them both. "The Midnight Moon Sword is sentient. It was formed from one half of the Pure Relic of Eternity. The other half remains as a relic, though its whereabouts are unknown."

"Can Pure Relics be split?" Cherry asked.

"Some can. I know of two off the top of my head: the Pure Relic of Eternity, and the Pure Relic of Security. I believe that Security had to be split because its two halves are too much an opposite of each other to remain connected safely. Eternity, I couldn't say why it was split. But it was split into the Daylight Sun and Midnight Moon Relics—known as Day and Night for short—with the Night Relic becoming the sword."

Ewan's brows lifted. "I see. That's why it can slay the undead. It holds its greatest power at night. But the Day Relic would be equally terrifying. It wouldn't even need to be a weapon. Its owner would be a weapon themselves." In a murmur, he said, "'The Night sky watches you with the eyes of Eternity.' So that's what she meant."

"All Vampires who go rogue live in fear of the Night and Day Relics. There have been quite a few rogues over the millennia, but there is a clan of Hunters that live in the Millennium Valley. They hunt everything from ghosts to rogues." Rourke sat back in his chair. "The strongest Vampire hunting clan would be the Kane Clan. We would want to enlist one of them to help us. They would have the knowledge we need for battle."

"Battle?" Cassie asked. She kept her hand lightly on top of Tyrian's relic hand. Under the table, he gripped her other hand like a lifeline.

Rourke nodded slightly. "Beelzebub can raise the dead."

Matthias grimaced. "The logistics of a battle against the undead are going to be messy indeed. You know where the Valley is, Ewan?"

"I do."

It said a lot about how much respect the Millennium Vampires had for Ewan. Very few knew the exact location of their homeland. You could find it on accident, but never know quite how you got there. Many normal races lived in the Valley peacefully, though they rarely emerged either. Some thought it might, as yet, have to do with Beelzebub.

"Speak with Tod. Have him send a message to the Kane Clan. Tell them to make haste. We can't know how much damage will be done before we can engage Beelzebub. I would say we find his castle and catch him while he is vulnerable," Matthias met Ewan's eyes, "however, you have more than earned the right to bring him down by your hand."

"While we wait for our Vampire Hunter," Samantha spoke up, "I say we track down that sword! Rourke, Ewan, do either of you have any idea where it is?"

"None," Ewan said.

"Nor I," Rourke said regretfully. "I'm a Scholar, not a researcher, so I can't even say I'd know where to look."

Scholars were repositories for knowledge, but they learned their knowledge from everything at hand. Rourke read every book he came across, but he didn't know where to look for the books to get knowledge he needed. A researcher would. It was another thing that Tyrian added to his mental list of needs. It was a list growing by leaps and bounds.

There was nothing more they could do that night, and it was a frightening feeling for everyone to think that with so many hours until dawn, there was much that Beelzebub could do. Come the dawn, he would be trapped within his castle, wherever that may be, and be forced to remain there until nightfall. It was little consolation to think that there had likely not been attacks in the time since the first; he would want to see if he had drawn out Tyrian before he went after another town.

Liang studied Tyrian's face and then left the room before anyone else did. The others were fairly sure no one would get any sleep, but they too parted ways to at least rest if possible. Rourke promised to go by the inn to make sure that the Healers were resting peacefully and that the victims were as yet recovering.

Tyrian remained standing tall until the elevator doors closed behind him and Cassie. As soon as they were away from prying eyes, he doubled over and pressed his face to her shoulder. Those stairs Ewan had spoken of had just become made of sharp stone. How much worse would it get? How much worse *could* it get?

With her uncanny knowledge of him inside her heart and soul, she said very softly, "Your father didn't know, Tyrian." She urged him into their tower room and kicked the door shut behind them. She firmly escorted him to the bed and made him sit down on the side. "Why do you think I wanted to speak with him that first day? I knew he would listen. He could be a Destined Star, too, for all we know."

His eyes focused on her as she firmly pulled off his shoes. "Ewan told me what happened at the Commune," he said softly. "I can't . . . I just can't fathom how any living being can wish that sort of devastation on anyone. Blaine is as evil as Beelzebub."

That he had doubted she was evil when Cassie had been sure all along just underscored the reason he was the Kaiten and she was the Kentei. He had wanted to believe that there was good inside everyone. She had known there wasn't and had therefore been ready to catch him when he fell.

She tugged him to his feet and he stood quietly as she helped get rid of his clothes. He was still freezing, the shivers seeming to come from his soul. She escorted him into the bathing room where the tub stood full of steaming hot water. As he blinked at it, she said, "Liang. Why do you think he left early? In you go."

He winced when the hot water touched his cold skin but he got in anyway and closed his eyes. Behind his lids danced macabre images of what he suspected the two towns must surely look like. Just thinking about it made his strength waver, and as it did, weakness rushed in from all sides. It was as if his energy just drained away.

"Tyrian!" Cassie grabbed his shoulders and kept him from slipping under the water. Her heart pounded hard and her mouth was dry. He had gone as pale as glass. "You need to sleep," she urged.

He had enough strength to stand, but she had to help him get out of the tub. She dried him briskly and then helped him make his way to bed. This was not simple relic weakness. She felt sure of it, though she wasn't sure of what it truly was.

She tucked him in and started to straighten but he grabbed her wrist.

"Don't go," he begged softly. "I need you to hold me, Cassie."

"I'm not going anywhere, Tyrian." She stripped off the clothes she had thrown on hastily when she had heard the alarm and then slipped into bed. He buried his face against her breast and she wrapped her arms around him tightly. He was warmer now, yet his hands still felt chilly where they curled around her waist.

It wasn't until he slept and she started to drift off that she realized she had gone out of the tower without covering her scar. She hadn't been wearing a scarf or her choker. She had completely forgotten it was even there.

Her arms tightened fiercely around Tyrian. He had healed her. It was up to her to heal him.

Chapter Twenty-One

"I want to believe in the power of many."

Cassie woke before Tyrian did, which was not an uncommon occurrence. He hadn't stirred once since falling asleep, proof of how badly he had needed the rest. He was often restless at night. He had never disturbed her sleep, but she had always been aware of his problems shutting off his thoughts. It had gotten much better since they had become lovers, yet there were times when even that could not bring him peace.

She didn't move from her position. She was content to hold him forever. He suddenly stirred slightly and his lips brushed across the inner curve of her breast. Her body heated instantly, her nipples tightening in anticipation of his touch. She always knew the difference in the way he touched her; she knew whether it was simply his need to hold her or if he was trying to seduce her. Part of it came from his relic hand. It burned and tingled much more obviously when he wanted her.

There was something dreamlike in the way he slowly caressed her. She was sinking before she knew she was in deep water. It seemed so easy to surrender when he was so tender. Giving up her control, giving over her body to his care, was not as frightening as it had once been. It was wonderful.

When he rose over her, she framed his face with her hands and drew him down for a kiss. He felt strong and secure, though she couldn't quite forget how fragile his heart was. It was her hands that held him together. "I love you," she breathed against his lips. "Never forget, Tyrian."

His green eyes looked velvety with a darkness that promised an oblivion of safety. There was a darkness inside him that offered rest to a weary monk, just as there was a light inside her that gave respite to a worn Kaiten Star. Protector and protected, entwined for eternity.

The sun was fully in the window when the door to the tower opened. "It's morning," Merilyne called. Her voice didn't have its usual cheer, but it was warm regardless. The events had affected everyone. "Lord Tyrian, Lady Cassie, please come to the meeting room as soon as possible. We have received a visitor."

Tyrian reluctantly sighed and disentangled himself from Cassie. He would have been quite content to stay in her arms all day. "When this is done," he told her softly, smoothing her hair from her eyes, "we're going away somewhere we can't be found and locking the door behind us. And we'll test out just how good your stamina is, my lady monk."

She had to grin as he got out of bed. "Is that a challenge, Lord Tyrian?" She sat up and slid her arms around his neck. His body was once more hot and wonderful, the chill of the night past. "So far you seem to be doing just fine."

He smiled as he ran his hands down her back. "I have incentive. I can't keep my hands off you."

She would have it no other way. "Good." She kissed him briefly and then got out of bed.

They got dressed and made their way down to the courtyard. When they got there, Evelyn waited for them with a tray. It had coffee and pastries on it. "I got up early," she said with a smile. "R.K. told me what happened. I wanted to be sure our new family had something good to eat, and so did you."

Tyrian gratefully took a cup of coffee and a pastry. He had no idea what she did, but her pastries were light, fluffy, and surprisingly filling for not being very big. Even when he wasn't hungry, he couldn't resist eating. Today's flavor looked like it had ham and cheese in it, and it had her secret sauce drizzled on top. "No one cooks like you do."

She winked sassily. "We all have our gifts." She headed off through the courtyard, and more than one guard trailed along wistfully on the scent of coffee and food.

In the meeting room, Matthias and Cherry were present with Ewan and a newcomer. The visitor was only a teenager, possibly sixteen or so, but held a sort of eerie calmness. He was a surprisingly imposing figure at one or two inches taller than Tyrian, and he wore head to toe black. Under the cloak fastened around his shoulders, a belt could be seen carrying an assortment of tools and weapons. A small crossbow tucked into a holster the way Shots carried his guns. On his right hand was a Resurrection Relic bearing the dark outline that meant it had been overclocked.

Tyrian took one look at him and knew two things. One, this was the hunter sent by the Kane Clan. How he had gotten there that fast was still a mystery, but Tyrian felt sure of his identity. The other thing he knew was that this Hunter was another Destined Star.

"Ah, Lord Tyrian." Matthias gestured to Tyrian. "Lord Tyrian, Lady Cassie, please meet Vladimir Kane, from the Kane Clan. Kane, the two before you are Tyrian Southerwind, our Kaiten Star, and Master Cassie from the Monk Clans, his Kentei protector."

"Master?" Tyrian murmured, noticing now that the title had been used more than once.

"Later," she murmured.

Kane turned and bowed gracefully. "Greetings." His voice suited the rest of him, sounding deep and calm all at the same time. "Mistress Selene of the Millennium Valley has sent me to give my aid."

"How did you get here so fast?" Tyrian asked.

"As soon as Beelzebub left his castle, Selene was aware of it. She knew he would be crossing your path and therefore sent me as assistance." He suddenly smiled and it lightened his face. "I am also a Destined Star, Lord Tyrian."

"I had noticed." Tyrian held out a hand and grasped Kane's tightly. "You've come at the right time. Has Matthias told you of what occurred when Beelzebub left his castle?" At the shake of Kane's head, Tyrian let out a long breath. "Then I think it's time you were told. Is Ewan coming?"

"I'll fetch him!" Cherry hurried out. She didn't want to hear the litany of destruction again. And she really didn't want to see the look on Tyrian's face when he talked about it.

By the time she returned with Ewan, the tale was done. Tyrian looked as calm as ever, but there was a flicker of darkness moving across his eyes. Kane's face was stony and he had one hand resting on his crossbow. He saw Ewan and instantly bowed. "Greetings, Ewan."

"Well met, Kane." Ewan looked at Tyrian. "One problem down. We have our Vampire Hunter. Now what the hell do we do about that sword?"

"I can help with that as well," Kane offered. When eyes swung toward him, he explained, "The Midnight Moon Sword sleeps within the Caves of Eternity that crawl underground between the Empire and Foresalia."

"Those caves are used all the time," Cassie said musingly. "I wonder how it was never found before."

"It's hidden." Kane glanced at Ewan. "But the first Midnight Moon Warrior could easily lead us there. I will go along in case Beelzebub knows where the sword is."

"We want to be discreet," Tyrian agreed. "Cassie and I will accompany you and Ewan." Matthias opened his mouth and Tyrian held up a hand. "No. I am going."

Recognizing that he had dug his heels in, Matthias just smiled ruefully. "Very well, Lord Tyrian. We will hold down things here."

"By horseback," Cassie said, "the closest entrance to the caves is a week away. Less if we ride without stopping. We will have to go slightly more south than normal because the western checkpoint sits inside the forest line that marks the border to the Highlights. There's a huge wall separating our two countries."

"With a casual war going on, little wonder," Tyrian muttered. "Hopefully I can get that fixed too!"

The others exchanged a smile. For someone born to walk a battlefield, he was unexpectedly passionate about hating war. But then, perhaps that was the very reason he was meant to blossom on the field. Sometimes ending a war meant fighting a war. They were words that Laia had once said, and again they rang true.

Tyrian led the way out of the meeting room, and the party of four headed downstairs. Evelyn waited for them when they reached the courtyard. She carried a large pack that she handed over to Ewan. "For the road," she said. "I want to make sure you're eating right out there!" she scolded Tyrian.

Tyrian looked down at himself in confusion. "Have I been losing weight?" He looked at Cassie. If anyone would know, it was her. "Well?"

She hesitated and then admitted softly, "Some. Nothing *alarming*, Tyrian. But it is showing that you don't sleep as much as you should and that you don't eat as much either." She had noticed it from that first night and had been intently monitoring it in the time since. He had lost about ten pounds and it added a stronger definition to the muscles of his body and the lines of his face. Any more and it would start to become dangerous. There was little to no fat on Tyrian's body to begin with; his body would have nothing to run on at all except his iron will.

Evelyn watched him with deep concern in her eyes, and Ewan looked slightly grim. With a sigh, Tyrian said, "I'm sorry, everyone. I can't promise to act normal, but I will at least try. There are times when I just can't stomach the thought of food, even yours, Eve."

She nodded. "I'll start looking for very light alternatives that will at least give you something." Her eyes lit with humor. "Rumor reached me to avoid ground-grown veggies unless they're very well hidden." When Tyrian's brows pulled together, she giggled. "It was Serentia, actually. She saw that you never went near that part of her garden and made Liang tell her. So she told me. I promise, we'll keep it a secret!"

"Do I want to know?" Kane asked dryly.

Ewan was grinning. "I certainly do. Remind me to bribe Liang later."

Tyrian just rolled his eyes. "Thank you, Eve."

With the food safely stashed away, the party headed for the stables to get horses from Beatrice. While Tyrian had usually been riding a normal brown stallion, he was unexpectedly surprised when Beatrice brought out a beautiful white mare who had a thick black mane and tail. "She's lovely!" He softly patted the horse's face when she butted against him. "Look at her." He stepped back and studied the mare closely. "She's thoroughbred, isn't she? City-State stock?"

Beatrice beamed like a proud mother. "That's right! You know your horses, Lord Tyrian."

He shook his head. "She must have cost you a fortune, Beatrice! The City-States raise the best horses in the world, and I can't imagine them cheerfully selling one to someone in the middle of a war, even if we're not their enemy." There was neither alliance nor enmity between Empire and the City-States.

"I didn't buy her," she protested. "She was found outside the gates this morning. There was a note on her mane that said she was expressly for you. As soon as I saw her, I knew why. She's been trained to be ridden by a war general. You can tell by how she carries herself. The note was signed, but I don't recognize the name."

He felt his heart skip a beat. "May I see the note?" It was handed over and he opened it quickly. There was nothing in the handwriting that looked familiar, but he instantly recognized the initials at the end. "DP," he said softly.

"DP?" Ewan asked.

Tyrian crushed the note. "Beatrice, burn this. All anyone knows is that it was a gift to me." He ran a hand down the mare's long face. She had calm, intelligent eyes; evidence that she was, indeed, from the best stock in the City-States. Some suspected that Unicorns ran with their horses and had permeated them with power.

"We're calling her Fay, if that suits you," Beatrice noted.

"I like it." Tyrian swung up onto Fay's back and she tossed her mane proudly.

Kane had to laugh. "I guess she knows just who is in charge around here."

Three more horses stood by, so the rest mounted up as well. It wasn't until they were on the road and well away from the base that Ewan said softly, "Okay, Tyrian. Give. Who sent the horse?"

Tyrian kept his eyes on the road. "It was a belated birthday gift. Or, considering the time that has passed, an early one. The DP stands for Donald Phiriead."

The last name was unfamiliar. The first name was not. And because Donald Southerwind was married, it didn't take a Scholar to guess his childhood family name. "Then that means he supports you, doesn't it?" Cassie asked softly. "Why else would he have expressly sent you a horse bred for carrying the head of an army into battle? And just looking at her demeanor, you know she was chosen for you."

"It's too much to try and think about," Tyrian admitted. "Whether he supports me or not, there will come a day when I have to face my father in battle. I'm not even sure if I will be able to handle that." He took a long breath. "Ben was with my family for ten years. Which means the Devourer, and me, were exposed to my family for ten years."

Ewan's hands tightened on his reins. "But isn't that only a concern if he dies? You're not going to kill him, Tyrian. It'll be like Gordon and Samantha. And no doubt the other Lower Generals as well. We'll outwit them and end things without bloodshed. And if you *do* have to duel him, you'll be able to win without killing him. Not without hurting him, maybe, but that's what Healers are for."

It didn't make it any easier for Tyrian to stomach. It was one thing to duel his father when they were training, as they had done for years. It was another entirely to face him in battle as enemies. Even if Donald was on his side. Even if he was supporting Tyrian. The battle would commence, and Tyrian couldn't bear it. Raising a weapon against a family member was sickening in his mind.

They rode hard during the day and rested only during the darkest hours of the night. It wasn't until they drew very close to approaching the caves that Tyrian asked Kane, "How did your family become Vampire hunters?"

"Accident." Kane smiled as he said it. "For as long as the Millennium Valley has existed, my family has worked alongside Selene. She's been a sort of surrogate aunt to me and is more like family than not. The first Vampire who went rogue surprised everyone. Until then, they hadn't even realized that the blessing was also a curse. My ancestor, also named Vladimir Kane, tracked the rogue down and destroyed him. Ever since, my family has been the most well-known of Hunters. We train expressly for it."

"How many Vampires are there?" Cassie asked.

"Hmm. A couple thousand total. We lose one or two to going rogue once every few years. The Millennium Vampires are very careful of who they convert, and they have to be strongly convinced sometimes. Even then, things happen. You can't have all good in any race."

"What about Beelzebub?" Ewan asked. "You can't tell me he was ever good."

"I don't know. Selene is the only one who knows the whole story, but she hasn't told anyone. I think it has to do with the Pure Millennium Relic that she possesses. There's a scar on her right hand and she carries the relic on her left."

Tyrian and Ewan looked at Cassie, the only one who seemed to know anything about Pure Relics. It was something that still had Tyrian suspicious as to her promised eternity. Slowly, she said, "Pure Relics can be removed from an owner, but the manner in which it is removed can be detrimental. If Selene had the relic fused and it was ripped from her without her will, it would have wounded both skin and soul. But say she wanted to pass it on willingly, and her recipient was willing. She'd suffer no physical effects and her recipient would have the normal pain of fusion."

"What I felt wasn't normal." Tyrian didn't bother making it a question.

"No. I can't tell you why exactly. I don't know *that* much. You should have felt some pain and some weakness, but nothing as debilitating as it was. And that's why I'm not even positive yours can be removed, Tyrian."

"How does that work for Selene?" Ewan asked. "Did the relic make her a Vampire?"

Kane hesitated. "Again, I'm not positive. It's from that time she doesn't talk about. *But* I do know that the vampirism is the price to be paid for having immortality without a relic. They're pretty well identical to Pure Relic users except for a tendency to sunburn and the need to drink blood."

"Until they go rogue," Tyrian murmured.

"Until then. Betraying what is a gift from the gods is only going to make you pay in the end. Hell, we're still not even done with the Era of Punishment, and that's been going on for a million years. Once we see these monsters starting to diminish, then we'll know we're finally forgiven."

Tyrian contemplated an eternity that eventually didn't have monsters to fight and slay and said wryly, "I'm going to get bored. Maybe the gods can cut back on the level of monsters that directly go after cities and leave the rest for bored combatants to mess with."

They reached the caves by nightfall, and as it was going to be dark inside the caves anyway, they went ahead and entered. The four horses stayed inside the entrance, and Fay kept the other three in line. Kane and Cassie lit torches to carry along, and they all moved deeper into the caves. Ewan and Tyrian walked with weapons in hand since no one knew what to expect.

Inexplicably, it wasn't long before Ewan began to feel a sharp tugging sensation inside. He stopped walking and looked down the path to the right. They had almost passed it up because the tunnel was so dark as to be invisible. The tug pulled in that direction. "Follow me. I think someone knows we're here."

They wound down more tunnels following the tug that he felt inside.

There were assorted beasts and monsters inside the caves, but they only attacked occasionally. The deeper into the caves that the party moved, the less inclined the monsters were to jump out. That, too, was a sign that they were on the right path.

One of the tunnels gave way abruptly to a room. There were torches along the walls, and Kane lit them from his. The light that flooded the room revealed it to be a perfect circle. In the very center rested a glowing orb of light. Hovering inside the orb was a sword. It was not, however, any normal sword.

It was the first sword that either Ewan or Tyrian had seen that put Mouse's craftsmanship to shame. The blade was almost three feet long, paper thin at the edges, and razor sharp. It was a much darker shade of silver, almost black even in the light. The hilt was stone and glass with not a bit of wood or metal to be seen. Where the hilt curved back to protect the wielder's hand, it looked like a Dragon claw. Holding the sword would look almost as if you held a Dragon's hand. At the center of the hilt where hilt met blade, a black relic had been embedded. Inside the relic swirled bits of midnight blue and silver like the night sky. The symbol in the relic was that of a serpentine Dragon—the eldest of all Dragons—wrapped around a crescent moon and sun fused together.

"Who disturbs my slumber?" a male voice asked in annoyance from the general vicinity of the sword.

Though sentient didn't always mean capable of speech, it certainly did this time. Ewan lifted his chin. "I am Ewan Grizmar. I seek your power to destroy the rogue Vampire known as Beelzebub. I would ask that you lend your power to the aid of my Kaiten Star."

There was a long silence and then the sword said softly, "Step forward, Ewan. I wish to see you." When Ewan stepped forward, the sword studied him in silence for a long while. His appearance was not an unfamiliar one, and the sight of it brought comfort to the Night Relic. He had waited a long time indeed.

The sword glowed softly, and an answering glow came from Ewan's shoulder. It was not, however, the star of his birth. The mark that appeared resembled the symbol of Eternity within the relic, but lacking in the sun half. "You are indeed the Midnight Moon Warrior I have been waiting for," the sword said in satisfaction. "And as your destiny binds you to Tyrian Southerwind, I will offer my services as well. Beelzebub is long overdue for a good smiting!"

Ewan grinned savagely. "Now you're talking my language!" He reached out and grabbed the Midnight Moon Sword and the orb of light exploded outward. The sword he had been using promptly shattered into dust. He turned sharply and held the Midnight Moon Sword in front of his face, and his brown eyes burned intently. "Tyrian Southerwind, by this sword, I will fight for you. You have my vow as a swordsman from the Commune of Soldiers."

Tyrian nodded. "I accept that vow."

"Hey, Night," Ewan said as he studied the sword, "I don't suppose you have transport capabilities."

"As a matter of fact, I can indeed perform one act of transportation. I can't promise it will work ever again. It only works because Lady Tanelia was at your base."

"And why would that be?" Cassie asked curiously.

"Long story," Night said dryly. "Best left told at another time. Transport now?"

"Hang on, we need the horses. Let's make our way out of this maze." Ewan sheathed Night and took the lead to get out of the caves as fast as possible. He couldn't shake the feeling that they needed to get out quickly. There was danger hovering nearby.

The answer as to what type of danger lurked was answered as soon as they got the horses and stepped out of the caves. The entrance had been surrounded by dozens of Imperial soldiers. Cassie, Kane, and Ewan instantly stepped together and protectively shielded Tyrian with their bodies. He didn't protest but he reached back to grab his staff. Like hell they would fight their way through without him.

"Surrender!" one soldier said sharply. "Put down your weapons and come quietly!"

Ewan snarled, "This has gone beyond the whole issue of the Rebellion! Lady Blaine sent out Beelzebub, the most evil of all creatures, just to get to Tyrian. Can you condone the brutal massacre of an innocent village just to stop someone who isn't doing harm to anyone except those who want to believe blindly in a decrepit old fool?"

There was no chance for a retort. Relic symbols suddenly appeared in the air over the soldiers. Over one half, the flame symbol of a Fire Relic appeared. Over the other, the vine symbol of a Land Relic. The sound of magic harmonizing echoed in the air and the fires of hell, literally, broke loose. The land cracked open violently under the feet of the soldiers and flames burst up from the depths. The double attack was more than doubly potent. Many soldiers fell and didn't get up again. The others were so busy trying to escape the effects that they didn't even notice the party scrambling out of the way.

Tyrian turned his head sharply and saw two figures running toward him. One was an older woman, and the other was a teenage male. Both wore the familiar clothes of a Magician, and both carried crystal topped wands specifically designed to enhance magical attacks. "Hurry!" he said urgently.

Kane grabbed the woman's hand and pulled her up onto the horse with him. Cassie grabbed the teenager. As soon as both mages were secured, Night let out a brilliant pulse of light that lit the night like the day. It blinded everyone. When the light faded, they stood outside the base.

The woman slid down to the ground and smoothed out her long jacket. It was worn rakishly over the top of a set of snug leggings and tunic. Her green eyes sparkled as she smiled at Tyrian. "Sorry about that. We're always dropping spells. You never know who might get caught up in a dropped spell."

Tyrian found himself grinning as he dismounted. "Tell me you specialize in attack magic."

The woman held up her hands. On one hand was a Fire Relic. On the other was a Water Relic. The boy had two Land Relics. It gave a double potency to any spell he cast. "I'm Verdure," he said as he hopped off Cassie's horse. He wore clothes not dissimilar from his partner, but everything fit much looser to give him room to grow. He gestured to the woman. "She's my mom, Crimson. We're both Magicians, and we're both ready to accidentally drop spells on enemy units, Lord Tyrian!"

Tyrian studied him. "Age?"

"Fourteen, sir."

Just old enough to enter a field of combat, and he was already quite powerful for being young. A minor weight lifted from Tyrian's shoulders. He held out his hands to them, and when they grasped on, the mark of destiny appeared on their shoulders. "You got here right when I needed you," he said softly. "Lend me your strength, and I know we can win."

"It's yours," Crimson said simply.

"One more and we have a full unit," Cassie said softly, her hand slipping into Tyrian's as he released the new Stars. "Laia's sword arm and your skill with a staff won't be wasted then."

The gate had been lowered, and everyone hurried inside. Verdure and Crimson followed a guard to get rooms, and Beatrice hurried to take care of the horses. It was night, but it wasn't late. Night's ability to transport them home had taken almost a week's worth of time off things, and it had potentially given them a strong advantage.

Even though it was night, the party moved swiftly toward the meeting room where they knew Matthias would be waiting. Tyrian walked into the room and said without preamble, "We have the Midnight Moon Sword and two elemental Magicians."

"Three," an unfamiliar man said curtly.

Tyrian arched a brow as he saw the newcomer standing next to the table. Matthias and Leonard were watching him warily, and Kyle looked distinctly unhappy. Cherry hid mostly behind Kyle, and her eyes were wide.

The man was handsome, fair-haired, and blue eyed. His age seemed indeterminate though he looked as if he was barely in his mid-twenties. Something far older lingered in his eyes, and when Tyrian glanced at his right hand, he realized why.

The man wore the Pure Relic of Wind.

"My name is Lane Aerian," the man said with a bored note in his voice. "I'm the great Lady Tanelia's apprentice. She told me I had to come here and help since you needed my aid." He scoffed. "Which was quite obvious when I saw the state of your magical reserves. Or lack thereof. Did you think you could play tricks the entire time?"

Ewan bristled. "Watch it, kid."

"Kid?" Lane smirked at him. "I'm over three hundred, *kid*, so I think I can say whatever I like. For a guy so big, you're not exactly smart, are you?"

Ewan looked at Tyrian. "I'm going to kill him, Tyrian. Tell me he's not a Destined Star."

Tyrian put a hand on his wrist in restraint. "I'm afraid so, Ewan."

Ewan hissed out a string of words that made Cherry's cheeks turn as red as her hair. Lane merely ignored him and turned back to Tyrian. "So you're the legendary destined Kaiten Star. You've definitely got strong potential as a sorcerer, but you haven't even tapped into a fraction of it. Are you just blathering around?"

Kyle and Ewan both bristled and went for their swords. Tyrian held up a hand sharply to stop them, his eyes never leaving Lane's. "Trying to make others feel small won't make you feel taller," he said very softly. "Stand down, Lane."

Cassie and Kane both backed up a few steps, and so did the others. They had never heard Tyrian speak quite like that before, and it seemed to be a warning sign of a considerable temper. As he had yet to lose his temper at all, it made everyone wary, even Cassie. This was much more deadly than when he had yelled at her for protecting him. That hadn't been real temper as much as frustration.

Lane rolled his eyes. "Please. You're just a kid compared to me, figuratively and literally. I'm here because I'm a Destined Star. Don't think that because I know you need me means I'm just going to respect you. Clear?"

"Clear."

Before anyone could blink, Tyrian's relic hand snapped up and a blast of raw black magic shot from his palm and streaked across the air. Lane tried to lift his hand to put up a shield, but he was nowhere near as fast as the Kaiten. The blast slammed into his chest and sent him tumbling backwards across the table only to crash onto the floor on the other side.

"Holy shit," Ewan said, eyes wide. "Damn, Tyrian."

Even Matthias was speechless. Cassie covered her mouth to hide a smile. Tyrian was a man of great passions. Temper was a passion. Just because he boiled slowly didn't mean he wouldn't boil over at some point and explode. Unfortunately for Lane, he had arrived a time where Tyrian had been on a slow boil for months. His attitude had been the last bit of heat needed to send Tyrian over the edge.

Tyrian shook off the excess power around his hand and then calmly walked across the room to kneel beside Lane. "Well?"

Lane looked up at him with grudging respect. "I'm impressed," he admitted. He even let Tyrian help him to his feet again. It was only pride that kept him from wincing as his body protested. That tumble across the table had not been any more pleasant than the landing at the end. "You're a much stronger sorcerer than I thought."

"For the magically stupid," Leonard said dryly, "what's a sorcerer? Is it different from a Magician or mage?"

"Mages are anyone who use a relic. Magicians are mages who specialize in using relics only. If they specialize in healing magic, they're a Healer," Lane explained. "A sorcerer is a mage who has above average magical capacity and output but chooses not to specialize in magic. A sorcerer who chooses to specialize in magic, like me, is typically called a Thaumoturge."

"What would Laia be?" Cherry spoke up curiously.

"Complicated," he muttered. Even he had no idea how Laia Mitakel could be a Magician, a Healer, *and* a warrior. She could effectively be called a Thaumoturge Warrior, and the idea alone was rather alarming for him. The possibilities were endless for what she could do. If he ever met another one, and one who could wear a Pure Relic, he had a feeling that the very world could be changed.

Tyrian turned toward the door. "You will be in charge of our magical unit. You will work with Verdure and Crimson to make sure our mages and Magicians are as well trained as they can be. Work with them tomorrow, and as hard as you can. Tomorrow night, we're going to the scene of the massacre. In the morning, Kane, I want to hear a full report on what to expect from Beelzebub's undead army."

"Yes, sir," Kane said instantly.

"Yeah, fine," Lane muttered. It still stung that a sorcerer that young had gotten the drop on him. The respect that tangled with his need to see Tyrian happy was an uncomfortable feeling for Lane. He had never really loved anyone except Tanelia.

Tyrian saw the sudden sadness in Lane's eyes but did not pry. He knew he would never have an answer. Instead, he said, "There's still a good deal of night left. Try to sleep if possible. Ewan, tomorrow morning, go see Mouse early on. If she can do anything for Night, let her do it."

"I haven't had a good sharpening in a while," Night admitted.

Cherry and Leonard stared at the sword Ewan wore. Kyle didn't bat a lash. "Naturally, Ewan would have a weapon with a big mouth."

Neither Night nor Ewan could take offense, much as they would have liked to. Like called to like, as they said.

Chapter Twenty-Two

"The wind and the stars have joined our fight; tell me how."

Cassie watched Tyrian critically as they made their way to their tower. He seemed to show no ill effects from using his relic in such a manner, and that was a good sign. Tapping raw relic power was no easy trick and could often be as draining as unlocking new levels. "I admit, I'm surprised he didn't challenge you to a Relic Duel," she said as they went into their room.

"Relic Duel?" He paused as he pulled off his shirt. "What's a Relic Duel?"

"It's where two relic users try to use the raw power of their relic to overwhelm their opponent. The idea being that all regular relics are equal in raw power, and Pure Relics are equal. It's the magical capacity of the wielder that makes them potent. So even though Lane probably has a fully unlocked relic and you don't, it wouldn't matter."

"Hmm."

She slid her arms around his waist and rested her hands on his bare stomach. Her lips feathered across his back. "It's normally only between enemies because it can be very dangerous, especially to outsiders. Relic users can feel the vibration in the air. Pure Relic users feel as if they're involved in the duel."

"You know a lot." He covered her hands with his.

"We collect information," she admitted. "And there are more Pure Relics in assorted people's hands than most think." She slowly slid her hands up over his chest and smiled as she heard his breath catch. It was a wholly different power to make such a powerful man tremble at her touch. "Am I distracting you?"

He turned and dragged her into his arms for a wild kiss. It almost seemed as if he wanted to devour *her*, and the feeling was thrilling. She bore a risk herself because there was no one closer to him than she, but if that was her eventual future, she did not care. As long as she stayed by his side, that was all she wanted.

Things were busy in the morning. Lane, Verdure, and Crimson began to work with the magic unit. Ewan went to see Mouse, and she proved her skill by sharpening Night's edge until it was as thin as a hair. When Ewan tested it on a broken pillar, he cleaved it straight in half without a single ragged mark or damage to Night. The combination of his skill and a legendary sword underscored why he had been born as the Midnight Moon Warrior.

Tyrian, Cassie, Gordon, and Samantha met up with Matthias and Kane in the meeting room. Ewan and Kyle joined them shortly thereafter, and so did Liang. As his mentor sat down, Tyrian leaned over and murmured, "I haven't seen you much. On one hand, your trust in Cassie is both welcome and justified. On the other . . ."

Color slowly climbed Liang's face. He had woken that morning to realize he was neglecting Tyrian, and that with the battle against Donald looming in the near future, Tyrian needed his support more than ever. "I am sorry, Tyrian."

"I'm not." Tyrian smiled when Liang looked at him in surprise. "You've been with Serentia and Tavi. I know you have. I've seen you helping in the garden and teaching Tavi the little things you used to teach me. And I'm glad," he said simply. "You've been like a father to me, Liang, and eventually, soon, we're going to have to part ways. You need to have a family. I love Tavi as if she were my baby sister. And Serentia . . ." He shook his head a little. "It's hard to get my head around. She's only eight years older than I am, but she's so much like a mother." Very softly, he said, "More of a mother than Annareal was."

The fact that Tyrian had not called Annareal his mother since Ophelia's death was evidence to the fact that he had never, and may never, forgive what she had done. Not unless Annareal ever truly regretted what she had done. If she showed true remorse, Tyrian might find forgiveness after all. He was more matured than Liang. He knew he would never forgive someone such a betrayal.

Evelyn showed up with breakfast and was serving it when the doors banged open and Tavi rushed in. She ran across the floor and climbed up onto Tyrian's lap without asking and then promptly buried her face against his shoulder.

Startled, he cuddled her close. "Tavi? What's wrong?"

She leaned back and her lower lip wobbled. "There's a family visiting the inn. The boy said I can't be a Destined Star because you don't need kids." Her eyes welled with tears as the others at the table bristled. "Yumi's ten but she's useful! I don't do anything!"

Gordon started to speak but Matthias shook his head. Tyrian gently cupped Tavi's chin. "You're here," he said softly. "My littlest Destined Star. You give me hope for the future, Tavi. It's your future that we're fighting for, and because you believe in me, I can have the strength to fight. That's why you're important too. If there was trouble, and you knew I needed you, then you'd come help me."

She rubbed at her eyes. She had known it, but she needed to hear Tyrian say it. She wanted so much to protect him! He always looked tired and it made her so mad that no one would let him rest. She tugged on his tunic, and when he leaned down, whispered in his ear, "If L'ang marries Mommy, will you be my big brother?"

He slowly smiled. He had suspected that she was eyeing Liang as her preferred choice of father. "I'd say so."

She held up her pinky. "Then we help!"

He solemnly linked pinkies with her and they shook on it. "Deal."

She climbed down and scampered out of the room as fast as she had entered. The doors almost banged shut again but the guards were quick enough to grab them. "Well," Matthias said. "It was inevitable, I suppose. It threw most of us off stride when we realized someone so young would be a Star, but we are much quicker to accept the ways of Destiny. Well handled, Lord Tyrian."

"It was the truth," he said simply. He leaned back in his chair. His green eyes remained calm but promised a dangerous anger. "I believe I'll need to have a word with everyone soon. There may as yet be more children to be Destined Stars. Yumi isn't as quickly noticed because she is 'useful' for her inventions. No one is going to belittle *any* of my Stars, no matter their age."

It wasn't the first time the others had noticed that the strong emotion between Kaiten Star and Destined Star went both ways. Tyrian was as fierce about them as they were about him. To him, his Stars belonged to him and nothing else mattered.

Evelyn had left with the cart, and everyone began to eat. While they did, Kane started talking. "It's probably not the best subject with food, but it can't be put off." He poked at the eggs on his plate. "Beelzebub has the ability to raise the dead. Any body that is deceased can potentially be raised as a soldier. The more recently dead come back as zombies. The older dead come back as just a skeleton. Both are equally unpleasant. Zombies are far worse for those involved because they, to some extent, retain features of their former self."

Ewan pushed his plate away. "Well, I'm done."

"Being dead," Kane continued, "they don't feel pain, so they can keep on attacking even if they lose limbs or take severe injuries. The only way to stop a zombie is to either remove the head or set it on fire. Skeletons are much trickier. They need to be cut in half through the chest."

Matthias frowned thoughtfully as he went over all strategies. "Our best hope for defeating the army Beelzebub will raise is to take our magic unit with Crimson in lead. Our ranged units are of no use. We'll want to have our close-range combat units all wearing Fire Relics if possible, or have Fire Scrolls if they can't wear a relic. How effective is Lightning magic?"

"Very," Kane said instantly. "If it is strong enough."

"Then Kyle and Laia will each be in a unit," Tyrian said. "We lack a Relic Master around here, but Beatrice has a lot of scrolls in supply."

Only Pure Relics could be equipped without the aid of a Relic Master. All others needed assistance from someone trained in relic application. Even though they had been amassing a great deal of relics in storage, there was no one to apply them. It went onto Tyrian's list of needs, along with everything else.

The Resurrection Relic also carried a lightning spell that was deliberately designed to be effective against the undead, so Kane, Marion, and Halkern were of equal importance in the coming battle.

They didn't know many units they would need at Beelzebub's castle, and they didn't even know precisely where it was located to begin with. It was said to be in the mountains, but that covered a lot of ground. That it hadn't been found in all these years was testament to how well it had been hidden.

"What do you hope to find at the massacre site?" Samantha asked Tyrian. "It's not going to be pleasant, Lord Tyrian."

"Beelzebub wants me. I can assume that means he will want to fight me on his turf. Well, I can hardly go on his turf unless I know where it is. That means there will be a clue left behind at the site." He looked at Matthias. "Is that your feeling?"

"It is indeed." It wasn't the first time they had thought similar. Tyrian was not much less of a brilliant strategist. "Persephone said her village was called T'que. If my memory serves, it was once an Elf city before others moved in and made it more diverse. It is to the northeast of Teasarn, fairly close to the mountains."

Tyrian drummed the fingers of his relic hand on the table. "We can't spare the time to get there by foot, or horse. We know Persephone and her family made it here in five days by running without stopping. Five days is an optimistic number, no doubt. It's about three to Teasarn alone."

Slowly, Ewan said, "Beelzebub likes things to be simple. He is, at his heart, a coward. I fully believe it. He is also confident in his own power. He wouldn't exert himself."

Matthias' eyes lit. "Ewan, you might very well be on to something. You are suggesting that the castle in the mountains might very well be close to T'que. It surely must be the closest city. Why would he go to some small town out of the way if something easier was closer?"

"So what should we do?" Cherry asked. She suddenly brightened. "Wait! You think we should use the Mechanoportal to send the units to T'que and then march the rest of the way once the castle is found?"

"Indeed! There is nothing stopping us from transporting in additional units once the castle is found. We can send a preliminary three, our magic unit and two close-combat, and then add more if needed. Lord Tyrian, name your unit leaders."

"For magic, Crimson will lead with Lane and Marion assisting. If Lane doesn't like it, he can get a damned Fire Relic himself." Ignoring the quick grins from the table, especially Ewan's, Tyrian continued, "The close-combat will consist of I, Cassie, and Kane in one unit, and either you or Cherry with Laia and Ewan in the other. If we find we need more units, I will choose the leaders at that time."

"I will ride," Matthias said. When Cherry frowned, he tugged on her braid. "My leg is doing much better today. I will be just fine."

Cherry was still obviously unsure, but she did not argue further. Since Matthias had told no one precisely what his ailment was, there was no one who could say definitively whether he was healthy or not. Tyrian *suspected* what was wrong and had ever since he had met his strategist, but it was Matthias' right to tell.

Units planned, everyone headed to where they belonged. Ewan's face stayed impassive as they waited for the Mechanoportal to power up, but Laia lightly rested a hand on his shoulder in silent support. He hesitated and then covered her hand with his in thanks. He knew he was about to revisit his nightmares.

When the transport ended and left the three units outside of T'que, a murmur of unease ran through the soldiers. In the late morning light, the village stood as a bloody wound on the land. Buildings were perfectly unharmed. The streets were immaculate. If it hadn't been for one small detail, it could have been a ghost town.

Blood stained every surface. It had splashed across walls and run down the streets. It was no longer normal hue after so many days, but the greyed color seemed somehow worse. There were no bodies in sight, yet their lack was not unexpected. Why find a graveyard to desecrate when there were newly fallen dead to make into an army?

Because they were there not just to wait for battle but to find a way to the undead castle, Laia and Ewan left their units to join Tyrian, Cassie, and Kane as they rode into the city. Even braced for it, Tyrian barely contained a flinch as he saw the lingering remnants of the massacre that had happened. How Persephone and her family had survived . . . somehow he knew it was only because Beelzebub had wanted them to carry his sadistic message.

"'He creeps in the night," Laia murmured, "feasting on the blood of the innocent. A path that crosses his will cross no more.'"

Cassie shuddered. "Thank you so much, Laia."

"It's a passage from an old text Rourke read once. It was never said it expressly meant Beelzebub. But you can be sure it likely did." Laia tilted her head slightly as if listening to something. "There's an area of dead air ahead."

"Dead air?" Ewan asked.

"An area where the air has been stripped of magic," Tyrian offered. "Laia has exceptionally sharp hearing, enough to hear where there is a pocket of silence."

"I didn't know air made noise," Kane said.

"It's not so much that it makes noise," Laia said softly. "When we get there, you'll notice it too."

The dead air was in the middle of what had once been the town center. A bloodstained teddy bear sat abandoned by a lamppost. A wagon had been overturned and the harnesses that had once been worn by horses were broken and tattered. From outside the center, the sound of a sign creaking in the wind was eerily audible. Once within the center, the creaking disappeared.

It wasn't the only thing to disappear. Until they entered that spot, none of them except for Laia had realized just how loud the world could be. Inside the dead zone was no sound at all. Even the faint background hum of magic that none of them had ever noticed before went away. Tyrian couldn't hear his heartbeat, couldn't hear the sound of them breathing. The horses' hooves made no sound on the stone.

A chill raced down Ewan's back. "I never realized that silence could be so frightening." Though audible, his voice carried an eerie cadence as it forced through the silence.

"There is a difference between natural and unnatural silence," Night said quietly. "A natural silence occurs when the magic in the air fades in and out from various locations. An unnatural silence, a dead zone, is what it sounds like. Beelzebub killed this piece of the air. It will always be dead. No magic can be used here."

If a clue was to be anywhere, it would be there. Tyrian swung off Fay's back and began to look around intently. He didn't know what he was looking for, but he knew he would know it when he found it.

The lamppost caught his attention. With a frown, he studied it. "There's something off."

The others looked and Laia's brows lifted. "There's no blood."

The lamppost was nearly pristine. Not a drop or splash of blood had marred the surface. Tyrian lightly ran his fingers over the post and felt what might have been faint carvings in the surface. "There's something here." He hesitated and then said, "Someone lend me their sword."

Laia dismounted. "Seeing you spill blood might make the rest of us violent," she said calmly. "I will do this instead." She drew her sword enough that the blade was visible and without a flinch she cut her palm so that blood welled.

Kane instantly looked at her speculatively. The others, too, looked at her a little curiously, though not with the same suspicion. Her blood was not the normal red of Humans, Mongra, and Grimalkin, nor was it the silvery color of Faeries, green of Elves, or blue of Dragons, Merfolk, and Fliers. Her blood was, in fact, a very dark shade of red that in the right light might have looked black.

"You're not Human," Tyrian noted.

"I'm half, actually," she told him. "The first pureblood Human in five generations was my mother. My father was a serious mutt, and yes, I include Mongra in that too. The fact that I lack wings, fur, or a tail of any kind is a, pardon the pun, bloody miracle."

"Fascinating," Kane murmured. If his suspicions were correct, then he thought he might very well have a better understanding of just how Laia Mitakel did what she did, and why her voice was so powerful even without her Music Relic.

Laia pressed her bloody palm to the lamppost and then slowly slid her hand downward so that her blood smeared the surface. The blood began to drip even further, but only from the smooth portions. The rough area that Tyrian had found revealed itself as words as her blood was trapped inside.

While she stepped out of the dead zone to heal the wound, Tyrian read, "'The sun never rises on the castle of the Vampire. At the moment of sunset, he awakes.'" He shook his head. "Anyone have any idea what that means?"

"It might be directions," Ewan offered. "There's got to be a cliff or something where it faces the west and is sheltered from the east. Think about it: if the mountains blocked the east, then the sun will literally never rise on the castle. But a clear view of the west would allow Beelzebub to know exactly when the sun set."

Laia and Tyrian both got onto their horses again, and Tyrian led the way toward the exit in town that headed directly into the mountains. The sun sat nearly directly overhead, and it was almost impossible to tell one direction from another. Luckily, after an hour of riding into the mountains, the sun began a distinct downward slope. With shadows for a compass, they began their search for a place where the sun would never rise.

It was unexpectedly found as sunset began. As they came around the side of a cliff, they found themselves standing on an enormous plateau. It tapered into a hillside rather than dropping off, and there were no trees to get in the way. The plateau ended against very high cliffs that would entirely block the sunrise. The sunset was perfectly seen as it set on the horizon like a ball of fire. In the light, Laia's hair seemed to turn to gold and the blue in Cassie's hair overtook the black. Even Tyrian's eyes seemed greener than usual.

Night suddenly said, "He's here. I can sense his presence. Ewan!"

"Way ahead of you!" Ewan leapt down to his feet and walked a few steps away from the party. He drew Night and swung him high in the air before slamming him point first into the ground. A shockwave ripped from the sword and tore across the land so violently that it cracked the stone and dirt.

Before the wave hit the cliffs, it hit something else. The shielding spell in place abruptly broke and crumbled like shards of glass. And there, hidden behind the safety of a shield that no longer existed, was the castle of the undead lord.

It was less of a castle than it was a mansion, and it stood like a decrepit mausoleum against the shelter of the cliff. The two highest points on the mansion barely skimmed the top of the cliff behind them. Everything was black and gray stone, and sinister gargoyles perched along the roofline to stare at visitors with hungry red eyes. Dead vines covered the walls, bars covered the windows. Burned into each window was an inverted pentagram in a perversion of a symbol used by Healers to promote life.

Kane rode closer to Laia. "Give me your strength." She held out her left hand and he took it with his right. His Resurrection Relic activated and so did her Music Relic. Like an amplifier, the power that he poured into the Music Relic greatly increased as a holy harmony seemed to swell on the air.

The wave of purple power swept across the land in what would normally be a spell to revive those close to death. Instead, it slammed into the mansion and shattered the windows. The unholy spells imbedded within were likewise shattered, removing all attempts to bar outsiders from entering.

As the sun sat behind them and darkness began to descend, the land began to shake and rumble. Bloody and decrepit hands with broken nails hooked like claws shoved up through the dirt. Grayed and gnarled skin hung loosely from bones. The hands grabbed the ground and pulled sharply. Dirt and rock flew as the zombies hauled themselves out of the land.

Ewan swung back up onto his horse's back and followed the others as they ran down the hill swiftly to escape the horde. When they reached the bottom and looked back, the swaying figures of violent undeath stood as sentries at the edge of the plateau.

Just as the zombies and skeletons started to run down the hill, fireballs began to rain from the sky. Tyrian turned sharply and saw the three units rushing up the hill toward where his party sat. The magic unit led the charge, and Crimson was readying them for another attack. With Lane's wind magic to increase the potency of all fire attacks, it was an inferno that rained down on the enemy.

Ewan and Laia rode over swiftly to join Matthias as Tyrian, Cassie, and Kane took command of their unit. "Magic!" Tyrian shouted. "Push back the tide! Let us pick off the stragglers! Swordsmen, focus on the finishing blows! All other combat is to focus on weakening the enemy! If you can take their arms off, they have nothing to attack with!"

Even with the Liberation Army working perfectly together, there seemed to be no end to the battle. For every undead that fell, another rose. After the first hour passed without anything changing and the Army beginning to tire, Matthias touched his Voice Relic. "Lord Tyrian, our best hope is for you to take Ewan, Kane, and Cassie into the castle itself and remove Beelzebub. This battle will not end unless you do. I will have replacement unit leaders called in."

"Done. I'm counting on you to give us the time we need." Tyrian looked at Cassie and Kane who nodded swiftly in understanding.

Ewan had been next to Matthias, and he already knew the orders. He rode quickly across the field, cutting apart anything stupid enough to try and get in his way. As soon as he reached the others, Tyrian pulled Cassie up onto the back of his horse. She had been dismounted for combat because her hands were her most lethal weapon.

With Kane shooting at anything that ran after them, and Ewan cutting apart anything in front of them, the party rushed back up the hillside toward the plateau and the mansion beyond. When they reached the doors, everyone leapt down and Cassie kicked the doors open. They ran inside, and Fay gathered the other two horses to run back down the hill toward the

Liberation Army. She knew that when her owner left a battlefield that she was to return to the strategist.

Cassie and Ewan slammed the doors behind them just as several skeletons jumped for them. The sound of bone hitting oak was both loud and sickening. A set of armor with a heavy axe stood nearby, so Ewan used the axe to keep the doors shut. Skeletal hands clawed under the bottom of the door but found nothing to grab onto.

The interior of the mansion was a far cry from the outside. It was opulent and decadent, fit more for a king than a mere noble. The tapestries and curtains were velvet and silk, and the floors had been made of polished stone. Jewels encrusted the statues and hung as part of the chandeliers. Lamps were finely crafted pieces of art, and expensive paintings hung on the walls.

Tyrian felt a shiver run all the way down his back. That someone who had such an appreciation for the finer things in life could be capable of such destruction . . . it was horrifying. Somehow, this beautiful manor looked more disgusting than the bloody remnants of T'que.

"Welcome," came a voice that Ewan had never forgotten. "Welcome to my home, Lord Tyrian Southerwind."

Tyrian turned sharply to see a man coming down the stairs toward them. The shiver spread through to his relic as his deepest soul recognized evil. Beelzebub was handsome, cultured, and polite. He wore the disguise of a man very well, but his eyes revealed the monster within. Knowing that Ewan had gouged out one of his eyes, Tyrian wondered just how much of Beelzebub's appearance was a lie. "You deliberately called for me," he said with a calm that impressed even Cassie. "I doubt it was to enjoy a cup of tea and discuss the weather."

Beelzebub chuckled. "Ah, spirit. Such a scarce commodity these days." He bowed with a mocking courtesy toward Cassie. "Lord Tyrian, your taste is impeccable. Lady Cassie has a beauty to rival the sunset." He shot a slight smirk at Kane. "And I see you've brought out the big weapons. Let's see . . . you would be the new Vladimir Kane. You look like your ancestor, boy, but I doubt you have his skill."

"Don't let my age fool you," Kane warned softly.

Beelzebub wasn't that stupid. Kane could have been six instead of sixteen and the Vampire would have treated him with caution. The Kane Clan's reputation was well earned, and any who went rogue feared the day when they looked back and saw the glint of a crossbow arrow.

He turned and looked at Ewan, and the hate could not be kept off his face. "Well, well," he said mockingly. "Look at this. What a blast from the past. You've gotten a little taller since I last saw you, Ewan. I do hope you've gotten a little stronger as well."

Ewan slowly drew Night from his sheath and had the deep satisfaction of watching the smugness drain from Beelzebub's face. The short sleeves of Ewan's tunic plainly revealed the mark of the Midnight Moon as he took an aggressive stance. "Stronger, better, and I've got a friend who has just been *dying* to meet you, Beelzebub."

"I don't think we need an introduction," Night said politely. "Lord Beelzebub knows just who I am, don't you, rogue?

Beelzebub hissed through his teeth as necrotic energy began to pulse around him. "Cursed Relic of Night."

"Oh, I'm not cursed," Night assured him. "Curses are overrated. I'm relatively normal for a half of a Pure Relic."

Beelzebub lunged for Ewan with claws extended. Ewan dodged to the side and swung Night as he did. The blade bit into Beelzebub's cheek and broke the illusion the Vampire had been wearing. His left eye seemed to disappear into a tangled mass of scarring. The scars had never healed properly; they were blackened and decayed rather than healthy.

Realizing that Ewan was, indeed, vastly better than he had ever been before, Beelzebub instead went after Tyrian. If Beelzebub was to go down, then he would take Ewan's beloved Kaiten Star with him!

Tyrian sidestepped gracefully and whirled his staff around so that it cracked into the back of Beelzebub's head. He promptly dissolved into bats before he ran into the wall and flew back to the center of the room. As soon as he reformed, Cassie seemed to appear from out of nowhere. She grabbed him by his tunic and flipped him entirely over her head. He barely managed to get his feet under himself to keep from slamming into the floor.

With a high-pitched scream of fury, he released a shockwave of power that sent Tyrian and Cassie flying into the wall. Kane was sent tumbling across the floor but rolled up to his feet and drew his crossbow. He began shooting at Beelzebub, and the Vampire had to dodge quickly. The arrows used by the Kane clan were not normal arrows. They were blessed by the Millennium Relic, and if they pierced a rogue's heart, the Vampire would be instantly destroyed.

The arrow barrage covered Ewan as he ran across the floor toward Beelzebub. "Block this, you bastard!" he snarled as he swung Night for Beelzebub's neck.

Beelzebub had no room to dodge, but in a morbidly humorous turn of events, he tripped on his own cloak and fell on the ground. The slash of the sword narrowly missed his head and sent Ewan stumbling before he caught his balance.

Tyrian hopped to his feet and his relic glowed brilliantly. The rolling wave of black power swept across the floor and consumed Beelzebub. It could not kill him, but when the dome of power ebbed, Beelzebub looked as if he had literally been through hell. His clothes and skin were ravaged, his energy depleted dangerously. He realized at last that he was outmatched and reached for his power as he began to dissolve into bats.

Kane's relic glowed. "Rapture!" he commanded.

Thick lightning bolts dropped from the sky and formed a proper pentagram around Beelzebub. He was forcefully thrown back into his normal body and fell to his knees as flickers of lightning leapt threateningly around him. "You think this is enough?" he snarled.

"Ewan, banish him!" Kane ordered. "Hurry!"

Ewan stepped forward and slammed the point of Night into the ground. Another shockwave was released that blew apart every bit of glass or crystal in the area. Beelzebub's voice rose on a horrendous scream as the wave tore through his body and then he abruptly disappeared. The pentagram dissolved peacefully as silence, natural silence, descended.

"Is he gone?" Cassie asked cautiously. She stood partially in front of Tyrian, keeping him between her and a wall for safety.

Tyrian's Voice Relic beeped softly and Matthias' voice said, "The battle is done. The zombies and skeletons have lost all power. We are undertaking the task of burying them where they are. It is the least we can do. Return and we will transport back."

"He's gone," Kane confirmed as he holstered his crossbow. "For good, though, I can't say. We dealt a big blow to him. It might be years before he recovers. When the war ends, I will track him. Unless I find proof that he is gone for good, I will assume he survived." He looked at Ewan. "Your battle with him may not be over. It may be just postponed."

"I can handle that." Ewan took a deep breath and then let it out again. "I faced him and won. That's enough for now. I know if I encounter him again, that that time I will be stronger still and be able to destroy him for good. At the least," he shot a grin at Tyrian, "we know he won't be after us again! Tyrian gave him Hell."

"I figured he must be acquainted with it, so he might have missed it." Tyrian let out a little breath as he and Cassie joined Ewan and Kane in the middle of the foyer. "At least we found some justice for T'que and the Commune."

A sudden sense that Tyrian was in danger had all three Destined Stars looking up sharply. They closed together, keeping Tyrian between them all, just as soldiers of the Imperial Army burst out of hiding. Their presence in Beelzebub's mansion was both confirmation of their suspicions of Blaine's involvement, and a vile testament to the corruption spreading through the Army itself.

"Surrender!" one soldier ordered sharply as he aimed a crossbow at them. Others were armed with regular bows, and some held close-range weapons. There were nearly twenty total in the area and they blocked every exit. "Put down your weapons and surrender, Rebellion scum!"

Fury began to churn inside Tyrian's heart and soul, and his relic began to glow softly. "You would call us scum," he said softly, "when you are the ones who stood aside and let a monster murder innocent civilians. Old men and women. Children. People who could not fight and had no desire to. You let them be slaughtered."

"It drew you out," a soldier said in satisfaction. "So what's a little blood here and there? They were just poor villagers anyway. Who cares what happened to them?"

Tyrian's eyes turned abruptly to black and the runic circle appeared around his feet as the symbol of the Devourer appeared over his head. In a lethally calm voice, he said, "Purgatory."

Black fire began to pour down the walls. It was so hot that it melted the stone it touched as it rolled across the floor. One by one, it engulfed the soldiers. Each began to scream in horror as the fires ate away at them. They were little more than ashes in moments, though their voices hovered in the air. It was a frightening display of power, but Cassie, Ewan, and Kane felt not one bit of remorse or guilt for the soldiers' painful destruction.

The flames evaporated and cool air swept into the manor. Tyrian went glassy white as his strength drained from him sharply. He wasn't even conscious as he fell, too weak to even resist the exhaustion. He landed safely in Cassie's arms and Ewan braced her so that she didn't fall. Together, they lowered Tyrian gently to the floor.

Kane knelt beside them and removed his cloak to wrap it around Tyrian. It suddenly seemed obvious to all of them just how tired Tyrian was. His pallor had revealed the vivid dark circles under his eyes. He looked impossibly fragile for someone so powerful.

Cassie gathered him closer against her heart, hoping the sound reached inside his sleep and comforted him. Tears seared her eyes and closed her throat. This could not go on for much longer. "Only the second level," she whispered.

Ewan brushed Tyrian's hair out of his eyes tenderly. "He'll be fine. It's why he has us to support him." He blew out a long breath and touched his

Voice Relic. "Matthias, we need someone to bring Fay to us. Tyrian is out. He unlocked the second level of his relic." Since all unit leaders could hear him, Ewan could hear Lane say something unpleasant. Because the tone held concern, Ewan asked, "What's wrong, Lane? If you know something, don't keep it to yourself!"

"It's too fast," Lane said in frustration. "He's leveling the relic too fast. His body is still adapting to the power it already has. I'll bring Fay to you. I might be able to help with my relic. I can't promise anything; I'm working purely on speculation based on my years of study with Lady Tanelia."

"Just hurry!"

Cassie buried her face in Tyrian's hair. She felt as if things were dragging on too long, and Tyrian was evolving too *quickly*? Just how long was he supposed to endure this? "Damn you, Destiny," she said softly. "Damn you to Hell."

Chapter Twenty-Three

"Blink and you'll miss it."

When Tyrian awoke, it was nighttime. He was in his bed, in his room, in his tower. There was a lamp lit on the sitting room side that spilled soft light around the top and sides of the short wall. The fire crackled softly to spread heat. The balcony doors must have been open because he could hear the sounds of the crickets outside. Everything was peaceful and calm . . . except for his heart.

His whole body still ached, though not as dramatically as it had when he had passed out. His strength was slowly rolling back in. The Devourer's presence loomed large inside his soul, but diminished as he grew stronger. He refused to let it devour him, if that was indeed what it tried to do. But confronting the reality of the power he wielded was an act of strength on its own. He couldn't even find remorse for burning the soldiers alive. He had wanted them to suffer the way they had made the villagers suffer.

The soft scent of strawberries reached him, and he opened his eyes to see Serentia standing at the edge of the wall. She smiled when she saw he was awake and walked over to sit on the side of the bed beside him. "Welcome back." She gently pressed a hand to his forehead and her fingers felt cool and comforting. "Hmm. Temperature is a little high still, but not alarming."

"Why are you here?" he asked softly. "Have you all been taking turns babysitting me? What day is it?"

"Easy." She pressed a finger to his lips. "You'll just get yourself worked up and waste all that rest. It's been two days since you were brought home. You've slept the entire time. Lady Cassie has been with you most of the time, though Marian and Halkern both took turns making sure you were all right. Lord Lane has been in a few times; he was able to feed you strength from his relic. It has a matching charge, so not much, but it helped."

Two days. He didn't feel as if he had slept for two days. It could have been mere hours. "Why are you here, Serentia? Not that I mind the company."

"Liang asked me to sit with you. He was insistent on it, though I can't say why." She smoothed his hair out of his face softly. "We've kept food warm in case you woke. I have some of Liang's porridge waiting. I won't ask if you're hungry," she scolded lightly. "You're going to eat and then go back to sleep. I can see you're still tired."

He didn't bother to argue. It felt foreign and yet wonderful to have someone mothering him in this way. He had never doubted his mother loved him until the scenario with Ophelia. In fact, part of the pain of her betrayal was because she had believed she had acted out of love. Yet even knowing that, he could see where she had never been as open and affectionate as Serentia. He had watched from the windows as Serentia and Tavi played together, and he had been a little wistfully jealous. Annareal had never known how to show love like that. Perhaps it was why she had been so easily fooled.

Serentia returned and put the bowl of porridge on the side table. She helped Tyrian prop himself up with pillows and then handed him the bowl. "There," she said. "Let me know if you need anything."

"Stay." He caught her wrist. "Please?"

Her eyes softened even as her heart did. He was only young enough to be her little brother, but she loved him the way she loved Tavi. "Alright." She went to collect the seed book she had been working on and brought it and a chair around to beside the bed. "But no talking. Eat your dinner."

He found himself hiding a smile. "Yes'm." He watched curiously as she sorted the packets of seeds she had in a basket and tucked them into pockets in the book. He was supposed to be eating, but he couldn't help but ask, "What are you working on?"

"It's how I keep track of what I planted and when. Some crops can be harvested in days. Others take weeks. I alternate what I plant so that we don't run out and so that something is always being harvested and planted. It keeps the soil healthy." She held up a packet of carrot seeds and smiled when he grimaced. "I heard a funny story not long ago."

He sighed. "Liang has a big mouth, and it was his fault anyway."

"Tavi hates carrots too." She put the packet away. "She says that they'll make her skin turn orange. I keep trying to tell her that she'd have to eat a *lot* of carrots for it to happen, but she's downright afraid of looking like a shroomling."

Shroomlings were orange forest monsters that looked like mushroom people. They were mostly docile though they could be hazardous to forest cities; they ate wood, a core component of buildings.

"You spend a lot of time with Liang." He smiled when her color rose. "I'm glad. If you don't mind, may I ask what happened to your husband?"

"Civ." She looked down at her hands. "Tavi was a few months old when the accident happened. Civ was so happy to be a father. We were so happy together. When I was pregnant, he panicked if I even went outside alone." She found herself smiling at the memories where she never had before. "He was a good man. A little quirky, a bit soft-spoken. We had known each other for a few years before he turned eighteen and I courted him. Tavi was born less than a year after we married."

He put his empty bowl to the side. "And brows wiggled across the village."

She laughed. "They did! And rightfully so. Civ and I had a wonderful marriage." She fell silent and then said softly, "We used to grow fruit trees in our garden. It was winter, and it was storming unexpectedly. We don't get a lot of storms in the Empire, but when they happen . . ."

"They happen hard."

"Yes. We had a tree that was our biggest producer. Our year's profit rode on it. Civ went out to try to put a shelter over it. Lightning struck the tree and broke it. It fell over on top of him. I didn't . . . I didn't even know initially. He was taking so long to come back inside. I looked out the window and saw the tree. I knew then," she said softly. "Some things . . . you just feel."

"Do your feelings for Liang scare you?"

She looked at him, unsurprised that he would know. "They did initially. I feel for him in a way I didn't feel for Civ. It was confusing. I didn't think I was strong enough to even consider being with someone again. It was Kyle who helped me get past it."

"Kyle?" His brows lifted.

"He said that the very fact I could even think about a relationship with Liang, that I could feel for him so strongly, was proof that I had healed. He said . . . he said that he couldn't even think about the idea of having someone else in his life other than Ophelia. He knows he will heal, but right now, healing means not dying whenever he thinks of her, not finding another love."

"He has another love in his future," he said quietly, "but that's between us, alright? His soul mate has yet to cross his path. He'll heal too, Serentia." He covered her hand with his. "Liang is the greatest man I've known. He was as much a father to me as my birth father was. I can't remember him not in my life. I want him to be happy. You make him happy. And he needs family." He smiled. "Tavi has him wrapped around her little finger."

"She's good at that." She sighed softly and laced her fingers with his. "He's very patient with me. I know he's waiting for a sign from me. I thought he was just being kind, but when I looked at him one day, I saw him watching me . . . well, he looked at me the way you look at Lady Cassie."

If Liang had for Serentia even a tenth of what Tyrian had for Cassie, Tyrian didn't blame him at all. It was impossible to hide that sort of feeling. "Follow your heart. That's what he would say. He'll wait a long time. He's very patient."

She suddenly smiled. "I wonder where you get it from." She stood and sorted the pillows out again. "No more talking. You need more rest, Lord Tyrian."

"Just Tyrian." He smiled as he lied down. "You're almost my mom, aren't you?"

She lightly tweaked his ear. "If so, then I can scold you for not resting. Hush and go to sleep." She leaned down and gently kissed his cheek and then took the chair and her book back to the sitting room.

Comforted by her presence, he fell asleep easily. When he woke again the next time, he felt fully back to his old self. His strength had completely returned and he actually felt rested. There was sunlight coming around the wall, and birds were chirping. Since they only chirped at sunrise, he knew it was still early. Cassie slept beside him with one arm thrown possessively across his chest.

He turned onto his side and studied her contentedly. He softly ran his fingers down her arm. She stirred and her eyes opened. Tender love filled her gaze as she lifted a hand to cup his cheek. "Better?" she asked softly.

"I am." He turned his head so he could softly nuzzle her hand. He teased her palm with the tip of his tongue and savored the way her breath hitched. "What day is it?"

"You slept four days total. You must be starving."

"Mm." He shifted and tumbled her onto her back. He pressed close, loving the way her eyes darkened to midnight pools. "Food can wait," he said huskily. "I'm hungry for something else entirely."

She sighed softly as she curled her arms around him. She loved when he was like this. When every kiss lasted forever. When every caress lingered until they were both breathless. When it seemed as if he accepted he had forever, and he wanted to spend forever touching her. She thrilled to the way desire could explode so hotly between them, but there were times when this lazy lovemaking was exactly what they both needed.

She was sprawled over the top of his chest, her ear over his heart, when they heard a knock on the door. After a brief pause, the door opened and Merilyne called, "Good morning, Lord Tyrian, Lady Cassie. I've brought coffee for you. There's a newcomer in the city and he's waiting at the inn for you."

She gathered up their dirty clothes and left, her soft whistling lingering in the air. Cassie just sighed. "I have to move, don't I?"

Tyrian tucked his hands under his head. "Not if you don't want to."

"I don't." She rubbed her cheek against his skin in tactile delight. "You scared me, Tyrian," she murmured. "You went so pale, looked so weak. Lane said you're evolving too fast, but that there's nothing we can do to stop it. You *have* to awaken your relic's full potential, though he won't say why it is so important."

"If I have to do it, why is he alarmed?"

She lifted her head to frown at him. "Because even though you have to evolve quickly, it was still much faster than you were supposed to be going. He said that there was something that could still happen that would lift the pressure off you, but he said it was impossible to explain. If it happens, then it'll happen."

"Did he at least give you a clue as to what it was?" He threaded his fingers through her hair.

"He said it was something only I could do, but, again, there's no way to explain. But he *did* say he was confident in it happening. And he wasn't being arrogant. His sincerity makes me believe him where his boasting wouldn't."

"He's just shy." He grinned when she looked at him skeptically. "He is. Remember, I know my Stars as well as they do. And from the minute I met him, I knew he was bluster. Being arrogant is a self-defense."

"And yet hazardous when in the vicinity of Ewan."

"And yet *humorous* when in the vicinity of Ewan."

She couldn't argue that. Ewan's infamous temper was the source of much amusement for everyone. Knowing she couldn't delay the inevitable, she reluctantly slid off his chest and got out of bed. It was no longer such a surprise to see her clothes in with his in the closet. Whimsically, she grabbed a pair of shorts and one of her snug tunics. She just didn't feel like putting all her gear on.

Tyrian watched her and wondered if she even realized that the small scars along her legs were as visible as the one on her neck. She had covered none of them, and the sight of it told him that she was growing stronger too. The knowledge was wonderful to him for two reasons. One, it meant she might soon claim her rightful eternity and that would take one fear off his shoulders. And two, well . . . she had a stunning body that he loved to admire. Her growing confidence meant a shrinking amount of clothing hiding her from his view.

He got dressed as well, in plain tunic and pants, because he didn't think they would be going anywhere just yet that day. He still put on his scarf though, and when she smiled, he said, "People wouldn't recognize me without it."

"Is this a bad thing?"

"I don't feel like enduring the teasing." He handed her one of the cups of coffee and took his own. With that in hand, they headed down the elevator to the courtyard.

The castle and city bustled around them. People who saw Tyrian clearly relaxed and went about things with more cheer. Everyone had been worried about him. He was a hero to the people not just for the deeds he did, but for the way he did them. You had to love Tyrian, Destined Star or not.

Aries and Yumi were having a lively discussion outside the inn when they spotted Tyrian. "Lord Tyrian!" Aries straightened with a relieved smile. "I'm glad you're up." He eyed Cassie's legs with interest. "Please don't hit me, but I must note that you have the best legs this side of the continent and it's a shame I couldn't notice until now."

She snorted softly. "Try your wiles on Taurus."

"That wasn't a wile. It was a statement of fact. And she would entirely agree with me anyway." He opened the door with a courtly bow.

Yumi hovered around Tyrian's side as he walked into the inn. "You're really okay, Lord Tyrian?" she asked anxiously. "You slept for a long time! I mean, I know you probably needed it but it was long and . . ." Her hat and goggles fell over her face and she stopped walking before she ran into something or someone.

Tyrian put them back into place on her head and then tugged on her braid. "Thank you, Yumi," he told her sincerely. "I'm alright now. Thank you for worrying about me."

"Of course I worried!" She hugged him fiercely. "I have to go help Tedium, but you come see us later, okay? We'll show you our new inventions! He isn't even blowing up anything this time!" She waved and ran off out the inn.

"Ball of energy," Aries said dryly. "If she could bottle that for her machines, they'd never malfunction."

Few seats were open in the pub of the inn. Persephone expertly manned the bar and poured drinks with a skill and technique that was on par with Myr's juggling. The bard was actually on the small stage with Taurus and Virgo, dancing to the melody the songstress sang. Virgo played an instrument and had one foot tapping along with the tune. Aries ran over and jumped up onto the stage to grab a guitar and join in.

Tyrian recognized everyone in the room except for one person. It was an Elf standing at the bar talking to Vee and Olan. He was tall, as was normal for the race, and he had very pale blue hair and blue eyes. He wore a Water Relic but carried no weapon. He also didn't wear any sort of armor or accessory; he was likely a civilian.

He was also a Destined Star. Tyrian and Cassie walked over to where the three stood, and Cassie slid onto the empty seat. Persephone winked and refilled her coffee mug. "Eve made it," she said cheerfully. "I know my limitations. I can make anything and everything except a decent cup of coffee."

"But I love you anyway," her husband said dryly as he went past with a tray balanced on one hand. The other hand used a crutch to take weight off his ruined foot. He would never walk on it again, but he didn't care. He was alive. His children and his wife were alive. It was enough for him.

Tyrian offered his relic hand to the Elf. "I'm Tyrian Southerwind, leader of the Liberation Army."

"Aquatico." He took Tyrian's hand and smiled as the glowing white star appeared on his shoulder. "And as is obvious, I'm a Star as well. I'm a bath maker! Hot springs, indoor water features; you name it, I do it! You've got direct access to fresh river water, and I bet I could make some nice hot springs for everyone to relax in." He winked. "Men's and women's. No need to make some people shy. You Humans have such modesty issues sometimes."

"At least we keep the rest of the species of the world entertained," Olan countered dryly.

The idea of actually relaxing in any shape appealed to Tyrian. "Done," he said. "Feel free to grab some people to help you build whatever you need." He sighed. "Damn, now I have to add builders to that list of people we need. We're still expanding, and we need specialists."

Sensing a man in dire need of a break, Aquatico beat a hasty beeline toward the Belowgrounds to find people who could swing a hammer. Much to his delight, he found several. He also recruited Ewan, Dylan, and Rourke to help haul lumber and supplies. Tavi helped too. She brought refreshments for everyone.

The hot springs had been built by evening. They had been made by diverting a portion of the river into a new area near the outer wall. Other walls had been built to divide the space into two separate baths, and a little landscaping with the help of Verdure's Land Relic had made both look as if they had always been there. A few Fire Relics planted in the floor of the springs shortly had the water steaming hot.

Since only six people could comfortably be in the bath on each side at any given time, lots were drawn among the Stars to see who went first. Tyrian and Cassie were, of course, automatically first. Among the men, Ewan, Kyle, Leonard, Halkern, and Gordon also won. Among the women, Emma, Myr, Taurus, Serentia, and Yhalenia won.

"No giggling over there!" Ewan called over the changing room wall. The changing rooms were built from the wall that separated the two sections, and as there was no roof, conversations had to be kept down or they would be heard by the other side.

"Why not?" Taurus retorted back. "It's not like we can see you."

"Hey, if you want to make Aries jealous, I can come over there. And you won't be giggling."

"There are tender eyes over here!" Serentia said dryly.

"Yours or mine?" Myr giggled.

Tyrian just rolled his eyes as he left his changing room. Towels were worn in hot springs, even if nothing else was. Even if Ewan walked over there, no one would get a show. It wasn't as if most of the men on grounds didn't go shirtless while doing hard work anyway. A fair chunk of women—humorously, mostly non-Humans—did as well. Myr had already seen quite a bit.

Content, Tyrian sank into the spring and sat down on a rock ledge. "Much better," he said with a sigh. "It's a brief respite, but it's a respite." He closed his eyes as he tilted his head back. "Someone tell me to stop thinking."

"Stop thinking," came eleven voices.

"He was talking to us, not you," Kyle called. He shook his head as he sat down in the spring next to Halkern. "Maybe there should be a roof over this thing anyway. We can sacrifice the sky for some non-nosy neighbors, right?" A sponge flew over the wall and smacked him in the head. "Hey!"

"Ooh! I hit who I was aiming for!" Emma's voice was full of laughter. "I was terrified I'd hit Lord Tyrian!"

Everyone laughed at that, and it felt good to just laugh for once. Tyrian knew that in the morning he would be meeting with Matthias and the others to go over the plan of attack for Dry Basin, and the brief respite would be over. The pause was as much for everyone else as it was for him. Everyone had been deeply affected by the events with Beelzebub.

He studied the scar on Ewan's chest curiously. He had seen it before, but knowing the story behind it just made it more impressive. The mark was several inches wide at the center and went in a straight line from his clavicle to just below his ribs. Ewan's will to live was great indeed.

There was a sudden burst of giggles from the women's side. Warily, Gordon called, "What are you doing over there?"

"It's rude to ask," Yhalenia retorted, which set off more giggles.

"Are you getting drunk over there?" Halkern asked.

"Nah, Cassie and I don't drink. We're working on Serentia. We want to throw her into Liang's room."

"They are not!" Serentia protested hastily.

"Well, if you have wine, you could have shared!" Leonard said in exasperation.

A few moments later, a hand appeared over the top of the wall holding a bottle. Ewan, being tallest, walked over to grab it. The wall stood only a foot higher than he was tall. "Thanks, Taurus!" he said cheerfully. She was the only one with a Music Relic over there, so the hand had to be hers.

"No problem. Whoops! Don't drop me, Emma!" There was a loud splash promptly after the words, followed by laughter from the other women.

"Normal life," Gordon murmured to Tyrian. "An unfamiliar but welcome thing. I suppose we're all a bit loopy after so much stress. We were bound to go a little nuts when we had a break." He sighed deeply. "I can't exactly stop thinking either. What the Imperial Army did . . ." He shook his head. "There is no excuse. If word reaches the other Lower Generals, I know they will abandon all pretenses and join us."

"Blaine won't let them know," Ewan said briskly. "We can be sure of that. But when we get a chance to talk to them, it will help convince them." He settled back against the edge of the tub. "You guys are smarter than I gave you credit for."

Gordon couldn't take offense. "We're trying, at the least. As I've said from the get-go, when the bounty was issued for Lord Tyrian, we knew something was funny. Alex asked the Emperor if the people had reason to rally around a rebellion, and he didn't give us a straight answer."

Comfortable silence fell, broken only by the sound of the water and the night. Tyrian had just passed the bottle of wine to Kyle when he felt an odd tingle in the air. He frowned and looked around. "Did anyone feel that?"

The men shook their heads. Tyrian glanced around again and then looked up at the sky. Even as he watched, a sudden swirl of clouds appeared directly over the middle of the spring. Before anyone could even think of moving, the clouds spit out a young woman who landed in the spring with a shriek and a splash.

Ewan and Leonard hastily grabbed her and pulled her back to the surface. She was dressed like a Magician, though her choice in clothing was a little old-fashioned since it consisted of an actual robe over the top of a slim dress. Her long black hair hung to her waist, and she defined 'cute' rather than 'lovely'. None of that really surprised anyone. What surprised them more than her entrance was the relic she wore.

It was a Pure Relic.

"Ohmygod!" she babbled. "How dib I ged here?" Since the stuffy sounding words were followed by a sneeze, and then another, she almost didn't have to say, "I hate gebbing colds!" She blinked the water out of her eyes and focused. As she did, her cheeks turned bright red. She was in a spring . . . with naked men. "Ohmygod! Ohmygod! I'm zo zorry, I dibn't mean to barge in, I jus' hab dis nasty cold and ib makes me sneeze and sneeze and den by relic went off and I was go'ng across da the sky ab den—ahchoo!—I got here and I'm zo zorry!" She yelped and covered her eyes as Tyrian and Gordon stood. "You're naked!"

"We're wearing towels," Tyrian said dryly, wryly resigned as he recognized the tug inside his soul. He grabbed a dry towel from the side and wrapped it around her shoulders. "Here. Let's get you out of here." He and Ewan helped her out of the hot spring, and she kept her face covered. Doing so revealed her relic more clearly, and it looked a bit like a mirror. Tyrian did not recognize it at all. "Now, what's this about your relic? Here." He helped her sit down on a bench and then glanced up at a sound to see the women peeked over the top of the wall. "Don't fall!" he scolded them.

"We're stable," Cassie promised.

The young woman cautiously peeked through her hands and saw that the men were, indeed, wearing towels. She dropped her hands as her shoulders slumped. "It's the Pure Echo Relic. Transports stuff. And me!"

"And you don't have full control." Kyle was trying not to laugh because he didn't want to hurt her feelings.

"I do . . . most of the time," she grumbled. She promptly sneezed and huddled in the towel. "I was go'ng to go find Lord Tyrian but den I gob sick." She snuffled and then covered her nose with the towel as she sneezed again. "Jus' by bad luck I geb dropped in a men's spwing! Uhm, doz anyboby know where I can find Lord Tyrian?"

Everyone pointed at Tyrian, and he slowly raised his relic hand. "Right here."

"Ooh." She hid her face in the towel. "I'm Miranda. Zorry 'bout dis."

Leonard disappeared into the changing room and shortly returned fully dressed once more. "Okay, missy." He paused. "Wait, a Pure Relic. How old are you?"

"Uhm." She squinted one eye closed. "Six hundred? I think. I . . . lost count."

She was older than Lane, which made several people, especially Ewan, rather gleeful. Leonard amended himself and said, "Okay, honey. Let's get you into the castle and find a room. Eve's restaurant should still be open, so we'll get you some soup to get rid of that cold." He scooped her up, towel and all.

Tyrian stood and smiled as Miranda looked at him askance. "Don't worry," he told her. "You're here. That's the important thing. We don't mind how you got here. Just lend me your strength, and we'll call it even."

She brightened and went from cute to almost pretty. It was a curious but enchanting sort of magic. "Dank you, Lord Tyrian! I pwomise I'll do whateber I can! Ahchoo!" She groaned as she kept her face buried in the towel. "Oooh. My heb."

Halkern also went to change clothes and then followed Leonard out of the spring. Magic didn't often do much for illnesses, but that didn't mean he wouldn't be able to help in some way. He might be able to alleviate some of the stuffiness with herbs; he wasn't a doctor, but a cold was part of basic care that anyone with a Medicine Relic learned.

"So." Emma propped her elbow on the wall with a wry smile. "How's that relaxing thing working, Lord Tyrian?"

"I think I need a break from my break," he grumbled.

Chapter Twenty-Four

"I scream and I beg but my pleas fall on deaf ears; why can't you hear me?"

Word of the decimation of the Imperial soldiers at the hands of Tyrian Southerwind was not something that could be kept under wraps. Nor could the battle against the undead be kept secret. All who lived in Trinan heard about the goings-on, and many began to wonder just who was truly the enemy.

Those closest to the kingdom, especially, heard the news. T'que's destruction had been earmarked as a casualty of combat, but Donald did not believe it. Not when he took in the facts. Tyrian *happened* to be fighting the undead and Beelzebub right after the destruction, and he just *happened* to destroy Imperial soldiers inside the rogue's castle?

Albanion and Blaine were in the throne room when Donald walked in unannounced. He didn't bow as he normally did. Instead, he crossed the room directly and said crisply, "I would like you to explain yourself, sire."

The Emperor lifted a brow. Because of his rank, Donald had many rights that no one else did. Such informality was one of them, but Albanion didn't like the tone of the High General's voice. "Explain what, General?"

"T'que. Intelligence reports that it was destroyed by Lord Beelzebub, the infamous rogue Vampire." He shot a look at Blaine that was icy. "Further information has reported that Tyrian engaged and defeated Beelzebub's undead army and then breached the castle itself with Ewan Grizmar and Vladimir Kane to banish Beelzebub himself. After that fight ended, Imperial soldiers tried to take him captive, but he destroyed them with the second level of his relic." His eyes narrowed. "What were Imperial soldiers doing in Beelzebub's castle?"

Blaine's nails bit into her palms as she curled her hands into fists. That cursed Kaiten Star! He and Ewan must have found the Midnight Moon Sword. And *Kane*. The Millennium Valley was throwing its weight behind the Rebellion, and that meant they might just lend a unit of soldiers too. A unit of Vampires was not a pleasant thought. It was almost a unit of Pure Relic users. Blaine hated Millennium Vampires with a vengeance. How dare they be given the gift of immortality?

Albanion's mouth opened and closed. "I have no idea," he said honestly. He looked at Blaine. "Do you know anything of this?"

Blaine lightly put a hand on his shoulder and purred, "No doubt they were there to take advantage of the situation."

He subsided. "Yes, of course." He looked at Donald. "Your son did the world a service by removing Beelzebub, but that does not excuse his other actions."

Disgust filled Donald's face. He had had enough. With a stiff bow, he said, "Of course it does not. Thank you for satisfying my curiosity." He turned on his heel and left the throne room. As soon as the doors shut behind him, he viciously grabbed the emblem on his cloak and removed it. He loved the Empire. The only way to save it was to end it. If the people wanted something new, as a General of the Empire, it was his duty to ensure it.

He had taken only a handful of steps down the hall when Blaine seemed to suddenly appear in front of him. Malevolence poured off her in waves, and her beautiful face no longer looked so appealing. Hatred glistened amid madness inside her eyes. "Move aside, monster," he told her. "Or I will cut you down."

She gave a bark of laughter. "I'm shaking in my boots, Southerwind. You can't even comprehend my power." Her hand lashed out and grabbed his neck. Power blasted from her fingers and into his body in a slimy and evil wave. "If you leave the castle grounds by other than my command," she snarled, "you will die instantly. And your life energy will be mine for the taking. There is much life in you, General. You were chosen well to be the father of the first Kaiten Star. Your energy might just give me the power to destroy him. Are we clear?"

Impotent fury welled inside him. "We are clear, Blaine." She released him and he pressed a hand to his throat. He could still feel her slimy touch, but he would be damned if he let her win.

She smirked as he stalked down the hall. A sound caught her attention and she moved swiftly to intercept the figure attempting to sneak away. "Lady Annareal," she purred. "What a pleasure. I've been intending to speak with you."

Annareal stared at her, her heart pounding hard. "What did you do to my husband?"

"Ensured his compliance. And you would do best not to cross me, bitch." Blaine's eyes narrowed sharply. "I would be happy to administer Kyle Raitels' justice for him."

Annareal fled down the hallway as fast as she could. Blaine was a monster. The Empire was full of monsters posing as feeling beings. The Imperial Army had abandoned a village to a massacre. Life as everyone knew it was crumbling to the ground, and Annareal had helped it happen.

Kyle Raitels might hate her, but not more than she hated herself.

She took a little breath and felt calmness descend. There was only one thing to do. Only one thing she could do to make amends. It was time to give back a life in exchange for the life she had taken.

She went out back to the gardens and over to a small flowerbed. There, sitting in the middle, was a little girl with a tiny pair of Faerie wings on her back. She was a ward of the Empire and had been since she was a baby. At six, she was frighteningly smart and serious. Annareal had always thought she reminded her of Tyrian as a child and that was why she loved her. "Raven," she said softly as she knelt beside the girl. "I need to talk to you about something."

Blaine didn't spare a thought for Annareal or Donald as she stalked toward her tower. The General would die soon enough, either at her hand or Tyrian's, and when he died, his life energy would be hers to control. And Albanion! She hissed softly under her breath. She was going to rip out what little spine he had. Useful as he may be, he was a pathetic weakling.

She had shut the door behind her when she felt a sudden sensation of power. She turned sharply and her eyes narrowed. Standing beside a window was a man. He was tall and powerful, golden haired and handsome. Beautiful, in fact, was a more apt term, though his eyes looked cold and cruel.

He wore a Pure Relic.

She bared her teeth. "Get out of my tower, whoever you are."

"Don't be so hasty," he said calmly. "I might just be able to help you, Lady Blaine. I believe we might just have similar goals." He offered a courtly bow. "Do allow me the time to at least explain myself."

Intrigued despite herself, she studied him. "Talk."

A slow smile touched his lips but did not warm his eyes. "Have you heard of the Summarians? They've left interesting relics around the world, and I might have the key to finding them."

Her interest was indeed caught. She remembered the Summarian race quite well. They had been beloved to Tanelia and so Blaine had hated them. 'Blessed by the gods.' What rubbish. But still . . . they had been powerful. Very powerful. She sat down on the opposing window ledge. "You have my attention."

Chapter Twenty-Five

"I can't say goodbye to yesterday, but I can't say hello to tomorrow."

Early in the morning, Tyrian and Cassie reported to the meeting room. Matthias was already there and he smiled when he saw Tyrian. "I understand we had a bit of an eventful evening, Lord Tyrian."

"That's one word for it," Tyrian said dryly. "Startled all of us when she appeared out of nowhere. I hope her cold is better this morning. I'd hate for her to transport herself away right in the middle of battle."

Lane walked in and said, "It's not likely to happen. Miranda's wildest transports tend to be more because of Destiny's whim than from her own lack of control. However, her lack of control doesn't help either. Partially it's because of the nature of the Echo Relic itself. It bounces its own power backwards sometimes. If she transports you, you might end up in a place *relative* to where she aimed rather than right on target."

Tyrian winced. "And there's nothing she can do about it?"

"Not really. She tried to take off the relic once and it transported her into the middle of the ocean." He shook his head wryly. "She trained with Lady Tanelia for a while. She's three hundred years older than I but has much less control over her relic. Then again, I have more natural talent."

The other three let that slide without comment. "Where can she transport us to?" Cassie asked. "Anywhere we want or are there limitations?"

"Anywhere you've been previously. She matches the magic you've left behind to send you there. And, again, it might be *relative* to that spot."

"As long as it's closer than walking or riding, I can handle that," Tyrian said. He sat down at the table and pulled the map closer. Thomas had been hard at work, and the map showed clearly what was still under Imperial control and what was now under Rebellion control. T'que had been crossed off with the universal symbol meaning a ghost town. It still infuriated Tyrian.

Evelyn arrived with breakfast right ahead of the others in the meeting. Ewan and Kyle took coffee gratefully while Gordon and Samantha took tea. Leonard opted for neither, and Cherry had juice. Plates were passed out, and Evelyn left the room with a cheerful step. She loved cooking for everyone.

"Dry Basin," Matthias began. He tapped a finger on the map where Dry Basin was located. "We stand at ten units, including two ranged and one magic. There are eight units at Dry Basin."

Kyle looked over in surprise. "Weren't there ten as of the last time we discussed this?"

"There were. Two units have been recalled to Trinan. Kell is investigating the reason why. We only found out this morning from Tod. One of his gossip partners is in Dry Basin and sent a pigeon to us. Something seems to be happening at the capitol, but information is scarce right now."

"So we could probably overwhelm them with sheer force." Samantha frowned. "That sounds too easy."

"It isn't as easy as it sounds. Among the eight remaining at Dry Basin are four magic units and two ranged. They only have one close-combat unit, but they don't really need more than that with their current set-up."

"We'd never have a chance to get in close to them," Ewan said. "Unless we could manage to put up some really good cover, we'd be picked off from a distance."

Cherry suddenly frowned. "Are they backed up against the city?"

"Yes." Matthias looked at her expectantly. "If you have an idea, I welcome it. I can't do everything alone."

"I was just thinking," she said slowly, "that we might be able to take advantage of our greater numbers if we can draw them away from the city. If we can clear enough space, we could just drop in an additional unit behind them. Say we distract them with our ranged and magic units. They won't be able to move in close-range either. But . . ."

"But if we can lure them into following us across the field, then we can drop in our close-range units right behind them." Gordon smiled at Cherry. "Very clever."

"And it might just work best." Matthias looked at Lane. "How much bluster can you make?"

"As much as you need."

"He *is* full of hot air after all," Ewan muttered.

Lane pointedly ignored him. Tyrian wisely hid a smile as he said, "Then we'll look at having you, Crimson, and Verdure each leading a unit. Laia will ride with you, and Halkern can ride with Verdure while Marian is with Crimson. Myr is good for helping enhance spell potency, so she can ride with you as well." He looked at Kyle. "It's a waste of your sword arm, but you're good with that relic. Ride with Verdure."

"You're the boss."

Suddenly speculative, Tyrian looked at Ewan. "Night? Just how much of you is still a relic?"

"Oh, I probably have one or two good spells inside me. Ewan's magically stupid, but he doesn't need to be a mage for this. If he points me at the enemy, I can do the rest."

"So just like normal?" Lane muttered under his breath.

Tyrian kicked Ewan under the table before he could open his mouth. "Don't encourage him. Ewan, you'll ride with Crimson. Samantha, will you ride with me and Cassie?"

"Gladly, Lord Tyrian."

"Emma and Olan can lead one ranged unit while Shots has the other. Matthias, will you ride?" At the nod, Tyrian drummed the fingers of his relic hand on the table. "Then you can ride with Emma and Olan. Yhalenia can ride with Shots. Cherry, I'd like you to ride along as well. Shots will need your guidance since he's acclimated for small combat."

"Okay. What about the ambush units?"

"Mine will be one of them. The other will be Dylan, Leonard, and Sean." Tyrian blew out a hard breath. "It's harder to play tricks on an enemy than it is to confront them head on."

"Which is why I prefer it," Samantha agreed dryly.

Dry Basin was one of the bigger cities in the Empire. It boasted a population of nearly thirty thousand and had six units to call its own. Because of its size, the effects of the tyranny were both easier and harder to see. If you looked at the upper class portion of town, it seemed as if nothing was happening at all. If you looked at the lower class, you realized it was low indeed. The middle class had been eliminated entirely.

But even the upper class was not happy. It was hard to eat breakfast when you knew people were starving. It was hard to go to sleep knowing people slept on the streets. The condition of the city was holding on by its teeth only by the benevolence of those few upper class people. They made the right noises to the capitol, got breaks on their taxes, and poured the extra money into their town.

The lieutenant leading the Imperial units had noticed what was happening but had said not a single word. Her duties were to guard the city, not tattle on people struggling to survive. She hated how people flinched when the soldiers went through town. She hated more that it was deserved. She even knew who in her own units could not be trusted. It was as if the water in Trinan had begun to poison everyone.

There was a bright flash of light and she straightened quickly. "The Liberation Army is approaching!" she snapped to her units. "Ready for engagement!"

Because she knew full well the Rebellion had more units on hand, she was understandably surprised when only five appeared on the field. She was more surprised to not see the familiar green scarf of Tyrian Southerwind. She lightly touched her Voice Relic. "And where stands Tyrian Southerwind?"

"Is there a rule against an army fighting without its leader?" Matthias said politely. "If there is, then your Emperor should be on every battlefield."

She couldn't argue with that, but she also couldn't help her suspicion. Tyrian had been on every other battlefield, so why not this one? "I see."

One of the other soldiers leaned over and said softly, "It is possible he has not recovered from the events in the mountains. I heard that he collapsed. I have no idea how long it takes to recover from evolving a Pure Relic, but you'd think it wouldn't be easy."

"Hmm." It was certainly plausible. "I suppose it would be a waste of time to ask for surrender," she said to Matthias.

"Quite."

"Very well, let the engagement commence."

The lieutenant's unit was the sole close-combat one, so she stayed to the back of the field as the other units began trying to lure each other closer. It ended up playing like a game of chesstac where only the king and queen were left. One couldn't win without losing at the same time. Not unless someone got aggressive.

She watched intently and realized that the range of the enemy magic units was not that great. They had to dance back after every attack. Sensing an opening, she began to move her unit across the field. If she could catch them in a back step, she could take out at least Matthias and end the battle.

No sooner had her unit moved away from the city than did a flash of light announce the sudden arrival of reinforcements. She turned sharply and stared in dismay at the sight of two more Liberation Army units standing right behind her. Riding at the front of one of them was a familiar figure. Sometimes being right wasn't enjoyable, she discovered then. And recognizing Samantha Yureny riding with Tyrian did nothing to make the defeat easier to swallow.

She could stand and be slaughtered, or she could surrender and spare what remained of her soldiers. Many had already fallen to the more potent magic on the other side. She threw her battleaxe on the ground with a sigh. "Yield."

All units stopped fighting. The three Healers on the field set about curing the wounded while the bodies of those who had fallen were retrieved. Casualties dotted both sides, but the lieutenant's swift surrender had ensured things did not get truly bloody.

Samantha and Cassie rode with Tyrian across the field toward the defeated lieutenant. Matthias and Cherry also rode closer. "Lieutenant . . . Araceli, correct?" Samantha asked. At the nod, she smiled. "Well met, Lieutenant. You've gotten much stronger since I last saw you."

"Apparently not strong enough," was the rueful response. She was silent for long moments as she weighed her choices and then lifted her chin distinctly. "Lord Tyrian, I would ask to join your fight. My soldiers are free to make their own choices, but I would lend my strength to you. I can't stomach what our Empire has become."

"Your skill will be appreciated," Tyrian said.

Ewan walked over and picked up the fallen axe. "You'll need this."

"Thank you." Araceli turned to her units and said, "Laws of engagement stand. Your choice needs to be made now as to whether you return to Trinan or follow me to the Liberation Army. My choice is a willing one."

Of those remaining on the field, five units' worth removed the emblems from their uniforms and switched sides. The rest did not and returned by magic to Trinan. The good news for the Liberation Army was that of the five they gained, they gained three magic and one ranged. The fifth was Araceli's close-range unit.

Ewan looked at Tyrian and asked, "Are you going into the city to look for Stars?"

"I am. I also wish to speak with the mayor about any strength that he or she can lend to us."

"Okay. We'll hold out here until you're done so you can transport back with us."

"That would be much appreciated." Tyrian glanced at Samantha. "Are you going with me and Cassie?" She arched a brow and he had to smile. "Alright, I suppose it was a silly question." He was also unsurprised when Dylan and Sean opted to go along as well. He was beginning to get used to everyone being overprotective.

A dramatic mood change had swept through the city. As Liberation Army soldiers moved in to start helping people, spirits immediately lifted. The six units belonging to Dry Basin were coming out of dormancy and talking to Liberation soldiers about obtaining uniforms and a flag to fly. It was a quick reminder to Tyrian that he needed an actual army symbol. Mouse and Myr were supposedly working on it. He would have to prod them along.

While they walked through the streets, he kept his senses alert. He had learned that not only did his Stars stand out in a crowd, but they also had a tendency to be in unlikely places as well. He wasn't discounting anyone or anything. It still baffled him that he had only a total of forty-eight Stars found. If he went on the theory that the remaining generals, including his father, were also Stars, then he could say that he had fifty-three. There were fifty-six to be found.

Commotion rose from inside a building and he glanced over curiously just as two kids came rushing out the doors. One was a girl with ashy blonde hair, roughly around the age of ten. The other was an auburn haired boy in the same age range. They came to a skidding stop in front of Tyrian, and the boy said, "You're Lord Tyrian!"

Tyrian smiled as he knelt down to be more on level. "I am."

The boy stuck out his hand. "I'm Mikey. This is Kami."

Tyrian shook his hand solemnly and then shook Kami's as well. That familiar tug was inside again, telling him even faster than the mark on their shoulder that they belonged to him. Neither looked to be anything more than a civilian, but there was an unquenchable spirit inside both that called to Tyrian. It was these children, these young ones who survived in the harshest climate, that he wanted to fight for. "It's nice to meet you," he said.

Kami took Tyrian's relic hand and studied the relic with immense curiosity. She had always been fascinated by relics, and she felt lucky to see a Pure Relic in her life. "My mom and dad were Relic Masters," she told Tyrian. "That's what I want to do when I grow up!" She got a speculative look in her eye. "Do you have anyone to take care of your relic supply?"

Cassie and Dylan shared a smile with Samantha and Sean. It was the familiar game to be played between Kaiten and Destined Star. That two such young children would know their destiny was not so surprising. The legend had spread rapidly.

"You know," Tyrian said, "I actually don't. We're looking for a Relic Master as well, but if you'd like to keep our relics safe, then I'd be glad for it. If we find our Master, you can help them with all the work. How old are you, Kami?"

"Twelve. I know, I'm small." She wrinkled her nose. "I turn thirteen in a few months. Mikey is almost eleven. We're not related," she added quickly, "but we've been friends since we were little. Uhm, littl*er*."

Mikey nodded firmly. "I can make beds and stuff at the inn. We can be helpful!"

"Well . . ." Tyrian hedged. He grinned when both gave him big-eyed pleading looks. "Alright." When they cheered, he added firmly, "You can't just go running off to the castle, though." Recalling the use of past tense that Kami had used, he asked gentler, "Are you orphans?"

Kami nodded. "Our parents were killed at one of the checkpoints a few years ago during a skirmish with Foresalia. The lady who runs the orphanage here has raised us. She's super nice and sweet! You have to meet her! We're the only orphans left, so she'll be glad to get rid of us. She's really old."

The kids grabbed Tyrian's hands and pulled him into the building they had run out of. "Grace!" Mikey called. "Guess what! Guess what! We're going to go with Lord Tyrian and we're gonna help him get freedom for the people!"

The old woman sitting in a rocking chair beside the fire just sighed. "Only months ago I would have thought you addled!"

Tyrian studied her and a little smile began to tug at his lips. Age had settled gracefully on the old woman for she was still lovely and fit. Her white hair softly curled around her dark face and her wrinkles seemed to emphasize her age beautifully. "I must ask," he murmured, "just how they knew about their destiny."

An impish light twinkled at the corner of her green eyes. "A good informant never reveals her sources." She got to her feet with surprising agility and let her cane lean against the wall. Without any hint of a physical ailment, she walked over to Tyrian and peered up into his face. "You're much more handsome than I expected," she told him. "You remind me of Kell in his youth."

"Ah! That's why your name is familiar." He took her offered hand and bowed over it as if she were nobility. "Your fans still speak of you highly."

Grace looked at Cassie and said blandly, "Watch this one. It's dangerous."

"I'd noticed," Cassie grumbled, causing Samantha to laugh and pat her shoulder in sympathy.

The white star appeared on Grace's shoulder, and Tyrian said, "Kell does a great job as an informant, but I think we could use a second sharp mind as well. How would you like to put your skills to work for the Liberation Army? They're wasted here, and I need your help." He tilted his head. "Tell me, did you ever marry after Kell chickened out?"

She smiled. "Love can wait patiently when it is needed."

He glanced at Cassie, thinking of the patience he had exerted for her sake. He would have waited a hundred years, even a thousand, to finally claim her for his own. "Indeed it can," he agreed softly.

The note of intimacy in his voice had a hint of pink climbing Cassie's cheeks. It took a lot of willpower not to kiss him in front of everyone. Not that she really had to worry about her reputation anymore; it was actually *growing* thanks to her being his Kentei Star. She mostly still just had to occasionally deal with her strict upbringing. Her orderly life had gone completely out the window, but she didn't regret it one bit.

Grace sighed contently; she remembered those days very well. She rubbed her hands together. She was old, but she didn't think that meant she had lost any right to claim the man she loved. "The kids and I will head out to the base," she decided firmly. "I'll help gather your intelligence, and I'll work on getting Kell's butt to an altar. I'll be married before I'm seventy or I'll toss him in the moat!"

"I want to be Grace when I grow up," Kami told Samantha solemnly.

The general grinned. "Me too."

Tyrian smiled at Sean and Dylan. "Dylan, can you help them get their things together? Sean, I want you to go talk to Ewan. Find three soldiers willing to make the trek back to the base on foot so that these three can go along."

"Four," Grace said. When Tyrian lifted a brow, she explained, "That old codger, Ted, is in town too. He and Tod are inseparable friends." She shook her head. "They and Tad courted me all at the same time. I was seeing Tod until Kell came along." She pointed a finger at Samantha. "You mark my words, young lady. When you see the right one, sit on him or her."

Dylan elbowed Samantha lightly and she coughed. Tyrian just smiled. "Alright. Sean, ask for four then. We'll find Ted on our way to talk to the mayor."

The problem with transport magic, whether relic or mechanical, was that it had max capabilities, Tyrian reflected as they headed outside. It couldn't transport more than a thousand soldiers at a time, nor could it do less than roughly nine hundred. Araceli's swift surrender had limited the number of casualties on both sides. Because of it, the units that had come to battle were going back at max even though they had lost some soldiers along the way. "Sometimes I wonder who tried to impose sanity on war," he murmured.

"That would be the people who knew it was an inevitable evil and were trying to limit the carnage," Cassie said softly. She slipped her hand into his and held on. "Someday, Tyrian. Someday we won't need rules of warfare. There won't even be war."

It was the hope that Ophelia had died for, and he was determined to do his part. And if there really were to be more Kaiten Stars, then he would damned well help them too. If someone was born under the same star as he was, then he or she would be a little brother or sister. He didn't want a need for more Kaitens, yet he couldn't help but wistfully think of how much fun it would be to have younger siblings. Especially a little sister. Tavi helped fill the void, but he felt the age gap too clearly.

The mayor's house was located near the center of town. Technically, of course, the mayor hadn't been mayor for more than a year, but the shift in control of the town had restored her to the position. When Tyrian arrived, she was standing outside her house issuing orders to people to work on restoring the city.

She was a slightly plump grandmotherly woman with riotously curly gray hair tied at the nape of her neck. When she spotted Tyrian, relief filled her eyes. "Lord Tyrian, thank you so much!" she said fervently. "We can't repay you for what you've done for us. If one more person lost their home, we would have all just collapsed entirely."

He shook his head slightly. "There is no repayment needed, but I would ask for your assistance. Dry Basin has six military units. I ask that you lend them to us."

"Done," she said instantly. "One can remain to hold the city, and the other five can go with you. One is a ranged unit, the rest are close-combat."

That would bring the total for the Liberation Army up to twenty units with five others in cities. Of the twenty, five were ranged and six were magic. Tyrian realized with a little chill that with numbers like that he was perfectly matched to the twenty units commanded by his father. It was not a welcome or pleasant thought. Necessary evils, he thought again. There were far too many in the world.

The mayor watched him and then said, "I would also ask a favor, Lord Tyrian." When he lifted a brow, she smiled. "Take my good-for-nothing husband with you. He's good for little except sending messages."

He found himself smiling back. "His name wouldn't be Ted, would it?"

"How did you guess?" Her tone was dry. She waved a hand for them to follow her. "Come with me. I'll show you where he roosts. Or where his pigeons roost. Damned little difference," she grumbled.

Samantha coughed to cover a laugh. Tyrian just followed along behind the mayor as she headed around behind her house. It wasn't hard to tell where Ted 'roosted.' The little shed behind the house was liberally covered in pigeons. An old man who certainly looked to be in Tod's age frame stood in the doorway and had pigeons all over his shoulders and head. "I'm not appreciated," he told Tyrian.

The mayor rolled her eyes expressively. Tyrian coughed lightly. "Well, we could use your assistance. If we could have more than one person to send and receive messages, it would be quite helpful." He offered his relic hand. "Tod is with my army, as is Kell, and now Grace."

"Just like old times," Ted said fondly. "I wonder if Grace will get that old coot to marry her finally. Ah well! Can't miss the fireworks, now can I? Count me in!" He took Tyrian's hand and the familiar white star appeared on his shoulder. He promptly wiggled his brows at his wife. "You'll miss me when I'm gone."

She turned her back with a flounce of her hair. "So you said when you visited your friends last year. I rather enjoyed the quiet!"

As she walked off, Ted said, "Pay her no heed. We've been married for fifty years for good reason." Fondly, he said, "Still my favorite girl."

Tyrian smiled at Cassie. They were at the other end of the spectrum from Kell and Grace. Sometimes it took fifty years to find that one person. But then, sometimes you were lucky. Even with everything else going on, Tyrian considered himself lucky. Now he just needed to figure out how to propose to his lady monk without making her get nervous. Unlike some people, he wasn't waiting fifty years to put a ring on her finger!

Chapter Twenty-Six

"The tragedy is that I loved you."

The increase in the size of the Liberation Army was seen as a sign to the other cities that freedom hovered close. The Imperial Army began to close ranks tighter around Trinan, stationing all spare units in that location to secure the castle and the Emperor. There were only eight cities left un-liberated in the Empire. Three cities of larger size than Dry Basin, Trinan, and the four checkpoints.

The checkpoints were as yet guarded by the other four Lower Generals. The Liberation Army outnumbered each general's army of eight units, but the individual checkpoints were also secured by other deterrents. Even as Matthias and Tyrian talked strategy for the checkpoints, they were talking strategy for the other three cities. Larksville and Pardue were still last on the list, to be handled after the checkpoints. It was Firmeza that they looked to next. It was fractionally bigger than Dry Basin, but not by much.

"In scope," Thomas said as he stood on a chair to point at the map he had just hung, "we're looking at Firmeza as having about thirty-five." He spoke the number with the understanding that he referred to thousands. "From what Kell and Grace have determined, we can sincerely look at Alphin, the eastern checkpoint, as the next target after Firmeza. It has forty in population. It's guarded by General Alexander Renduex and his eight units."

"Alex gets seasick," Gordon noted. "I never did understand why he ended up with a coastal checkpoint."

Ewan was sitting with his feet propped on the chair that held Thomas. The weight kept the boy balanced. "Someone has a poor sense of humor."

"Fair enough."

Thomas pointed to another city, very happy that he could be helpful in this way. "After that, there's Betane, the southern checkpoint. It has fifty, and it is guarded by General Diamond Cutter."

"That's a good thing, actually," Samantha told Matthias. "If we have Alex on our side before we go after Di, then he will definitely increase our chances of getting in without a fight. Let's put it this way: at their rate, they're going to turn into Kell and Grace."

Matthias hid a smile. The budding romance between the two informants had become a source of much entertainment for everyone over the last week. A new betting pool had even started. Tod was having a grand time flirting with Grace, and Kell was not a happy camper over it. "I see."

"After Betane, there's Gammine, the western checkpoint near the border to Foresalia. General Marcus Quint is guarding it, and it stands at sixty. The last checkpoint is the northwestern Deltine. It stands at seventy-five, and it is guarded by General Vincent Martine." He hopped down off the chair. "Larksville is after Deltine. It has one hundred ten. Pardue is close after with one hundred fifteen. Both are guarded by twenty units each, and these are *elite* units."

"The Special Forces," Gordon said. "They are the next rank higher than our own units. They're on par with the units that General Southerwind commands. To be honest, I'm surprised that they haven't been recalled to Trinan and replaced by the regular units."

"It might as yet happen," Tyrian said. He was drumming his fingers on the table again. "We can't even hope to guess what Blaine is doing. We still can't even confirm why those units were yanked from Dry Basin at the last minute." He got to his feet, unusually agitated. There was a slimy sensation running down his back, and his relic seemed to be hotter than usual. Something was wrong. It felt as if he was getting excess energy for no good reason.

The others watched him in concern. Tyrian was so calm, so serene. This restless pacing and moving from window to window was very unlike him, and it alarmed everyone. "Tyrian?" Ewan asked softly as he straightened up. "What's wrong?"

"I don't know." He tried to force himself to stand still, but he couldn't. "I feel like I can't sit still. Too much energy." He pressed his hands to his head as a headache began to throb behind his eyes and his stomach rolled. "I feel sick."

"Fetch Lane," Matthias ordered Thomas, who scrambled out the door as fast as he could.

Cassie moved to Tyrian's side and grabbed his hands with hers. "Breathe. Look at me." His eyes met hers, and she could see the darkness swirling inside that was a mark of his powers moving as much as it was a mark of his mood. This restless energy had been happening for two days. There was something indeed wrong.

Lane walked into the meeting room and he was frowning. "What's going on? Why was Thomas so panicked?" He took one look at Tyrian and his frown deepened. "I see." He took a breath and then said bluntly, "Someone exposed to Tyrian for a long enough time has died and their energy has been consumed by the Devourer. As Tyrian is at full strength, it's like overdosing on sugar."

It was an unpleasant and unsettling thought. Worse still, there was any number of people it could have been. Living in Trinan as Tyrian had, he had been around a good deal of people for a long time. It might as yet have been from Ben's time carrying it. There was no knowing.

"Will it burn itself off normally? It's been two days," Kyle said.

"At this rate, it could be weeks. Whoever it was had a lot of life energy." Lane tucked his hands in his pockets, wishing there was more he could do. "I'm not a doctor, but I've watched assorted relic users over the centuries. Tyrian's under a lot of pressure to begin with." He still had the aches to prove he had gotten the wrong end of Tyrian letting off steam. He looked at Matthias. "Call it for today. Let him be."

Matthias nodded instantly. "There's nothing we can do like this." He looked at Cassie. "Take him to your tower so he can have some peace."

Cassie hauled Tyrian toward the door, and the Kaiten muttered distinctly, "As if I'm not even here!" He didn't bother to resist. The nausea had faded back into the agitated feeling inside. The headache kept coming and going.

When they got into the tower, he shrugged off Cassie and began to pace back and forth across the floor. Even with boots on, his feet stayed soundless. His body moved with sleek danger and rippling power. Just watching him made something hot and needy clench inside her body. She never stopped wanting him. What was it about him that pulled at everything inside her?

He suddenly looked at her and his eyes darkened with fierce hunger. With a predatory stride, he walked toward her. "I think I know how to get rid of the energy." The words were little more than a rumble.

She stopped breathing entirely as she watched him approach. Hunger swelled fiercely inside until she burned with agony for him to touch her. His hot hands closed around her arms, and the magic of his relic hand blasted all the way into her soul. It was both relief and desperation entangled. There was something inside him that she had never seen before. Something that tore past all layers of civilization, all the years of self-control and holding herself back emotionally. She had thought she was free in his arms, but the side of herself that she saw then had been so deeply buried that she had never known it was there.

The sudden rush of blue taking over the black in her eyes was highly erotic. He fisted a hand in her hair and dragged her up for a bruising kiss. Her lips parted eagerly as a low moan caught in her throat that seared every nerve. His hands streaked down her body, curved around her perfect bottom, and dragged her against his aching body. In response, she grabbed his shoulders and hoisted herself with a sexy surge of strength until her legs could wrap around his waist.

He whirled and dropped her on the top of the table. He couldn't release her mouth long enough to remove her tunic so he simply ripped it from her body instead. Her hands yanked at his shirt in response and it too tore as they wrested it off. Her hands were everywhere, her nails scraping over his skin.

She felt frenzied in a way she never had before. If she didn't hold him inside her body, she was going to fade away. The blind leap into mindless craving was shocking and thrilling and wonderful. Some instinct swelled inside and she grabbed his relic hand. She pressed a kiss directly to the relic mark and his entire body shuddered. "The most sensitive place," she teased huskily as she hotly caressed his hand with little kisses and nips of her teeth.

His green eyes glowed like gemstones. "Not *the* most sensitive place." He lifted her and scraped his teeth over the curve of her breast. When she moaned, he captured in his mouth the tight nipple desperately begging for attention. She burned inside him like a light inside his darkness. "Mine!" It was barely more than a snarl. "I want you to be mine!"

"I'm not?" The words ended on a sob of need as his relic hand caught her other breast and the magic teased her as terribly as his touch. She was going to burn alive. She couldn't burn hot enough, fast enough. "Tyrian!"

He dropped her back down on the table and nearly tore away what remained of her clothes. Her black hair was wild and rumpled, her skin flushed with desire. He had never wanted or needed anything more. The energy that drove him was life energy, and there was no life for him without this woman. *Damn* the curse of the Pure Relic. He wanted to see her holding their child, wanted to watch her be the incredible mother he knew she would be. "Mine, Cassie! No one else will ever have you!"

Half-mad with desire, she could only lie there as he tried to remove what was left his clothing. He couldn't get his pants off all the way, but that didn't matter. The sight of his fiercely aroused body sent another wave of need through her body. He was so beautiful, so starkly and impossibly beautiful!

He dragged her to the edge of the table and buried his throbbing erection deep inside her body. The hard thrust dragged a cry from her lips that thrilled him. He drove into her again and again, harder with every thrust, needing her to go out of control, needing to know she wanted him as badly as he wanted her. *Eternity*. He felt it looming on the horizon. An eternity of love and laughter if she was there. "Marry me, Cassie."

Her eyes opened, dark and shocked. "What?" It ended on a gasp as he dragged her up and buried his mouth against her hammering pulse, his hips stopping entirely so that he stayed motionless within her aching body. Ecstasy hovered and beckoned but there was no end to the terrible pleasure. Her nails bit into his shoulders in pleading.

The hot suckling kisses moved up her neck to her ear. His breath was heated and sultry, his voice a rasp of sin wrapped in velvet. "Marry me."

A shudder went through her entire body that made her clench around him. The green of his eyes seemed to disappear as his pupils expanded. Unable to bear any of it—the plea, the demand, the desperation—she managed to say, "Yes! So, please . . . !"

He drove into her fiercely and the tension snapped wildly. Ecstasy roared down through her body, her soul, emptying her until there was nothing left but the desperation to hold him close. She wrapped her arms and legs tighter around him, holding him as he held her, clinging on when the world melted and dissolved around them until only they remained, drowning in wicked pleasure.

After, there was only the sound of them trying to catch a breath. Not only was the excess energy gone, he didn't think he had any energy at all left. All he could do was brace his hands around her hips on the table and try to stay on his feet. Her body quivered as hard as his did, and the little aftershocks rippled through them both.

It took a few moments for her to find her voice, and when she did, it was still husky. "Did you propose to me in the middle of all that?"

"I did." He tasted the curve of her neck and lingered. His tongue soothed a little mark he had made unintentionally. "You said yes. You can't go back on it."

"I would like to note that I have no intention of going back on it, but being proposed to by a man who didn't remember to take his boots off before he made love to me was *not* in my list of wistful fantasies." She paused and then said, laughter in her voice, "My imagination was never that good."

He lifted his head and smiled at her. "Admit it. You never expected to marry at all."

"I admit it." She framed his face in her hands. "I could never have possibly thought up anything that has happened." She softly kissed him and smiled. "Do I get a ring?"

He brought her fingers to his lips. "Since you accepted my proposal, yes. You'll get it when I find one that won't get in the way of how you fight." He slowly and reluctantly withdrew from her body and then pulled his pants back up before removing his boots as he should have before. "My boots are off so I can make love to you again properly. But I will never look at that table quite the same way again."

She wouldn't either, that was for certain. She got to her feet and winced wryly as muscles protested. "I'll feel that for a while." She looked at the tattered remains of her clothing and hastily gathered them up. "I'll throw these away. I'm not sure Merilyne could handle the shock."

As he sat down at the table, he watched her with a slow smile that brought in a fresh surge of heat to her body. His smile just increased as if he knew. "Someday we'll live hidden away and go naked all the time."

She contemplated that. "As long as wherever we are doesn't have mosquitoes." He laughed, and her heart fluttered. It was his first laugh in quite a while. She went over to him and slid onto his lap to cuddle close. "Do you feel better?"

"The excess energy is certainly gone, but my relic still feels warmer than usual. And I still feel that odd sense of dread."

A heavy fist suddenly pounded on the door. "Tyrian!" The voice was Kyle's. "You need to hurry! Come down to the city! *Hurry!*"

Cassie leapt to her feet and grabbed the first clothes she found. Tyrian yanked on a new shirt but didn't fasten it as he ran to the door. He also forgot his shoes, but the urgency in Kyle's voice meant that whatever had happened was seriously bad. If he had to fight, he would just do it barefoot.

The elevator seemed to take forever, but Tyrian and Cassie shortly left the castle and ran out into the city. There was a crowd gathered near the gate, which was lowered, and Tyrian felt his stomach clench with dread for the worst. He shoved his way through the crowd, expecting to see someone dying, yet that was not at all what he saw.

He saw a tiny little girl with delicate Faerie wings sitting on a horse that wore Imperial colors. She was barely more than six, if that, and her pale mossy colored hair hung in a messy braid. Her eyes, one blue and one green, seemed too old and serious in her tiny face. She looked at him and her lower lip quivered . . . and he fell instantly in love. "Hi," he said softly as he walked closer. "I'm Tyrian."

Raven looked at him closer and was instantly intrigued. There was something about him that made her want to protect him and make sure he was happy. Yet there was something else as well. Something that made *her* feel safe too, and it wasn't a familiar feeling. "Hi," she said softly, and the sweetly innocent cadence to her voice belied her bloodline as surely as her wings. "I'm Raven."

He looked at her iridescent black wings and found the name very apt. He held up his hands, and when she leaned down, he lifted her off the back of the horse. She curled her arms around his neck and burrowed closer, unintentionally burrowing into his heart. She felt impossibly tiny, and sudden terror gripped him. "How did she get here?" he asked Kyle.

His friend shook his head. "We don't even know, Tyrian. The guards spotted the horse before they saw her. As soon as they realized there was a baby on its back, they rushed to get her inside."

"I'm not a baby!" came a fierce and stubborn mutter against Tyrian's neck, making several people smile.

Kyle wasn't one of them, and the sight of his face made Tyrian tense for the worse. "What else, Kyle?" he asked softly.

"She was wrapped in this cloak." Kyle held out the black velvet material. "There's a note inside it."

Tyrian almost didn't need to see the note. He recognized the cloak instantly as one of his mother's favorites. Hands trembling slightly, he handed Raven to Cassie and then took the cloak to retrieve the note.

Raven rested her head on Cassie's shoulder and closed her eyes, content to be held by the pretty lady with the blue-black eyes. She felt safe and warm, just like Tyrian did. She almost didn't believe they were real. They were so much like the parents she had secretly dreamed of finding. She hadn't liked the Emperor, and she really hadn't liked Lady Blaine. She had wanted to be adopted to leave the stuffy palace. She had known someone needed her.

Tyrian slowly opened the note and recognized Annareal's handwriting. The sight of it was painful nostalgia, and as he read, the pain slowly spread.

My beloved Tyrian,

I'm sorry. The words are inadequate, but they're the only ones I can find. If I could go back in time and take back what I did, I would do it instantly. Tell Kyle Raitels that when the war ends, he may choose to take my life if he wishes as payment for what I did. I have earned whatever judgment the gods may bring.

The girl is named Raven. She is a ward of the Empire. Her parents were, obviously, Faeries. Forest and Water Faeries, to be precise. I have been caring her for these last few months. She reminds me so much of you at that age. Serious and smart and so curious for the world.

When the war reaches the castle, Blaine will kill her. I know she will. There is much power inside Raven's body, and her life, short as it has been, is full of energy and spirit. I send her to you on the fastest horse, praying the stars will lead her to you safely. The stars blessed you, Tyrian. And they blessed me to be your mother. I only pray that someday you will ever forgive me.

Your loving mother, Annareal Southerwind

The pain seemed to be slowly welling up from the depths of his soul. She had learned. She had understood. She had given back a life in payment for the one she had taken. She had made atonement for the children she had traumatized. He needed to tell her she was forgiven, that all he had ever wanted was for her to realize what she had done. There had to be a way to get a message to her!

The sound of a cane on stone preceded Matthias. His face seemed older suddenly, and there was a palpable heavy air around him. Grace and Ted were at his side, and both seemed to look their age for once. "Lord Tyrian?" Matthias asked softly.

Tyrian looked at him. "My mother sent Raven to me for her own safety. She knows what she did to Ophelia was wrong."

"Yes." Matthias' eyes closed. "And so, it would seem, does the Empire know." He took a deep breath. "She was executed for treason two days ago."

The words fell like stones into the silence. The note slid from Tyrian's fingers and softly fluttered to the ground. Two days. "Treason?" His voice sounded eerily calm to even him. Inside, screams slowly built as the pain tore at his soul.

"She was caught trying to send you a message. We don't know the contents. But Ted just received the notice, and Grace's contacts in Trinan confirmed it. Without telling anyone beforehand, the Emperor had her executed. Death by beheading as a traitor to the Empire. General Southerwind was not even notified until after the event occurred."

There was a roaring inside Tyrian's ears. Two days ago, his mother had been murdered for trying to help him. It was a bitterly ironic ending for the woman who had murdered another whose only crime was helping others. And because she had been with him all those years, been with Ben, been exposed to the power of the Devourer . . . her life energy had been consumed by the relic.

Somehow, he held onto his strength. Somehow, he held onto his composure. He handed the cloak to Winifred and said, "Please preserve this." His voice was still unnaturally calm. He looked at Beatrice. "Tend to the horse."

"What of Raven?" Kyle asked softly.

"She's a Destined Star." The roaring was getting louder. It almost seemed as if he couldn't hear what anyone said. "Let me be." He walked calmly, evenly, serenely, back toward the castle even though every instinct urged him to run. Run and never stop running.

Cassie handed Raven to Laia and rushed to Tyrian's side. Other Stars closed in as well, intently watching him as he walked into the courtyard. There was terror inside all of them as they recognized he stood again at the edge of the breaking point.

His strength lasted until he was on the elevator, and he did not say a word as Cassie and Liang got on it with him. When the doors closed, the strength left his body all at once. It was only Cassie and Liang's speed that kept him from falling on the ground. The pressure of the pain was swelling inside, but it wouldn't break. Why wouldn't it break? He could feel the tears but they never reached his eyes. He wanted to cry. He wanted to scream. He didn't want to be strong.

They helped him into the tower room, and he sank down to sit against the short wall. He buried his face in his hands and said raggedly, "Leave me be."

Cassie knelt and wrapped her arms around him, and he buried his face against her breast. A single bloody red tear slid down his cheek though he did not truly cry. He simply held onto her, his only sanity, with all his strength. If she let go of him, then he would break into a million pieces. He just couldn't handle this event on top of everything else.

Liang sat down without a word; he refused to leave Tyrian's side through this lowest point. He felt sick to his stomach with the knowledge that it could, and likely would, get worse yet. There was no knowing what would happen with Donald. If this event drove him to leave the Empire, what would Blaine do to him?

It seemed to be forever until Tyrian relaxed in Cassie's arms. As he did, she let out a soundless breath of relief. The worst had passed. He was clawing his way back from the edge again, but he would never return to where he had begun. The breaking point would simply move further out.

It was obvious to both Cassie and Liang that Tyrian had exerted all his will on keeping his mind blank. He didn't say anything at all, though he remained aware of their presence. Liang glanced at Cassie and she nodded. He left the tower without a word to tell the others Tyrian would be fine.

Tyrian stirred and slowly pulled back from Cassie though his hands didn't let go entirely. She said nothing as she helped him get to his feet. She smoothed his hair out of his eyes and then cupped his cheek. "You don't have to see anyone just yet," she said softly. "You're in no condition to talk to anyone about anything."

His eyes focused on her. "How is this fair, Cassie?"

"We believe in an eye for an eye among the monks. The instant she committed murder, she set herself up for celestial payback. Her understanding of what she did, her regret, means she will have a chance to be reborn." She sighed softly as she urged him around the wall and made him sit on the bed. "Would we be talking about this if it had been an assassin doing the deed? No, because that is what they do. Ophelia wanted a non-violent end to things, so her assassination would have been wrong either way. But it wouldn't have been murder."

It was little comfort, but he accepted it because he had to. His biggest pain, and he was sure Cassie knew, was that he had not gotten a chance to talk to Annareal before she died. He had lost her as his mother months before and had moved past. That grief was done. He grieved now for the lost chances at the future.

The rest of the day stayed quiet at the castle. People spoke in murmurs and children were unusually somber. Tyrian's pain had rippled into every one of his Stars and then it had rippled further. Slowly but surely, this fight for independence was becoming personal to the Kaiten Star, and that made it personal to everyone. It had gone past the simple tyranny of a foolish emperor.

Even late that night, Tyrian was still not able to sleep. Cassie was snuggled into his arms, and he took what comfort he could from having her there. At a soft fluttery sound, he lifted a brow. He gently disentangled himself from his fiancée's arms and got out of bed. He grabbed the first pair of pajama pants he found and pulled them on.

On silent feet, he crossed to the balcony doors. He knelt down and then peeked the curtain aside. He was promptly nose-to-nose with a little girl wearing a pink nightshift. "Gotcha," he said softly. He opened the door further so that she could scoot inside out of the cold. "What are you doing, Raven?" He ushered her over to the fireplace for warmth and sat down beside her. "Did you fly up here?"

She nodded solemnly and rubbed at her eyes. "I can't fly far," she admitted. "But I can fly up and down. I can't go sideways yet. I start doing circles."

At six, her wings were still developing just like everything else about her. He scooped her up and settled her on his lap where she could snuggle close. The way she spoke was far advanced compared to her age, and he was reminded of not just himself, but of Cassie as well. That willingness to confront her own shortcomings even if she was afraid. "You could have used the elevator." He rubbed his cheek over her soft hair.

"I didn't know if the guards would let me in." She rested her cheek over his heart and the beat sounded comforting. "I had a nightmare. The monsters were chasing me again."

Not for the first time that day, terror prowled through him at the very idea of her having made it from Trinan to the base by herself. A week, out alone, unprotected. The packs on the saddle had held plenty of food and water, but there had been nothing and no one there for her in the night. No one to protect her. "Did they chase you a lot?"

She nodded. "Lady Anna said they would, but if I was brave and thought about you, I would be okay. So I was brave, and I thought about making it here. The horse ran fast when he saw monsters, and I held on." She frowned suddenly. "When can I learn to fight so I can protect myself?"

A moment of déjà vu made him nostalgic in a good way. He remembered saying those exact words to Liang and Donald in response to being kept from doing the things he wanted because it wasn't safe. Donald had promptly started him training with a staff. "What do you want to learn?"

She thought about it. "I like watching berserkers and how they swing axes."

The thought of a tiny Faerie trying to swing an axe was both amusing and frightening. "Let's start small and work our way up." He held out his hand and she placed hers on top of it. Her whole hand was smaller than his palm. "When your fingers can touch mine," he said, "then you can try an axe. Well, if your parents want you to. You'll be adopted after the war, I'm sure." It was a painful thought, more than Kami and Mikey. He wanted them to find families. He didn't want to share Raven.

It was a mutual thought. She held onto him tighter and said intensely, "I don't want another family. Can't you adopt me? You could be my dad. Cassie could be my mom. I don't want to be adopted by anyone else!"

"Shh." Emotion closed his throat and the well of love seemed to erase the lingering grief that had held him all day. That dangerous edge of no return moved further away. Annareal had given back far much more than she had taken. She had made amends for everything. "If Cassie wants to be a mom, I would like to be your dad."

"I could be persuaded," Cassie said softly from where she leaned against the short wall and watched them. She wore the other half to the pajamas that Tyrian wore, and the ends of the shirt went to her knees. Her heart ached as she watched them. They were wonderfully beautiful together. It seemed impossible to think she had an entire family right there before her. A daughter, of all things. "Do you think Liang will be surprised to be a grandfather at his age?"

Tyrian smiled. "He was a father to me when he was barely sixteen. I think he can take it in stride." He released Raven when she straightened and smiled as she crossed over to Cassie. He had wanted to have a child with Cassie, and he had been given that gift.

Cassie knelt down and lifted Raven into her arms. The little girl cuddled close and wrapped her arms around Cassie's neck. There was something really safe and secure about Cassie that Raven loved. She was warm and smelled like what Raven had always thought a mommy should smell like. She couldn't describe it, but Cassie just smelled like a mommy, just like Tyrian smelled like a daddy. Feeling safe for the first time in a long time, Raven fell asleep with the ease of a child who trusted implicitly that the one who held her would protect her.

Cassie looked at her contented face and fell hopelessly in love. Her lips trembled as she looked at Tyrian with tears shimmering across her eyes. It was a terrifying feeling to love so much so fast for someone so small and fragile. It hadn't been that frightening to love Tyrian, and he was arguably just as fragile if not more. "How is it possible?"

He got to his feet and walked over to draw them both into his arms. He softly smoothed Raven's hair out of her face. "You've never told me what eternity is yours to claim," he said softly. "But I am fairly sure if I guessed, I would be right. Even if we removed that from the picture, I bear a Pure Relic. The damage has been done. Even if I somehow took off this relic, I will never have children of my blood. We could never have a child together, no matter how we wished. Enter Raven."

Cassie softly rubbed her cheek over her daughter's fine hair. "Not ours by blood, but ours the same. Oh, Tyrian. She's just like you! She's so intense and serious and smart."

He smiled. "But she has her mother's fearlessness. Rather than take the elevator, she flew on barely-grown wings to a several story high balcony."

"Let's call that stubborn more than fearless."

"As I said, she's just like her mother." He cupped Cassie's cheek and leaned down to kiss her softly. "Should we take her back to her room?" he asked softly.

"She could sleep with us tonight. It wouldn't hurt her, would it?"

"Why should it?"

Neither had ever gotten the chance to sleep in their parents' bed after a nightmare, though for differing reasons. They knew what it was like to be young and afraid and alone. There was no need to make her go back to her room by herself when she was no doubt sleeping truly for the first time in a long time.

They tucked Raven into bed between them where she was safely snuggled against them both. Her wings had folded against her back, evidence of a deep and true sleep. As she was drifting off herself, Cassie murmured, "We're going to need to sleep in pajamas from now on. I get this feeling she'll sneak in through the balcony more than once."

"Like I said." Tyrian softly smoothed his hand down both of their hair in turn. "She's like her mother." With a sigh of contentment, he closed his eyes. It was constant ups and downs. In the space of one day, he had been up, then down, then up again. There would be another down around the corner, and if the pattern held true, it was going to be worse still.

Cassie was thinking the same thing, and a certainty had gelled inside her heart. It was time for her to return to the Monk Clans. She would demand their promised aid in battle, and she would claim the legacy that was rightfully hers. Any fear of the trials she would face was completely eclipsed by the fear she had felt as she watched Tyrian hover at the edge of breaking. Lane had told her what she needed to do. She was going to do it.

Period.

Chapter Twenty-Seven

"The wheels spin and I am where I began; nothing changes."

Tyrian woke the next morning to the sound of knocking on the bedroom door. With a mutter, he pulled the pillow over his head. On a delicate yawn, Raven asked Cassie sleepily, "Why's Daddy hiding?"

Dryly, her mother answered, "He hates the morning."

There was another knock and Raven scrambled up. "I get it!" She narrowly avoided kicking both her parents and would have fallen over the side of the bed if her wings hadn't caught her. She scurried to the door and opened it to find Serentia on the other side. "Hi!" she said. "Who're you?"

Serentia felt a smile tugging at her lips. "I'm Serentia," she said as she knelt down. "Interestingly, I was here to ask Tyrian and Cassie if they knew where you were, little one. I went to your room, but you weren't there. You panicked the guards when they realized you'd gotten out."

"Oh." Raven rubbed at her eyes. She liked Serentia's smile and manner. "I had a nightmare." She brightened. "Guess what!"

"What?" Serentia itched to pick her up for a cuddle.

"Tyrian and Cassie are going to adopt me, so they're my daddy and mommy now!"

"Oh my." Not entirely surprised, she glanced up to see Tyrian standing at the edge of the short wall. "Congratulations," she said dryly. "You may say goodbye to what remains of any sanity you have."

"That makes you her grandmother almost, doesn't it?" he asked calmly.

Raven brightened. "Can I call you Gramma?" She hugged Serentia happily around the neck, delighted to be finding the family she had always wanted. "Do I have a Grampa too?" she asked Serentia seriously. "Uncles? Aunts? Cousins?"

The gardener blinked and then began laughing. "We're all doomed. She's too much like you, Tyrian." She stood with Raven held securely in her arms. "You have a Grampa Liang," she said gently, "but he's not my husband."

Raven blinked. "Why not?"

"Out of the mouths of babes," Tyrian murmured. Taking pity on Serentia because she looked flustered, he told Raven, "Liang and Serentia are like my mom and dad in the way I'm your dad now. Liang helped raise me, and Serentia has been like a mother. I don't call them 'Mom' and 'Dad', but that's what they're like. So they're like your grandparents. And if you assume that we're all family, you have a *lot* of aunts and uncles and cousins." Marian would be wrapped around Raven's finger before the day was done.

"Let's go get you cleaned up!" Serentia looked at Tyrian gratefully and then turned back to Raven. "You're older than my daughter, but about the same size. Tavi says you can have some of her clothes to wear."

Raven cocked her head. "If you're my Gramma, and Tavi is your daughter, then she's my aunt, right? I'm older than my aunt." She contemplated that and nodded. "Okay, that's fair."

Tyrian managed to keep the grin off his face until the door had shut behind them. As soon as it was closed, he promptly started chuckling. He turned to look at Cassie and found her grinning at him. "I dread the day when she is old enough to be courted," he confessed.

She laughed at him. "Why should you? She'll be swinging a battleaxe by then, and I have no doubt it'll be enough to intimidate everyone in a five-mile radius even if her father's legend does not." She got out of bed and went to wrap her arms around his waist with a smile. "And that's providing anyone manages to get past 'Uncle Ewan' and 'Uncle Kyle.'"

He snorted softly. It was indeed a good thing Raven had so much of his personality. She would be smothered by her overprotective family if she didn't. He still wasn't sure how he so easily accepted the way his Stars were always protecting him and overreacting to danger. He was just glad he *could* accept it. They weren't likely to ever stop.

Because it was a new day, and a war was waiting, they got dressed and headed down the elevator. Tyrian told the guards at the bottom, "Cassie and I are adopting Raven. She'll be coming here a lot. I know you don't bar the Stars from entering, but even if I've said I don't want visitors, she is permitted anyway."

Puzzled, one asked, "How did she get up there anyway?"

"She flew over the balcony." Tyrian smiled wryly when they both winced. "At least she can't fly sideways yet." When she could, there would be no stopping her if she had her mind set. It could be left for debate as to which parent she was more like in that.

He and Cassie were halfway to the meeting room when there came a flutter of wings and Raven suddenly latched onto his shoulders. "Daddy!" She held on as he continued walking. "Gramma says that since I'm growing, we need to get me more clothes. She says I'm growing like a weed. I'm a Faerie. Do we get that big?"

"Well, Faeries are smaller than average among all races, but you're not going to be *that* small. I think most Faeries average around five-two or so, male or female. I can't say if you're small for your age or not, since relative to other children, you're going to be small anyway." He spoke to her as he would an adult, knowing her intelligence deserved the respect.

The rest of those in the meeting had already arrived when Tyrian and Cassie walked in with Raven. Ewan instantly grinned. "Tyrian, you have a growth."

"But a cute one," Kyle said with a matching grin.

Liang just smiled. Serentia had told him what had occurred, and it did not surprise him at all. He had seen the look on Tyrian's face when he had met Raven. The tiny girl in a dress the color of pink roses was the princess of the castle, and she had been from the moment she had arrived. "Hello, Raven," he told her when she looked at him. "I'm Liang."

She brightened. "You're my grampa, right?" She released Tyrian and flew woozily across the room to hug Liang. She could fly up and down and forwards. Flying backwards would follow the side-to-side motion. "Can I call you 'Grampa'?" she asked. Very seriously, she said, "I know you're not supposed to be old enough to be a grampa, but that's not important, right?"

She was so much like Tyrian that he couldn't help but love her immediately. "Right," he said softly. He hugged her for a moment and then let go so she could fly back to Tyrian.

Halfway there, she lost stability and would have landed on the table if Ewan hadn't quickly caught her. She appeared positively tiny beside him, but she looked at him without a single concern as she dangled in his hands. "I'm not small. You're big."

Kyle coughed into his coffee. Matthias, rather wisely, hid a smile. Ewan could take no offense. "You are correct," he told her, though he kicked Gordon under the table when the general smirked. "My name is Ewan. You remember Kyle from yesterday." He turned her around. "That's Matthias, Gordon, and Samantha." He put her down on the chair beside him. She could see onto the table if she stood rather than sit.

There wasn't a single thought in anyone's mind to exclude her from the meeting. Her age did not mean she didn't have a right to be there to help her Kaiten, especially because he was also her father now. If anything, like Cassie, Liang, and Marian, Raven now had *more* right to be there.

"Can I see a map?" she asked Matthias.

"Certainly." He handed her one of the smaller ones. He then smiled at Tyrian and Cassie as she began to avidly study it. "A future Scholar, Lord Tyrian?"

He smiled. "She wants to learn to use a battleaxe."

Every person at the table winced. Raven just ignored them as she contemplated the map. What was scary about her wanting to use an axe? She wasn't going to be that small forever, and it would make up for the height difference. And it would be fun.

"How are you this morning?" Gordon asked Tyrian.

"Better than can be expected." He glanced at Raven and then back. "I'm learning to accept that there's a balance for everything." His eyes briefly flicked to Cassie. "And the excess energy was gone even before we found out what had caused it."

"I imagine it was," Samantha murmured.

Cassie felt her cheeks warm slightly. Tyrian just smiled. "So, Firmeza," he said. "That's our next goal, correct?"

Matthias nodded. "Indeed. There's only one way to access Firmeza, and that is from the eastern side. They're backed up near the Y Border. Too far north or south and we enter into the territory of a checkpoint."

"As soon as Firmeza has been reclaimed," Cassie said quietly, "I wish to take a brief journey back to the hidden city in the mountains where the Monk Clans reside. If we are going after Alphin first, I can journey to that battle, and as soon as it ends, I can head into the mountains. We were promised units that have not been delivered." Something powerful moved in her eyes. "And I am rightfully owed something that I am ready to claim."

"Done," Tyrian said instantly. He covered her hand with his. "I will go with you." He brought her fingers to his lips. "I really should have a chance to meet your father before we get married and force him to accept me in his family."

"Hot damn," Gordon said. "Does that mean it's official at this point?"

"It does indeed." Tyrian laced his fingers with Cassie's. "I think that means we have a plan for our next few steps. We take Firmeza, and then take Alphin. When it is secured, Cassie and I and no doubt a few others will travel to the Clans and make the alliance formal. As soon as we return, we can look at Betane."

"There's something funny about the cities," Raven suddenly said.

She instantly had everyone's attention, and both Matthias and Ewan leaned closer to see since they were on either side of her chair. "Like what, Raven?" Matthias asked. "Do you see something we haven't?"

She grabbed the pencil on the table and drew very careful lines connecting the four checkpoints. The very spot where all four connected was the exact location of Trinan and the castle. "Was it on purpose?" she asked.

Gordon slowly shook his head. "I do not know. I don't think either

Sam or I ever noticed there was such a thing."

"Indeed, I did not."

Matthias sat back with a thoughtful frown. "I think that is something for Grace to look into. I want Kell to look into where the Dragonist Clan stands in all this. If we're in the mountains already, we might as well make contact with them too. They would be very powerful allies, and having aerial capabilities in combat will put us ages ahead of the Empire."

"Dragonists?" Raven's ears perked up. Seeing it, the others smiled. The long and pointed ears marked her Forest Faerie blood and gave a greater range of hearing. No one had realized they could move independent of each other.

"Dragonists are a specialized classification of combatant, as well as an actual title," he explained. "They are warriors on par with the skill of the Commune of Soldiers, so they are talented in battle like Ewan, Kyle, and General Yureny. But the Dragonists have a powerful alliance with the assorted Dragon clans across the world—hence the name. They form partnerships and work as units. A Dragonist is therefore technically *two* warriors in one, though the Dragon he or she works with might actually be adept as a Magician or Healer."

"Oh, I met one!" She brightened. "He was really nice. His name was Ryu. He came to the palace a few months ago. He had a meeting with . . ." She wrinkled her nose as she thought. "The general with the pretty face."

Samantha tried not to smile. "Alexander Renduex?"

"Yeah! They had a meeting. The general saw me in the hall after and he smiled. He had a nice smile, not like the Emperor. And he told me that everything would be okay." She nodded firmly, not noticing the sudden speculation on faces. "The Dragonist came out next. He also smiled at me. I liked him too. He even let me meet his partner! Her name was Celestial. She had pretty white hair and she cast magic. And she made such a pretty white Dragon! She said when everything was safe that she and Ryu would come take me for a ride."

"Interesting," Tyrian murmured softly.

Matthias looked at Raven very seriously. "You have given us some very important information. I think there may be more still that you know and just don't realize. If at any time, you think of something, or you remember something when we're talking, tell us."

"Alex was meeting with the Dragonist Clan." Gordon tapped a finger on the table. "Interesting, indeed. And to tell Raven everything would be okay . . . Also, that Ryu, telling Raven that everything would be safe."

"Raven," Cassie asked her daughter, "did you feel the same sort of way near Alex that you do near Gordon or Samantha? Or Ewan and Kyle?" At the nod, she asked, "Did you feel that near Ryu?"

Raven tilted her head, one ear quirked. "Yes."

"We were fairly sure General Renduex and the other generals are Destined Stars," Liang noted. "But if a Dragonist is also a Destined Star . . . we can't dismiss how Raven felt near them. Like calls to like."

"And that means we do, indeed, want to make contact with them." Matthias crossed his arms as he thought. "Particularly when the Dragonists are known for standing up for the rights of people, just as the Monk Clans do. I believe during the coup in Melodina a few years back, the Dragonists aided the side of the people. They didn't win, but they made an effort."

"Did you ever meet Blaine?" Tyrian asked Raven.

She wrinkled up her nose. "No. I ran if I saw her. She was *ugly*."

It was a curious statement to hear when Blaine's only redeeming quality was her beauty, but Tyrian still had Ben's memories swirling in his mind. He knew Blaine's true self. That a child, a Faerie child, could see through the illusion to reality was not a stretch. Raven was very special for many reasons.

"Firmeza, then." Ewan didn't bat a lash as Raven climbed onto his lap to look at the map in front of him. It was covered with the notes he had taken over the course of the meetings. "It holds six personal units, all close-combat. Guarding the city are ten close-combat units. Shit, why don't we just go in and kick their asses?"

"That's a bad word," Raven told him.

"Then don't repeat it until you're older."

"The idea has merit," Matthias said. "We've played so many tricks and used so many clever tactics that to hit them with blunt force would be a trick of its own. They would be expecting a surprise and perhaps not focus as fully on the fight as they should. They might think we intend to pull back at the last minute."

"We've got plenty of strong unit leaders. Strictly speaking, close-combat leaders don't have to be that close." Kyle was mostly thinking out loud. "Hell, we could plant Emma or Olan in a unit and take advantage of stealth arrows. It's not illegal."

"The important thing is to limit damage to the city." Matthias nodded. "That is our plan, then. We're going to overpower them. Lord Tyrian, neither I nor Cherry will ride this time. We would be a hindrance, and I think you will do just fine without us."

"How come the units in the city don't just . . . kick the bad guys out?" Raven pointed at Ewan's map. "You have a 'six' in the city, and a 'ten' around it. Wouldn't the surprise make up the difference?"

"Your child is beginning to frighten me," Samantha told Cassie.

"She takes after her father," was the dry retort.

"You know . . ." Matthias contemplated Raven. "It wouldn't be a trick to rally the units inside the city. We could catch the Imperial units in a crossfire and perhaps force a concession before things get too bloody. Soldiers are willing to give their lives in battle for what they believe. It is up to us to make sure that they do not fall when there is no need."

While the others began to assemble the unit leaders and prepare the troops, Tyrian went to find Ted and Tod. The latter was happily flirting with Grace at the pub, and she kept fluttering her lashes with a dexterity a younger woman would envy. Kell, sitting a few tables away, looked like one grumpy old informant. He even harrumphed when he heard Tod praise Grace's eyes.

"Sorry to interrupt," Tyrian said dryly, "but I need your assistance, Tod. We need to get a message into Firmeza."

"I'm your man, then!" He blew Grace a kiss and then got to his feet to follow Tyrian out of the pub. Once outside, he laughed richly. "I must say, I'm having the time of my life. It's just like old times!"

"Well, don't push it. I'd like Kell to avoid a heart attack."

"Oh, pish. He's strong as a mule. Stubborn too. Now, what message am I delivering? My buddy Tad lives in there, so it'll get in right as rain without a single suspicion. Actually, you'll want to talk to him. Trouble comes in threes."

So did good things, and Tyrian found all three gossips to be not only lively, entertaining, and useful, but knew they were always honest and never malicious. If you caught a rumor from one of them, you could be sure it was true. "Here's the plan."

* * * * *

Firmeza stood in a condition not dissimilar from Dry Basin. The pointed difference lay in the response of the Imperial Army that had captured it. For the most part, they simply did not care. They had their orders and followed them. It didn't matter what happened to these ignorant citizens as long as the Emperor continued to pay the army. If he was gone, then so went the lifestyle. Lady Blaine had assured them that it was so.

Others within the Imperial Army were not that certain. They were sickened by the events, tired of fighting against the will of the people they were sworn to defend. Cities *cheered* for the Liberation Army. Wasn't that a sign of needed change?

It was nearly a relief to see the Liberation Army suddenly appear on the field. They appeared with only ten units, all close-range, and the lieutenant in charge of the Imperial Army was instantly suspicious. Where was the catch? Since when did the Rebellion try to match brawn instead of brain? The lack of a strategist on the field seemed to imply they really were there to blunt force it through, but Tyrian Southerwind was no slouch in the strategy department himself.

Both General Yureny and General D'terio were on the field as well, and they led different units. For some of the Imperial army, it was a disgusting sight. For others, it was a sign that the time had come for things to change.

The engagement commenced, and it became nearly a bloody free-for-all. Unit matched to unit, and the Liberation Army slowly began to overpower the enemy. Things moved ever quicker as Imperial Army soldiers threw down arms and surrendered even before their unit was defeated. Some even removed their emblems, switched sides, and promptly helped fight against their former allies.

The lieutenant's unit had secretly been filled with mages among its close-range soldiers. He moved swiftly and steadily toward Tyrian's unit with the intent of taking him down. When he was still just out of range, there came a shout from within the city and six more units appeared on the field. All six wore the emblem marking them as city militia.

The Imperial Army was not only overpowered, they were also outnumbered and surrounded. The lieutenant saw a red haze of fury. In that fury, he rushed several of his men across the field toward Tyrian. The Kaiten Star looked at him and lifted his relic hand. The symbol of the Devourer appeared in the air, and it was large enough to be seen by all. Black waves of energy appeared in the middle of the lieutenant's party and rolled upward until all the soldiers were encased in the black dome. When the light faded, not a single soldier remained.

Any enemies left on the field threw down arms. "Laws of engagement," Tyrian said quietly, steel in his voice. "You may stand and fight for the people you swore to protect, or you may retreat to Trinan and cling to the false promises of a woman who is as evil as Beelzebub himself."

When all was said and done, the Liberation Army gained five units. The rest of the soldiers that were still standing retreated back to Trinan. The captain riding at the front of Firmeza's militia saluted Tyrian crisply. "Lord Tyrian, we were glad to answer your call. We are also glad to lend our strength to yours to bring back peace to our land!"

"Leaving one unit here," Myr said to Tyrian, "doesn't that mean we now have thirty units?" She whistled softly. They had expanded the castle with the intent of holding fifty thousand units. They were already at thirty, and there were other cities and generals that would be joining. She frowned. "We need a bigger castle."

Tyrian smiled wryly. "Indeed. Well, there's room. We can push the walls out further when we get there. Hopefully, we will have professional builders by then." He dismounted Fay and handed her reins over to a soldier. Cassie and Myr followed him as he headed for the city and made their way through the field of soldiers who were beginning to tend to the fallen as well as incorporate the newly acquired forces.

Like most of the towns in the Empire, Firmeza was a cross between a desert town and an oasis. Copious amounts of drought resistant trees had been planted around buildings to offer relief from the sun. With the exception of the upper class portion of town, the city showed the signs of abuse and neglect. People were already rushing to repair and revive; boarded up homes were being opened once more and shops actually put up 'open' signs.

Myr spotted a scroll shop and brightened. "Lord Tyrian! Look!" She grabbed his arm and pointed at the universally recognized shop sign with the scroll etched into it. "Now we have another source to buy scrolls from! Lupine has tried to keep up, but it's been hard."

Tyrian eyed the shop speculatively. "Let's go in," he said.

The inside of the shop was incredibly well stocked, which didn't come as a surprise since business would have been suffering. It was also warm and welcoming with the little tingle that meant a lot of relics existed in the same place at the same time. The long counter at the end of the shop was covered with scroll racks, and each rack had been organized by element.

The young woman behind the counter had the pointed ears of an Elf, yet she had a shorter height that meant some other blood had mixed in to her bloodline. She was frowning as she looked at a record book, but when she looked up and saw the three in her doorway, she promptly smiled. "Welcome! I'm Melianne. Are you from the Liberation Army?" She broke off as she saw Tyrian's green scarf and the relic on his hand. "Oh. Oh!" She covered her mouth with her hands. "Oops."

"This is Lord Tyrian!" Myr said cheerfully. "The monk is Lady Cassie. I'm Myrroria."

"It's an honor to meet all of you," Melianne said sincerely. "And thank you for routing those jerks out there! Some of them were actually nice, but there were some that I wouldn't trust any further than I could throw my shop!"

"Rightfully so," Cassie noted. She glanced at Tyrian and inclined her head as if asking a question.

Tyrian nodded slightly. Melianne was indeed a Destined Star, just as his gut had told him she would be. "Melianne," he said gently, "I could use your help in this war." When she stared at him, he gestured to the shop. "We have a limited supply of scrolls, and without a Relic Master, our soldiers have no way to equip relics without trying to get to another city and back quickly. It's been more expeditious to just stock scrolls. But the other cities are struggling to keep up with demand. We need our own Scroll Master."

"Oh. Oh my." She didn't know what it was, but something about him made her feel as if he really did need her help. She needed to be there to help him make it through this ordeal, to help him fight for all of them. She nodded firmly. "Alright! You can count on me, Lord Tyrian! I look forward to keeping up with the demands of the Liberation Army a lot more than I did selling stuff to the Imperials!"

"We'll even pay you," he agreed dryly.

She giggled, unsurprised he would know that the Imperial Army demanded free supplies as if it were their due. "But not the full price. That'd be silly." She held out a hand. "I'll get my stuff together to get out to the base!"

He took her hand and his relic glowed softly. An answering star glowed from her shoulder, and she stared at it in shock. *She* was a Destined Star? Was that why she felt as if she was needed? How had she been chosen as one of the blessed ones?

Myr stayed to help Melianne start boxing up things, and Tyrian and Cassie caught some soldiers outside. They were from Firmeza, but they already wore Tyrian's colors. They promptly went to help Melianne as well. It was one more thing that could be crossed off Tyrian's mental list, and it made things a little easier. Anything he could need, Destiny would provide. It almost made up for everything.

Much to his surprise, a massive library had been built in Firmeza. He spotted it as he and Cassie were on the lookout for Tad. Libraries were a rare commodity in the world and typically reserved only for the biggest of cities. To his knowledge, Trinan was supposed to have the only library in the Empire. In a way, he wasn't surprised to discover another one. People in the capitol liked to pretend they were the only ones to have a lot of things.

Cassie followed with a smile as he headed into the library. He had such a curious mind! She couldn't imagine where Raven had gotten it from.

Truthfully, even though it had been barely a day, she didn't really remember that Raven was not theirs by blood. In another couple years, she would probably forget entirely. Serentia and Persephone had teasingly told her how lucky she was to get out of childbirth, but Cassie envied them more. She would have loved to carry Raven and give her life.

The library was even bigger inside than it looked from the outside. The ceilings stood at over twenty feet high, and the bookcases went all the way to the roof. A balcony ran around the room at about ten feet in the air, and ladders could be used to reach every possible shelf. Smaller bookcases were spaced across the floor and formed into rows and lines. There was a large area with tables for study, and a professional copyperson sat to the side to make a duplicate of passages from books for Scholars and researchers.

Tyrian spotted a book that had a Faerie on the cover and picked it up curiously. It was a history of the Faerie race written by actual Faerie researchers. It chronicled all types of Faeries, covering every element, and also noted the common traits among the various subspecies. He had always found it fascinating that the most versatile of races—the Humans—were the only species without subspecies. Perhaps it was that fact that lent to their versatility. "Raven would like this."

A young face wearing glasses suddenly peered over the top of the bookcase. "It has some violence in it. Most racial histories do. Not suitable for kids."

"My daughter has seen more than her share already. She's very smart for her age." Tyrian glanced at the face and began smiling. The speaker was probably not that much older than Raven, so it was very much a case of the pot and kettle. "May I check this out?"

"Well, of course—gah!"

The face dropped suddenly out of view amid the sound of a chair falling. It was followed by a thud. Tyrian and Cassie rushed around the side of the bookcase to discover the boy had landed on the floor in relative safety, though he was rubbing his hip. He shoved his glasses back onto his face from where they had slid off and sighed. "Hi."

Tyrian wisely hid a smile as he knelt to offer the boy a hand up. "Hi." As he tugged the boy up, he asked, "Are you a researcher-in-training?"

"Yes, sir." He eyed Tyrian, already thinking of the things he wanted to write when he wrote the story of Tyrian Southerwind. He was more personable than Merlot had been expecting, and though he was supposedly not yet nineteen, he looked and acted with a maturity beyond his years. It would be worth noting. "My cousin, Zin, is the primary researcher here." He winced as he heard footsteps. "Speaking of."

A brown haired whirlwind came around the side of the bookcase and propped her hands on her hips. "Merlot!" she scolded. "How many times do I have to tell you to not stand on chairs! That's what we have ladders for." She blew out a breath and then looked at Tyrian and Cassie. "Welcome to Firmeza's library, Lord Tyrian and Lady Cassie! I'm Zinfandel." She caught her cousin in an affectionate headlock. "This is Merlot. He's my apprentice, but he's really smart. He'll be a great researcher."

Merlot looked up at her with hero worship in his eyes. It was clear he loved his cousin a great deal and the affection was returned. Zinfandel was probably only a year or two younger than Tyrian, so it said a lot for the family line that she had already become a full researcher.

Ask and ye shall receive. Both were Destined Stars. "How attached are you to the library?" he asked softly.

The cousins exchanged a smile. "Not that attached," Zinfandel said gently. "We would be honored to come fight at your side, Lord Tyrian. If you need any information, we can find it." She held up her right hand to show a Listening Relic. "Recorded within our relics are every book in this library. We can call up copies of any text. If we can't find it, then it doesn't exist."

"Thank goodness!" he said with feeling. "We have a Scholar on hand, but without a researcher, we were limited in what we could find. I even have an immediate task for you. Please start researching information on the prophecy of the Kaiten Star. I'd like to start knowing as much as everyone else does."

Neither cousin could blame him. Being the last to know something about yourself would not be pleasant. "We're on it!" Merlot said firmly. "We'll find ourselves a nice place to set up shop and we'll bring a bunch of our books too."

"No chairs," Cassie scolded him.

Zinfandel giggled as Merlot scowled. While they got to work, Tyrian and Cassie headed out of the library with the Faerie History book tucked safely into Tyrian's backpack. They both knew that Raven would love it. The idea of reading it to her one evening when they had a brief respite was appealing.

"Where do you want to live?" Cassie asked softly. "When this is done. We both love the Empire, but I know you won't be happy in a city. I don't think you ever were."

"Those days growing up in Teasarn were my happiest days. I suppose I'm a farm boy at heart." He would have tucked her under his arm, but she wore her full monk gear and he didn't want to block her access to the hidden places where she stashed her throwing stars. He had already learned the hard way that she would guiltlessly knock him flat to keep him safe if she couldn't reach her projectiles. "What are the mountains like?"

"Beautiful," she said simply. "There's this one place where the sun rises and sets on each side of a hidden niche. You have to be deliberately looking for it to find it. I found it a few years ago. Stayed there for a few days to live off the land. It was wonderful."

"How would a home fit there?"

"I think it would fit well. We can spend some years traveling with Raven and then we can have our home until she is ready to fly on her own. I will be leader of the Monk Clans in not too long a future, and being close would be convenient." She looked up at him, wanting nothing more than to hide him away in her secret retreat so that he was always safe and smiling. "Does that suit you?"

"It does indeed." He brought her fingers to his lips and then leaned down to softly kiss her. Public displays of affection were usually frowned on by monks in full gear, but he didn't really care what the rest thought as long as she was happy.

"Ahem."

At the elderly voice, he sighed and lifted his head. "You had better have a good reason." He glanced to the side, saw the old man with pigeons on his shoulders, and sighed a second time. "You have a good reason."

"I think I like you." Tad nodded firmly. "So you're Lord Tyrian. I'm Tad. I'll be joining you at the base. Between me and my buddies, we can get your messages out to anywhere, and we can bring in messages too! I can also help twist Kell's arm." He wiggled his brows. "I courted Grace once too."

"I've decided," Cassie told Tyrian. "I want to be Grace when I grow up, too."

He grinned. "With the pointed exception of being married well before seventy?"

Her eyes twinkled, the blue chips sparkling merrily. "Naturally."

Chapter Twenty-Eight

"Snow White's red, red apple; Juliet's sweet, sweet poison; feast to the memories."

With Firmeza liberated, a palpable air of burgeoning hope hung over the Empire. Even people in Trinan waited with their breath held for the next step. The entire country knew what was next: the checkpoints.

Word was spreading even further than the borders of the Empire. It had reached the other societies of the world. Melodina was still recovering from its own inner turmoil, but watched intently for the outcome. The City-States and the Moors even further to the west remained mostly ambivalent, though they did pay attention. Foresalia watched attentively. If Tyrian Southerwind won, and the Empire was lost, the king in Foresalia had absolutely no desire to start war with a man who had single-handedly revolutionized a country. Fight against destiny? No one was that insane.

People worked hard and fast at the Liberation Army base. The three gossips pulled in as much information as they could on the checkpoints and their multitude of specialized defenses. That information was fed to Merlot and Zinfandel who teamed with Rourke to go through every book they could to find an answer. Rourke was a happy camper with that system; it gave him free access to more books to read. Laia just laughed at him.

As the information came in, meetings were held from dawn until dusk. Raven attended all of them. If she wasn't standing on a chair to watch them talking over the maps, she was under the table reading her Faerie book. She was fascinated to learn about her own race, and she really hoped that her bloodline had longevity. Faeries with longevity could live up to a thousand years. Some were even nearly immortal. She wanted a lot of time with her mommy and daddy.

The first real bit of news that hit the meeting room ended up having nothing to do with the checkpoints. Ted came bursting into the meeting room and blurted, "Albanion married Blaine!"

"Here comes the bride," Ewan muttered, "all covered in blood."

"Let me guess," Kyle said curtly. "It's being touted by Albanion as the great romance of the millennia, how after so long he finally found true love. Where's Shots? Someone needs to shoot me before I choke on the hypocrisy."

Only the two Lower Generals at the table looked remotely pleased with the news. They both remembered when Albanion's first wife had been alive. The Emperor had loved her very dearly, and their happy marriage had been salt in the wounds of those who couldn't be with loved ones because of 'distractions.' That Albanion was now married and miserable was, perhaps pettily, satisfying.

"There's something more," Ted said. "One of my contacts in Trinan saw a man in Blaine's tower."

"A butler?" Cassie asked.

"It was the middle of the night, and he wasn't wearing a shirt. There's this new blond general in the Imperial Army. That's why the units were called back. He first took over the Prime Duke's duties and is now slowly taking over General Southerwind's duties, but the consensus is that he's not nearly as good as the High General is. The name was . . . Reyu. Strange name. Rather old-fashioned, actually. Merlot says it was in style about a thousand years ago. Guy must have one hell of a family history."

Matthias lightly tapped a finger on the table. "So Blaine marries Albanion to secure her position and then promptly makes the new general her lover. Perhaps part of her lethality is that very cleverness. She knows full well what she's doing. Now she has the Emperor and the, potentially, new High General under her control."

"And she removed the Prime Duke from the picture entirely, shortening the number of people she needs to keep under her heel." Ewan snorted, hard. "No sadness for losing that ass, though. He was not much better than the Emperor. Is he alive?"

"He had a heart attack."

"How convenient!"

Tyrian held up a hand to forestall more commentary. "How is my father?" he asked softly.

Ted hesitated and then sighed. "Terrible, Lord Tyrian. He has been utterly devastated by all these events. He has not left the castle. Few have seen him at all."

Unease churned in Tyrian's stomach. That didn't sound right at all. His father had never suffered in silence before. He could clearly remember when his grandmother had died, how Donald had vented all his grief by intensely training. Even if he took into account the fact that Donald loved Annareal a great deal, it just felt out of character. "Something's wrong," he said softly.

He instantly had everyone's attention. Gordon and Samantha were also frowning. "It's not like General Southerwind," Gordon said softly. "When I saw Lord Tyrian's reaction to losing Lady Annareal, my first thought was 'oh, he doesn't handle things the way his father does.'"

Tyrian closed his eyes for a moment and then opened them again. "Ted. Get a message to my father. Tell him that he is a grandfather and that I'm not going to let him hide like a coward and shame my daughter's legacy."

Ted's brows shot up. "Er, as you command, Lord Tyrian." He hurried out, and the pigeons fluttered along in his wake.

Even Matthias and Cassie looked at Tyrian warily. "What do you hope to accomplish?" Matthias asked quietly. "I thought you did not want to face him in battle."

"I don't." His hands curled together under the table. "But there is something wrong. I don't know what. I suspect Blaine, and no doubt rightfully so. Father . . . he was teasing me when I turned eighteen. He said that if I would take pity on him, he would like to be a grandfather before he was too old to play with his grandchild. It wasn't saying much; he's only forty. But I know that if Blaine did something, this might give him the will to fight against her. I am *not* losing my father."

The distinct ring of steel in his voice was a testament to his powerful will and intense nature. If the power of a Kaiten Star's spirit alone could make things happen, Donald Southerwind would be on their side in no time.

Thinking about ages and the time that had passed, Cassie found herself a little surprised to look at a calendar and realize she had turned twenty a few days back. She had been so caught up in everything that she had completely forgotten her own birthday. For the next few months, Tyrian would be two years younger. She could only pray that the war ended before his nineteenth birthday, though the symbolism of it was oddly apt.

She was brought back to the conversation as Matthias said, "Resuming our discussion about Alphin, we can't be certain of what the external defenses consist of. They are kept inactive unless an army is physically approaching. The same is true of other checkpoints. Zinfandel informed me that she has some books on the origins of the checkpoints on their way to her from a secret source in Trinan."

"So we have to show up and see what we're facing right there in the open. You and Cherry will have to almost literally fly by the seat of your pants," Ewan summarized.

"In a nutshell, yes." Matthias looked at Tyrian. "You do not need to worry, Lord Tyrian. We won't let you down."

"I never thought you would."

Because Alex's army units included two magic and two ranged, Tyrian brought two of each of his as well. He assigned unit leaders without much thought behind it, automatically assigning positions based on the strengths of his Stars, something he knew intimately. The regime of war had become so second nature to him that he no longer even acknowledged there was any other way of life. It was too painful to do anything else.

He was just getting ready to mount Fay when Raven came running through the middle of the courtyard and skidded to a stop beside him. He knelt down to her height and ran a hand over her hair. "I'll be fine," he promised softly.

She shook her head, her eyes distressed. "I feel like something is bad, Daddy. I can't remember what I heard, but I heard something." She held out a pin that had a spray of *rubentia* flowers on it. The tiny vibrant red desert flower was where the city got its name. "Please wear this. Gramma helped me make it. It will keep you safe."

He didn't question her instincts or her need to protect him. He pinned the small clutch of flowers to the side of his shirt. None of the Stars wore uniforms into battle, and that was what made them distinct. Not a single one wore anything alike, though there were assorted similarities between same-type warriors. In fact, most wore something loosely based on what was considered the traditional style of clothing for the weapon they used.

He hugged Raven and then nudged her back out of the way as he swung up onto Fay's back. "Be good," he told her. "Mind your grandmother."

She nodded and ran over to where Serentia and Tavi stood. Both little girls huddled against Serentia's legs, and she did not blame them. It was hard to watch someone they loved as much as they loved Tyrian ride into battle and not be able to protect him.

The Mechanoportal was in fine working form and didn't seem to be spewing smoke that morning, for which all soldiers were grateful. It was only a matter of moments before all eight units landed in the fields that led to the coastal city known as Alphin. They had opted to land out of immediate range for fear of instantly triggering any number of dangerous traps that might be placed around something as valuable as a checkpoint city.

As they approached, no one noticed anything unusual at first. One soldier in every unit had been assigned the duty of lookout and was the person most intimately acquainted with reading the land and sky. Something was *off* but not necessarily instantly wrong.

All of that changed within a heartbeat. The army crossed some sort of invisible barrier and every flower in the land began spewing a sort of green fog into the air. There was no immediate response from most people, but anyone wearing a relic was instantly affected with everything from sneezing to violent nausea.

"Back the mages out!" Matthias ordered sharply into his Voice Relic. "Everyone else retreat!"

The Liberation Army backpedaled as the two magic units disappeared from the field. Lane willingly resisted the transport and instead used his Wind Relic to keep the fog from getting to him. Even still, his stomach churned and a headache pounded behind his eyes viciously as he tried to make it across the field toward his Kaiten, arguably another at the most risk.

They managed to get away from the fog, and those wearing relics sat down hard in the grass. Fear rose sharply inside Matthias as he swiftly looked around and took stock. It was not hard to determine that those of the highest magical capacity had been the ones affected the worst. Laia, riding with Samantha, was completely incapacitated. She had lost all ability to walk or ride, and Ewan was carrying her to a safer location while Samantha checked her vital signs.

A sudden thud followed by Cassie screaming Tyrian's name froze everyone on the field. Without even really being conscious of it, Matthias rushed his horse toward where Tyrian's unit had been. When he saw the tableau, he paled sharply. "Lord Tyrian!"

Tyrian had fallen off Fay's back and was lying in the grass. He looked as pale as salt. Cassie knelt beside him with Dylan, who had been in the unit as well. The swordsman looked as terrified as Matthias felt. "What happened?" Matthias demanded.

"We don't know! He seemed fine initially as we were retreating. Some nausea, a headache. Same as anyone else. But then he suddenly went white and collapsed." Cassie's voice was even, but tears shimmered across her eyes. She pressed a hand to Tyrian's forehead and hissed softly. "He's burning up."

"Let me through!" Lane shoved past the soldiers and knelt beside them. He instantly lifted Tyrian's relic hand to look at the mark. When he saw the pale and fading image, his breath hissed out in a string of curses in another language. "His relic is poisoned," he said flatly. "It's called Soul Fog. It goes directly to the magical capacity of a soul, and it poisons from inside out."

"I didn't think it was deadly!" Dylan snapped. "I've heard of Soul Fog being used in battle before. It incapacitates mages. No one has ever died from it, and you can't tell me that Tyrian and Laia aren't at risk of dying!"

"Laia will recover eventually. She was speaking coherently, if sluggishly, and stayed conscious. Think of it as her having caught a particularly nasty influenza. Tyrian is different." Lane's hands curled into fists at his side. "Don't you idiots realize what the Devourer really is? It's a parasite! If it wasn't for Tyrian's iron will, it would have consumed him a dozen times by now! The influenza that Laia caught is much more deadly in Tyrian. With all his strength suddenly gone, the Devourer leapt to consume him. All his focus is on fighting the relic, and that means nothing is left to fight the influenza. One or the other is going to kill him unless we do something!"

A rising tide of terror began to move through the soldiers. The Stars still on the field shoved their way through to join the others. "Laia has been recalled to the base," Ewan told Matthias curtly. "She was coherent, but there was absolutely no strength left in her physically or magically. Halkern says it could be weeks before she recovers. Our other mages and Magicians are suffering from much milder symptoms. A week or less and they'll be back to normal."

"How'd you escape it?" Cherry asked Lane.

"I recognized it the instant it appeared. I used my Wind Relic to keep it off. I was trying to get to Tyrian to protect him when I heard him fall." Lane shook his head sharply. "We have to purify his relic, and through it, his soul. It has to be done with another Pure Relic."

"Then do it!" Ewan snapped at him.

"I can't! Both the Wind Relic and the Devourer have negative charges inside. They repel. I can't do anything for him at all."

"Miranda!" Matthias said. "The Echo Relic?"

"Negative charge." The frustration was in Lane's voice. "But maybe together we can do something, anything."

Cassie, who had been silent the entire time, asked softly, "The Pure Shrieking Relic. Is it positive or negative?"

He paused as he thought about it. "Positive. It would certainly be able to aid Tyrian, but it hasn't been seen in a few hundred years. The nature of the Shrieking Relic is to create silence that nullifies sound, so you can't even sense it, no matter how powerful you are." He suddenly stopped as another thought occurred to him. "Wait. How did you know about the Shrieking Relic?"

She looked at him, and a spirit that was not much less for strength than Tyrian's stirred in her eyes. "It has been in the possession of the Monk Clans, passed down from leader to leader, for those hundred years you mentioned. It has never been worn. No leader ever felt the need for it. My adopted father is currently its keeper."

"That's the eternity you said was yours to claim," Dylan said softly. "If you were strong enough. Why wouldn't you be, if it is rightfully yours?"

"There is a trial for me to face." She gently brushed Tyrian's hair from his eyes. She could feel the battle waged within his soul, but she would never let him be devoured by his relic. She would never let him go. "It may bring me to the breaking point. It may break me entirely. I still have to try. I will go now." She straightened.

"Hold up!" Leonard held up a hand. "Not alone, you won't. We're going to support you. Your father owes us some army units, and we need to collect on that debt too."

It was against the rules to bring in outsiders, but the rules could go to hell. Cassie nodded instantly. "We will bring Tyrian there as well. We have a clan doctor, Doctor Kelan, who will be able to care for him while I face my trials."

Matthias nodded briefly. "You, Leonard, Ewan, Dylan, and Lord Lane will take Lord Tyrian to the Monk Clan stronghold. While you are there, we will research how to either get around the Soul Fog or find another way into the city entirely. Hurry," he urged softer. It made him sick to think none of them had realized just how heavy Tyrian's burden was.

"What's the quickest way to get there?" Ewan asked Cassie as he lifted Tyrian. He instantly grimaced. Tyrian weighed less than the last time he had been carried, and that was not a good sign at all. Perhaps his lack of hunger was as much a product of the relic as it was the stress of the entire situation.

Cassie didn't get a chance to answer. A swirl of clouds appeared in the air and Miranda tumbled out. She was right over Leonard, but the mayor was quick on his feet and caught her before she fell far. "Honey," he told her, "your aim needs improvement." He gently put her down.

She waved her hands in agitation and narrowly missed hitting Lane in the head with her wand. Luckily, he was well used to her and smart enough to move out of the way. "The soldiers coming back said you were going to take Lord Tyrian somewhere and I was hoping I could make it faster because I really don't like him being sick and if where you're going is somewhere you've been before then I can transport you!"

"It is," Cassie told her. "It's my hometown. The Monk Clan Stronghold. Do you know where it is?"

"No, but that's not important. Long as *you* know where it is, I can send you." She swung her wand in a looping arc that narrowly missed hitting more than one person. "Here we go! Hang on tight!"

There was a bright flash of light that made everyone blink rapidly as everything around them started looking like a double—or an echo—of itself. When the light faded, they stood at the edge of what looked like a small city in a mountain valley. As the others continued to stare in fascination at the lingering double-echo, Lane said, "And now you know where the relic got its name. It'll fade quickly enough."

It had cleared just as a young man suddenly appeared from out of nowhere, and he wore the familiar gear of a monk. "Master Cassie!" he said sharply. "Why have you brought these outsiders?" He planted himself physically in the middle of the path to block them. "Leave!" he said heatedly. "You don't belong here."

"Ernest," Cassie said softly, her voice cool, "get out of my way. I wish to see Doctor Kelan, and I wish to speak with my father."

He shook his head. "Master Kotan will not permit you to come into town with these . . . these heathens!"

"Stand aside." It was no less than a sharp order. "Stand aside, Second Class. You would prevent us from bringing in an ill man just because it isn't protocol? You are an embarrassment to our code."

Ashamed color climbed his face as he actually saw that the very large man was carrying another person. In fact, when he looked a second time, the color left his face as he recognized Tyrian's dark hair and green scarf. "Doctor Kelan!" he shouted as he whirled and ran into the city. "Hurry!"

"He's not very controlled for a monk," Dylan noted.

"He's only a Second Class. He has a long way to go." Cassie lifted her chin and led the way into the city. "Stay with me."

The others, even Lane, couldn't help but look around curiously at the city. It was even smaller than Teasarn, and built with a style that none of them had ever seen. The buildings had been elevated and made from interesting pieces of round wood. Many children ran around, but it was obvious that every person who called the city home was either a monk or a monk-in-training.

At the end of the city, against the mountain, sat a much larger building. Cassie glanced toward it but diverted to go into one of the regular buildings first. Inside, Ernest stood talking to a man in his mid-twenties. He wore the familiar white coat of a doctor. "Doctor Kelan," Cassie said. "Please."

"Bring him in," Kelan urged. He looked at Tyrian's face as Ewan put him on one of the medical beds and promptly grimaced. He recognized Soul Fog poisoning. "I've never seen a case so severe." He spotted the flowers pinned to Tyrian's shirt and also recognized them instantly. "Well, interesting."

"What?" Cassie asked.

"Those flowers. *Rubentia* are a flower known to negate the effects of Soul Fog. They might well have saved his life." He picked up Tyrian's wrist to check his pulse and saw the state of the Devourer. He also recognized the relic symbol. "I see. Ernest, fetch the Land and Water Relics from the cabinet."

"Why me?" The monk gulped as Kelan glared at him. "Yes, sir." He hastily scrambled over and opened the cabinet to pull out the two relics. He handed them over and asked, "What for?"

"They're positively charged," Lane said. "They might help stabilize the Devourer long enough for Cassie to get the Shrieking Relic."

Ernest bristled. "You told them about it?"

"Would you shut up?" Cassie snapped at him, causing his eyes to widen significantly. "I don't have the time for you to play stupid games. Tyrian needs me to save him, and I'm going to do whatever it takes."

"You're sleeping with him!" It was an accusation.

"I'm marrying him!" she shot back.

His mouth opened and then closed several times in utter shock. He had never seen her like this before. "What's wrong with you? You should never have gone to the capitol! It's completely ruined your life!"

Ewan had had enough. He grabbed Ernest by the back of his scarf and lifted him a foot off the floor. As the monk kicked and flailed, Ewan snarled, "Kid, you have one hell of a big mouth, and coming from me, that's saying something!" He swung him around and forced him to look at Tyrian. "Just look at him, would you?"

Ernest didn't want to look at anyone, but Ewan wasn't putting him down anytime soon, so he gave in and looked at Tyrian. Emotion immediately punched into his heart. He could just somehow *see* that Tyrian needed Cassie. And he couldn't shake the feeling that Tyrian needed him too. He stopped struggling and lowered his gaze. "What is that?" he asked, visibly subdued.

Ewan put him down, suspicions confirmed. Those of the Destined Stars who had been around the longest were beginning to recognize each other in the way Raven did because of her age. "Destiny," he said simply. "Tyrian's our Kaiten Star. We share the skies with him. You were born under a star, meant to be there to support him. But it's more than that. He loves us as much as we love him. If he believes in you, then you can do anything."

Ernest said nothing. He had nothing he could say. He felt small and petty. Cassie barely spared him a look as she headed for the door. "Ernie," she said softly, "his life is priceless. Do we have an understanding?"

He straightened up and bowed deeply. "Yes, Master Cassie."

"Is there anything we can do?" Leonard asked Cassie.

"Just stay here and protect Tyrian." Without looking back, she walked out of the doctor's office.

In a murmur, Leonard said, "I can't imagine why she's the Kentei Star."

Even Ernest had to agree with that.

Chapter Twenty-Nine

"If it was for you I could fly the skies; I'd always be looking over you from above."

Cassie moved swiftly and surely toward the pagoda in the distance where her trial awaited her. Her stomach was already churning.

Standing on the steps of the pagoda was an older man with hair that had already gone white. He was as fit and strong as a man half his age, and though he and Cassie shared no blood, she had clearly grown up in his image. "The prodigal daughter," Kotan said with a touch of wryness.

She planted her hands on her hips and demanded, "Why the hell haven't you responded to any of my messages? We're fighting a damned war out there! We struggled to get up and running; those promised units would have been useful, Father!"

He held up his hands placatingly. "Your messages only arrived just a few days ago. I was preparing to have the units start toward your base on the morrow." He studied her with a parent's knowing eye. "We have, of course, been pulling in information and rumor as they spread. I must say, you seem like an entirely different person. A year ago, you'd have never had an outburst like that." She set her chin in a stubborn line and he smiled. "It's good for you." He sighed. "Not that I was entirely happy when I first heard the phrase 'Tyrian Southerwind's lover' in reference to you."

"Does it help to know he was courting me the entire time and has since proposed marriage? And that we've adopted a little Faerie girl as our daughter?"

"Indeed! Ah, well. I can't imagine there's any person less likely to break your heart. I will journey with you to the base so I may meet my granddaughter properly." He took a deep breath and then let it out. "So you come for the Shrieking Relic. And not to merely take over my position. You will fuse it."

"The instant Tyrian got the Devourer, I knew that this was my future." Her gaze lowered. "I just needed the courage for it. I was intending to come here even before he was affected by Soul Fog." She paused and then frowned. She would need to ask Lane if by chance either of them, or both, might as yet be able to help Laia. Losing one of their best unit leaders for weeks was not good for anyone.

Kotan stepped aside. "Come inside, then. We must hurry." He glanced up as he heard murmuring, and he saw people gathering as they realized what was occurring. At twenty, Cassie was the youngest ever to challenge for leadership. But then, she had been the youngest to become a First Class—at seven!—and youngest to be a Tenth Class at the age of fifteen. Without question, she was the finest monk that had ever been born. Kotan had already decided that an Eleventh Class needed to be invented just for her.

The pagoda was oddly welcoming to Cassie as she walked inside. It felt like forever since she had been there. The straw mat on the floors, and the wooden walls, were nostalgic. She had spent so much time there. And though she would claim it as her own, she knew she would never live there again.

She went to the center of the main room and waited. Kotan placed Seeing Relics at each of the four corners of the large straw mat she stood on. Even though he would not see what she did, he already knew what she would confront. A year ago, he would have doubted she was ready. Now he held no doubt that she would survive.

The Seeing Relics activated and the pagoda went away from around Cassie. Her entire body tensed as wispy images began to fill the air. The Seeing Relics were attuned specifically to access the memories of the one confronting the trial. The trial was simple enough when it was pared down to the most basic component: the challenger had to face the moments in their life that defined them.

Kotan had passed a fairly simple trial when he had taken it on. The hardest thing to face had been the death of his wife to a plague. But Cassie . . . too much tragedy had lined her young life.

The memories were average enough at first. Cassie saw herself starting monk training at the age of three; again, young for it, but showing promising skill. It was one of the most defining parts of her life, and it did not surprise her to see it.

But then the screaming started. It was as raw and fresh as the day it had occurred. She watched herself as a child, running away through the forests between Foresalia and Empire. She was clutching her mother's hand while stumbling over roots and branches. The screams tore apart the trees as the soldiers chased them. An accident. Her family had come upon a secret village of Faeries and Elves in the forest just as Foresalia had.

Blood began to seep up under her feet. A shudder ran through her body as she watched her father fall right in front of her. She wanted to run. She wanted to run and hide and not see this ever again. She even found herself backing up, but she forced herself to stop.

Her mother had fallen trying to protect her. The way the sword cut into her body was burned into her eyes. The sound of her body hitting the ground was engraved in her ears. This feeling, this helpless horror, had been part of her rage with Annareal's actions. Those children now carried some of the scars Cassie lived with.

She saw herself staring at a soldier whose sword dripped with the blood of her parents. It was war. There was no mercy based on age when the enemy was already ruthless enough to slaughter a town indiscriminately. The soldier had stabbed her a little in the shoulder, just to make her cry. She had just stared at him. Even now, she didn't know if it was shock or defiance.

He had upped the ante by lightly stabbing her in the side. Just little stabs, barely half an inch deep. Enough to hurt. Enough to bleed. When she had still stared at him, he had slowly and carefully sliced along her neck. Not deep enough to kill. Not yet.

She pressed her hand to her throat as she felt the pain as sharply as if it had just occurred. She couldn't breathe! She fell to her knees as she struggled to drag in a breath. It was just an illusion trying to trick her into thinking she was there again. She threw her will into fighting back, into letting go of the memories. She had *survived.* They hadn't won. Somehow she had escaped. She had lived, she had thrived. She was better than this!

The screaming abruptly stopped and she could breathe again. The pain became a dull throbbing. She gulped in air gratefully as her ears continued to ring and spots swam before her eyes. At a sound, her shoulders tensed for what was next, but when she looked up, she saw Tyrian. Shocked, there was nothing she could say. He was walking through the Imperial Palace with Liang and Marian pacing at his side. He walked into a room, and she saw . . . herself.

Everything seemed to align. Calm descended. That tragedy of her youth had led her to train harder and longer to never be weak again. That training had led her to reaching such a high rank before she was in her twenties. That rank had led her to be the delegate chosen to help Ophelia Goldwind . . . and led to her destined meeting with her Kaiten Star.

She slowly got to her feet and lifted her chin. The illusions splintered around her, leaving her alone in the middle of the floor. There was nothing more to be seen. "Everything happens for a reason," she said quietly. "We all obey the whims of Destiny."

Kotan started breathing again. He hadn't been breathing the entire time, and certainly his heart had stopped when she had fallen. Getting out of the trial once it started only happened one of two ways. You passed, or you were destroyed by your own memories. It could happen to even strong people. He had watched it happen to his elder brother when he had tried to take leadership from their mother. "I would think," he said softly, his voice gruff, "that the Kentei Star does not lack much less of an iron will than her Kaiten Star."

"Well, *someone* has to keep him line." She took a deep breath and turned around. "I'd be lying to say that I won't have nightmares. But . . . I'm okay. And I'm finally ready to ask you just what happened to me. How I was saved. I never could before."

"The Imperial Army had already been rushing to the scene," he said willingly. He had always hoped there would come a day when she would be strong enough to know it all. "The High General, though he was still just a Lower General then, reached the scene first. It was he who tended your wounds and carried you away."

In a way, it was not as shocking as it should have been. Threads tied all of them together in some way or another. "I wonder if he knows who I am," she mused mostly to herself. She would have to tell Tyrian. It might lift his spirits to think his father had saved her life. And thinking of Tyrian brought back the sharp reality of why she was there. "I claim by family right and right of trial the leadership over the Monk Clans."

"Come with me, daughter." He led the way past the mat to a door in the wall. Instead of opening it, he pushed on the wall panel beside it. The panel rotated open to reveal a short hall and a tiny room at the end. "Inside there is what you seek."

She ducked into the hall and moved swiftly to the end. In the center of the small room was a slim pedestal. On the top of that was a blue cushion. Settled into the center of the cushion was a glass sphere. It glowed with a soft sapphire color, and within the center of the relic hovered a symbol reminiscent of a broken musical note. There was no mistaking it for a Music Relic. Though the symbol was *like* a note, it was also entirely different. The symbol of silence. The mark of the Pure Shrieking Relic.

She held out her left hand without hesitation. Though most single relics were worn on the right hand, she felt the sharpest pull of her magical capacity flowing through her left hand. The few times she had worn a relic, she had always worn it on her left hand. As Tyrian wore his on his right, she couldn't help but wonder if her relic hand choice was also destiny.

The Shrieking Relic floated up into the air and then hovered over her left hand. She immediately became aware of the emptiness inside her soul. It was a shocking feeling to realize just how deep her own capacity went. She had been primed for that moment without ever knowing it.

With a flash of light, the relic fused to her hand. The pain was sharp and ambushing, welling up from her very soul as the relic forced itself inside and rooted deep. Her head went light and she fell to her knees as she sought for her stability. She felt positively stuffed, as if her soul had become tangible and could be physically experienced. Her magical capacity was not only great, but it was also now thoroughly utilized.

The pain faded to a dull throbbing and the dizziness ebbed. The swiftness of the recovery only confirmed her feelings that it had been the nature of the Devourer itself that had been detrimental to Tyrian. She felt exhausted, certainly, but not nearly as drained and weakened as he had been.

When she returned to Kotan's side, he hugged her tightly. "I'm very proud of you," he said roughly.

The display of affection was only a little surprising. She had always known he loved her, though he'd had trouble expressing it. "Thank you," she said softly. She hugged him back and then let go. "Don't think you can retire yet. You need to handle day-to-day things for me."

"I can do so." He released her. "Go now to his side," he urged. He watched her hurry out of the room and let out a long sigh before following at a slower pace. Retirement and a granddaughter. He was getting old after all.

It seemed as if everyone in the city had gathered outside the pagoda. Cassie brushed past all of them as she ran back toward the doctor's office. No one tried to stop her, though many swarmed around Kotan with eager questions and congratulations. Yet again, Master Cassie had proven why she was their greatest monk.

When Cassie burst into the doctor's office, the others glanced at her in surprise, even Ernest and Kelan. They had all thought it would take much more time for her to confront her trial; it had only been an hour. Lane glanced at her hand and saw the Shrieking Relic, and he felt some of the knots in his stomach unclench. The feeling of being terrified of losing Tyrian was not entirely pleasant. He had never experienced so much emotion for anyone other than Lady Tanelia, and she had always been like a mother to him.

"What do I do?" Cassie asked Lane. "And don't take an attitude with me. Just tell me what to do."

He forced himself to bite his tongue. Honestly, these fledgling sorcerers could be very vexing! "Take Tyrian's hand and place the mark of your relic directly against the mark of his relic. Try to call a spell to start the power flowing. You shouldn't have the first level unlocked yet, so you'll just get raw magic."

She sat beside Tyrian on the bed and gently lifted his relic hand. She pressed the back of their hands together and felt a sudden jolt all the way to her soul. The sensation was very, very intimate. She couldn't guess at whether it happened because of what was already between her and Tyrian, or if it was normal. She also didn't have the nerve to ask.

She reached for her power, not yet even knowing what to call it. Her relic glowed softly and the symbol of Shrieking appeared over her head. Though she did not initially intend to cast an actual spell, she felt it well up inside. "Silence," she said softly.

The entire room went dead silent as all magic nullified from everyone except for her and Tyrian. Lane opened his mouth and then closed it, at a true loss for words. If she was going to evolve at Tyrian's rate, then things could be deadly for them both. Tyrian needed Cassie to be his anchor. Lane swiftly ducked outside. This was over his head, but Tanelia would have the answers.

Power welled from inside Cassie and moved freely without being impeded by other forces in the air. It flowed directly into the Devourer and then moved beyond, purifying the lingering effects of the Soul Fog and returning strength to Tyrian's body. With the Shrieking Relic providing the strength to heal, Tyrian's will was enough to fight the Devourer. Balance was once more achieved and color returned to his face, though he did not wake.

The silence ended and sound returned. Softly, Ewan said, "So that's what you meant, Night. A natural silence versus an unnatural one. This wasn't that unnerving. It was a bit soothing."

"Particularly for you because you do not wear a relic. Natural silence is quite peaceful, though it is an effective weapon against an enemy." Without missing a beat, Night added, "You might want to catch her."

Ewan could be quick for his size. He moved forward just in time to catch Cassie as she fell over the side of the bed. "I should have realized that would happen," he said with a sigh. "So much for Lane thinking he knows everything." He stood and gently handed Cassie to Dylan. "You take her. I'll get Tyrian." He looked at Kelan. "Do they need to remain here?"

"No. Only rest can help them at this point. Ernest, show them to where Cassie's home is located." When the monk sulked, Kelan narrowed his eyes. "Do as I say, Second Class."

Ernest jumped. "Yes, Master Kelan!" He beat a hasty retreat out the door.

"*Master* Kelan?" Leonard lifted his brows.

Kelan smiled. "I'm a Fifth Class, the lowest you can be to become a

Master. But I prefer to heal wounds rather than inflict them. That doesn't mean I can't. I just prefer otherwise."

Cassie's home sat not far from the pagoda. The door was unlocked, which made Ewan frown at Ernest. As he held the door, the monk said, "We never lock doors here. Outsiders don't come here, and stealing from each other would just be silly. We lock them if we're home and don't want visitors, though."

Ewan and Dylan put Tyrian and Cassie in her room and then followed Ernest toward the pub. Monks didn't get drunk, but that didn't mean they didn't like to drink. After the emotional upheaval, both Ewan and Dylan were glad for it. They needed booze.

Tyrian awoke feeling stronger than he had in quite a long while. The room was dark and quiet though some light spilled in through the window curtains. Cassie slept beside him, which was normal enough, but the bed they slept on was not as big as the one in their tower. The general feel of the room seemed soothing but not in the same way.

Shadows fell in an unusual pattern across the floor. He got to his feet and walked silently over to the window to look out. The darkened village was unfamiliar in shape and size, and snow softly fell. Snow only fell in the higher mountains, so he could take a fairly decent guess as to their current location.

A lamp lit behind him. "Tyrian?"

He turned immediately and went back over to the bed. "I'm right here." He sat down as Cassie sat up, and he cupped her cheek in his hand. "What did you do?" he asked softly. "I was so busy fighting the Devourer that it shocked me when I saw your power. I can still feel it to some extent."

She held up her left hand where the stark image of the Shrieking Relic was clearly visible. "I am now the leader of the Monk Clans," she said softly. "That is what this relic represents. Until I met you, I never thought I'd ever be strong enough to face the trial of leadership. This was why I wanted to come here. When you fell . . . Lane said that only a Pure Relic with a positive charge could save you. That's what this has."

There was a steadiness inside her, a sense of calm, that had become only more powerful now. It was a seductive lure to Tyrian, offering a promise of peace and quiet and sanctuary. Eternity. It was theirs to share. She would always be by his side. "I love you," he vowed intensely. "I would never have made it this far without you. And if millennia with you is my reward for this burden, then I'll do it again and again."

"Then understand why I don't regret what I faced to reach this point.

I am the lucky one, Tyrian." She pressed her relic hand against his and sparks leapt and flew between their palms. In the way the positive and negative charges of the relics could fuse, so too were their owners meant to be one. "Are you truly better?" she asked softly, searching his face intently.

In answer, he drew her relic hand to his lips and teasingly skimmed a kiss across the mark. Her breath caught as the shock of pleasure streaked through her entire body. Even expecting it didn't prepare her for how strong it felt. "Should I apologize for teasing you that time?" she asked huskily.

His lips slowly curved. "How about I simply return the favor?" He tumbled her over onto the bed, his heated breath sensitizing her skin until she shivered from the inside out with hunger. As he trailed soft kisses down her arm, her hand curled around his neck. Her touch was hot and powerful, the magic inside tingling against his skin. "Do you think it's just us, or any relic?" he asked softly.

The little rasp to his voice made her breath catch. She loved when he sounded like that, when he had no will to resist her and it reflected in his voice. "We could ask Laia," she said teasingly. "She's the only one who could answer without embarrassing herself or us equally."

His laugh teased her ears and clenched her heart. "True, I can't see us asking Lane. He'd start getting arrogant and know-it-all." He worked on removing her gear as he spoke; his nimble fingers were now intimately familiar with every fastening and how to remove it in the fastest way possible. "Think he'll get his someday?"

"Oh, I think so. And we'll even get to see it." She tugged at his shirt and pulled it up over his head when he lifted his arms. Even with her body aching for his, there was no desire to rush. Already she could feel that time had stopped for them. There was a war waiting with the dawn, and there was no knowing what every day would bring. More Destined Stars, more battles, and even a confrontation with Donald Southerwind loomed ahead.

It didn't seem that frightening anymore for either of them. Tyrian knew that this was what Lane had meant when he had said there was something only Cassie could do to lift his burdens. The enemy couldn't defeat him. The Devourer couldn't consume him. Not so long as they were together.

It wasn't until they lay tangled together that he finally realized something he had subconsciously sensed all along. There had always been something deeper between them, some mysterious element that encompassed love and desire and yet was more than both together. This time, finally, he thought he knew what it was. It was eternity.

It had been there all along.

Part Three

"Dreams are like stars...you may never touch them, but if you follow them they will lead you to your **destiny**."

- Anonymous

Chapter Thirty

"We are only as strong as our hearts decide."

Tyrian woke in the morning to the smell of breakfast. For a moment, he was left completely disoriented as he tried to figure out why he was sleeping in the courtyard so close to the restaurant. Or was Evelyn just cooking up a storm and the smells drifting into the tower?

Cognizance returned when he tried to roll over in bed and instead fell out. The landing on the floor reminded him quite distinctly that he was not in his tower and assuredly not in his bed. A pair of rather sexy feet stepped in front of him and he looked up at Cassie with a sigh. "Your bed is too small."

"It was never intended to hold a six foot male," she pointed out dryly. She knelt down and tried not to smile. The instant she had heard the thud, she had known what had happened. "If we ever want to stay here, we'll need to have a bigger bed."

He rolled nimbly to his feet and tugged her into his arms. She was wearing a blue silk robe that he approved of wholeheartedly. "Bring this with you," he urged softly. He nuzzled at her neck and then tasted the curve of her jaw. "I like it."

"I noticed." She rubbed a hand over his jaw. It was slightly rough to the touch, as it had been from the beginning of the war. Ceasing to age had started to cause his ability to grow hair to slow down. "Get cleaned up. Breakfast will be ready soon. The others will be worried and want to see that we're okay."

He slowly and reluctantly released her. "If you insist."

"I do," she said firmly.

His lips curved. "Yes'm, Master Cassie."

As he sauntered into the bathing room, she found herself grinning. At least he appreciated that there was someone who didn't let him have his way all the time. And because it was better to remove temptation from sight, she quickly got dressed in her regular gear before going to finish making breakfast.

Tyrian had also gotten dressed when he joined her, and he was very happy to be fed. He felt positively ravenous, and that was a good sign to them both. A returning appetite meant that he could better handle his physical health. It humbled Cassie to think she alone was so critical to this man who was so critical to everyone else.

After breakfast, they headed toward the doctor's place. It was the mostly likely place to find the others since there wasn't exactly an inn located in town. Halfway toward their destination, a young teenager wearing an eye patch got in their way and planted her hands on her hips.

On one look, Tyrian knew she wasn't Human. Her bright red hair matched with a dark red eye, the second of which was an impossible color for Human blood without something else added in. Truthfully, Laia's purple eyes had been the first clue all along that she wasn't fully Human. This girl was also quite powerful, enough that he could sense it plainly. "Hello," he said.

"Hi." She studied him critically. "So that's what Ernie meant. That feeling he felt." She nodded firmly. "Okay, then I'm going with you too!" She belatedly remembered her manners and looked at Cassie sheepishly. "If that's alright with you, Master Cassie."

"You might try an introduction first," her teacher said dryly.

"Oh!" She winced. "Right. I'm sorry, Lord Tyrian. Everyone calls me Squint." She smiled as she said it. "For the obvious reasons." She tapped her eye patch. "Don't worry about this or my age. I'm fourteen, but I'm strong. And what I can't see, I can darned well smell a mile away!"

"You are . . .?"

"A Dragon."

Tyrian blinked. "Well, then." He knew that Dragons could take a smaller form to make walking in other cities easier, but he had never met one so young. Suddenly, he smiled. He had a Kraken as a Destined Star. Really, a Dragon wasn't all that unusual in the end. That little tug inside was a little stronger than it had been, and with it came an eerie sense of knowledge. Where he had subconsciously known things about his Stars before, it was now more consciously known. "I know you won't let me down," he said softly.

Squint hesitated and then hugged him fiercely before running off to her home to pack. Bemused, Tyrian said to Cassie, "I think Dragons maintain their strength even in a smaller form. That was like being hugged by Ewan."

"She's a special girl," she agreed. "She was in her natural form when she was found as a baby, but hasn't been back in that form since. Doctor Kelan suspects that with a severe enough need, she'll manage it."

"What was this about an 'Ernie'?" he asked curiously.

"Me." Ernest had come from out of nowhere and stood in the path in front of them. His cheeks were bright pink but he made himself meet Tyrian's eyes. "I'm Ernest. I'm one. I'm a Destined Star too. Ewan was right. And . . . I'm proud of it. I want to help you too. I'm sorry for being so rude to everyone. I know you'll hear about it."

Tyrian studied him for long moments before promising softly, "You can trust me with her heart, Ernest. I cherish it a great deal."

Ernest lowered his gaze, a bit embarrassed but a bit relieved that Tyrian would understand why he had been hostile. "Okay. Then, I'll see you at the base. I'm going to help Squint." He hurried off through the village past them.

Cassie frowned at Tyrian. "Just what were you talking about?"

He skimmed his thumb down her cheek. "He's in love with you." She stared at him in shock and he kissed her in front of everyone, uncaring that he made a scene in the last place where a scene would be welcome. To his delight, there came a distinct burst of applause from those observing. "Will I go to Hell for that?" he asked against her lips.

Her lips curved. "You are a terrible man, Tyrian Southerwind." Putting aside the issue of Ernest's feelings—and how had she missed that?—she continued to lead the way toward Kelan's building. If they were lucky, they would get there before sunset.

And yet, she wasn't wholly surprised when Tyrian stopped outside the accessory shop and studied it with a familiar look in his green eyes. She followed amiably as he went inside, and she smiled when she saw the familiar disaster. "Do you never clean, Yaegi?" she asked fondly.

The woman behind the counter sighed deeply. "I gave up. Every time I thought I had it under control, it was shortly a disaster again." She propped her elbows on the counter and smiled. "How do you feel, Master Cassie?"

"Remarkably normal, relatively speaking."

Tyrian studied Yaegi and noticed that she bore a very strong resemblance to Yagi in not just name but in appearance as well. "Are you any relation to Yagi?"

"He's my twin brother," she confirmed. She sighed. "Is he still always fighting with Sharmie?" At the wry nods, she dropped her head onto her arms. "Ugh! They've been friends as long as I remember, but they've *always* bickered. I tried to tell them that they fought because they're too much alike, but it fell on deaf ears."

"Would that we all had deaf ears," Tyrian murmured dryly.

She studied him and then smiled. "I could come out and play mediator. And sell accessories." She pointed to the bracer he wore. "I made that, so you've seen my work."

"Done," he said instantly. "I'll be glad to have your help. There's been a general jealousy among the fighting types that they don't have something as good as my bracer. Hopefully we'll get an Armorer and Tailor as well and have all the bases covered."

She gave a quick and graceful bow. "Alright then! I'll head out when Squint and Ernest do." She winked. "Monks are horrible at keeping secrets in town."

Tyrian was still smiling about that as they approached Kelan's place at last. Monks had a very powerful, and well-earned, reputation in the world. Clans were located in all five countries with the one in the Empire considered the main base. Monks, like the Dragonists and Gunners' Guild, had particularly special gifts, and they had the respect that such a thing deserved. But, truly, they were not much different from the ordinary person, if you discounted their lethality.

As if she was reading his mind, Cassie murmured, "You could pass one of us on the street and never know what we were unless we were in our gear. And that's the whole point of what we do. Part of why we're deadly is how we can hide in plain sight."

"And with this," he swung her relic hand to his lips, "you'll be even more dangerous. We'll have to pit you and Laia against each other and see if her ears can still find you." His eyes suddenly darkened as he remembered something Cassie had told him that morning while getting him caught up. "Do you think she will have recovered from poisoning before we get back?"

"Probably not. Lane said she was recovering, but it could take weeks. I want to ask him if we can help her somehow."

"Yes, you can," Lane said from the doorway to the office. "She's a Thaumoturge, but she doesn't wear a Pure Relic, so two Pure Relics will have more than enough punch to help restore her." He added in a mutter, "I wish Lady Tanelia would tell me what the hell she is. She has a magical capacity that surpasses mine."

Lane, being a Thaumoturge with a Pure Relic, was in possession of a larger capacity than average. It said something, indeed, about Laia's capabilities. "What did she say when you asked her?" Cassie asked.

He sighed and quoted, "'Lane, you know well that answers come with time. You need only be patient. In less than twenty-five years, it will make sense.'"

The fact that twenty-five years didn't feel all that long to Tyrian or Cassie was another sign that they already felt the effects of eternity. It didn't seem such a frightening concept anymore for either of them. Eternity was only a burden if you were alone.

"Well don't stand there," Kelan said in exasperation from behind Lane. "Do come in." He smiled as Tyrian and Cassie walked in, and he looked knowingly toward where their relic hands clasped together. "I see everything is settled properly." He bowed with a grace that underscored his monk class. "I am Doctor Kelan, Lord Tyrian. Many kids call me 'Doc' for short. I answer to it as well as to my name, so feel free to take your pick."

Ewan, Dylan, and Leonard were sitting at a table to the side, and they had looked over as soon as they heard Tyrian's name. Tension left all three pairs of shoulders as they saw how well Tyrian looked. In fact, he looked better than Ewan or Dylan had ever seen him, and they had been by his side from the start of the ordeal. "Welcome back to the living, Tyrian," Ewan said.

"How was near-death?" Dylan asked, amusement in his voice.

"Not entirely pleasant. I'd as soon not visit it again." Tyrian shook his head at Kelan. "I apologize for the heathens you've been entertaining. I'll take them away with me."

"That's not a nice thing to call Ewan," Leonard noted.

"He meant you, too," the taller male grumbled.

Kelan just smiled at Tyrian. "They were perfectly decent houseguests. And as we both know I am a Destined Star, we also know I can't fully escape them anyway. I will be packing my bags to come along to the base. I am sure my services will be needed. Magic can only do so much, but my skill is vast."

"I've been hoping to find a doctor to join the Liberation Army. I couldn't ask for better. I know you won't let me down, Doc." His mind ran swiftly over everyone at base, and he knew of several people that could be served immediately by Kelan's skills. Persephone's husband was one of them. Matthias was another. "There is a lot to be done," he said simply. "But I know you will take care of things."

It was a strangely empowering feeling to have Tyrian believe in him, Kelan discovered. Perhaps that was the true power of the Kaiten Star.

"How are we getting out of here?" Leonard asked Cassie. "How far are we relative to where we left the Army? They were going to leave a unit there to pick us up."

"If we take the shortcuts I know, we're only two days away. I will send a message before we leave so that they know we will have four more people to come back with us." Cassie sighed. "Where's Miranda when you need her? She could just transport all of us to the base."

"We'd land in the moat," Dylan muttered.

Lane suddenly looked up, and so did Tyrian and Cassie. A familiar swirl of clouds appeared in the middle of the room and Miranda came tumbling out. She was only a few feet over the ground, and she landed with a thump on her bottom. "Ouch! Oooh." She rubbed her sore posterior and blew her hair out of her eyes. "Darn you, Tedium!"

"Tedium?" Tyrian repeated, trying not to smile as he knelt and offered a hand to her. He tugged her to her feet and kept her balanced as she brushed out her robes. "What does Tedium have to do with this?"

She waved her free hand. "He said he could tune the Mechanoportal to my power and then if I tried to focus on your power then I could probably get transported to where you were so that I could bring everyone home but there was a lot of smoke coming out of the machine and if it broke it isn't my fault!" she finished in a rush.

"We have plenty of mages running around now, and Samantha brought a transporting mage with her," Ewan said soothingly. "So if it's broken, then we'll be fine anyway. At least you got here safely. You could have gotten stuck in a wall."

"Again," Lane noted with a smirk.

Miranda whirled and aimed her wand at his face. "You shush, Lane Aerian! I may have been stuck in a wall, but I still beat your butt in that Relic Duel! And you can bet if I ever meet Sienna, I'll tell him!"

Lane shut his mouth very quickly. "Sienna?" Tyrian asked.

Miranda beamed. "The High Priest of Melodina. He's the possessor of the Pure Relic of Land, and he and Lane are old rivals. I've never met him, but, ooh. I've heard the stories! Lady Tanelia said they were like little boys whenever they got near each other."

"Shut up, Miranda," Lane muttered.

"Then stopping sassing me." She stuck out her tongue and turned her back on him. "Well, I'm here, so I can definitely port everyone back to base! You all come talk to me when you're ready. I'm gonna go take a peek around. Is that okay?" she asked Cassie anxiously.

Miranda, for all her flightiness and absent-minded tendencies, was both personable and charming. Cassie predicted at least half the village being smitten with her before they left. "Go for it," she said. "They'll know you're here for Tyrian."

"Yay!" She hurried out the door quickly.

"Is there anything else we need to do?" Lane asked Cassie. "What about those units you said were promised to us? Do we get them now that you're in charge?"

"My messages were being delayed. The units were to deploy tomorrow anyway. Monk soldiers will be coming in from all five corners over the next few days. Two units' worth." She looked at Tyrian. "My father wishes to come along as well. He will make a fine unit leader even though he isn't a Star himself. And that leaves me free to remain at your side."

"I trust your judgment." He skimmed his thumb over her cheek with a smile. "You being so much older and wiser." He lightly kissed her smile because it was irresistible and then caught sight of movement in the doorway. He glanced up, studied the older man standing there, and said, "Greetings. I would have noticed you sooner, but I was kissing your daughter."

Kotan instantly liked him for the greeting alone. "A suitable distraction," he agreed. He bowed. "Greetings, Tyrian. I've been looking forward to meeting you."

"The honor is mine," Tyrian said sincerely. "Thank you for sending Cassie to me, however unintentionally it was done. I would not have made it this far without her. She says you wish to join us in battle."

Kotan eyed Cassie. "I said I wished to come along to meet my granddaughter."

She rolled her eyes. "As if you would stay out of the combat!" She knew her father too well to think he would just sit idly by when he was still one of the strongest monk warriors on Oriku. Tenth Classes didn't come along every day.

It took only a few hours for everyone to be ready to go. They all gathered together in the middle of the village where Miranda waited by a fountain. "Okay," Miranda warned as she hefted her wand, "I haven't transported this many people before, so I don't know how it's going to work out. I'm going to try really hard to be accurate!"

"Pray for us," Dylan muttered under his breath to Ernest.

"Here we go!" She swung her wand in an arcing loop and her relic activated. One bright flash of light later and they all stood in the courtyard of the castle. Well . . . *almost* everyone stood in the courtyard of the castle. Lane landed in a tree, and Yaegi ended up in the Belowgrounds on top of a house.

"You know," Leonard said, "only missing two people out of a group that size isn't that bad. Maybe there were too many people for the power to reflect back and throw things off."

"Hee." Miranda felt quite pleased herself. Maybe she should start 'porting units. Then nobody would get lost. Well, maybe.

As people began to disperse to find rooms or quarters to claim, the sound of wings fluttering filled the air. Tyrian was quick. He caught Raven just as she zoomed into his arms and held on fiercely. "They said you were sick!" she said fretfully against his neck. She clung on tighter. "If Mommy didn't help you, you might die!"

The honesty despite Raven's age didn't surprise anyone. You couldn't sugarcoat things for the children involved, not when they, too, lived to support Tyrian. In many ways, the children had not remained children for long. "I'm fine now," Tyrian said softly as he buried his face in her soft hair. "I'm just fine, baby. Hey." He tugged her back until she looked at him. "See? I'm fine. Those flowers you gave me saved my life just as much as what Cassie did."

She stared at him, as if deciding for herself if he was really okay, and looked so much like him that those observing hid smiles. She suddenly nodded and wiped at her eyes. "Okay. I believe you." She promptly turned and grabbed onto Cassie. She hadn't missed the Pure Relic on her mother's hand. "You need to be okay too! I don't want to be an orphan again. You two have to stay around for*ever*."

Cassie cuddled her close with a smile. "I'm fine too, Raven. I promise. I was a little tired from the first use of my relic, but I'm perfectly fit now. Lane has assured us that I should develop at a normal rate, so I won't deal with my next relic spell for at least a few years. Plenty of time to recover." She turned her daughter toward Kotan. "Meet your other grandfather."

Raven blinked as she stared at Kotan and then she looked up at her parents and said solemnly, "My grampas are scary."

"Wait until she meets General Southerwind," Gordon said dryly from where he had approached.

Raven held out her arms to Kotan and he scooped her up. When she hugged him, he fell in love. It was like seeing Cassie as a child again. Too smart and too quiet for her age, but he could see the intensity Raven had inherited from Tyrian. She would be a force to be reckoned with. "Do you want to be a monk too? Or are you going to follow in your dad's footsteps?"

She shook her head. "I want to use a battleaxe!" As he stared at her, she scowled. "You all do that! Why's it so bad?" Honestly, it was like they had never before seen a Faerie who wanted to swing an axe! It wasn't that unusual, was it?

"Lord Tyrian, welcome back," Matthias said as he approached. "You had all of us quite terrified. Most of our mages have recovered completely, though the Magicians are still 'foggy' as it's called."

"What about Laia?" Tyrian asked quietly. "How is she recovering?"

"Very slowly." Matthias slowly shook his head. "I've never seen the like. If there is anything you can do for her, this is the time to do it. We can't spare one of our best combatants when we're preparing to take on a checkpoint. Once you've seen to her, come meet me in the meeting room. We may have found a backdoor into Alphin."

Raven led Kotan on a tour, and Gordon followed Matthias. Tyrian and

Cassie were left as the only two in the immediate area, and they began to head toward where Laia and Rourke's room resided located in the eighth wing of the castle grounds. Partway there, they ran into Liang and Serentia. Liang grabbed Tyrian in a fierce hug. "Are you okay?" he demanded.

"I'm fine." Tyrian was beginning to feel a bit like a parrot, but he didn't begrudge anyone the question, least of all Liang. "Cassie was able to cure me, and we're about to see if we can help Laia." He sighed as Liang released him and Serentia hugged him instead. Honestly, he hoped they would just make their relationship official so that he could say they were his adopted parents and be done with it. That and he could collect on the betting pool. It was almost as big as the one between Grace and Kell.

"We just needed to reassure ourselves," Serentia told him. She released him and studied him with a mother's eye. He looked much better than he had in a very long while. "Come see Tavi when you have a chance. She was very worried too."

"I will."

She looked at Liang. "You stay with him. I have gardening to tend to." She lightly touched his hand and then headed away down the hall.

Liang longingly watched her walk away, still breathing the scent of her skin and feeling the warmth of her hand. His feelings for her grew stronger every day. "I'm in love with her," he said softly.

"Am I blind?" Tyrian asked softly. Liang looked at him in surprise and he shook his head. "Marian and I knew from the get-go that it was more than just a bad case of attraction. We all knew. You can't hide it, Liang."

"Serentia doesn't know," he murmured.

"Yes, she does," Tyrian disagreed softly. "She told me that she had realized you were being more than kind. She saw you watching her the way I watch Cassie. She's working her way there, Liang. She told me that she feels for you in a way she never felt for her husband, and they were happy together. It's not her heart that's in question. It's her mind. Just give her a little more time. I know she's in love with you too."

Liang didn't question him. Hope stirred inside and made him feel as if the patience would be worth it. But, dear gods, it was so difficult! "I'm going to be insane before this is done," he muttered.

"Been there," Tyrian agreed dryly, "done that. And cold showers don't help."

Cassie coughed, more amused than embarrassed. Looking back on the events that had occurred, even she could find the humor in the entire situation.

Liang stayed with them as Tyrian lightly knocked on the door to the room. It was opened by Rourke; he looked relatively unscathed despite his wife being in such terrible condition. When he saw Cassie eyeing him, the brawler said wryly, "Let's just say that Laia has assuredly kept my life interesting. Her paladin nature makes her willing to put down her life to protect others, so she's had more near-death scares than I care to remember. This is minor compared to other things. Someday I'll tell you about the incident in the Moors. I should have gray hair."

There was no rebuttal from the vicinity of the bed, but when Tyrian walked over, he saw that Laia was asleep. Her skin looked frighteningly pale and nearly as translucent as her hair. Her veins showed dark under her skin and no longer looked deceptively blue. The marks of her three relics were faded and dull. "How has she been this last day?"

"Sleeping. She woke once and managed to eat some broth that Eve brought her, but she was asleep almost instantly after. Merlot looked up the Soul Fog poisoning in one of his books and he said this was relatively normal for someone as strong as she is. This is what would have happened to Lane if he hadn't managed to block, or to you if the Devourer hadn't been involved."

"She has a strong spirit." Tyrian picked up her left hand and pressed her relic against his as he called on his power. It felt nothing like when he and Cassie touched relics together. There was a feeling of being connected, certainly, but it wasn't as intimate. Curiously enough, by actually touching Laia's soul, he was able to see indeed that she was no normal Thaumoturge. And though she had half-Human blood, she did not feel Human at all. "What are you?" he murmured.

"Complicated," Rourke said dryly.

The color returned swiftly to Laia's face, and she had started breathing much more evenly. The marks of her relics regained some clarity as if to prove her body moved swiftly to eliminate the last of the threat. "We'll have Doctor Kelan come look at her as well," Tyrian said. "Just to be on the safe side. She'll be up and giving you more gray hair in no time."

"I'd have it no other way," Rourke murmured.

There was nothing more they could do at that time, so Rourke headed to find where Kelan was setting up his clinic, and Tyrian, Cassie, and Liang made their way to the meeting room. When they got there, two very relieved guards opened the doors for them. "Welcome back, Lord Tyrian!" one said happily.

Matthias, Cherry, Kyle, Ewan, and Gordon waited for them inside the meeting room. Because Kyle had been on the field as well, Tyrian looked at him and asked, "How are you feeling?"

"Perfectly normal," Kyle answered. He could only shake his head. It was just like Tyrian to ask about his friends first.

As Tyrian took his seat, Matthias began, "We've been studying Alphin. The land approach, as we so painfully discovered, is lined with Soul Fog that triggers when an army unit approaches. We don't dare approach from that direction. However, Alphin sits on the ocean. We can approach from the water."

"We're not equipped for water battle, unless you count Infine," Tyrian noted. "And aren't the waters around Alphin too violent this time of year for most ships to pass through?"

"Indeed, but I believe that we may have found the perfect captain to sail us through. He's got quite a reputation as being the best on the sea."

Kyle's brows shot up. "You mean Theo?"

"Theo?" Tyrian asked.

"Theo. He and his brother, Mayo, are amazing sailors. I've never known better. They're technically surrogate members of the Rebellion since Ophelia had them on call in case things went onto the seas. They surely know by now that she's gone and you're in charge, but you might be able to play on that loyalty to get them to help us."

Tyrian drummed the fingers of his relic hand on the table. "But that would be just one ship. We can't fit even a whole unit on a single ship. Are we thinking to employ some subterfuge again?"

"We know going in," Cherry explained, "that General Renduex is one of us, and he's already made motions that prove he's on the side of the people. What Raven overheard is proof of it. We're not going to attack the checkpoint at all. We're going to sneak inside with Theo as our cover."

"The great Theo, out testing a new ship," Matthias said gravely. "He was trying it against the shores of Alphin since they're so dangerous. He has full access to all cities since he's not known as a part of the Rebellion. You, General Yureny, Kyle, Ewan, Liang, and Cassie will stow away on his ship and sneak into town to find General Renduex. If anything, this might culminate in a duel, but there is no doubt of your success, Lord Tyrian."

"Yeah, but there's a problem," Ewan said. "We have to convince Theo to help us under new management, and he's a pain in the bloody ass. Where's he holed up anyway?"

"A very small ocean city to the far south of Alphin. It's not dissimilar from Acre in many ways, including being so small as to not be considered an official city. Maybe a hundred people live there." Kyle nodded briefly. "I've been there. Miranda can send us. Once we convince Theo, he can sail us right up to Alphin."

"Why would he be so difficult to convince?" Cassie wondered.

"You should have seen what Ophelia went through to convince him," Ewan said in aggravation. "He's got this picky thing about respect. He needs to respect someone before he's willing to help them, rather than help and grow to respect them. It took her, what, a month? Tyrian's going to have to work fast to convince him in a short time."

A little smile touched Tyrian's lips. "I think I can handle it." He glanced at Matthias. "We'll leave this afternoon."

Chapter Thirty-One

"If you can't believe then you can't dream; if you can't dream then you can't believe."

When they left the meeting room, Kyle detoured to go find Samantha. The others headed to the courtyard where Miranda hung out if people wanted a transport somewhere. Liang felt very glad to be fighting alongside Tyrian once more. He was still kicking himself for not being on the field during the Soul Fog incident. Even if he hadn't been able to help, he could have supported Cassie in her efforts to save Tyrian.

Marian was there waiting for them when they reached Miranda. She looked relatively back to normal despite being in the mage unit that had taken the biggest slap from the Fog. Mostly she looked as if she was recovering from a bad cold. Tyrian lightly pressed his hand to her forehead and frowned. "Should you be up?" He knew she was quite powerful, enough to have been hit harder.

"Doc said I was perfectly fine for getting up, don't worry." She hugged her cousin tightly and hid her face against his shoulder. He was like a brother to her, and the thought of losing him after losing Ben terrified her. It had nothing to do with her destiny. It was Tyrian. She would be there either way. "You scared me."

"I know." He hugged her for a moment and then let go. "It wasn't intentional. And it shouldn't be such a worry for the future now."

She reluctantly let him go only to turn and hug Cassie, surprising the younger woman greatly. "You're my family now, too," Marian scolded her, "so you have to stop doing dangerous things as well!" The fact that Cassie was arguably one of the hardest people in the world to kill was a moot point. She was Marian's sister-cousin now.

"I can't promise that," Cassie told her. "Remember, I have to keep your cousin safe, too. And with his stubbornness, I'm going to be getting us out of a lot of trouble, to be sure! Eternity certainly won't be boring."

Tyrian just smiled. Marian sighed. "I can't begrudge you that, I suppose. But, still! You're a mother, so you need to be more careful, okay?" She hugged them both, and Liang, and then hurried off before Kelan scolded her for doing too much.

In a murmur, Ewan said, "She holds onto family very tightly."

"I'm all she has," Tyrian said simply. "At least until we get my father back." He frowned. "I wonder if my message will have had any impact on him." He still couldn't shake the feeling that something terrible would happen. That something terrible might have already happened. It took much effort to shrug it off.

Kyle and Samantha joined them, and Miranda focused on Kyle. "Next stop, Seabank!" She swung her wand in a looping arc, narrowly missing Liang, and her relic activated. "Hang on!"

A few seconds later, Kyle, Tyrian, and Cassie landed on the dock of the tiny town called Seabank. The other three landed in the ocean beside the dock with a splash big enough to scare away the seagulls. Ewan surfaced and slung his hair out of his eyes. "I wish I could get mad at her about that, but I know it's not her fault."

As he hauled himself out, Kyle helped Samantha out, and Liang let Tyrian and Cassie tug him onto the dock. While those who had gotten a dunk wrung out their clothes, Tyrian looked around the area. The small dock of Seabank had a handful of small dinghies and rowboats. At the end of the longest part of the dock sat a much larger ship that looked like it would carry at least ten people comfortably. He would have bet money on it belonging to Theo; he had never before seen a ship in that good of condition.

He led the way off the dock and into what was the only road in the town and therefore the center as well. Even using the word 'village' to describe Seabank was being generous. It was little more than a hub. There was a lone grocer, Item Shop, and an inn with a tavern attached. All homes had their own gardens or ranches. The Item Shop was no doubt just in case travelers came through, just like the inn.

It was to the tavern that Tyrian headed. It looked fairly busy inside despite the size of the town, but many people were distinctly visitors. He swept his gaze over the room and then settled on a corner where a lively game of dice went on. Kyle followed his gaze and said, "That's him. The shorter haired blond is Theo. The longer is Mayo."

The brothers were obvious identical twins, but Theo's blond hair stayed extremely short while Mayo's hung longer and tied at the nape of his neck. They were both attractive, though more weathered than handsome, and they had the obvious strength of men used to a life at sea. Age-wise, Tyrian guessed them to be a few years older than Ewan.

A giggling bellhop brought towels to Ewan, Liang, and Samantha, and Tyrian went with Kyle over to the game. Mayo wasn't playing; he watched absently while he whittled a piece of wood into something or another. Theo looked distinctly smug, and rightfully so since he had most of the gold coins on his side. The other three at the table didn't look quite as happy.

Theo glanced up and recognized Kyle instantly. "Well, look what the

Grimalkin dragged in." His blue eyes filled with empathy. "How are you?"

"As well as can be expected, I suppose." Kyle rested a hand lightly on Tyrian's shoulder. "Theo, Mayo, meet Tyrian Southerwind."

"'lo." Mayo glanced at Tyrian curiously and decided he liked the younger man's serene nature. It was such an oxymoron to the intensity that seemed to permeate everything else about him. The dark green eyes that looked back at Mayo held a fierce glitter as bright as the stars that would no doubt burn just as eternally. A leader's eyes.

"This is no place for kids," Theo told Kyle in annoyance after a cursory study of Tyrian. "Take him back to your little castle and let him play general somewhere else."

The room fell silent. Samantha slowly arched a brow and then shared a quick smirk with Ewan. Cassie and Liang said nothing. Kyle bristled slightly. "This isn't the time to be an asshole, Theo," he said curtly. "You want to say that Tyrian's not carrying out Ophelia's wishes, and doing a better job than we might have ever hoped?"

"Hold on, Kyle," Tyrian said softly, though his voice carried. "If he wishes to be a coward, then let him. There is no shame in his fear."

Theo shot to his feet so sharply that he jostled the table and sent dice and coins flying. "Who are you to call me a coward?" he snarled at Tyrian. "You don't even know me, kid!"

Tyrian met his eyes directly. "And you do not know me. Therefore you can't rightfully call me a kid." He stepped closer, and though he was fractionally shorter, he suddenly seemed much taller. "You can stay here," he said softly, intensely, "and pretend that your world is perfect. You can hide in this little town and say that because you are spared then the rest of the world must be fine. But you *know* it's not. I came looking for a great captain. A man said to confront any and every challenge. All I see is a coward wasting his time cheating at dice and pretending he's as good as he used to be."

"Cheating!" another player yelped.

"The dice are weighted." Tyrian turned and walked out of the tavern without looking back, and he clearly ignored the sudden ruckus as people realized Theo hadn't won fairly.

"Oh nice one," Mayo told Theo in annoyance. "Real smart. I've never known anyone who could piss off that many people at once."

"Just take your damn money back!" Theo snapped at the people yelling at him. "And Mayo, shut up!" He shot to his feet and ran out of the tavern, anger and shame boiling inside his heart. How *dare* that punk call him a coward? And how dare he show up like that, making Theo feel as if he was needed? Just who did Tyrian think he was?

He was so blinded to his anger as he ran onto the dock that he didn't see the staff stuck in his path until he tripped over it and stumbled. He couldn't catch himself in time and fell headfirst into the ocean with a big splash. When he surfaced, Tyrian knelt on the edge of the dock with his staff propped over his shoulder. "Cool off," he suggested mildly.

Theo scowled at him. "As if that was mature!" He sputtered as Tyrian shoved him underwater. When he surfaced again, Tyrian was sitting down on the side of the dock. It would have been very easy to grab his ankle and yank him in, but it would have also been petty and immature.

On a sigh, he hauled himself out of the water and onto the side of the dock. It had become hard to hang onto his anger. "Do a lot of people have a problem hating you?" he asked.

Tyrian thought about it. "For the most part, yes. Mostly because I really don't hate anyone in return. It takes a lot to get me to that level." His eyes darkened as shadows churned inside. "In my life, there have been three people I hated. Only one of them have I forgiven." He leaned back on his hands. "I suppose it doesn't mean much considering my age. I'll be nineteen in a few months."

Theo looked at him in surprise. "I thought you were older than that. Huh." He turned his gaze to the ocean. "So why don't you tell me just what's going on, Tyrian? Even out here, we've heard the legend spreading. How did all this happen?"

By the time Tyrian had told him everything, Theo felt sick to his stomach. That Tyrian was still sane seemed shocking. He also didn't need to ask to know that Blaine and Beelzebub would be the two people Tyrian still hated. Forgiving Annareal was mind-blowing. "You're a better person than I am," he said softly.

Tyrian slid a look at him. "But not a better sailor or captain."

"No one is." It was said without conceit, just simple fact. He blew out a hard breath. "Crap. I'm one of those Destined Stars, aren't I? Me and Mayo. There's no other reason for the way I feel like you really need my help."

"I can't do it without you," Tyrian said simply. He clapped Theo on the shoulder with his relic hand, and the glow of the star came visibly. "We share the skies, Theo. Now I need you to share the seas as well. A man of your skill is wasted in that pub cheating at dice."

"How did you know that anyway?" the captain muttered.

Tyrian grinned. "I guessed."

"Son-of-a . . ." He broke off as he realized the epithet was not, actually, that inaccurate. He would never forgive Annareal for what she had done, that was for damn sure. "Alright," he decided briskly. "You've got yourself a captain, Tyrian!"

"And your respect?"

"Hell, kid, you had that when you called me out in the tavern. Not many have that kind of guts, and I have to admire it." He contemplated Tyrian. "So what's the plan?" After Tyrian told him, he could only admire him all the more. "Damn, you definitely have guts. You want to just sail right into Alphin like it's nothing."

"You can't do it?"

"I've never tried," Theo said cheerfully. "This will be fun!"

The others had walked up, and Kyle looked at Tyrian in bemusement. "Only you," he said. "What'd you do to him?"

"Threw me in the ocean," Theo admitted. He elbowed Ewan when his friend snorted. "You'll be next, Grizmar, if you don't watch it!"

"Already had a dunking," Ewan said politely. "I don't need another."

Tyrian and Mayo shared a smile. There were no words needed between them. Sometimes it really was that simple.

Theo was in distinctly higher spirits as he headed down the dock toward his ship. "All aboard!" he announced cheerfully. As people filed on, he asked, "And who the hell is everyone anyway?" He eyed Samantha with interest. He had always liked women, no matter their race, height, shape, or skill set.

Tyrian gestured to Liang. "This is Liang. He's been with me since I was a child." He smiled at Cassie. "The monk is Cassie. She is my Kentei Star as well as my fiancée." He grinned as he saw Theo eyeing Samantha. "That would be General Samantha Yureny."

The name triggered and Theo's eyes widened. "Greetings, ma'am," he said respectfully. "No offense meant."

She grinned. "None taken."

Mayo untied the ship and then hopped aboard. Theo took the wheel and they set out into the ocean. The sail from Seabank to Alphin took only a few hours, and the trip was spent planning just how they would sneak inside. There was never any question of Theo getting them there safely. It was merely the determination of the after that kept them occupied.

"Lord Tyrian is too recognizable," Samantha said. "And I don't mean the scarf, though it doesn't help. The relic does it too. And if anyone looks at his eyes, they're going to know who and what he is."

"What about disguising him in Healer robes?" Mayo asked. "They have hoods, right? Just cover his hands with gloves, and keep the hood down, and no one will be the wiser. But Cassie's kind of going to stick out too."

"No one will see me," Cassie noted mildly. "I assure you of that. And we can't discount anyone's face, frankly. Everyone knows Samantha, and you can be sure a lot of people will know Ewan by now after what happened in Trinan and with Beelzebub. Night is too conspicuous as well."

"And Kyle," Ewan reminded her. "His pretty mug was slapped on posters a while back."

"Great, so we walk into the city and cause mass hysteria. Oh, that's going to be so stealthy." Kyle frowned thoughtfully. "And we can't all disguise ourselves without standing out even more. Six mages would be too obvious, and anyway, any other mage will sense that you, Liang, and Sam don't have relics."

"We could hide in plain sight," Samantha said.

"Hide in plain sight?"

"Just walk into the city as we are. No one is going to believe that Lord Tyrian would just walk into an enemy stronghold without an army. If Lady Cassie is hidden, then it will be even more believable. We disguise Liang as the Healer and just walk in. Alex might be the only one suspicious, frankly, but that's not an issue."

Cassie nodded. "I can retrieve the robe and hood without being seen, as well as other clothes for everyone. I think you might be right, Samantha. You'd make a good monk yourself."

Samantha grinned a bit at the compliment. It was high praise coming from someone of Cassie's caliber.

The ship began to rock back and forth with more than the normal movement of natural waves. Tyrian got to his feet and went onto the deck. The ocean seethed restlessly, and it grew only more unhappy the further they sailed. He walked over to Theo whose face was calm but arms were taut with the strength of controlling the ship. "What causes this anyway?"

"There are tons of theories, up to and including some sort of conspiracy by the Emperor to employ Merfolk to keep the ocean unstable during the low point of trade season. I've often thought there might be an underwater vein of Water Relics causing the disturbance. We've mined Fire Relics from volcanoes, so . . ."

Since Tyrian didn't see Merfolk being inclined to help the Emperor with anything, he leaned toward Theo's theory too. The Merfolk weren't often found in Imperial waters anyway. They lived much further to the east, toward the western edge of the Moors. Though only one ocean wrapped around the large landmass of Oriku, it was a given that the waters were warmest near the Moors and coldest near Melodina.

The sea was getting more violent. Tyrian grabbed onto the railing as a particularly large wave nearly lifted the ship entirely off the ocean. Alphin was a line on the horizon, just big enough and close enough that it became a shaped line rather than a flat one. The sky stayed perfectly clear with no storms about. The ocean was simply impassible for these two months of the year.

Impassible to normal ships. Theo had built this baby from scratch, and he wouldn't let some pissy waves ruin all his work. He pulled his hat low over his eyes and said, "Better hang on tight, Tyrian! I'm going to start fighting back! I play to win!"

Tyrian made his way to the cabin door and went inside. As he stumbled across the floor and Ewan caught him, he said dryly, "Let's hope he weighted the dice again."

Theo stopped trying to go through the waves. He started going around them. Mayo headed up to the deck and added his help by using the Wind Relic he wore. The timing between the twins was critical. If Mayo hit the sails too soon or too late, they ran the risk of capsizing the boat entirely.

No one inside the cabin had any idea what was going on. They had realized that staying on their feet was potentially suicidal, so all laid flat on the floor and hoped that the lower altitude might save them a few bruises.

Abruptly, the shaking and bouncing stopped. The boat went back to rocking softly and rhythmically. It was peaceful and calm once more. "Are we dead?" Liang asked warily.

"Ewan's here," Kyle said, "so if we are, it's in hell."

"You made the reservations, friend."

"We're not dead," Tyrian said dryly. He got to his feet carefully and then helped pull Kyle up as well. Both males could only watch with wistful envy as Cassie flipped to her feet. It would be much more convenient to learn how to do that. Laia could even do it in plate armor while carrying her claymore; both Kyle and Ewan were determined that she teach them how she did it.

Cassie pulled on her hood and facemask, obscuring her entire face from view except for her eyes. As soon as she put on her gloves as well, there was no telling her apart from any other monk. She disappeared into the shadows and went onto the deck to wait until they docked. Theo was whistling as if he hadn't just sailed them through the worst waves on the world. Alphin was getting to be more than a line, and the cityscape was much more distinct. It was only minutes before he pulled in to the dock where several wide-eyed soldiers stood.

Cassie disappeared into the city quickly, and Theo tossed the ropes to one of the men. "Here, tie me off!" he said.

"You . . . but how . . . where . . ." The soldier was completely lost for words though he did tie off the boat properly.

"Whew!" Theo sat down on a bench on the deck and lit his pipe. "I need a breather! That was hell out there. But look at that! Not a mark on this baby!" The soldiers were still staring at him and he winced. "My apologies, my good men. I'm Theo."

"Oh. Oh!" The soldiers promptly saluted, awe on their faces. Everyone who had ever been on a boat knew the name of Theo. His skills as a captain were legendary, and the Empire had tried for many years to recruit him for a sea assault on Foresalia. A staunch pacifist, he had always turned them down. "Welcome to Alphin," one soldier said. "I can't believe you made it through those waves!"

"Well, I had some travelers who wanted to get to the city, and I wanted to test the boat, so I figured it was a win-win." He felt a little draft that was Cassie slipping back into the cabin and had to be impressed. He was sure no one else had noticed her at all. Monks could be sneaky creatures. "Told 'em that if I capsized us, they didn't owe me any money."

"I guess that's fair," someone grumbled.

The cabin door opened and Kyle cautiously peered out. A blue bandana covered his blond hair, and he now wore clothes more suited to a farmer. His sword was safely hidden in his backpack and nowhere in sight. "We're alive, right?"

The soldiers frowned, thinking he looked familiar, and their frowns deepened as Ewan, also dressed like a farmer, stepped out. He was familiar too. And so was the woman who followed, though she dressed like a bard rather than a farmer. More than one of the soldiers eyed her long legs and luscious figure wistfully.

A Healer followed the bard, and he was completely indistinct. It was the fifth person to step out that had the soldiers starting to be alarmed. Even without a green scarf and fighting clothes, the young man in the clothing of an inventor looked a damned lot like Tyrian Southerwind. "Hang on here," one soldier muttered.

"He's not who you think he is!" Samantha complained. She turned on Tyrian and scolded, "I *told* you that you looked like that guy, but *no* you never listen to me!" She grabbed Ewan's hat and shoved it on Tyrian's head. "You wanted to come here, so hide your pretty face and not cause hysteria, got it?"

There was no way the guy was Tyrian. Seriously, the leader of the

Liberation Army taking that sort of abuse from anyone? Not likely. The soldiers saluted, and one smiled apologetically. "Our sincere apologies, travelers. Things have been tense as of late. Welcome to Alphin." He helped Samantha step onto the dock and then sighed as the tall male pointedly pulled her closer. The good ones were always taken, damn it.

"Anyone want to play some dice?" Theo asked the soldiers innocently as the party made their way casually into the city.

"I feel like an idiot," Samantha muttered.

"Just smile and accept the adoration of the people whose tongues are dragging on the ground as you pass," Ewan said. He kept his arm around her shoulders and glared at several admirers for good measure. "I'll keep away the idiots for you."

"Can't I just use my sword for that?"

"Not without blowing our cover. Down, girl."

Tyrian kept his hat pulled low over his face so that his features stayed hidden from view. He could feel Cassie close by even though he couldn't see her at all. Knowing she was there let him feel safe enough to look around the city with intense curiosity.

The general state of the city was no different from Firmeza or anywhere else. The size of a city dictated only that the problems spread out over a larger space, not that they were eliminated. There were simply that many more people to lose homes and businesses. The abuse had spread out across the city, so immediately seeing the depression was not possible. Someone could fool themselves into believing everything was okay.

Visually, however, Alphin appeared very different from other cities. Built on the ocean, it was made of stone and mortar to stand against the salty sea air. Some buildings were impressively tall, and every road had been paved with stone to make travel easier. There was little wood to be had in any construction, but there were a lot of beach trees around to soften the landscape.

If it was this lovely in this state, he could only imagine how beautiful it would be once restored. He couldn't help but feel they had arrived just in time. A sort of tension hovered in the air as if the city hovered on the verge of collapse. "The city that smiles even though the dagger sinks deeper," he murmured.

"Wars are expensive," Liang said quietly. "And with this many cities liberated, Albanion and Blaine will have to depend harder on those who remain to support their troops and their cushioned lifestyle."

Tyrian nodded slightly. "Let's find General Renduex."

Finding Alex turned out to be slightly easier than they had thought.

While they had expected to find him at the inn where he was supposed to be staying, they actually found him while on their way there. They also found him arguing with a grocer about the price of the supplies he was trying to buy.

Samantha walked up behind him and asked politely, "Problem?"

"He won't charge me!" he said in annoyance. "I don't want things for free, damn it!" He blinked as he realized the voice was familiar and then turned around sharply. He stared at Samantha for several seconds before his lips began to curve. "Sam, you've never looked lovelier."

"Oh, shut up!" She glared at the grocer. "Just take his money. He's a penny-pincher anyway."

"Thanks a lot!" her friend muttered as he handed the snickering grocer a handful of coins. He hefted his bag and looked at the other four people standing near. He recognized Ewan and Kyle instantly, was fairly sure he knew who the Healer was, and he felt positive he knew the young man hiding his face from view. "Should we do this the easy way, or the more formal way?"

"Let's make it formal." Samantha's sword suddenly appeared in her hand and she pressed the blade under his chin lightly. "Alexander Renduex, under laws of engagement, I demand you surrender or die, by the order of Tyrian Southerwind, leader of the Liberation Army."

People who were observing quickly cleared the area. Soldiers spotted the commotion and came running, drawing weapons as they approached. Alex held up a hand sharply. "Stop!" he ordered. "The laws of engagement have been declared!"

It was the exact same situation as with Gordon and Shots, except it was off the field of battle. Typically, the sniper was an archer, or gunner, but a close-range combatant could be just as effective if they could get close enough. Samantha had her sword against Alex's neck—she was more than close enough.

Tyrian pulled off his hat and tossed it to the side. Pointedly, he removed the gloves he wore. The mark of the Devourer glowed brightly in the sunlight as he held his hand in the air. "Do you stand or yield?" he asked Alex.

The tinniest of smiles touched Alex's lips. "Yield." He glanced at his soldiers. "You may retreat or remain."

There wasn't really a decision to be made. Every soldier in the vicinity removed their emblems and tossed them on the ground. At the sight of the army switching sides, the people of Alphin began to cheer loudly.

It took several seconds for the enormity of what had just happened to sink into Tyrian. When it did, he felt staggered emotionally. He had just claimed a checkpoint. He now controlled the eastern border of the Empire. When the turbulent season ended, trade would be coming in from the other countries, and he would be the one claiming it. The capitol was almost completely cut off from trade with Melodina and the Moors.

Cassie suddenly appeared at his side and tangled the fingers of her relic hand with his. The familiar sensation helped ground him though his head still spun lightly. "Let's talk," he told Alex.

"Indeed." Alex gestured toward the inn down the road. "After you." He grinned at Samantha. "Bards first."

"Kiss my ass." She stalked past him, and the soldiers cleared her path quickly. None of them trusted a woman that skilled when she was that pissed off and armed.

"Why did you pick that anyway?" Tyrian asked Cassie softly.

"It was the only thing in her size that would hide her identity," she said just as softly. She winced wryly. "I had a feeling she wouldn't like it."

Alex watched Samantha shove two gawking guards out of the way and also winced. "You have a mastery of understatement, my lady."

Chapter Thirty-Two

"Wind me down the unending road; reflect the travels I've taken."

When they got to the inn, Samantha wasted no time in going to change clothes. Liang just removed his hood, and Kyle and Ewan put their swords back on. On a long-suffering sigh, Night said, "Your backpack is dusty. When did you last clean that thing?"

"It's not my fault that you're so distinctive," Ewan said reasonably. "And it's a backpack. You expect it to be pristine and clean?"

Tyrian ignored them as he and Cassie sat down at a table with Alex. "It's been a while," he said. "You look like you're doing well, General Renduex."

"I think we can dispense with some formality, Lord Tyrian. Just Alex will suffice." He sat back with a sigh. "I can't say as this moment truly surprises me. I think I knew it would happen the instant I heard you had joined the Rebellion. Certainly, I knew it when Gordon and then Sam joined you."

"Is that why you spoke with the Dragonists?" Cassie asked.

He looked at her in surprise. "How did you hear of that?"

"Raven. Tyrian and I have adopted her. She told us that you met with Ryu of the Dragonists clan and that both of you promised her that everything would be alright. She felt the same near you as she does near any other Destined Star, so . . ."

Alex was entirely unsurprised to hear that they had adopted Raven. When he had learned that Lady Annareal had sent Raven away, he had wondered. "I've actually known Ryu a few years," he admitted. "He's seventeen now. I met him when he was thirteen and first gained his partner, Celestial. Once I figured out what was happening, I asked him to meet with me. I told him what was going on, and I told him my intent to side with you when the time came. I asked him to let the Dragonist Clan know that you might be seeking their aid to save our people. He promised that he would speak with Draco Silver, their leader, and make sure they were ready when we were."

"That was very risky," Tyrian said quietly. "How did you explain meeting with him to the Emperor?"

"I said I was making sure you hadn't called on their assistance yet." His hands tightened around his cup of coffee. "Blaine terrifies me," he admitted in a low voice. "She's . . . not quite sane, Lord Tyrian. Ever since

General Reyu joined, she's steadily gotten worse. She does not trust any of us Lower Generals, and I'm not sure we're safe near her. I ordered Di not to return to the palace at all."

"Oh, I'm sure she appreciated that!" Samantha said as she sat down, once more in her regular clothing. "Or did she sense your reasoning?"

"I flat out told her why. I know better than to tell her to do something without having a reason for it. I got her response a few days ago. She concurred with me wholeheartedly, and she also sent a warning to Vincent and Marcus." His eyes closed. "I can't believe how fast things have changed. It scares me more that so much had already changed without us realizing."

"But we're making the right change now." Tyrian held out his relic hand. "Join your strength with mine, Alex. Serve the people when they need you most. I can't do this without you."

Alex took his hand tightly and the white star glowed from his shoulder. It was merely a visible recognition of what he had already understood. He had always thought there had to be a good reason why he and the other Lower Generals had been so fiercely protective of him all these years. Tyrian was damned easy to love to begin with. Perhaps Destiny had merely taken advantage of that fact. "I'll do whatever I can," he promised. "And to begin with, I'll help your strategist out-think Diamond."

"If anyone can," Samantha agreed with a smile, "it's you."

Strong personalities needed to be matched with equally strong partners, Tyrian thought as he glanced at Cassie with a smile. It was just the way of nature, and Nature was nearly as picky a master as Destiny. She just didn't rule on Oriku.

Samantha and Ewan stayed to help Alex gather his soldiers. With the tide changed, the Imperial flags were already being replaced with the flag that had Tyrian's colors. He *really* needed a symbol on it. But what symbolized liberation?

The other good thing about the city being under the Liberation Army's control was that units belonging to the army were no longer considered an enemy and wouldn't trigger the Soul Fog defense. A unit transported in outside the city so that it could transport back with Alex's units.

Alphin possessed ten units of its own, but Tyrian wanted them to remain in the city to hold onto it. The checkpoint was far too valuable to lose right after getting it. However, despite staying, the militia units would also wear Tyrian's colors and be considered a part of the Liberation Army. In the final siege on Trinan, they would be called in. That the final siege was actually within sight also boggled Tyrian.

Cassie's hand slipped into his and he tangled their fingers together. "How do you know these things?" he asked her softly. "I don't even need to tell you."

She smiled up at him. "I just do."

Kyle felt a little twist of pain in his heart as he watched them, but the pain was not as sharp as it had been in the past. Whether it was healing or numbness, at the least it was a change. He wanted to be happy to see other couples together. He didn't want to grieve forever. Ophelia would have hated it. Just a little longer, he thought to her spirit. Let me love you just a little longer.

Tyrian had no particular destination in mind as he walked the streets. He was just looking around, talking to the people and seeing what was what. He liked to be approachable to people. He didn't want them to think of him as some indistinct figure. If there were problems, he needed to know so he could fix them.

He rounded a corner near some new construction that was already being begun and found himself face-to-face with a tiny woman sporting a cap of riotous red hair. She wore the rugged clothing of a worker, and a tool belt hung around her hips. "You're Tyrian," she said. She aimed a hammer at him. "I hear you need a builder or two." Before he could say anything, she blithely continued, "You've come to the right place! My husband and I are the best in the soon-to-no-longer-be-Empire. I'm Jacqueline, so you know. We'll be taking ourselves off to your castle and getting everything into shape!"

Tyrian could only blink as she turned and walked off with a stride that had many clearing her way before they were run over. Even before he belatedly realized she was a Destined Star, a man came hurrying out of the half-built building. "I'm Peter! Nice to meet you! Jackie!" The last was added in aggravation as he hurried after his wife. "Damn it, quite leaving me behind!"

"Uhm, Tyrian." Kyle really couldn't find anything else to say.

"Yeah." Tyrian rubbed the side of his head. "I'm not really sure either. To each his own?"

"It takes all kinds?" Liang offered.

"That might be more accurate, true."

There was one more surprise waiting for Tyrian when he finally got outside to where the unit waited. Miranda had come along to transport all those who weren't in a unit and therefore couldn't go back the other way. When Tyrian, Liang, Kyle, and Cassie got to her, she was avidly talking with a man wearing sturdy farm clothes. Several cows stood nearby, as did a flock of chickens. A sheepdog sat at the man's ankle.

"Lord Tyrian!" Miranda waved happily. "You did it oh my god I can't believe you did it, I mean, I can, 'cause it's you, but you did it!"

"Yes I did," he said dryly. "And thank you." He smiled at the newcomer. "I'm Tyrian."

The man removed his hat respectfully. "I'm Findley," he said. "It's an honor to meet you, Lord Tyrian. I was moving my animals back toward the city when I saw all the commotion. Alphin is my home, and I'm grateful for your help in freeing it. I'd like to repay the favor by helping you. I'm a rancher, if you have need of one."

"I do," Tyrian said instantly. "Our gardener has tried to keep the animals in line, but it's just not her skill. And the sheep are still slightly traumatized, so they don't trust anyone except me."

"Traumatized?" Findley asked warily, and even his dog looked slightly nonplussed at the choice of words.

"Don't ask. Just, don't ask," Kyle muttered.

"Righto. Well, I'll be glad to get those babies in line for you. Leave it to me and Savon to take care of things. Right, girl?" He patted her on the head and she woofed happily in agreement.

Tyrian knelt and ruffled her fur and then laughed as she began to enthusiastically lick his face. It was the first time Kyle or Miranda had actually heard him laugh, and it made both of them lose a little tension in their shoulders. Never laughing was, to them, just as bad as never crying. Tyrian had too much of a love for life, too much humor, to be so serious all the time.

Even Findley, just meeting him, felt a similar sense of relief. Just looking at Tyrian told him that the younger man walked a fine line every day of his life. He obviously needed someone to help him lift some burdens, and Findley knew he was the only one who could help in this way.

Once everyone had gathered, Miranda transported them back to the base. Miraculously, they landed safely without mishap. Unfortunately, she started sneezing when they landed and promptly transported herself somewhere. The loud splash that followed indicated it was likely either in the hot spring—again—or the dock area.

Findley headed off to meet Serentia, with Liang following to make the introductions, and the flock of animals followed in their wake much to the amusement of all. Several guards hurried to help urge the larger cows along and had to help shove them out a few doors. "Maybe Miranda should have been less accurate with them," Kyle groused.

Alex had arrived with his units, and he waited for them at the stairs.

"I can get settled in later," he said. "Time is getting to be of the essence. I also have information about Betane and its defenses. We'll need to retrieve an artifact in order to break through."

Tyrian nodded. "That can be done." He smiled as he heard the flutter of wings. He was already turning around before Raven reached him, and he caught her safely in his arms with a smile. "There you are! You're late," he chided teasingly.

She wrapped her arms around his neck. "I was with Eve. She made me taste her new cookies."

"*Made* you, did she?" Cassie asked.

Raven nodded firmly. "She said to tell you it was all her fault and she coerced me, so you can't get mad if I ruined my dinner." She spotted Alex and brightened. "Hi! You're going to fight for Daddy now, right?"

"It's actually formal now," he agreed with a smile.

She climbed over into Cassie's arms and held onto her mother contentedly. She had to be fair with her parents 'cause she didn't want them to think she preferred one over another, 'cause she didn't. But parents were sensitive to those things and she knew she had to be careful. Adults could be so delicate! She just liked Tyrian to carry her 'cause Cassie needed her hands free to protect them if something happened. Compromising, she clung onto her mother's back.

Matthias and Cherry waited for them in the meeting room, and both smiled as the entourage entered. "Well done, Lord Tyrian!" Matthias praised. "We just took the level of this war to an entirely new place. General Renduex, welcome to the Liberation Army. Your skill will be very welcome."

"Thank you, Professor Matthias. And it's an honor to meet you."

Everyone grabbed their seats, and Raven stood on a chair between Tyrian and Cassie. She liked being at these meetings. They talked about interesting things, and she could help them.

"Go for it, Alex," Samantha said. "You said you had intelligence we could use. Let's hear it. It's getting late in the day. If we can get the plan hammered out, we can get started tomorrow morning."

"Betane," Alex began, tapping a finger on the city on the map, "controls the southern oceanic entry into the country. To claim it would cut off all sea trade for the Empire and effectively land lock it. The mountains go all the way from the Y Border to the sea to the north of Alphin, so nothing could come that way. And the only other way in would be through Foresalia, which, given the current status quo, is not a given."

"Where *does* Foresalia stand in this?" Kyle asked. "I don't think there's been a peep from them since the Rebellion started."

"Marcus will have a better idea since he's stationed at Gammine. If we're lucky, the kingdom of Foresalia won't want to cross into what will be considered Lord Tyrian's land even if he isn't in charge of it. Cross the path of someone chosen by Destiny? No one is that insane." Alex crossed his arms on the table. "As for Betane, there's a very complicated barrier of light that surrounds it. You don't actually see it until you walk into it, and if you do, you're instantly blinded. Sometimes permanently. It only affects hostile forces, and as good as our intentions are, we're still the hostile force in the current scenario."

"I assume that means it goes around the entire city, so even with Theo, we can't approach from the sea." Matthias tapped a finger on the table as he thought quickly. "What generates the light barrier?"

"Light Relics. But someone would have to be inside to turn them off, and I'm positive they're guarded. Our best bet is to simply reflect back the light from the way it's coming."

"Yeah, but don't Light Relics break mirrors?" Ewan asked. "The power is too concentrated. We'd need one hell of a massive mirror for it to be strong enough to reflect back that much power from that many relics."

"That's why we need the Echo Mirror."

"Echo . . . ?" Tyrian's brows lifted. He looked at Raven. "Go find Miranda."

"Kay!" She fluttered off quickly. Even when she ran on the ground, she still seemed to hover slightly.

"So what's the Echo Mirror?" Cassie asked. "I assume it's related to Miranda's relic."

"I couldn't say," Alex admitted, "but I do know that it's a mirror that can't break. Di told me that it's hidden in the mountains, but that she hadn't bothered to send anyone to retrieve it. I figure that's probably our cue to do so."

Miranda came hurrying into the room with Raven clinging to her hand. She still appeared a bit soggy and had a towel around her shoulders. "You called for me?" she asked. "Whatever you need, I can do!"

"The Echo Mirror," Matthias said.

"Oh that thing!" She cocked her head. "I made it a couple hundred years ago. After a really bad 'porting accident, I removed the Echo Relic to see if Lady Tanelia could help me. Long story short, we chipped off a bit of the relic and it seemed to help. I turned the chip into a mirror because it was too pretty to lose. I then promptly lost the mirror, darn it!"

"Since it was made from the relic, does it have power?"

"Sure! It can return the user and their party back to their home, wherever that may be. So like if Lord Tyrian used it, he would come back here 'cause it's his home. No one has been able to test the theory, though. It's super picky and won't let just anyone use it. It's not *sentient* per se, but it has a particularly finicky power."

"Having that mirror would be doubly handy," Cherry told Matthias. "Not only to get into Betane, but then we wouldn't need to send Miranda to fetch Lord Tyrian from the cities. He could just come back with whomever he's found. Is there a limit to how many it can bring?"

"Hmm, dunno. I'd guess no more than twenty 'cause it isn't big, but in a worst-case scenario, it'd just not work. It wouldn't blow up or anything. That's Tedium's job."

The sound of a distant explosion seemed to imply he was still hard at work. Tyrian just ignored it. "Alex says it's in the mountains. Do you have any idea where that might be?"

"Hmm." She thought about it. "No, I don't know."

"The mountains are huge," Ewan sighed. "We can't just go combing over the damn things."

Raven held up her hand. With a smile, Matthias asked, "Yes?"

"If it hasn't been found, that means it's got to be somewhere it can't be seen, right? 'Cause it's pretty distinctive, right?" At the nods, she asked, "Well, why wouldn't it hide inside something else reflective? Like a river or something. Lady Blaine dropped a mirror into the pond at the castle once and she was so mad 'cause she couldn't see it in the water. I had to find it 'cause I was the only one who could see it 'cause I'm a Faerie." She wrinkled her nose. "I made a maid give it to her because I didn't want to see her!"

"Rivers." Tyrian grabbed the map and pulled it closer. He flipped to the detailed layout of the mountains and began to search through the landscape. Thomas did his job very well; there was no question of the accuracy of the map.

"There was a small stream near Acre," Cherry offered. "I'm not sure of any other water sources. Any near the Monk Clans?" she asked Cassie.

"It's all underground except for a hot spring further north."

"Here we go." Tyrian found where Acre had been handwritten in and then moved slightly north to the stream. It stretched for roughly a mile in total length, starting near the town and then moving east. There were no other sources of water that ran aboveground in the mountains. None of the rivers ran through. They either stopped short or diverted past.

"I believe Raven has a sound idea," Matthias said. "She is correct that something so obvious should have been found by now. I think if it is any place, it will be in the stream. And that is convenient because Miranda can transport you to Acre, Lord Tyrian. Once you have the mirror, you can return back."

"I want to go!" Raven said firmly. When the protests started immediately, she crossed her arms and set her chin. "I'm not going to do any fighting! That's *your* job. But I have to go 'cause I can see the mirror in water. I *have* to help!"

"If she comes along as a convoy member," Tyrian said, "then I can still bring five others with me in case we either encounter monsters or the Imperial Army has a nasty surprise waiting for us. I don't like it either," he admitted, "but she has as much right to be there as any of you do. More, perhaps."

To be in the convoy of a party meant that you were a non-combatant or incapable of battle. It was a signal to enemies that the convoy was considered civilian, and therefore they were protected under the laws of engagement. When it came to monsters, there were no rules, but as long as Raven stayed close, she would be safe from them as well.

It was shortly determined that in addition to Cassie going along, Liang, Marian, Lane, and Shots would also join the party. It gave them a wide breadth of skills, including magic of both healing and attacking variant, and Shots, being a ranged fighter, would be solely dedicated to protecting Raven. He could attack from a distance, which would remove Raven from the danger zone as well.

Bright and early the following morning, the party met up with Miranda to be transported. When Marian arrived, she also arrived with good news. "Laia's back to normal," she said happily. "I was with Doc yesterday afternoon when he checked up on her, and she was awake and alert. She's been lifted from restricted combat, so if we need her, she's back on call."

"Hot damn," Shots said. "That was one leggy lass that we didn't want t'be without for long. I right reckon she was happy to be back to normal too." He winked. "And her husband was happy too, no doubt."

"They were arguing like usual. All was indeed well." Marian knelt down and smiled at Raven. "You're starting to look like you mean business, little wings."

Raven beamed. She hadn't wanted to wear a dress because it was inconvenient, so she got to wear clothing much closer to that of a combatant. The tunic and leggings made it much easier to move around, and it was much lighter so she could even fly better. But because she liked pretty things, the tunic had open sleeves that held on at her wrist and shoulder. Her gramma said once they had a tailor, then she could get something even better, too. "And boots!" She held up a tiny foot proudly.

"Look at those things." Shots squinted at her feet and then at his. "Well, shoot and damn, little bit, you got better boots than I do." He scooped her up and settled her on his shoulder. "But since those feet aren't quite as made for walking as your boots, let's make this trip easy on you. Let me know if you see any low branches."

She grabbed his hat and pulled it on her own head. It was too big, but she pushed it back where she could see. "Kay!"

Even Lane was grinning. "She'll be breaking hearts," he warned Tyrian.

Tyrian thought of his daughter's desire to learn combat via big axes. "And heads, so it doesn't worry me that much."

Miranda giggled. "Okay, are we ready to go?" At the nods, she swung her wand up. "Okay, here we go! Hang on tight!"

Whether she was getting better or her relic was disinclined to misbehave with a child around, no one knew, but they all landed quite safely on the outskirts of Acre. The entire place had been gutted from the fire, and in the time since, rain had come through to add to the wreckage. Quite a bit of land around the town had been decimated as well, but there were already signs of new growth starting. It wouldn't take too long for the people to get things back into proper condition.

Knowing that didn't take any of the bitterness from Tyrian's mouth as they walked through the remains of the town. Just to get to him, the Imperial Army had been willing to kill innocent civilians and destroy their lives. If they even remembered the laws of engagement anymore, it would be a surprise.

The stream started beyond the town, and it was less than ten feet wide and only about two feet deep. Not even Raven, small as she was, was in any danger of falling in and drowning. And while the crystal clear water was obviously quite drinkable, the very clarity of the water became a problem. It reflected the landscape before it revealed what lay underneath.

"If I was a persnickety mirror," Lane decided, "I'd hide in there too."

Shots walked right along the bank with Raven tucked under his arm like a sack of potatoes. It allowed her to see into the water without any effort, and since she weighed next to nothing, it was no effort for him either. The others looked as well, but held little hope of spotting anything before the Faerie did. She was attuned to trees and water in a way none of the rest of them ever would be.

They had gotten halfway down the course of the river when Shots suddenly lifted his head sharply. "We've got company, y'all. And it ain't the neighborhood watch, if you get my meaning. T'ain't nothing stealthy 'bout this group."

Cassie and Liang instantly put Tyrian behind them even as Shots ducked down and hid Raven under the edge of his long coat. Marian and Lane both drew their wands as they moved closer as well.

From out of the trees burst three people, and Cassie groaned softly as she recognized them. "By the stars," she muttered as she covered her face with her hand.

The three bandits were enough alike in appearance to be related, for they shared similar ordinary features and blue eyes. The female was taller than her brothers, but they all wore the familiar gear of bandits or thieves, including the hipsacks for carrying their stolen loot.

The female was also armed with a handful of throwing knives, which she aimed toward Shots. "Hands up, gunner!" she said warningly.

He slowly lifted his hands. "Easy there." He felt movement under his coat but didn't dare glance down to see what that frighteningly smart little Faerie was doing. The last thing he wanted was to call attention to her. Bandits rarely operated by any rules.

A shot suddenly rang out and the female bandit ducked on a yelp as strands of her hair were clipped. "Hey!"

Her brothers hit the dirt as well though no one had shot at them. "Oh for crying out loud!" Marian stalked over and firmly took away the males' daggers. "You have to be the dumbest bandits I've ever met!"

"You would be correct," Cassie agreed dryly. She sighed as she stepped forward and cracked her knuckles lightly. "Now, didn't we have a talk about this sort of thing?" she asked the girl.

The bandit scowled. "Only Imperial soldiers have been around here, and I didn't see you! What were we supposed to think?" She sighed deeply. "Alright, how did you do that?" she demanded of Shots. "Your hands were in the air!"

"I think we might need to ask the tiny gunslinger." He opened his jacket to reveal Raven still holding his gun. "Clever little mite."

"Raven!" Marian was more astonished than horrified.

Shots fingered the hole in his jacket. "Hmm. I can just see me trying t'explain this one to the Guild. Gimme that." He took the gun from her gingerly and put it back in his holster. "Now how'd you do that, little lady?"

She set her chin in a stubborn line. "I saw you use it, so I thought I could too. I just thought the shot would surprise them. I didn't intend to actually hit her."

"Damn fine shootin' for no aimin'." He shook his head. "Let's just keep this a secret, y'all. We don't want the Guild to know 'bout our little gunslinging lady. Natural talent is highly coveted."

For the first time, Tyrian began to realize just how much his daughter would keep him on his toes. Liang glanced at his face and suddenly laughed. "Congratulations, Tyrian. I do believe you're officially a father." He clapped him lightly on the back. "Don't worry. She has enough of Cassie in her to follow rules." He grinned. "And enough of you to know how to bend them."

Cassie ignored that, true though it was. "Allow me to make introductions. Everyone, meet Ninehvi, Nihvent, and Nicran. I'm not going to bother going the other way; I think you three know who the man in the scarf is."

"Uhm, yeah." Nihvent got to his feet and tugged his brother up and then both helped their sister stand. "Can we be let go with a warning and be on our way?" he asked hopefully. "We've been messing with only Imperial soldiers. We wouldn't have jumped you if we'd realized you were the good guys. Or that you had a pint-sized gunner in convoy."

Tyrian felt a smile tugging at his lips as he realized just why they had been drawn there. It did, indeed, take all types. "I could use your help," he said, surprising everyone except Cassie. Little surprised her anymore. "Admittedly, your subterfuge could use some work, but to be honest, we lack unit leaders with any sort of subterfuge skill. We have three, but we have more than one unit that needs leaders. I think with some training, you'll be exactly what I need. Will you help me? Of course, you'll have to clean up your act if you do."

"Are you kidding?" Nicran blurted. "We'd love to help you!" He grinned at his sister. "You *did* read the tea leaves right! Whoops!" He hastily covered his mouth as he realized what he had said.

Tyrian glanced at Ninehvi. "You're a fortuneteller?"

She fidgeted. "Of a sort. Sometimes I see things in my tea. Usually things in the future, but no one believes me. My brothers do, but no one else. It's why we started living like this. The town was starting to look at me weird."

"You won't get that at the castle!" Shots said cheerfully. "We're all weird!"

"Sad, but true," Tyrian agreed. He held out his hand. "I'm thinking that your skills will be in high demand, Ninehvi. Do you tell love fortunes as well?" When she nodded, he smiled. "Then you'll assuredly be needed. There are so many betting pools going on at once that people are going to be looking for ways to hedge their bets."

There was no question that joining Tyrian was the right thing. All three siblings could feel that he really did need them. A home. The idea was astonishing. *Belonging*. They had never had that either. That Tyrian would trust them . . . they absolutely had to help him. "Okay!" Ninehvi took his hand and smiled as her brothers put their hands on hers. "We're going to do our best!"

Tyrian's relic glowed softly, and the white stars appeared on their shoulders. Inside, Tyrian felt the familiar sensation that meant he had passed another milestone. Every Star he had found was engraved inside his heart. He had found seventy Destined Stars. Only thirty-nine remained. So close. They were getting so close.

The bandits tagged along with them as they continued to move down the stream. With luck, they would be able to go back via the mirror too. "What're you calling your base anyway?" Nihvent asked curiously. "Does it even have a name? It kind of needs one."

"He's right, Tyrian," Marian reminded her cousin. "We can't keep calling it 'the castle' or 'the base.' It needs a name!"

He frowned as he thought about it. "Aon Castle," he finally said. "Taurus was teaching me Elfish, and she said that the word '*aon*' is the word they use when they are referring to the feeling of freedom."

"That's perfect," Cassie decided. "Aon Castle it is!"

"It does have a nice ring to it," Liang agreed.

Raven suddenly stopped walking and grabbed Shots' hand. "I see something in the water!" she said excitedly. She jumped into the stream before anyone could stop her and ducked underwater. When she came up, she held what looked like an ordinary hand mirror. She waded out and handed the mirror to Tyrian. "Is that it?" she asked excitedly. "It has magic!"

It certainly did. Tyrian could feel the magic pulsing inside the mirror, though in appearance it was rather unremarkable. The mirror face set into a plain green backing engraved with clouds. On first glance, he wouldn't have thought it was any sort of powerful artifact, but when he looked into the mirror at the reflection, he could actually see the soft dark swirl that was the Devourer inside him. It no longer seemed ominous.

Shots took off his jacket and wrapped Raven up snuggly as he picked her up. "You might as well keep it," he told her. "Since you broke it in for me. But you'll have to grow into it, got it? So you better get taller."

She nodded firmly. Getting taller was definitely high on her list of plans for the future. Getting a puppy and learning to fight were up there too. She was holding out on the former as a birthday wish from her parents. Savon was going to have babies; maybe she would get to keep one of them.

Tyrian held up the mirror and said softly, "Aon Castle."

The mirror glowed brightly and the familiar flash of light occurred. When they could see again, they stood near Miranda in the courtyard. She brightened when she saw them. "You did it! Oh, wow! Yep, that's the mirror. Wow, it's a lot prettier than I remembered it was, but I thought maybe I didn't remember it well because it was so long, so maybe it was always this nice. And since it likes you, that means it's yours, Lord Tyrian!"

"For now," he conceded. "After the war, we'll see if there's a better use for it." He tucked it safely into his backpack where it wouldn't get lost or damaged. "Shots, take Raven to Serentia, please. She's going to need to get warmed up and into dry clothes."

"You're the boss." He tossed Raven over his shoulder and ambled off toward the gardens. "Never explain this to anyone," he grumbled again as he disappeared out the doors to the back.

The three bandits were staring in awe at the sheer scale of the castle and the city, and they scampered off quickly to explore it fully. They had never gotten to be inside a big city, and this was definitely big. Once they had the lay of the land, they would have to see about that training. There was no knowing when Tyrian would need them!

"What about us?" Marian asked.

"Don't go far. Cassie and I are going to briefly check in with Matthias. We'll need Alex, which is another reason I let Shots go. With a little luck, we'll have another checkpoint under our belt by dinner."

And if Cassie had her way, he would be sleeping after said dinner. The breakneck pace of the last few days was beginning to show its toll on him once more. As his Kentei, it was her duty to ensure his health and safety. As his lover, it was her privilege to bully him into doing what she told him when she told him.

Whether he liked it or not.

Chapter Thirty-Three

"What lies beneath the hearts of mankind: salvation or sin?"

The infuriated scream was heard all the way through Trinan. More than one person cringed. Many others wished they could leave, but there was no escaping Trinan. No one entered. No one left. The gates were permanently guarded by soldiers, and other units stood stationed in the lands around the capitol. The safe walls had become a prison. Nearly everyone prayed for Tyrian Southerwind to arrive. He had seen sooner than anyone else just what monster lurked inside the palace.

Blaine's scream was still echoing off the throne room as she whirled away from the messenger who had brought her the news. Alphin had fallen. Betane would be next. Then Gammine. She had no illusions that all would fall. There was no stopping the tidal wave that the Kaiten Star had begun.

The messenger scrambled out of the throne room in fear for his life, but Blaine didn't notice. She stared at her hands and saw them wrinkled and gnarled, crabbed with age as merciless Time dragged at her.

"Blaine," Albanion said as he moved to her side, "this is unbecoming behavior for a lady of your quality." She whirled on him, and belatedly he finally saw the emptiness inside her eyes. Too late he saw the madness. "Blaine." For a moment, his voice regained its authority.

Her hand shot out and closed around his neck. Her power blasted down her arm and into his body and began to suck out every bit of life. "You are a weak worm," she hissed as he began to sag in her grip. "One year ago, I told you to have Tyrian Southerwind killed. Did you listen? No. Your usefulness is done, Albanion. Think of this as me saving the Kaiten Star the trouble!"

His lifeless body dropped to the floor and she stared at her suddenly perfect hands. They were smooth and flawless. Young and beautiful. She didn't have much longer. The life energy didn't last as long as time passed. She needed that Pure Relic!

The doors opened behind her and Reyu sauntered in. "Ah. I figured you'd eventually do that." He came up behind her and wrapped an arm around her waist. His lips brushed at her nape in a falsely tender caress. "Things are not yet over, Blaine. We can find the power to match him."

"You can't even find someone to use that disgusting thing you brought. 'Pure of heart.' Feh!"

"Not just pure of heart, but powerful. And there happens to be just such a person in the Liberation Army. No doubt she will take to the field if I am there. She will be compelled to respond by the very blood in her veins."

Blaine found herself reluctantly interested. She turned away from her husband's dead body and studied Reyu. "Alright. I'm listening."

Chapter Thirty-Four

"Sing to me sweet melodies of war and peace."

"What exactly is the plan?" Alex asked Tyrian as they walked downstairs to where Miranda waited with the others. "We can break through the light barrier, but are we taking units for a full battle, or are you planning something else?"

"Matthias' plan has several 'if/thens' as he calls them. If something happens, then we do something else. It's mostly contingent on how General Cutter reacts to our arrival. We're going as a party, but there are units on standby. Just follow my lead."

"That's simple enough," the general murmured. "You're as natural a leader as your father is."

"Thank you." When they had joined the others, he told Miranda, "Use Alex as the one to get the signature from. We need to land outside the city, not in. I'm asking for some very precision transport power from you, but I know you can do it."

"Leave it to me!" She focused on Alex. "Here we go!"

Moments later, they stood in the sandy desert outside the city of Betane. It was only a few hundred yards away and clearly distinct in the afternoon light. Equally distinct were the eight units sitting outside the city limits. It was impossible to see their expressions at that distance, but a low murmur of surprise moved in the air.

Di, riding at the front of the main ranged unit, recognized Alex across the distance of the field. Truthfully, she would recognize him anywhere at any distance. A part of her wanted to go running to him and jump in his arms. The sane part told her that doing so would be stupid. The man was a predator. If she showed weakness, he would move in. It wouldn't be the first time, frankly. Instead, she settled back on her horse and prepared to see just what Tyrian had up his sleeve. This was certainly bound to be interesting.

There was no sign of any sort of barrier around the area, but that was the entire point of it. Tyrian pulled out the Echo Mirror and held it like a shield as he walked forward. Beams of light suddenly shot through the air and lit the area brilliantly. The others had covered their eyes in preparation so were not blinded. Tyrian didn't have to protect himself. The beams struck the mirror and bounced back the way they had come. Distant explosions inside the city seemed to indicate that the relics themselves had been broken.

He put the mirror away and then touched the Voice Relic he wore. "Greetings, General Cutter."

"Quite an entrance, Tyrian," she countered. "I see you found the Echo Mirror. I can't say as I'm surprised, though. But I must ask just what you're doing out here without an army. You're just a *bit* outnumbered."

"I thought perhaps you might want to solve this whole issue with a duel. General Renduex tells me you're brilliant with a bow and sword equally. He speaks very highly of you, General Cutter."

"I imagine so," Di's second lieutenant murmured dryly.

"Shut up," she muttered. She tried to ignore the reflexive flutter of her heart at the idea that Alex would be singing her praises. This was one large farce, certainly, but the knowledge still warmed her. Thirty years. Was she never going to get past him? "I suppose a duel would be a nice, civilized way to end this." She dismounted her horse and handed off her bow. She carried a sword in her pack and removed it as she began to cross the field. "Laws of engagement have been claimed," she told her soldiers. "A duel is commencing."

Tyrian lightly nudged Alex and he realized Tyrian's game. He calmly drew his sword and crossed the field to stand even with the woman he loved. Judging by the way her eyes widened, she also realized quickly the plan. "I have been asked to stand as a surrogate combatant," he told her. "Lord Tyrian knows that we're more evenly matched."

It was an unfortunate turn of events for Di. She was left with the options of raising a sword against the man she loved, or surrendering without a fight. There was no one she could call in as a surrogate. Not a single soldier in her units would have any chance of defeating Alex.

"Clever," she muttered as she realized the situation they had created. On one hand, she wouldn't have minded kicking Alex's ass for forcing her to make a scene; on the other, this was not the time or place for rebelling. There was a very viable way to surrender without bloodshed, and because they were all on the same side anyway, that was the route to take. She took a deep breath. "Tyrian, I ask that you fight me yourself or choose another surrogate. I can't fight Alex."

"Fight or surrender, General." Tyrian's voice was cool and calm, the voice of a man who had led more than his fair share of combat and would give no quarter to an enemy. "You accepted the duel. Laws of engagement stand."

She slowly lifted her sword and then threw it on the ground. "Yield," she said softly. "I can't raise a weapon against this man." She turned toward her soldiers. "Choose," she ordered. "I stay to fight on the side of the Rebellion to bring back peace to our land and freedom for our people."

Every single soldier either removed their jacket or removed the emblem from their jacket. From within the city came a cheer of joy as the citizens realized what had just occurred outside the border.

A unit from the Liberation Army appeared on the field and moved forward to meet up with Di's units. Riding at the forefront of the unit were Laia, Samantha, and Kyle. Seeing them told Di that her suspicions had been correct and that Tyrian had never really been alone on the field. "Your strategist is quite clever," she told Tyrian as he approached. "If I hadn't yielded and had kicked this smug bastard's ass, what would you have done?"

"Well, if you *had* decided to fight him, I would have told Alex to use dirty tactics."

"Dirty tactics? This guy? Like what?" She got her answer as Alex caught her by the back of the neck and dragged her close for a kiss that melted every muscle in her body. She thought she heard whooping and catcalling from the soldiers, but her hearing had gone away with her ability to think clearly.

"Dirty tactics," Marian said gravely, trying not to giggle. "Of the type most effective between couples. Is that why you don't train with Tyrian?" she asked Cassie. "You don't trust him?"

"I trust him about as far as I can throw Aon Castle," the monk retorted dryly. "He plays to win. Which, of course, is one of the reasons I love him."

"All's fair," he reminded her. He cleared his throat politely. "Alex? You may let her go now."

With obvious reluctance, Alex released Di. Life was hell with her, but it wasn't worth living without her. "Missed you," he said against her lips. "And whether you admit it or not, I know you missed me. Damn it, Di. Put us out of our misery."

She dropped her head against his shoulder. She just didn't feel like fighting with him right now. Not when her heart and body ached equally for him. "Damn you," she said against his shoulder. She looked around his arm at Tyrian and scowled. "And damn you for bringing him to me!"

"He was miserable," Liang noted dryly.

Lane just snorted softly. They wouldn't see *him* acting like that much of an idiot over any woman. Eternity thing notwithstanding, he had yet to meet any woman that he felt was worth becoming an idiot over. Any woman who was *available*, he amended in all fairness. The good ones were always taken, as they said.

"I want to head into the city," Tyrian announced as Laia, Samantha, and Kyle approached. "I'm trying not to be some nameless, faceless figure. I want to talk to the people and get a feel for the situation. I'm sure it's no different from Alphin, but I want to see it. I also can't be sure there aren't any Destined Stars here."

"Did you sense anyone you felt a kinship to?" Samantha asked Di.

"Not that I noticed."

"It's still worth looking," Laia said. "You've got the mirror, so we—" She broke off and lifted her head sharply as her purple eyes darkened to nearly black. A chill visibly raced over her body and all three of her relics flickered.

"Laia!" Kyle and Tyrian both moved to grab her and keep her on her feet when she staggered. "Maybe you're not fully recovered after all," Kyle said with a frown. "We need to get you to Doctor Kelan. With how strong you are, there's no knowing the permanent effects of the Soul Fog."

"No." She shook her head. "It's not that."

She was still shivering even in her plate armor, and Alex removed his jacket to put it around her shoulders and block where a draft could enter. Marian lightly touched Laia's Music Relic and instantly realized what had happened. "How odd. Another power deliberately touched her. It threw off her equilibrium."

"Something evil comes." A shimmer of power, stronger than usual, flickered through Laia's voice.

Bright flashes of light announced the arrival of more troops. This time, they were Imperial troops. Riding at the forefront was a handsome man with golden hair that, for some reason, seemed very distasteful to all three Pure Relic users who were present. Laia, when she saw him, felt a low pulse of power in her blood that seemed to be urging her to battle. She hated him, and she couldn't even say why.

"General Reyu," Di said in a low voice. Without even thinking about it, she moved when the others did to keep Tyrian safely protected behind them. "No one has any idea where he's from. He just showed up one day and started taking General Southerwind's duties after Lady Annareal was murdered."

There were nine units on the field behind Reyu. There were a total of nine on the Liberation Army side. Reyu made a slight gesture and all of his soldiers began to rush toward the Liberation Army. Realizing he wasn't going to play by the rules—and thereby forfeited any right to them—Tyrian turned toward his soldiers. "Don't give any mercy! Hold them off!"

The bloody battle began and was little more than a free-for-all. It was disgusting for those who abided by the rules. This very chaos was the entire reason the laws of engagement stood. No one would really win today.

"We have to end this fast," Samantha said to Tyrian. "More reinforcements?"

"Let me take out Reyu."

Tyrian looked at Laia in surprise. "Are you sure?"

She looked at him, and her eyes still looked dark. Never before had the power inside her been more visible. Somehow, it was a strangely familiar power to those present. "I demand right as a Destined Star. This is not your fight."

"I'll leave it to you," he said quietly.

Reyu was enjoying the fight immensely when he felt a chill race down his back. He turned sharply to discover that Laia stood less than twenty feet away, a sword in one hand and her other propped on her hip. His lips curled into a smile that was more of a sneer. "So there you are, little girl."

"I hate to tell you," she retorted coolly, "but only two men have ever had the right to call me little. Put up or shut up, *little boy*. You called me for a challenge, and we both know it."

She wore the mantle of her ancestors well, he noticed, even though her body only housed a fraction of her ancestors' blood. Of course, it was powerful blood, so it would never fully dilute from her bloodline. The crystal clarity of her purple eyes was a welcome sign to him. As was the way of the species, the purity of her heart was there in her eyes. The perfect subject.

He drew his sword and moved forward to match her, but she suddenly shot forward and attacked before he could blink. To his surprise, he was forced to block and dodge, never able to get in an attack of his own as she kept him on a constant retreat. One of her strikes bit through his armor and into the flesh beyond. The pain was a shocking reminder to him that he was not invulnerable.

Showing the classic predatory nature of her ancestry, she didn't loosen on her assault even though he was wounded. The next attack cut through his armguard, but missed the flesh beneath. Following blows stopped just shy of actually wounding him. Mercilessly, she closed in on the kill.

He was outmatched, and he knew it. He instead gathered his power and blasted her in the chest. The blow sent her tumbling across the field but she let her body go with the force and rolled right back up into a crouched position. Her armor was damaged, seared off in places, and she had distinctly been wounded for dark blood slid down her sword arm. As he took a gliding step forward, she switched her sword to her other hand and straightened to her full height.

He stopped on a vile curse. There would be no taking her through battle. Not unless it was the end of a much longer battle against many more enemies. She was simply too skilled and too powerful. "We're done for the day," he told her stiffly.

She laughed, and the musical sound grated on his ears. "Why? Is the 'little girl' too much for you?"

His teeth clicked together. "I'll see you in Trinan!" he snarled. He made a sharp gesture and both he and his troops disappeared from the field entirely.

The instant it was clear, the others ran over to Laia. Tyrian caught her when her legs buckled, and he gently lowered her to the ground where Marian could examine her. "That was one hell of a bluff," he said softly. He lightly brushed a kiss over her forehead.

Her lips curved. "Who said it was a bluff? I'm ambidextrous." She opened her eyes and looked at him seriously. "Do not face him in battle, Tyrian. For all your power as a Kaiten, you would not beat him. You're stronger than I, but the power is different. Do you understand?"

"I sure don't," Kyle muttered.

Lane shook his head. "There are different aspects to power. Like positive and negative charges. That's one aspect. Elements are considered another aspect. Tyrian has a Dark element. Cassie has a Light element. I'm a Wind element . . . etcetera. I was watching the fight. Reyu has a full-elemental spectrum. Might be the Pure Eight-Fold Relic he wears; there's no knowing. But that means he can defend himself against anything Tyrian throws at him. Laia is also full spectrum. It takes a serious versatility to have that sort of thing. I'm shocked that we've now to see two, and one doesn't have a Pure Relic."

"So I may be stronger than Laia, but I lack the same defenses she possesses." Tyrian nodded. "I understand. I don't have any intention of facing Reyu alone." He frowned. "Why did he come directly after Laia? Was it because of that elemental spectrum?"

"The Golden Scourge," Laia murmured. Her eyes closed. "The Bloody Scourge is more likely."

Tyrian felt his heart skip a beat as he remembered his mysterious meeting with the man called Agrime. He was looking for the 'Golden Scourge.' That meant he was looking for Reyu. He didn't doubt Laia's sixth sense any more than he doubted Ninehvi's ability to see fortunes in her teacup. "Agrime," he said quietly. "I need to go back for Agrime. I think I know who he hunts."

There were other things to be done first, however. Once Laia regained her feet, she joined Kyle and Samantha in assessing the losses to the units on the Liberation Army. They were mercifully few considering the mania of the prior battle. Laia's quick action in confronting Reyu had limited the casualties. Di and Alex assessed the other units and found few losses there as well.

"I wonder if he came here looking for you or for Laia," Cassie said softly as she stood beside Tyrian and watched the wounded be tended. "She said he deliberately challenged her, and you can be sure she was definitely called out directly. He didn't even seem to take note of you, really."

"I also didn't like his parting shot at her." He crossed his arms. "'I'll see you in Trinan.' That seems to mean he will wait for the final battle to come after her again. I just wish we knew *why* he wanted her. Perhaps Agrime will have that answer. It's got something to do with her power, of that we can be sure."

She glanced at his face and saw the dark circles under his eyes. This latest development was just another burden on his shoulders. It was, perhaps, a heavier burden because he loved his Stars very deeply. Though the Destined Stars lived to love, support, and protect him, it was a two-way street because he wanted to do the same to them. This situation was made even worse because Laia was one of his most beloved Stars.

She stayed close by his side as he made his way through the troops and met the new soldiers. She was there when he briefly spoke with his older soldiers, and she was there when he began to make his way into the city. Liang and Marian went with them while the others returned with the units back to Aon Castle.

Betane was a flurry of activity. People were starting to take back their lives, and the militia of the city was already switching to Tyrian's colors. They, like in Alphin, would remain to hold the city.

It was a staggering thought anew to think that there were two checkpoints under his control, Tyrian realized. The Empire was now entirely cut off from trade unless someone came in through the Y Border, which, given the current state of affairs, was probably not necessarily safe either.

By the time they had gone through most of the city, he was sure there were no more Destined Stars to be found there. That didn't mean there might not be one later, but there weren't any right now. It was just as well. The sun was setting and it was getting late. If he wanted to fetch Agrime, he needed to do it now.

After talking briefly with the mayor of Betane, and assuring him that he was back in charge of the day-to-day business, Tyrian took out the Echo Mirror so he and his bodyguards could return to the castle.

The first thing they heard when they landed in the courtyard was the sound of Di shouting at, presumably, Alex. Tyrian lifted a brow at Miranda and she giggled. "So, like, General Renduex told the guards that General Cutter would share his room which she completely didn't like but, you know, I think she's mad because she *wants* to but doesn't want to say so, so anyway she's now yelling at him about being arrogant, heavy-handed, and presumptuous."

The yelling stopped rather abruptly, and it was followed by the sound of cheering from the castle staff. "Dirty tactics?" Cassie asked Tyrian dryly.

He had to smile. "It works, doesn't it?" He kissed her lightly and then tugged her close. He had no doubts as to Alex winning the fight eventually. Di's only real problem was the certainty that they would fight for the rest of their lives. What was so wrong with that? It would keep things interesting. He liked fighting with Cassie because it meant they were equals. They never said anything that would hurt each other, and every fight inevitably ended with laughter.

"I need dinner," Marian decided. She pointed at Tyrian. "Don't be out late! Get Agrime and come right back for dinner." She turned on her heel and walked off toward the restaurant, her hair swinging around her shoulders. She obviously expected to be obeyed.

"I'll go with you two," Liang said.

Tyrian didn't bother to argue. "Miranda, please send us to Caschin."

They landed outside the city, but it was close enough that they didn't quibble the details. Tyrian headed directly into the city and toward the alley where he remembered meeting Agrime before. A part of him didn't expect to find him still there, but more of him was sure that Agrime wouldn't make things difficult for him.

He sensed the other man's power long before he was close. He stepped into the entrance to the alley and spotted the familiar figure in plate armor leaning against the wall. It was as if he had never moved in all the time since, as if he had simply remained there waiting for Tyrian's return. "Agrime," Tyrian said quietly, "I have need of your strength."

"So he shows his face." Agrime straightened. "The Golden Scourge. It is a pity that a face so beautiful should mask a heart so evil. He kills without remorse, Tyrian. There is no mercy inside him. He doesn't break the rules: rules don't even exist inside his world. His is a false existence. All those vile desires inside have only been amplified by the Eight-Fold Relic he wears."

"He came directly after my paladin. Laiaeariel Mitakel."

"That is to be expected. In his possession is a very powerful artifact of the Summarian race. The most powerful, perhaps. It is . . . finicky. The people who could use it are few indeed. Only two currently live that I am aware of. Laia is one of them. The other lives in the City-States."

"What is Laia?"

Agrime's smile entered in his voice. "Complicated. And that is all that can be said at this time." He drew his sword and held it before his face in a knight's gesture of fealty. "Please accept my dedication as a Destined Star. When the battle is taken to Trinan, it will be I who confronts Reyu. His false life will end by my blade."

"Laia has a grudge," Cassie warned.

"She will let me fight in her place. She will know who I am just as I know who she is."

"Glad someone knows what's going on around here," Liang said under his breath. Things just seemed to keep getting more and more complicated. It was beginning to feel a lot like the future peace of the entire world hung on the outcome of this battle. How many more burdens would be put onto Tyrian's shoulders?

They returned back to Aon Castle via the Echo Mirror, and Agrime went to find Laia. Liang went to get dinner, and Tyrian found himself dragged by his lover through the courtyard toward the tower. Since he had long before learned that she outclassed him in raw strength let alone skill, he let her tow him along. "I can walk," he said mildly.

"And would likely go wandering off to check on everyone. You're going to eat some dinner and rest, Tyrian." Her tone booked no argument as they got on the elevator. "Tomorrow will arrive soon enough. These last few days have taken a harder drain on you, particularly coming on top of the Soul Fog."

He thought about arguing, but he knew his Kentei was just as stubborn as he was, and he didn't feel like trying to out-stubborn her. It felt too good to let her take over. With a sigh, he sank down onto the floor in front of the fireplace. It was already burning cheerfully. "I just want this to be over, Cas," he said softly. "I don't want anyone else to be afraid. I'm so damn frightened of what Blaine might do next. You can be sure Reyu is dangling that artifact in front of her like a lure. And what if he *did* find someone to use it? The most powerful relic of the most powerful race in history." He shook his head. "We'd be doomed."

She knelt beside him. "It won't happen." She caught his face in her hands and forced him to look at her. "We can only fight the battles that are here before us right now. If another battle comes, then we will lend our strength and our experience to whoever is in charge. Agrime will handle Reyu. So long as we save the people of the Empire, that is what is important right now. Saving the world will fall on someone else's shoulders."

His eyes closed and he leaned his head against her shoulder. "Thank you," he said softly. "Sometimes it all gets jumbled in my head. I find myself thinking of the future a lot now. Maybe it is because our future will be very long." He tugged her down onto his lap and buried his face in her hair. "So many questions still to be answered," he said softly.

"The answers will come." She rested her relic hand lightly over his heart and closed her eyes as his relic hand covered hers. "Don't always think about the bad things in the future. Think of the good." Her lips curved. "Like trying to raise a Faerie who wants to use a battleaxe, has the brain of a strategist, and natural gunner talent."

As far as futures went, that was a pretty nice one, though equally terrifying in its own way. He sighed and let himself stop thinking about things he couldn't change. If answers were to be found, then Merlot and Zinfandel would find them. They were closing in on the origins of the legend of the Kaiten Star, and perhaps that would bring the last of the answers.

He had a feeling the story was only just beginning with him.

Chapter Thirty-Five

"When me and you become we; that is when it all begins."

Word arrived the following morning while Tyrian and Cassie were having breakfast with Raven in the restaurant. Squint came bursting into the room and blurted, "The Emperor is dead!"

Everything came to a screeching halt. The Lower Generals, sitting a few tables over, looked up sharply and then shared a long look between them. As voices began to rise, Tyrian held up a hand for silence. "What is being said caused it?" he asked Squint.

"The message that Tad got said that Albanion's heart gave out and he just toppled over. Lady Blaine is so grief-stricken that she has allowed no one but General Reyu to tend to her."

"Grief-stricken, my ass!" Ewan muttered distinctly. "She's probably the one who killed the old bastard."

"Have all of our informants confirmed the information?" Matthias asked as he gingerly limped up. His leg had steadily been paining him more lately, a surer barometer of the coming end of the war than anything else. "All three gossips as well as Grace and Kell?"

"They've checked and double-checked. Word is spreading rapidly through the remaining cities under lockdown. The soldiers are talking about it. The Emperor is definitely dead." Squint sat down on a bench under the nearest window, and her one eye blazed with temper. "He didn't even have the decency to live to see the end of the war he caused!" As her breath puffed out, a ring of smoke came with it, proof positive of her ire. Any Dragon that got angry enough tended to breathe out their element—a hazardous thing when the Dragon happened to be a temperamental Fire type!

Alex drummed his fingers on the table. "Blaine," he said curtly.

"To be sure," Matthias agreed. "But we can't really see this as changing anything. We have known all along that Lady Blaine was the driving force behind events. That the status quo changed with her arrival is no coincidence. We must simply carry on as before. Perhaps, if anything, this is more impetus to continue. Should we fall, there is no knowing what Lady Blaine will do to the people."

"Well, this bites!" Squint muttered under her breath.

Evelyn shoved a pastry into her mouth. "You're breathing fire. Calm down, Squint." She held her tray against her chest as she looked at Tyrian.

"We stand beside you, Lord Tyrian. Whatever you need of us, you have only to ask. We believe in you."

"On that token, Eve, will you please bring a pot of coffee up to the meeting room?" Matthias turned toward the Generals as Evelyn hurried into her kitchen. "General Cutter, General Renduex, I ask that you join this meeting. Ewan, Kyle, your presence is required as well."

"How'd we get dragged into this?" Kyle groused as he got to his feet.

"You've been here the longest," Tyrian reminded him. "You're senior soldiers in the Liberation Army."

"I don't like the sound of that," Ewan complained. "I'm only three years older than you are." He grabbed another pastry from the buffet as he went past and scooped up Raven when she grabbed his leg. "Come on, kiddo. You've proven to be pretty useful. That and you keep us from swearing too much."

"You mean *you* swear too much," she told him primly, and made the entire room start snickering.

Together as a group, they headed for the elevator. Once the doors shut, Tyrian asked Di softly, "Whose room were you in last night?"

"Mine," she muttered.

Based on the slightly smug smile on Alex's face, she hadn't been alone in her room. Tyrian just smiled. Alex had his full sympathy and support, and everyone knew it. "Just don't turn into Grace and Kell," Tyrian murmured. "No one wants to wait that long to collect on the bet."

The best Di could say to that was, "Shut up, Tyrian."

Cherry waited for them at the meeting room and hopped to her feet to help Matthias into his chair. "I've been doing some research," she said as everyone sat down. "Our next stop is Gammine, which we know is in the forests that mark the border to Foresalia. To be precise, the city is built on top of a lake. The only way you can access it is via a sole road in. That road is currently entirely defended by Marcus Quint's units."

"To make matters worse," Di picked up, "the lake itself is impassible for boats. The water contains a property that completely eats through wood within a matter of moments. Our only hope of storming the city is to attack via the road, but there's no way we could muscle through."

"The complication," Matthias said, "is that while we are sure that General Quint, and General Martine, are both Destined Stars as well, as of this moment, they are still our enemies. We want to avoid bloodshed if at all possible, but we cannot expect them to simply hand over the keys to the checkpoint."

"Why not?" Kyle asked. "We're all after the same thing."

"It's a test." Alex settled back in his chair. "I believe I speak for all the Lower Generals when I say that we want to see Lord Tyrian test his mettle against us. If he can't get past the meager defenses we offer, then there's no way he can take on Trinan. It is also a test of you, Professor Matthias, as you are the strategist. If you two cannot work to take a checkpoint, the Rebellion stands no chance."

"I had begun to suspect that was so," Matthias said. "And you are correct. I may formulate the plan, but it is Lord Tyrian who must execute it. And should something go wrong, he must think on his feet. But I trust him to do so. He almost doesn't need me."

Tyrian smiled at him. "Sure I do. Knowing you're taking care of this part means I can focus on all the rest. My place is on the battlefield, not in the war room. I'm just the weapon to be wielded. And I am perfectly fine with that. I was born to be a warrior. I would never have lasted long if I had become a Lower General. I am sure of that now."

No one could argue with him. They had all watched him bloom on the battlefield like the rarest of flowers. Quite literally, he had been born for this very moment. But Matthias also knew that while Tyrian needed him, his presence was not what would ensure victory. There was no Rebellion without Tyrian. He represented the hopes of every person who lived in the Empire.

"What do we want to do?" Ewan asked Matthias. "I doubt we can sneak someone inside like we've done before. Quint is probably on to that tactic by now. None of us would be able to get past the gate."

Matthias lightly drummed his fingers on the table as he thought quickly over the possible recourses. "I believe the simplest thing to do is to tackle the lake. We'll sail up to the back door."

"What part of 'the water eats wood' did you miss?" Kyle asked.

"The part where she said the water eats stone."

"Oh!" Raven brightened. "Ships of stone!"

"Correct!" Matthias couldn't help but wistfully wish for a future where she could have been his student as well. There was much he would have loved to teach her. He would have to be content with Cherry carrying on his tutelage, perhaps with Raven, perhaps not. "I propose we make some boats out of stone and sail across the waters. We can breach the city from behind quite easily."

"But you still have to deal with Marcus," Alex reminded him. "Getting in is only half the battle."

"I think we're going to make a little switch in the décor. Wouldn't our flag look lovely flying from the highest tower?"

"Ah, I get it." Tyrian smiled. "We fly our flag even before we've got General Quint on our side. The entire city is going to think we've already won. He won't have any choice but to surrender."

"You'll have to be fast." Di shook her head. "Marcus has a strong sixth sense for magical power. He'd feel you or Cassie the instant you were inside the city."

"Then maybe we need to distract him," he said. "We send in someone to find and distract him, and when they have him occupied, then we'll take care of the flag. What sorts of things distract General Quint?"

In one voice, Alex and Di said, "Women."

Ewan grinned. "I'm going to like him."

Tyrian began to mentally run through the women in the Destined Stars who were of the right age frame and personality to successfully distract a battle-hardened general. A smile touched his lips. "I do believe this might be the perfect task for my cousin."

Kyle's brows lifted. "True, she did a damned good job of flirting us into quite a store of scrolls that first battle. She's beautiful, and she's personable. She gets my vote."

"She's also a Healer," Matthias noted, "which means that she automatically gets overlooked by others as being no threat. Never mind that she swings that mace pretty hard and her aim with her Resurrection Relic's lightning rivals Kane's." He nodded. "I agree. Lady Marian is a good choice for this task. Do you think she'll be a good choice?" he asked the two Lower Generals.

Di grinned. "You couldn't have picked better, I assure you. Let's just say that if it hadn't been for the rules about military members being distracted by significant others, Marcus might very well have come knocking on her door the instant she was eighteen."

Curiously, Tyrian found that unsurprising. He hadn't seen anything expressly obvious over the years after Marian had turned eighteen, but there had just been something in the way General Quint acted when she was around. Perhaps that had subconsciously fueled his decision. "Then Marian is indeed the proper choice."

"Well, that takes care of that issue," Alex said, "but what do we do about the boats? Can Theo build a boat of stone? And how do we sail up to the back of the city without being noticed, anyway?"

The meeting room doors opened at that point and Theo walked in. At his side was a woman of roughly the same age who had short red hair and lovely features, and the telltale pattern of scales over her skin to imply she had Merfolk blood; she also possessed fins for ears. She wore the familiar rugged clothes of someone used to working hard for her living. "I brought a present," Theo said gravely. "I hope I'm not interrupting."

"Not at all." Tyrian got to his feet with a smile. It was there again, that little tug inside. "I'm Tyrian," he told the woman. "Welcome to Aon Castle. Did Theo drag you here?"

"He's cute, so it's not a hardship." She waved a hand in the air and then propped her hands on her hips. "My name is Paola, Lord Tyrian. I'm a ship builder. Theo said that since you have the two port cities, you might be needing my services."

Ewan looked at Kyle. "I'm not so unnerved by that happening anymore."

Kyle shook his head. "We'll stay sane longer if we don't ask."

"You couldn't have come at a better time," Tyrian said honestly. "We have need of your immediate services, Paola." He looked at Theo. "Can you see to finding her a room? She'll be staying with us a while."

"Ha, knew it." He grinned at Paola. "You don't want to share my room?"

She sniffed. "I don't sleep with ship rats."

With a whistle, clearly un-offended, he left the meeting room. Tyrian hid a smile as he gestured for Paola to take one of the empty seats. There was obviously nothing romantic between the two. He could only liken it to the way Marian and R.K. flirted just for the fun of it. It was just as well. There were too many betting pools already anyway.

"Welcome to the Liberation Army, Paola," Matthias said. "All those present are also Destined Stars, even young Raven. You are welcome at any time to join us in any meeting if you feel you are needed. We have all learned that we know when Lord Tyrian needs us, just as he knows when we need him."

"That works just fine for me." She pulled a pad of paper out of a pocket and retrieved the pencil stuck over her left fin. "So what are we talking?" The explanation was brief, and she could only whistle lightly when they finished. "You're right, you do need me. Let's see . . . a ship made of stone. It's not as hard as you think. It just needs to be scaled properly to whatever it's sailing in. There's also the option of not making it *solid* stone. A stone cover over wood might work as well."

"We're also concerned about visibility," Alex said. "We don't expect them to start shooting at us, but we're trying to be covert. Sailing up to the back door is enough of a problem to begin with."

"Not that much so," she disagreed. "There's actually another bridge back there that can be lowered. The higher nobility *never* use the main road because it's so *dirty*. I've known some narcissists who would pitch a fit if they so much as looked at dirt."

"Narcissist?" Raven asked Tyrian. "That's a weird word."

"For some weird people," he conceded. "A narcissist is a person of higher nobility who is so full of him or herself that they think only they are important. They tend to be very vain, very snobby, and *very* condescending to lesser beings." His brows suddenly lifted and he looked at Matthias.

The strategist was already thinking of the same thing. "You know," he said musingly, "wouldn't it be perfectly normal for a high class lady to be traveling to Gammine to escape the dirty reconstruction in other cities? And wouldn't it be perfectly normal for her to demand they let her in the back so she doesn't have to deal with those messy soldiers?"

"And while she's making this huge scene, wouldn't it be too bad if a small boat just happened to slip under radar and get into the checkpoint?" Tyrian murmured.

"How many people in the boat?" Paola asked.

"Three. Lord Tyrian, Lady Cassie, and General Cutter," Matthias said.

"Then it can be pretty small . . . I think a stone cover on the wood would be fine." She sketched across her paper swiftly and accurately, mapping out the dimensions as well as the supplies she would need. "If I blackmail Theo and Mayo and grab those two builders as well, we can have it ready by the morning. It won't be pretty, but it doesn't have to be."

"I'll leave it to you," Tyrian told her. "I know you'll get it done." He looked at Matthias. "Tomorrow would be ideal anyway. I still need to get Marian up to speed on the plan, and we need to transform her into a narcissist." He frowned thoughtfully. "Where are we going to get her the proper clothes? We don't have a tailor yet."

"Myr?" Cherry asked. "She has quite the collection of clothing since she's a bard. She might have something that Serentia can alter for Lady Marian."

"Then that's the plan," Matthias said. "Lord Tyrian, if you will speak with Myr, Serentia, and Lady Marian, we will help Paola get everything she needs to have our stone boat ready by morning."

"Done." Tyrian got to his feet and smiled as Raven climbed onto his back. "If anything, this will be amusing," he said to Cassie as they headed out of the meeting room to go find Marian. This time of day, she would no doubt be with Kelan. She and Halkern worked with the doctor to help tend to everything from broken bones to runny noses.

"You know," Cassie said wryly, "in a way, I'm glad one of us ended up with a Pure Relic before we, uhm, cemented our relationship." The tact was only for the presence of their daughter's tiny ears, though both parents were fairly sure she already knew the basics. She was turning into quite the Scholar with the way she read books. "I'm fairly hard to embarrass, but asking your *cousin* for herbs to prevent pregnancy might have been more than I could take in stride."

"She would have giggled," he conceded, "but she wouldn't have made it difficult for you."

"Yes, but she's your cousin, and is nearly a sister. Can you imagine if I had a sister and you had to ask her for birth control?"

"Depends on how much like you she was." He grinned. "If she was exactly like you, then I wouldn't need to ask. She'd just give them to me and tell me to behave myself."

She found herself laughing. She really couldn't find fault with that argument.

Marian was indeed in the doctor's office, and she was organizing the herbs when Tyrian and Cassie walked in without their daughter. Raven had abandoned them when she heard Savon just had her new puppies. "Good morning," Marian said as she finished stacking a few boxes. She dusted off her hands and walked over to hug Tyrian. "Word has spread," she said. "But I know you'll be okay. You have us."

"I know." He hugged her back and then caught her hands. "I need to ask you to do something."

"Name it," she said simply.

"Walk with us to find Myr, and we'll explain."

By the time they got to Myr's room, Marian was both impressed by the plan and humbled to be trusted with something so important. She was also slightly flustered, but she kept that well hidden. They wanted her to distract Marcus Quint? The accepted playboy of the Imperial Army? She had never seen him with the same woman twice! Not, of course, that she had been *watching* or anything.

When Tyrian knocked on Myr's door, she opened it immediately. She brightened when she saw who stood outside. "Lord Tyrian! Hi, come in!" She stepped back to let all three enter. "What's going on?"

One explanation later and she leapt to her feet to go over to her closet. "Oh, I have the perfect thing! When we went to Rubentia, I picked up a whole lot of my stuff, and I know there's a dress in here that'll look *amazing* on you, Lady Marian! It was a gift from a fan of my caravan, and he's a great tailor, so it should be high enough quality."

The dress she emerged with certainly spoke of high fashion. The skirt was excessively voluminous, the material was silk, and the top would perfectly frame and flatter the wearer's curves. There was also quite a bit of lace and ruffle, enough to make anyone think the owner had a high opinion of herself.

While on one hand, Marian was slightly nonplussed by the decadence, she was also taken with the pale pink material. She normally couldn't wear pink because of her rusty hair color, which was more orange than red. This pink had a bit more yellow than normal, and it would be flattering.

"Let's see if it fits!" Myr said. She grinned at Tyrian. "Turn around so we can surprise you. If *you* can be impressed, then we know the general will!"

He obligingly turned around. "If it doesn't fit, we can ask Serentia to adjust it," he reminded them after a few moments.

"It laces, so it fits." Myr sighed happily. "You look so pretty, Lady Marian!"

Tyrian turned around and began smiling. The dress was indeed beautiful, and it did indeed flatter Marian's figure and coloring, but in some strange way, it just didn't seem to suit her. She was a Healer of high caliber, and her regular leggings and jackets suited her much better. "You look like a real lady," he told her. "But not quite like my cousin."

"I'd rather be your cousin," she admitted with a smile. "But there's a tiny part of me that's enjoying itself entirely."

"Well, good. There are no rules about taking your enjoyments where you find them." He contemplated her hair and its thick braid. "What about her hair, Myr? Isn't it in style for the high class to wear their hair down?"

"Down with ribbons," she agreed. She grabbed a brush and handful of pink ribbons. "You're going to knock General Quint on his butt! He'll be so distracted that Lord Tyrian could probably sneak everyone out of the city!"

Thirty minutes later, Marian was able to escape back into her own clothes for the rest of the day. The dress had been handed off to Persephone for a good washing and ironing so that it looked absolutely pristine by morning. Several people from the higher class in the city got into things, and matching shoes, gloves, and a very excessively frilly parasol were also borrowed and set aside.

Peter and Jacqueline worked around the clock with Paola, Theo, and Mayo, and come the morning, they had completed the small boat. It had been designed to be as small as it could while still holding three people. With the thin veneer of stone over the wood, not only would it resist the properties of the lake water, but it would also blend in much better.

Tyrian and Cassie left their tower right after dawn to meet up with Di and Marian. Raven was sleeping in their bed, having snuck in the night before. The guards were aware of her presence, and they knew to have Serentia or Liang fetch her if she wasn't up by breakfast. Both felt impressed with their Kaiten and Kentei; parenting was hard enough without doing it in the middle of a war.

A very sleepy eyed Miranda waited for the party in the courtyard, and she had a cup of coffee. "Eve is up," she said. She held out a plate with pastries. "She said to eat something before you go."

Marian, looking every inch the narcissist, shook her head. "My stomach is full of nerves. I couldn't eat anything right now." She did, however, accept a sip of Miranda's coffee just so she actually had something in her stomach. "I can do this," she said firmly. "I know I can. I don't look stupid, do I?" she asked her cousin.

He shook his head. "You look beautiful, Marian. Stop worrying." He looked at Di. "You've been to Gammine." At the nod, he turned to Miranda. "Focus on Di, and use her to get us to the city. We need to land behind it, and inside the woods enough to not be seen. I know you can do it."

That belief made Miranda surer in herself, and she lifted her wand with more confidence. "Here we go!"

A few moments later, the party landed safely inside the woods behind the city and out of sight. "Of course," Cassie noted dryly, "that means that the next time she ports us, we're going to land *in* the trees."

"Naturally," Tyrian said. He glanced out of the trees and saw that the boat was exactly where it was supposed to be. It had been transported there in the middle of the night under the cover of darkness. If he hadn't been looking for it, he would have never seen it. "Are you ready?" he asked Marian.

She opened her parasol and took a quick breath. "I'm ready."

General Marcus Quint was the youngest of the Lower Generals, but he was by far one of the more skilled. Even Samantha looked on his skill with a sword with respect, something he took as a high compliment. He was also highly sensitive to the fluctuations of magic in the air to the point that he always knew what relics were worn by what people in his immediate vicinity. The stronger the user, the further away he could sense them.

So, truthfully, he *felt* the commotion at the back road long before he heard it. In the middle of writing down more notes on buildings in need of immediate repair, he looked up with surprise as he sensed a strong healing type magic not far away. Curiously, it was a familiar magic.

A few moments later, he heard a woman's voice say, "Just lower the bridge before any more dirt gets on my dress!"

He sighed. It wasn't the first narcissist to enter the city in such a fashion. "Lower the bloody bridge," he muttered to the soldiers as he joined them. "Just get it done with before she makes a bigger scene. I'll escort her to the inn and smooth her feathers."

Marcus had a way with women of all ages; playboy notwithstanding, he was also a true gentleman. He just always knew exactly how to handle any given female at any given time. His soldiers, including his female soldiers, were both impressed and amused by it—and had often begged him to act as a wingman on their behalf.

The bridge lowered and a young woman in a lovely pink gown hurried across it with her parasol held to shade her face from the sun and prying eyes alike. The closer she got, the more Marcus' eyes narrowed. Suspicions churned as he walked forward. The very fact that he couldn't find the right thing to say was as much proof of who he looked on as the sight of beautiful rusty colored hair.

He offered a hand, and when she lightly placed hers on it, he drew her fingers to his lips with a bow. "Welcome to Gammine," he said. In a very soft voice, he added, "Lady Marian."

Her heart began to beat harder. For a moment, she was terrified that she had messed the entire plan up, but he simply tucked her hand into the crook of his elbow and began to escort her into the city. He acted as if everything was normal, yet she had a frightening image of being thrown in jail. Not that she thought he *would*, but there was no knowing what he thought!

"Don't be afraid," he said quietly. "I am the last person you should be afraid of, Marian. Are you here to infiltrate the defenses and find a weakness?" He suddenly smiled wryly. "Or was this Alex and Di's not so subtle way of exploiting *my* weakness?" He fully admitted that he had a fondness for women. Since he didn't use, abuse, or hurt them in any fashion, he didn't see it as such a bad fondness to have.

"Yes," she admitted softly.

"Then you have to come with me on a tour of town and see what you can pry out of me." He brought her fingers to his lips again and smiled. It was pure gut instinct when it came to Marian. He could only guess if he was making the right move or saying the right thing. He felt certain he was making a fool of himself half the time, but she never noticed. "Will you bat your lashes and flirt?"

She found herself smiling at him. He always made her smile. "That was the plan." She fluttered her lashes playfully. "Should I hang on your arm, or would that be overkill? I wouldn't want to make anyone jealous. I'm sure you've been breaking hearts all over town."

"I have never broken a heart," he told her. "Perhaps dented a few, but never broken." He took a breath and grabbed for courage. This slim Healer always seemed to take it all away. "Marian," he said quietly, seriously, "is there anyone in your life?"

Her heart started pounding again. "If you mean whether or not I am courting or have been courted, the answer is no. I've been continuously single for five years." A sad smile touched her lips. "I've never met an eligible man I wanted to court, and certainly none have come by my door."

"Would you allow me to be the first?"

She stopped dead in her tracks and looked at him in shock. "What?"

"Would you let me court you?" he asked. He brushed her hair out of her face softly. As beautiful as she looked, he missed the way she looked in her Healer's clothing. It suited her much better. "I'd have asked five years ago, but," he shrugged lightly, "I did not want you to be miserable by having a beau, possibly a husband, who you could almost never see."

"Why are you telling me now?"

"Because things are changing. And because it finally occurred to me that the reason I never quite know what to say to you has to be because you're the one who really counts. This isn't a line, Marian. The man before you is the real one. It always has been."

She took a deep breath. "Something for which I'm grateful. I've always liked the real General Marcus Quint. I'd watch you with girlfriend after girlfriend and always be so . . . so . . . so *jealous*." She found a smile though her lips trembled. "I would be very happy if you courted me, Marcus."

He bent his head to lightly brush her lips with his and lingered long enough that she softly sighed into his lips. It was the sweetest sound he had ever heard. He kissed her again, a little deeper, and heard a very distinct cheer in the background. "Is that at us?" he asked huskily.

Her body aching for his touch and her lips tingling, she still found she could be amused by the whole situation. Her lips curved. "No, that's at the flag."

"The flag?" He lifted his head quickly and looked to the tower. There, distinctly, flew the flag of the Liberation Army. He couldn't help it. He started laughing. "Checkmate, Marian. That was a very adept distraction!"

She grinned teasingly. "I was just supposed to flirt. You're the one who got so serious." She went up on her toes and kissed him quickly. He was quite a bit taller because she was short, but she had always liked that about him. A Healer should always have a good warrior to protect them.

Tyrian had to smile as he watched the scene from the tower. "I think they were both distracted," he said to Di and Cassie.

Di grinned. "Couldn't have happened to a better man."

Tyrian led the way down out of the tower, and by the time they got to the bottom, Marcus and Marian waited for them. "Greetings, General Quint," Tyrian said. "I believe that the entire city now thinks that I'm in charge instead of you. What say you to that?"

"I say you're one sneaky bastard, and you're very much like your father. And I say that with a great deal of respect." Marcus bowed gracefully. "Consider this a formal surrender, Tyrian. I will inform my troops that they are free to make their decision as to stay or return. I know my soldiers though; you can count on adding my eight units to your total count. They serve the people. The people want change."

"At this point," Tyrian said quietly, "we can say they *need* change. It's become so much more than a rebellion, Marcus. Blaine is evil. Left to her own devices, there is no one who will be safe. She's murdered indiscriminately, and she will do it again. All she wants is a Pure Relic. The Empire is nothing more than a tool. If we don't free the people from her grasp, then there won't be anything left. I need you to help me do this. Lend your strength to mine."

"It's yours," he said simply as he took Tyrian's hand. "Please accept my dedication as a Destined Star." He didn't need to see the star on his shoulder to know what he was. It was that feeling inside him that told him. The feeling that had always been there all along. He would always be grateful for the gift he had been given. "Let's go to the inn to talk, and we can get Marian out of that dress." He blinked and then sighed. "That came out wrong."

Marian giggled, and Tyrian just smiled. "Lead the way."

Chapter Thirty-Six

"The baited breath, lured by the promise of an end, held inside my heart."

Halfway toward the inn, two men hurried down the street and caught up with everyone. Marcus smiled as he saw them. "Di, you no doubt remember my lieutenants. Tyrian, Marian, please meet Dorian and Caleb. They're two of my best. Dorian, Caleb, please meet Lord Tyrian Southerwind and his cousin, Lady Marian."

Tyrian smiled. The phrase 'coming out of the woodwork' was beginning to come to mind as time passed. Here were two more Destined Stars. Better still, Dorian was a Magician with Lightning and Wind relics, thus adding more force to the magic side. Caleb carried a staff on his back in a way not dissimilar from Tyrian. "Greetings," Tyrian said. "Are you choosing to stay and fight for freedom?"

Caleb grinned. "Better than fighting for that evil broad in the castle."

"Shush!" his brother scolded. He sighed. "I apologize for my elder brother, Lord Tyrian. He has no manners."

"Why do you think General Quint appreciates me?" Caleb retorted. "I say it like it is, thank you." He eyed Marian with interest. "And we share similar hobbies."

"Hands off," Marcus told him dryly. He shook his head. "Tyrian, you can kick them out. These heathens are almost more trouble than they're worth." It was said affectionately; he considered his lieutenants to be equals and friends alike.

Dorian said, "But we earn our keep, right?"

"Most of the time."

The elder of the two brothers just smiled, his green eyes warming. "Well, I don't think Lord Tyrian can *quite* get rid of us, Marc. Dorian and I share the same star in the sky, and it is a star that follows the Kaiten's path."

"And you didn't mention this?" Marcus complained.

"You didn't ask."

"How did you know?" Tyrian asked curiously. "I'm finding that more and more people are beginning to know what they are even before I say something. And I don't think this is something you've only *just* figured out. The longer time goes on, the more it seems as if the Kaiten Star legend wasn't such a secret as we thought."

They had walked into the inn by that point, and Marian hurried off to change clothes. She had been carrying her regular stuff in her backpack so she could go back to normal quickly. She had full sympathy for Samantha and the bard incident, that was for sure.

The others sat down at a table in the dining room, and Caleb said slowly, "It's not something that's *common* knowledge, exactly. At least, it wasn't. It's getting that way now. We figured it out a few years ago when we were with Marcus in Firmeza. A traveling storyteller knew the legend and told us about it."

"Does it bother you that we know before you do?" Marcus asked.

"It doesn't bother me that you know more than I do. It bothers me that I don't know anything about my own destiny. I feel a little like I'm stumbling around in the dark."

Marian returned at that point and sat down between Marcus and Tyrian. "What's the next course of events?" she asked.

"I want to take a quick tour of the city and talk to the mayor about the city militia holding the town for us," Tyrian said, "and then we need to return to Aon Castle. We will want to meet with Matthias and Cherry to discuss how to approach Deltine." He let out a long breath. "The last checkpoint."

Following which, there were only two cities to be claimed before the movement toward Trinan. It was a staggering realization. More staggering was the thought that at any given moment, he could be forced to face his father in combat. It wasn't any surety, but his gut told him that Blaine had done something to Donald. There was no reason for him to be shut away as he was. He was not an idiot, and as much a servant of the people as the Lower Generals. More, perhaps. He would have come to the Liberation Army half a dozen times by now if something wasn't stopping him.

Cassie saw his fingers drumming on the table and softly covered his hand with hers in support. "One day at a time," she reminded him. "Stop thinking so far ahead, Tyrian. It's only going to make things harder. We need to focus on what we can change now, not what might never happen."

He let out a long breath. "Thank you," he said softly. He turned his hand over so that their fingers laced together. "With your units," he told Marcus, "the Liberation Army stands at an immediate fifty-six. We also have more than thirty additional units to call upon from their stations at the checkpoints and other cities. Do you believe that this will be enough to engage the Special Forces at Larksville and Pardue?"

"Absolutely," Marcus said. "Once we have added Vincent's units to our army, we Lower Generals can start training everyone in the specialized combat that SF soldiers get." He hesitated and then admitted, "It will also prepare them for battle with General Southerwind's troops if needed. They are entirely made of SF soldiers."

"It's not something we can pretend won't happen," Tyrian said calmly. Despite the tone, his fingers tightened with Cassie's. "And I will deal with it if and when it happens."

There was nothing anyone else at the table could say. Marian wanted to cry at the very idea of her beloved uncle and cousin having to cross weapons under any circumstance. She hadn't even liked watching them train together! Marcus, Caleb, and Dorian could do nothing except willingly shoulder the pain they felt from their Kaiten. All they could do was support him through it all.

A unit from the Liberation Army had arrived by that point, and the city was in changeover mode. The three newest Stars and Di opted to transport back with the units, so Tyrian, Cassie, and Marian were the only ones to make a tour of the city. They stopped to talk to the mayor—who promised her city militia would hold the checkpoint and be ready anytime Tyrian needed—and made the time to speak with shop owners and civilians to make sure that they would be able to recover. Many were already expressing a desire to move to Aon Castle, if only to help maintain it until the end of the war. It was the least they could do.

Tyrian returned to the castle by afternoon. With his two-woman bodyguard set, he headed immediately for the meeting room. When he walked inside, he said, "That was slightly easier than expected. Marian did her job very well." He smiled at his cousin. "And got herself a beau at the same time."

"Ha!" Alex grinned. "Good for you, Lady Marian! And good for Marcus."

Under his breath, Liang groused, "Took him damn long enough."

Marcus suddenly stepped into the doorway and lightly rested a hand on Marian's waist. "You are not wrong," he told Liang. "I suppose I just happen to be slow on the uptake." He grinned at Alex. "Though not as slow as some."

Alex saluted lightly. "She'll marry me by the end of the war."

Tyrian was no longer nonplussed by all the romances going on while a rebellion was in full swing against an evil tyrant. When he had lamented on it to Laia and how it didn't make sense, she had told him that in the midst of hate, love was the only sure weapon. That the Destined Stars would be, however unconsciously, wielding such a weapon was not a surprise. It would be more surprising if it didn't happen.

She had said something else, too. Something that still tickled his mind. "The bonds of the Destined Stars will save the world," he murmured.

"Pardon?" Matthias asked.

"Something Laia said to me. She was being mystical and all-knowing, as is her way." He sat down at the table and smiled when Marcus promptly sat down between Marian and Liang. Marcus didn't lack for nerve, which was why he was so good at his job. "On our way in," he said, "I stopped to talk to Zinfandel. She's still searching the archives for the full legend. It might hold some more answers for me. And because it won't be a secret for long, I'll say it out loud: there will be more Kaiten Stars."

"Huh." Ewan sat back in his chair. "Well, there are other countries, all with their own issues. Couple hundred years and there could be more outbreaks of war. If it happens, it happens. Other Kaitens mean other Destined Stars and other Kentei Stars. They'll be just fine."

"Was that reason from Ewan?" Kyle asked Leonard.

Leonard snorted. "A sure sign the world is ending."

Matthias hid a smile. "Welcome to the Liberation Army, General Quint. I would apologize for the underhanded tactics, but I don't see that you're overly upset to have your weakness exploited."

Marcus smiled. Under the table, he skimmed his fingers over Marian's hand. "I find myself both gratified and amused. I have no shame for liking women. They're beautiful works of art." It wasn't said as a line. He truly believed it. Because it was no different from someone who admired paintings, Marian couldn't be jealous. "I can't say I was expecting anything specific to happen, though I had a hunch the back road would be involved. Just how did you get in?" he asked Tyrian.

"Boat made of stone. While Marian was making a scene, we just sailed right up to the 'beach.' You were so busy focusing on her that you didn't even notice two Pure Relic users slipping into the city. Which was the intent, of course." Tyrian hooked an arm over the back of his chair. "All's well that ends well. Three down, one to go. There are many metaphors to be used. But they all point to the same destination."

"Deltine." Marcus nodded. "Vincent Martine is the last of the Lower Generals, and he's currently stationed there. The city is located near the Y Border, at the place where the forest collides with the mountains. The proximity of the two landscapes has created a particularly potent area of magic."

"Ah," said Night. "You refer to the Living Wood. I was wondering if it was still around."

"Living Wood?" Matthias repeated.

"The magic in the area has caused the trees of the Living Wood surrounding Deltine to become sentient. They cling to peace, and they reject any who enter with hostile intentions. All of the checkpoints, at some time, have been claimed by an enemy except for Deltine. Hell, bandits can't even get in," Marcus said. "And from what Vincent said in his last message to me, the trees have responded rather harshly to the climate of the country. They won't let anyone at all in."

"Where's the backdoor?" Matthias asked. "There is always a backdoor."

"By skipping through the Y Border, you can circle around to behind the city. The woods back there aren't alive, but they're a nasty maze. There's a branch of the Commune of Soldiers just on the outside of the maze. Supposedly, they know the way through."

Kyle nodded. "I know the branch you speak of. I am sure they would be willing to help us. I've been there, and so has Ewan, so Miranda can easily send us there. But once we get through the woods, what are we supposed to do about the city itself? I doubt just getting there will be impressive enough to get us in."

"Vincent is unpredictable," Alex said slowly. "There's really no knowing what direction he'll go. This may be one of those situations where Lord Tyrian will need to think on his feet. All I can say with certainty is that Vincent *abhors* bloodshed. His troops are brilliant and so is he, make no mistake, but he prefers to end things without battle. That's why he was best suited for Deltine."

"So even if he throws a wrench in the plan, as Tedium might say, it won't involve the risk of someone's life." Tyrian nodded slightly. "I think that will make things easier. Matthias, if you're willing to trust me, I would like to see if I can't handle this on my own. I would normally ask you to go along, but I don't want you to put undue stress on your leg." His eyes met Matthias'. "Doctor Kelan has kept me updated on your condition."

"What exactly *is* wrong with your leg?" Kyle asked bluntly. "You're beginning to alarm me, Matt."

Matthias took a long breath, and Cherry looked away. "It's a condition I've had since birth," he admitted. "For lack of any other way to describe it, there is a leak in my lifeforce."

A sudden slicing pain cut into Kyle's heart. He didn't even realize he wasn't breathing until Ewan slapped him on the back and forced him to take in a breath. "You're dying," he said flatly. "Why didn't you tell anyone?!"

"It can't be stopped," Matthias said gently. "I have long learned to live with it. It can be prolonged, but it cannot be stopped. And, frankly, the older I get, the less it can be prolonged. My leg is already dead. It's slowly making its way through the rest of me. I will see the end of the war, but I will not live much beyond it." He looked at Tyrian. "I would like to be buried near Ophelia."

Tyrian nodded. There was pain inside his heart as well, but he had suspected from the day he had met Matthias just what was wrong and what was happening. He had accepted it. "I will see to it myself," he promised. "And I will always be grateful for everything you've done, Matt. Your life would have been longer had you not been here with me."

The strategist smiled. "But my life would not have been nearly as fulfilling. I am honored that this is my last task to accomplish."

Kyle said nothing. It was like salt in a wound that had not yet healed. Matthias had been like his brother as well. From the day Ophelia had accepted Kyle's suit, Matthias had opened his heart to the younger man and become family. To lose not just Ophelia but also Matthias was excruciatingly painful, particularly close together.

Cassie had been suspicious for a long while; there were no secrets between her and Tyrian. To hear it said plainly was still daunting. She curled her hand around Tyrian's under the table. It was little comfort to think that Matthias would have died anyway, even if he hadn't been part of the Destined Stars.

Tyrian brought the subject back around with a visible exertion of his iron will. "I will take Cassie, Ewan, Kyle, and Marian with me to the Commune of Soldiers. The sixth place will be reserved for whomever our escort turns out to be. Once we're through the woods, I'll play it by ear."

"We will have General Quint and a few others standing by," Matthias said, "just in case we need Miranda to transport in reinforcements."

"Good." Tyrian got to his feet. "In that case, I say we get moving now. Depending on what information we get from the Commune, we might be best going through the woods at night, anyway."

Those going with him also got to their feet. Marian briefly kissed Marcus and then grinned when Liang muttered under his breath. "Don't grouse," she scolded. "He can beat you at arm-wrestling, and you know it." With a flounce of rusty hair, she followed her cousin out of the meeting room. The doors shut behind her, and her smile faded as she hugged Kyle. "I'm sorry," she said softly.

He let out a long breath. "I can handle this. It's settling in a little easier than it did when he first said it. Maybe because somehow I always knew. It was just this feeling inside." He hugged her back and then gratefully gripped Tyrian's hand when it settled on his shoulder. "Thank you," he said quietly. "I'm sorry I can't be a better support for you, Tyrian."

"You're here," Tyrian said simply. "And you and Ewan are two of my best friends now. I think it's fair to say we have a give-and-take relationship. We're even."

It was more of a comfort than Kyle had expected. Even with so many tragic things happening, there were still bright moments. A part of him couldn't help but wonder if their appreciation for the brighter moments was *because* of the tragic ones.

Miranda was more than happy to transport them to the Commune of Soldiers. There was only one tiny problem, though. When she swung her wand around, she smacked a passing guard and completely lost her concentration. The party found themselves landing inside the city alright, but they landed *in* the trees. Dangling upside down by his knees, Tyrian just sighed. "Cassie, let it be known this is the only time I've ever wanted you to be wrong."

His lover also sighed from where she was caught between two branches. "So noted."

"Nice of you to drop in," a female voice said dryly. "Most use the gates, you know."

Tyrian turned his head and found himself nose-to-nose with a slender young woman possessing a mane of curly, tawny colored hair. She wore the familiar short bodice and split skirt of a dagger user, and she had two of the blades equipped. One on her hip, and the other in a sheath around her upper leg. "Our transporter seems to have a problem with her aim," he told her. "We were aiming for the gates."

"I'd hate to see what would have happened if you'd aimed for the trees!" She grinned. She knew full well who the green-eyed male in the tree was, and she liked him a lot more than she had expected. He was such a fascination! He seemed really serious and mature, but there was a really strong intensity inside him that commanded attention. "I'm Tandy," she said. "You're Tyrian."

"Correct. Hang on." He pulled himself up onto the branch properly and then swung his legs around and dropped to the ground. The others were slowly disentangling themselves as well, and Cassie was luckily close enough to help Ewan. Men of his size did not belong in trees. "Greetings, Tandy," Tyrian said. "It's nice to meet you."

"Well met, indeed!" She propped her hands on her hips as she studied him. "You're my age. I wasn't expecting that. And you're really attractive, so I guess some rumors were doing you justice."

He didn't bat a lash. "Thank you."

She laughed. "Wow, nothing fazes you. That's really awesome." She linked her hands behind her back as she leaned forward to peer up into his face. There was a strong tug inside her heart that told her this was someone in serious need of a laugh or two. He needed her levity to help him get through things. "I'm one of your Stars, aren't I?"

He held out a hand and smiled when she took it firmly. There was nothing shy about Tandy, and he couldn't help but adore her for it. His relic glowed softly and the answering star glowed from her shoulder. "Seems so. I need your strength, Tandy. Help me win this fight."

"Done," she said instantly. "It's so boring here anyway!"

"Tandy!" a young man scolded as he approached. "Now what trouble are you getting into?"

She sniffed and turned up her nose. "You have no say in my life, Hiro. You won't even court me because you can't name your sword! You have forfeited all right to tell me what to do."

The young man shot her a look of combined frustration and exasperation. He made a striking contrast to Tandy in all ways. Where she didn't hold still and moved with vibrant energy, he was very quiet and serene. Even in coloring, they were perfect opposites. He stood roughly the same height as Tyrian, but he held a slimmer physique.

He was also a Destined Star. Tyrian smiled at him. "I'm Tyrian Southerwind."

"Well met." The young man caught a handful of Tandy's skirt before she flounced off. Even when she glared at him, he kept hold and kept her tethered. "I'm Hiro." He spotted Ewan and Kyle finally getting out of the trees, and his eyes widened as he recognized them. "You're Kyle Raitels and Ewan Grizmar!"

"The same," Ewan said with a salute.

"Hiro!" Tandy said in annoyance. "Let go of my skirt! I have no compunctions about ripping it to get away, and if you want to strip me, you'd better be courting me first!" Her skirt was promptly let go and she walked off in a huff.

Hiro sighed. "My apologies, Lord Tyrian. Tandy is . . . temperamental."

"That would be why I liked her," Ewan noted with a grin. "So am I."

"More's to the pity of Tyrian's sanity," Cassie said dryly as she helped Marian out of the tree as well. "Thankfully there aren't too many of you."

Temperamental types were known for being unpredictable and liable to lose their temper on a moment's notice. There was nothing wrong with such a thing, but they certainly kept their friends and families on their toes! It was another reason that many looked at Ewan with anticipation: seeing him end up with a temperamental daughter would be icing on the cake, and suitable revenge.

Tyrian just shook his head. "Don't worry, Hiro. I think she's a very lively and lovely young woman. But you can't court her yet because of naming your sword?"

"Yes and no," Kyle offered. "Technically, Hiro has every right to court her as long as both are eighteen. *But* he won't be able to actually marry her until he's an adult in the eyes of the Commune. A lot of swordsmen and women will refrain from courting anyone until they're adults because they don't want their loved one to wait indefinitely."

Hiro nodded. "Exactly so. I just turned eighteen, so I am the right age to court someone. But I have yet to prove my worth. And, well." He sighed. "It would be my unfortunate luck that Tandy is the daughter of the Commune leader and his wife."

Ewan winced. "Yikes. That would add a new level of stress. Who is your instructor?" At Hiro's helpless look, Ewan whistled softly. "Damn, kid. You really got yourself into a pickle. So the Commune leader is your instructor *and* a parent of the girl you want. Nice."

Tyrian lifted his brows at Kyle who obligingly explained, "Every new swordsman or woman is taken under the wing of an experienced adult. Only that instructor can determine when the new Soldier is ready to be an adult. Normally, the instructor is in agreement with the Commune leader, but there have been disagreements in the past. The instructor typically wins."

"But since Hiro's instructor *is* the Commune leader," Tyrian surmised, "he was already having to prove himself twice without adding Tandy to the mix." He smiled wryly. "Ewan's right. That's some pickle to be in." He cocked his head as a new thought occurred to him. "How is it that only those who use swords are required to go through such a rigorous testing? Is Tandy more of an adult or less of one because she uses daggers?"

Kyle shook his head. "The easiest way to say it is to say that Tandy is a regular soldier, and those who name their swords are special forces. Anyone who comes out of a Commune is damned good, but the Commune was originally founded on just swords users. So if you use a sword, you've got a much higher standard to live up to. You have to prove you're worthy of carrying on the Commune name."

"That makes sense," Tyrian decided. "And thank you for the explanation. I've been wondering for a while how it all worked." He looked at Hiro. "Will you be allowed to join my fight even if you haven't named your sword? You're one of mine as well, Hiro." It was said simply and was all the more powerful for the simplicity.

"Likely so," Hiro said. "Perhaps it will be what earns me the right to be an adult." He frowned. "Were you here looking solely for Tandy and I?"

"That was the welcome side benefit. We need to get through the woods to the back of Deltine. Supposedly people here know the way."

"I know it," Hiro offered. "So does Tandy. Either of us can show you the way." He suddenly went very still, his head turning sharply. "Tandy. She's in trouble." He took off like a shot through the Commune and ducked around people and buildings as he headed for the entrance to the woods. "Did anyone see Tandy?" he asked urgently, but no one had noticed her going past. That alone was odd; Tandy was always noticeable.

By the time Tyrian and the others caught up, Hiro had gotten partway into the woods. He was standing next to a tree and staring at a note pinned to it. Tyrian gently put a hand on his shoulder in support and Marian yanked the note free. "'I have the girl,'" she read. "'Come and get her before it's too late.' It's signed by General Martine." She frowned. "Wait. That's odd."

"Let me see." Cassie took the note and briefly studied it. "This is his handwriting, I am sure of it. Huh. Interesting. Marcus and Alex swore that Vincent would never hurt someone, and Tandy is innocent of anything except having a temper."

"The back door," Tyrian said softly. "I see. He's giving us an excuse to come into Deltine. If we can make it to the city, we have a legitimate excuse to go inside to negotiate."

"You're sure he won't hurt Tandy?" Hiro asked.

"Positive," Tyrian said instantly. "But that doesn't mean we can take our time. She's not going to be happy, and I'd like to find Vincent whole and healthy so that he can join us as well. Temperamental types tend to act before thinking."

Night snorted. "Ewan's picture is next to the word in the dictionary."

"And you're one to talk," his wielder muttered.

"I'm going with you." Hiro's hands curled into fists at his side. "I have to go along to get her back. I can't claim her as my own yet, but I love her more than anything. And she'll have my ass if I don't rescue her," he added on a wince.

As they said, Tyrian thought, sharing a smile with Cassie, opposites attracted.

Chapter Thirty-Seven

"Reach out; you can touch the stars."

Because they had planned ahead for the sixth spot, it was easy for Hiro to fall into the party. He took the point position as they headed into the woods, and it didn't take very long for the others to realize why it was such a good idea to have a guide. The woods looked identical no matter where they went, and the path twisted in a million directions.

It also didn't take very long for the monsters to find them. Tyrian found himself once more in the position of sorcerer, and it greatly amused him. He didn't mind too terribly the role, but he knew his relic was made more for specialized attacks than actually doing general magical damage. Still, with three swordsmen, it made more sense for him to move back in the lineup, even if he only used raw magic instead of the actual spells.

As they finished one set and continued down the path, Ewan noted to Hiro, "You're good, kid."

Indeed, there was no denying Hiro had many skills with a sword. "Skill isn't everything," he said with a wry smile and a shrug. "I think part of my problem is that I'm not very assertive. I prefer to listen rather than take command."

"There's nothing wrong with that," Marian said staunchly. "Being quiet doesn't mean you're not mature!"

Cassie glanced at Tyrian with a smile. "We are who we are because we are what Tyrian needs to support him. So the fact that you are a quiet type means you balance for those with the biggest voices. And I don't mean just Ewan. We have quite a few, hmm, *forceful* Stars too."

Tyrian thought about Laia and Liang and a few others as well. "Bossy is another word." He stopped walking suddenly and covered his relic hand as he felt a strong presence.

He wasn't the only one to notice. Cassie made the same gesture, and Kyle and Marian looked around. Night was the one who first realized what they had sensed. "There's a mage in the vicinity. A strong one too. But non-elemental; they must have a non-combat relic or two."

Feeling a light tug inside, Tyrian turned off the path and moved deeper into the woods. The trees were much thicker in this area, and it was hard to see clearly where he went. He didn't worry about getting lost. Hiro would easily get them re-sorted again.

To his immense shock, when he pushed between some trees, he

found himself looking at a tiny clearing, and in the middle of it lay a baby griffin. The beast reached no higher than his hip, and it was still covered in the soft down of fledgling years. Its paws were proportionately too big, making it both gangly and adorable.

Kyle went for his sword but Tyrian held up a hand. "Hold," he said.

"You don't have a Listening Relic," Cassie reminded him. "You can't know what it is thinking."

"I don't need one." Tyrian walked without fear over to the griffin and knelt down beside it. "Hi," he said softly. He gently rubbed his fingers over the griffin's beak and was rewarded by a sound that blended both purr and trill. "All types," he said. "It really does take all types."

"A griffin is a Destined Star?" Hiro asked incredulously.

"Remind me to tell you about the Kraken in the river," Ewan said dryly.

"*Kraken*?!"

The griffin clearly seemed to know where it belonged. It very happily rubbed against Tyrian and made its trilling noise. It hopped to its feet and ran around in loping circles before flying into the air and doing a loop. It landed again and sat happily at Tyrian's side like a large dog might. "You've been claimed," Kyle said warmly. "Griffins are very possessive of their prides and all members within."

"Her name is Xero."

The soft feminine voice surprised all except Tyrian. He had sensed her presence as soon as he had gotten close. "Come out," he said softly. He looked toward the trees and held out a hand. "It's alright," he coaxed. "You know I won't harm you."

A slender figure stepped out of the trees but clung close to their sheltering branches. If she was over thirteen, it wasn't by very much. She was a lovely young girl, and the presence of canine ears and a fluffy tail were distinct traits marking her as at least half-Mongra. The tail, her ears, and her hair had the same cobalt blue color as her doe-shaped eyes. She had a relatively Human-like appearance otherwise, which came as no surprise. Fliers, Mongra, and Grimalkin—the avian, canine, and feline races in the world—could be more or less Human in appearance depending on their personal genetics, even among full-bloods. Hazards of many, many millennia of cross-breeding.

The presence of durable shorts and a sleeveless tunic seemed to indicate she lived in the woods. On her right hand was a Listening Relic. On her left was a Voice Relic. She clung to the trees, and her legs trembled with visible fear. "Are you taking Xero with you?" she whispered.

Tyrian stepped closer slowly as if approaching a wild animal. It broke his heart that she would be afraid of them. It didn't take his insight to guess she had been abused and run away. "You can come with her," he offered gently. "What's your name?"

"Lupe." She looked at his hand with a combination of longing and fear. She could feel that he wouldn't hurt her. He would be there to protect her, and she could protect him. She just somehow knew that he needed her. But it was so scary! "Are . . . are you Imperial soldiers?"

Ewan bit back a particularly violent oath so that he didn't alarm Lupe further. His hands curled into fists at his side, and he was barely aware of both Cassie and Marian grabbing his wrists. If he found out which soldiers had traumatized this puppy, he would bust heads.

"No," Tyrian told Lupe. "We're from the Liberation Army. We're trying to save the Empire." He was close enough to touch her, but all he did was kneel down to be less of an imposing figure. "My name is Tyrian," he told her. "I swear on the relic I wear that you will *always* be safe at Aon Castle. The monk is Cassie. The Healer is Marian. The blond is Kyle. The slender swordsman is Hiro. And the big guy is Ewan. He's not as scary as he looks. He loves kids. How old are you, Lupe?"

"Fourteen." In a soft rush of breath she said, "Please take me with you! I won't take up a lot of space! I can be in the convoy for now, can't I? Xero and I. We won't get in the way!" She shook her head and her thick hair flew around her face. Her eyes looked wide and distressed. "Just don't sell me!"

"Sell . . ." He choked on the words, horrified at the very idea. Very, very softly, he asked, "Who tried to sell you, Lupe?"

The intensity in him was suddenly palpable, but it didn't frighten her. If anything, it began to reassure her. "I was orphaned in Foresalia," she said softly. "The Imperial Army brought me home as a slave. But I wasn't useful. They were going to sell me back to Foresalia as . . . as some sort of bargaining chip."

Ewan and Kyle both walked away in different directions. They were quiet, but Cassie's hearing had enhanced thanks to her relic and she heard them both quite clearly. She also learned several new ways to use words she had already known. She hardly blamed them. Her hands fisted over her stomach as if to combat the knot of sheer fury inside. Incidents like the one Lupe described were incredibly rare across the world as a whole, but they did happen. If word reached the monks about such a thing, someone would be dispatched to free the one in captivity.

Fiercely, Marian burst out, "You would never be sold, Lupe! Tyrian loves his Destined Stars, and I know you have to be one! You can come to the castle and everyone will love you, too! When the war is over, you'll be able to choose your own destiny!"

Xero trilled fiercely and butted against Tyrian. She then flapped her wings and butted Lupe. The young mage took a quick breath and said, "She says that you have a beautiful heart. That you couldn't hurt anyone at all. And she says . . . says that you need us. So please take us with you."

Tyrian held out his hand and hers cautiously settled onto his palm. She was a foot and a half shorter than he was, and a great deal smaller with it. The back of her hand from her lower knuckles and her lower arms to her elbows were covered in the same soft fur as her tail and ears. He curled his hand around hers gently, and the white star appeared on her shoulder as well as Xero's wing. "There," he said. "Now you know you belong."

She hesitated and then hugged him around the neck tightly. He hugged her back gently and got to his feet. There was something so pure, so beautiful about Lupe's heart that he had no doubt the entire castle would love her instantly. Her ability to communicate with animals and beasts would also be *very* useful.

Ewan and Kyle had rejoined them, and though both found real smiles for Lupe, it was fairly obvious both were still very pissed off. Tyrian counted himself exceedingly lucky that it was only Ewan who got loud and violent. Kyle got quiet, and then he got revenge.

Lupe clung close to Tyrian's side, staying just behind him so he was free to attack anything that came after them. Xero flew beside Lupe though she occasionally landed and walked as well. Hiro once more took point, and they continued through the woods. The going proved much easier this time; the monsters recognized Lupe and diverted rather than attack.

They didn't bother to stop and camp when night fell. A lantern gave them plenty of light to see by, and none of them felt excessively tired. There were also thoughts of Tandy as well. Not as much her safety as Vincent's, though. Unless the general had been talking fast, there was no doubt that he would be the one worse the wear for snagging the temperamental dagger thrower.

"Temperaments and projectiles." Kyle shook his head wryly. "If that ever gets combined with someone who can also use a sword, I'll be hiding in a bunker."

They reached the edge of the woods just as dawn arrived and they could see the city line. As expected, the soldiers in Vincent's eight units were not actually standing guard anywhere. There was no need for it, frankly: the two parts of the woods provided plenty of protection. But the soldiers were still visible as they wandered around. All of them either helped citizens or oversaw reconstruction.

"Is it just me," Marian whispered, "or did they jump the gun, as Shots would say? This looks like what happens *after* we've freed a city!"

"For all intents and purposes," Cassie whispered back, "we have. With no worry for the Imperial Army getting in here, General Martine was free to capitalize on the events of other checkpoints. He's had plenty of time to gain the trust of the people and prove he isn't a bad guy."

"I wonder where he's holding Tandy," Hiro said softly.

Rather suddenly, they all heard a familiar voice yell, "That's the stupidest thing I've *ever* heard! Couldn't you have come up with something *smarter* than this? Why me!? Ooh! I'm going to stab you! My boyfriend's going to kill you!"

Ewan barely muffled a snort of laughter as he clapped a resigned Hiro on the back. "Her confidence in you is heartwarming."

"At least we found her," Cassie said dryly.

"Bloody hell!" a man was heard saying in distinct exasperation as he walked out of a building not far away. Marian, Tyrian, and Cassie recognized him as being the general they sought. His short hair looked slightly frazzled, and the reason why was explained when he raked his hands through it and mussed the locks more. "I just had to grab the fireball," he muttered loudly.

"I heard that!" Tandy yelped from inside the building. "Untie me!"

Vincent Martine eyed the building with rueful and reluctant amusement. He had grabbed her because he had seen her talking to Tyrian. He hadn't quite expected to discover that she had a temperament fierier than a volcano and just about as unpredictable too. He had tried to explain the situation, but she wasn't listening.

When he saw the party approaching him, he was relieved for more than the simple fact of freeing the city. Even with his soldiers working quickly, the people knew that they were still technically under Imperial control, and at any given time, Vincent could be yanked and replaced. Morale was higher than when he had arrived, but not by much. He walked forward a few steps and smiled. "Greetings, Lord Tyrian."

"Greetings, General Martine." Tyrian smiled wryly. "I believe you bit off more than you can chew."

"Tyrian!" Tandy shouted as she recognized his voice. "Get me out of here!"

Vincent winced. "You may be right, Lord Tyrian." He swept his gaze over those present and recognized all except the griffin and the girl. The slim swordsman was familiar from the Commune. "You are Hiro, correct?"

he asked. "Your taste is . . . interesting."

Hiro lifted his chin, his courage bolstered by the way Kyle and Ewan moved to stand behind him. He knew they trusted him. "There's a match for everyone. Tandy is mine." He drew his sword and took an offensive stance. "I swore by my sword to defend her. Draw your weapon and fight me!"

Inside the house, Tandy's jaw dropped. Was that *her* Hiro out there? He was challenging the *general* on her behalf?!

Vincent studied Hiro for long moments and then drew his sword as a little smile tugged at his lips. He had been friends with Samantha for many years. He knew the intricacies of the Commune of Soldiers as well as a member did. "If I decided to let her go without a fight," he asked mildly, "would you stay your blade?"

"No."

"Don't throw the fight," Kyle warned Vincent. "Don't shame Hiro's duty as Tandy's sworn defender."

Lupe ducked behind Ewan to avoid watching the fight. Cassie and Marian moved back a few steps with Tyrian and Kyle to remove themselves from any flying sparks. Xero sat at Ewan's side, her ears back. If she didn't like the outcome, someone would get bitten!

The duel began, and Vincent realized very swiftly that there was no need to throw the fight. Hiro was *damned* good. His smaller frame gave him an added agility that made up for his slightly lesser strength. It was only slightly, though; he swung a sword almost as hard as Samantha did.

It took only a handful of minutes before Hiro managed to disarm Vincent, though it was a very tense few minutes. Both men bore the wounds of strikes that had gotten through defenses. Hiro aimed the tip of his sword at the general's neck and said, "Yield or die." His blue eyes sharpened like shards of glass.

"Yield," Vincent said. He held out a key. "Free your lover. She might go for my eyes."

Hiro snatched the key out of his hand and ran into the house quickly. Vincent only then winced and pressed a hand to his ribs where Hiro's foot had landed. "Damn, that kid is good. Why hasn't he named his sword yet?"

Marian hurried forward to heal him, and Tyrian said, "He is not yet an adult in the eyes of the Commune. Hopefully, that will change now." He stepped forward and lifted his chin slightly. His green eyes glittered fiercely and made him look every inch the hero that he was. "We can consider his win as my win, or you can now engage *me* in a duel, General Martine. You blatantly challenged me to find you. I did. It's your move."

Vincent held up his hands. "Yield, Lord Tyrian," he said softly. "You know I could never raise a weapon against you." He pressed his hand to his heart and bowed gracefully. "Please accept my dedicated service as a Destined Star." He blew out a quick breath. "And thank you for making sense of everything."

"Yay Tyrian!" Tandy had come out of nowhere and jumped and hugged Tyrian happily. "You have all the checkpoints!"

Tyrian actually staggered a step when that sank in. The enormity of what he had done simply boggled his mind. He controlled all four checkpoints. He controlled nearly all cities of the Empire. He could lay claim to an army of nearly one hundred units—one hundred thousand solders. He had eighty-one out of one hundred and nine Destined Stars.

That he would find twenty-eight Stars in the final two cities was an impossibility. A part of him feared he might have missed someone. A bigger part was afraid that this meant the war was not nearly as close to being completed as he thought.

Tandy released him and frowned. "Tyrian?"

Cassie moved to take Tyrian's arm. "He's fine," she said softly. "Go into the city. We'll meet you there." She waited until the footsteps had faded before framing Tyrian's face with her hands. "Tyrian?"

His eyes focused on her. "I just . . . it just hit me. What I've done. What I've yet to do. I can't shake the feeling, Cassie. Something terrible is about to happen. I can't be close to winning when I've got so many other Destined Stars to find. We still don't have the rest of the Kaiten legend, and Kell still can't find anything on Blaine. I just . . . there are too many questions left. I wanted it to be over. But even saying there are only three cities left including Trinan . . . it's not over."

"No it isn't," she agreed readily. "But, Tyrian, stop thinking about how long it has to go. Look at how fast it's gone. It hasn't yet been a year, and we've come so far." She went on her toes and kissed him softly, lingering until the tension fled his body and his hands curled around her waist. "I'm here," she promised. "I won't let you break."

He let out a long breath and rested his forehead against hers. There was nothing in his world that was as important as Cassie and Raven. If they had needed it from him, he would have walked away from this burden without hesitation. But then, perhaps that was the very reason they stood there beside him. "I'll be fine," he said softly. He kissed her tenderly and then teasingly nipped at her lower lip. "Monks are indeed lethal," he added huskily.

Her lips curved. "You better believe it."

By the time they caught up with the others, they had already gotten to the inn. Lupe was very nervous of all the people coming and going, and she stayed hidden behind Ewan. If his posture was any indication, only a real idiot would try to get to the little Mongra. Kyle and Marian sat at a table with Vincent, and Hiro attempted to keep Tandy from arguing with the innkeeper. Xero tried to help too; she had a beak full of Tandy's skirt and kept tugging.

"I've notified my troops," Vincent told Tyrian. "They stand by you as well. The mayor is on his way to speak with you about the city militia holding down the fort, so to speak. And I believe that the Commune leader is on his way as well."

Hiro grimaced. "I'm doomed."

"You are not!" Tandy grabbed onto his arm and scowled at him. "You were *amazing*, Hiro! And I know that Kyle and Ewan and Tyrian will completely stand by what you did! You didn't even hesitate to take up arms against a guy bigger and older than you!"

"Not sure I like the older part," Vincent grumbled. He glanced at the door as two Magicians hurried in, and he smiled. "You're late."

"Sorry!" The female smiled, and her pale brown eyes sparkled. A cap of auburn hair was cut close around her lively features. On her hip rested a heavy-duty wand with a crystal at the top. One hand bore a Fire Relic. The other bore a Light Relic. The second was known mostly for its ability to give light, but it could also produce powerful attacks. "Klint and I were tangled up with trying to figure out why we can't get that one house back onto its foundation."

Her brother—he had to be related considering they shared matching coloring—sighed. He was dressed in a similar fashion to his sister, and his right hand had a Water Relic while the left had a Dark Relic. Its presence alone indicated he was skilled; few could successfully equip a Dark Relic. "Kris tried everything she could, but it won't budge."

"Hmm. It may need to be rebuilt from scratch." Vincent gestured to Tyrian. "Kris, Klint, meet Tyrian Southerwind. Lord Tyrian, allow me to introduce you to two of my unit leaders. They're the best Magicians I have."

Kris looked at Tyrian curiously, having been wondering all along just what sort of person he was. What she saw looked somehow familiar. She just felt as if she had always intended to meet him. Having heard about all the goings-on, she suspected she knew just what the surprising punch of emotion inside meant. "I think we've met."

"I think you're right," Tyrian agreed. "I would ask that you and Klint lend me your strength not just for Vincent, but for me as well. I can't do this without you two. My magical troops are limited for skilled unit leaders."

"You can count on us!" Klint said fiercely. "We won't let you down, Lord Tyrian!"

A sudden commotion at the door had everyone turning to see a swordsman arguing quite loudly with a soldier. "Where is my daughter?" he demanded in a near roar. "Kidnapped! I'll have the head of whoever did it!"

Very blandly, Kyle said to Hiro, "So it's genetic? You have my future sympathies."

"Daddy!" Tandy said in exasperation. "I'm right here and I'm fine! Hiro saved me! Didn't he, Lord Tyrian?" She looked at Tyrian pleadingly as her father stormed into the inn, hoping he would help Hiro stand up to her father.

To her surprise, however, Hiro took a step forward and said, "I battled Vincent Martine to retrieve Tandy. I swore by my sword to defend her, and I did so. Whether you think I should have or not, I don't particularly care. Nothing will stop me from being by her side."

"You can't marry her," the Commune leader reminded him. "You're not an adult."

"So be it. If she wants me, I am still hers. I'll court her for however long it takes until I can marry her." He looked at Tandy and found himself smiling at the way her mouth hung open. It happened very rarely that she was speechless. "Would you be happy with that, Tandy?" he asked her.

Her response was to jump into his arms and knock him onto his ass. Wildly happy, she kissed him in front of everyone. All she had *ever* wanted was for the silly man to just let her make the choice. She would wait forever for him. If it was for Hiro, she could learn patience.

"I think that was a yes," Ewan said with a grin.

"So it would seem." A tiny smile tugged at the Commune leader's lips. "Hiro?" When the young man looked up at him, the leader said, "You have shown bravery, skill, and maturity all within the space of a few hours. You prove yourself an adult, not a child, in your words and manner alike, and as is my right as your instructor, I declare you to be a full adult with the right to name your sword and walk the world with the respect you deserve."

Shy Lupe let out a happy cheer and then hastily covered her mouth. Ewan just laughed and ruffled her hair. "I couldn't have said it better myself, pup!"

Calling a Mongra a pup or puppy was no different from calling one a kid. It could be endearment or insult. Lupe knew full well that Ewan meant it as an endearment. He had a very beautiful heart beneath his gruff exterior.

"When are you going to marry me?" Tandy demanded of Hiro.

"Soon enough," he managed to say. Shock was written all over his face. "I . . . I was not expecting that."

"You never are," Kyle said simply. "It's why we have instructors, Hiro. They see much clearer than we do when we hit that invisible point where we are an adult. I've often thought maybe that point happens when we're not looking for it, rather like finding love."

"Yeah. Wow."

"What're you going to name your sword?" Tandy asked eagerly. "We can go get it engraved!" Her heart skipped a beat and her pulse fluttered as he gave her one of those looks that made her feel as if she was the only woman in his world. His eyes were *so* unfair. "Hiro?" It dawned on her, and her lips trembled. "You wouldn't."

"I've planned for it since we were five," he said simply. "My sword will be named *Tandy*, just like the woman I love."

Tyrian rested a hand on Kyle's shoulder in silent support. The blond swordsman said nothing, but he did cover Tyrian's hand with his own. He focused only on his happiness for Hiro and Tandy. The pain seemed to lessen a little more every day as he found new reasons to smile and live.

The mayor arrived only moments later and was more than happy to sit down with Vincent and Tyrian. While they conferred, Hiro and Tandy went to find the Weaponsmith in town so that he could get his sword engraved. Kris and Klint went along to show the way. Ewan and Kyle went to meet up with the Liberation Army unit that was transporting in. As soon as Vincent had yielded, Kyle had sent the beacon signal to the castle.

One hour later, Tyrian held up the Echo Mirror. Most everyone was going back with the units, but Lupe, Xero, Cassie, and Marian had stayed with Tyrian. Deltine was officially liberated now, and the flag of the Liberation Army flew high from the tops of the towers and buildings. All militia soldiers now wore Tyrian's colors as well.

When they arrived back at the castle, Tyrian was surprised to find Merlot waiting for him. "Merlot, is something wrong?"

"We don't know, but we found some writings of Lady Tanelia's," Merlot explained. "It might have some information that you can use. We skimmed through it, but we didn't read it, and we're not sure what's in it. We thought you should be the first to look inside."

Tyrian nodded. "I'm on my way. Marian, can you take Lupe to get a room? Xero can go with her; she's not too big to be in the castle." He smiled when Xero chirped. He didn't need a Listening Relic to understand his Stars. "You're welcome."

Lupe was happy to go with Marian, and Cassie followed Tyrian as he pointedly headed for the Belowgrounds where the Library had been placed. Merlot and Zinfandel were working on filling the shelves with their copies of books, but there were still stacks all over the place, and it was even more of a disaster than usual with the recent search.

"Where did you find it?" Tyrian asked as he walked in.

"In the history section, of all places." Zinfandel shook her head as she put the slim twilight colored book down on a table. "It belatedly makes sense. I mean, Lady Tanelia lived through history, so her memoirs could be taken as fact."

Tyrian lightly ran a finger over the embossed lettering on the front of the book. It was truly a beautiful volume. Whoever had bound the writings had done it with a great deal of respect for Lady Tanelia. With a little breath, he sat down and opened the book. He was aware of Cassie's presence as she stood behind him, and he felt grateful for the way her hands rested on his shoulders.

The first few pages detailed the legend of the mirror in the sky. Tanelia had been there to see it happen. Awe filled him as he realized that rumor was right. Tanelia was over one million years old. Her Pure Time Relic was the first Pure Relic to exist. She was the oldest living being . . . and she was alone. It broke his heart.

The next few pages detailed the reactions of her town and family. A little shiver went down his back.

My sister . . . my sister was not happy. She felt that she should have received a gift from the gods too.

The sudden suspicion inside him was horrible to think, and should have been impossible to be true. But . . . it would make sense of everything. He needed to ask Tanelia.

Her prophecy of the Kaiten Stars was written down as well, but he suddenly didn't have any desire to read it. He closed the book. "I'll wait," he said. "Reading this now is just going to agitate me. I know it. I can barely think about *my* war, let alone future wars for future Kaitens. When this is done . . . then I'll read it. I have to focus on now."

"We'll put the book somewhere safe," Merlot promised. "Did it have anything useful though?"

"It might have," Tyrian said softly. He looked up at Cassie. "We need to find Lane and ask him how to contact Lady Tanelia. I have some questions for her. She might very well know exactly what is going on and who Blaine is."

Cassie shook her head. "It's mid-morning and you haven't slept in nearly twenty-four hours. You're going to eat something and get some rest. We're back into the planning stages. Our next stop is Pardue. Matthias and Cherry can start the process without you."

He stood with a frown. "But . . ."

"But nothing!" She began to haul him along behind her as she headed out of the library. "They can wait until tomorrow morning." She pointedly rubbed her thumb over the mark of his relic and watched his eyes darken with intense hunger that seemed to only get stronger as time passed. It was a blatant seduction, but she had no qualms about using every weapon at her disposal to make her lover take the breaks he needed in order to survive the coming days.

As her fingers lightly skimmed the mark again, he snatched her up into his arms with a speed that made her pulse happily flutter. "You've convinced me," he said, his voice husky as he headed back to ground level and carried her toward the castle and their tower. "You, my lady monk, are a tease. You won't always get your way by seducing me."

Her lips curved. "No, but I will most of the time." She nipped at his jaw. "The rest of the time, you can have your way by seducing me. Fair enough?"

He could find nothing to argue with about that. Who would have thought bargaining with someone as stubborn as he was, and losing, would be so rewarding in the end?

Chapter Thirty-Eight

"Sometimes the sun doesn't set; sometimes the stars don't shine."

Tyrian's rest was cut much shorter than expected. He was awakened before dawn the following morning by the sound of shouting from the tower watch points. "To arms!" a guard shouted. "The Imperial Army approaches!"

Both Tyrian and Cassie leapt out of bed and rushed into their clothes. Tyrian's mouth was dry, his pulse pounding hard. He almost couldn't breathe as they rushed the elevator down to the courtyard and then ran across to the closest tower. He took the steps three at a time, his feet barely touching the stone. "Where?" he demanded when he got to the top.

The guard handed over the telescope. "To the north," he said. His face was drawn and his eyes deeply alarmed. It wasn't fear for the Rebellion. It was fear for Lord Tyrian and what he was about to see.

Tyrian looked to the distance and his stomach rolled violently. There were twenty units slowly approaching, and all wore the colors of the High General. At this distance, even with the scope, he couldn't make out who rode at the front. But . . . he knew. "We have half an hour at most," he said, and his voice somehow stayed calm. "Gather the Lower Generals and Professor Matthias. I also want Ewan, Kyle, and Lane. I will meet them at the meeting room."

"Yes, sir!" The guard saluted and hurried down out of the tower. The entire city and castle was waking, soldier and civilian alike beginning to rally and prepare for war.

Tyrian's legs gave out and he sank down onto the ground. Cassie leapt forward and held onto him fiercely, her heart breaking. "Tyrian."

"Why?" His voice broke on the word as he pressed his face to her stomach. "Why, Cassie? Why is this happening? All I wanted . . . all I wanted was to stop the Emperor from destroying our country. Why did Blaine have to get involved?"

A soft lavender light filled the air and Tanelia walked out of it. Her eyes looked dark and sad. "I'm sorry, Tyrian," she said softly. "In the end, this may well be my fault." Her gaze lowered. "Blaine . . . is my twin sister. I am sure you had guessed from my memoirs."

"If Kyle can't blame me for what my mother did, then I can't blame you for your sister." His hands curled into fists at his side. He was only dimly aware of Cassie's presence as a glowing light inside that he clung onto with all his will. He wanted to scream that any of this had ever happened, but the screams remained locked inside. "She hates you for your eternity."

"And has sought for a million years to have her own. There is nothing good inside her, Tyrian. Too late, I saw that she was evil. She has . . . she has destroyed my happiness as well." Tanelia shook her head slightly. "It matters not what she has done to me. I knew, many years ago, that she would cross the path of the first Kaiten. And I can only say . . . I'm so sorry."

"No." The word was low and forceful. "Do not *dare* apologize for the evil of your sister. She does not even deserve to be called your kin." He looked up, and his green eyes blazed with a spirit that could not die. "There is nothing but good inside you, Tanelia. I can feel it. You have done everything you could to help me. You did not have to tell me the shame of your family, but you did." He got to his feet carefully. "She will *never* have a Pure Relic. Not mine, not anyone else's."

"I believe in you," she said simply. "I always have."

He very nearly asked her how the coming battle would play out, but he did not want to make her tell him the one thing he didn't want to hear if it was true. He would give everything he had, fight as hard as he could, and find the strength to accept whatever outcome would occur.

Tanelia took her leave, and Cassie held onto Tyrian. "I'm here," she vowed. "I'm not going anywhere."

"If you weren't here . . ." He didn't need to finish the thought. They both knew what not having her would mean for his sanity.

The Lower Generals, Kyle, Ewan, and Lane had assembled with Matthias and Cherry when Tyrian and Cassie walked in. Without preamble, Matthias said, "As soon as I heard, I had Shots run reconnaissance. High General Southerwind is riding at the front of his army. He commands twenty units, all of which are Special Forces. Two knights, Sir Janus and Sir Juniper, are also riding with General Southerwind. They are considered to be amongst the best of those under his command. They each sub-command ten of the twenty units."

"I've never met them," Tyrian said. "But I do know of them. They're roughly Laia's age. I remember when they joined my father. They were knighted young for extreme acts of bravery and heroism when confronting Foresalia."

"They are indeed formidable," Samantha agreed. "It does not surprise me that they would have come with General Southerwind. What surprises me is that he is even here like this." She shook her head. "Unless he is here to do what I did."

"It's not his style," he said very quietly. "He would not attack us unless he was intent on fighting. If he wanted to join us, there would be no farce. He would have simply shown up at the door and asked to be let in." He laughed, but it was self-mocking and made everyone wince. "Can't imagine where I get that from."

The doors opened and Hawke walked in. Her eyes glittered fiercely in her face. "Lord Tyrian," she said, "every Destined Star that is capable of field combat is joining you in this battle. We are gathering with the troops. All you have to do is tell us what you need us to do and who we are to follow. If you need us as unit leaders, we will do that too. You won't go into this alone."

Tyrian closed his eyes for a moment. "Thank you," he said softly. Their support meant nearly as much as Cassie's did. For the first time, he thought he truly understood why the Kaiten Star needed so many Destined Stars. His eyes opened and he looked at Kyle and Ewan. "You are in command of all sword based combatants. I leave the selection of troops and unit leaders to you. Samantha, I ask that you give them your aid."

"Done," Samantha said instantly.

The three hurried out, and Tyrian turned to Gordon. "You and Hawke will take command of ranged combat. Have Emma and Olan help you select the best archers." His gaze turned to Lane. "Have Verdure and Klint help you select our magical reserves. Rely also on Laia's skill if needed. Marian and Halkern are to have a full unit of Healers if at all possible. Doctor Kelan can ride with them."

"Consider it done." Lane hurried out of the room, his stomach sick with the knowledge of what occurred.

The other Lower Generals were given their orders as well, and Alex was chosen to personally select Tyrian's own troops. Yhalenia and Kotan were already assembling the two monk units, and the three former bandits would be working with them.

Matthias looked at Tyrian and said, "I will ride with you. Cherry will ride with Marian. All of us who can be on that field will be there, Lord Tyrian. I have already requested that Fay be readied for you so your unit can be mounted."

With a deep breath, Tyrian said, "There's nothing more to be done then. Let's get this over with."

The High General's army was vastly outnumbered by the total number of troops that the Liberation Army commanded. However, his troops were also much better trained than any except the Destined Stars. As such, Donald was not surprised to see thirty units emerge from the walls of the city and move forward into position. His heart felt heavy, and it had been ever since Blaine's vile order had come to him. Yet under the heaviness came incredible pride as he saw his son riding at the front of the Liberation Army. Tyrian had become a hero among soldiers, and he was every bit deserving of the mantle of Destiny's hero.

With a little smile, Donald touched his Voice Relic. "Hello, Tyrian."

"Hello, Father." Tyrian's voice was calm and unruffled, as it always seemed to be. Donald had always envied and admired his son's absolute serenity. "I admit," Tyrian said, "that I was expecting you sooner. Are you slowing down in your advanced age?"

"Well, being as I am apparently a grandfather now, I suppose I am entitled to my slower speed." He shifted his gaze to the black haired woman who rode beside Tyrian. "Master Cassie," he said, "I could not have asked for a better mate for my son. I find I can't say I am sorry I was not able to meet with you that first day. Watch out for my boy. He's too much like his old man."

Cassie's hand curled around Tyrian's wrist and held on as she sensed the inner shaking inside her lover. "If he is, then it's no wonder he is such an amazing man." She took a breath and urged, "General Southerwind, please. Lay down your arms. Join us. You know that we are not the enemy!"

"I can't." It was the simple truth. He had carefully planned every movement of this battle. He would not let Blaine win. This would be his final gift to his son. Everything was up to Tyrian now. He would save the Empire they loved. "I ask for a battle of skill."

Tyrian's brows lifted and he looked at Matthias. The strategist had a speculative look on his face. "A battle of skill," Matthias said slowly, "is a normal battle, but the intent is not to kill your enemy. Think of it as a unit sized duel. Everything is done the same way, but all soldiers know that they are to disarm, not kill. It matches range to range, mage to mage, and so on. I've never seen one done on this scale, but it is a surefire method of avoiding bloodshed."

"His troops are better trained," Tyrian said quietly. "Doesn't that swing the battle to his favor?"

"Under normal circumstances, I would say yes. But this is hardly normal, Lord Tyrian. I can't put my finger on it, but there is something about General Southerwind that has me on guard. There's something wrong. I can't determine why from this distance. It just feels . . . familiar." He nodded slightly. "General Southerwind," he said to the opposing leader, "we will accept your request. The engagement will be a battle of skill. But do not underestimate us."

"Ewan Grizmar," the black haired male riding beside Donald said, "I would ask that you match your sword against mine."

Ewan grinned. "Night, you up for smacking a knight around?"

"Not nearly as interesting as rogues, but I can be convinced," Night answered sassily.

The brunette on Donald's other side looked at Kyle. "Kyle Raitels, I would have you challenge me."

Kyle smiled. "Very well."

All other units matched up, and the extra ten units of Tyrian's stood by. If one of Tyrian's units was defeated, a unit of matching type could step in. There would be no calling strategy in this battle. The strategy was solely up to the soldiers on the field as they paired off one-by-one. Tyrian took a deep breath and said, "Let the engagement commence."

The battlefield became a cacophony of sound as the fights began. In some places, it was obvious that Tyrian's soldiers and unit leaders were stronger. In others, the favor was for Donald's side. The troops that Tyrian personally commanded pitted directly against the ones that Donald personally commanded. The unit leaders on each side met in the middle. Two lieutenants rode with Donald, and one looked at Matthias. "I yield without lifting a blade as you cannot enter combat."

Matthias inclined his head. "My thanks, lieutenant."

The other lieutenant smiled wryly at Cassie. "I am not so foolish as to engage a Tenth Class monk. I yield, Master Cassie."

Cassie nodded in acceptance, but her gaze remained solely on Tyrian. His face was calm, yet his fingers clenched so hard around the reins that his knuckles had gone white. They knew there was no way Donald would yield. The entire battle would end if either Tyrian or Donald was defeated.

Close up, Matthias felt more certain than ever that there was something wrong with Donald Southerwind. He still couldn't determine what it was, but he knew that the High General was not well. He glanced across the field and saw that Lane's unit stood idle after defeating its opponent. "Lord Lane," he said into his Voice Relic. "I require your knowledge."

Neither Donald nor Tyrian noticed. "Well," Tyrian said. "I suppose it would be foolish to ask for a surrender."

"I trained you better than that." Donald swung down off the back of his horse with the agility of a man half his age. He looked older than he had before, but he still moved like the warrior he was.

It was doubly painful for Tyrian as he dismounted and drew his staff. This close to his father, he did not feel the tug he felt when near a Destined

Star. That left Donald's future as one empty slate. It was up to Tyrian to decide the outcome. There was no way for this to miraculously become right.

Donald drew his sword and swung it lightly through the air. "Let's see what you've learned over the last few months." Without waiting for a response, he lunged toward Tyrian on a shout.

This was no quick battle with an easy win. Father and son were almost equally skilled. Tyrian was more powerful magically, but he refused to use the Devourer. Even though they used different types of weapons, it made neither of them more or less lethal. Blood was drawn on both sides when the right strike managed to sneak past a guard.

Slowly, the rest of the battle ended around them. Enough of Tyrian's army had been victorious to be considered the winner, but it was no longer important. Ally and enemy stood side by side as they watched the duel that raged. No one liked what they witnessed. No matter who took a blow, everyone winced.

Tyrian suddenly seemed to take in a surge of extra strength from out of nowhere. He ducked under Donald's guard and slammed his staff into his stomach. The blow sent the older man flying to the dirt and he rolled several feet before stopping. Breathing hard, his eyes burning, Tyrian nearly shouted, "Yield, damn you!"

Donald didn't immediately get up, and when several seconds passed, Matthias said softly, "The engagement is over. Lord Tyrian is the victor."

There was no chance for anyone to cheer. Donald surged to his feet and went after Tyrian once more. A shout rose among the army as they realized Donald had broken the laws. Ewan and Kyle went for their swords but Lane ordered harshly, "Stand down!!"

The discontent flowed through both sides of the field, but no one moved. It was only Liang and Laia holding Cassie back that kept her from leaping forward.

Tyrian didn't notice. He had his hands full trying to fend off Donald. He didn't know what was wrong, what was happening. His father would *never* break the rules of engagement! It was as if he had deliberately forfeited his life. "Stand down!" he shouted.

Donald didn't respond with words, and his eyes looked fierce and determined. One particularly sharp swing of his sword cut clean through the middle of Tyrian's staff. He kicked the Kaiten in the stomach and sent him tumbling back across the ground. Without any obvious hesitation, he raised his sword and went in for the kill.

The deepest instincts inside Tyrian, the ones that made him survive in the harshest times, rose hotly. Encoded in his very soul was the indomitable spirit of a Kaiten Star, a spirit that above all else would always want to live. His hand closed around the closest half of his staff and he lunged upward just as Donald got close.

The severed end of the staff was a sharp as a blade. It slammed into Donald's stomach and went far enough through that it came out the back. The High General staggered past Tyrian as his sword fell to the ground. His legs gave out and he collapsed onto the dirt as blood began to flow.

Marian's scream of anguish ripped through the field and she tried to shove her way through. Marcus and Di found her and forced soldiers aside to let her run to where Tyrian knelt beside Donald. Liang and Cassie also ran as fast as they could to get to the scene.

Tyrian's face was white, his eyes so dark that the pupils disappeared. Dully, he said, "Why did you do that?" He didn't see Liang or Marian, was only dimly conscious of Cassie's presence. Something inside shook violently. "You forced me to do that. Why?"

Lane knelt beside Marian. "Blaine cursed you," he told Donald. "I could see it from across the field. That's why Matthias thought something was familiar about you. He recognized the way your lifeforce was being bled out. No matter what happened here, Blaine set you up to die."

Donald nodded slightly. There was almost no pain to be felt. There was nothing but relief that it was over. Blaine would not win. "I was going to leave," he admitted softly. "After Beelzebub. But she cursed me. I knew what she wanted. I won't let her have it."

Marcus pulled Marian into his arms and she buried her face against his shoulder as her entire body shook with her sobs. The other Lower Generals had come forward as well, and so had Janus and Juniper. "Why can't I heal him?" Marian wailed into Marcus' shoulder. "It's not in the critical zone! Not my spells, not even my raw magic—why?!"

Magicians and Healers *became* the magic they commanded. Marian's relics had changed her magic capacity to pure healing force, allowing her to use her raw capacity as another way to heal when her spells alone might not be enough. She had done it before; she and Halkern had both exhausted themselves by using up their capacities in such a way to heal Persephone's family. They could only use their magic within the range of the spells they had unlocked, but Marian had fully unlocked relics and a higher than average capacity. She should have been able to do *something*!

Lane slowly shook his head. "It's not just the wound he was dealt. His lifeforce is being recalled to Blaine. And there is a lot of life inside him. He was chosen well to be the father of a Kaiten Star. You can't heal lifeforce,

Marian, I'm sorry." He looked at Tyrian. "You can stop this. You have to, Tyrian. You know you can't let Blaine have his life energy. You're not killing him. He was dead long before he ever stepped onto this field."

Tyrian's relic hand curled into a fist. "Bring Raven," he said evenly. "She deserves to meet her grandfather. Give me your cloak, Janus." He issued the order without hesitation.

Janus removed his cloak and spread it over Donald to hide the horrid wound. Even with the staff removed, it was a violent reminder of the task Tyrian had been forced to do. He and Juniper knelt side by side. They had been given specific orders, and having met Tyrian, they knew now why. Something told them that they, too, were destined to fight beside this man with the eyes of a hero. Neither could bear the sight of his suffering.

Ewan walked up with Raven in his arms and knelt to put her down. Donald focused on her, and he suddenly found a smile. "No wonder. No wonder Annareal loved her so. She's so much like you, Tyrian."

"Then she's just like her grandfather too." Tyrian took a deep breath. Time was running out. Even he could now feel the energy fleeing Donald's body. Already his legs and lower body were dead. There was no stopping what happened. "I love you," he said softly. "I'm proud to be your son."

"Hell, Tyrian." Donald closed his eyes. "I'm the one who's proud. There was never a day I wasn't proud of you." He grimaced as the numbness encountered his wound and the pain returned with a vengeance. He could now feel his body dying and the fleeing lifeforce was more painful than the wound itself.

"Hurry!" Lane urged Tyrian.

Tyrian's eyes closed and the runic circle opened around his body. The symbol of the Devourer appeared in the air over his head, visible to all who watched. He couldn't stand the idea of sending Donald to Hell, and he had done nothing to deserve Purgatory. His eyes opened suddenly and they had turned solid black. "Effervesce."

Ribbons of green and black power emerged from the symbol of the Devourer and flowed down to consume Donald. A bright glow emerged from his body and began to flow back up the ribbons to the symbol. When there was no more glow to be taken, the symbol and circle disappeared and the ribbons dissolved.

The High General was dead.

"He's smiling," Marian whispered.

Marcus held her tighter. "He's happy," he said roughly. "He died as a general. He gave his life for his people, just as every soldier who joins the army knows he or she might. There is no shame in that. There is no higher honor than dying for your country, or, for us, dying for our Kaiten."

Janus drew his cloak up over Donald's face. "Lord Tyrian," he started quietly, "Juniper and I were given orders contingent on General Southerwind's death. Those orders are to fight by your side. Please accept our vow as knights of the Empire to help you save our country and our people."

"Please also accept our dedication as Destined Stars," Juniper added. "We will fight by your side and give you our strength. If you need anything of us, it is yours." His voice broke and then steadied. He couldn't stand seeing Tyrian so quiet and pale. It was terrifyingly clear how close Tyrian walked to the edge of shattering.

One by one, then more, until it was a wave spreading across the field, soldiers began to kneel in respect for Donald and allegiance for Tyrian. Imperial and Liberation soldier alike, they were united as one. Tyrian slowly lifted his head as the wave spread and he watched as all fifty units on the field gave and re-gave their vow to fight under his flag.

It was too much all at once. Exhaustion came rushing in and he slumped over. He was almost pitifully grateful for the welcoming black of unconsciousness. Cassie caught him quickly and held him cradled in her arms. Tears slid slowly down her cheeks. "Tyrian." She buried her face in his hair and held on tight.

Quietly, Matthias said, "Prepare a hero's burial for General Southerwind. Sir Janus, Sir Juniper, I welcome you as a fellow Destined Star." He looked at Liang. "Can you carry Lord Tyrian?"

"I haven't tried since he was ten," Liang said. It seemed as if he had aged dramatically over the last few hours, with lines appearing at the corner of his eyes and mouth. "But I'm still a bit bigger than he is." It was just enough bigger that he was able to lift Tyrian from the ground to carry him on his back toward the castle. Cassie went with him, and Ewan picked up Raven to follow.

The Lower Generals, minus Marcus, took charge of the new twenty units. Marcus took Marian back to her room and stayed by her side as she suffered through a rage of grief that was both hers and her cousin's. She knew he could not cry, and so she cried for him as well. Why was Destiny so bitterly unfair to a man as wonderful as Tyrian?

The day passed quietly. Tyrian remained asleep while Cassie and Raven stayed near his side. Liang, with Serentia and Tavi's support, selected a space inside the city that would be the perfect place for Donald to be buried. Tavi then, with Yumi, Kami, and Mikey's help, picked out the prettiest stones they could find to be used as a grave marker.

It was several days before Tyrian finally awoke, and when he did, he woke to a pain that was more emotional than physical. It was not even dawn, if the sounds from outside were a clue, and he couldn't move his left arm since both Raven and Cassie were lying on it. He didn't mind. Their presence was welcome and comforting.

After a few minutes, he carefully extracted his arm and got out of bed. It was cold on the balcony since he only wore pajama pants, but he didn't care. He leaned on the rail and looked up at the stars. His burned as steadily as ever, and he could see how the others clustered much closer than usual as if to protect him.

He heard a sound behind him and said softly, "If it is the last thing I ever do, I will personally introduce Blaine to the Devourer Relic. She wants it so badly, I'll be glad to demonstrate its powers."

Cassie stepped up beside him and covered his hand on the rail. Even before he had awakened, she had sensed that the war was no longer about the Rebellion. It had become very personal for Tyrian. "I think if anyone deserves to be devoured," she concurred quietly, "then it would be her. I believe in an eye for an eye, but Laia put it better. 'Let the punishment fit the crime.'"

His fingers tightened on the rail. "A part of me just wants to go straight to Trinan and storm the castle. But I know I can't." He turned to look at her, and the natural intensity inside him seemed to roll off him in waves. "I will not lose. I am going to find my Stars, I'm going to end this war, and I'm going to kill Blaine. She will die by my hand."

"Good." She softly rubbed her relic hand over his with the intent to soothe rather than seduce. "That third spell in the Devourer. It was somehow beautiful to see. You called it Effervesce. Do you know what it means?"

"No."

"According to Zinfandel, to effervesce is to be reborn. While you can say that the spell is as deadly as the rest, how it does it is something else entirely. A mercy killing, perhaps, is a way to view it."

"It's little comfort, but it is some." He let out a long breath. "I've almost never used my spells except for the first time I've gained them; I just use raw magic. I don't think I ever will use them commonly. It needs to be an extreme situation for me to feel justified."

"There's nothing wrong with that, Tyrian." She ducked under his arm and wrapped her own around his waist. "You're a sorcerer, not a Thaumoturge. Same as me. If you were a Thaumoturge, you'd have a different Pure Relic entirely, and a different burden to bear."

He turned and held her closer. His hands skimmed over her back, enjoying the tactile feel of her silk robe and the warm skin beneath. Blaine was slowly taking away the people he loved, but he would *never* let her lay a hand on any of those that were left.

In a similar vein, Cassie was thinking of how terribly Blaine wanted Tyrian dead. She would stoop to anything to get him and his relic. Nowhere except the castle would ever be safe, not as long as that psychopath was still around. "I will *never* let her touch you," she vowed softly. "I swear I will die first."

He didn't bother to point out that if she was gone, then he had no reason to continue. He needed that fierce defense. He needed to know she was there to protect him. There were so many other things to think of that his own safety hovered low on the list.

He shivered suddenly and she smiled. "Inside with you." She caught his hand and drew him back into the warmth of the tower room. She shut the balcony doors and curtains and then caught her breath as his hands curled around her waist. The magic in his skin burned and tingled with intent. "Raven's asleep in our bed," she said breathlessly. "You wouldn't dare seduce me with our daughter in the room."

"You'll just have to be very quiet." He pressed his lips to the curve of her neck and tasted her skin. "She won't wake up."

"What if she does?" The protest was getting weaker as his hands and lips set fire to her body. She barely caught a moan as his hands slid up to cup her breasts. "Tyrian."

He lowered her slowly to the floor, needing the life she offered freely. He found salvation in her arms, and he needed it more than air. "She won't wake up," he said huskily as he unwrapped the robe.

Much to her mother's relief, Raven did indeed remain peacefully asleep until well after dawn. By the time she did stir, Tyrian and Cassie were dressed and preparing to go downstairs to meet with the others. She peeked around the corner to watch them put their shoes on and then asked, "Daddy?"

"I'm alright, honey." Tyrian picked her up and rubbed his cheek over her hair. "I'll be fine now. Do you want to come with us?" When she nodded firmly, he put her on her feet. "Then scoot back to your room and get dressed."

"Okay!" A thought occurred to her and she frowned thoughtfully. "Was there a funny noise last night?"

Cassie felt her cheeks heat. "I didn't notice anything."

"Oh. Okay." Raven hurried out of the tower and hopped into the elevator, unconcerned with strange noises since her parents hadn't heard them.

Tyrian's grin looked more than a little wicked as he curled his hand around the back of Cassie's neck. He kissed her hard and hungry and then murmured against her lips, "I *told* you to be quiet."

"Oh shut up." Despite herself, she found herself smiling. He had a terrible devilish streak, but she wouldn't have changed him at all.

Chapter Thirty-Nine

"Tomorrow begets the mystery of destiny."

Janus and Juniper waited for Tyrian and Cassie when they reached ground level. Tyrian was able to actually focus on them this time. He had only been dimly aware of their presence and their position as Stars in his sky. "Hello," he said. He studied Juniper and then Janus, and a smile tugged at his lips. "I apologize for not saying anything sooner."

"Please don't," Juniper disagreed. "We are the ones who wish to apologize, Lord Tyrian. There was nothing we could say or do to sway General Southerwind from his intent. We understood when he said that his life was already lost, but we didn't want the task to be on your shoulders."

Tyrian shook his head slightly. "There was no one else it could be," he admitted simply. "This was not simply some illness he had." His hands clenched at his sides for a moment and then relaxed. "I'm handling it. I can't say everything is alright because it isn't. But this has only made me more determined to remove Blaine entirely."

Juniper pulled a face. "I never liked her when she came on the scene. She just never looked . . . pleasant to me."

"I still say your Faerie blood is to blame for that, thin as it is," Janus said. "And I'll admit she fooled me initially, but it didn't take long to realize she was bad to the core."

"At the least, you listened to me about that," Juniper groused.

"I *always* listen to you. I just don't always *act* like I do."

Cassie's brows slowly raised and she looked at Tyrian. He just smiled. A bit bemused, she linked her hands behind her back. "How long have you two known each other?" she asked the knights.

"Years," Janus offered. "When I enlisted, Juniper decided to join me. When we were in our early twenties, we found ourselves in a battle with Foresalia." He shook his head. "We don't really talk about what we saw. But General Southerwind had us knighted."

"It's been more of an annoyance than anything," Juniper added dryly.

Never one to beat around the bush, Tyrian asked, "Why? Because it's much harder to keep your marriage a secret when you're constantly in the public eye?"

"I told you he'd notice," Janus said dryly as Juniper stared at Tyrian.

"I know my Stars," Tyrian said simply. "And, well, you *do* sound a bit like an old married couple." He smiled as he said it. "To be sure, just friends can bicker all the time, but they don't usually have that . . . particular look in their eyes, or tone in their voice."

Juniper winced a bit wryly. "There is no law saying you have to disclose your marital state, and I listed my next-of-kin as my sister." He had to grin. "Janus listed *his* husband, though. So, no one has ever questioned that Janus and I are best friends and always together; after all, Janus is married to a farm boy from our hometown whom he loves so very much. He talks about him all the time."

Janus grinned as well. "Do admit I stay close to the truth, other than changing your name. I have to have *some* way of bragging about you, don't I?" He added to Tyrian, "We were always lucky, too. General Southerwind always deployed us together."

"He knew the truth," Tyrian said simply. He cocked his head. "By your preference, do you want it to remain a secret, or be out in the open? You know that the laws will change, so choose what will make *you* happy."

The couple exchanged a look and then nodded. "In the open," Juniper decided. "I've never liked hiding how I feel, especially when Janus is his most frustrating. I keep wanting to kiss him to shut him up!" He snorted. "And, anyway, there are not enough married knights around. There's a strange stigma to knights that implies most of us stay unwed."

"I have a married lady in mind for knighting when the dust settles," Tyrian assured him. He opened his mouth to say more when he heard a sudden commotion from the direction of the kitchen. He had never heard Evelyn squeal like a child before, therefore his attention was understandably caught. "Pardon me?"

"Certainly. We're due to train soldiers anyway. If you need us, call us." Janus bowed gracefully and walked away with Juniper at his side as his equal. Though there was nothing intimate in their body language, Tyrian had a feeling that everyone knew Janus' beloved husband was actually not far from his side. He also had no doubt that respect for both knights meant no one spoke of what they saw so that they would not be separated for fear of a 'distraction'.

When Tyrian and Cassie got to the kitchen, they found Evelyn being swung around in the arms of a tall young man. Tyrian knew two things on one look. One, the two of them were either brother and sister or cousins, and two, the young man was also a Destined Star. The entire restaurant was happily buzzing, and he asked Aquatico, "What happened?"

The bath maker grinned. "Eve was flipping pancakes when this guy came out of nowhere. She dropped the pan and jumped on him. They've been talking so fast we can't understand a word of it, but they're both really happy."

Cassie hastily scooted over to the kitchen and saved the pan from catching fire. The pancakes were beyond repair, and she worked on prying them out. Lane was in the vicinity and created a quick breeze to blow through the area to remove the smoke and the smell. Tyrian walked over to his chef and cleared his throat.

Evelyn glanced at him and then laughed. "Oh, Lord Tyrian!" She wiped at her eyes and stood on her own feet. "This is Terrence Summers. He's my oldest friend; we went to cooking school together! We're cousins too, but we've been friends from the time we were babies. We're even the same age!"

"Our mothers had a bet on who would be older." Terrence grinned quickly and it lit up his handsome face. "Evie beat me out by two days, the brat."

"You were just lazy," she sniffed in return.

Tyrian found himself smiling. He knew how they felt because Marian had always been his friend as well as his cousin and surrogate older sister. "Welcome to Aon Castle, Terrence. Are you here to help Eve?"

Terrence gave a jaunty salute. "I'm here to help you, Lord Tyrian. Eve and I have stars that are cousins as well, so I am also a Destined Star. You can count on me to help feed the masses. I hate vegetables, though, so you won't see them in my dishes."

Whether it was destiny, a guess, or Evelyn being a tattletale, Tyrian had no idea, but he felt exceptionally grateful. "I'm not fond of them either," he admitted. "I will be glad to have your help. Eve has done a brilliant job keeping up with everyone, but she needs your help." He held out a hand that Terrence clasped. The white star instantly appeared on the new chef's shoulder. "Thank you."

"No, thank you," Terrence said softly. He released Tyrian's hand and rubbed his own together. "Let's make some breakfast!" A cheer rose in the restaurant and he laughed at Evelyn. "You have them trained."

"Of course!"

Tyrian smiled as he watched them take control of the kitchen with seamless teamwork. Glad for it, he grabbed a seat at a table with Emma, Dylan, and Thomas. All three were watching him very closely, and he found a smile for them as Cassie sat down beside him. "I'm handling it," he told them. "We're just here for some coffee. Matthias and the others are waiting for us." He cocked his head slightly. "How did Terrence get here safely, anyway? I thought he and Evelyn came from Larksville."

"Me!" a male voice said behind Tyrian. When the Kaiten turned around, the Grimalkin behind him grinned. "My name is Grimwell, though lots call me Grim. I have no idea why; I'm rarely ever grim."

Tyrian believed it. He smiled again as he felt the tug inside. In his moment of lowest hope and deepest despair, Stars had surged forward to surround him safely. He needed them and they responded. It was the miracle of his birth and he would always be grateful for it. "Thank you, Grim," he said, "for bringing Terrence here safely." He studied the sheath with daggers on the taller male's hip. "Medium or long range?"

"Medium, long, and if someone gets too close, I stab fairly hard too. I'm better on a large combat scale than a small combat, but if you point me at something, I can hit it." He saluted sassily, and his silvery eyes looked a lively compliment for his silvery hair and fur. His tail swung merrily behind him, covered in the same silver fur as his ears and hands. "Just leave it to me." He wiggled his brows. "I hear there's a lovely bard running around here who also uses daggers."

"Who happens to be good friends with another dagger user named Vee," Dylan noted dryly.

Grimwell winced. "Oops. I know Vee. She's a protective sort. I hope she at least lets me smile at the bard." He sighed wistfully. "I love watching bards dance. They're as free as the stars." He saluted Tyrian again. "Count me in the army, Lord Tyrian. I even wash dishes if needed."

"I bribe him with crepes," Terrence called, and set the room off into laughter.

Grimwell wandered off with a whistle, and Thomas said, "Myr's only fifteen!" He scowled. "He can't court her yet."

"He may only wish to flirt with her," Cassie said gently, "and that is perfectly acceptable at her age. He could even date her if she was interested back. He's a Star, Tom, just as you are. He won't hurt Myr." She smiled. "We should be more worried she'll break *his* heart." Certainly it seemed she had captured Thomas' heart as well!

Coffee was served shortly thereafter, and Tyrian and Cassie took their leave. Halfway to the meeting room, Raven caught up with them and rode along on her mother's back. She was wearing her leggings and tunic again, and this time a jaunty cap had been added that rested delicately on her pointed ears. "Fluffy slippers!" She stuck out a foot happily to show off the ridiculous, yet comfortable, house shoes a lot of people wore inside the castle.

"Indeed!" Tyrian tapped the bottom of her foot. "Very nice ones, too."

The six Lower Generals, Matthias, Cherry, Ewan, and Kyle waited inside the meeting room. Leonard was also present. He was slowly taking on more tasks and duties; as a mayor, he was well used to being in charge, and Tyrian guiltlessly took advantage of his organizational skills. He also intended to take advantage of his leadership skills soon enough, though he suspected only Matthias knew his intent. He sat down beside Marcus and asked quietly, "How is Marian?"

Strain still lurked on the general's face. "Doing better than she was the first day or two. She's a strong woman, and she's pulling herself up for you. She told me that she refuses to let you worry about her when you have your own pain to handle."

"I've turned my pain into determination." His green eyes burned as he looked around the table. "I want Blaine's head. This isn't about the Rebellion anymore. If you told me that I could lead the Rebellion or go after Blaine, then I would walk away."

"Lane said that this would happen," Kyle said quietly. "And we support you without question, Tyrian. You know that. I, more than any other, support you. When you go after Blaine, I will be by your side."

"And so will I," Ewan promised softly.

Tyrian nodded briefly. "Good." He looked at Marcus. "Blaine is after me. She will strike at the ones I love. I am trusting you to be Marian's protector. If she isn't with me, she will be with you. On the field of battle, she will ride with your unit or mine. If she has to be in a healing unit, you will ride with her instead."

"Done," Marcus said instantly.

Tyrian turned to Matthias. "I am removing Liang from active duty in battle unless absolutely needed. I want him here to protect Serentia, Tavi, and Raven. If something happens to Liang, the task of guarding my family will fall to Kyle, Ewan, or Laia. There is no one else I would ever trust with the task of guarding my daughter's life."

No one took offense. They understood entirely why he felt the way he did. Matthias linked his hands together on top of the table. "Then there is no time left to waste. Larksville is our next target. It stands protected by twenty units of Special Forces. We are now in a position to engage them thanks to the addition of General Southerwind's troops. Sir Janus and Sir Juniper have already begun enhanced training of our other troops. They make a . . . remarkable team, I must say."

"Yeah, I noticed that," Ewan said. "To be fair, they reminded me a bit of Laia and Rourke, how they can just read each other's mind."

Tyrian smiled. "Rightfully so. Janus and Juniper are married."

"Called it," Ewan told Kyle. "Pay up."

The Lower Generals also felt no surprise; most of them had become suspicious if not outright sure, and they had kept their silence for the same reason everyone else had. If a couple found a way to get around the ridiculous law, then they deserved the respectful silence of those around them. As Tyrian had noted, the knights were not the only married or engaged pair within the ranks of the Imperial Army who put up a lie about their relationship status.

Matthias just shook his head in sympathy. "Then their accomplishments are all the more note-worthy; it is very hard to hide a secret so significant when you are in the public eye."

"What do we do next?" Leonard asked. "Do we even know where the Special Forces stand in this whole scenario?"

"The SF are now under control of General Reyu." Vincent made a slight gesture. "We can't be sure if he has corrupted them or not."

Kell walked into the meeting room at that point and said, "Larksville has ceased to pay taxes to the capitol." As brows lifted, he grabbed the seat beside Cherry. "My sources have informed me that as soon as word was official that General Southerwind was dead, they promptly cut off all funds flowing to Trinan. Grace is checking on the state of Pardue to see if they have done the same. However, we have found no sign that the Special Forces have struck back at the cities for their sudden 'betrayal.'"

"Interesting." Matthias frowned thoughtfully. "Can we be sure the SF know that the taxes have been stopped and simply don't care? Or is it something they're unaware of?"

"They know." Grace walked in and sat down beside Kell. She deliberately bumped her shoulder against his, causing most everyone in the room to hide grins. "I have gotten confirmation that Pardue also ceased to pay their taxes. Supposedly, the lieutenant in charge of the forces outside Pardue 'accidentally' lost a missive from General Reyu. Coincidentally, the missive was found by someone in town. It specifically said to retaliate against Pardue for treason."

"And Reyu doesn't dare actually organize the attack himself," Tyrian said, "because he knows that he would be outnumbered at this point. If Pardue's militia joined with the SF, they'd be thirty-five strong. Reyu commands only twenty. He'd have to pull everyone off Trinan to take them down, and that would give *me* an open shot at the capitol."

"It wouldn't be worth his effort. At best, he can try to squeeze the city and hope that the lieutenant is as big an asshole as he is." Ewan huffed out an annoyed breath. "Which, obviously, they aren't. We might finally be culling the bad apples out of the barrels. By the time we get to the capitol, it's going to *reek*."

"And the people will be casualties," Matthias noted. "We will have to investigate possible ways of evacuating the people as the battle commences. For now, our eyes are set on Larksville." He grew thoughtful as he considered the possible ramifications. "With the current status quo, I do not think we need to play along with the farce of resistance. We played along with the checkpoints because it was time for Lord Tyrian to prove himself."

"I think he's proven himself time and time again," Kyle muttered distinctly. He held nothing against the Lower Generals for needing to be sure, but he was tired of the hoops Tyrian had to jump through. "If they're on our side, they can damned well just join us! The cities are safe from retaliation if the units outside are already proving to protect them."

Samantha opened her mouth and then closed it. She was silent for moments before saying slowly, "The Special Forces were under General Southerwind's control until Lady Annareal's death. We can no doubt assume that his reaction to the events was as much because of the curse he bore as it was her actual death."

Tyrian looked at her quickly. "You suspect that Father may have issued final orders to the Special Forces like he did to Janus and Juniper? Orders contingent on his death. If he is dead, then they are to join me in my battle." His hands gripped together under the table as he felt a sharp stab of pain inside. His father had left the fate of the country in his hands with the full knowledge that only he could save it. It had hurt to think his father had stopped loving him for following his heart. It hurt deeper to know he had never loved him more.

Cassie covered his hands with hers and held on. "Then we may only need to talk to the lieutenant in charge of the forces outside Larksville and Pardue." She drew his hands to her lips and held them there. His fingers felt like ice. "He said it himself, Tyrian," she reminded him. "He was going to join you to fight against Albanion and Blaine. He knew he couldn't so he made sure in every way he could that you would succeed. He believed in you the entire time."

Tyrian took a deep breath. "Thank you," he said quietly. He looked at Matthias. "I will take a party with me to Larksville. Have units on standby just in case we're wrong. At my side, I will take Cassie, Ewan, Vee, Kris, and Halkern." He turned to Raven and ran his hand down her hair. "Stay with your grandpa and grandma," he said softly.

She nodded and hugged him tight around the neck. It took a lot of willpower to let him go, and it was only when the door shut behind him that her lower lip began to quiver. "I hate this!" she shouted. She turned on Kyle as tears welled in her eyes. "It's not fair!"

Kyle scooped her up and cuddled her close as she cried against his neck. "I know, honey." He sighed as he looked at the other adults. They all felt the same way. "I know."

The uncanny connection between Destined Star and Kaiten was a strong and profound thing. Because of it, the rest of Tyrian's party waited for him near Miranda. They had felt his need for them and they had responded. "Larksville, huh?" Vee said. "It's been a while since I was back. Is that why you asked for me, to make the trip shorter?"

"One of the reasons. The other is how good your aim is." Tyrian looked at Miranda. "Vee has been to Larksville, so use her as a beacon."

"Okay, here we go! Gah!" The last was added as she narrowly missed beaning Rourke as he was going by.

Sadly, it threw her aim off, and it therefore threw off her magic. The party landed, literally, in the middle of the Special Forces units. Kris and Vee found themselves at the feet of a couple startled archers. Halkern landed somewhere near a mage unit. Ewan ended up in the middle of puzzled swordsmen. Cassie and Tyrian landed in the main unit, and Tyrian found himself at the feet of the lieutenant in charge.

The elder soldier studied Tyrian for long moments and then asked, "Have you ever had one of those days?"

"I'm having one of those years," Tyrian admitted on a sigh. "And despite the inelegant entrance, I hope you would still consider joining my forces. I'm not really in the mood to play games anymore. Either you stand beside me, or you stand beside Blaine."

The lieutenant dismounted his horse and offered a hand to Tyrian. "We stand beside the people," he said calmly. "General Southerwind told us that if we are to save the people, we must join with you. He fully believed you are the only one who can save this land. And I believe it too."

Tyrian took his hand and got to his feet gracefully. "Despite my entrance."

If anything, the lieutenant thought, it was only a further testament to Tyrian's character that he still looked every inch a leader even while sitting on the dirt. There was a fierce glitter in Tyrian's eyes that spoke of a spirit strong enough to lead thousands, if not millions. It was a glitter not unfamiliar to the older man. "You remind me of my son," he admitted. "Though if *he* had landed there, he would have asked me to join him before we started the conversation."

Tyrian smiled at that. "He sounds like a fascinating character."

"That he is. Rihou's only a few years younger than you." He bowed with all the grace of a long-time warrior. "My name is Divan Royaltine, Lord Tyrian. My skills are yours to command, as are my soldiers."

"Divan." Tyrian frowned thoughtfully. Around them, things had become a flurry of activity as the transition from Imperial to Liberation was made. Several of Tyrian's units transported in to help make the change, and Tyrian's party was making its way back to him. "I know that name." It dawned on him suddenly. "Wait, I remember. You were fighting on the side of Foresalia during a skirmish with Melodina."

Divan smiled. "Indeed! I was lamenting not getting to see my family one last time when your father came out of nowhere." He shook his head. "He told me to either fight beside him or sit out of the way. I chose to fight. From that day forward, he had my friendship. Not even a year ago, he contacted me and asked me to come join the Special Forces as a lieutenant."

Tyrian felt his stomach clench with fresh pain. "Roughly ten months ago?"

"Indeed." Divan's smile faded. "I arrived at Trinan just as you claimed Aon Castle. To be honest, a part of me thought Donald had called me out here to fight you. It was not long before I realized he expected me to eventually fight *beside* you. His final orders to us confirmed what I had known all along."

Cassie slid her hand into Tyrian's as she stepped up beside him. "I find it interesting that a Lower General from an enemy country would be allowed to come fight on behalf of the Empire. Or at least the people."

"King Utheron is not a fool," Divan said. "From the moment the Rebellion gained momentum over here, he has been watching. He knew of my friendship with Donald but did not argue against it. As long as it did not interfere with war, he didn't care. When I told him that Donald had asked me to come join the fight, he said that as long as I reported to him the goings-on, he was amiable."

"And where does Utheron stand now?" Ewan asked. He had come up behind Tyrian with Kris, Vee, and Halkern. "Is he going to start crap with the country protected by the legendary Kaiten Star?"

"No," Divan said instantly. "It is obvious now who the winner will be. Foresalia may not be an *ally* to whatever the Empire becomes, but they will assuredly not be enemies any longer."

Tyrian let out a little breath. It was one less pressure on his shoulders. He had hated all along the idea that two countries could so casually be at war for so long. He had no doubt that Foresalia would have its own troubles with the ruthless nature of so many soldiers, but the troubles would not touch the Empire. "Good."

"Only Pardue and Trinan after this," Kris murmured.

"For which I am also glad," Divan admitted. "I miss my family."

"Your wife and son?" Tyrian asked.

"My son and daughter. She's slightly older than Rihou. It's just Rihou, Naomi, and me since my wife died many years ago. While I am here, my kids have been staying with the family of Rihou's best friend." He shook his head on a wry smile. "The terrible two. I dread when they are adults. There will be no stopping them."

"Sounds like someone else we know," Halkern said dryly.

Tyrian ignored him. "Let's touch base inside the city before we head back to Aon Castle." There was a whisper in the wind, a sort of feeling in the air, that told him more friends waited inside the borders of the city that was even then beginning to hum with an air of excitement. Not paying taxes was one thing. Being officially liberated was another.

Larksville looked like Trinan but on a grand scale. It covered many square miles and had people everywhere. Some buildings were even three stories in height, a feat seen only in the highest level of cities. There were at least three or four of every kind of shop, and musicians played on several corners.

Both Tyrian and Cassie had a sudden feeling of being boxed in by all the people moving around them. Automatically, their relic hands clasped together in mutual support. It was a very disorienting sensation to feel as if you watched time move past while you held still. With every passing day, eternity affected them more strongly. Even Miranda, for all her vivacious and social personality, preferred to live out of the way of cities. It was simply another price to pay for bearing a Pure Relic.

A young man with short and spiky brown hair suddenly came out of nowhere and planted himself in front of Tyrian. "Tell me you know where my irresponsible band members are," he demanded.

Tyrian had to smile. "They're at my castle. You must be Capricorn."

"Cap for short." Cap sighed. "Taurus sent me a letter a while back saying that destiny bound her and Aries and Virgo to your side. Rather than risk my hide trying to get to the castle, I figured eventually you'd find me. I mean, obviously we're a package deal." He saluted with the guitar he carried. "You can count on me to help play the music that inspires you!"

"And keep the other three out of trouble?" Vee asked dryly.

Cap winced. "That too." He was almost afraid to ask what his friends had been up to lately. They had a knack for getting in trouble if he wasn't there to pull the reins. "Should I set out for the castle?" he asked.

"Wait for us," Tyrian suggested. "I have a mirror that can take us all home. I want to see if there's anyone else here waiting for me. I also want to speak with the mayor."

"Fair enough. I'll be waiting here for you." He sat down on a bench with a smile.

The party didn't get much further into the city before they were assailed by the sudden scent of perfume. It was two scents, in fact, and in clashing odors. It was so strong and potent that Ewan felt his eyes water. "Holy hell, are we somewhere near the city brothel?"

By tacit agreement, no one asked how he knew what the city brothel smelled like.

"Over there." Kris pointed over Tyrian's shoulder.

He followed her direction and barely hid a wince. Descending on the party like perfumed steamrollers were two excessively well dressed women. From the top of their curled hairstyles to the bottom of their fancy shoes, everything about the women screamed they were not only high society, but narcissists as well. Resigned, he stopped walking. Raven would get to see firsthand just why narcissists were considered vexing to everyone else.

"You!" The blonde pointed her fan directly in his face. "You are Tyrian Southerwind, correct?" Before he could speak, she rolled on, "Obviously you must know who I am! Everyone knows the name of the De Jardin family! Tell this . . . uncultured cow beside me that you are here looking for us! Of course you are, aren't you?"

The redhead snapped before he could speak, "Oh, come down off your ivory tower, Marigold! Obviously a man of such refined taste as Tyrian Southerwind would never stoop to wanting your kind in his castle! Only a Kween family member would ever bring some culture to that drab army!"

Marigold sniffed loudly. "Do not mind Frances. She is only sore because she has been stood up at the altar five times. Why, you would think there was something wrong with her!" She tossed back her perfectly curled ringlets. "You do not mind if I come out and bring some style, do you? Of course not! I will make my way there immediately!"

Frances sniffed back. "Of course you would think to walk when there is an army outside! *I* will simply make them take me along. Lord Tyrian is in need of style, not catastrophe, which is all you would bring." She turned on her heel and walked away, her fluffy silk skirts swirling around her legs.

Marigold went chasing after her and blessed silence descended. "Did you get a word in edgewise?" Halkern asked. "If you did, I missed it."

"I didn't try," Tyrian admitted. "I've discovered that it's better to let you all make your own decisions about your reasons for joining me. I'm simply too grateful that you're there. No matter how snobby those two are, there's a reason for them to be Stars. Something about them is what I need."

"A headache?" Vee grumbled.

Tyrian smiled. "You might be surprised. Come on. There's more to be seen."

The size of the city meant that seeing all of it in a few hours was near impossible. By the time evening approached, they had only covered half the landscape. The city was not in the same disrepair as other cities, but there was still a much more jubilant air. People believed that the war was already won, and conversations already flowed about what sort of new government they wanted. A republic seemed to be the general wish, but everyone was already putting Tyrian in charge.

"If they try," Kris promised, "we Destined Stars will sneak you and Lady Cassie and Raven out under the cover of darkness. They'll never find you."

They had been walking past a rather plain looking little building while she spoke, and Ewan abruptly stopped in his tracks. "Whoa. Tyrian, you need to see this."

Curious, Tyrian stepped closer. He instantly caught his breath in wonder. Hanging in the window of the small shack was a painting. It wasn't just any painting, though. It was a brilliant depiction of the battle outside Lupine when Tyrian had dueled the dishonest lieutenant. There was a great deal of love in every brushstroke, and he immediately went into the building. The others followed.

Paintings stood stacked all over the place inside the front area of the shop. Nearly all of them depicted Tyrian. The one that caught his eye in particular, though, was not only of him. It was of him and Cassie. It showed them dancing together at the inn during their one date, and the background had been blurred away until it was as if they were in their own world. "So that's what I look like," he said softly as Cassie knelt beside him. "That's how I look when I look at you."

It almost seemed as if the eternity that bound them was visible in the painting. Cassie could hardly believe she was looking at her own image, but she recognized the look on her face as she looked at Tyrian. She had never seen how she looked either, but it looked exactly as it felt. Powerful, unstoppable. A bit terrifying to love someone that much, to need him to be safe and smiling and believing in her. "Amazing," she breathed softly.

"Thank you."

At the voice, they turned to see a slim young woman standing behind them. The feline ears, fluffy tail, and tilted eyes spoke of her Grimalkin bloodline. Her paint streaked shorts and tunic spoke of her skill. Like others of the animalistic species, some Grimalkin looked more like a cat than a Human. Others looked more like a Human than a cat. The artist was caught in a strange and exotic middle ground that made her surprisingly beautiful.

Tyrian stood and fully faced her, and her eyes went wide. With a smile, he said, "May I buy this painting?" He gestured to the one showing him and Cassie.

She shook her head. "It's not for sale." She walked over and picked up the painting and then turned and held it out to him. "But it is a gift." She smiled and her pale green eyes crinkled at the corner. "I'm Catherine."

Since she knew well who he and Cassie were, he only gestured to the others. "Ewan, Kris, Halkern, and Vee."

She gave a little salute. "It's nice to meet you." She linked her hands behind her back and began to circle Tyrian while she studied him intently. She had seen him in her dreams for a long time, but there was nothing like having a model on hand. She nodded decisively. "You need family portraits. You're a dad, right?"

"I am."

She held up a finger. "Then you need portraits! And you need the best, so you need me! I'll illustrate your story, Lord Tyrian, and I'll bring color to the Liberation Army. You can count on me to show you the way we see you even when you're feeling oppressed."

"I have every confidence in you," he said firmly. "But watch out. Raven will become one of your favorite subjects."

The painter giggled. "I like kids because they're expressive. I don't mind at all!"

"We'll stay and help her pack up," Halkern told Tyrian and Cassie. "Come get us before you leave. You can probably cover a bit more ground."

Tyrian didn't mind at all. It seemed as if he never quite got enough time alone with Cassie, and he firmly tangled her fingers with his as they walked down the street. "I suppose some things even eternity can't stop." He brought her fingers to his lips. "My desire is to be alone with you. Preferably somewhere private and away from prying eyes. I tell myself that when this is done that we'll have millennia to be alone together, but I think I'm a greedy man."

If he didn't stop looking at her with that familiar heat in his eyes, she was going to find a private place to drag him off to at that very moment.

"I'm greedy too," she admitted. "I'm not *jealous* of the other Destined Stars, exactly, but I also don't like to share. It's a very strange thing to feel. I want to hide you away where no one can find you."

"You promised you would once the war was done. I'll hold you to it." He stopped walking and tugged her into his arms for a lingering kiss. People who were going past began to whistle and giggle at the sight, but no one had the nerve to actually interrupt. There was something incredibly beautiful about the way Kaiten and Kentei glowed together under the halo of the stars. Protector and protected, hero and guardian . . . something was familiar about the image they presented though no one could put their finger on it.

"Ahem."

Tyrian reluctantly lifted his head, and his fingers glided over Cassie's cheek. Her eyes shimmered like melted blue gems, her lips begging for another kiss. It was highly tempting to just find the inn and stay there for the night. Having a six-year-old who could sneak into their room at any time certainly made things interesting. He wanted to take his time loving Cassie. He would happily take forever.

"*Ahem*." The feminine voice sounded highly amused.

With a sigh, he turned his head and found himself looking at a hauntingly beautiful young woman with a toddler perched on her shoulders. Both mother and daughter had matching powder blue hair and eyes and the elegantly pointed ears of ancient Elf blood. The woman wore a slim silver dress inlaid with relic symbols, but she wore no relics of her own. Instead, there were delicately tattooed symbols over her lower arms in the many symbols of lesser relics.

She was also a Destined Star.

She smiled as she saw the recognition in his eyes. "Hello, Lord Tyrian. My name is Jeanine Tallium. This is my daughter, Zellanna. I am one of the hundred and nine, and my star is a fixed position. I have known for many years that my path would cross yours. I am a Relic Master. It is my honor to offer my services."

"It is my honor to accept them," he said simply. "You are greatly needed, Jeanine."

Cassie studied Zellanna, feeling a distant sense of kinship not dissimilar from what she felt toward Jeanine. "Is Zellanna . . .?"

"Not yet," Jeanine offered readily. "Her path follows another for the future." She sighed fondly. "She wants to be a Scroll Master."

Zellanna beamed. "Like Daddy!"

"Yes, like your daddy." Jeanine shook her head in amusement. "Once the war is done, we will go back to the City-States to see him." She gave a graceful bow not at all marred by the child perched on her shoulders. "We will see you at the castle, Lord Tyrian." A little shimmer of light swirled around her and she disappeared.

Startled, Tyrian looked at Cassie. She smiled. "Relic Masters, by nature of what they do, tend to absorb bits of power from every relic they ever fuse to someone. That's why all those tattoos are on her arms. She can use a little bit of power from every relic. The flipside to that is that she will never be able to equip a relic herself."

"It seems a fair trade." He let out a long breath. "A future Destined Star," he murmured. "You recognized her but I didn't. That means the Kentei Star is considered a fixed position. An unusual fixed, I suppose, as Laia said fixed stars usually only belonged to one person. I wonder why."

Cassie thought about it. "Because fixing the position of the Kentei ensures that I, and therefore you, will be drawn to aid future Kaitens in whatever way we can, perhaps keeping them from stumbling around the way we have so often." She slid a glance up at him. "I suppose it is just as well. I'll have to give guidance to future Kenteis on how to handle stubborn, overworked, and bossy Kaitens."

He just smiled. "And I can give guidance on how to handle pushy, overprotective, possessive Kenteis." He stole another kiss. Against her lips, he said, "Should we stay here tonight or go home? I want to be alone with you."

Her fingers framed his face tenderly. "Let's have Unca Ewan distract Raven so we can be home. Our bed is much more comfy than any inn."

"It's a date," he agreed. He glanced around and let himself 'feel' the air of the city. It told him that there was no one else waiting for him. "Let's talk to the mayor then go home." With a little sigh, he said, "Ninety-two found."

The end was, finally, in sight.

Chapter Forty

"What is there to fight over when we are the same inside?"

After speaking with the mayor of Larksville, Tyrian was reassured that the fifteen militia units of the city would hold it while the Special Forces units came back with him to the castle. He and Cassie collected the other Stars from their waiting locations and returned via the mirror to their base. Ewan, tactful soul that he was, noticed rather pointedly that Kaiten and Kentei wanted to be alone. He intercepted Raven as she came to greet her parents and spirited her off to the pub to get a sundae from Persephone.

Tyrian and Cassie's need to be together was fairly obvious to one and all. Catherine stood with Marigold and they watched as their leaders headed for their tower. They weren't walking quickly, and it wasn't as if they deliberately ignored anyone else. But there was so much intimacy in the way their fingers brushed together that Catherine felt a little embarrassed to be watching them.

"There's an old story," Marigold murmured softly. "About how the swan became the symbol of peace."

Catherine looked at her curiously, her ears quirked. "What is it?"

"There was a black swan who lived among a flock of white swans," Marigold began. "He was a bit different, obviously, but he was accepted. One day, hunters came looking for feathers for sale in a town. The black swan rallied his family and spirited them away safely. In the process, he was wounded by a hunter. Before he could be killed, a female panther came out of the trees and went after the hunters for her next meal."

"And?"

"The hunters fled obviously. The panther, deprived of her meal, turned her attention on the swan, which was easy prey." She shook her head. "No one knows why she didn't kill him. Instead, she took care of him. She fished for the both of them, and let the swan ride on her back if his wing hurt too much for him to fly. Well, those hunters came back looking for the panther to get her claws. They found her hunting for food, and they threw a net over her. Before they could kill her, the swan came out of nowhere and protected her."

"And the sight of two natural enemies living together peacefully shook them up." Catherine was holding her breath. It seemed like a children's story, but she could believe it had happened.

"It was said that a few days later, there was a fight between two cities. Before the soldiers could come to blows, the swan and panther arrived. The swan knocked weapons out of hands and caused general mayhem before returning to the panther's side. And seeing them made people realize that peace *could* be found between such opposites." She smiled. "So the swan became the symbol of peace, and the panther became the symbol of hope."

"That's it!" Catherine waved her hands excitedly. "That's it! Marigold, that's *it*! Come with me!" She grabbed Marigold's wrist with her tail and dragged the narcissist behind her as she ran off to find where her art supplies had been stashed.

"You're getting me dirty, you lousy feline!" Marigold complained as she saw dirt splattering all over her clean clothes.

"Shut up and help me!" She snagged the sleeve of a bard going past. "Hey, are there any messengers around here?"

Myr blinked. "Yeah, the old guys." Curious, she followed along as Catherine dragged Marigold toward the small building that had been designated an art space. "Can I help with something?"

"Yeah!" Catherine briefly and concisely explained what was in her mind and knew she had gotten both of the other two females' assistance when they began grinning. "I'll get started on the flag! Marigold is great with a needle. You go send my message!"

"Okay!" Myr happily dashed off to find one of the three old gossips. She had been trying for months to come up with the symbol of the Liberation Army. Finally, they would have a proper flag for the cities to fly.

Come the dawn, Tyrian and Cassie were reluctantly watching their alone time disappear with the rising sun. They were sitting together in front of the fire with Cassie leaning against Tyrian and enjoying the feel of his arms around her. A thick blanket kept the wind from the open balcony doors from chilling them.

Tyrian combed his fingers through Cassie's hair and watched the strands glide over his fingers. When they had met, it had hung close around her face. It now fell to the tops of her shoulders. There wasn't a hint of curl in her hair, but that was to her advantage since it was so thick. "Are you going to cut it?" he asked as he rubbed his cheek against her hair.

"Not really," she said. "It seems to have stopped since I got my relic, so I figure I'll keep it." She smiled up at him. "Your hair is getting a little shaggy too."

He ran a hand through his hair. Unlike his need to shave, his regular hair had only slowed down a little in its ability to grow. Lane had told him it would taper off within another few months. Some people with Pure Relics just took longer for all growth processes to cease. Others like Cassie ceased right from the start. "Should I grow a ponytail?" he teased.

After a moment of thought, she said, "Maybe a small one. I think it would be very good on you." At the speculative look on his face, she sat up to turn around and face him. Her fingers trailed over his face to memorize the lines. "You never considered it before?"

"Actually, no." He smiled. "I'll give it a try. If it looks bad, I just need to get rid of it. It's not like I'd be stuck with it." He stretched largely and sighed. The sun was distinctly coming in the window. "Let's wash up and get dressed. By the time we're done, it'll be about right for heading to the meeting room. We can grab food along the way."

They had only just gotten dressed and pulled on their shoes when they heard the voice-box beginning to beep. Tyrian walked over and pressed the button. "We're on our way to the meeting room," he said.

"Detour," Matthias suggested. "Come down to the city center. We have something to show you."

Tyrian quirked a brow. "Alright." He looked at Cassie but she shook her head; she had no idea either.

Hands linked, they took the elevator down to the courtyard. To their surprise, it was pretty well vacant. It was as if everyone had gone to the city center as well. More intrigued than ever, Tyrian and Cassie made their way to the city center. It wasn't easy. They had to make their way through the crowd. Even with people trying to move out of the way, there wasn't much room to move to begin with.

It certainly seemed as if everyone in Aon Castle was present. Tyrian spotted all of his Stars as well as every civilian that could possibly fit. Soldiers sat on rooftops and packed the walls. He didn't worry that kids would be lost in the crowd; most rode on someone taller's shoulders. Laia had Raven perched on her shoulder, and Lupe sat on Ewan's; she waved when she saw Tyrian.

In the center of the crowd was an opening that Tyrian and Cassie finally reached. There they found Matthias with Myr, Catherine, and Marigold. Frances was also close at hand, and she and her fellow narcissist held onto the edges of some giant swatch of material in Tyrian's familiar black and green colors. He thought it might be a flag, but couldn't be sure. "What's the occasion?" he asked curiously.

"It would seem that Catherine had a moment of brilliant inspiration when she was speaking with Marigold," Matthias began. He lifted his voice so that everyone could hear him. "With Myr's help, she has created the symbol of the Liberation Army, and when she brought it to me, I knew she had finally realized what we'd all subconsciously known all along."

"Let's see it then," Tyrian said with a smile. "I trust you both."

Marigold and Frances opened up the flag with great flourish so that everyone could see it. Most realized instantly what they were looking at, but it took Tyrian and Cassie a few moments. When they did realize, they both felt greatly humbled.

The image in the center of the flag showed a black panther sitting with one paw in the air. Perched gracefully on the panther's paw was a black swan. It seemed almost impossible to tell who was supporting who. Though the panther held the swan in the air, the swan's body was arched protectively, his wings sheltering his love.

"Well." It was all Tyrian could say.

Catherine linked her hands together behind her back. The surprise in his eyes made her exasperated. Didn't he realize how they all saw him? "I have a friend named Jeo. He's a sculptor. Tod sent him a message for me last night. He lives in Pardue. I sent him my sketches so he can make a statue to go here too. Is . . . do you like it?"

"I love it," he said simply. "And I'm glad you were in charge, Catherine. Do you know how long it took me to *name* this place? Left to me, the war would be done and gone and Raven would have kids herself before I came up with a design!"

Laughter rippled through the crowd. Matthias smiled. "We have also sent the design to the other cities so that tailors can update the flags we already have flying. We lack our own tailor, so we must rely on others."

"Hopefully we find one soon," Persephone grumbled from where she stood in the crowd. She and Serentia shared mending and altering duties for the time being, and it was quite a lot on top of everything else they did.

The flag was absconded by some soldiers to be flown from the top of the castle itself, and the crowd began to disperse. Tyrian, Cassie, Matthias, Cherry, Ewan, and Kyle (the usual suspects, as Laia called them) made their way back into the castle and took the elevator up to the second floor.

Tyrian had no idea how Evelyn and Terrence had done it—he swore he had seen them in the crowd—but there were pastries, coffee, and other breakfast items waiting on a cart in the meeting room. They were still piping hot. Tyrian got a cup of coffee and decided to call it another quirk of his Stars' varied and sundried abilities.

They had only just seated themselves when Raven showed up with Divan. Though he was not a Star himself, Tyrian felt a strong kinship to the older man. Divan reminded him a great deal of Donald; he was not surprised that they had been such good friends. "Good morning," he said.

"Good morning." Divan put Raven down on the chair beside Tyrian and then took a seat as well. "I feel honored that I am being included here."

"You hold a skill on par with the Lower Generals," Matthias reminded him. "In fact, you *are* a Lower General, though it is for Foresalia. Your skill is very welcome, as is your knowledge of the Special Forces. That is something that not even our generals can provide to us. It was Lord Tyrian's request to have you here, and I concur wholeheartedly."

Divan smiled wryly at Tyrian. "Never meet Rihou. You'd take over the world."

The statement just made Tyrian more determined to meet the other boy, but he kept that to himself. "So noted," he said dryly. He saw Raven eyeing his coffee and offered her the mug. Caffeine didn't affect Faeries, thankfully. The last thing he needed was his daughter buzzed on an energy rush. "Pardue," he said. "We're past the games stage. I want to do there what we did at Larksville."

"Drop in unannounced in the middle of enemy units?" Ewan grumbled.

"Alright, I'd like to do *most* of what we did at Larksville," Tyrian conceded. "To be more specific, I want to talk to the lieutenant in charge of the units. He has the same orders that Divan did, and we know already that they refused to retaliate against the city for ceasing to pay taxes."

"How do we get there without transporting units?" Kyle asked. "Has anyone been to the city recently?"

"I know Olan's been there," Matthias supplied. "He ran reconnaissance for me not very long ago. Miranda could use him to take you to the city. Relatively speaking, of course."

Tyrian nodded. "Then we'll be on our way now." He took a deep breath. "I can't shake the feeling that there's something bad looming. The people in Trinan are in danger, of that I can be sure." He shook his head. "There's also that business of the checkpoints forming distinct paths right across the city."

"To the best of Kell and Grace's investigating," Cherry offered, "we know for a fact that it is a defensive mechanism. But even the people who live in the checkpoints aren't sure just what it is, what it does, or how it is triggered."

"It might be like the defenses on the checkpoints themselves," Cassie suggested. "Triggered only by hostile forces invading. We might even want to test it. Miranda could take Yhalenia out that that way and see how close they get before something happens. Yhalenia can shield both herself and Miranda from being seen, and if something happens, Miranda can bring them both back."

"Agreed." Matthias looked at Cherry. "Go talk to Yhalenia. As soon as Miranda has transported Lord Tyrian, she can take herself and Yhalenia near to Trinan. And they are to be very careful."

Cherry hurried out, and Tyrian got to his feet. "In addition to Olan, I'll take Kyle, Kris, and Yumi." Cassie went without saying, and he had stopped mentioning her. "Yumi deserves a chance to come along."

They had all noticed that the younger Stars were feeling the strain of not being able to help their Kaiten as much as they wanted. It surprised no one that Tyrian had picked up on it as well and was doing whatever he could to show them they were all just as important.

Kyle and Cassie followed Tyrian out of the meeting room, and none were surprised that the other three had already gathered near Miranda. They always knew when Tyrian needed them. The bond only got stronger as time passed.

Yumi was almost bouncing on her toes in excitement. When she saw Tyrian, she threw her arms around his waist. "I'm so glad I get to go along!" She beamed up at him and her hat fell over her eyes.

He put her hat back into place and then lightly tweaked her nose. "Since we're not going to have any field combat, you can help me get things done." He looked at Miranda. "Focus on Olan to send us to Pardue, please."

"Okay!" Miranda studied Olan and swung her wand into the air. "Here we go!"

The magic kicked in and sent everyone winging across the land. The good news was that they didn't land in the middle of the Special Forces. The bad news was that they landed in the river right next to the city.

Kyle was the first to surface, and when he didn't immediately see Yumi, he dove back under to find her. He caught her under the arms and propelled her to the surface quickly. Her belt with its tools added more weight than she could overcome by swimming. "You okay?" he asked her.

She held onto his shoulders and sighed. "Yes, thank you."

The others surfaced as well and they made their way to the shore. As they were climbing out, Tyrian realized a hand was being offered to assist. He looked up quickly to discover several soldiers from the Special Forces standing nearby. The lieutenant in charge was the one offering her help. "Thank you." He took her hand and let her pull him up out of the water. He then turned and helped Cassie and Kris.

"You certainly have a way of making an entrance," a soldier said dryly.

"We've done worse," Kyle sighed.

Tyrian studied the lieutenant before saying, "I'm beyond the point where I want to play games. A monster sits in Trinan, bloated by the promise of power. If she isn't stopped, then there will be nothing left. Rebellion? We're beyond that. Either you stand and fight for the people, or you fight for Blaine."

"We fight for the people," the lieutenant answered calmly as she removed the emblem from her jacket. "But we fight for you as well, Lord Tyrian. General Southerwind's last orders to us were clear. You may count on our strength joining yours. We will help you save our country."

His breath unraveled softly. So far. He had come so far. Every city in the Empire save the capitol was now under his protection. He held command over more than a hundred and twenty units. There were barely twenty total left at Trinan. For all intents and purposes, he commanded what had once been the entirety of the Imperial Army, and then some.

Kyle lightly rested a hand on his shoulder and looked at the lieutenant. "Rally your troops and have them switch to Tyrian's colors. Send a signal flare to Aon Castle and a unit will come to meet you. They will bring a flag to fly over Pardue."

"Done." The lieutenant saluted and then walked away with her soldiers.

"Thanks," Tyrian said softly.

"That's what friends are for." Kyle took a deep breath. "And I need to thank *you*, Tyrian. Seeing this happen . . . seeing what Ophelia wanted to happen actually start to occur . . . it makes her death easier to bear."

"I'm glad." Tyrian covered his hand for a moment and smiled. "Well, let's go into the city. By the time we've made the rounds, we should be dry again."

"Speak for yourself," Kris groused as she continued trying to wring out her robes. "You're not wearing ten layers of cloth!"

"You could be wearing ten layers of metal, you know," Olan reminded her.

She snorted. "I wouldn't have surfaced without help. At least cloth makes me buoyant. Most of the time, anyway. Remind me to tell you about when Klint and I went spelunking the hard way."

Lucky for all of them, the sun was high enough and hot enough that they had mostly dried by the time they entered the city. Kris and Cassie, wearing the most layers, were still slightly soggy but took it with good nature.

A palpable air of cheer lingered everywhere inside the city. Despite a different layout, Pardue looked quite similar to Larksville in many ways. The soldiers and the city militia were moving quickly, and the flags were being changed out. People were beginning to gather supplies and prepare for the final battle looming in the distance. No matter how you looked at it, Trinan would be devastated. Pardue citizens had every intention of giving the escapees and survivors every aid they could.

The party hadn't gotten very far into the city before they were assailed by a sudden cloud of strong cologne. "Euuw." Kris wrinkled her nose. "Who bathed in the perfume bottle again?"

A horse suddenly skidded to a stop beside them, and Tyrian sensed as much as heard the groans from those with him. He just smiled. "Greetings," he said.

The dandy perched on the back of the horse wore almost as many laces and ruffles as Frances did, had hair curlier than Laia's after the infamous Mechanoportal incident, and exuded a strong aura of self-importance. He peered down at Tyrian and nodded decisively. "You must be Lord Tyrian! I hear my cousin is at your palace." At the lifted brow, he sighed dramatically. "Frances Kween. I am Francis Garmint. And if you have the Kween branch, you simply *must* have the Garmint branch! We're so much more cultured than they are, you know. Of course you know!"

With all the frankness of childhood, Yumi said, "You smell like the bottom of a cologne bottle. Is your nose broken?"

Kyle and Olan choked and turned in different directions. Francis' face turned several shades of red before settling on an embarrassed pink. "I'll forgive your lack of taste because of your age," he decided graciously. "Only a mature woman of refined taste would ever appreciate my fine scent and masculine air."

Yumi looked at him for long moments and then looked at Tyrian. "If that's a refined gentleman, can I marry a Northman?"

Francis sputtered, then said, "Y-you would prefer a Northman to likes of me?!"

"They don't smell like perfume stores," she countered reasonably.

Knowing full well that Francis stood no chance against the pragmatic scientist, Tyrian took pity on him. "Francis, your aid is very welcome. I would be glad to have you on my side. You may wait for us to finish our rounds and go back with us, or you can go back with the soldiers."

"Soldiers?! Ugh. I'll wait here." As they walked away, he muttered, "How can she prefer a Northman to me? I'm cultured! I'm fashionable. I'm on a horse, damn it!"

"Don't worry," Kris told Yumi solemnly. "It's not your age. I wasn't that impressed either."

"Tell me there won't be any more narcissists in the Stars," Olan pleaded with Tyrian. "I know they have as much value as the rest of us, but they can be a bit trying, Lord Tyrian. The girls were enough without adding *him* to the mix. No offense to Catherine and Grim, but the catfights are pretty terrible."

Tyrian found himself laughing. "I can't promise anything, Olan. Everyone has a purpose. If we hadn't found Marigold and Frances, we'd have no flag to fly. We might not even have a symbol yet. They gave the inspiration to Catherine."

"Yes, but still." The archer sighed. "If I shoot that puffed up pink marshmallow in the ass, you can't blame me."

"So noted," his leader said dryly. He tugged Yumi's hat down slightly over her eyes. "I think Yumi has fine taste, personally."

She grinned up at him impishly. "Think Rourke has a little brother?"

"In fact, he has several." Tyrian smiled as he saw the looks on Kris and Kyle's faces. "But you're scaring your surrogate big siblings with these plans for being an adult. Enjoy being a kid, Yumi. It doesn't last long enough." Cassie slipped her hand into his without a word, and he laced their fingers together, his other hand resting companionably on Yumi's shoulder.

A young man suddenly popped out of a building. "Lord Tyrian!" Bits of dust and stone clung to his dark skin and dirty apron. In one hand was a chisel and in the other was a hammer. "I'm Jeo!" he said excitedly. "Cat's friend! I'm almost done with your statue! Come in and see it!"

"Ooh! Let me see!" Yumi darted into the building quickly.

The others followed, and Jeo turned on more lights than just his working ones. The statue sat in the middle of the main room, and it was being carved from black marble that held blue and green veins. The base was all that was left to be completed; the panther and the swan rose from the marble gracefully, so realistic that it was as if they were live animals posing for the artist.

The marble was still rough on the surface and in need of polishing, but Jeo's skill couldn't be missed. "It's amazing," Tyrian murmured. It was also very big, he realized. It stood a foot higher than he did. It would look amazing in the middle of the courtyard. "Transporting this will take some doing," he admitted. "It must weigh a ton."

Yumi held out her hands to Jeo. "Paper, please!" He handed her a notepad and a pencil, and she promptly began writing down what looked like complicated mathematical equations. "Height? Weight?" she asked Jeo. He supplied them and she wrinkled her nose as she studied her numbers. "I can get it there," she said decisively.

"Dare we ask how?" Kyle asked dryly.

"It won't blow up," she noted reasonably, "so you don't have anything to worry about, y'know. It'll get there just fine! I'm going to hijack the Mechanoportal through my Mechanobot. A bit of remote finagling and it'll be perfect."

Jeo grinned at Tyrian. "I have no idea what she's talking about, but she sounds like she knows what she's doing."

"She does," Tyrian assured him. He held out his relic hand with a smile. "I can't wait to see what else you create, Jeo. Are statues your specialty?"

"Nah, I do all kinds of carving." He took Tyrian's hand and smiled as the star appeared on his shoulder. "I do everything from tiny stuff to big stuff." His eyes flicked to Cassie, to her hands, and then back to Tyrian. "I'm versatile."

"Good to know," Tyrian murmured. "I might have a commission for you. And you'll let me pay you," he scolded. He turned to Olan and Kris. "Can you stay to help Yumi and Jeo? He'll no doubt have other things to bring with him as well."

"Can do!" Olan said with a salute.

Yumi was already issuing orders, and Tyrian, Cassie, and Kyle took their leave. Their next stop was to talk to the mayor, and since he currently worked out of the inn, they found themselves going to the fourth floor where he tried to keep out of the way of the travelers and tourists.

That the inn was four stories in height seemed impressive enough. It was the tallest building in the entire city, and the view from the top floor was spectacular. As they walked down the hall, Kyle studied the sparkling windows and said, "One wonders how they keep them clean."

A figure suddenly popped up on the other side of a window. He opened the bottom and leaned on the edge. "That'd be my job." When all three jumped in surprise, he winced. "Sorry about that. Aw, no worries," he added as they stared at him in shock, "My name is Amos. I'm a Flier! I'm not levitating." He grinned. "So, Lord Tyrian, you got windows you need cleaned?"

Tyrian walked closer to actually see the other male. He was indeed a Flier since there were large and elegant avian wings affixed to his back. His face seemed to be shaped more like a Human, but his bare feet were the familiar talon shape of his bloodline. He also didn't have hair; soft feathers covered his head and went around his neck like a collar. "You don't run the risk of being chased by Grimalkin, right?"

"Are we talking about the lovely Catherine?" Amos sighed gustily. "If only she would. Nah, Grimal don't chase Fliers. We've had some interesting histories together, but we're pretty peaceful to each other. The only cross-species feud I even know about is the Air Dragons and the plains Grimal of the Grasslands. Got me as to why, but they don't like each other at all."

"In that case, I have plenty of high windows for you to take care of," Tyrian assured him. "The top levels of the castle were getting a bit grungy from the outside since no one could figure out how to get there safely."

"Wings." Amos nodded sagely. "The only way to fly." He saluted with the scrub brush he carried. "I'll see you there, Lord Tyrian!" With a flutter of his wings, he flew off.

"He nearly gave me heart failure," Kyle complained. "There are no ledges around this place, so I couldn't figure out how he'd gotten there."

"Fliers are notorious for playing pranks like that on Humans," Cassie said ruefully. "I'm sure he'll catch many others unaware at Aon Castle too." She suddenly laughed. "Maybe we should warn Ewan."

Kyle grinned wickedly. "Now why would we do that, Cassie? It would serve him right!"

Tyrian just shook his head. After a meeting with the mayor—who was very happy to lend whatever help he could—Tyrian led the way back out of the inn. It was getting later in the day and he wanted to get back to the base to find out if they had learned anything about the barrier on Trinan and how it was triggered.

He started to turn back toward the road leading to the entrance where Francis was no doubt waiting with Jeo and the others, but his attention got caught by the sight of an armory shop. Something tugged at him insistently and he recognized the feeling immediately. He went over to the shop and stepped into the open doorway.

The woman inside the shop had been working over a forge, but when she sensed Tyrian's presence, she lowered her mallet and lifted her visor. She studied Tyrian for several moments and then smiled. "I'm Oruqui." The name belied her Elfish blood as strongly as her pointed ears and delicately coiled pink hair did. "I'll pack up my things."

To Cassie and Kyle's mutual fascination, it was that simple. Oruqui stuck the piece of plate she had been working on into a bucket of water and began to pack up tools. Tyrian stepped back onto the street and said, "I think that's everyone here." He saw the looks on their faces and smiled. "You're not used to it yet?"

"It's fascination more than surprise," Kyle decided. "I think of the hoops you've jumped through for some of us, then how easy it is for others. Mouse told me that there was a balance in all of life, but I don't think it sank in until now. Ah, well." He tucked his hands into his pockets. "Let's head back before Olan snipes Francis with an arrow. That'd be bad form, right?"

"Afraid so," Tyrian said dryly. "Keep that up and you'll turn into Ewan."

"Bite your tongue."

Chapter Forty-One

"Curse me not for my heart; curse me not for my way."

After picking up those waiting for them, Tyrian used the Echo Mirror to transport everyone back to the castle. Whatever Yumi had done had been successful, and the statue waited in the courtyard for Jeo to finish it. It wasn't the only thing waiting. Squint and Ewan waited, too.

"Tyrian," Ewan said, "you need to come to the meeting room, quickly."

Squint's entire body seemed to be vibrating with anger, and smoke puffed from her nose. "I'm going to eat Blaine!" she vowed fiercely.

"You'd get indigestion." Tyrian wrapped an arm around her shoulders and urged her along as he followed Ewan. He could smell, never mind sense, the Dragon magic rumbling through his Star's body. It grew stronger every passing day.

Inside the meeting room, Matthias and Alex stood talking with three newcomers. Two were female, one was male. The male was a teenager wearing the clothes of a Dragonist; clothes that fit more snug than usual to cut down on wind resistance, but actual plate armor on the top in the form of a half breastplate and shin guards. A lance was sheathed on his back.

One of the females had pure white hair and snowy white eyes. She wore casual clothing normally suited to a civilian, but her body was strong despite being slender, seeming to imply she was a combatant of some type. Around her left wrist rested a silver bracer identical to one worn by the young man. Power permeated the air around her in a familiar way.

The other female wore full plate armor and had a battleaxe on her back. Her helm sat on the table beside her, so her short black hair and lively brown eyes were visible. She wasn't lovely by the normal definition, but her features seemed pleasing to look at. She looked not much older than the Dragonist.

Tyrian knew two things on one look. One, he knew that he was looking at the Dragonist that Alex had met with. And two, he knew that the Warrior and the berserker were both Destined Stars. The white haired female, he was sure, was Ryu's Dragon partner, Celestial. "Greetings," he said. "I understand there's something wrong."

"You understand right." Ryu looked at him sadly. "I am so sorry, Lord Tyrian. I wanted to come and offer the assistance of the Dragonist clan. Instead, I must ask for yours."

"I have a feeling I'm not going to like this." Tyrian sat down at the table with a sigh. He raked his hands through his hair. "Let's start at the top."

Everyone except for Squint sat down. She was pacing off her agitation. Because it helped her stay calm, the others didn't argue. "To begin with," Alex said, "let me introduce you to Ryu and Celestial. They are the Dragonist pair that I met with long ago. With them is Tamari. She isn't a Dragonist, but she came with Ryu in case something happened to Celestial."

"And other reasons," Tamari admitted. "Obvious ones."

"Indeed. I'm glad for your aid. There aren't enough axe users around here." Tyrian found a smile. "And watch out for my daughter. She'll be peppering you with questions."

"So noted."

Matthias linked his hands on top of the table. "Yhalenia and Miranda returned from their reconnaissance an hour before Ryu arrived. As soon as they were within a mile of the city, they triggered the defense mechanism. Beams of light came from the directions of the four checkpoints and encased the entirety of Trinan in a powerful barrier. It blocks everyone and everything from getting in or out. Miranda examined the barrier before they came back, and she is certain that Dragon magic could break it."

"Dragon magic," Celestial offered, "is not necessarily *stronger* than the magic belonging to anyone else, but it tends to be more *potent*, possibly because we live such long lives. We average a few centuries in age. Ryu is my third partner in my life. I might have three or four more."

Tyrian closed his eyes. "And with a barrier only breakable by Dragon magic, it would stand to reason that that would provoke me to seek out the Dragonist clan sooner rather than later. And on the basis that Ryu is here for my help, and there was concern for Celestial's health, I can assume that Blaine has made the first strike against you."

"We're not even sure what's wrong." Ryu stared at the table blindly. "Dragons are just . . . dying. Left and right. It's a curse of some kind. And because we're linked to our Dragons, the rest of us are getting violently sick. I don't even know why Celestial and I have been spared. There's supposed to be a doctor somewhere who can break curses, but none of us can be spared to find them. I'm so sorry, Lord Tyrian, that we must ask this of you on top of everything else."

"It's not your fault!" Ewan snapped. "Kid, it's no one's fault except for Blaine!"

"I agree," Tyrian said firmly. Even saying it, he couldn't help but feel his own share of guilt. It was Cassie's hand on his leg that kept him steady. This had to end before anyone else died. "I'll go with you to the Dragonists stronghold. I'll speak with your leader and make things formal. I'll break the curse and you can lend whatever help you can to breaking the barrier."

Squint's hands hit the table with a thump. "I'm going!" She stuck her chin out in a stubborn angle. "It's my kind that's being hurt! I have to help, Lord Tyrian! I know I'll be in danger of getting sick, but I have to do this!"

"Easy," he said. "I won't stop you." He smiled. "Why would I turn down the help of my Dragon monk? Tamari, I'd like you to go along as well since you're familiar with the landscape. For the sixth, we'll bring Dylan. I'm not sure I want to expose Magicians or Healers to whatever's going on there until we're sure it is racially confined and not simply targeting powerful magic."

"It'll be easy enough to get there," Kyle noted. "Miranda can use her magic to transport you there. We'll begin preparing for the final battle while you're gone." He stopped and shook his head. "What an odd thing that is to say."

There were ten Destined Stars to be found. Somehow, Tyrian had no doubts that he would find all of them before he returned to the castle the next time. He could feel them calling to him. He was so close to unlocking his relic's full potential that he could feel the magic brimming over inside. On one hand, he wasn't looking forward to the final spell's effects, but on the other, he knew it would be needed.

Dylan waited for them by the time the group reached Miranda. He asked no questions. All he said was, "Where to, Tyrian?" Interest lit his eyes as he spotted Tamari. "Hello." He smiled. "I don't often meet female berserkers. It's a nice change."

"I was bored with just swords," she admitted dryly. "And I have a tendency to be, uhm, a bit out of control when I start fighting, so it just fit."

"She's not legal," Ryu told Dylan dryly.

Dylan grinned at him. "But not by enough that I'm not allowed to appreciate her." He offered a hand. "Dylan."

"Ryu." He shook Dylan's hand and decided he would like the hard-edged berserker; he had a good heart. "This is Celestial, my partner. And that's Tamari. She's not a Dragonist, though. She hasn't met a Dragon she was comfortable with."

"It must be like having a twin," Cassie murmured. "Someone you have to be able to trust implicitly and understand wholly."

Celestial crooked an arm around Ryu's neck. Both stood roughly the same height as Cassie did. "So far Ryu's been my favorite partner," she said. "I'm going to miss him like hell when he's gone." Without hesitation, she admitted, "He might well be my last partner. Sometimes it happens that way. That one partner is so special you can't replace him or her."

Ryu smiled at her. "You're just glad I let you cheat at chesstac."

"That too."

Tyrian smiled. He was not really surprised that Celestial wasn't a Star herself. She and Ryu were a package deal; only one needed to be a Star. And Ryu was the one who needed Tyrian as much as Tyrian needed him, and therefore that was where Destiny swayed. Tyrian often felt that life was a tapestry that Destiny wove with careful threads; he was still figuring out the pattern to his.

"Okay, who's the victim this time?" Miranda asked curiously.

"Him." Squint pointed at Ryu. "We're going to the Dragonists' stronghold in the mountains." She frowned at Cassie suddenly. "How come we've never run into each other?"

"Different ends of the mountains," Cassie explained. "And deliberately so. Would *you* want to have two such powerful factions in close proximity? It would cause more trouble than it was worth."

"Fair enough."

Miranda swung her wand up and focused on Ryu. "Hang on everyone! Here we go! Please work!" she added under her breath as her relic began to glow brightly.

It might have been simply that asking nicely was all that was needed, but when everyone landed outside the stronghold, they landed safely. Everyone was intact, together, and not in a tree or river. "Holy hell," Dylan said. "She did it."

"Follow me," Ryu said. "We'll go talk to Draco Silver. He's the leader of the Dragonists."

The party fell into step behind him and Celestial, and Tyrian looked around curiously. The stronghold was built directly into the cliffs of the mountains, and caves served as homes and shops alike. It gave them added shelter from the sometimes bitter winters that came to the peaks this high, and it also allowed for structures big enough to accommodate Dragons in either their natural form or their chosen smaller shape.

Most chose to take a Human shape when they wanted to be smaller, but others opted for Elf. Curiously, they couldn't take a Faerie or Flier shape. Squint's best guess was that it had to do with their wings. In any shape, a Dragon retained his or her strength, so it was just as well they couldn't become a delicate Faerie.

The entire stronghold felt quiet and somber. Only a handful of people walked around. Doors were shut up and down the cliffs. The only door that stood open was the one for the infirmary. Several Healers were coming and going as quickly as possible. Beyond the main area, tucked behind some trees, was what looked like a new, and alarmingly large, graveyard.

"How many lost?" Tyrian asked quietly.

Ryu took a long breath. "The Dragonist clan stood at two units in strength. We're down to one on active duty, and half a unit in various stages of illness. We've lost over five hundred thus far. It seems to simply grow faster and spread quicker the more people we lose. That's why we weren't even sure Celestial would make it. She's an older Dragon, and they seem more vulnerable."

The guards outside the leader's domain were glad to move aside to let the party enter. The strain showed visibly on their faces as well. The Dragonists were as close as the monks were, and because of it, they all suffered.

Ryu led the way to the meeting room, and as he walked inside, he said, "I've brought Tyrian Southerwind. He's here to help us so that we can help him as well."

The man sitting at the table with his head in his hands couldn't have been much older than Ewan, but worry for his people had aged him rapidly. Without looking up, Draco Silver said, "I'm sorry, Tyrian. I would not have asked you to come here in this way."

Somehow unsurprised by the tug inside, Tyrian walked over and knelt down beside him. "It was inevitable that I come here to help," he said softly. "Even if you hadn't sent for me, I would have known you needed me. Ryu and Tamari are Destined Stars . . . and so are you. There may be others as yet here. That means all of you are mine to protect. Perhaps that as much as the threat to the barrier is why Blaine came after you. I'm going to make everything right. I promise it."

Draco straightened up with a little smile. "You make me believe the impossible."

"He's good at that," Dylan agreed.

"How is Peyn?" Tamari asked Draco. "Is he still okay?" At the curious look from Squint, she explained, "Peyn is Draco's partner."

"He's fine so far. He's been tending to the youngest, trying to keep their spirits from lagging." Draco drew a deep breath. "Lord Tyrian, I cannot offer my service to you until my people are whole once more. Please. I beg of you to find a cure. There's supposed to be a hidden city somewhere in the Empire where people have escaped the tyranny. If the doctor who can cure curses is anywhere, then that is where he or she will be."

"We've covered most every inch of the Empire," Cassie said softly. "We've been through the forest, and we've seen most of the mountains.

Where else could there be left to be hidden? With so much flat land, there is no hiding a town of any size in the Empire."

"We'll have to figure out something." Tyrian got to his feet. "I'd like to talk to everyone here, if that's okay. Perhaps there will be more pieces to the puzzle that I can use to find this hidden city. Someone will always know something. Ryu, would you show me and Cassie around?"

"Gladly."

Celestial nodded slightly. "I will secure rooms for everyone. It is late enough that we couldn't leave today if we wanted to."

Dylan decided to stay to talk to Draco, and Squint went with Tamari for a tour of the training grounds. Tyrian and Cassie followed Ryu out of the building and into the main area of the stronghold. They went up one level to a row of doors and Ryu said, "This is where our civilians reside. We have shops and the like, of course. We even have a Tradesmaster. It's where we get a lot of our supplies. Oh, and we have a tailor and a teacher. We have kids here too."

He pushed open the door to a shop to let Tyrian and Cassie in and then followed them calling, "Anyone home?"

"Ouch!"

He winced as he heard the yelp. "Sorry, Dart. Did I startle you?"

With a scowl, an older woman with blonde hair only just starting to go gray came out of the back room shaking out her hand. "Stabbed myself with a needle, dang it." She propped her hands on her hips as she surveyed the two that he had brought in. "So what have we here? What have you brought me, Ryu?"

"A hero." He nodded firmly.

"A friend," Tyrian corrected. He smiled. "I'm only a hero on my off days. Most of the time I'm just running around trying to keep people from doing stupid things. And stopping the inventor from blowing up stuff." He sighed. "Or traumatizing the sheep."

"Oh my." Dart decided she liked him. "So you're Tyrian Southerwind, eh? Hmm. You're cuter than I expected."

"Thanks," he said dryly.

There was something about him that tugged sharply at her. He looked like a man in serious need of someone to take burdens off his shoulders. She could practically see the ropes tying him down! And she was sure, positive, that she could help him in some way. He needed her. "Who does your tailoring out at that castle of yours?"

"Our barkeep and our gardener."

"Well, that won't do!" She nodded firmly. "I'll have to come out there and take over. You can't be fighting a war while worrying that you'll split your pants or something." She went over to the door and leaned out. "Tyler!" she shouted. She pulled her head back in and grinned. "Don't suppose you need a teacher, too, do you? I can't very well leave my husband here. He'd whine."

A gray haired older man walked in the door with a rueful smile. Though climbing in age, he was still trim and fit, well able to keep up with the little hooligans he tried to teach. "You bellowed?" he asked dryly.

"We're going to Aon Castle."

"We are?" He blinked at his wife and then looked at Tyrian. Instantly, he realized what she was thinking and why. If this was Tyrian Southerwind, then he definitely needed their help. Tyler could feel it inside. And there was sadness as well. Why were the heavy burdens put on the shoulders of the young? "If you need a teacher, I'm glad to help as well, Lord Tyrian."

"We have a lot of kids running amok," Tyrian said frankly. "If you can corral them, I welcome you with thanks."

"Not that they idolize their Kaiten Star," Cassie murmured drolly. "Someone *else* would run amok if I wasn't there to keep him out of trouble on a daily basis."

"Shush."

Dart and Tyler exchanged a grin. They had been married for thirty years and they still bickered like that. It spoke well for a good, long life together. Bickering with the one you loved was half the fun. Making up was the other half. "We'll start packing," Tyler promised. "By the time the curse is gone, we'll be ready to go." There was no doubt in him at all that Tyrian would find a way. The green-eyed Kaiten could do anything he set his mind to.

"Wow," Ryu said softly as they left the shop. "I mean, I felt it myself, but it's sort of amazing to watch it happen to someone else. I wish I could have been there for you for longer, Lord Tyrian."

"You're here now. It's enough."

They stopped by the item shop and armory, the owners of which were glad to see Tyrian as well. There wasn't anyone in the Empire who didn't know that he was the only one who could make everything right again.

It was evening by the time they got to the trade shop, and the young Flier who ran it was in the process of turning over the closed sign. When she saw who approached, she opened the door for them with a smile that lit her blue eyes. "Come in anyway."

"Not if you're closed," Tyrian protested.

"Nah, it's okay. I don't mind. I'm just keeping the kids out." She let the door close behind them and walked over to begin closing cabinets and displays that showed wares from around the world. The brown and blue feathers that covered her head and wings fluttered lightly in the air as she moved. "There's so little to be happy about right now. The kids come here to look at the toys from other countries and think about when things were so much better. There's no one who hasn't lost a loved one. And we lose more by the day. Oh." She turned around quickly. "I'm so sorry to rattle on like that."

"Don't be," Tyrian disagreed.

"I'm Cleo." She smiled as she said it. "I took over the shop from my parents." Her gaze lowered. "Dad was a Dragonist," she whispered. "His partner was one of the first to fall ill. It took him and my mother fairly quickly too." She lifted her chin. "Lord Tyrian, if you'll help us, I want to help you. Aon Castle could use a trade shop too. I mean, it's become a hub for the Empire, right? You can't sustain commerce on just regular shops. Stuff has to go outside the country. I can help you do it."

"Done," Tyrian said instantly. "I know I can count on you, Cleo."

She beamed. "Okay then! I'll get my stuff together." She hesitated and then hugged him tightly. "You just looked like you needed that."

Oddly, he had. "Thank you," he said softly.

When they had made their way back to the inn situated in the middle of the stronghold, it was no longer evening and had finally become night. Tyrian felt exhausted to his soul, evidence that he had hit the ground running from the moment he had woken. Claiming a city and arranging to fight a curse could be tiring.

Dylan and Squint sat in the nearly empty dining room with Celestial and Tamari. The female berserker and younger Dragon were having a lively conversation while their older companions relaxed over ale. Somehow, Tyrian wasn't surprised that Tamari and Squint had bonded quickly. They suited each other very well. Whether they partnered or not, he didn't particularly care. He just wanted them to be happy.

As Tyrian sat beside him, Dylan said wistfully, "I wish she was legal."

"Sixteen isn't *that* far off from eighteen. Just date her until you can court her. Patience can be rewarding, Dylan." Tyrian grimaced as he took the glass of brandy that Cassie offered. "I just had another of those weird Pure Relic moments. I realized my birthday was in roughly a month and a half, and that I would only be nineteen. I don't feel it. I feel old."

"You are old," Dylan retorted bluntly. "Inside. Before I went to meet up with you, I ran into Yumi. She was crying because you'd told her to enjoy being a child, and she'd realized that you'd been cheated out of it."

Tyrian didn't deny the charge. It had nothing to do with the events on his birthday, and it had nothing to do with the fact that most people were at least mostly mentally and emotionally mature by eighteen. His whole life, he had always been older inside. Perhaps partially because of being bound to the Devourer at nine, perhaps partially because of his father's job. "I suppose so," he agreed quietly.

"Dinner!" The announcement came from a lovely brunette carrying a tray with plates on it. She passed out the plates and then put down a basket of bread. "I'm C.J.," she said with a smile to Tyrian. "I'm the innkeeper here. Well, sort of," she added on a laugh. "I'm more like a denmother! I'm always taking care of others. But I enjoy it, so they indulge me." Tamari had pointedly pulled over an extra chair, and she sat down with a sigh. "I have beds to turn down."

"And yet she doesn't move." Tamari happily broke open a loaf of bread.

"My feet are too grateful." She propped her elbows on the table and smiled as she watched everyone dig into their food. Especially Tyrian. The poor thing looked as if he simply didn't have enough time to think let alone sit and relax. She wasn't that much older, but she definitely got the feeling he needed someone to take some pressure off his shoulders. "Do you have an inn for travelers out where you are?"

"Sure do." Tyrian dunked a piece of bread into his soup. "We have an innkeeper named R.K. He's been with me from the beginning." He sighed. "Poor guy wears too many hats. He was doing the cooking and the cleaning on top of everything else until we found other people to take over. He's single-handedly running that inn, and with the massive foot traffic, I'm worried he's going to work himself to death."

"I could help him. I'm good at bossing people around until they take a break."

"She is," Ryu assured Tyrian.

"Then your help is greatly appreciated. And I know I speak for R.K. as well." Tyrian shook his head wryly. "I worry about all my friends to begin with. I don't need you all working yourselves into the ground for my sake or anyone else's either!" He smiled at her. He had a sneaking suspicion that R.K. would be putty in her hands, and he couldn't have been happier. "Thanks, C.J."

"Anything I can do," she said simply as she got to her feet and picked up her tray. "And I'd feel that way even if I wasn't a Destined Star."

As she walked away, Tamari asked. "Did anyone know anything?"

"The item seller said something that caught my attention," Tyrian admitted. "When I mentioned that I was going to be looking for this hidden city, he said that if he was going to hide a city, he'd go to ground. It made me think about my castle. What if the hidden city is *underground*?"

"That makes sense," Celestial said slowly. "It would certainly be off detection of the capitol."

Squint groaned and put her head on the table. "How do you find something underground?"

"Let's be logical," Cassie said. "If you're going to live underground, you still need a way to get supplies. You're also going to need water. If you emerge, you need to emerge in a place where you're not going to be immediately seen."

Dylan tapped a finger on the table. "Isn't there a really small lake in the forest, other than Gammine's? It's too close to Foresalia for a city to be built there, so it hasn't been tapped as a source of water. If I was hiding, that'd be a good place for it."

"From where we are, we're close to the Commune of Soldiers," Ryu said. "A day or two out. Relative to that and the checkpoint further south, how far are we from that spot?"

"By foot, we're talking a few days."

"What about by flight?"

"I have no idea. How long does it take you to fly to the Commune?" Dylan asked Celestial.

"A few hours. We'd be flying downhill, so it goes faster. Most Dragons can cover in a few hours what people can cover by foot in a day. Not only are we faster to begin with, we also don't have to deal with monsters."

"Then we're probably a day's flight away from the lake." He eyed Celestial. "I don't know how big Dragons can get, but can you carry all of us at once?"

"I can certainly try. At the worst, I can literally carry two of you in my claws while everyone else rides." She glanced at Squint and then back again. "We might also be able to recruit another Dragon to help us out."

Because it was getting late, and they wanted an early start, they split up for the night. Tyrian said little as he went down the hall with Cassie; his mind was buzzing in a million directions with everything left to be done. "It seems like the closer we get to being done," he said softly, "the more I want to run away. I hate myself for that."

Her arms slid around his waist and she pressed against his back. "That's only natural. The pressure is just getting stronger. Externally and internally." She feathered her lips over his shoulder. "I can feel the magic inside you getting hotter. Not just when we make love, but at all times. We can do this, Tyrian."

"We?"

She smiled. "You're not alone, remember?" She caught her breath as he turned suddenly and his arms banded around her waist. He buried his face against her neck and she wrapped her arms around him. "I'm here," she promised softly. "I could never leave you. And you have the others as well. Whatever you need from us, we provide."

He turned and tumbled her down onto the bed. "Right now, I need only you. Don't let go of me, Cassie. I'm safe in your arms."

Let go of him? There was no letting go of him. She knew it and accepted it. She would hold onto him for eternity.

In the morning, just before dawn, they met up with the others in the dining room. C.J. had suspected they would be up early, and she had coffee and food waiting for them. Squint was more restless than usual, unable to sit still. Finally she blurted, "I want to help! I'm going to help fly us there!"

"But!" Tamari stopped when Dylan held an arm in front of her and shook his head silently. She clung onto his arm tightly, her eyes dark with distress. Squint had told her everything. She knew why this was dangerous.

Tyrian walked over to Squint and put his hands on her shoulders. "Are you sure?" he asked her quietly. "I know full well what this means, and what it might do to you."

"Well, I don't!" Ryu said. "What's wrong with Squint taking her natural shape?"

"She hasn't done it since she was a baby," Cassie explained softly. "We found her in her natural shape, but she transformed into a Human one while we were transporting her to safety. She's never changed back. The eye that was lost was her focal point."

"Her . . ." Ryu took a sharp breath. Every Dragon had a focal point where their power was strongest. Losing that point was like losing all control over their power. Squint's choice not to transform back to her natural shape was not that much of a choice after all. It would be something she had no control over. "You're still a kid," he told her fiercely. "Especially by Dragon standards! We can figure something else out."

"I have to do this!" She shook her head so hard that her red hair flew around her face. "I have to help Lord Tyrian! Doc said that if I tried hard, I could control my power again. I'm going to do it!"

Losing control of her power would destroy not only Squint, but also potentially anyone in the area. Tyrian knew it. But he also had full faith in her. He knew she had the strength for this. "If you think you can do this, then I *know* you can."

Knowing he believed in her made it easier for her to calm her nerves. She had to do this. She could do this. Tyrian believed in her and he needed her.

"Let's go where there is more room," Celestial said. "Down to the landing area would be best."

She led the way, and everyone stayed back as far as they could so that Squint had plenty of space. She seemed impossibly young as she stood in the center of the landing zone and looked at the places where claws had dug into stone for purchase. She had never felt a lack of her Dragon origins. The monks had made her one of them. But, now, it was time to claim her true shape.

The fire that billowed into the air around her was not unexpected. Her red coloring and smoky breath belied a Fire Dragon heritage. She closed her eye and concentrated fiercely on willing her power to do what she wanted it to do. She didn't even know *what* she was doing. It was all instinct. She thought she could see the spell she had used to take her Human shape, and thought that undoing it might be what she needed.

The magic began to go rogue. Sparks leapt over her skin as the fire burned out of control. "Get back!" Celestial shouted. She shifted into her Dragon shape with a surge of white, cloudy light and covered Ryu, Tamari, and Dylan protectively with her wings. She managed to wrap her tail around Cassie and bring her closer for safety, but Tyrian moved forward before she could stop him. "Lord Tyrian!"

"Get back!" Squint cried at Tyrian. "I can't do this!"

"Yes, you can." He stood only feet in front of her, his green eyes calm. "You were chosen to share the skies with me, Squint. That means that you have something only you can do. This is that something. You *can* do this, and you will."

Tears welled in her eye and she found a tremulous smile. "I can do anything."

The power engulfed her and surged outward in a red sea. Tyrian dove to the side and rolled several feet to safety. When he cautiously lifted his head, he found himself nose to snout with a lovely red Dragon. She was lying in front of him with her head on her claws, her good eye almost shy. The other, no longer covered by a patch, showed the mark of vicious scars where someone had deliberately attacked her.

He rolled nimbly to his feet and wrapped his arms around her neck to gently kiss the scars. She wasn't very big compared to an adult Dragon, though that was to be expected; at most, her length was ten feet from tip to tail, with her wings that and a half. Celestial was half that larger. "You make a beautiful Dragon," he told her. Teasingly, he added, "I hope I won't have to scare off your Dragon admirers. I think I'd be outmatched."

She rubbed her head against him contentedly. "Nah, I'm okay with being a kid for now." Her ears perked up and she lifted her head to look at the others. "It's okay now. I think I have control. But I can't change too frequently."

"That's normal," Celestial told her as she lowered her wing so the others were freed. "Even with a focal point, young Dragons can't change shape often. Actually, the fact that you changed shape successfully as a baby without your focal point is evidence of your natural skill. You'll do just fine, Squint."

"You look amazing!" Tamari hurried over to hug Squint as well, her eyes bright with excitement. "I can't believe how amazing you look! Don't worry about flying. I've heard the other Dragons say it's as natural as breathing."

"Squint, if you can carry Lord Tyrian and Lady Cassie, I can carry the other three," Celestial said as she offered a claw to help Ryu climb nimbly up onto her back.

"Okay!" Squint lay down again to make it easier for Tyrian and Cassie to climb onto her back. She barely felt their weight, and they were just enough smaller to fit perfectly. "Will I get bigger?" she asked wistfully.

"Of course you will. You're of average height for your age, hon." Tamari wistfully eyed her and then went over to join Ryu and Dylan. She really wanted to ride with Squint, but there was no room for a third person.

Having never flown, the three newcomers had no idea what to expect. The two Dragons got a running start and then suddenly took off up into the air. Squint was a little wobbly, but as soon as she caught the wind, her balance steadied. "I can't see to my left," she told Tyrian and Cassie. "Please watch out for me."

"No worries." Celestial flew down onto Squint's left. "I can block this side."

"This is amazing!" Tyrian exclaimed. "I've always wondered what it would be like to fly!"

Hearing the happiness in his voice just made Squint feel even better about her accomplishment. *She* had given him this wish, and had made him happy. Something only she could do. She had done it damn well.

Chapter Forty-Two

"A secret, down in the deep."

Covering the land by air was not only quick, but it felt even faster. The ground was little more than a blur below them, and animals and monsters seemed like little dots. They weren't very high in the air, only a few hundred feet, but it was an awe-inspiring sight to those not used to it.

They stopped only for a break around noon so that they could eat. Squint was very hungry because she wasn't used to being in her natural shape and burned much more energy in it. Quite used to traveling with a Dragon, Ryu had brought plenty of food.

Once refueled, they got on their way again. Celestial kept to Squint's left so that she didn't worry about something approaching from that direction. There was no concern for monsters or enemy attacks, but something as innocuous as a bird might startle her and throw her off balance.

Evening had begun to fall as they flew over the top of the trees that encircled the lake. They found a safe place to land, and the riders slid down to ground level. Tamari, grinning, had to hold Dylan up since his legs were shaky. "Amateur," she teased. "That's why Ryu and I were always shifting our weight. Keeps from cutting off the blood to our legs."

"Now she tells me," the taller male groused. Not that he complained about getting to lean on her though, and if the flirty way she kept looking up at him was any clue, she was not complaining either. He would *definitely* have to ask her to date him—if she didn't ask him first.

Tyrian and Cassie were only slightly unbalanced since both had seen what Ryu and Tamari did and had guessed why. Celestial changed into her Human shape, and Squint cautiously reached for her magic to do the same. It took two tries, but she did manage to go back into Human form. Unfortunately, her legs gave out and she sat down hard on the ground. "I'm dizzy."

"You're exhausted." Dylan knelt beside her. "I'll carry you, okay?" She wrapped her arms around his shoulders and he stood with her perched on his back. It fascinated him that someone who could be such a large creature would feel that small in this form. He almost couldn't believe she was a Dragon at all.

Cassie was the best tracker of the lot, and she began to scout out the area for anything unusual. She wanted to find signs of civilized life since it was not an area normally frequented by people. She finally found it in the shape of a bed of leaves and moss. It had been too precisely placed to have been made by nature, and as she pushed it aside, she realized why. It was a carefully constructed cover that went over the top of a set of stairs leading down into the land. "Here we go. This looks promising."

She went first, followed by Tamari. The others went down after them with Ryu bringing up the rear after putting the covering back in place. The tunnel was obviously well used since it was lit nicely with a series of Light Relics imbedded in the walls. At the end of the tunnel was what looked like a larger light leading into what might have been a hidden city.

A guard stood at the end of the tunnel and she straightened as she saw the group approaching. Her eyes went directly to Tyrian and she brightened visibly. "You're Lord Tyrian!" She turned and hurried into the city beyond. "Lord Tyrian is here!" she called happily. "Everyone, come out!"

All manner of people began to emerge from the catacomb-like rooms as Tyrian and the others walked into the area. It was a *very* tiny village and boasted a population of less than fifty. The entire 'city' could have fit into the courtyard of Aon Castle. Every manner of age and race was represented, as well as a blend of civilian and combatant alike. To Tyrian's utter shock, he found himself looking at more than one face that struck that familiar chord inside. Though Draco had not formally joined, he counted as found, so there had been only six Destined Stars left.

All six stood before him.

One was a female Grimalkin who was more feline than Human in appearance, and she clapped her hands together happily. Though she had distinct fingers, they were short enough that they almost looked like paws. Her hair, tail, and soft fur were orange with white tabby stripes. At her feet sat two tame Dire Wolves, evidence that she was a Beastmaster. "You made it!" she said happily. "I'm Solei!" She scampered forward and clasped Tyrian's hand. "Shadi said if we waited, you'd find us when you needed us! You can count on me and Van to tame any monsters we meet!"

Tyrian found himself smiling at her. He glanced over her head to where a male Human stood with a winged monster perched on his shoulder. Both Beastmasters wore similar sturdy traveling clothes and leather bracers around their arms for taloned creatures to land without harm. "Since I lack any methods of dealing with monsters other than killing them, I'm grateful for you both."

Van grinned. "Solei can be a bit of a handful, but I'm fairly good at taming her too."

She stuck her tongue out at him and made everyone laugh. An Elf with golden hair stepped forward with a smile. She wore lightweight chain armor with casual elegance. On each hip was a scimitar. "I'm Honey," she said. "I'm normally at home on the seas, so if you need me to do any sea battles, just let me know."

"So far we haven't needed any, but that might as yet change," Tyrian told her. The river ran close enough past Trinan that it would certainly allow for an unexpected angle to attack from. He and Matthias had discussed it more than once.

"Well," another Human girl said, "I'm not a fighter, but I make some darned pretty stained glass. My name is Sierra!" She looked barely older than Yumi, and her green eyes were just as lively. Her hands showed the soot stains and abrasions from her art. "I don't know if you need any stained glass windows, but that's my specialty."

Tyrian thought of the dull and boring windows that Amos kept clean and decided, "Considering the lack of color around the castle, you are certainly needed! In fact, if you want to go after my balcony doors first and foremost, I'd be grateful. I leave the art in your hands. I have no taste."

"Liar," Tamari said with a snort.

Sierra grinned. She knew he was lying too, but she appreciated that he did it to make her know that he trusted her completely. She actually had several pieces in mind that she really wanted to give him. She had seen him in her dreams for a long time, and she had been making things with him in mind for months.

A Human woman in her mid-thirties stepped forward and said, "Alright, everyone, start the packing process again. Let me talk to Lord Tyrian." She smiled as most everyone scampered off. "My name is Shadi. I'm a Healer by choice and a doctor by trade."

Ryu caught his breath. "Wait, can you cure curses?" When she nodded, he began to breathe again. "We need you," he said urgently. "The Dragonists have been cursed and our Dragons are dying!"

"Please," Tyrian said. "I know you're the only one who can do this."

She smiled at the others in bemusement. "Is it always like that?"

As one, the others said, "Yes."

She shook her head. "Well, obviously I'm not about to say no. When I was gathering survivors, I was deliberately looking for those who shared the same destiny as me. We settled here knowing that when you needed us, you would find us. We come from nearly all the cities in the Empire. Ceredine is a survivor of T'que."

Tyrian's head swung to where the slender redheaded Mongra stood nearby; unusually for her race, the fur of her ears and tail was an orange color different to her red hair. She wore no armor or relic, and her flowing clothing marked her as a dancer or bard of some type. The dance shoes on her feet showed long use. In age, she was probably only slightly older than he was, and her eyes had been haunted by a familiar look. "I'm glad," he told her softly. "You'll have to teach me how to dance so I don't embarrass my fiancée at our wedding."

Ceredine's black eyes brightened. "I would be honored," she said. "And I will be glad to dance at the celebration party as well, to renew the strength and spirit of our soldiers. Do you have any bards?" At the nod, she smiled. "I used to be one, so I'll be able to dance with them properly. Leave it to us to keep morale high."

Myr and Café Latte had already been doing a spectacular job of that very thing, and he knew Ceredine would be the perfect addition. Such a simple thing as providing music and dance shouldn't have been able to soothe soldiers who had seen too much trauma, but it really did help lift spirits. Tyrian always felt better when he could simply sit and watch them perform. For just a while, the world could be normal.

After a bit of thought, he gave Dylan the Echo Mirror to take everyone to Aon Castle. It initially didn't want to be used by him, but after a stern scolding from Tyrian, the mirror began to glow. Once Dylan had taken everyone there, he could have Miranda send him and the mirror back to the stronghold to pick the others up.

Squint found herself back on her own feet again, but she was much more alert than she had been. She felt even better when Solei gave her cup of amber colored liquid to drink. "Syrup!" She drank the whole thing in a single gulp.

Solei grinned. "Dragons and their sweet teeth. I've never known such bottomless pits."

"This from the cat who chews on sugar cubes," her partner countered politely.

With Squint happily refueled, Shadi grabbed the things she would need and joined the party to head up to ground level where the Dragons could transform and they could all be on their way. There was no time to wait and rest, not when that many lives hung in the balance. They could get back to the stronghold by dawn if they hurried, and that might just make the difference for at least a few people.

Dawn was indeed creeping over the horizon as they climbed the mountains at last, but it brought with it more than just a stunning sunrise. It brought the sight of smoke and the smell of fire. It also brought to Cassie's sensitive ears the sound of vicious fighting. "Hurry!" she shouted. "The stronghold is under attack!"

The closer they got, the more visible the fighting became. Mounted Dragonists struggled to drive back aerial beasts and monsters, while others still fought on the ground against the Imperial soldiers swarming the area. There was no rhyme or reason to the battle, no sense that there were even any laws to engagements at all. It was a bloody horror show.

Celestial flew down close to the ground and Tamari and Shadi jumped down. The white Dragon promptly turned and flew into the air with Ryu as he drew his lance. Their communication was seamless and absolute to the point that Ryu only had to use his hands for battle. Celestial focused on magic as well as keeping him secure on her back.

Squint landed to let Tyrian and Cassie down, and they promptly went rushing into battle. For the first time, Tyrian actually used his relic in combat, unhesitatingly unleashing Hell on the enemies foolish enough to get too close. When you broke the laws, you were not protected by them any longer, and there was no guilt in his heart. He wasn't passing judgment. He was simply sending the offenders on to a higher power who would.

Tamari stayed close by Squint, and her axe cut through monsters and soldiers alike. A brassy taste of fear lingered in her mouth. She had never been in large-scale combat, but she knew that this was worse than a real battlefield. Squint blew fire and used her tail like a whip before realizing how silly she was being. She focused as hard as she could, dropped back into Human form, and slammed her fist into a soldier's jaw hard enough that he went flying. "That's more like it!" she decided.

Tyrian had a very specific destination in mind. He was looking for the person controlling the monsters. When he spotted the vile Beastmaster at the top of the living area, he immediately changed course and began fighting his way through. He lost Cassie in the crush but didn't pay it any mind. He not only trusted her to defend herself, he also trusted that she would find him if he needed her.

When he reached the rooftop where the Beastmaster stood, he spun his staff one handed and aimed the end at the other male. He recognized him from his life in Trinan and knew that he was one of the better Beastmasters that the Imperial Army had. It saddened him to realize the corruption had spread this far. "This is your last chance to end this," he said icily. "Unless you wish to visit Purgatory sooner rather than later." The Devourer glowed briefly even as he spoke.

The Beastmaster threw his arms wide on a maniacal laugh. "Go ahead! Kill me in cold blood, Southerwind!" The color abruptly left his face as the mark of the Devourer appeared in the air and flames began to whip around Tyrian's body. "You would do it."

Tyrian's green eyes were as hard as stone and glittered as fiercely as the stars only then sinking from sight in the skies. "What is coldblooded about removing someone who fights only for devastation? You deliberately attacked a cursed people just to make them suffer more. I have no reason to show you mercy."

With no options for escape that would not end in death anyway, the Beastmaster's hand filled with fire magic. "Let's see the Liberation Army survive without its precious Kaiten Star!" he snarled. He hurled the magic into the middle of the rooftop and it exploded with such force that it not only killed the Beastmaster instantly, it also sent Tyrian flying backwards off the top of the roof.

A collective shout lifted as everyone realized what had happened, and Cassie felt her heart stop. A blue streak shot through the air overhead and underneath Tyrian when he was only feet from hitting the ground. The landing knocked the breath out of him, and as his sight cleared, he realized he had landed on the back of a Dragon.

"Nice of you to drop in," Draco muttered. "Damn it, Tyrian, you scared the shit out of all of us with that stunt. You're damned lucky that Peyn's so fast!"

The Dragon muttered equally, "I'm too old for this." He flew down to ground level and landed gracefully beside other Dragons that were coming in. He angled his wing to help Tyrian down and then offered a claw to Draco. With the Beastmaster gone, the monsters had instantly retreated, and the soldiers, then outnumbered, had done so as well.

"You idiot!" Cassie shouted at Tyrian as she seemed to appear from out of nowhere.

He somehow dodged the punch she aimed for his face but stumbled a step as she threw herself into his arms. Her entire body trembled violently and he held her fiercely close. He couldn't apologize for what he had done. Even if he had known the Beastmaster would attempt a suicide bomb, he would have still gone up there to take him out. Every minute counted when lives were on the line. He looked over her head to where Tamari and Squint stood. Both looked slightly ragged, though otherwise fit. "Are you okay?" he asked gently.

"Dragon monks are scarier than Dragonists," Tamari said. Her legs felt shaky, but she kept that a secret. "Squint was actually knocking those guys back twenty feet! It's horrible of me, but I found it very funny and very satisfying."

"That's not horrible," Cassie assured her. "I've seen her do it too, and

I also find it very funny. Especially because she's very small in this shape." She ran her hand down Squint's hair gently. "Well done. I'm very proud of you."

Draco stepped closer and said, "Did you return just to help us, or did you find the doctor you were seeking?"

"I'm right here," Shadi said as she came back down to the ground from the second level. "I was trying to get out of the way when C.J. and Tyler grabbed me and made me hide with them and the kids. Take me to one of the cursed Dragons. I need to see exactly what I'm dealing with."

The others dispersed to tend to wounds, and Draco led the way toward the hospital. Tyrian, Cassie, and Shadi went with him while the others helped with the beginning of the cleanup. Dylan had arrived just as the fight was ending, and he was very glad to see everyone intact. He joined Ryu in transporting the wounded to a more sheltered location.

There were no unoccupied beds in the hospital, and Shadi went immediately to where the first person rested. The young woman seemed unconscious but stirred while Shadi examined the lesions along her arms. Her lashes lifted and she said in a slurred voice, "They appear last."

"She's correct." Draco's arms were tightly crossed, his knuckles white with his effort to control himself. He hated seeing his people in this condition. "It begins with a regular fatigue but swiftly drains all lifeforce from the ill. The last stage before death is the appearance of those red marks."

Tyrian's lashes flinched slightly yet his voice remained neutral. "Is it possible that Blaine is collecting the lifeforce as it is drained?"

"It's no doubt a certainty." Shadi straightened and said in satisfaction, "But she obviously didn't put too much effort into this curse. I can actually read the spell in the lesions. The trick to curses is to learn the spell and then cast it backwards."

The Medicine Relic on her right hand began to glow as did the Resurrection Relic on her left. Slowly, carefully, she began to recite the spell backwards. It sounded like utter gobbledygook to everyone present but the effects were apparent. The lesions instantly disappeared from the woman's skin and she took a sudden deep breath. "I can breathe!" she said. Strength poured back in rapidly, evidenced as she sat up cautiously. "It's like the last few days didn't happen."

"Give it another one or two and you'll be just as good as new." Shadi looked at Draco. "I need every Healer you have. In fact, even mages with Medicine or Resurrection Relics will do. I'll teach them the reversal and we'll get everyone before the hour is done. No one dies on *my* watch!"

True to her word, in less than an hour, every person who had been cursed was no longer in that condition. Those in the earliest stages were as good as new almost instantly, but those who had been suffering longer wouldn't be better without at least a day or two of rest. It seemed to lift the cloud that had hovered over the stronghold. People began to smile again, and the doors opened once more.

Draco stood with Tyrian inside the inn and looked out at the city as it began to bustle with activity. "Thank you," he said quietly. "I know you'll say Shadi did the work, but you're the one who took a leap of faith to find her. We would never have found her on our own."

"You couldn't expect me to walk away," Tyrian noted. "It's just not in me. How do you think I got caught up in all this anyway? I joined the Rebellion before I knew anything about being the Kaiten Star. Even before Ophelia died. As soon as I understood what was happening, I couldn't stand by."

"I suppose that's one of the reasons all of us love you." Draco turned from the window, and his silvery eyes burned intently. "Tyrian, please accept my dedication as a Destined Star. I and Peyn will join you in battle, and so will every able-bodied Dragonist. We fight for those who are being oppressed. My alliance is yours until the day I die. Perhaps beyond. I am honored to share the skies with you."

Tyrian let out a long breath as he felt the sudden wellspring of magic inside. He had done it. He had finally done it. He had gathered all one hundred and eight of his companions. The one hundred and nine Destined Stars were joined at last.

Cassie wrapped her arms around his waist and held on tightly. "You did it," she said softly.

Draco lightly squeezed Tyrian's shoulder. "I'm sure others feel the same, but I am sorry I couldn't be there for longer."

"It's what I told Ryu." Tyrian took a deep breath. "Being here now is what matters. Everyone has something to give, and I fully believe I found my Stars at the moment when I needed them. Some came to me, knowing I needed them. As long as we can share the land as we share the skies, then everything is okay."

They went to help the others with whatever packing and gathering they had left to do, and then Tyrian used the mirror to take them all back to the castle. While he and Draco had been talking, a unit from the Liberation Army had arrived to help the Dragonists regroup, and they returned to the castle not long after Tyrian did. The half unit of Dragonists would blend into a half unit of Special Forces with Divan and Draco in charge.

Matthias waited for Tyrian in the hall of the second floor. "We begin our assault on Trinan tomorrow," he said. "The strongest of the Dragons are preparing the spell that they can use to bring the barrier down. While they are doing that, we will launch our attack via the river and land from two directions while our Dragonist unit comes in from the skies."

Tyrian nodded and followed him down the hall, toward the balcony at the end that had once been used by a monarch for royal speeches. He had never been out on it since he had never felt a need to give a speech. "What about evacuations of the people?" he asked.

"Yhalenia and Master Kotan are preparing to take one of our monk units into the city under stealth and get everyone out. Grace got one last message into the city before it was locked down, and the people will know to be ready to escape. We can't waste any more time, Lord Tyrian. Tomorrow is the final battle." He opened the balcony doors. "I asked for everyone to gather so you can speak to them."

Tyrian glanced over his shoulder but somehow wasn't surprised to realize that Cassie had disappeared. He had sensed the instant she was no longer in the vicinity. She couldn't hide from him in any fashion anymore. They had relic bonded, made love with their magic, and fragments existed inside each of them of the other's power. With a breath, he stepped onto the balcony and looked out at the field that had once been used as the barracks.

It was a sea of faces. Every soldier and every citizen had gathered. He saw all one hundred and eight of his Destined Stars, and the smaller ones sat on the shoulders of the taller. Dragons hovered in the air with as many people as they could carry on their backs. Several people held the flag of the Liberation Army and waved it happily when they saw Tyrian. It was a dizzying sight for Tyrian. He could never have imagined such a sight even among all the other amazing things he had seen so far.

"Tomorrow," he said clearly, "we fight against evil. When the barrier is brought down by our Dragon allies, we will attack from the land, water, and sky. The people will be evacuated. All of you will have your orders; all of you will have something important to do. Even those who are civilian, who are not going to be there on the field, will be fighting as well. You give us someone to fight for, someone to come home to. Too many lives have been lost for the freedom we all crave. What started as a struggle for rights against tyranny has become something bigger than we imagined. We've come too far to stop now. We *will* win tomorrow."

The cheer that filled the air was deafening. It rang off the rooftops and bounced off the beautiful stained glass that had begun to be installed in windows. Tyrian sensed her power before she appeared and turned as the lavender colored light swirled into appearance and brought Tanelia. "What say you, Great Sage?"

She smiled as pride shined in her eyes. "I am very proud of you, Tyrian. You have fulfilled your destiny. The one hundred and nine Destined Stars are together at last. Inside you, the final spell of your relic has unlocked. It possesses a power the likes of which no other has ever controlled. It will serve its place in the battle tomorrow and will bring you victory."

Tyrian felt the stirring of power inside and firmly grabbed control in the way only a fully powered Kaiten Star could. His iron will, that great thing that had saved his sanity and kept him from being devoured by his relic, was a palpable force around him, intense and forceful. The Devourer sensed it and turned docile. No longer would it seek to claim its owner. To claim so great a lifeforce would be instant destruction for even a Pure Relic that powerful.

"Celebrate," Tyrian told the gathered people. "Tonight, celebrate. Cherish your lives and your loved ones. Tomorrow night, we will celebrate again. But tomorrow, we will be celebrating victory!" The cheers lifted once more and he closed his eyes. "Thank you," he said softly to Tanelia.

"No," she countered just as soft. "Thank you, Tyrian." With a swirl of light and spark of lightning, she disappeared from the balcony.

He looked out over the crowd and then walked off the balcony. He had some important things to do that night as well. He would not enter the battle with regrets or loose threads. One loose thread could ruin the entire tapestry. He had spent too damn long unraveling them to begin with!

Chapter Forty-Three

"The weaving that makes the fabric of destiny."

People took celebrating so seriously that not only were Evelyn and Terrence kept busy in the kitchen, but R.K. and C.J. also found themselves chipping in. Or rather, C.J. chipped in. She made R.K. wait tables so he wouldn't burn his hands on the stove again. All of Aon Castle and the city around it filled with music and lively laughter. It was almost as if the war was already over, just as Tyrian had wanted.

Matthias and Cherry had dinner together at the inn since the restaurant was packed to overflowing. Persephone brought over a large milkshake and put it in front of Cherry with a wink. "In three years, I'll serve you something more grownup."

Cherry grinned up at her. "I'd still prefer your milkshakes." She happily sipped her drink and watched the room around her. It was a whirl of voices and light.

In a murmur, Matthias said, "I wish I'd be here to see you be an adult."

She immediately looked at him with a frown. "I wish it too," she said frankly, "but I've come to accept the things I can't change. I've watched Destiny for almost a year now. I understand that we all have a place to be." She let out a little breath. "Laia said my star is fixed. I'll still be fighting on your behalf." Sadly, she added, "I wish Seymour was still here. He'd have learned from all this."

"That can't be certain, Cherry." He sighed and covered her hand with his. She was too young and too smart for these worries. "It will take something far bigger than even this war to make him find his heart. I'm not sure he'd even understand what being a Destined Star is. But I believe that someday he will find himself. And when he does, he will be the greatest strategist ever known. Even more than me."

"I hope so," she said softly. Though she had never said out loud that she cared for Seymour as much as she did, she knew Matthias understood. It was going to be very lonely without him around. She was not quite fourteen yet, and not in possession of enough skills to be on her own; she would have to be given to another legal guardian. "Where will I go?" she wondered.

"Well," he said softly, "I was talking with Kris and Klint. If you like, they will be your guardians. They've also expressed a desire to retire from military life and travel, which I know you'd like to do."

She brightened. She loved Kris and Klint. They had become an instant big sister and big brother to her from the moment they had met. "I'd like that."

"Good." He got to his feet with a sigh. Even a cane couldn't take the weight off his bad leg. His other leg had begun to go as well. His time wouldn't last much longer than the war, but he would make the end. That was enough for him. "Don't be up too late."

When he got outside, he found himself bumping into Kyle as he entered. "Sorry, Matt," Kyle said. He paused for a moment. "Mind walking with me?"

"Not at all as long as you don't mind my leaning on you."

"Anytime." Kyle offered his arm to give him added support. They walked slowly through the city, working their way through the crowds of people moving in all directions. "When everything is done," Kyle said slowly, "Ewan and I are talking about a journey through the City-States. We love the Empire, but there are too many painful memories here right now."

"Should I be mad at you? Kyle, if you were perfectly fine with everything, then you would not have truly loved Ophelia. And you and Ewan have struggled almost as hard as Lady Cassie to help keep Lord Tyrian steady." Softer, he added, "I once wanted to travel. Knowing my little brother travels in my place will be enough for me. Live the life I and Ophelia were not allowed, Kyle. Love again someday. You have so much to give."

Kyle let out a long breath. It somehow made things easier to know Matthias believed in him. "Thanks, Matt."

On the other side of the castle grounds, Di was perched in one of the towers watching the stars when she sensed Alex approaching. "Go away," she said without turning.

"Di, that hasn't worked for three decades. What makes you think it will work now?" He leaned on the window ledge beside her. She wasn't looking at him, but he didn't mind. Her profile was as beautiful as the rest of her. "Do you really want to turn into Grace and Kell?" he asked her after a moment. "Because I'm damned well prepared to wait another fifty years if that's what it takes. Of course, we'll have grandkids by then, wondering why their grandparents aren't married, but that's fine with me."

The absurd image made her laugh. She dropped her head onto her arms as the laugh became a groan. "Damn it, Alexander. I'm going to make your life hell. You know that and yet you persist."

He tangled his fingers in her hair and drew her closer. "Because life is worse without you," he said softly. He ran the fingers of his other hand over her lips. "Di, we might as well be married. You boss me around, yell at me for being late, and refuse to listen to me when I think you're wrong. You might as well get a new name out of the deal."

He was really too incorrigible for words. "Maybe I like having an illicit affair with you. It's exciting."

"Oh, I'm sure I can keep you entertained even if our affair isn't illicit." His hands curled around her waist to tug her closer. "Say it, Di."

She could only sigh. "Fine. I'll marry you. But you have to stop being such a jerk." She stifled a yelp as she found herself suddenly hoisted and thrown over his shoulder. "Alexander!" She beat her hands on his back, mortified as she was carried out of the tower past many soldiers, most of whom were in her units. All were grinning. "I'm going to kill you!"

"You wanted excitement," her fiancé murmured without guilt. "I'm obliging you." He saw Marcus coming down the hall and said as he passed, "Di's going to marry me."

Marcus didn't bat a lash. "I always knew you were perfect for each other."

"You're next!" Di snapped at him. "I'm telling Marian all your weaknesses!"

"She already knows them." Marcus grinned and waved as his friends disappeared into Alex's room. As soon as the door was shut, his smile faded. His other hand, hidden behind his back, clutched a bouquet of flowers he had begged Tavi and Raven to pick for him. He didn't know if Marian even liked flowers, but it never hurt to be bearing them when you were about to put your honor and heart on the line.

He knocked on the door and it was opened as if she had been waiting for him. He stopped breathing as he stared at her. It always happened that way. If he hadn't seen her for at least a few hours, when he did, it was like being reminded all over again how beautiful she was inside and out.

"Marcus." She had been hoping so hard that he would come to her. She had been all but sitting by the door in the hopes that she would hear his knock. She always knew who was at her door. She would know this man anywhere. "Do you want to get dinner?" she asked hopefully. If they could, they had been eating most meals together.

"No, I . . ." He cleared his throat and held out the flowers while he desperately searched for the words to say. "Here."

"Oh." Her eyes softened. He had picked *rubentia* and *arconile*, her two favorite flowers. The second was also a Healer's flower, able to mend some of the most persistent burns. The scent was as soothing as its balm.

"Thank you."

Feeling a bit silly standing in the doorway, he rubbed the back of his neck. "Can I come in?"

"Of course." She stepped back so he could enter and then shut the door behind him. She put the flowers in the vase on her dresser, well aware that he was trying to figure out how to say something important. Nerves began fluttering inside her stomach. Was he going to say that he had changed his mind and no longer wanted to court her? How would she handle that? She loved him terribly.

Determination firmed her heart. If he had changed his mind, she would take a page from Grace's book and sit on him until he realized they were perfect for each other. When the silence finally got to be too much, she asked hesitantly, "Are you . . . upset with me?"

"No!" He grabbed her hands and held onto them tightly. "Never that, Marian. I just . . . damn it!" He scowled. "Why can't I find the right words for you? The one person it means the most with, I can't find the words for!"

"You always say the right thing to me, Marcus," she countered softly. "Maybe because you do speak from your heart when you can find the words. Now, let's see if I can help. What would be the general subject you're trying to broach?"

He found himself smiling. "Marriage."

Her fingers quivered inside his as her hopes lifted. "Would this be in general or specific?"

"Specific. Very specific." He released one of her hands so he could reach into his pocket. The ring he pulled out was a simple thing with a small but fiery orange gem in the center. "We've braved hell together, Marian," he said softly. "We've seen the best and worst in each other in such a short time. I need you in my life. I love you, and I want you to marry me." When her lips trembled, he frowned. "I didn't ask right. I didn't actually *ask*, did I?"

"No!" She gave a hiccupping laugh and freed her hand so she could throw her arms around his neck. "Don't you dare take it back!" She kissed him wildly, beyond happy, feeling as if her entire world might finally be aligning itself. After watching her beloved cousin, her little brother, suffer so terribly, she had thought she would never be happy until he was freed from his horrible burden. But here . . . she had never been happier.

He held her fiercely and then slowly let her go. He slid the ring over her finger and smiled as it sparkled. "It reminded me of you."

"Small and sassy?" she asked.

"Beautiful to the core," he countered softly. "Forged in adversity, but still incredibly beautiful." He kissed her again tenderly and slowly released her. "Now we can get dinner," he said huskily. "I didn't want to walk in there unless we had settled this."

As he turned, she smiled. "Marcus?" When he turned around again, she slid her arms around his waist and pressed close. "I don't want to go out." She eased up to teasingly nip at his chin. "We can get dinner later."

It would take a stronger man than Marcus Quint to turn down the woman he loved when she offered herself freely. He lifted her into his arms and moved toward the bed with purpose. "I'm sure Eve or Terrance would be happy to deliver to your room. They might laugh at us, but even that doesn't seem to be enough to make me turn you away."

"That's because you know they'd only be laughing because they were happy for us." She kissed him tenderly. "I'm going to make your life interesting, General Quint. You need to be kept on your toes. You'd be bored otherwise."

He smiled. "And you would get away with murder if you didn't have me."

"Bossiness runs in the family."

The littlest of the children, Destined Star or not, had a lot of trouble settling down as the night grew longer. By tacit agreement, adults let the kids run wild until they fell asleep on their feet. Some took longer than others, but a wave of sleepiness ran through everyone ten and under by eleven. Taurus and Aries took charge of Yumi, and more than one person smiled to see them walking out with Yumi asleep in Aries' arms with her head on his shoulder; most already knew the musical couple would be adopting the little scientist. Kami and Mikey lasted not much longer, and Grace and Kell ushered them along home. The patient old woman had won her battle: Kell had proposed in the middle of the dining room and promised to go through with it this time. No one, least of all Grace, doubted him.

Raven eventually fell asleep as well, and Samantha took charge of getting her to her room since her parents were in high demand. Tavi held out the longest but literally fell asleep in the middle of running across the restaurant to see what Lupe was playing with Amos. She toppled over and landed safely in Liang's arms. He had been watching her closely, fairly sure she would give out soon. As he lifted her, she snuggled in contentedly. "Daddy." It was little more than a drowsy mumble, her eyes not opening. Simply a subconscious recognition of who she thought carried her.

It fiercely grabbed his heart. He made his way through the crowd to where Serentia was collecting her cloak. "I'll walk you to your rooms," he told her. "I don't think Tavi will let go just yet."

Serentia smiled as she saw the grip her daughter had on his shirt. "I think you're right." She fell into step beside him as they left the restaurant and took a deep breath as the quiet of the halls sank in. "It was a bit riotous in there. Were Rourke and Ewan trying to out-drink each other?"

"They were."

"Who won?"

"Laia."

She laughed. "That doesn't surprise me." She fell silent for a few moments and then said softly, "Tavi loves you a great deal, Liang. When she realized that the end of the war meant you'd leave, she was inconsolable. She wants us to move to Trinan so we can be near you. That is where you said you were going."

"Mm. Tyrian won't be mine to guard for much longer," he admitted. "I've decided I want to take a chance at that restaurant Marian and Tyrian say I need. Evelyn and Terrence are sure I can do it, and they're the pros. They even asked I not work in their city else I take away business."

"I think it would be perfect for you." Casually, she said, "I suppose it wouldn't hurt Tavi and me to move to Trinan. After all, a gardener can find work anywhere. And you said you like working with the things I grow."

The idea of having her close at hand but not being able to keep her for his own was a painful one for him. He had no idea how Grace had been patient for fifty years. He wasn't even sure how Tyrian had been patient for a few weeks. Being patient for as long as he had was getting harder and harder for Liang. "I do indeed. And you know I wouldn't mind spending time with you and Tavi."

"Indeed." She leaned in the doorway to Tavi's room and watched with a smile as he tucked Tavi into her nightclothes and then into her bed. He seemed to have no idea just how perfectly he had become a part of their lives. No one would ever think Tavi wasn't his by blood; their bond was simply that strong and deep. "Would you like to join me for a drink before bed?" she asked as they stepped into the hall again.

His hands tightened at his sides. "I shouldn't."

"Why not?" She glanced up at him from under her lashes.

He let out a ragged breath. "Serentia . . . I'm beginning to get the feeling you're flirting with me."

"I might be." Absolutely, she was. "I haven't tried to flirt for a while, so I'm a bit rusty." She moved closer, let her body brush against his. That wonderful powerful body that made her feel feminine and safe. She had become used to the way she felt hot and breathless if he was near. She was beginning to thrill to it. She hoped to feel the thrill for at least a few more decades. "Flirting is first, isn't it?"

"First before what?" He was losing the train of the conversation. She was soft and shapely and beautiful, haunting him with things he wanted more than air. Physically and emotionally alike, he wanted her until there was no room to want anything else. His knuckles turned white as he struggled not to grab her.

"Courting, of course." She let her hands rest lightly on his chest where her fingers kneaded at his muscles. The man was built like a god. To be wanted by such a man was a heady feeling. "I've decided I'm going to court you."

His hands shot up and grabbed her wrists. "Serentia," he warned softly, "you're teasing a very frustrated man. You've been nearly kissed senseless more times than I can count, and the tally is rising as we speak."

"Well, we could skip the courting then." She eased up to lightly brush his lips with hers. "You could just marry me. I have your ring in my pocket." His grip tightened and she wanted to laugh. "Liang, I'm in love with you. How can you not know that? Everyone knows it! I want to have a lover again. To have someone to hold onto at night, to have someone there by my side. Until I met you, I didn't miss it. Be my husband. Let me share my daughter with you, and have more children with you. Unless you don't love me as well."

His response to that was a kiss that walked the edge of self-combustion. If he hadn't been holding her wrists, she would have melted into a puddle on the floor. It had been a long time since she had been kissed like that. In fact, she wasn't sure she had *ever* been kissed like that.

"I warned you," he said roughly as he lifted his head enough to speak. He released her wrists to grip her hips and pull her close against his aching body.

"I'm not quite senseless yet. You need to try again."

He let his forehead rest against hers as he began to smile. "I didn't stand a chance, Serentia. From the day I saw you, I was lost. You and that little terror of yours had me wrapped around your fingers from the beginning. Only you didn't seem to know I was in love with you. Do you have any idea how hard it was to be patient?"

She framed his face with her hands and kissed him softly. "I have some idea. Stay with me tonight, Liang. Tomorrow I will watch you go into battle. And when you come home, you'll come home to me." She pulled the stone ring with its embedded green gem out of her pocket and slid it over his finger. As Jeo had promised, it fit perfectly, and would not impede Liang's fighting. "We'll raise vegetables and kids and puppies and enjoy having a granddaughter at our ages. You'll own a restaurant and feed hungry people, and I'll muck around my gardens and come home filthy so that we just have to bathe together." She smiled as he cupped her cheek with his ringed hand and the gem sparkled. "How does that sound?"

To him, it sounded like heaven. "Deal."

Cassie had been near to Tyrian's side for most of the evening, but when she turned from a conversation with Kotan, she was surprised to discover that her lover had disappeared. It both fascinated and alarmed her equally that he could be quiet enough that even she didn't hear him coming and going. The longer she wore her relic, the sharper her hearing became. Laia was helping her learn to control it, but it was something that would take years to master. "Did you see Tyrian leave?"

"Mmm." Her father smiled. "A while ago, in fact. He looked tired. He may have gone to the tower to escape the crowd. I would think even he needs some peace. Perhaps him more than any other." He lightly patted her shoulder. "Go to him, daughter. I'm going to turn in soon myself. I think we're all winding down."

Indeed people were beginning to file out to go home. Cassie saw couples walking holding hands, and she was especially happy to see Janus and Juniper finally being open in their relationship. But then, she fully understood the couple for what they had done. She would have done the same if it had been the only way to stay by Tyrian's side.

She made her way to the courtyard and then to the tower. The guards saluted as she went past and she smiled wryly to herself. The one thing she hadn't gotten used to was the guilt by association aspect that had everyone treating her like nobility.

When she walked into the tower room, she found Tyrian crouched in front of the fire and staring into it as if it had the secrets of the universe. He was half-undressed and the firelight rippled over his beautiful body. She walked over to him and leaned down to lightly rub his shoulders. "You abandoned me," she said. "It always worries me when you run off without me. I imagine all sorts of trouble you could get into."

He smiled and got to his feet. He turned and tugged her into his arms just so he could savor how she felt against him. "I've only once gotten into trouble when I've lost you."

She snorted. "And promptly gave Draco gray hair with that stunt! I nearly had a heart attack." She sighed and rested her head on his chest to hear the steady sound of his heart. It seemed impossible that a heart so giving could even be contained within one man. "But I suppose I can forgive you this time." Her arms tightened around his waist. "Tomorrow, then."

"I'm not afraid." He threaded his hands into her hair. "In a way, I'm glad. Tomorrow is the end of this nightmare. Our people will be free and so will we. Well . . . to some extent. We won't be able to escape immediately."

"Oh and why's that?"

"I think there would be mass mutiny if we got married where no one could attend. And on that note . . ." He slowly released her and reached into his pocket. "I ran off so I could find Jeo. I did the asking in our courtship, so I had to get the ring." He brought her left hand to his lips and then slid the aforementioned ring over her finger. "How's this suit you?"

Startled, she turned her hand so she could see what she wore. It was made of a lightweight black stone that she barely noticed wearing, but the stone had the familiar veins running through it that meant it would be impossible to break. It was more flat than rounded though there were no sharp edges, and the small blue gemstone in the center was actually imbedded into the band itself.

Tears began to shimmer in her eyes. The ring would in no way hamper her monk training, and Tyrian's acceptance and acknowledgement of her skill had always been something she cherished. "It's perfect," she said softly. She slid her hands slowly up his chest and felt a little thrill as she watched the ring sparkle. "Are there matching wedding rings?"

"He's working on them." He cupped her cheek tenderly. "There's no knowing what tomorrow will bring," he said softly. "But I'm not afraid. As long as you're there, I can do anything."

"I'm not going anywhere. Not tonight, not tomorrow." She caught her breath as he lifted her into his arms and carried her to their bed. "You never seem to remember that I have feet. I'm more than happy to walk here under my own power."

He smiled as he let her slowly slide down his body. "But then I'd have to let you go. And I don't have the willpower for that, Cassie. I can handle anything except losing you."

There was something almost reverent in the way he touched her. Words suddenly seemed to be unimportant. The heat that burned between them started as soft flames that leapt without warning into an inferno. Clothes were thrown aside without care for where they landed and he fiercely tumbled her down onto the bed.

With a husky laugh, she twisted and rolled until he was pinned and she was on top. She couldn't get enough of his taste and feel, couldn't seem to imprint him deep enough inside her soul. Her hands traced every beloved line of his body, her lips following in their wake until he trembled as hard as she did.

When he couldn't take it anymore, he caught her close and rolled again so that he could savor how it felt to feel her body against his. There was no inch of her body that he didn't know, no secret he had not found. He sought all of them, fueled the fire in them both. And when he finally slipped inside her welcoming heat, his world was perfect.

They slept curled together with their relic hands linked together over his heart. What had started as a burden had become a gift. Destiny never asked more than could be given, and she always gave as much as she asked. No matter what happened on the morrow, the day would end with the start of eternity.

Neither Tyrian nor Cassie could have asked for more.

Chapter Forty-Four

"Free me from the chains that bind me to an unreasonable future."

Tyrian and Cassie were awakened early in the morning by the sound of Merilyne arriving. As she set out their clothes, she called, "I have new clothes for you to wear as well as some food. Lord Matthias asks that you eat and come down to the meeting room as soon as you can."

The door shut behind her as she left, and Tyrian sat up in bed. The moment had finally arrived and there were no nerves left at all. "Ready?" he asked Cassie softly.

"I am." She sat up and eased up to kiss him. No matter what happened, it would happen while they were together. "Let's go free our people."

They ate the light breakfast that had been made, both grateful that their chefs had thought to prepare something that was filling but wouldn't sit heavy on their stomachs. Once fueled, they turned their attention to their new clothes. They were made in their normal styles yet had been created of entirely new material.

Cassie's monk gear looked virtually no different, but the cloth was both stronger and lighter to give her greater range of motion. Stitched into the back of her top layer was the now familiar symbol of the Liberation Army. The embroidery was done in dark green thread so that she now wore the colors of the army.

Likewise, Tyrian's clothes looked much the same, but green threads visibly stitched the black material together, and his green scarf had been borrowed so the symbol could be stitched in black onto the end. When he equipped his staff on his back, he barely noticed the presence of his clothes at all. New bracers had been included as well, courtesy of Yaegi and Oruqui's combined skill.

Matthias was not the only one waiting in the meeting room. Ewan, Kyle, and the Lower Generals were present as well. All wore new clothes as well, keeping their personal style but now bearing Tyrian's colors. When he saw Tyrian, Matthias said, "All Stars who are field combatants will be fighting. All wear your colors with one pointed addition."

Tyrian glanced at his Stars and realized that each wore a star embroidered into their clothing somewhere. It was both humbling and empowering to know they would willingly be marked as his companions. "Thank you."

"None of that," Ewan said firmly.

Tyrian smiled briefly before turning back to Matthias. "Where do we stand?"

"Infine, Honey, and Dylan are leading the attack by river. The aerial attack is being led by Ryu, Tamari, and Squint. The land attack will be led by you. Name your third."

Without question, Tyrian said, "Liang. When we breach the castle, I want Kyle, Ewan, and Marian to join us. What about Reyu? We know he will be coming after Laia, but Agrime has the right of battle with him."

"Laia will be setting herself as bait to lure Reyu out. When he has shown himself, Agrime will handle things. General Yureny will be riding in their unit and has been briefed on the situation. I and Cherry will be on the field as well, but the commands are yours to give, Lord Tyrian."

With a little breath, Tyrian said, "Let's bring down that barrier."

* * * * *

Those who were still inside Trinan did not know what to expect or when to expect it. The barrier that encased the city cut off the sky and the sun alike. No one knew what day it was or what time it was. Civilians stayed inside with the doors locked. Shops were closed. Supplies had been cautiously divided, but there was no knowing when they would run out. There was no going to get more. The city was overrun with monsters who didn't know right from wrong and soldiers who didn't care.

The sudden crack of power striking the shield made many scream in fear. People rushed to windows and watched as the shield broke into billions of pieces in the onrush of familiar Dragon power. When the shield came down, it revealed the sea of Liberation Army soldiers on the other side. Units were approaching from the land and pouring in from the river. More still came in from the air as the Dragonist aerial unit began to launch warning attacks at the castle itself.

Though the Imperial Army numbered far fewer soldiers, it made up the difference with monsters and beasts of all shapes and sizes. There were no laws of engagement to be had in this battle. The Liberation Army spared no quarter and gave no mercy. Tyrian, with the ruthless determination of a Kaiten Star who would never give in, directed his units toward whatever he knew they could defeat and pulled back those being overwhelmed.

The monk units swept into the city under the cover of the chaos and rounded up the citizens. They were either transported away or escorted as far from the city as possible. The fighting moved from the fields into the city itself, and while buildings became part of the casualties, there were no innocent lives lost.

Reyu watched the fight from a window in the castle with a little smirk on his lips. His hordes of monsters kept the fight even, neatly distracting the Liberation Army so that they could not simply rush into the castle. Better still, there was no end to the monsters that could be summoned.

Without warning, a sudden crack of power seemed to slap across his face as if from the palm of a hand. It was a humiliating sensation that he had never before experienced, and his smirk became a snarl as he realized what had happened. "So she has the arrogance of her bloodline as well." He turned away from the window sharply. "I'm going to retrieve our songbird."

Blaine's nails bit into her arms as she watched him walk out. She hated him. Hated his arrogance and his power. Hated more that she had no choice but to comply with what he wanted because she lacked the power to resist. She wanted the Devourer for her own and she wanted Tyrian Southerwind dead. But if Reyu was killed by Laiaeariel Mitakel, she wouldn't really care one way or another. She was more than ready to deal with things herself.

Laia was cutting through a monster when she felt an answering slap of power coming for her. She blocked it with her relic and turned to see Reyu advancing across the field toward her. The cocky swagger to the way he walked seemed to indicate that he thought he had already won.

"Surrender," he told her.

"Get stuffed," she retorted. She swung her sword lightly through the air. "If I was the type to surrender so easily, I wouldn't be a Destined Star."

He hated it, but he couldn't argue with that logic. Those locusts swarming around the Kaiten Star possessed strong wills and spirits that well suited their leader. "You can't defeat me."

She laughed openly in his face. "Honey, if you recall, I didn't exactly *lose* our last battle." She took an offensive stance. "You want me? Come and get me. Unless you're not enough of a warrior," she taunted.

He snarled and lunged toward her across the field. She ran forward to meet him, but she leapt into the air at the last moment and flipped over the top of his head. Before he could process why she had done it, he realized there was a different figure rushing toward him with a sword drawn. He didn't recognize the man in the armor, but a sudden fear came from out of nowhere.

He jerked to the side and rolled across the field just as the oncoming warrior attacked. The blade narrowly missed Reyu's head. He got nimbly to his feet, caution in his eyes and body. The figure, now that he looked, was not unfamiliar. He didn't know the man, but he knew he had been following Reyu for centuries. "You."

"Me," Agrime said in satisfaction. "I've hunted you a long while, Scourge." He saluted Laia with his sword.

She returned the salute. "I yield this battle to you. Destined Stars stick together."

Reyu watched her walk away as hate and fury churned inside his body. He had been set up. He would never get his hands on Laia Mitakel and he knew it. He needed to get away from this hunter and look for his next target. Blaine and her lust for power were doomed and he didn't care. The power of the Summarian race *would* be his.

Agrime attacked without warning and Reyu worked fiercely to dodge. When he finally saw an opening, he blasted the other man and sent him tumbling across the field. By the time Agrime got his feet under himself again, Reyu had disappeared into the sea of battle around them. "Damn him!" Agrime snarled, though he was not truly surprised.

Reyu cut his way through the field as quickly as he could to find a place it would be safe to escape from. He removed anything that got in his path, Imperial or Liberation or monster. The beasts would continue to appear on the field until the Beastmasters fell.

Unexpectedly, he found himself entering an open area where Tyrian was fighting. He and his lover fought back-to-back and expertly defeated their enemies. The Kaiten Star was not only fighting, he was also issuing commands into his Voice Relic. Even Reyu couldn't help but reluctantly appreciate Tyrian's cool head in the middle of chaos.

He sensed Agrime closing in and felt fury whip through the shriveled weed that passed for his soul. He would make any victory a hollow victory. His relic activated and the symbol for the Eight-Fold appeared over his head. He let the power well and snarled viciously when Tyrian and Cassie turned. "Die!"

The blast streaked through the air with deadly intent. Dozens saw it, but no one was close enough to stop it. A collective shout raised in the air as Star and soldier alike leapt forward. Liang, who had moved away to fight a monster, was closest but knew he would be too late. Cassie threw herself over Tyrian and knocked him down, uncaring if she traded her life for his.

Just before it would have struck them, Divan leapt down off the back of a Dragon and landed directly in the path of the blast. It slammed into his chest, tore out through the back, and dissipated as it lost its charge. With shocking strength of will and spirit, Divan gathered his Light Relic's power and sent an answering blast at Reyu that was so potent it gouged the

Scourge's armor and into the flesh beneath.

Reyu abandoned the field entirely and Divan collapsed. Tyrian pushed Cassie aside and scrambled over to where Divan had fallen. "How could you do that?!" Tyrian shouted at him. "Your family is waiting for you!"

Divan found a smile. "Couldn't seem to help myself. You remind me of Rihou." He grasped Tyrian's hand tightly. "Please. I want you to be the one to tell him and Naomi. I regret nothing, Tyrian. I knew coming here that this could be my future. Maybe this is just a way for me to get in that fishing time Donald and I swore we'd find." His breath caught and then slowly sighed out. "You'll do just fine, kid."

Tyrian sensed the instant he was gone both externally and internally. The Devourer stirred and, for the first time, he willingly let it consume the life energy leaving someone who had died. It was a great deal of lifeforce. Divan had shared more than a love of fishing with Donald. The lifeforce flowing into the Devourer didn't just refresh Tyrian; it woke the final level of his spell.

He slowly straightened. The runic circle opened around his feet and the symbol of the Devourer opened over his head. His green eyes burned with the indomitable will that was his by birth and destiny. "Fissure!"

A shockwave tore from his body and swept outward across the battlefield. Monsters were blown instantly to bits. Enemies were drained of energy so sharply that some simply collapsed where they stood. Allies were left untouched by the shockwave though they assuredly felt it as it passed through their bodies. With the monsters gone, it took no time at all for the Liberation Army to take out the rest of the Imperial soldiers. Solei and Van themselves removed the evil Beastmasters.

The quiet that followed the end of the battle was both eerie and welcome. Tyrian sensed Matthias' approach and said, "Have Divan's body moved to a secure location. I intend to personally escort his body home to his family to tell his son and daughter what happened. They will hear from me, and no one else, that their father died a hero."

"It will be done," Matthias said quietly.

"His will be the last life taken. That I promise." Tyrian glanced to the side as he sensed Ewan, Kyle, and Marian approaching. All looked relatively unscathed, though Ewan and Kyle had clearly been in the thick of things. Marian, having been with Marcus, was unharmed. "Heal Ewan and Kyle," he told her.

She did so without hesitation. "You two can't go getting yourselves into too much trouble," she scolded. "Who will attend Marcus' bachelor party and tell all the bad jokes?" She smiled toward Liang. "You won't kill him, will you?"

Liang had noticed the instant he had seen Marian and Marcus what had happened the night before. He had, in fact, been hoping for just such an event to occur. "I suppose not, but you may want to check with your cousin more than me."

"Since he clearly treated you well," Tyrian decided, "he can live." He turned his gaze toward the castle that sat not far away.

"It begins and ends in the same place," Kyle murmured. He nodded decisively. "Lead the way, Tyrian. We'll cover your back the entire time."

Tyrian turned without hesitation toward the castle and the other five fell into step behind him. They walked with weapons drawn, though no one expected to encounter resistance. All those who had been able to fight had been on the field. The monsters had stopped appearing the instant the Beastmasters fell.

It was quiet as a tomb inside the palace. It seemed perfect and immaculate, as if nothing that had happened over the last year had ever occurred. Tyrian could practically feel Blaine's presence, and he knew it was because of Ben. She had taken his life energy, but his spirit lingered near Tyrian.

The throne room doors were bolted and locked. That didn't stop Ewan. He drew Night and hacked clean through the middle of the doors. The pieces crumbled to the floor and the chains went with them, useless without something solid to hold. He started to step into the room, but a bolt of magic suddenly streaked out and slammed into his chest. It sent him reeling into the hall wall and he slumped to the floor.

"Ewan!" Tyrian nearly leapt to his friend's side. The wound was bloody and ugly, but it wasn't as bad it initially looked, and it wasn't in the critical zone. "Are you okay?"

"Fuck." Ewan's breath hissed out. "Sucker punched me. But I've dealt with worse." He waited only long enough for Marian to heal the worst of the wound before getting to his feet. "That's it. I'm separating her head from her shoulders!"

They rushed as a group through the doors and scattered in several directions to make it impossible to hit them all at once. Blaine barely spared a glance for the Destined Stars. Her malevolent eyes fixed on Tyrian. She couldn't even be sure which reason made her hate him the most. His relic, his rebellion, or his importance to Tanelia. "The legendary Kaiten Star," she snarled. "Your story ends here!"

"I wouldn't be so sure," he told her icily. "I believe Lady Tanelia prophesized that I would be the *first*. That means there will be *more*." He spun his staff with one hand and began to advance toward her. "You know why you weren't chosen by the gods and she was? Because the gods pick those who are *worthy*."

She shrieked and began throwing blasts at him. She was so focused on her determination to kill him that she didn't see Kyle and Ewan until they were right beside her. She managed to dodge Kyle's attack entirely, but Ewan's cut clean across her chest. If she hadn't dodged as much as she had, she would have been cut in half. The pain was a shocking reminder of her mortality.

She scrambled away as her blood spilled onto the floor and made it slippery. She stumbled twice before she got her feet under her. She knew she was outmatched. Tears of bitter rage filled her eyes as she screamed, "The gods chose the wrong sister! I will prove it! I'll destroy all of you!"

Kyle and Ewan leapt in front of Tyrian and crossed their blades to form a barrier as wild blasts of magic fired from Blaine's fingers. The entire palace was beginning to shake and rumble. "Get Marian out!" Kyle shouted at Liang. "We'll protect Tyrian!"

Marian didn't want to go, but she was given no choice. Liang threw her over his shoulder and ran her out. He too wanted to stay by Tyrian's side, but he had full faith in those who remained.

Cassie dodged several blasts and came up with her throwing stars in hand. Several missed Blaine. Others struck flesh. None could seem to hit anything vital. She dove across the floor and rolled up beside Tyrian. "Fissure," she told him. "It's the only thing that will work!" She broke off abruptly as her sensitive ears caught the sound of screaming. Her breath caught. "There are still servants in the palace!"

Blaine laughed maniacally. "And when they die, their energy will be mine!" She stopped throwing magic blasts and shot up through the ceiling as a blur of necrotic energy to find higher ground. The palace continued to shake warningly despite it.

"Over our dead bodies!" Kyle sheathed his sword. "Ewan and I will get the people out. You two get rid of Blaine."

Tyrian grabbed both his and Ewan's arms. "If you die," he told them softly, "I am going to be extremely pissed off. And you both know that I get violent when I finally get mad."

"Well, we can't have that." Ewan grinned. "Unless you'd be targeting that windbag again." He sheathed Night. "Don't worry. We've got too much left to do. After the things we've lived through, no crumbling castle is going to be our end."

He and Kyle ran out the throne room doors, and Tyrian took a quick breath. It was up to him and Cassie. This was a matter of the Kaiten and Kentei Stars. With her at his side, he ran out of the throne room as well. He knew the castle like the back of his hand and took several hidden shortcuts to make it to the stairs. They took the stairs two or three at a time as they raced up toward the roof. When they burst into the rooftop garden, they found Blaine kneeling in the middle. The sight of her stopped both Kaiten and Kentei short.

Gone was the beautiful woman's façade. All the energy she used in trying to destroy them only served to drain whatever was left of her stolen lifeforce. She had aged decades before their very eyes. Time had not been any kinder to her than Destiny had. Tyrian remembered this appearance from Ben's memories. It was curiously satisfying to see that the evil inside was finally visible.

In a low hiss, Blaine said, "Always sticking your nose where it doesn't belong. Standing in my way. You're just like your father!"

He inclined his head slightly. "Thank you."

She gave a high-pitched shriek of fury and lunged for him. He didn't move. At the last moment, Cassie stepped in front of him and slammed her fist into Blaine's stomach. The old woman gasped and choked as blood stained her lips. She staggered back and looked down to see a throwing star imbedded in her flesh. It bled even faster than the vicious gash across her chest. Desperately she reached for her power. She needed to get away!

The runic circle opened under Tyrian's feet as the mark of the Devourer appeared. "Fissure!"

The shockwave tore through Blaine's body and hurled her over the side. She dropped like a stone to the ground below with a sickening thud and did not move. Tyrian walked over to the edge of the roof and looked down at her with calm green eyes. "I ought to take your lifeforce," he said quietly, knowing she would hear him. "It would be a fitting punishment. But you don't deserve it."

She stared up at him, bloody tears running down her face, but said not a word. The last of the energy fleeing her finally left, and her entire body crumbled into dust. Not even a trace of her was left behind.

The castle shook ever more violently, warning that a collapse somewhere was imminent. Cassie ran over to Tyrian to find a way out, but it proved unnecessary. Squint and Tamari flew down and hovered beside the roof so that they could scramble onto Squint's back. They shot away from the palace just as the first floor gave way and the second floor came crashing down on top of it. Dust and debris spewed into the air and onto the field as Squint landed beside where the other Stars had gathered.

Tyrian slid off her back and looked around sharply. There was no sign of Ewan or Kyle. But then, even as he watched, he saw them walking out of the dust cloud. They looked none the worse for the wear, though both sported more wounds than when they had left the throne room. Following them was a handful of servants.

A cheer rose in the air as they were seen, and Marian ran over to hug Ewan fiercely. "Ooph!" He laughed and ruffled her hair. "Easy on the ribs." He looked at Tyrian. "Is it done?"

"It's done," Tyrian confirmed.

The cheering grew even louder. It would be a long and hard rebuild to get the cities back on their feet and to get their new government up and running. But it would be *their* government. The tyranny had ended.

They were free.

EPILOGUE

"From this moment, eternity begins."

Tyrian woke a few days later to a restless feeling inside his soul. For the first time, he didn't bother to rein it in. The world was his to explore. There were things to do first, but there were no longer any chains binding him. No war to be fought. No fear for his friends, no fear for the people.

He glanced to the side, yet he had known the moment he woke that Cassie was not there. He knew she was not far away, and he was fairly sure he knew where she was and what she was doing. He smiled. It was a comforting feeling to have someone who knew him so well. He would never get away with anything, but he had his own ways of dealing with his stubborn Kentei wife.

For the last time, he got out of bed and got dressed. Most everything had already been packed. He walked over to the door and then glanced back at the room. He had been promised that it would always be cared for so that he could come back at any time. The same promise had been made for his home in Trinan. When he was ready to rest from travels, there would be a place for him.

He took the elevator down to the courtyard, went into the castle, and headed for the meeting room. The guards opened the doors for him, and when he walked inside, he saw Ewan, Kyle, Leonard, the Lower Generals, and Cherry . . . but no Matthias. "I see," he said softly. He had wondered. When he had gone to bed the night before, he had seen one of the stars in the sky flickering rapidly as if to go out.

Cherry's lips trembled but she managed to smile. "He made the end of the war. That was what he wanted. And he . . . didn't want to say goodbye to you because that means you'll never see him again." Vincent wrapped an arm around her shoulders and she gulped back her tears. "He was smiling."

"As he should be," Tyrian said simply. "He did a lot of great things, and his legacy lives on in you." He leaned against the table. "I'm preparing to leave," he announced calmly. "I'm going to take Divan home to his family. Cassie is going with me. For now, Raven will stay with her grandparents. When we come back for Liang and Serentia's wedding, we'll pick Raven up to travel with us."

No one was surprised by the news. Tyrian and Cassie had married the day before to an immense celebration that had doubled as an end-of-war party. They were combining their honeymoon trip with the journey to

Foresalia, and that was why their daughter would be staying behind for a few months. Raven didn't mind; she was learning all kinds of fun things from Tamari. The recently promoted Dragonist Tamari, no less. She and Squint were formally partners, and Ryu and Celestial had started training them.

"I wish you'd reconsider leading," Leonard said. "I am honored that I've been chosen to be the first president of our republic, but the position is rightfully yours."

"I don't want it." Tyrian smiled as he said it. "I was planning to put you in charge all along, Leo. What're we naming our republic anyway?" He laughed, and the sound grabbed at everyone's hearts. They had heard him laugh more in the last few days than they had over the last year. "I want you in charge to take that issue off my hands too."

"We've decided on the Republic of Taron." Marcus grinned. "It's a blend of your name and Aon Castle, so you're not getting out of the issue entirely."

"That I can handle." Tyrian looked at Leonard. "Since you're now in charge of the country, I have a request for you, President. Something only someone of your position or higher can do: I want Kyle and Ewan knighted."

"What!" Ewan almost yelped.

"No, really, that's okay!" Kyle protested hastily. "Really, Tyrian. It's appreciated but not needed."

Tyrian arched a brow. "It's not? I seem to recall that either extensive years of experience *or* 'extreme acts of heroism and bravery' are sufficient for knighting, and you two have done *more* than your share of those. You were there by my side from the beginning and more than once you two saved my sanity. You two suffered more than any and you continued to push forward. In the middle of a falling castle, you detoured to save innocent lives. You've earned the right to be seen with the highest of honor from more than the Commune of Soldiers."

"Okay, fine." Ewan crossed his arms. "But if you want us knighted, you have to do it yourself. And you can't do it unless you're in charge. So I guess it won't happen."

Tyrian sighed. Really, didn't they know him better than that? He looked at Leonard. "I want to be in charge."

Leonard was grinning outright and so were the Generals. "Okay, you're in charge."

"*Damn* you," Kyle muttered.

"Give me your swords." Tyrian held out his hand. "Come on."

Still muttering under their breath, the two swordsmen drew their swords and held them out. Tradition stated that a swordsman could only be knighted with their own sword. If they had known this would happen, they would have hidden their swords. Night, though, was tickled by the entire thing. "I've never knighted anyone."

"So glad you're enjoying things," Ewan told him in annoyance. "I don't want to be knighted. It's a pain in the ass."

"Shut up, Ewan." Tyrian lightly touched his heart with the tip of Night. "For acts of heroism and bravery, for the risk of life to ensure the safety of innocents, let it be known you have been given the highest of honors, Sir Ewan Grizmar. Let it be acknowledged."

"So acknowledged," the Lower Generals chorused.

Tyrian handed Night back to Ewan and then lightly touched Kyle's heart with the tip of *Ophelia*. "For acts of heroism and bravery, for the risk of life to ensure the safety of innocents, let it be known you have been given the highest of honors, Sir Kyle Raitels. Let it be acknowledged." He handed the sword back over as that too was acknowledged. "There we go." He looked at Leonard. "You're in charge again."

"Why, thank you. Anyone else you want knighted, since we're on the subject?"

"I can think of one. I also think she would make a perfect High General. Let me know if she balks. I'll come back and be President for a day again."

Ewan suddenly laughed and grabbed Tyrian in a headlock. "I wish I could hate you for that." He hugged him for a moment and then let go. "You'd better visit," he said gruffly. "It'd be boring not to see your face around. Maybe our paths will cross again. Kyle and I are headed out to the City-States."

"Taking Night with you?"

"Yes," Night said.

"No," Ewan said.

Tyrian winced. "Okay, I'm not staying for that fight." He glanced at Marcus. "When you and Marian are ready to marry, let me know. I'll drop everything and come back for it."

"Of course," Marcus said.

A sound at the window made everyone turn, and they smiled to see Amos flying past with Sierra to judge where to put her new stained glass. It was freshly made, depicting images of the final battle. When they all turned back to where Tyrian had been, none of them were surprised to see that he had slipped out.

They moved over to the window as a group and watched as Tyrian crossed the courtyard toward the stables. They wanted to stop him because they were all going to miss him madly, but they loved him enough to let him go. He had earned his freedom, perhaps more than any other in Taron had. "Goodbye, Tyrian," Di murmured.

"Not goodbye." Cherry smiled at her. "It's 'see you again.'"

"Right you are." Di rested her head on Alex's shoulder. "Right you are."

When Tyrian walked into the stables, he found Cassie attaching the supply packs to her horse. Fay was already saddled, and both horses were ready to be hitched to the wagon they would pull. The wagon was specially made to transport the deceased, and it would be in that wagon that Divan would make his final journey. "I hope he won't be offended to be traveling with newlyweds," Tyrian said teasingly.

Cassie smiled at him. She wanted to laugh and to dance with the happiness of the last few days. She had lost count of the times he had smiled and laughed. She couldn't even name all the ways that he had shown them all that, finally, he was whole. They would never again worry that he might break. "I'm sure he'll forgive us."

They took the horses outside and hitched them to the wagon. Flowers and tokens asking for a safe rebirth were all over the casket that held Divan. He had come from Foresalia, but he had died a champion of Taron. No one would forget his bravery.

Dozens turned out to watch Tyrian and Cassie leave, and children chased after them down the road to throw flowers and confetti. When finally the castle had disappeared into the distance behind them, Tyrian took a deep breath. Even the air seemed freer. "I'd like to say I've never been happier," he said softly, "but I have."

"Do tell."

He smiled at her. "When you were finally mine. That moment was my happiest." Her eyes softened, and he leaned over to kiss her when he suddenly sensed a familiar presence. He straightened and stopped their horses just as lavender light appeared and heralded Tanelia. Though there still lurked an eternal sadness in her eyes, it seemed as if her burdens had lightened some. "It's done," he told her simply.

"It has only begun," she countered softly. "The prophecy you would not read. I will tell you now. There will be three Kaiten Stars. Two more wait on the horizon. A war for sanity will rise next. In the future beyond that time, there will be a war to end wars. A war for the peace of the world. As you realized already, Cassie's star is fixed. She will follow these two Kaiten Stars. They will need you too, Tyrian."

"Is that the future Ophelia died for?" Tyrian asked.

"It is. When the third arrives, you will finally find the answers to the many questions I know you still have."

He considered his words and then said, "I suppose the most important thing I can offer my younger siblings is advice on how to handle their Kentei Stars."

Laughter suddenly lit Tanelia's twilight colored eyes. "Perhaps you should learn to handle yours first." With a swirl of light, she disappeared once more.

"That could take eternity," Cassie murmured. She laughed as Tyrian firmly reached over and lifted her onto the horse in front of him. She framed his face with her hands and knew she would never tire of having him there to have and hold. "Do you mind taking eternity to learn how to handle me?"

He rubbed his thumb over her cheek tenderly. "It'll be a difficult task, but I think I'm up to the challenge. Do you mind if I take my time?" His lips brushed hers.

She sighed happily. She had grown very, very fond of his patience. It was rewarding for both of them. "Take all the time you need."

All around them, the desert was hot and dry and dusty, but it was free from fear and oppression. Across the cities and towns that claimed to be part of the Republic of Taron, the Kaiten Star would be spoken of as a hero who had ended a war fraught with danger and pain and fear. Lives had been taken. Lives had been lost.

Yet, even in the darkest moments, it had been a war filled with love. The love of one hundred and nine stars who shared the skies. The love of a general's son for his land and his people. And the love of two souls born under the Kaiten and Kentei Stars. No one would ever forget their destiny.

No one would ever forget their story.

Author Notes

Where do I start with this story? Fans of the old Suikoden video games will surely recognize the resemblance—something done deliberately, for I wanted to do my own take on that type of story, no more or less than I did in the District series. How would *I* tell the tale of a hero ordained by Destiny to gather so many companions? Well, I clearly deviated pretty far from the original in *many* ways, but I am thoroughly happy with the way I've told Tyrian's tale. The Threads Series is my love song to all the role-playing games that have shaped my life from my childhood on.

If you were paying attention, you no doubt can guess who the next Kaiten Star will be! UNRAVELING LEGENDS will tell the tale of the second Kaiten, and his epic journey to thwart the madness festering within Foresalia as it attempts to spill over into the City-States.

Also coming in 2018 will be the first book of The Kingdoms Series, which is also a love song—but to the magical girl stories that also shaped my imagination. In THE TWO KINGDOMS, another universe ruled by Destiny own lays out worlds like flowers in a garden, and only the ones known as Cultivators can keep the weeds of evil at bay. Be they Ruler or Defender, the Cultivators tend their worlds and the universe beyond—but always at a high price, for history is stained with their blood.

If you loved this story, or any of my stories, please leave me a review on Amazon! Reviews are the bread and butter of an author's life, and even a simple "More, please!" will keep us going.

You can keep up with me on www.facebook.com/stacyjgarrett or www.stacyjgarrett.com or follow my blog at stacyjgarrett.wordpress.com. I sometimes lurk on Twitter (@stacyjgarrett), and Tumblr as well (stacyjgarrett.tumblr.com).

I can't wait to share more stories with you. Until we meet again in Foresalia, or perhaps another galaxy, keep dreaming of those happy endings.

Stacy J Garrett

Stacy J. Garrett was made in England but born in Sacramento, California, and like the redwoods of the state, her roots have dug deep. Her destiny as a bard was somewhat inevitable. Little else can explain how she constantly told her mother tall tales so outlandish that she couldn't even get grounded for them. Her mother and grandmother had her reading by age three, and that love of a good story propelled her through so many books that Scholastic Books gave her a medal. A love of worlds created by others eventually brought out the desire to create her own, and she has never looked back.

Stacy has seen both good and evil in her life, and her stories, like life, have no half measures. Even in a fantasy world of dragons and faeries, even in a modern city where magic abounds, she knows that the constants of real emotion never change. Dreams come true, love can be found at first sight, princesses can rescue their princes, and maybe there really can be happily ever after. Her happy endings never come without cost, though, for she truly believes we can't appreciate the good and the joy without the bad and the pain along the way.

Her current haunt is a comfy house in her beloved Sacramento where she wrangles three feline fur-kids and consumes peppermints like mana in order to balance a calendar filled with more creative venues than a sane person should realistically undertake. If she's not chained to her desk, she's stomping through the scenery in search of equally fantastical photographs.